Miles,
Mystery
&
Mayhem

BAEN BOOKS by LOIS McMASTER BUJOLD

The Vorkosigan Saga:
Cordelia's Honor
The Warrior's Apprentice
The Vor Game
Young Miles
Cetaganda
Miles, Mystery & Mayhem
Borders of Infinity
Brothers in Arms
Mirror Dance
Memory
Komarr
A Civil Campaign
Diplomatic Immunity (upcoming)

Ethan of Athos
Falling Free

The Spirit Ring

Miles, Mystery & Mayhem

LOIS McMASTER BUJOLD

MILES, MYSTERY & MAYHEM

Cetaganda copyright © 1996; *Ethan of Athos* copyright © 1986; "Labyrinth" copyright © 1989; "Author's Afterword" copyright © 2001; all by Lois McMaster Bujold.

A Baen Books Original

Baen Publishing Enterprises
P.O. Box 1403
Riverdale, NY 10471
www.baen.com

ISBN: 0-671-31858-6

Cover art by Patrick Turner
Interior map by Eleanor Kostyk

11/2001 Gen Fund 24.-

First printing, December 2001

Library of Congress Cataloging-in-Publication Data

Bujold, Lois McMaster.
    Miles, mystery & mayhem / by Lois McMaster Bujold.
      p. cm.
    "A Baen Books original"—T.p. verso.
    Contents: Cetaganda — Ethan of Athos — Labyrinth
    ISBN 0-671-31858-6
    1. Vorkosigan, Miles (Ficticious character)—Fiction. 2. Science fiction, American.
    I. Title: Miles, mystery, and mayhem. II. Title.

PS3552.U397 A6 2001
813'.54—dc21   2001043348

Distributed by Simon & Schuster
1230 Avenue of the Americas
New York, NY 10020

Production by Windhaven Press, Auburn, NH
Printed in the United States of America

10 9 8 7 6 5 4 3 2 1

Contents

Cetaganda 1

Ethan of Athos 237

"Labyrinth" 419

Author's Afterword 499

Vorkosigan Saga Timeline 503

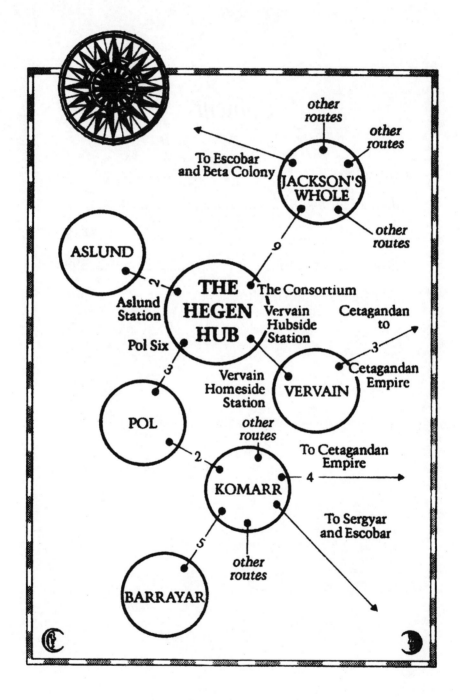

other
routes

other
routes

To Escobar
and Beta Colony

JACKSON'S
WHOLE

other
routes

other
routes

ASLUND

9

THE
HEGEN
HUB

The Consortium

2

Aslund
Station

Vervain
Hubside
Station

Cetagandan
to

Pol Six

3

Vervain
Homeside
Station

Cetagandan
Empire

3

VERVAIN

POL

other
routes

To Cetagandan
Empire

2

KOMARR

4

To Sergyar
and Escobar

5

other
routes

BARRAYAR

Cetaganda

To Jim and Toni

Chapter One

"Now is it, 'Diplomacy is the art of war pursued by other men,'" asked Ivan, "or was it the other way around? 'War is diplo—'"

"All diplomacy is a continuation of war by other means," Miles intoned. "Chou En Lai, twentieth century, Earth."

"What are you, a walking reference library?"

"No, but Commodore Tung is. He collects Wise Old Chinese Sayings, and makes me memorize 'em."

"So was old Chou a diplomat, or a warrior?"

Lieutenant Miles Vorkosigan thought it over. "I think he must have been a diplomat."

Miles's seat straps pressed against him as the attitude jets fired, banking the personnel pod in which he and Ivan sat across from each other in lonely splendor. Their two benches lined a short fuselage. Miles craned his neck for a glimpse past the pod pilot's shoulder at the planet turning below them.

Eta Ceta IV, the heart and homeworld of the sprawling Cetagandan empire. Miles supposed eight developed planets and an equal fringe of allied and puppet dependencies qualified as a sprawl in any sane person's lexicon. Not that the Cetagandan ghem-lords wouldn't like to sprawl a little farther, at their neighbors' expense, if they could.

Well, it didn't matter how huge they were, they could only put

3

military force through a wormhole jump one ship at a time, just like everybody else.

It was just that some people had some damned *big* ships.

The colored fringe of night slid around the rim of the planet as the personnel pod continued to match orbits from the Barrayaran Imperial courier vessel they had just left, to the Cetagandan transfer station they were approaching. The nightside glittered appallingly. The continents were awash in a fairy dust of lights. Miles swore he might read by the glow of the civilization, as if from a full moon. His homeworld of Barrayar seemed suddenly a dull vast swatch of rural darkness, with only a few sparks of cities here and there. Eta Ceta's high-tech embroidery was downright . . . gaudy. Yes, overdressed, like a woman weighted down with too much jewelry. Tasteless, he tried to convince himself. *I am not some backcountry hick. I can handle this. I am Lord Vorkosigan, an officer and a nobleman.*

Of course, so was Lieutenant Lord Ivan Vorpatril, but the fact did not fill Miles with confidence. Miles regarded his big cousin, who was also craning his neck, eyes avid and lips parted, drinking in their destination below. At least Ivan looked the part of a diplomatic officer, tall, dark-haired, neat, an easy smile permanently plastered on his handsome face. His fit form filled his officer's undress greens to perfection. Miles's mind slid, with the greased ease of old bad habit, to invidious comparison.

Miles's own uniforms had to be hand-tailored to fit, and insofar as possible disguise, the massive congenital defects that years of medical treatments had done so much to correct. He was supposed to be grateful, that the medicos had done so much with so little. After a lifetime of it he stood four-foot-nine, hunchbacked and brittle-boned, but it beat being carried around in a bucket. Sure.

But he *could* stand, and walk, and run if need be, leg braces and all. And Barrayaran Imperial Security didn't pay him to be pretty, thank God, they paid him to be smart. Still, the morbid thought did creep in that he had been sent along on this upcoming circus to stand next to Ivan and make him look good. ImpSec certainly hadn't given him any more interesting missions, unless you could call Security Chief Illyan's last curt ". . . and stay out of trouble!" a secret assignment.

On the other hand, maybe Ivan had been sent along to stand next to Miles and make him *sound* good. Miles brightened slightly at the thought.

And there was the orbital transfer station, coming up right on schedule. Not even diplomatic personnel dropped directly into Eta Ceta's atmosphere. It was considered bad etiquette, likely to draw an admonition administered by plasma fire. Most civilized worlds had similar regulations, Miles conceded, if only for purposes of preventing biological contaminations.

"I wonder if the Dowager Empress's death was really natural?" Miles asked idly. Ivan, after all, could hardly be expected to supply the answer. "It was sudden enough."

Ivan shrugged. "She was a generation older than Great Uncle Piotr, and he was old since forever. He used to unnerve the hell out of me when I was a kid. It's a nice paranoid theory, but I don't think so."

"Illyan agrees with you, I'm afraid. Or he wouldn't have let *us* come. This could have been a lot less dull if it had been the Cetagandan emperor who'd dropped, instead of some tottering little old haut-lady."

"But then we would not be here," Ivan pointed out logically. "We'd both be on duty hunkering down in some defensive outpost right now, while the prince-candidates' factions fought it out. This is better. Travel, wine, women, song—"

"It's a State *funeral*, Ivan."

"I can hope, can't I?"

"Anyway, we're just supposed to observe. And report. What or why, I don't know. Illyan emphasized he expects the reports in writing."

Ivan groaned. "How I spent my holiday, by little Ivan Vorpatril, age twenty-two. It's like being back in school."

Miles's own twenty-third birthday would be following Ivan's soon. If this tedious duty ran to schedule, he should actually be back home in time for a celebration, for a change. A pleasant thought. Miles's eyes glinted. "Still, it could be fun, embroidering events for Illyan's entertainment. Why should official reports always have to be in that dead dry style?"

"Because they're generated by dead dry brains. My cousin, the frustrated dramatist. Don't get too carried away. Illyan has no sense of humor, it would disqualify him for his job."

"I'm not so sure. . . ." Miles watched as the pod wove through its assigned flight path. The transfer station flowed past, vast as a mountain, complex as a circuit diagram. "It would have been interesting to meet the old lady when she was still alive. She witnessed a lot of history, in a century and a half. If from an odd angle, inside the haut-lords' seraglio."

"Low-life outer barbarians like us would never have been let near her."

"Mm, I suppose not." The pod paused, and a major Cetagandan ship with the markings of one of the out-planet governments ghosted past, on and on, maneuvering its monstrous bulk to dock with exquisite care. "All the haut-lord satrap governors—and their retinues—are supposed to be converging for this. I'll bet Cetagandan imperial security is having fun right now."

"If any two governors come, I suppose the rest have to show up, just to keep an eye on each other." Ivan's brows rose. "Should be quite a show. Ceremony as Art. Hell, the Cetagandans make blowing your nose an art. Just so they can sneer at you if you get the moves wrong. One-upmanship to the nth power."

"It's the one thing that convinces me that the Cetagandan haut-lords are still human, after all that genetic tinkering."

Ivan grimaced. "Mutants on purpose are mutants still." He glanced down at his cousin's suddenly stiff form, cleared his throat, and tried to find something interesting to look at out the canopy.

"You're so diplomatic, Ivan," said Miles through a tight smile. "Try not to start a war single . . . mouthed, eh?" *Civil or otherwise.*

Ivan shrugged off his brief embarrassment. The pod pilot, a Barrayaran tech-sergeant in black fatigues, slid his little ship neatly into its assigned docking pocket. The view outside shrank to blank dimness. Control lights blinked cheery greetings, and servos whined as the flex-tube portals matched and locked. Miles snapped off his seat straps just a shade more slowly than Ivan, pretending disinterest, or savoir faire, or something. No Cetagandan was going to catch him with his nose pressed to the glass like some eager puppy. He was a Vorkosigan. His heart beat faster anyway.

The Barrayaran ambassador would be waiting, to take his two high-ranking guests in hand, and show them, Miles hoped, how to go on. Miles mentally reviewed the correct greetings and salutations, including the carefully memorized personal message from his father. The pod lock cycled, and the hatch on the side of the fuselage to the right of Ivan's seat dilated.

A man hurtled through, swung himself to a sudden halt on the hatch's handlebar, and stared at them with wide eyes, breathing heavily. His lips moved, but whether in curses, prayers, or rehearsals Miles wasn't sure.

He was elderly but not frail, broad-shouldered and at least as tall as Ivan. He wore what Miles guessed was the uniform of a station employee, cool gray and mauve. Fine white hair wisped over his scalp, but he had no facial hair at all on his shiny skin, neither beard nor eyebrows nor even down. His hand flew to his left vest, over his heart.

"Weapon!" Miles yelled in warning. The startled pod pilot was still snaking his way clear of his seat straps, and Miles was physically ill-equipped to jump anyone, but Ivan's reflexes had been honed by plenty of training, if not actual combat. He was already moving, rotating around his own hand-hold point-of-contact and into the intruder's path.

Hand-to-hand combat in free fall was always incredibly awkward, due in part to the necessity of having to hang on tightly to anybody one wanted to seriously hit. The two men quickly ended up wrestling. The intruder clutched wildly, not at his vest but at his right trouser pocket, but Ivan managed to knock the glittering nerve disruptor from his hand.

The nerve disruptor tumbled away and whanged off the other side of the cabin, now a random threat to everyone aboard.

Miles had always been terrified of nerve disruptors, but never before as a projectile weapon. It took two more cross-cabin ricochets for him to snatch it out of the air without accidentally shooting himself or Ivan. The weapon was undersized but charged and deadly.

Ivan had meanwhile worked around behind the old man, attempting to pinion his arms. Miles seized the moment to try to nail down the second weapon, dragging open the mauve vest and going for that lump in the inner pocket. His hand came away clutching a short rod that he first took for a shock-stick.

The man screamed and wrenched violently. Greatly startled and not at all sure what he'd just done, Miles launched himself away from the struggling pair and ducked prudently behind the pod pilot. Judging from that mortal yell Miles was afraid he'd just ripped out the power pack to the man's artificial heart or something, but he continued to fight on, so it couldn't have been as fatal as it sounded.

The intruder shook off Ivan's grip and recoiled to the hatchway. There came one of those odd pauses that sometimes occur in close combat, everyone gulping for breath in the rush of adrenaline. The old man stared at Miles with the rod in his fist; his expression altered from fright to—was that grimace a flash of triumph? Surely not. Demented inspiration?

Outnumbered now as the pilot joined the fray, the intruder retreated, tumbling back out the flex tube and thumping to whatever docking bay deck lay beyond. Miles scrambled after Ivan's hot pursuit just in time to see the intruder, now firmly on his feet in the station's artificial gravity field, land Ivan a blow to his chest with a booted foot that knocked the younger man backward into the portal again. By the time Miles and Ivan had disentangled themselves, and Ivan's gasping became less alarmingly disrupted, the old man had vanished at a run. His footsteps echoed confusingly in the bay. Which exit—? The pod pilot, after a quick look to ensure that his passengers were temporarily safe, hurried back inside to answer his com alarm.

Ivan regained his feet, dusted himself off, and stared around. Miles did too. They were in a small, dingy, dimly lit freight bay.

"Y'know," said Ivan, "if that was the customs inspector, we're in trouble."

"I thought he was about to draw on us," said Miles. "It looked like it."

"You didn't see a weapon before you yelled."

"It wasn't the weapon. It was his eyes. He looked like someone about to try something that scared him to death. And he did draw."

"*After* we jumped him. Who knows what he was about to do?"

Miles turned slowly on his heel, taking in their surroundings in more detail. There wasn't a human being in sight, Cetagandan, Barrayaran, or other. "There's something very wrong here. Either he wasn't in the right place, or we weren't. This musty dump can't be our docking port, can it? I mean, where's the Barrayaran ambassador? The honor guard?"

"The red carpet, the dancing girls?" Ivan sighed. "You know, if he'd been trying to assassinate you, or hijack the pod, he should have come charging in with that nerve disruptor already in his hand."

"That was no customs inspector. Look at the monitors." Miles pointed. Two vid-pickups mounted strategically on nearby walls were ripped from their moorings, dangling sadly down. "He disabled them before he tried to board. I don't understand. Station security should be swarming in here right now. . . . D'you think he wanted the pod, and not us?"

"You, boy. No one would be after me."

"He seemed more scared of us than we were of him." Miles concealed a deep breath, hoping his heart rate would slow.

"Speak for yourself," said Ivan. "He sure scared *me*."

"Are you all right?" asked Miles belatedly. "I mean, no broken ribs or anything?"

"Oh, yeah, I'll survive . . . you?"

"I'm all right."

Ivan glanced down at the nerve disruptor in Miles's right hand, and the rod in his left, and wrinkled his nose. "How'd you end up with all the weapons?"

"I . . . don't quite know." Miles slipped the little nerve disruptor into his own trouser pocket, and held the mysterious rod up to the light. "I thought at first this was some kind of shock-stick, but it's not. It's something electronic, but I sure don't recognize the design."

"A grenade," Ivan suggested. "A time-bomb. They can make them look like anything, y'know."

"I don't think so—"

"My lords," the pod pilot stuck his head through the hatch. "Station flight control is ordering us not to dock here. They're telling us to stand off and wait clearance. Immediately."

"I *thought* we must be in the wrong place," said Ivan.

"It's the coordinates they gave me, my lord," said the pod pilot a little stiffly.

"Not your error, Sergeant, I'm sure," Miles soothed.

"Flight control sounds very forceful." The sergeant's face was tense. "Please, my lords."

Obediently, Miles and Ivan shuffled back aboard the pod. Miles refastened his seat straps automatically, his mind running on overdrive, trying to construct an explanation for their bizarre welcome to Cetaganda.

"This section of the station must have been deliberately cleared of personnel," he decided aloud. "I'll bet you Betan dollars Cetagandan security is in process of conducting a sweep-search for that fellow. A fugitive, by God." Thief, murderer, spy? The possibilities enticed.

"He was disguised, anyway," said Ivan.

"How do you know?"

Ivan picked a few fine white strands from his green sleeve. "This isn't real hair."

"Really?" said Miles, charmed. He examined the clump of threads Ivan extended across the aisle to him. One end was sticky with adhesive. "Huh."

The pod pilot finished taking up his new assigned coordinates; the pod now floated in space a few hundred meters from the row of docking pockets. There were no other pods locked onto the station for a dozen pockets in either direction. "I'll report this incident to the station authorities, shall I, my lords?" The sergeant reached for his com controls.

"Wait," said Miles.

"My lord?" The pod pilot regarded him dubiously, over his shoulder. "I think we should—"

"Wait till they ask us. After all, we're not in the business of cleaning up Cetagandan security's lapses after them, are we? It's their problem."

A small grin, immediately suppressed, told Miles the pilot was amenable to this argument. "Yes, sir," he said, making it an order-received, and therefore Miles's lordly officer's responsibility, and not that of a lowly tech-sergeant. "Whatever you say, sir."

"Miles," muttered Ivan, "what do you think you're doing?"

"Observing," said Miles primly. "I'm going to observe and see how good Cetagandan station security is at their job. I think Illyan would want to know, don't you? Oh, they'll be around to question us, and take these goodies back, but this way I can get more information in return. Relax, Ivan."

Ivan settled back, his disturbed air gradually dissipating as the minutes ticked on with no further interruptions to the boredom in the little pod. Miles examined his prizes. The nerve disruptor was of some exceptionally fine Cetagandan civilian make, not military issue, in itself odd; the Cetagandans did not encourage the dispersal of deadly anti-personnel weapons among their general populace. But it did not bear the fancy decorations that would mark it as some ghem-lord's toy. It was plain and functional, of a size meant to be carried concealed.

The short rod was odder still. Embedded in its transparent casing was a violent glitter, looking decorative; Miles was sure microscopic examination would reveal fine dense circuitry. One end of the device was plain, the other covered with a seal which was itself locked in place.

"This looks like it's meant to be inserted in something," he said to Ivan, turning the rod in the light.

"Maybe it's a dildo." Ivan smirked.

Miles snorted. "With the ghem-lords, who can say? But no, I don't think so." The indented seal on the end-cap was in the shape of some clawed and dangerous-looking bird. Deep within the incised figure gleamed metallic lines, the circuit-connections. Somewhere somebody owned the mate, a raised screaming bird-pattern full of complex encodes which would release the cover, revealing . . . what? Another pattern of encodes? A key for a key . . . It was all extraordinarily elegant. Miles smiled in sheer fascination.

Ivan regarded him uneasily. "You are going to give it back, aren't you?"

"Of course. If they ask for it."

"And if they don't?"

"Keep it for a souvenir, I suppose. It's too pretty to throw away. Maybe I'll take it home as a present to Illyan, let his cipher-laboratory elves play with it as an exercise. For about a year. It's not an amateur's bauble, even I can tell that."

Before Ivan could come up with more objections, Miles undid his green tunic and slipped the device into his own inner breast pocket. Out of sight, out of mind. "Ah—you want to keep this?" He handed the nerve disruptor across to his cousin.

Ivan plainly did. Placated by this division of the spoils, Ivan, a partner in crime now, made the little weapon disappear into his own tunic. The weapon's secret and sinister presence would do nicely, Miles calculated, to keep Ivan distracted and polite all through the upcoming disembarkation.

At last the station traffic control directed them to dock again. They locked onto a pod pocket two up from the one they had been assigned before. This time the door opened without incident. After a slight hesitation, Ivan exited through the flex tube. Miles followed him.

Six men awaited them in a gray chamber almost identical to the first one, if cleaner and better lit. Miles recognized the Barrayaran ambassador immediately. Lord Vorob'yev was a stout solid man of about sixty-standard, sharp-eyed, smiling, and contained. He wore a Vorob'yev House uniform, rather formal for the occasion Miles thought, wine-red with black trim. He was flanked by four guards in Barrayaran undress greens. Two Cetagandan station officials, in mauve and gray garb of similar style but more complex cut than the intruder's, stood slightly apart from the Barrayarans.

Only two stationers? Where were the civil police, Cetagandan military intelligence, or at least some ghem-faction's private agents? Where were the questions and the questioners Miles had been anticipating dissecting?

Instead, he found himself greeting Ambassador Vorob'yev as if nothing had happened, just as he'd first rehearsed. Vorob'yev was a man of Miles's father's generation, and in fact had been his appointee, back when Count Vorkosigan had still been Regent. Vorob'yev had been holding down this critical post for six years, having retired from his military career to take up Imperial service on the civil side. Miles resisted an urge to salute, giving the ambassador a formal nod instead.

"Good afternoon, Lord Vorob'yev. My father sends you his personal regards, and these messages."

Miles handed across the sealed diplomatic disk, an act duly noted by a Cetagandan official on his report panel. "Six items of luggage?" the Cetagandan inquired with a nod, as the pod pilot finished stacking them on the waiting float pallet, saluted Miles, and returned to his ship.

"Yes, that's all," said Ivan. To Miles's eye, Ivan looked stuffed and shifty, intensely conscious of the contraband in his pocket, but apparently the Cetagandan official could not read his cousin's expression as well as Miles could.

The Cetagandan waved a hand, and the ambassador nodded to his guards; two of them split off to accompany the luggage on its trip through Cetagandan inspection. The Cetagandan re-sealed the docking port, and bore off the float-pallet.

Ivan anxiously watched it go. "Will we get it all back?"

"Eventually. After some delays, if things run true to form," said Vorob'yev easily. "Did you gentlemen have a good trip?"

"Entirely uneventful," said Miles, before Ivan could speak. "Until we got here. Is this a usual docking port for Barrayaran visitors, or were we redirected for some other reason?" He kept one eye on the remaining Cetagandan official, watching for a reaction.

Vorob'yev smiled sourly. "Sending us through the service entrance is just a little game the Cetagandans play with us, to re-affirm our status. You are correct, it is a studied insult, designed to distract our minds. I stopped allowing it to distract me some years ago, and I recommend you do the same."

The Cetagandan displayed no reaction at all. Vorob'yev was treating him with no more regard than a piece of furniture, a compliment he apparently returned by acting like one. It seemed to be a ritual.

"Thank you, sir, I'll take your advice. Uh . . . were you delayed too? We were. They cleared us to dock once and then sent us back out to cool."

"The runaround today seems particularly ornate. Consider yourselves honored, my lords. Come this way, please."

Ivan gave Miles a pleading look as Vorob'yev turned away; Miles shook his head fractionally, *Wait. . . .*

Led by the expressionless Cetagandan station official and flanked by the embassy guards, the two young men accompanied Vorob'yev up several station levels. The Barrayaran embassy's own planetary shuttle was docked to a genuine passenger lock. It had a proper VIP lounge with its own grav system in the flex tube so nobody had to float. There they shed their Cetagandan escort. Once on board the ambassador seemed to relax a little. He settled Miles and Ivan in luxuriously padded seats arranged around a bolted-down comconsole table. At Vorob'yev's nod a guard offered them drinks of choice while they waited for their luggage and departure clearances. Following Vorob'yev's lead they accepted a Barrayaran wine of a particularly mellow vintage. Miles barely sipped, hoping to keep his head clear, while Ivan and the ambassador made small talk about their trip and mutual Vorish friends back home. Vorob'yev seemed to be personally acquainted with Ivan's mother. Miles ignored Ivan's occasional raised-brow silent invitation to join the chat, and maybe tell Lord Vorob'yev all about their little adventure with the intruder, yes?

Why hadn't the Cetagandan authorities been all over them just now, asking questions? Miles ran scenarios through his heated brain.

It was a setup, and I've just taken the bait, and they're letting the line play out. Considering what he knew of Cetagandans, Miles placed this possibility at the head of his list.

Or maybe it's just a time lag, and they'll be here momentarily. Or . . . eventually. The fugitive must first be captured, and then made to disgorge his version of the encounter. This could take time, particularly if the man had been, say, stunned unconscious during arrest. If he was a fugitive. If the station authorities had indeed been sweeping the docking area for him. If . . . Miles studied his crystal cup, and swallowed a mouthful of the smoky ruby liquid, and smiled affably at Ivan.

Their luggage and its guards arrived just as they finished their drinks, experienced timing on Vorob'yev's part, Miles judged. When the ambassador rose to oversee its stowage and their departure, Ivan leaned across the table to whisper urgently to Miles, "Aren't you going to tell him about it?"

"Not yet."

"Why not?"

"Are you in such a hurry to lose that nerve disruptor? The embassy'd take it away from you as fast as the Cetagandans, I bet."

"Screw that. What are you up to?"

"I'm . . . not sure. Yet." This was not the scenario he'd expected to unfold. He'd anticipated bandying sharp exchanges with assorted Cetagandan authorities while they made him disgorge his prizes, and trading for information, consciously or unconsciously revealed. It wasn't his fault the Cetagandans weren't doing their job.

"We've got to at least report this to the embassy's military attaché."

"Report it, yes. But not to the attaché. Illyan told me that if I had any problems—meaning, of the sort *our* department concerns itself with—I was to go to Lord Vorreedi. He's listed as a protocol officer, but he's really an ImpSec colonel and chief of ImpSec here."

"The Cetagandans don't know?"

"Of course they know. Just like we know who's really who at the Cetagandan embassy in Vorbarr Sultana. It's a polite legal fiction. Don't worry, I'll see to it." Miles sighed inwardly. He supposed the first thing the colonel would do was cut him out of the information-flow. And he dared not explain why Vorreedi shouldn't.

Ivan sat back, temporarily silenced. Only temporarily, Miles was sure.

Vorob'yev joined them again, settling down and hunting his seat straps. "And that's that, my lords. Nothing taken from your possessions, nothing added. Welcome to Eta Ceta Four. There are no official ceremonies requiring your presence today, but if you're not too tired from your journey, the Marilacan Embassy is hosting an informal reception tonight for the legation community and all its august visitors. I recommend it to your attention."

"Recommend?" said Miles. When someone with a career as long and distinguished as Vorob'yev's recommended, Miles felt, one attended.

"You'll be seeing a lot of these people over the next two weeks," Vorob'yev said. "It should provide a useful orientation."

"What should we wear?" asked Ivan. Four of the six cases they'd brought were his.

"Undress greens, please," said Vorob'yev. "Clothing is a cultural language everywhere, to be sure, but here it's practically a secret code. It is difficult enough to move among the ghem-lords without committing some defined error, and among the haut-lords it's nearly impossible. Uniforms are always correct, or, if not exactly correct, clearly not the wearer's fault, since he has no choice. I'll have my protocol office give you a list of which uniforms you are to wear at each event."

Miles felt relieved; Ivan looked faintly disappointed.

With the usual muted clinks and clanks and hisses, the flex tubes withdrew and the shuttle unlocked and undocked from the side of the station. No arresting authorities had poured through the hatch, no urgent communications had sent the ambassador hurrying forward. Miles considered his third scenario.

Our intruder got clean away. The Station authorities know nothing of our little encounter. In fact, no one knows.

Except, of course, the intruder. Miles kept his hand down, and did not touch the concealed lump in his tunic. Whatever the device was, that fellow knew Miles had it. And he could surely find out who Miles was. *I have a string on you, now. If I let it play out, something must surely climb back up it to my hand, right?* This could shape up into a nice little exercise in intelligence/counter-intelligence, better than maneuvers because it was real. No proctor with a list of answers lurked on the fringes recording all his mistakes for later analysis in excruciating detail. A practice-piece. At some stage of development an officer had to stop following orders and start generating them. And Miles wanted that promotion to ImpSec captain, oh yes. Might he somehow persuade Vorreedi to let him play with the puzzle despite his diplomatic duties?

Miles's eyes narrowed with new anticipation as they began their descent into the murky atmosphere of Eta Ceta.

Chapter Two

Half-dressed, Miles wandered across the spacious bedchamber–
sitting room the Barrayaran embassy had assigned to him, turning the glittering rod in his hand. "So if I'm meant to have this,
am I meant to stash it here, or am I meant to carry it on my
person?"

Ivan, neat and complete in the high-collared tunic, side-piped
trousers, and half-boots of fresh undress greens, rolled his eyes
ceilingward. "Will you quit fooling with that thing and get dressed,
before you make us late? Maybe it's a fancy curtain-weight, and
it's *meant* to drive you crazy trying to assign it some deep and
sinister significance. Or drive me crazy, listening to you. Some
ghem-lord's practical joke."

"A particularly subtle practical joke, if so."

"Doesn't rule it out." Ivan shrugged.

"No." Miles frowned and limped to the comconsole desk. He
opened the top drawer and found a stylus and a pad of plastic
flimsies embossed with the embassy seal. He tore off a flimsy and
pressed it against the bird-figure on the rod's cap-lock, then traced
the indentations with the stylus, a quick, accurate, and to-scale
sketch. After a moment's hesitation, he left the rod in the drawer
with the pad of flimsies, closing it again.

"Not much of a hiding place," Ivan commented. "If it's a bomb, maybe you ought to hang it out the window. For the rest of our sakes, if not your own."

"It's not a bomb, dammit. And I've thought of a hundred hiding places, but none of them are scanner-proof, so there's no point. This should be in a lead-lined blackbox, which I don't happen to have."

"I bet they have one downstairs," Ivan said. "Weren't you going to confess?"

"Yes, but unfortunately Lord Vorreedi is out of the city. Don't look at me like that, I had nothing to do with it. Vorob'yev told me the haut-lord in charge of one of the Eta Cetan Jumppoint stations has impounded a Barrayaran-registered merchant ship, and its captain. For importation infractions."

"Smuggling?" said Ivan, growing interested.

"No, some complicated cockeyed Cetagandan regulations. With fees. And taxes. And fines. And a level of acrimony that's going asymptotic. Since normalizing trade relations is a current goal of our government, and since Vorreedi is apparently good at sorting out haut-lords and ghem-lords, Vorob'yev detailed him to take care of it while he's stuck here with the ceremonial duties. Vorreedi will be back tomorrow. Or the next day. Meanwhile, it won't hurt to see how far I can get on my own. If nothing interesting turns up, I'll bounce it over to the ImpSec office here anyway."

Ivan's eyes narrowed, as he processed this. "Yeah? So what if something interesting does turn up?"

"Well, then too, of course."

"So did you tell Vorob'yev?"

"Not exactly. No. Look, Illyan said Vorreedi, so Vorreedi it is. I'll take care of it as soon as the man gets back."

"In any case, it's *time*," Ivan reiterated.

"Yeah, yeah . . ." Miles shuffled over to his bed, sat, and frowned at his leg braces, laid out waiting. "I have to take the time to get my leg bones replaced. I've given up on the organics, it's time to go with plastic. Maybe I could persuade them to add a few centimeters of length while they're at it. If only I'd known I had all this dead time coming up, I could have scheduled surgery and been recovering while we traveled and stood around being decorative."

"Inconsiderate of the dowager empress, not to send you a note and warn you she was dropping dead," Ivan agreed. "Wear the damn things, or Aunt Cordelia will hold me responsible if you trip over the embassy cat and break your legs. Again."

Miles growled, not very loudly. Ivan could read him entirely too well, too. He closed the cool steel protection around his lumpy, discolored, too-many-times smashed legs. At least the uniform trousers concealed his weakness. He fastened his tunic, sealed the polished short-boots, checked his hair in the mirror over his dresser, and followed the impatient Ivan, already at the door. In passing he slipped the folded flimsy into his trouser pocket, pausing in the corridor to re-key the door lock to his own palm. A somewhat futile gesture; as a trained ImpSec agent Lieutenant Vorkosigan knew exactly how insecure palm locks could be.

Despite, or perhaps because of, Ivan's prodding, they arrived in the foyer at almost the same moment as Ambassador Vorob'yev. Vorob'yev was wearing his red and black House uniform again. Not a man who liked making a lot of decisions about clothing, Miles sensed. He shepherded the two younger men into the embassy's waiting groundcar, where they sank into soft upholstery. Vorob'yev politely took the rear-facing seat across from his official guests. A driver and a guard occupied the front compartment. The car ran on the city net's computer control, but the alert driver sat ready to hit the manual override in case of some non-natural emergency. The silvered canopies closed, and they oozed out into the street.

"You may regard the Marilacan embassy as neutral but non-secured territory tonight, gentlemen," Vorob'yev advised them. "Enjoy yourselves, but not *too* much."

"Will there be many Cetagandans present," Miles asked, "or is this party strictly for us off-worlders?"

"No haut-lords, of course," said Vorob'yev. "They're all at one of the late empress's more private obsequies tonight, along with some of the highest-ranking ghem-clan heads. The lower-ranking ghem-lords are at loose ends, and may be out in force, as the month of official mourning has reduced their usual social opportunities. The Marilacans have been accepting a great deal of Cetagandan 'aid' in the past few years, a greediness I predict they will come to regret. They think Cetaganda won't attack an ally."

The groundcar climbed a ramp, and swung around a corner offering a brief vista down a glittering canyon of high buildings, strung together with tubeways and transparent walks glowing in the dusk. The city seemed to go on forever, and this wasn't even the main center.

"The Marilacans aren't paying sufficient attention to their own wormhole nexus maps," Vorob'yev went on. "They imagine they are at a natural border. But if Marilac were directly held by Cetaganda, the next jump would bring them to Zoave Twilight, with all its cross-routes, and a whole new region for Cetagandan expansion. Marilac is in exactly the same relationship to the Zoave Twilight crossings as Vervain is to the Hegen Hub, and we all know what happened *there.*" Vorob'yev's lips twisted in irony. "But Marilac has no interested neighbor to mount a rescue as your father did for Vervain, Lord Vorkosigan. And provocative incidents can be manufactured so easily."

The alert rush in Miles's chest faded. There was no personal, secret meaning in Vorob'yev's remarks. Everyone knew of Admiral Count Aral Vorkosigan's political and military role in creating the swift alliance and counter-attack that had driven off the attempted Cetagandan capture of its neighbor Vervain's wormhole jumps to the Hegen Hub. No one knew of the role ImpSec agent Miles Vorkosigan had played in bringing the Admiral to the Hegen Hub in so timely a fashion. And what no one knew, no one got credit for. *Hi, I'm a hero, but I can't tell you why. It's classified.* From Vorob'yev's and practically everybody else's point of view, Lieutenant Miles Vorkosigan was a low-ranking ImpSec courier officer, a nepotistic sinecure that shuffled him off into routine duties that took him out of the way. *Mutant.*

"I thought the Hegen Alliance gave the ghem-lords a bloody enough nose at Vervain to keep them subdued for a while," said Miles. "All the expansionist party ghem-officers in deep eclipse, ghem-General Estanis committing suicide—it was suicide, wasn't it?"

"In an involuntary sort of way," said Vorob'yev. "These Cetagandan political suicides can get awfully messy, when the principal won't cooperate."

"Thirty-two stab wounds in the back, worst case of suicide they ever saw?" murmured Ivan, clearly fascinated by the gossip.

"Exactly, my lord." Vorob'yev's eyes narrowed in dry amusement. "But the ghem-commanders' loose and shifting relationship to the assorted secret haut-lord factions lends an unusual degree of deniability to their operations. The Vervain invasion is now officially described as an unauthorized misadventure. The erring officers have been corrected, thank you."

"What do they call the Cetagandan invasion of Barrayar in my grandfather's time?" Miles asked. "A reconnaissance in force?"

"When they mention it at all, yes."

"All twenty *years* of it?" asked Ivan, half-laughing.

"They tend not to go into the embarrassing details."

"Have you shared your views on Cetagandan ambitions toward Marilac with Illyan?" Miles asked.

"Yes, we keep your chief fully informed. But there are no material movements at present to support my theory. I'm just reasoning on principle, so far. ImpSec is watching some key indicators for us."

"I'm . . . not in that loop," said Miles. "Need-to-know and all that."

"But I trust you grasp the larger strategic picture."

"Oh, yes."

"And—upper-class gossip is not always as guarded as it should be. You two will be in a position to encounter some. Plan to report it all to my chief of protocol, Colonel Vorreedi. He will be giving you daily briefings, as soon as he returns. Let him sort out which tidbits are important."

Check. Miles nodded to Ivan, who shrugged acquiescence.

"And, ah . . . try not to give away more than you gain?"

"Well, *I'm* safe," said Ivan. "I don't know anything." He smiled cheerily. Miles tried not to wince, nor mutter *We know, Ivan,* under his breath loud enough to be heard.

Since the off-planet legations were concentrated in one section of Eta Ceta's capital city, the drive was short. The groundcar descended a street-level, and slowed. It entered the Marilacan embassy building's garage and pulled into a brightly lit entry foyer made less subterranean by marble surfaces and decorative plants trailing from tiers of tubs. The car's canopy rose. Marilacan embassy guards bowed the Barrayaran party into the lift tubes. Doubtless they also discreetly scanned their guests—it seemed Ivan had mustered the good sense to leave that nerve disruptor in his desk drawer, too.

They exited the lift tube into a wide lobby, opening in turn onto several levels of connected public areas, already well populated with guests, the volume of their babble invitingly high. The center of the lobby was occupied by a large multi-media sculpture, real, not a projection. Trickling water cascaded down a fountain reminiscent of a little mountain, complete with impressionistic mountain-paths one could actually walk upon. Colored flakes swirled in the air around the mini-maze, making delicate tunnels. From their green color Miles guessed they were meant to represent Earth tree leaves even before he drew close enough to make out the realistic details of their shapes. The colors slowly began to change, from twenty different greens to brilliant yellows, golds, reds and black-reds. As they swirled they almost seemed to form fleeting patterns, like human faces and bodies, to a background of tinkling like wind chimes. So was it meant to be faces and music, or was it just tricking his brain into projecting meaningful patterns onto randomness? The subtle uncertainty attracted him.

"*That's* new," commented Vorob'yev, his eye also caught. "Pretty . . . ah, good evening, Ambassador Bernaux."

"Good evening, Lord Vorob'yev." Their silver-haired Marilacan host exchanged a familiar nod with his Barrayaran counterpart. "Yes, we think it's rather fine. It's a gift from a local ghem-lord. Quite an honor. It's titled 'Autumn Leaves.' My cipher staff puzzled over the name for half a day, and finally decided it meant 'Autumn Leaves.' "

The two men laughed. Ivan smiled uncertainly, not quite following the in-joke. Vorob'yev formally introduced them to Ambassador Bernaux, who responded to their rank with elaborate courtesy, and to their age by telling them where to find the food and pointedly turning them loose. It was the Ivan-effect, Miles decided glumly. They mounted stairs toward a buffet, cut off from getting to hear whatever private comments the two older men went on to exchange. Probably just social pleasantries, but still . . .

Miles and Ivan sampled the hors d'oeuvres, which were dainty but abundant, and selected drinks. Ivan chose a famous Marilacan wine. Miles, conscious of the flimsy in his pocket, chose black coffee. They abandoned each other with a silent wave, each to circulate after his own fashion. Miles leaned on the railing overlooking the lift-tube lobby. He sipped from the fragile cup and wondered where its stay-warm circuit was concealed—ah, there on the bottom, woven into the metallic glitter of the Marilacan embassy seal. "Autumn Leaves" was chilling down to the end of its cycle. The water in the trickling fountains froze, or appeared to, stilled to silent black ice. The swirling colors faded to the sere yellow and silver-gray of a winter sunset, the figures, if figures they were, now suggesting skeletal despair. The chime/music faded to discordant, broken whispers. It was not a winter of snow and celebration. It was a winter of death. Miles shivered involuntarily. *Damned effective.*

So, how to begin asking questions without revealing anything in return? He pictured himself buttonholing some ghem-lord, *Say, did one of your minions lose a code-key with a seal like this . . . ?* No. By far the best approach was to let his . . . adversaries find him, but they were being tediously slow about it. Miles's eye swept the throng for men lacking eyebrows, without success.

But Ivan had found a beautiful woman already. Miles blinked as he registered just how beautiful. She was tall and slim, the skin of her face and hands as delicately smooth as porcelain. Jeweled bands bound her blond-white hair loosely at the nape of her neck, and again at her waist. The hair did not trail to its silky end until halfway to her knees. Her dress concealed rather than revealed, with layers of underslips, split sleeves, and vests sweeping to her ankles. The dark hues of the over-garments set off the pallor of her complexion, and a flash of cerulean silk underneath echoed her blue eyes. She was a Cetagandan ghem-lady, without question— she had that attenuated-elf look that suggested more than a tinge of haut-lord genes in her family tree. True, the look could be mimicked with surgeries and other therapies, but the arrogant arch to her brow had to be genuine.

Miles sensed the pheromones in her perfume while still spiraling in from three meters away. It seemed redundant; Ivan was already on overdrive, his dark eyes sparkling as he decanted some story featuring himself as hero, or at least protagonist. Something about training exercises, ah, of course, emphasizing his Barrayaran martial style. Venus and Mars, right. But she was actually smiling at something Ivan had said.

It wasn't that Miles enviously sought to deny Ivan his luck with women; it would simply be nice if some of the overflow would trickle down his way. Though Ivan claimed you had to make your own luck. Ivan's resilient ego could absorb a dozen rejections tonight for some smiling thirteenth payoff. Miles thought he would be dead of mortification by Attempt Three. Maybe he was naturally monogamous.

Hell, you had to at least achieve monogamy before you could go on to larger ambitions. So far he had failed to attach even one woman to his sawed-off person. Of course, nearly three years in covert ops, and the period before that in the all-male environs of the military academy, had limited his opportunities.

Nice theory. So why hadn't similar conditions stopped Ivan?

Elena . . . Was he still holding out for the impossible, on some level? Miles swore he wasn't nearly as choosy as Ivan—he could hardly afford to be—yet even this lovely ghem-blonde lacked... what? The intelligence, the reserve, the pilgrim soul...? But Elena had chosen another, and probably wisely. Time and past time for Miles to move on too, and carve out some luck of his own. He just wished the prospect didn't feel so bleak.

Spiraling in from the other side a moment or two after Miles came a Cetagandan ghem-lord, tall and lean. The face rising up out of his dark and flowing robes was young; the fellow was not much older than Ivan and himself, Miles guessed. He was square-skulled, with prominent round cheekbones. One cheekbone was decorated with a circular patch, a decal, Miles realized, a stylized swirl of color identifying the man's rank and clan. It was a shrunken version of the full face paint a few other Cetagandans present wore, an avant-garde youth fashion currently being disapproved of by the older generation. Was he come to rescue his lady from Ivan's attentions?

"Lady Gelle," he bowed slightly, and "Lord Yenaro," she responded with a precisely graded inclination of her head, by which Miles gathered that 1) she had a higher status in the ghem-community than the man, and 2) he was not her husband or brother—Ivan was probably safe.

"I see you have found some of the galactic exotics you were longing for," said Lord Yenaro to her.

She smiled back at him. The effect was downright blinding, and Miles found himself wishing she'd smile at him even though he knew better. Lord Yenaro, doubtless inoculated by a lifetime of exposure to ghem-ladies, seemed immune. "Lord Yenaro, this is Lieutenant Lord Ivan Vorpatril of Barrayar, and, ah—?" Her lashes swept down over her eyes, indicating Ivan should introduce Miles, a gesture as sharp and evocative as if she'd tapped Ivan's wrist with a fan.

"My cousin, Lieutenant Lord Miles Vorkosigan," Ivan supplied smoothly, on cue.

"Ah, the Barrayaran envoys!" Lord Yenaro bowed more deeply. "What luck to meet you."

Miles and Ivan both returned decent nods; Miles made sure the inclination of his head was slightly shallower than his cousin's, a fine gradation alas probably spoiled by the angle of view.

"We have an historical connection, Lord Vorkosigan," Yenaro went on. "Famous ancestors."

Miles's adrenaline level shot up. *Oh, damn, this is some relative of the late ghem-General Estanis, and he's out to get the son of Aral Vorkosigan. . . .*

"You *are* the grandson of General Count Piotr Vorkosigan, are you not?"

Ah. *Ancient* history, not recent. Miles relaxed slightly. "Indeed."

"I am in a sense your opposite number, then. My grandfather was ghem-General Yenaro."

"Oh, the unfortunate commander of the, uh, what do you folks call it? The Barrayaran Expedition? The Barrayaran Reconnaissance?" Ivan put in.

"The ghem-general who lost the Barrayaran War," Yenaro said bluntly.

"Really, Yenaro, must you bring him up?" said Lady Gelle. Did she actually want to hear the end of Ivan's story? Miles could have told her a much funnier one, about the time on training maneuvers when Ivan had led his patrol into gluey waist-deep mud, and they'd all had to be winched out by hovercar. . . .

"I am not a proponent of the hero-theory of disaster," Miles said diplomatically. "General Yenaro had the misfortune to be the last of five successive ghem-generals who lost the Barrayaran War, and thus the sole inheritor of a, as it were, tontine of blame."

"Oh, well put," murmured Ivan. Yenaro, too, smiled.

"Do I understand that thing in the lobby is yours, Yenaro?" the girl inquired, clearly hoping to steer the conversation away from a fast downslide into military history. "A trifle banal for your crowd, isn't it? My mother liked it."

"It is but a practice piece." A slightly ironic bow acknowledged this mixed review. "The Marilacans were delighted with it. True courtesy considers the tastes of the recipient. It has some levels of subtlety only apparent when you walk through it."

"I thought you were specializing in the incense contests."

"I'm branching out into other media. Though I still maintain scent is a subtler sense than sight. You must let me mix for you sometime. That civet-jasmine blend you're wearing tonight absolutely clashes with the third-level formal style of your dress, you know."

Her smile went thin. "Does it."

Miles's imagination supplied background music, a scrape of rapiers, and a *Take that, varlet!* He tamped down a grin.

"Beautiful dress," Ivan put in earnestly. "You smell great."

"Mm, yes, speaking of your craving for the exotic," Lord Yenaro said to Lady Gelle, "did you know that Lord Vorpatril here is a biological birth?"

The girl's feather-faint brows drew in, making a tiny crease in her flawless forehead. "All births are biological, Yenaro."

"Ah, but no. The original sort of biology. From his mother's body."

"*Eeeuu.*" Her nose wrinkled in horror. "*Really*, Yenaro. You are so obnoxious tonight. Mother is right, you and your *retro-avant* crowd are going to go too far one of these days. You are in danger of becoming someone not to know, instead of someone famous." Her distaste was directed at Yenaro, but she shifted farther from Ivan, Miles noticed.

"When fame eludes, notoriety may serve," said Yenaro, shrugging.

I was a replicator birth, Miles thought of putting in brightly, but didn't. *Just goes to show, you can never tell. Except for the brain damage, Ivan had better luck than I. . . .*

"Good *evening*, Lord Yenaro." She tossed her head and moved off. Ivan looked dismayed.

"Pretty girl, but her mind is so unformed," murmured Yenaro, as if to explain why they were better off without her company. But he looked uncomfortable.

"So, uh . . . you chose an artistic career over a military one, did you, Lord Yenaro?" Miles tried to fill the breach.

"Career?" Lord Yenaro's mouth quirked. "No, I am an amateur, of course. Commercial considerations are the death of true taste. But I hope to achieve some small stature, in my own way."

Miles trusted that last wasn't a double entendre of some sort. They followed Lord Yenaro's gaze over the rail and down into the lobby, at his fountain-thing gurgling there. "You absolutely should come see it from the inside, you know. The view is entirely altered."

Yenaro was really a rather awkward man, Miles decided, his prickly exterior barely shielding a quiveringly vulnerable *artiste*'s ego. "Sure," he found himself saying. Yenaro needed no further encouragement, and, smiling anxiously, led them toward the stairs, beginning to explain some thematic theory the sculpture was supposed to be displaying. Miles sighted Ambassador Vorob'yev, beckoning to him from the far side of the balcony. "Excuse me, Lord Yenaro. Ivan, you go on, I'll catch up with you."

"Oh . . ." Yenaro looked momentarily crushed. Ivan watched

Miles escape with a light of ire in his eye that promised later retribution.

Vorob'yev was standing with a woman, her hand familiarly upon his arm. She was about forty-standard, Miles guessed, with naturally attractive features free of artificial sculptural enhancement. Her long dress and robes were styled after the Cetagandan fashion, though much simpler in detail than Lady Gelle's. She was no Cetagandan, but the dark red and cream colors and green accents of her garments worked as cleverly with her olive skin and dark curls.

"There you are, Lord Vorkosigan," said Vorob'yev. "I've promised to introduce you. This is Mia Maz, who works for our good friends at the Vervani Embassy, and who has helped us out from time to time. I recommend her to you."

Miles snapped to attention at the key phrase, smiled, and bowed to the Vervani woman. "Pleased to meet you. And what do you do at the Vervani Embassy, ma'am?"

"I'm assistant chief of protocol. I specialize in women's etiquette."

"That's a separate specialty?"

"It is here, or should be. I've been telling Ambassador Vorob'yev for years that he ought to add a woman to his staff for that purpose."

"But we haven't any with the necessary experience," sighed Vorob'yev, "and you won't let me hire you away. Though I have tried."

"So start one without experience, and let her gain it," Miles suggested. "Would Milady Maz consider taking on an apprentice?"

"Now there's an idea. . . ." Vorob'yev looked much struck. Maz's brows rose approvingly. "Maz, we should discuss this, but I must speak to Wilstar, whom I see just hitting the buffet over there. If I'm lucky, I can catch him with his mouth full. Excuse me. . . ." His mission of introduction accomplished, Vorob'yev faded—how else?—diplomatically away.

Maz turned her whole attention gratefully upon Miles. "Anyway, Lord Vorkosigan, I wanted to let you know that if there's anything we at the Vervani Embassy can do for the son or the nephew of Admiral Aral Vorkosigan during your visit to Eta Ceta, well . . . all that we have is at your disposal."

Miles smiled. "Don't make that offer to Ivan; he might take you up on it personally."

The woman followed his glance down over the railing, to where his tall cousin was now being guided through the sculpture by Lord

Yenaro. She grinned impishly, making a dimple wink in her cheek. "Not a problem."

"So, are, uh . . . ghem-ladies really so different from ghem-lords as to make a full-time study? I admit, most Barrayarans' views of the ghem-lords have been through range-finders."

"Two years ago, I would have scorned that militaristic view. Since the Cetagandan invasion attempt we've come to appreciate it. Actually, the ghem-lords are so much like the Vor, I'd think you'd find them more comprehensible than we Vervani do. The haut-lords are . . . something else. And the haut-ladies are even more something else, I've begun to realize."

"The haut-lords' women are so thoroughly sequestered . . . do they ever do anything? I mean, nobody ever sees them, do they? They have no power."

"They have their own sort of power. Their own areas of control. Parallel, not competing with their men. It all makes sense, they just never bother explaining it to outsiders."

"To inferiors."

"That, too." Her dimple flashed again.

"So . . . are you well up on ghem- and haut-lord seals, crests, marks, that sort of thing? I can recognize about fifty clan-marks by sight, and all the military insignia and corps crests, of course, but I know that just scratches the surface."

"I'm fairly well up. They have layers within layers; I can't claim to know them all by any means."

Miles frowned thoughtfully, then decided to seize the moment. There was nothing else going on here tonight, that was certain. He drew the flimsy from his pocket and flattened it out against the railing. "Do you know this icon? I ran across it . . . well, in an odd place. But it smelled ghemish, or hautish, if you know what I mean."

She gazed with interest at the screaming-bird outline. "I don't recognize it right off. But you're correct, it's definitely in the Cetagandan style. It's old, though."

"How can you tell?"

"Well, it's clearly a personal seal, not a clan-mark, but it doesn't have an outline around it. For the last three generations people have been putting their personal marks in cartouches, with more and more elaborate borders. You can practically tell the decade by the border design."

"Huh."

"If you like, I can try to look it up in my resource materials."

"Would you? I'd like that very much." He folded the flimsy back up and handed it to her. "Uh . . . I'd appreciate it if you wouldn't show it to anyone else, though."

"Oh?" She let the syllable hang there, *Oh . . . ?*

"Excuse me. Professional paranoia. I, uh . . ." He was getting in deeper and deeper. "It's a habit."

He was rescued from tripping further over his tongue by the return of Ivan. Ivan's practiced eye summed up the attractions of the Vervani woman instantly, and he smiled attentively at her, as sincerely delighted as he had been with the last girl, and would be with the next. And the next. The ghem-lord artiste was still glued to his elbow; Miles perforce introduced them both. Maz seemed not to have met Lord Yenaro before. In front of the Cetagandan, Maz did not repeat to Ivan her message of boundless Vervani gratitude to the Vorkosigan clan, but she was definitely friendly.

"You really ought to let Lord Yenaro take you on the tour of his sculpture, Miles," Ivan said ruthlessly. "It's quite a thing. An opportunity not to be missed and all that."

I found her first, dammit. "Yes, it's very fine."

"Would you be interested, Lord Vorkosigan?" Yenaro looked earnest and hopeful.

Ivan bent to Miles's ear to whisper, "It was Lord Yenaro's gift to the Marilacan embassy. Don't be a lout, Miles, you know how sensitive the Cetagandans are about their artsy, uh, things."

Miles sighed, and mustered an interested smile for Yenaro. "Certainly. Now?"

Miles excused himself with unfeigned regrets to Maz the Vervani. The ghem-lordling led him down the stairs to the lobby, and had him pause at the entrance of the walk-through sculpture to wait for the show-cycle to begin anew.

"I'm not really qualified to judge aesthetics," Miles mentioned, hoping to head off any conversation in that direction.

"So very few are," smiled Yenaro, "but that doesn't stop them."

"It does seem to me to be a very considerable technical achievement. Do you drive the motion with antigrav, then?"

"No, there's no antigrav in it at all. The generators would be bulky and wasteful of power. The same force drives the leaves' motion as drives their color changes—or so my technicians explained it to me."

"Technicians? I somehow pictured you putting all this together with your own hands."

Yenaro spread his hands—pale, long-fingered, and thin—and stared at them as if surprised to find them on the ends of his wrists. "Of course not. Hands are to be hired. Design is the test of the intellect."

"I must disagree. In my experience, hands are integral with brains, almost another lobe for intelligence. What one does not know through one's hands, one does not truly know."

"You are a man capable of true conversation, I perceive. You must meet my friends, if your schedule here permits. I'm hosting a reception at my home in two evenings' time—do you suppose—?"

"Um, maybe . . ." That evening was a blank as far as the funeral formalities went. It could be quite interesting, a chance to observe how the ghem-lordlings of his own generation operated without the inhibitions of their elders; a glimpse into the future of Cetaganda. "Yes, why not?"

"I'll send you directions. Oh." Yenaro nodded toward the fountain, which was starting up with its high-canopied summer greens again. "Now we can go in."

Miles did not find the view from inside the fountain-maze all that much different from the outside. In fact, it seemed less interesting, as at close range the illusion of forms in the flitting leaves was reduced. The music was clearer, though. It rose to a crescendo, as the colors began to change.

"Now you'll see something," said Yenaro, with evident satisfaction.

It was all sufficiently distracting that it took another moment for Miles to realize that he was *feeling* something—tingling and heat, coming from his leg braces lying against his skin. He schooled himself not to react, till the heat began to rise.

Yenaro was babbling on with artistic enthusiasm, pointing out effects, *Now, watch this*— Brilliant colors swirled before Miles's eyes. A distinct sensation of scalding flesh crept up his legs.

Miles muffled his scream to a less-edged yell, and managed not to jump for the water. God knew, he might be electrocuted. The few seconds it took him to pelt out of the maze brought the steel of his braces to a temperature sufficient to boil water. He gave up dignity, dove for the floor, and yanked up his trouser legs. His first snatch at the clamps burned his hands, too. He swore, eyes watering, and tried again. He tore off his boots, snapped loose the braces, and flung them aside with a clatter, and curled up momentarily in overwhelming pain. The braces had left a pattern of rising white welts surrounded by an angry red border of flesh on shin, knees, and ankles.

Yenaro was flapping about in distress, calling loudly for help. Miles looked up to find himself the center of an audience of about fifty or so shocked and bewildered people, witnessing his display. He stopped writhing and swearing, and sat panting, his breath hissing through clenched teeth.

Ivan and Vorob'yev shouldered through the mob from different directions. "Lord Vorkosigan! What has happened?" asked Vorob'yev urgently.

"I'm all right," said Miles. He was not all right, but this was not the time or place to go into details. He pulled his trouser legs quickly back down, concealing the burns.

Yenaro was yammering on in dismay, "What happened? I had no idea—are you all right, Lord Vorkosigan? Oh *dear* . . ."

Ivan bent and prodded at a cooling brace. "Yes, what the hell . . . ?"

Miles considered the sequence of sensations, and their possible causes. Not antigrav, not noticeable to anyone else, and it had slid right past Marilacan embassy security. Hidden in plain sight? Right. "I think it was some sort of electro-hysteresis effect. The color-changes in the display are apparently driven by a reversing magnetic field at low level. No problem for most people. For me, well, it wasn't quite as bad as shoving my leg braces into a microwave, but—you get the idea." Grinning, he got to his feet. Ivan, looking very worried, had already collected his flung boots and the offending braces. Miles let him keep them. He didn't want to touch them just now. He blundered rather blindly closer to Ivan, and muttered under his breath, "Get me out of here. . . ." He was shivering and shocky, as Ivan's hand on his shoulder could sense. Ivan gave him a short, understanding nod, and swiftly withdrew through the crowd of finely dressed men and women, some of whom were already turning away.

Ambassador Bernaux hurried up, and added his worried apologies to Yenaro's one-man chorus. "Do you wish to stop in to the embassy infirmary, Lord Vorkosigan?" Bernaux offered.

"No. Thank you. I'll wait till we get home, thanks." *Soon, please.*

Bernaux bit his lip, and regarded the still-apologizing Lord Yenaro. "Lord Yenaro, I'm afraid—"

"Yes, yes, turn it off at *once*," said Yenaro. "I will send my servants to remove it immediately. I had no idea—everyone else seemed to be enjoying—it must be re-designed. Or destroyed, yes, destroyed at once. I am so sorry—this is so embarrassing—"

Yes, isn't it? thought Miles. A show of his physical weakness, displayed to a maximum audience at the earliest possible moment . . .

"No, no, don't destroy it," said Ambassador Bernaux, horrified. "But we certainly must have it examined by a safety engineer, and modified, or perhaps a warning posted. . . ."

Ivan reappeared at the edge of the dispersing crowd, and gave Miles a thumbs-up signal. After a few more minutes of excruciating social niceties, Vorob'yev and Ivan managed to get him escorted back down the lift tube to the waiting Barrayaran embassy groundcar. Miles flung himself into the upholstery and sat, grinning in pain, breath shallow. Ivan eyed his shivering form, skinned out of his tunic, and tucked it around Miles's shoulders. Miles let him.

"All right, let's see the damages," demanded Ivan. He propped one of Miles's heels on his knee and rolled back the trouser leg. "Damn, that's got to hurt."

"Quite," agreed Miles thinly.

"It could hardly have been an assassination attempt, though," said Vorob'yev, his lips compressed with calculation.

"No," agreed Miles.

"Bernaux told me he had his own security people examine the sculpture before they installed it. Looking for bombs and bugs, of course, but they cleared it."

"I'm sure they did. This could not have hurt anyone . . . but me."

Vorob'yev followed his reasoning without effort. "A trap?"

"Awfully elaborate, if so," noted Ivan.

"I'm . . . not sure," said Miles. *I'm meant to be not-sure. That's the beauty of it.* "It had to have taken days, maybe weeks, of preparation. We didn't even know we were coming here till two weeks ago. When did it arrive at the Marilacan embassy?"

"Last night, according to Bernaux," Vorob'yev said.

"Before we even arrived." *Before our little encounter with the man with no eyebrows. It can't possibly be connected—can it?* "How long have we been scheduled for that party?"

"The embassies arranged the invitations about three days ago," said Vorob'yev.

"The timing is awfully tight, for a conspiracy," Ivan observed.

Vorob'yev thought it over. "I think I must agree with you, Lord Vorpatril. Shall we put it down as an unfortunate accident, then?"

"Provisionally," said Miles. *That was no accident. I was set up. Me, personally. You know there's a war on when the opening salvo arrives.*

Except that, usually, one knew *why* a war had been declared. It was all very well to swear not to be blindsided again, but who was the enemy here?

Lord Yenaro, I bet you throw a fascinating party. I wouldn't miss it for worlds.

Chapter Three

"The proper name for the Cetagandan imperial residence is the Celestial Garden," said Vorob'yev, "but all the galactics just call it Xanadu. You'll see why in a moment. Duvi, take the scenic approach."

"Yes, my lord," returned the young sergeant who was driving. He altered the control program. The Barrayaran embassy aircar banked, and shot through a shining stalagmite array of city towers.

"*Gently*, if you please, Duvi. My stomach, at this hour of the morning . . ."

"Yes, my lord." Regretfully, the driver slowed them to a saner pace. They dipped, wove around a building that Miles estimated must have been a kilometer high, and rose again. The horizon dropped away.

"Whoa," said Ivan. "That's the biggest force dome I've ever seen. I didn't know they could expand them to that size."

"It absorbs the output of an entire generating plant," said Vorob'yev, "for the dome alone. Another for the interior."

A flattened opalescent bubble six kilometers across reflected the late morning sun of Eta Ceta. It lay in the midst of the city like a vast egg in a bowl, a pearl beyond price. It was ringed first by a kilometer-wide park with trees, then by a street reflecting silver, then by another park, then by an ordinary street, thick with traffic. From this, eight wide boulevards fanned out like the spokes of a wheel, centering the city. Centering the universe, Miles gained the impression. The effect was doubtless intended.

"The ceremony today is in some measure a dress rehearsal for the final one in a week and a half," Vorob'yev went on, "since absolutely everyone will be there, ghem-lords, haut-lords, galactics and all. There will likely be organizational delays. As long as they're not on our part. I spent a week of hard negotiating to get you your official rankings and place in this."

"Which is?" said Miles.

"You two will be placed equivalently to second-order ghem-lords." Vorob'yev shrugged. "It was the best I could do."

In the mob, though toward the front of it. The better to watch without being much noticed himself, Miles supposed. Today, that seemed like a good idea. All three of them, Vorob'yev, Ivan, and himself, were wearing their respective House mourning uniforms, logos and decorations of rank stitched in black silk on black cloth. Maximum formal, since they were to be in the Imperial presence itself. Miles ordinarily liked his Vorkosigan House uniform, whether the original brown and silver or this somber and elegant version, because the tall boots not only allowed but required him to dispense with the leg braces. But getting the boots on over his swollen burns this morning had been . . . painful. He was going to be limping more noticeably than usual, even tanked as he was on painkillers. *I'll remember this, Yenaro.*

They spiraled down to a landing by the southernmost dome entrance, fronted by a landing lot already crowded with other vehicles. Vorob'yev dismissed the driver and aircar.

"We keep no escort, my lord?" Miles said doubtfully, watching it go, and awkwardly shifting the long polished maplewood box he carried.

Vorob'yev shook his head. "Not for security purposes. No one but the Cetagandan emperor himself could arrange an assassination inside the Celestial Garden, and if he wished to have you eliminated here, a regiment of bodyguards would do you no good."

Some very tall men in the dress uniforms of the Cetagandan Imperial Guard vetted them through the dome locks. The guardsmen shunted them toward a collection of float-pallets set up as open cars, with white silky upholstered seats, the color of

Cetagandan Imperial mourning. Each ambassadorial party was bowed on board by what looked to be senior servants in white and gray. The robotically-routed float-cars set off at a sedate pace a hand-span above the white-jade-paved walkways winding through a vast arboretum and botanical garden. Here and there Miles saw the rooftops of scattered and hidden pavilions peeking through the trees. All the buildings were low and private, except for some elaborate towers poking up in the center of the magic circle, almost three kilometers away. Though the sun shone outside in an Eta Ceta spring day, the weather inside the dome was set to a gray, cloudy, and appropriately mournful dampness, promising, but doubtless not delivering, rain.

At length they wafted to a sprawling pavilion just to the west of the central towers, where another servant bowed them out of the car and directed them inside, along with a dozen other delegations. Miles stared around, trying to identify them all.

The Marilacans, yes, there was the silver-haired Bernaux, some green-clad people who might be Jacksonians, a delegation from Aslund which included their chief of state—even they had only two guards, disarmed—the Betan ambassadress in a black-on-purple brocade jacket and matching sarong, all streaming in to honor this one dead woman who would never have met them face-to-face when alive. *Surreal* seemed an understatement. Miles felt as if he'd crossed the border into Faerie, and when they emerged this afternoon, a hundred years would have passed outside. The galactics had to pause at the doorway to make way for the party of a haut-lord satrap governor. *He* had an escort of a dozen ghem-guards, Miles noted, in full formal face paint, orange, green, and white swirls.

The decor inside was surprisingly simple—tasteful, Miles supposed—tending heavily to the organic, arrangements of live flowers and plants and little fountains, as if bringing the garden indoors. The connecting halls were hushed, not echoing, yet one's voice carried clearly. They'd done something extraordinary with acoustics. More palace servants circulated offering food and drinks to the guests.

A pair of pearl-colored spheres drifted at a walking pace across the far end of one hall, and Miles blinked at his first glimpse of haut-ladies. Sort of.

Outside their very private quarters haut-women all hid themselves behind personal force-shields, usually generated, Miles had been told, from a float-chair. The shields could be made any color, according to the mood or whim of the wearer, but today would all be white for the occasion. The haut-lady could see out with perfect clarity, but no one could see in. Or reach in, or penetrate the barrier with stunner, plasma, or nerve disruptor fire, or small projectile weapons or minor explosions. True, the force-screen also eliminated the opportunity to fire out, but that seemed not to be a haut-lady concern. The shield could be cut in half with a gravitic imploder lance, Miles supposed, but the imploders' bulky power packs, massing several hundred kilos, made them strictly field ordnance, not hand weapons.

Inside their bubbles, the haut-women could be wearing anything. Did they ever cheat? Slop around in old clothes and comfy slippers when they were supposed to be dressed up? Go nude to garden parties? Who could tell?

A tall elderly man in the pure white robes reserved for the haut- and ghem-lords approached the Barrayaran party. His features were austere, his skin finely wrinkled and almost transparent. He was the Cetagandan equivalent of an Imperial majordomo, apparently, though with a much more flowery title, for after collecting their credentials from Vorob'yev he provided them with exact instructions as to their place and timing in the upcoming procession. His attitude conveyed that outlanders might be hopelessly gauche, but if one repeated the directions in a firm tone and made them simple enough, there was a chance of getting through this ceremony without disgrace.

He looked down his hawk-beak nose at the polished box. "And this is your gift, Lord Vorkosigan?"

Miles managed to unlatch the box and open it for display without dropping it. Within, nestled on a black velvet bed, lay an old, nicked sword. "This is the gift selected from his collection by my Emperor, Gregor Vorbarra, in honor of your late Empress. It is the sword his Imperial ancestor Dorca Vorbarra the Just carried in the First Cetagandan War." One of several, but no need to go into that. "A priceless and irreplaceable historical artifact. Here is its documentation of provenance."

"Oh." The majordomo's feathery white brows lifted almost despite themselves. He took the packet, sealed with Gregor's personal mark, with more respect. "Please convey my Imperial master's thanks to yours." He half-bowed, and withdrew.

"*That* worked well," said Vorob'yev with satisfaction.

"I should bloody think so," growled Miles. "Breaks my heart." He handed off the box to Ivan to juggle for a while.

Nothing seemed to be happening just yet—organizational delays, Miles supposed. He drifted away from Ivan and Vorob'yev in search of a hot drink. He was on the point of capturing something steaming and, he hoped, non-sedating, from a passing tray when a quiet voice at his elbow intoned, "Lord Vorkosigan?"

He turned, and stifled an indrawn breath. A short and rather androgynous elderly . . . woman?—stood by his side, dressed in the gray and white of Xanadu's service staff. Her head was bald as an egg, her face devoid of hair. Not even eyebrows. "Yes . . . ma'am?"

"Ba," she said in the tone of one offering a polite correction. "A lady wishes to speak with you. Would you accompany me, please?"

"Uh . . . sure." She turned and paced soundlessly away, and he followed in alert anticipation. A lady? With luck, it might be Mia Maz of the Vervani delegation, who ought to be around somewhere in this mob of a thousand people. He was developing some urgent questions for her. *No eyebrows? I was expecting a contact sometime, but . . . here?*

They exited the hall. Passing out of sight of Vorob'yev and Ivan stretched Miles's nerves still further. He followed the gliding servant down a couple of corridors, and across a little open garden thick with moss and tiny flowers misted with dew. The noises from the reception hall still carried faintly through the damp air. They entered a small building, open to the garden on two sides and floored with dark wood that made his black boots echo unevenly in time with his limping stride. In a dim recess of the pavilion, a woman-sized pearlescent sphere floated a few centimeters above the polished floor, which reflected an inverted halo from its light.

"Leave us," a voice from the sphere directed the servant, who bowed and withdrew, eyes downcast. The transmission through the force screen gave the voice a low, flat timbre.

The silence lengthened. Maybe she'd never seen a physically imperfect man before. Miles bowed and waited, trying to look cool and suave, and not stunned and wildly curious.

"So, Lord Vorkosigan," came the voice again at last. "Here I am."

"Er . . . quite." Miles hesitated. "And just who are you, milady, besides a very pretty soap-bubble?"

There was a longer pause, then, "I am the haut Rian Degtiar. Servant of the Celestial Lady, and Handmaiden of the Star Crèche."

Another flowery haut-title that gave no clue to its function. He could name every ghem-lord on the Cetagandan General Staff, all the satrap governors and their ghem-officers, but this female haut-babble was new to him. But the Celestial Lady was the polite name for the late Empress haut Lisbet Degtiar, and that name at least he knew—

"You are a relative of the late Dowager Empress, milady?"

"I am of her genomic constellation, yes. Three generations removed. I have served her half my life."

A lady-in-waiting, all right. One of the old Empress's personal retinue, then, the most inward of insiders. *Very* high rank, probably very aged as well. "Uh . . . you're not related to a ghem-lord named Yenaro, by chance, are you?"

"Who?" Even through the force-screen the voice conveyed utter bafflement.

"Never mind. Clearly not important." His legs were beginning to throb. Getting the damn boots back off when he returned to the embassy was going to be an even better trick than getting them on had been. "I could not help noticing your serving woman. Are there many folk around here with no hair?"

"It is not a woman. It is ba."

"Ba?"

"The neuter ones, the Emperor's high-slaves. In his Celestial Father's time it was the fashion to make them smooth like that."

Ah. Genetically-engineered, genderless servants. He'd heard rumors about them, mostly connected, illogically enough, with sexual scenarios that had more to do with the teller's hopeful fantasies than with any likely reality. But they were reputed to be a race utterly loyal to the lord who had, after all, literally created them. "So . . . not all ba are hairless, but all the hairless ones are ba?" he worked it out.

"Yes . . ." More silence, then, "Why have you come to the Celestial Garden, Lord Vorkosigan?"

His brow wrinkled. "To hold up Barrayar's honor in this circu—um, solemn procession, and to present your late Empress's bier-gift. I'm an envoy. By appointment of Emperor Gregor Vorbarra, whom *I* serve. In my own small way."

Another, longer pause. "You mock me in my misery."

"*What?*"

"What do you *want*, Lord Vorkosigan?"

"What do *I* want? You called me here, Lady, isn't it the other way around?" He rubbed his neck, tried again. "Er . . . can I help you, by chance?"

"You?!"

Her astonished tone stung him. "Yeah, me! I'm not as . . ." *incompetent as I look.* "I've been known to accomplish a thing or two, in my time. But if you won't give me a clue as to what this is all about, I can't. I will if I do know but I can't if I don't. Don't you see?" Now he had confused himself, tongue-tangled. "Look, can we start this conversation over?" He bowed low. "Good day, I am Lord Miles Vorkosigan of Barrayar. How may I assist you, milady?"

"Thief—!"

The light dawned at last. "*Oh.* Oh, no. I am a Vorkosigan, and no thief, milady. Though as possibly a recipient of stolen property, I may be a fence," he allowed judiciously.

More baffled silence; perhaps she was not familiar with criminal jargon. Miles went on a little desperately, "Have you, uh, by chance lost an object? Rod-shaped electronic device with a bird-crest seal on the cap?"

"You have it!" Her voice was a wail of dismay.

"Well, not *on* me."

Her voice went low, throaty, desperate. "You still have it. You must return it to me."

"Gladly, if you can prove it belongs to you. I certainly don't pretend it belongs to me," he added pointedly.

"You would do this . . . for nothing?"

"For the honor of my name, and, er . . . I *am* ImpSec. I'd do almost anything for information. Satisfy my curiosity, and the deed is done."

Her voice came back in a shocked whisper, "You mean you don't even know what it *is*?"

The silence stretched for so long after that, he was beginning to be afraid the old lady had fainted dead away in there. Processional music wafted faintly through the air from the great pavilion.

"Oh, shi—er, oh. That damn parade is starting, and I'm supposed to be near the front. Milady, how can I reach you?"

"You can't." Her voice was suddenly breathless. "I have to go too. I'll send for you." The white bubble rose, and began to float away.

"Where? When—?" The music was building toward the start-cue.

"Say nothing of this!"

He managed a sketchy bow at her retreating maybe-back, and began hobbling hastily across the garden. He had a horrible feeling he was about to be very publicly late.

When he'd wended his way back into the reception area, he found the scene was every bit as bad as he'd feared. A line of people was advancing to the main exit, toward the tower buildings, and Vorob'yev in the Barrayaran delegation's place was dragging his feet, creating an obvious gap, and staring around urgently. He spotted Miles and mouthed silently, *Hurry up, dammit!* Miles hobbled faster, feeling as if every eye in the room was on him.

Ivan, with an exasperated look on his face, handed over the box to him as he arrived. "Where the hell were you all this time, in the lav? I looked there—"

"Sh. Tell you later. I've just had the most bizarre . . ." Miles struggled with the heavy maplewood box, straightening it around into an appropriate presentational position. He marched forward across a courtyard paved with more carved jade, catching up at last with the delegation in front of them just as they reached the door to one of the high-towered buildings. They all filed into an echoing rotunda. Miles spied a few white bubbles in the line ahead, but there was no telling if one was his old haut-lady. The game plan called for everyone to slowly circle the bier, genuflect, and lay their gifts in a spiral pattern in order of seniority/status/clout, then file out the opposite doors to the Northern Pavilion (for the haut-lords and ghem-lords), or the Eastern Pavilion (for the galactic ambassadors) where a funereal luncheon would be served.

But the steady procession stopped, and began to pile up in the wide arched doorways. From the rotunda ahead, instead of quiet music and hushed, shuffling footsteps, a startled babble poured. Voices were raised in sharp astonishment, then other voices in even sharper command.

"What's gone wrong?" Ivan wondered, craning his neck. "Did somebody faint or something?"

Since Miles's eye-level view was of the shoulders of the man ahead of him, he could scarcely answer this. With a lurch, the line began to proceed again. It reached the rotunda, but then was shunted out a door immediately to the left. A ghem-commander stood at the intersection, directing traffic with low-voiced instructions, repeated over and over, "Please retain your gifts and proceed directly around the outside walkway to the Eastern Pavilion, please retain your gifts and proceed directly to the Eastern Pavilion, all will be re-ordered presently, please retain—"

At the center of the rotunda, above everyone's heads on a great catafalque, lay the Dowager Empress in state. Even in death outlander eyes were not invited to look upon her. Her bier was surrounded by a force-bubble, made translucent; only a shadow of her form was visible through it, as if through gauze, a white-clad, slight, sleeping ghost. A line of mixed ghem-guards apparently just drafted from the passing satrap governors stood in a row from catafalque to wall on either side of the bier, shielding something else from the passing eyes.

Miles couldn't stand it. *After all, they can't massacre me here in front of everybody, can they?* He jammed the maplewood box at Ivan, and ducked under the elbow of the ghem-officer trying to shoo everyone out the other door. Smiling pleasantly, his hands held open and empty, he slipped between two startled ghem-guards, who were clearly not expecting such a rude and impudent move.

On the other side of the catafalque, in the position reserved for the first gift of the haut-lord of highest status, lay a dead body. Its throat was cut. Quantities of fresh red blood pooled on the shimmering green malachite floor all around, soaking into the gray-and-white palace servitor's uniform. A thin jeweled knife was clutched rigorously in its outflung right hand. *It* was exactly the term for the corpse, too. A bald, eyebrowless, man-shaped creature, elderly but not frail . . . Miles recognized their intruder from the personnel pod even without the false hair. His own heart seemed to stop in astonishment.

Somebody's just raised the stakes in this little game.

The highest-ranking ghem-officer in the room swooped down upon him. Even through the swirl of face paint his smile was fixed, the look of a man constrained to be polite to someone he would more naturally have preferred to bludgeon to the pavement. "Lord Vorkosigan, would you rejoin your delegation, please?"

"Of course. Who was that poor fellow?"

The ghem-commander made little herding motions at him— the Cetagandan was not fool enough to actually touch him, of course—and Miles allowed himself to be moved off. Grateful, irate, and flustered, the man was actually surprised into an unguarded reply. "It is Ba Lura, the Celestial Lady's most senior servitor. The Ba has served her for sixty years and more—it seems to have wished to follow on and serve her in death as well. A most tasteless gesture, to do it *here* . . ." The ghem-commander buffeted Miles near enough to the again-stopped line of delegates for Ivan's long arm to reach out, grab him, and pull him in, and march him doorward with a firm fist in the middle of his back.

"What the hell is going *on*?" Ivan bent his head to hiss in Miles's ear from behind.

And where were you when the murder took place, Lord Vorkosigan? Except that it didn't look like a murder, it really did look like a suicide. Done in a most archaic manner. Less than thirty minutes ago. While he had been off talking with the mysterious white bubble, who might or might not have been haut Rian Degtiar, how the hell was he to tell? The corridor seemed to be spinning, but Miles supposed it was only his brain.

"You should not have gotten out of line, my lord," said Vorob'yev severely. "Ah . . . what was it you saw?"

Miles's lip curled, but he tamped it back down. "One of the late Dowager Empress's oldest ba servants has just cut its throat at the foot of her bier. I didn't know the Cetagandans made a fashion of human sacrifice. Not officially, anyway."

Vorob'yev's lips pursed in a soundless whistle, then flashed a brief, instantly stifled grin. "How *awkward* for them," he purred. "They are going to have an interesting scramble, trying to retrieve *this* ceremony."

Yes. So if the creature was so loyal, why did it arrange what it must have known would be a major embarrassment for its masters? Posthumous revenge? Admittedly, with Cetagandans that's the safest kind. . . .

By the time they completed an interminable hike around the outside of the central towers to the pavilion on the eastern side, Miles's legs were killing him. In a huge hall, the several hundred galactic delegates were being seated at tables by an army of ser-vitors, all moving just a little faster than strict dignity would have preferred. Since some of the bier-gifts the other delegates carried were even bulkier than the Barrayarans' maplewood box, the seating was going slowly and more awkwardly than planned, with a lot of people jumping up and down and re-arranging themselves, to the servitors' evident dismay. Somewhere deep in the bowels of the building Miles pictured a squadron of harried Cetagandan cooks swearing many colorful and obscene Cetagandan oaths.

Miles spotted the Vervani delegation being seated about a third of the way across the room. He took advantage of the confusion to slip out of his assigned chair, weave around several tables, and try to seize a word with Mia Maz.

He stood by her elbow, and smiled tensely. "Good afternoon, m'lady Maz. I have to talk—"

"Lord Vorkosigan! I tried to talk with you—" they cut across each other's greetings.

"You first." He ducked his head at her.

"I tried to call you at your embassy earlier, but you'd already left. What in the world happened in the rotunda, do you have any idea? For the Cetagandans to alter a ceremony of this magnitude in the middle—it's unheard of."

"They didn't exactly have a choice. Well, I suppose they could have ignored the body and just carried on around it—*I* think that would have been much more impressive, personally—but evidently they decided to clean it up first." Again Miles repeated what he was beginning to think of as "the official version" of Ba Lura's suicide. He had the total attention of everyone within earshot. To hell with it, the rumors would be flying soon enough no matter what he said or didn't say.

"Did you have any luck with that little research question I posed to you last night?" Miles continued. "I, uh . . . don't think this is the time or place to discuss it, but . . ."

"Yes, and yes," Maz said.

And not over any holovid transmission channel on this planet, either, Miles thought, *supposedly secured or not.* "Can you stop by the Barrayaran Embassy, directly after this? We'll . . . take tea, or something."

"I think that would be very appropriate," Maz said. She watched him with newly intensified curiosity in her dark eyes.

"I need a lesson in etiquette," Miles added, for the benefit of their interested nearby listeners.

Maz's eyes twinkled in something that might have been suppressed amusement. "So I have heard it said, my lord," she murmured.

"By—" *whom?* he choked off. *Vorob'yev, I fear.* " 'Bye," he finished instead, rapped the table cheerily, and retreated back to his proper place. Vorob'yev watched Miles seat himself with a slightly dangerous look in his eyes that suggested he was thinking of putting a leash on the peripatetic young envoy soon, but he made no comment aloud.

By the time they had eaten their way through about twenty courses of tiny delicacies, which more than made up in numbers what they lacked in volume, the Cetagandans had reorganized themselves. The haut-lord majordomo was apparently one of those commanders who was never more masterly than when in retreat, for he managed to get everyone marshaled in the correct order of seniority again even though the line was now being cycled through the rotunda in reverse. One sensed the majordomo would be cutting *his* throat later, in the proper place and with the proper ceremony, and not in this dreadful harum-scarum fashion.

Miles laid down the maplewood box on the malachite floor in the second turning of the growing spiral of gifts, about a meter from where Ba Lura had poured out its life. The unmarked, perfectly polished floor wasn't even damp. And had the Cetagandan security people had time to do a forensics scan before the cleanup? Or had someone been counting on the hasty destruction of the subtler evidence? *Damn, I wish I could have been in charge of this, just now.*

The white float-cars were waiting on the other side of the Eastern Pavilion, to carry the emissaries back to the gates of the Celestial Garden. The entire ceremony had run only about an hour late, but Miles's sense of time was inverted from his first whimsical vision of Xanadu as Faerie. He felt as if a hundred years had gone by inside the dome, while only a morning had passed in the outside world. He winced painfully in the bright afternoon light, as Vorob'yev's sergeant-driver brought the embassy aircar to their pickup point. Miles fell gratefully into his seat.

I think they're going to have to cut these bloody boots off, when we get back home.

Chapter Four

"Pull," Miles said, and set his teeth.

Ivan grasped his boot by the ankle and heel, braced his knee against the end of the couch upon which Miles lay, and yanked dutifully.

"Yeow!"

Ivan stopped. "Does that hurt?"

"Yes, keep going, dammit."

Ivan glanced around Miles's personal suite. "Maybe you ought to go downstairs to the embassy infirmary again."

"Later. I am not going to let that butcher of a physician dissect my best boots. Pull."

Ivan put his back into it, and the boot at last came free. He studied it in his hand a moment, and smiled slowly. "You know, you're not going to be able to get the other one off without me," he observed.

"So?"

"So . . . give."

"Give what?"

"Knowing your usual humor, I'd have thought you'd be as amused by the idea of an extra corpse in the funeral chamber as Vorob'yev was, but you came back looking like you'd just seen your grandfather's ghost."

"The ba had cut its throat. It was a messy scene."

"I think you've seen messier corpses."

Oh, yes. Miles eyed his remaining booted leg, which was throbbing, and pictured himself limping through the corridors of the embassy seeking a less demanding valet. No. He sighed. "Messier, but no stranger. You'd have twitched too. We met the ba yesterday, you and I. You wrestled with it in the personnel pod."

Ivan glanced toward the comconsole desk drawer where the mysterious rod remained concealed, and swore. "That does it. We've got to report this to Vorob'yev."

"If it *was* the same ba," Miles put in hastily. "For all I know, the Cetagandans clone their servants in batches, and the one we saw yesterday was this one's twin or something."

Ivan hesitated. "You think so?"

"I don't know, but I know where I can find out. Just let me have one more pass at this, before we send up the flag, please? I've asked Mia Maz from the Vervani embassy to stop in and see me. If you wait . . . I'll let you sit in."

Ivan contemplated this bribe. "Boot!" Miles demanded, while he was thinking. Somewhat absently, Ivan helped pull it off.

"All right," he said at last, "but after we talk to her, we report to ImpSec."

"Ivan, I *am* ImpSec," snapped Miles. "Three years of training and field experience, remember? Do me the honor of grasping that I may just possibly know what I'm doing!" *I wish to hell I knew what I was doing.* Intuition was nothing but the subconscious processing of subliminal clues, he was fairly sure, but *I feel it in my bones* made too uncomfortably thin a public defense for his actions. *How can you know something before you know it?* "Give me a chance."

Ivan departed for his own room to change clothes without making any promises. Freed of the boots, Miles staggered to his washroom to gulp down some more painkillers, and skin out of his formal House mourning and into loose black fatigues. Judging by the embassy's protocol list, Miles's private chamber was going to be the only place he could wear the fatigues.

Ivan returned all too soon, breezily trim in undress greens, but before he could continue asking questions Miles couldn't answer or demanding justifications Miles couldn't offer, the comconsole chimed. It was the staffer from the embassy's lobby, downstairs.

"Mia Maz is here to see you, Lord Vorkosigan," the man reported. "She says she has an appointment."

"That's correct. Uh . . . can you bring her up here, please?" Was his suite monitored by embassy security? He wasn't about to draw attention by inquiring. But no. If ImpSec were eavesdropping, he'd certainly have had to deal with some stiff interrogation from their offices below-stairs by now, either via Vorob'yev or directly. They were extending him the courtesy of privacy, as yet, in his personal space—though probably not on his comconsole. Every public forum in the building was guaranteed to be bugged, though.

The staffer ushered Maz to Miles's door in a few moments, and Miles and Ivan hastened to get her comfortably seated. She too had stopped to change clothes, and was now wearing a formfitting jump suit and knee-length vest suitable for street wear. Even at forty-odd her form supported the style very nicely. Miles got rid of the staffer by sending him off with an order for tea and, at Ivan's request, wine.

Miles settled down on the other end of the couch and smiled hopefully at the Vervani woman. Ivan was forced offsides to a nearby chair. "Milady Maz. Thank you for coming."

"Just Maz, please." She smiled in return. "We Vervani don't use such titles. I'm afraid we have trouble taking them seriously."

"You must be good at keeping a straight face, or you could not function so well here."

Her dimple winked at him. "Yes, my lord."

Ah yes, Vervain was one of those so-called democracies; not quite as insanely egalitarian as the Betans, but they had a definite cultural drift in that direction. "My mother would agree with you," Miles conceded. "She would have seen no inherent difference between the two corpses in the rotunda. Except their method of arriving there, of course. I take it this suicide was an unusual and unexpected event?"

"Unprecedented," said Maz, "and if you know Cetagandans, you know just how strong a term that is."

"So Cetagandan servants do not routinely accompany their masters in death like a pagan sacrifice."

"I suppose the Ba Lura was unusually close to the Empress, it had served her for so long," said the Vervani woman. "Since before any of us were born."

"Ivan was wondering if the haut-lords cloned their servants."

Ivan cast Miles a slightly dirty look, for being made the stalking horse, but did not voice an objection.

"The ghem-lords sometimes do," said Maz, "but not the haut-lords, and most certainly never the Imperial Household. They consider each servitor as much a work of art as any of the other objects with which they surround themselves. Everything in the Celestial Garden must be unique, if possible handmade, and perfect. That applies to their biological constructs as well. They leave mass production to the masses. I'm not sure if it's a virtue or a vice, the way the haut do it, but in a world flooded with virtual realities and infinite duplication, it's strangely refreshing. If only they weren't such awful snobs about it."

"Speaking of things artistic," said Miles, "you said you had some luck identifying that icon?"

"Yes." Her gaze flicked up to fix on his face. "Where did you say you saw it, Lord Vorkosigan?"

"I didn't."

"Hm." She half-smiled, but apparently decided not to fence with him over the point just now. "It is the seal of the Star Crèche, and not something I'd expect an outlander to run across every day. In fact, it's not something I'd expect an outlander to run across *any* day. It's most private."

Check. "And hautish?"

"Supremely."

"And, um . . . just what is the Star Crèche?"

"You don't know?" Maz seemed a little surprised. "Well, I suppose you fellows have spent all your time studying Cetagandan military matters."

"A great deal of time, yes," Ivan sighed.

"The Star Crèche is the private name of the haut-race's gene bank."

"Oh, that. I was dimly aware of—do they keep backup copies of themselves, then?" Miles asked.

"The Star Crèche is far more than that. Among the haut, they don't deal directly with each other to have egg and sperm united and the resulting embryo deposited in a uterine replicator, the way normal people do. Every genetic cross is negotiated and a contract drawn between the heads of the two genetic lines—the Cetagandans call them constellations, though I suppose you Barrayarans would call them clans. That contract in turn must be approved by the Emperor, or rather, by the senior female in the Emperor's line, and marked by the seal of the Star Crèche. For the last half-century, since the present regime began, that senior female has been haut Lisbet Degtiar, the Emperor's mother. It's not just a formality, either. Any genetic alterations—and the haut do a lot of them—have to be examined and cleared by the Empress's board of geneticists, before they are allowed into the haut genome. You asked me if the haut-women had any power. The Dowager Empress had final approval or veto over every haut birth."

"Can the Emperor override her?"

Maz pursed her lips. "I truly don't know. The haut are incredibly reserved about all this. If there are any behind-the-scenes power struggles, the news certainly doesn't leak out past the Celestial Garden's gates. I do know I've never heard of such a conflict."

"So . . . who is the new senior female? Who inherits the seal?"

"Ah! Now you've touched on something interesting." Maz was warming to her subject. "Nobody knows, or at least, the Emperor hasn't made the public announcement. The seal is supposed to be held by the Emperor's mother if she lives, or by the mother of the heir-apparent if the dowager is deceased. But the Cetagandan emperor has not yet selected his heir. The seal of the Star Crèche and all the rest of the empress's regalia is supposed to be handed over to the new senior female as the last act of the funeral rites, so he has ten more days to make up his mind. I imagine that decision is the focus of a great deal of attention right now, among the haut-women. No new genomic contracts can be approved until the transfer is completed."

Miles puzzled this through. "He has three young sons, right? So he must select one of their mothers."

"Not necessarily," said Maz. "He could hand things over to an Imperial aunt, one of his mother's kin, as an interim move."

A diffident rap at Miles's door indicated the arrival of the tea. The Barrayaran embassy's kitchen had sent along a perfectly redundant three-tiered tray of little petit fours as well. Someone had been doing their homework, for Maz murmured, "Ooh, my favorite." One feminine hand dove for some dainty chocolate confections despite the Imperial luncheon they'd recently consumed. The embassy steward poured tea, opened the wine, and withdrew as discreetly as he had entered.

Ivan took a gulp from his crystal cup, and asked in puzzlement, "Do the haut-lords marry, then? One of these genetic contracts must be the equivalent of a marriage, right?"

"Well . . . no." Maz swallowed her third chocolate morsel, and chased it with tea. "There are several kinds of contracts. The simplest is for a sort of one-time usage of one's genome. A single child is created, who becomes the ... I hesitate to use the term *property* ... who is registered with the constellation of the male parent, and is raised in his constellation's crèche. You understand, these decisions are not made by the principals— in fact, the two parents may never even meet each other. These contracts are chosen at the most senior level of the constellation, by the oldest and presumably wisest heads, with an eye to either capturing a favored genetic line, or setting up for a desirable cross in the ensuing generation.

"At the other extreme is a lifetime monopoly—or longer, in the case of Imperial crosses. When a haut-woman is chosen to be the mother of a potential heir, the contract is absolutely exclusive— she must never have contracted her genome previously, and can never do so again, unless the emperor chooses to have more than one child by her. She goes to live in the Celestial Garden, in her own pavilion, for the rest of her life."

Miles grimaced. "Is that a reward, or a punishment?"

"It's the best shot at power a haut-woman can ever get—a chance of becoming a dowager empress, if her son—and it's always and only a son—is ultimately chosen to succeed his father. Even being the mother of one of the losers, a prince-candidate or satrap governor, is no bad deal. It's also why, in an apparently patriarchal culture, the output of the haut-constellations is skewed to girls. A constellation head—clan chief, in Barrayaran terminology—can never become an emperor or the father of an emperor, no matter how brightly his sons may shine. But through his daughters, he has a chance to become the grandfather of one. Advantages, as you may imagine, then accrue to the dowager empress's constellation. The Degtiar were not particularly important until fifty years ago."

"So the emperor has sons," Miles worked this out, "but everyone else is mad for daughters. But only once or twice a century, when a new emperor succeeds, can anyone win the game."

"That's about right."

"So ... where does sex fit into all this?" asked Ivan plaintively.

"Nowhere," said Maz.

"Nowhere!"

Maz laughed at his horrified expression. "Yes, the haut have sexual relations, but it's purely a social game. They even have long-lasting sexual friendships that could almost qualify as marriages, sometimes. I was about to say there's nothing formalized, except that the etiquette of all the shifting associations is so incredibly complex. I guess the word I want is *legalized*, rather than formalized, because the rituals are intense. And weird, really weird, sometimes, from what little I've been able to gather of it all. Fortunately, the haut are such racists, they almost never go slumming outside their genome, so you are not likely to encounter those pitfalls personally."

"Oh," said Ivan. He sounded a little disappointed. "But . . . if the haut don't marry and set up their own households, when and how do they leave home?"

"They never do."

"Ow! You mean they live with, like, their mothers, forever?"

"Well, not with their mothers, of course. Their grandparents or great-grandparents. But the youth—that is, anyone under fifty or so—do live as pensioners of their constellation. I wonder if that is at the root of why so many older haut become reclusive. They live apart because they finally *can*."

"But—what about all those famous and successful ghem-generals and ghem-lords who've won haut-lady wives?" asked Miles.

Maz shrugged. "They can't all aspire to become Imperial mothers, can they? Actually, I would point out this aspect particularly to you, Lord Vorkosigan. Have you ever wondered how the haut, who are not noted for their military prowess, control the ghem, who are?"

"Oh, yes. I've been expecting this crazy Cetagandan double-decked aristocracy to fall apart ever since I learned about it. How can you control guns with, with, art contests? How can a bunch of perfumed poetasters like the haut-lords buffalo whole ghem-armies?"

Maz smiled. "The Cetagandan ghem-lords would call it the loyalty justly due to superior culture and civilization. The fact is that anyone who's competent enough or powerful enough to pose a threat gets genetically co-opted. There is no higher reward in the Cetagandan system than to be Imperially assigned a haut-lady wife. The ghem-lords are all panting for it. It's the ultimate social and political coup."

"You're suggesting the haut control the ghem through these wives?" said Miles. "I mean, I'm sure the haut-women are lovely and all, but the ghem-generals can be such hard-bitten cast-iron bastards—I can't imagine anyone who gets to the top in the Cetagandan Empire being that susceptible."

"If I knew how the haut-women do it," Maz sighed, "I'd bottle it and sell it. No, better—I think I'd keep it for myself. But it seems to have worked for the last several hundred years. It is not, of course, the *only* method of Imperial control, to be sure. Only the most overlooked one. I find that, in itself, significant. The haut are nothing if not subtle."

"Does the, uh, haut-bride come with a dowry?" Miles asked.

Maz smiled again, and polished off another chocolate confection. "You have hit upon an important point, Lord Vorkosigan. She does not."

"I'd think keeping a haut-wife in the style to which she is accustomed could get rather expensive."

"Very."

"So . . . if the Cetagandan emperor wished to depress an excessively successful subject, he could award him a few haut-wives and bankrupt him?"

"I . . . don't think it's done quite so obviously as all that. But the element is there. You are very acute, my lord."

Ivan asked, "But how does the haut-lady who gets handed out like a good-conduct medal feel about it all? I mean . . . if the highest haut-lady ambition is to become an Imperial monopoly, this has got to be the ultimate opposite. To be permanently dumped out of the haut-genome—their descendants never marry back into the haut, do they?"

"No," confirmed Maz. "I believe the psychology of it all is a bit peculiar. For one thing, the haut-bride immediately outranks any other wives the ghem-lord may have acquired, and her children automatically become his heirs. This can set up some interesting tensions in his household, particularly if it comes, as it usually does, in mid-life when his other marital associations may be of long standing."

"It must be a ghem-lady's nightmare, to have one of these haut-women dropped on her husband," Ivan mused. "Don't they ever object? Make their husbands turn down the honor?"

"Apparently it's not an honor one can refuse."

"Mm." With difficulty, Miles pulled his imagination away from these side-fascinations, and back to his most immediate worry. "That seal of the Star Crèche thing—I don't suppose you have a picture of it?"

"I brought a number of vids with me, yes, my lord," said Maz. "With your permission, we can run them on your com-console."

Ooh, I adore competent women. Do you have a younger sister, milady Maz? "Yes, please," said Miles.

They all trooped over to the chamber's comconsole desk, and Maz began a quick illustrated lecture on haut crests and the several dozen assorted Imperial seals. "Here it is, my lord—the seal of the Star Crèche."

It was a clear cubical block, measuring maybe fifteen centimeters on a side, with the bird-pattern incised in red lines upon its top. *Not* the mysterious rod. Miles exhaled with relief. The terror that had been riding him ever since Maz had mentioned the seal, that he and Ivan might have accidentally stolen a piece of the Imperial regalia, faded. The rod was some kind of Imperial gizmo, obviously, and would have to be returned—anonymously, by preference—but at least it wasn't—

Maz called up the next unit of data, "And *this* object is the Great Key of the Star Crèche, which is handed over along with the seal," she went on.

Ivan choked on his wine. Miles, faint, leaned on the desk and smiled fixedly at the image of the rod. The original lay some few centimeters under his hand, in the drawer.

"And, ah—just what *is* the Great Key of the Star Crèche, m'la—Maz?" Miles managed to murmur. "What does it do?"

"I'm not quite sure. At one time in the past, I believe it had something to do with data retrieval from the haut gene banks, but the actual device may only be ceremonial by now. I mean, it's a couple of hundred years old. It has to be obsolete."

We hope. Thank God he hadn't dropped it. Yet. "I see."

"*Miles . . .*" muttered Ivan.

"Later," Miles hissed to him out of the corner of his mouth. "I understand your concern."

Ivan mouthed something obscene at him, over the seated Maz's head.

Miles leaned against the comconsole desk, and screwed up his features in a realistic wince.

"Something wrong, my lord?" Maz glanced up, concerned.

"I'm afraid my legs are bothering me, a bit. I had probably better pay another visit to the embassy physician, after this."

"Would you prefer to continue this later?" Maz asked instantly.

"Well . . . to tell you the truth, I think I've had about all the etiquette lessons I can absorb for one afternoon."

"Oh, there's *lots* more." But apparently he was looking realistically pale, too, for she rose, adding, "Far too much for one session, to be sure. Are your injuries much troubling you? I didn't realize they were that severe."

Miles shrugged, as if in embarrassment. After a suitable exchange of parting amenities, and a promise to call on his Vervani tutor again very soon, Ivan took over the hostly duties, and escorted Maz back downstairs.

He returned immediately, to seal the door behind him and pounce on Miles. "Do you have any idea how much trouble we're in?" he cried.

Miles sat before the comconsole, re-reading the official, and entirely inadequate, description of the Great Key, while its image floated hauntingly before his nose above the vid plate. "Yes. I also know how we're going to get out of it. Do you know as much?"

This gave Ivan pause. "What else do you know that I don't?"

"If you will just leave it to me, I believe I can get this thing back to its rightful owner with no one the wiser."

"Its rightful owner is the Cetagandan emperor, according to what Maz said."

"Well, ultimately, yes. I should say, back to its rightful keeper. Who, if I read the signs right, is as chagrined about losing it as we are in finding it. If I can get it back to her quietly, I don't think she's going to go around proclaiming how she lost it. Although . . . I do wonder how she *did* lose it." Something was not adding up, just below his level of conscious perception.

"We mugged an Imperial servitor, that's how!"

"Yes, but what was Ba Lura doing with the thing on an orbital transfer station in the first place? Why had it disabled the security monitors in the docking bay?"

"Lura was taking the Great Key somewhere, obviously. To the Great Lock, for all I know." Ivan paced around the comconsole. "So the poor sod cuts its throat the next morning 'cause it lost its charge, its trust, courtesy of us—hell, Miles. I feel like we just killed that old geezer. And it never did us any harm, it just blundered into the wrong place and had the bad luck to startle us."

"Is that what happened?" Miles murmured. "Really . . . ?" *Is that why I am so desperately determined for the story to be something, anything, else?* The scenario hung together. The old ba, charged with transporting the precious object, loses the Great Key to some out-lander barbarians, confesses its disgrace to its mistress, and kills itself in expiation. Wrap. Miles felt ill. "So . . . if the Key was that impor-tant, why wasn't the ba traveling with a squadron of Imperial ghem-guards?"

"*God* Miles, I wish it *had* been!"

A firm knock sounded on Miles's door. Miles hastily shut down the comconsole and unsealed the door lock. "Come in."

Ambassador Vorob'yev entered, and favored him with a semi-cordial nod. He held a sheaf of delicately colored, scented papers in his hand.

"Hello, my lords. Did you find your tutorial with Maz useful?"

"Yes, sir," said Miles.

"Good. I thought you would. She's excellent." Vorobyev held up the colored papers. "While you were in session, this invitation arrived for you both, from Lord Yenaro. Along with assorted profound apologies for last night's incident. Embassy security has opened, scanned, and chemically analyzed it. They report the organic esters harmless." With this safety pronouncement, he handed the papers across to Miles. "It is up to you, whether or not to accept. If you concur that the unfortunate side-effect of the sculpture's power field was an accident, your attendance might be a good thing. It would complete the apology, repairing face all around."

"Oh, we'll go, sure." The apology and invitation were hand-calligraphed in the best Cetagandan style. "But I'll keep my eyes open. Ah . . . wasn't Colonel Vorreedi due back today?"

Vorob'yev grimaced. "He's run into some tedious complications. But in view of that odd incident at the Marilacan embassy, I've sent a subordinate to replace him. He should be back tomorrow. Perhaps . . . do you wish a bodyguard? Not openly, of course, that would be another insult."

"Mm . . . we'll have a driver, right? Let him be one of your trained men, have backup on call, give us both com links, and have him wait for us nearby."

"Very well, Lord Vorkosigan. I'll make arrangements," Vorob'yev nodded. "And . . . regarding the incident in the rotunda earlier today—"

Miles's heart pounded. "Yes?"

"Please don't break ranks like that again."

"Did you receive a complaint?" *And from whom?*

"One learns to interpret certain pained looks. The Cetagandans would consider it impolite to protest—but should unpleasant incidents pile high enough, not too impolite for them to take some sort of indirect and arcane retaliation. You two will be gone in ten days, but I will still be here. Please don't make my job any more difficult than it already is, eh?"

"Understood, sir," said Miles brightly. Ivan was looking intensely worried—was he going to bolt, pour out confessions to Vorob'yev? Not yet, evidently, for the ambassador waved himself back out without Ivan throwing himself at his feet.

"*Nearby* doesn't cut it, for a bodyguard," Ivan pointed out, as soon as the door sealed again.

"Oh, you're beginning to see it my way now, are you? But if we go to Yenaro's at all, I can't avoid risk. I have to eat, drink, and breathe—all routes for attack an armed guard can't do much about. Anyway, my greatest defense is that it would be a grievous insult to the Cetagandan emperor for anyone to seriously harm a galactic delegate to his august mother's funeral. I predict, should another accident occur, it will be equally subtle and non-fatal." *And equally infuriating.*

"Oh, yeah? When there's been one fatality already?" Ivan stood silent for a long time. "Do you think . . . all these incidents could possibly be related?" Ivan nodded toward the perfumed papers still in Miles's hand, and toward the comconsole desk drawer. "I admit, I don't see how."

"Do you think they could possibly all be unrelated coincidences?"

"Hm." Ivan frowned, digesting this. "So tell me," he pointed again to the desk drawer, "how *are* you planning to get rid of the Empress's dildo?"

Miles's mouth twitched, stifling a grin at the Ivan-diplomatic turn of phrase. "I can't tell you." *Mostly because I don't know yet myself.* But the haut Rian Degtiar had to be scrambling, right now. He fingered, as if absently, the silver eye-of-Horus ImpSec insignia pinned to his black collar. "There's a lady's reputation involved."

Ivan's eyes narrowed in scorn of this obvious appeal to Ivan's own brand of personal affairs. "Horseshit. *Are* you running some kind of secret rig for Simon Illyan?"

"If I were, I couldn't tell you, now could I?"

"Damned if I know." Ivan stared at him in frustration for another moment, then shrugged. "Well, it's your funeral."

Chapter Five

"Stop here," Miles instructed the groundcar's driver. The car swung smoothly to the side of the street and with a sigh of its fans settled to the pavement. Miles peered at the layout of Lord Yenaro's suburban mansion in the gathering dusk, mentally pairing the visual reality with the map he had studied back at the Barrayaran embassy.

The barriers around the estate, serpentine garden walls and concealing landscaping, were visual and symbolic rather than effective. The place had never been designed as a fortress of anything but privilege. A few higher sections of the rambling house glimmered through the trees, but even they seemed to focus inward rather than outward.

"Com link check, my lords?" the driver requested. Miles and Ivan both pulled the devices from their pockets and ran through the codes with him. "Very good, my lords."

"What's our backup?" Miles asked him.

"I have three units, arranged within call."

"I trust we've included a medic."

"In the lightflyer, fully equipped. I can put him down inside Lord Yenaro's courtyard in forty-five seconds."

"That should be sufficient. I don't expect a frontal assault. But I wouldn't be surprised if I encountered another little 'accident' of some sort. We'll walk from here, I think. I want to get the feel of the place."

"Yes, my lord." The driver popped the canopy for them, and Miles and Ivan exited.

"Is this what you call genteel poverty?" Ivan inquired, looking around as they strolled through open, unguarded gates and up Yenaro's curving drive.

Ah yes. The style might be different, but the scent of aristocratic decay was universal. Little signs of neglect were all around: unrepaired damage to the gates and walls, overgrown shrubbery, what appeared to be three-quarters of the mansion dark and closed-off.

"Vorob'yev had the embassy's ImpSec office make a background check of Lord Yenaro," Miles said. "Yenaro's grandfather, the failed ghem-general, left him the house but not the means to keep it up, having consumed his capital in his extended and presumably embittered old age. Yenaro's been in sole possession for about four years. He runs with an artsy crowd of young and unemployed ghem-lordlings, so his story holds up to that extent. But that thing in the Marilacan embassy's lobby was the first sculpture Yenaro's ever been known to produce. Curiously advanced, for a first try, don't you think?"

"If you're so convinced it was a trap, why are you sticking your hand in to try and trip another one?"

"No risk, no reward, Ivan."

"Just what reward are you envisioning?"

"Truth. Beauty. Who knows? Embassy security is also running a check on the workmen who actually built the sculpture. I expect it to be revealing."

At least he could make that much use of the machinery of ImpSec. Miles felt intensely conscious of the rod now riding concealed in his inner tunic pocket. He'd been carrying the Great Key in secret all day, through a tour of the city and an interminable afternoon performance of a Cetagandan classical dance company. This last treat had been arranged by Imperial decree especially for the off-planet envoys to the funeral. But the haut Rian Degtiar had not made her promised move to contact him yet. If he did not hear from his haut-lady by tomorrow . . . On one level, Miles was growing extremely sorry he had not taken the local ImpSec subordinates into his confidence on the very first day. But if he had, he would no longer be in charge of this little problem;

the decisions would all have been hiked to higher levels, out of his control. *The ice is thin. I don't want anyone heavier than me walking on it just yet.*

A servant met them at the mansion's door as they approached, escorting them into a softly lit entry foyer where they were greeted by their host. Yenaro was in dark robes similar to the ones he'd worn at the Marilacan embassy's reception; Ivan was clearly correct in his undress greens. Miles had chosen his ultra-formal House blacks. He wasn't sure how Yenaro would interpret the message, as honor, or reminder—*I'm the official envoy*—or warning—*don't mess with me.* But he was fairly certain it was not a nuance Yenaro would miss.

Yenaro glanced down at Miles's black boots. "And are your legs better now, Lord Vorkosigan?" he inquired anxiously.

"Much better, thank you," Miles smiled tightly in return. "I shall certainly live."

"I'm so glad." The tall ghem-lord led them around a few corners and down a short flight of steps to a large semicircular room wrapped around a peninsula of the garden, as if the house were undergoing some botanical invasion. The room was somewhat randomly furnished, apparently with items Yenaro had previously owned rather than by design; but the effect was pleasantly comfortable-bachelor. The lighting here, too, was soft, camouflaging shabbiness. A dozen ghem-types were already present, talking and drinking. The men outnumbered the women; two bore full face paint, most sported the cheek-decal of the younger set, and a few radical souls wore nothing above the neck but a little eye makeup. Yenaro introduced his Barrayaran exotics all around. None of the ghem were anyone Miles had heard of or studied, though one young man claimed a great-uncle on staff at Cetagandan headquarters.

An incense burner smoked on a cylindrical stand by the garden doors. One ghem-guest paused to inhale deeply. "Good one, Yenaro," he called to his host. "Your blend?"

"Thank you, yes," said Yenaro.

"More perfumes?" inquired Ivan.

"And a bit extra. That mixture also contains a mild relaxant suitable to the occasion. You would perhaps not care for it, Lord Vorkosigan."

Miles smiled stiffly. Just how much of an organic chemist was this man? Miles was reminded that the root word of *intoxication* was *toxic*. "Probably not. But I'd love to see your laboratory."

"Would you? I'll take you up, then. Most of my friends have no interest in the technical aspects, only in the results."

A young woman, listening nearby, drifted up at this and tapped Yenaro on the arm with one long fingernail glittering with patterned enamel. "Yes, dear Yenni, results. You promised me some, remember?" She was not the prettiest ghem-woman Miles had seen, but attractive enough in swirling jade-green robes, with thick pale hair clipped back and curling down to her shoulders in a pink-frosted froth.

"And I keep my promises," Lord Yenaro asserted. "Lord Vorkosigan, perhaps you would care to accompany us upstairs now?"

"Certainly."

"I'll stay and make new acquaintances, I think." Ivan bowed himself out of the party. The two tallest and most striking ghem-women present, a leggy blonde and a truly incredible redhead, were standing together across the room; Ivan somehow managed to make eye contact with both, and they favored him with inviting smiles. Miles sent up a short silent prayer to the guardian god of fools, lovers, and madmen, and turned to follow Yenaro and his female petitioner.

Yenaro's organic chemistry laboratory was sited in another building; lights came up as they approached across the garden. It proved to be a quite respectable installation, a long double room on the second floor—some of the money that wasn't going into home repairs was obviously ending up here. Miles walked around the benches, eyeing the molecular analyzers and computers while Yenaro rummaged among an array of little bottles for the promised perfume. All the raw materials were beautifully organized in correct chemical groupings, betraying a deep understanding and detailed love of the subject on the owner's part.

"Who assists you here?" Miles inquired.

"No one," said Yenaro. "I can't bear to have anyone else mucking about. They mess up my orderings, which I sometimes use to inspire my blends. It's not all science, you know."

Indeed. With a few questions, Miles led Yenaro on to talk about how he'd made the perfume for the woman. She listened for a while and then wandered off to sniff at experimental bottles, till Yenaro, with a pained smile, rescued them from her. Yenaro's expertise was less than professorial, but fully professional; any commercial cosmetics company would have hired him on the spot for their product development laboratory. So, and so. How did this square with the man who'd claimed *Hands are to be hired*?

Not at all, Miles decided with concealed satisfaction. Yenaro was unquestionably an artist, but an artist of esters. Not a sculptor. Someone else had supplied the undoubted technical expertise that had produced the fountain. And had that same somebody also supplied the technical information on Miles's personal weaknesses? *Let's call him . . . Lord X.* Fact One about Lord X: he had access to Cetagandan Security's most detailed reports on Barrayarans of military or political significance . . . and their sons. Fact Two: he had a subtle mind. Fact Three . . . there was no fact three. Yet.

They returned to the party to find Ivan ensconced on a couch between the two women, entertaining them—or at least, they were laughing encouragingly. The ghem-women fully matched Lady Gelle in beauty; the blonde might have been her sister. The redhead was even more arresting, with a cascade of amber curls falling past her shoulders, a perfect nose, lips that one might . . . Miles cut off the thought. No ghem-lady was going to invite *him* to dive into her dreams.

Yenaro departed briefly to oversee his servant—he seemed to have only one—and expedite the smooth arrival of fresh food and drinks. He returned with a small transparent pitcher of a pale ruby liquid. "Lord Vorpatril." He nodded at Ivan. "I believe you appreciate your beverages. Do try this one."

Miles went to alert-status, his heart thumping. Yenaro might not be a sculptor-assassin, but he would undoubtedly make a great poisoner. Yenaro poured from the pitcher into three little cups on a lacquered tray, and extended the tray to Ivan.

"Thanks." Ivan selected one at random.

"Oh, zlati ale," murmured one of the junior ghem-lords. Yenaro passed the tray to him, taking the last cup himself. Ivan sipped and raised his brows in surprised approval. Miles watched closely to be sure Yenaro actually swallowed. He did. Five different methods for presenting deadly drinks with just that maneuver and still being sure the victim received the right one, including the trick of the host consuming the antidote first, flashed through Miles's mind. But if he was going to be that paranoid, they ought not have come here in the first place. Yet he'd eaten and drunk nothing himself so far. *So what are you going to do, wait and see if Ivan falls over first, and then try it?*

Yenaro did not, this time, pause to confide to the two women bracketing Ivan the repulsive biological history of his birth. Hell. Maybe the incident with the fountain really had been an accident, and the man was sorry, and trying his very best to make it up to the Barrayarans. Nevertheless, Miles circled in, trying to get a closer look at Ivan's cup over his shoulder.

Ivan was in the process of the classic *I'm just resting my arm along the back of this couch* test of the redhead on his right, to see if she was going to flinch from or invite further physical contact. Ivan swiveled his head to repel his cousin with a toothy smile. "Go have a good time, Miles," he murmured. "Relax. Stop breathing up my neck."

Miles grimaced back in non-appreciation of the height-humor, and drifted off again. Some people just didn't want to be saved. He decided instead to try to talk with some of Yenaro's male friends, several of whom were clustered at the opposite end of the room.

It wasn't hard to get them to talk about themselves. It seemed that was all they had to talk about. Forty minutes of valiant effort in the art of conversation convinced Miles that most of Yenaro's friends had the minds of fleas. The only expertise they displayed was in witty commentary upon the personal lives of their equally idle compatriots: their clothes, various love affairs and the mismanagement thereof, sports—all spectator, none participatory, and mainly of interest due to wagers on the outcome—and the assorted latest commercial feelie dreams and other offerings, including erotic ones. This retreat from reality seemed to absorb by far the bulk of the ghem-lordlings' time and attention. Not one of them offered a word about anything of political or military interest. Hell, *Ivan* had more mental clout.

It was all a bit depressing. Yenaro's friends were excluded men, wasted wastrels. No one was excited about a career or service— they had none. Even the arts received only a ripple of interest. They were strictly feelie dream consumers, not producers. All in all, it was probably a good thing these youths had no political interests. They were just the sort of people who started revolutions but could not finish them, their idealism betrayed by their incompetence. Miles had met similar young men among the Vor, third or fourth sons who for whatever reason had not gained entry to a traditional military career, living as pensioners upon their families, but even they could look forward to some change in their status by mid-life. Given the average ghem life span, any chance of ascent up the social ladder by inheritance was still some eighty or ninety years off for most of Yenaro's set. They weren't inherently stupid—their genetics did not permit it—but their minds were damped down to some artificial horizon. Beneath the air of hectic sophistication, their lives were frozen in place. Miles almost shivered.

Miles decided to try out the women, if Ivan had left any for him. He excused himself from the group to pursue a drink—he might have left without explanation just as easily, for all anyone seemed to care about Lord Yenaro's most unusual, and shortest, guest. Miles helped himself at a bowl from which everyone else seemed to be ladling their drinks, and touched the cup to his lips, but did not swallow. He looked up to find himself under the gaze of a slightly older woman who had come late to the party with a couple of friends, and who had been lingering quietly on the fringes of the gathering. She smiled at him.

Miles smiled back and slid around the table to her side, composing a suitable opening line. She took the initiative from him.

"Lord Vorkosigan. Would you care to take a walk in the garden with me?"

"Why . . . certainly. Is Lord Yenaro's garden a sight to see?" *In the dark?*

"I think it will interest you." The smile dropped from her face as if wiped away with a cloth the moment she turned her back to the room, to be replaced with a look of grim determination. Miles fingered the com link in his trouser pocket, and followed in the perfumed wake of her robes. Once out of sight of the room's glass doors among the neglected shrubbery, her step quickened. She said nothing more. Miles limped after her. He was unsurprised when they came to a red-enameled, square-linteled gate and found a person waiting, a slight, androgynous shape with a dark hooded robe protecting its bald head from the night's gathering dew.

"The ba will escort you the rest of the way," said the woman.

"The rest of the way where?"

"A short walk." The ba spoke in a soft alto.

"Very well." Miles held up a restraining hand, and drew his com link from his pocket, and said into it, "Base. I'm leaving Yenaro's premises for a while. Track me, but don't interrupt me unless I call for you."

The driver's voice came back in a dubious tone. "Yes, my lord . . . where are you going?"

"I'm . . . taking a walk with a lady. Wish me luck."

"Oh." The driver's tone grew more amused, less dubious. "Good luck, my lord."

"Thank you." Miles closed the channel. "All right."

The woman seated herself on a rickety bench and drew her robes around herself with the air of one preparing for a lengthy wait. Miles followed the ba out the gate and past another residence, across a roadway, and into a shallow wooded ravine. The ba produced a hand-light to prevent stumbles on rocks and roots, politely playing it before Miles's polished boots, which were going to be a lot less polished if this went on very far . . . they climbed up out of the ravine into what was obviously the back portion of another suburban estate in an even more neglected condition than Yenaro's.

A dark bulk looming through the trees was an apparently deserted house. But they turned right on an overgrown path, the ba pausing to sweep damp branches out of Miles's way, and then back down toward the stream. They emerged in a wide clearing where a wooden pavilion stood—some ghem-lord's former favorite picnic spot for *al fresco* brunches, no doubt. Duckweed choked a pond, crowding out a few sad water-irises. They crossed the pond on an arched footbridge, which creaked so alarmingly Miles was momentarily glad he was no bigger. A faint, familiar pearlescent glow emanated from the pavilion's vine-veiled openings. Miles touched the Great Key hidden in his tunic, for reassurance. *Right. This is it.*

The ba servitor pulled aside some greenery, gestured Miles inside, and went to stand guard by the footbridge. Cautiously, Miles stepped within the small, one-roomed building.

The haut Rian Degtiar or a close facsimile sat, or stood, or something, the usual few centimeters above the floor, a blank pale sphere. She had to be riding in a float-chair. Her light seemed dimmed, stopped down to a furtive feeble glow. *Wait. Let her make the first move.* The moment stretched. Miles began to be afraid this conversation was going to be as disjointed as their first one, but then she spoke, in the same breathless, transmission-flattened voice he had heard before. "Lord Vorkosigan. I have contacted you as I said I would, to make arrangements for the safe return of my . . . thing."

"The Great Key," said Miles.

"You know what it is now?"

"I've been doing a little research, since our first chat."

She moaned. "What do you want of me? Money? I have none. Military secrets? I know none."

"Don't go coy on me, and don't panic. I want very little." Miles unfastened his tunic, and drew out the Great Key.

"Oh, you have it *here!* Oh, give it to me!" The pearl bobbed forward.

Miles stepped back. "Not so fast. I've kept it safe, and I'll give it back. But I feel I should get something in return. I merely want to know exactly how it came to be delivered, or mis-delivered, into my hands, and why."

"It's no business of yours, Barrayaran!"

"Perhaps not. But every instinct I own is crying out that this is some kind of setup, of me, or of Barrayar through me, and as a Barrayaran ImpSec officer that makes it very explicitly my business. I'm willing to tell you everything I saw and heard, but you must return the favor. To start with, I want to know what Ba Lura was doing with a piece of the late Empress's major regalia on a space station."

Her voice went low and tart. "Stealing it. Now give it back."

"A key. A key is not of great worth without a lock. I grant it's a pretty elegant historical artifact, but if Ba Lura was planning on a privately funded retirement, surely there are more valuable things to steal from the Celestial Garden. And ones less certain to be missed. Was Lura planning to blackmail you? Is that why you murdered it?" A completely absurd charge—the haut-lady and Miles were each other's alibis—but he was curious to see what it would stir up in the way of response.

The reaction was instantaneous. "You vile little—! I did not drive Lura to its death. If anything, you are responsible!"

God, I hope not. "This may be so, and if it is, *I must know.* Lady—there is no Cetagandan security within ten kilometers of us right now, or you could have them strip this bauble off me and dump my carcass in the nearest alleyway right now. Why not? *Why* did Ba Lura steal the Great Key—for its pleasure? The ba makes a hobby of collecting Cetagandan Imperial regalia, does it?"

"You are horrible!"

"Then to whom was Ba Lura taking the thing to sell?"

"*Not* sell!"

"Ha! Then you know who!"

"Not exactly . . ." she hesitated. "Some secrets are not mine to give. They belong to the Celestial Lady."

"Whom you serve."

"Yes."

"Even in death."

"Yes." A note of pride edged her voice.

"And whom the ba betrayed. Even in death."

"No! Not betrayed . . . We had a disagreement."

"An honest disagreement?"

"Yes."

"Between a thief and a murderess?"

"No!"

Quite so, but the accusation definitely had her going. Some guilt, there. *Yeah, tell me about guilt.* "Look, I'll make it easy for you. I'll begin. Ivan and I were coming over from the Barrayaran courier jump-ship in a personnel pod. We docked into this dump of a freight bay. The Ba Lura, wearing a station employee uniform and some badly applied false hair, lumbered into our pod as soon as the lock cycled open, and reached, we thought, for a weapon. We jumped it, and took away a nerve disruptor and this." Miles held up the Great Key. "The ba shook us off and escaped, and I stuck this in my pocket till I could find out more. The next time I saw the ba it was dead in a pool of its own blood on the floor of the funeral rotunda. I found this unnerving, to say the least. Now it's your turn. You say Ba Lura stole the key from your charge. When did you discover the Great Key was missing?"

"I found it missing from its place . . . that day."

"How long could it have been gone? When had you last checked it?"

"It is not being used every day now, because of the period of mourning for the Celestial Lady. I had last seen it when I arranged her regalia . . . two days before that."

"So potentially, it could have been missing for three days before you discovered its absence. When did the ba go missing?"

"I'm . . . not sure. I saw Ba Lura the evening before."

"That cuts it down a little. So the ba could have been gone with the key as early as the previous night. Do the ba servitors pass pretty freely in and out of the Celestial Garden, or is it hard?"

"Freely. They run all our errands."

"So Ba Lura came back . . . when?"

"The night of your arrival. But the ba would not see me. It claimed to be sick. I could have had it dragged into my presence, but . . . I did not want to inflict such an indignity."

They were in it together, right.

"I went to see the ba in the morning. The whole sorry story came out then. The ba was trying to take the Great Key to . . . someone, and entered into the wrong docking bay."

"Then *someone* was supposed to supply a personnel pod? Then *someone* was waiting on a ship in orbit?"

"I didn't say that!"

Keep pressing her. It's working. Though it did make him feel faintly guilty, to be badgering the distraught old lady so, even if possibly for her own good. *Don't let up.* "So the ba blundered onto our pod, and—what was the rest of its story? Tell me exactly!"

"Ba Lura was attacked by Barrayaran soldiers, who stole the Great Key."

"How many soldiers?"

"Six."

Miles's eyes widened in delight. "And then what?"

"Ba Lura begged for its life, and head and honor, but they laughed and ejected the ba, and flew away."

Lies, lies at last. And yet . . . the ba was only human. Anyone who had screwed up so hugely might re-tell the story so as to make themselves look less at fault. "What exactly did it say we said?"

Her voice grated with anger. "You insulted the Celestial Lady."

"Then what?"

"The ba came home in shame."

"So . . . why didn't the ba call on Cetagandan security to shake us down and get the Great Key back on the spot?"

There was a longer silence. Then she said, "The ba could not do that. But it confessed to me. And I came to you. To . . . humble myself. And beg for the return of my . . . charge and my honor."

"Why didn't the ba confess to you the night before?"

"I don't know!"

"So while you set about your retrieval task, Ba Lura cut its throat."

"In great grief and shame," she said lowly.

"Yeah? Why not at least wait to see if you could coax the key back from me? So why not cut its throat privately, in its own quarters? Why advertise its shame to the entire galactic community? Isn't that a bit *unusual*? Was the ba supposed to attend the bier-gifting ceremony?"

"Yes."

"And you were too?"

"Yes . . ."

"And you believed the ba's story?"

"Yes!"

"Lady, I think you are lost in the woods. Let me tell you what happened in the personnel pod as *I* saw it. There were no six soldiers. Just me, my cousin, and the pod pilot. There was no conversation, no begging or pleading, no slurs on the Celestial Lady. Ba Lura just yelped, and ran off. It didn't even fight very hard. In fact, it scarcely fought us at all. Strange, don't you think, in a hand-to-hand struggle for something so important that the ba slit its own throat over its loss the next day? We were left scratching our heads, holding the damned thing and wondering what the hell? Now you know that one of us, me or the ba, is lying. I know which one."

"Give the Great Key to me," was all she could say. "It's not yours."

"But I think I was framed. By someone who apparently wants to drag Barrayar into a Cetagandan internal . . . disagreement. *Why?* What am I being set up *for?*"

Her silence might indicate that these were the first new thoughts to penetrate her panic in two days. Or . . . it might not. In any case, she only whispered, "Not yours!"

Miles sighed. "I couldn't agree with you more, milady, and I am glad to return your charge. But in light of the whole situation, I would like to be able to testify—under fast-penta, if need be— just *who* I gave the Great Key back to. You could be anyone, in that bubble. My Aunt Alys, for all I know. Or Cetagandan security, or . . . who knows. I will return it to you . . . face-to-face." He held out his hand half-open, the key resting invitingly across his palm.

"Is that . . . the last of your price?"

"Yes. I'll ask no more."

It was a small triumph. He was going to see a haut-woman, and Ivan wasn't. It would doubtless embarrass the old dragon, to reveal herself to outlander eyes, but dammit, given the run-around Miles had suffered, she owed him something. And he was deathly serious about being able to identify where the Great Key went. The haut Rian Degtiar, Handmaiden of the Star Crèche, was certainly not the only player in this game.

"Very well," she whispered. The white bubble faded to transparency, and was gone from between them.

"Oh," said Miles, in a very small voice.

She sat in a float-chair, clothed from slender neck to ankle in flowing robes of shining white, a dozen shimmering textures lying one atop another. Her hair glinted ebony, masses of it that poured down across her shoulders, past her lap, to coil around her feet. When she stood, it would trail on the floor like a banner. Her enormous eyes were an ice blue of such arctic purity as to make Lady Gelle's eyes look like mud-puddles. Skin . . . Miles felt he had never seen skin before, just blotched bags people wore around themselves to keep from leaking. This perfect ivory surface . . . his hands ached with the desire to touch it, just once, and die. Her lips were warm, as if roses pulsed with blood. . . .

How old was she? Twenty? Forty? This was a haut-woman. Who could tell? Who could care? Men of the old religion had worshipped on their knees icons far less glorious, in beaten silver and hammered gold. Miles was on his knees now, and could not remember how he'd come to be there.

He knew now why they called it "falling in love." There was the same nauseating vertigo of free fall, the same vast exhilaration, the same sick certainty of broken bones upon impact with a rapidly rising reality. He inched forward, and laid the Great Key in front of her perfectly shaped, white-slippered feet, and sank back, and waited.

I am Fortune's fool.

Chapter Six

She bent forward, one graceful hand darting down to retrieve her solemn charge. She laid the Great Key in her lap, and pulled a long necklace from beneath her layered white garments. The chain held a ring, decorated with a thick raised bird-pattern, the gold lines of electronic contacts gleaming like filigree upon its surface. She inserted the ring into the seal atop the rod. Nothing happened.

Her breath drew in. She glared down at Miles. "What have you done to it!"

"Milady, I, I . . . nothing, I swear by my word as Vorkosigan! I didn't even drop it. What's . . . supposed to happen?"

"It should open."

"Um . . . um . . ." He would break into a desperate sweat, but he was too damned cold. He was dizzy with the scent of her, and the celestial music of her unfiltered voice. "There are only three possibilities, if there's something wrong with it. Someone broke it—not me, I swear!" Could that have been the secret of Ba Lura's peculiar intrusion? Maybe the ba had broken it, and had been seeking a scapegoat upon whom to shuffle the blame? "—or someone's re-programmed it, or, least likely, there's been some kind of substitution pulled. A duplicate, or, or . . ."

Her eyes widened, and her lips parted, moving in some subvocalization.

"*Not* least likely?" Miles hazarded. "It would surely be the most difficult, but . . . it crosses my mind that maybe someone didn't think you would be getting it back from me. If it's a counterfeit, maybe it was meant to be on its way to Barrayar in a diplomatic pouch right now. Or . . . or something." No, that didn't quite make sense, but . . .

She sat utterly still, her face tense with panic, her hands clutching the rod.

"Milady, talk to me. If it's a duplicate, it's obviously a very good duplicate. You now have it, to turn over at the ceremony. So what if it doesn't work? Who's going to check the function of some obsolete piece of electronics?"

"The Great Key is not obsolete. We used it every day."

"It's some kind of data link, right? You have a time-window, here. Nine days. If you think it's been compromised, wipe it and re-program it from your backup files. If that thing in your hand is some kind of a non-working dummy, you've maybe got time to make a real duplicate, and re-program *it*." *But don't just sit there with death in your lovely eyes.* "Talk to me!"

"I must do as Ba Lura did," she whispered. "The ba was right. This is the end."

"No, why?! It's just a, a *thing*, who cares? Not me!"

She held up the rod, her arctic-blue eyes fixing on his face at last. Her gaze made him want to scuttle into the shadows like a crab, to hide his merely human ugliness, but he held fast before her. "There is no backup," she said. "This is the sole key."

Miles felt faint, and it wasn't just from her perfume. "No backup?" he choked. "Are you people *crazy*?"

"It is a matter of . . . control."

"What does the damn thing really do, anyway?"

She hesitated, then said, "It is the data-key to the haut gene bank. All the frozen genetic samples are stored in a randomized order, for security. Without the key, no one knows what is where. To re-create the files, someone would have to physically examine and re-classify each and every sample. There are hundreds of thousands of samples—one for every haut who has ever lived. It would take an army of geneticists working for a generation to re-create the Great Key."

"This is a real disaster, then, huh?" he said brightly, blinking. His teeth gritted. "Now I *know* I was framed." He climbed to his feet, and threw back his head, defying the onslaught of her beauty.

"Lady, what is *really* going on here? I'll ask you one more time, with feeling. What in God's green ninety hells was the Ba Lura *ever* doing with the Great Key on a *space station?*"

"No outlander may—"

"*Somebody made* it my business! Sucked me right into it. I don't think I could escape now if I tried. And I think . . . you need an ally. It took you a day and a half just to arrange this second meeting with me. Nine days left. You don't have *time* to go it alone. You need . . . a trained security man. And for some strange reason, you don't seem to want to get one from your own side."

She rocked, just slightly, in frozen misery, in a faint rustle of fabrics.

"If you don't think I'm worthy of being let in on your secrets," Miles went on wildly, "then explain to me how you think I could possibly make things any *worse* than they are right now!"

Her blue eyes searched him, for he knew not what. But he thought if she asked him to open his veins for her, right here and now, the only thing he'd say would be *How wide?*

"It was my Celestial Lady's desire," she began fearfully, and stopped.

Miles clutched at his shredded self-control. Everything she'd spilled so far was either obviously deducible, or common knowledge, at least in her milieu. Now she was getting to the good stuff, and knew it. He could tell by the way she'd stalled out.

"Milady." He chose his words with extreme care. "If the ba did not commit suicide, it was certainly murdered." *And we both have good reason to prefer the second scenario.* "Ba Lura was your servitor, your colleague . . . dare I guess, friend? I saw its body in the rotunda. A very dangerous and daring person arranged that hideous tableau. There was . . . a deep mischief and mockery in it."

Was that pain, in those cool eyes? So hard to tell . . .

"I have old and very personal reasons to particularly dislike being made the unwitting target of persons of cruel humor. I don't know if you can understand this."

"Perhaps . . ." she said slowly.

Yes. Look past the surface. See me, not this joke of a body. . . . "And I am the one person on Eta Ceta *you know* didn't do it. It's the only certainty we share, so far. I claim a *right* to know who's doing this to us. And the only chance in hell I have to figure out who, is to know exactly *why.*"

Still she sat silent.

"I already know enough to destroy you," Miles added earnestly. "Tell me enough to save you!"

Her sculpted chin rose in bleak decision. When she blessed him with her outward attention at last, it was total and terrifying. "It was a long-standing disagreement." He strained to hear, to keep his head clear, to concentrate on the words and not just on the enchanting melody of her voice. "Between the Celestial Lady and the Emperor. My Lady had long thought that the haut gene bank was too centralized, in the heart of the Celestial Garden. She favored the dispersal of copies, for safety. My Lord favored keeping it all under his personal protection—for safety. They both sought the good of the haut, each in their own way."

"I see," Miles murmured, encouraging her with as much delicacy as he could muster. "All good guys here, right."

"The Emperor forbade her plan. But as she neared the end of her life . . . she came to feel that her loyalty to the haut must outweigh her loyalty to her son. Twenty years ago, she began to have copies made, in secret."

"A large project," Miles said.

"Huge, and slow. But she brought it to fruition."

"How many copies?"

"Eight. One for each of the planetary satraps."

"Exact copies?"

"Yes. I have reason to know. I have been the Celestial Lady's supervisor of geneticists for five years, now."

"Ah. So you are something of a trained scientist. You know about . . . extreme care. And scrupulous honesty."

"How else should I serve my Lady?" She shrugged.

But you don't know much, I'll bet, about covert ops chicanery. Hm. "If there are eight exact copies, there must be eight exact Great Keys, right?"

"No. Not yet. My Lady was saving the duplication of the Key to the last moment. A matter of—"

"Control," Miles finished smoothly. "How did I guess?"

A faint flash of resentment at his humor sparked in her eyes, and Miles bit his tongue. It was no laughing matter to haut Rian Degtiar.

"The Celestial Lady knew her time was drawing near. She made me and the Ba Lura the executors of her will in this matter. We were to deliver the copies of the gene bank to each of the eight satrap governors upon the occasion of her funeral, which they would be certain to all attend together. But . . . she died more suddenly than she had expected. She had not yet made arrangements for the duplication of the Great Key. It was a problem of considerable technical and cipher skill, as all of the Empire's resources went into its original creation. Ba Lura and I had all her instructions for the banks, but nothing for how the Key was to be duplicated and delivered, or even when she had planned this to happen. The ba and I were not sure what to do."

"Ah," Miles said faintly. He dared not offer any comment at all, for fear of impeding the free flow, at last, of information. He hung on her words, barely breathing.

"Ba Lura thought . . . if we took the Great Key to one of the satrap governors, he might use his resources to duplicate it for us. I thought this was a very dangerous idea. Because of the temptation to take it exclusively for himself."

"Ah . . . excuse me. Let me see if I follow this. I know you consider the haut gene bank a most private matter, but what are the *political* side-effects of setting up new haut reproductive centers on each of Cetaganda's eight satrap planets?"

"The Celestial Lady thought the empire had ceased to grow at the time of the defeat of the Barrayar expedition. That we had become static, stagnant, enervated. She thought . . . if the empire could only undergo mitosis, like a cell, the haut might start to grow again, become re-energized. With the splitting of the gene bank, there would be eight new centers of authority for expansion."

"Eight new potential Imperial capitals?" Miles whispered.

"Yes, I suppose."

Eight new centers . . . civil war was only the beginning of the possibilities. Eight new Cetagandan Empires, each expanding like killer coral at their neighbors' expense . . . a nightmare of cosmic proportions. "I think I can see," said Miles carefully, "why perhaps the Emperor was less than enthused by his mother's admittedly sound biological reasoning. Something to be said on both sides, don't you think?"

"I serve the Celestial Lady," said the haut Rian Degtiar simply, "and the haut genome. The Empire's short-term political adjustments are not my business."

"So all this, ah, genetic shuffling . . . would the Cetagandan Emperor, by chance, regard this as treason on your part?"

"How?" said the haut Rian Degtiar. "It was my duty to obey the Celestial Lady."

"Oh."

"The eight satrap governors have all committed treason in it, though," she added matter-of-factly.

"*Have* committed?"

"They all took delivery of their gene banks last week at the welcoming banquet. Ba Lura and I succeeded in that part of the Celestial Lady's plan, at least."

"Treasure chests for which none of them have keys."

"I . . . don't know. Each of them, you see . . . the Celestial Lady felt it would be better if each of the satrap governors thought that he alone was the recipient of the new copy of the haut gene bank. Each would strive better to keep it secret, that way."

"Do you know—I have to ask this." *I'm just not sure I want to hear the answer.* "Do you know to *which* of the eight satrap governors Ba Lura was trying to take the Great Key for duplication, when it ran into us?"

"No," she said.

"Ah," Miles exhaled in pure satisfaction. "Now, *now* I know why I was set up. And why the ba died."

Fine lines appeared on her ivory brow as she stared at him.

"Don't you see it too? The ba didn't hit us Barrayarans on the way out. It hit us on the way *back*. Your ba was suborned. Ba Lura *did* take the key to one of the satrap governors, and received in return not a true copy, because there was no time for the extensive decoding required, but a decoy. Which the ba then was sent to deliberately lose to us. Which it did, although not, I suspect, in quite the manner it had originally planned." *Almost certainly not as planned.*

He found himself pacing, keyed up and hectic. He ought not to limp before her, it brought attention to his deformities, but he could not keep still. "And while everybody is off chasing Barrayarans, the satrap governor quietly goes home with the only real copy of the Great Key, getting a large jump-start on the haut-competition. After first arranging the ba's reward for its double-treason, and incidentally eliminating the only witness to the truth. Oh. Yes. It works. Or it would have worked, if only . . . the satrap governor had remembered that no battle-plan survives first contact with the enemy." *Not when the enemy is me.* He stared into her eyes, willing her to believe in him, striving not to melt. "How soon can you analyze this Great Key, and support or explode these theories?"

"I will examine it immediately, tonight. But whatever has been done to it, my examination will not tell me *who* did it, Barrayaran." Her voice grew glacial with this thought. "I doubt you could have created a true duplicate, but a non-working forgery is certainly within your capabilities. If this one is false—where is the real one?"

"It seems that is just what I must discover, milady, to, to clear my name. To redeem my honor in your eyes." The intrinsic fascination of an intellectual puzzle had brought him to this interview. He'd thought curiosity was his strongest driving force, till suddenly his whole personality had become engaged. It was like being under—no, like *becoming* an avalanche. "If I can discover this, will you . . ." *what?* Look favorably upon his suit? Despise him for an outlander barbarian all the same? ". . . let me see you again?"

"I don't . . . know." Reminded, her hand drifted to the control on her float-chair for the concealing force-screen.

No, no, don't go. . . . "We must have some way of communicating," he said hastily, before she could disappear again behind that faintly humming barrier.

Her head tilted, considering this. She drew a small com link from her robes. It was undecorated, utilitarian, but like the nerve disruptor he'd taken from Ba Lura perfectly designed in what Miles was beginning to recognize as the haut style. She whispered a command into it. In a moment, the androgynous ba appeared from its guard post beside the pond. Did its eyes widen just slightly, to see its mistress without her shell?

"Give me your com link, and wait outside," haut Rian Degtiar ordered.

The little ba nodded, turning the device over to her without question, and withdrew silently.

She held the com link out to Miles. "I use this to communicate with my senior servitors, when they run errands outside the Celestial Garden for me. Here."

He wanted to touch her, but scarcely dared. He instead extended his cupped hands toward her like a shy man offering flowers to a goddess. She dropped the com link into them gingerly, as into the hands of a leper. Or an enemy.

"Is it secured?" he dared to ask.

"Temporarily."

In other words, it was the lady's private line only as long as no one in higher-level Cetagandan security troubled to break in. Right.

He sighed. "It won't work. You can't send signals into my embassy without causing my superiors to ask a whole lot of questions I'd rather not answer just now. And I can't give you my com link either. I'm supposed to turn it in, and I don't think I can get away with telling them I lost it." Reluctantly, he handed the link back to her. "But we have to meet again somehow." *Yes, oh yes.* "If I'm going to be risking my reputation and maybe my life on the validity of my reasoning, I'd like to prop it up with a few facts." One fact was almost certain. Someone with enough wit and nerve to murder one of the most senior Imperial servitors under the nose of Cetaganda's own emperor would hardly balk at threatening a decidedly un-senior female Degtiar. The thought was obscene, hideous. A Barrayaran scion's diplomatic immunity would be an even more useless shield, no doubt, but that was merely the price of the game. "I think you could be in grave danger. It might be better to play along for a bit—don't reveal to anyone you have obtained this key from me. I have a funny feeling I'm not following his script, y'see." He paced nervously back and forth before her. "If you can find out anything at all about Ba Lura's real activities in the few days before it died—don't run afoul of your own security, though. They have to be following up on the ba's death."

"I will . . . contact you when and how I can, Barrayaran." Slowly, one pale hand caressed the control pad on the arm of the float-chair, and a dim gray mist coalesced around her like a fairy spell of seeming.

The ba servitor returned to the pavilion to escort not Miles but its mistress away. Miles was left to stumble back through the dark to Yenaro's estate alone.

It was raining.

Miles was not surprised to find that the ghem-woman was no longer waiting on the bench by the red-enameled gate. He let himself in quietly, and paused just outside the lighted garden doors to brush as many of the water droplets as possible off his formal blacks, and to wipe his face. He then sacrificed the handkerchief to the redemption of his boots, and quietly dropped the sodden object behind a bush. He slipped back inside.

No one noticed his entry. The party was continuing, a little louder, with a few new faces replacing some of the previous ones. The Cetagandans did not use alcohol for inebriation, but some of the guests had a late-party dissociated air about them similar to over-indulgers Miles had witnessed at home. If intelligent conversation had been difficult before, it was clearly hopeless now. He felt himself no better off than the ghemlings, drunk on information, dizzy with intrigue. *Everyone to their own secret addictions, I suppose.* He wanted to collect Ivan and escape, as swiftly as possible, before his head exploded.

"Ah, there you are, Lord Vorkosigan." Lord Yenaro appeared at Miles's elbow, looking faintly anxious. "I could not find you."

"I took a long walk with a lady," Miles said. Ivan was nowhere to be seen. "Where is my cousin?"

"Lord Vorpatril is taking a tour of the house with Lady Arvin and Lady Benello," said Yenaro. He glanced through a wide archway at the room's opposite side, which framed a spiral staircase in a hall beyond. "They've been gone . . . an astonishingly long time." Yenaro's smile attempted to be knowing, but came out oddly puzzled. "Since before you . . . I don't quite . . . ah, well. Would you care for a drink?"

"Yes, please," said Miles distractedly. He took it from Yenaro's hand and gulped without hesitation. His eyes almost crossed, considering the possibilities of Ivan plus two beautiful ghem-women. Though to his haut-dazzled senses, all the ghem-women in the room looked as coarse and dull as backcountry slatterns just now. The effect would wear off with time, he hoped. He dreaded the thought of his own next encounter with a mirror. What had the haut Rian Degtiar seen, looking at him? A simian black-clad gnome, twitching and babbling? He pulled up a chair and sat rather abruptly, the spiral staircase bracketed in his sights. *Ivan, hurry up!*

Yenaro lingered by his side, and began a disjointed conversation about proportional theories of architecture through history, art and the senses, and the natural esters trade on Barrayar, but Miles swore the man was as focused on the staircase as he was. Miles finished his first drink and most of a second before Ivan appeared in the shadows at the top of the stairs.

Ivan hesitated in the dimness, his hand checking the fit of his green uniform, which appeared fully assembled. Or re-assembled. He was alone. He descended with one hand clutching the curving rail, which floated without apparent support in echo of the stair's arc. He jerked a stiff frown into a stiff smile before entering the main room and the light. His head swiveled till he spotted Miles, toward whom he made a straight line.

"Lord Vorpatril," Yenaro greeted him. "You had a long tour. Did you see everything?"

Ivan bared his teeth. "Everything. Even the light."

Yenaro's smile did not slip, but his eyes seemed to fill with questions. "I'm . . . so glad." A guest called to him from across the room, and Yenaro was momentarily distracted.

Ivan bent down to whisper behind his hand into Miles's ear, "Get us the hell out of here. I think I've been poisoned."

Miles looked up, startled. "D'you want to call down the lightflyer?"

"No. Just back to the embassy in the groundcar."

"But—"

"*No*, dammit," Ivan hissed. "Just quietly. Before that smirking bastard goes upstairs." He nodded toward Yenaro, who was now standing at the foot of the staircase, gazing upward.

"I take it you don't think it is acute."

"Oh, it was cute all right," Ivan snarled.

"You didn't murder anybody up there, did you?"

"No. But I thought they'd *never* . . . Tell you in the car."

"You'd better." Miles clambered to his feet. They perforce had to pass Yenaro, who attached himself to them like a good host, seeing them to his front door with suitably polite farewells. Ivan's good-byes might have been etched in acid.

As soon as the canopy sealed over their heads, Miles commanded, "Give, Ivan!"

Ivan settled back, still seething. "I was set up."

This comes as a surprise to you, coz? "By Lady Arvin and Lady Benello?"

"They *were* the setup. Yenaro was behind it, I'm sure of it. You're right about that damned fountain being a trap, Miles, I see it now. Beauty as bait, all over again."

"What happened to you?"

"You know all those rumors about Cetagandan aphrodisiacs?"

"Yes . . ."

"Well, sometime this evening that son-of-a-bitch Yenaro slipped me an *anti*-aphrodisiac."

"Um . . . are you sure? I mean, there are natural causes for these moments, I'm told. . . ."

"It was a *setup*. I didn't seduce them, they seduced me! Wafted me upstairs to this amazing room—it had to have been all arranged in advance. God, it was, it was . . ." his voice broke in a sigh, "it was *glorious*. For a little while. And then I realized I couldn't, like, *perform*."

"What did you do?"

"It was too late to get out gracefully. So I winged it. It was all I could do to keep 'em from noticing."

"*What?*"

"I made up a lot of instant barbarian folklore—I told 'em a Vor prides himself on self-control, that it's not considered polite on Barrayar for a man to, you know, before his lady has. Three times. It was considered insulting to her. I stroked, I rubbed, I scratched, I recited poetry, I nuzzled and nibbled and—cripes, my fingers are cramped." His speech was a bit slurred, too, Miles noticed. "I thought they'd *never* fall asleep." Ivan paused; a slow smirk displaced the snarl on his face. "But they were smiling, when they finally did." The smirk faded into a look of bleak dismay. "What do you want to bet those two are the biggest female ghem-gossips on Eta Ceta?"

"No takers here," said Miles, fascinated. *Let the punishment fit the crime.* Or, in this case, the trap fit the prey. Someone had studied his weaknesses. And someone just as clearly had studied Ivan's. "We could have the ImpSec office do a data sweep for the tale, over the next few days."

"If you breathe a *word* of this I'll wring your scrawny neck! If I can find it."

"You've got to confess to the embassy physician. Blood tests—"

"Oh, yes. I want a chemical scan the instant I hit the door. What if the effect's *permanent*?"

"Ba Vorpatril?" Miles intoned, eyes alight.

"Dammit, I didn't laugh at *you*."

"No. That's true, you didn't," Miles sighed. "I expect the physician will find whatever it was metabolizes rapidly. Or Yenaro wouldn't have drunk the stuff himself."

"You think?"

"Remember the zlati ale? I'd bet my ImpSec silver eyes that was the vector."

Ivan relaxed slightly, obviously relieved at this professional analysis. After a minute he added, "Yenaro's done you now, and he's done me. Third time's a charm. What's next, do you suppose? And can we do him first?"

Miles was silent for a long time. "That depends," he said at last, "on whether Yenaro's merely amusing himself, or whether he too is being . . . set up. And on whether there's any connection between Yenaro's backer and the death of Ba Lura."

"Connection? What possible connection?"

"We are the connection, Ivan. A couple of Barrayaran back-country boys come to the big city, and ripe for the plucking. Somebody is using us. And I think somebody . . . has just made a major mistake in his choice of tools." *Or fools.*

Ivan stared at his venomous tone. "Have you got rid of that little toy you're packing yet?" he demanded suspiciously.

"Yes . . . and no."

"Oh, *shit.* I *knew* better than to trust—what the hell do you mean by *Yes and no*? Either you have or you haven't, right?"

"The object has been returned, yes."

"That's that, then."

"No. Not quite."

"*Miles* . . . You had better start talking to me."

"Yes, I think I better had." Miles sighed. They were approaching the legation district. "After you're done in the infirmary, I have a few confessions to make. But if—when—you talk to the ImpSec night-duty officer about Yenaro, don't mention the other. Yet."

"Oh?" drawled Ivan in a tone of deep suspicion.

"Things have gotten . . . complex."

"You think they were simple before?"

"I mean complex beyond the scope of mere security concerns, into genuine diplomatic ones. Of extreme delicacy. Maybe too delicate to submit to the sort of booted paranoids who sometimes end up running local ImpSec offices. That's a judgment call . . . that I'll have to make myself. When I'm sure I'm ready. But this isn't a game anymore, and it's no longer feasible for me to run without backup." *I need help, God help me.*

"We knew *that* yesterday."

"Oh, yes. But it's even deeper than I first thought."

"Over our heads?"

Miles hesitated, and smiled sourly. "I don't know, Ivan. How good are you at treading water?"

Alone in his suite's bathroom, Miles slowly peeled off his black House uniform, now in desperate need of attention from the embassy's laundry. He glanced at himself sideways in the mirror, then resolutely looked away. He considered the problem, as he stood in the shower. To the haut, all normal humans doubtless looked like some lower life-form. From the haut Rian Degtiar's foreshortened perspective, perhaps there was little to choose between him and, say, Ivan.

And ghem-lords did win haut wives, from time to time, for great deeds. And the Vor and the ghem-lords were very much alike. Even Maz had said so.

How great a deed? *Very great.* Well . . . he'd always wanted to save the Empire. The Cetagandan just wasn't the empire he'd pictured, was all. Life was like that, always throwing you curveballs.

You've gone mad, you know. To hope, to even think it . . .

If he defeated the late Dowager Empress's plot, might the Cetagandan emperor be grateful enough to . . . give him Rian's hand? If he advanced the late Dowager Empress's plot, might the haut Rian Degtiar be grateful enough to . . . give him her love? To do both simultaneously would be a tactical feat of supernatural scope.

Barrayar's interests lay, unusually, squarely with the interests of the Cetagandan emperor. Obviously, it was his clear ImpSec duty to foil the girl and save the villain.

Right. My head hurts.

Reason was returning to him, slowly, the astonishing effect of the haut Rian Degtiar wearing off. Wasn't it? She hadn't exactly tried to suborn him, after all. Even if Rian were as ugly as the witch Baba Yaga, he'd still have to be following up on this. To a point. He needed to prove Barrayar had not filched the Great Key, and the only certain way of doing *that* was to find its real thief. He wondered if one could get a hangover from excess passion. If so, his was apparently starting while he was still drunk, which did not seem quite fair.

Eight Cetagandan satrap governors had been led into treason by the late empress. Optimistic, to think that only *one* could be a murderer. But only one possessed the real Great Key.

Lord X? Seven chances of guessing wrong, against one of guessing right. Not favorable odds.

I'll . . . figure something out.

Chapter Seven

Ivan was taking a long time, downstairs in the infirmary. Miles shrugged on his black fatigues and, barefoot, fired up his com-console for a quick review of the eight haut-lord satrap governors.

The satrap governors were all chosen from a pool of men who were close Imperial relations, half-brothers and uncles and great-uncles, in both paternal and maternal lines. Two current office-holders were of the Degtiar constellation. Each ruled his satrapy for a set term of only five years, then he was required to shift—sometimes to permanent retirement back at the capital on Eta Ceta, sometimes to another satrapy. A couple of the older and more experienced men had cycled this way through the entire empire. The purpose of the term limitation, of course, was to prevent the build-up of a personal local power base to anyone who might harbor secret Imperial pretensions. So far so sensible.

So . . . which among them had been tempted into hubris by the dowager empress, and Ba Lura? For that matter, how had she contacted them all? If she'd been working on her plan for twenty years, she'd had lots of time . . . still, that long ago, how could she have predicted which men would be satrap governors on the unknown date of her death? The governors must have all been brought into the plot quite recently.

Miles stared narrow-eyed at the list of his eight suspects. *I have*

to cut this down somehow. Several somehows. If he assumed Lord
X had personally murdered the Ba Lura, he could eliminate the
weakest and most fragile elderly men . . . a premature assumption.
Any of the haut-lords might possess a ghem-guard both loyal and
capable enough to be delegated the task, while the satrap governor lingered front and center in the bier-gifting ceremonies, his
alibi established before dozens of witnesses.

No disloyalty to Barrayar intended, but Miles found himself
wishing he were a Cetagandan security man right now—
specifically, the one in charge of whatever investigation was progressing on Ba Lura's supposed suicide. But there was no way
he could insert himself inconspicuously into that data flow. And
he wasn't sure Rian had the mind-set for it, not to mention the
urgent necessity of keeping Cetagandan security's attention as far
from her as possible. Miles sighed in frustration.

It wasn't his task to solve the ba's murder anyway. It was his
task to locate the real Great Key. Well, he knew in general where
it was—in orbit, aboard one of the satrap governors' flagships. How
else to finger the right one?

A chime at his door interrupted his furious meditations. He
hastily shut down the comconsole and called, "Enter."

Ivan trod within, looking extremely dyspeptic.

"How did it go?" Miles asked, waving him to a chair. Ivan
dragged a heavy and comfortable armchair up to the comconsole,
and flung himself across it sideways, scowling. He was still wearing his undress greens.

"You were right. It was taken by mouth, and it metabolizes
rapidly. Not so rapidly that our medics couldn't get a sample,
though." Ivan rubbed his arm. "They said it would have been
untraceable by morning."

"No permanent harm done, then."

"Except to my reputation. Your Colonel Vorreedi just blew in,
I thought you might like to know. At least *he* took me seriously.
We had a long talk just now about Lord Yenaro. Vorreedi didn't
strike me as a booted paranoid, by the way." Ivan let the implication, *So hadn't you better go see him?*, hang in the air; Miles left
it there.

"Good. I think. You didn't mention, ah—?"

"Not yet. But if you don't cough up some explanations, I'm
going back to him for another pass."

"Fair enough." Miles sighed, and steeled himself. As briefly as the complications permitted, he summed up his conversation with the haut Rian Degtiar for Ivan, leaving out only a description of her incredible beauty, and his own stunned response to it. *That* was not Ivan's business. That *especially* was not Ivan's business.

" . . . so it seems to me," Miles ran down at last, "that the only way we can certainly prove that Barrayar had nothing to do with it is to find which satrap governor has the real Great Key." He pointed orbit-ward.

Ivan's eyes were round, his mouth screwed up in an expression of total dismay. "We? *We?* Miles, we've only been here for two and a half days, how did *we* get put in charge of the Cetagandan Empire? Isn't this *Cetagandan* security's job?"

"Would you trust them to clear us of blame?" Miles shrugged, and forged on into Ivan's hesitation. "We only have nine days left. I've thought of three strings that could maybe lead us back to the right man. Yenaro is one of them. A few more words in our protocol officer's ear could put the machinery of ImpSec here into tracing Yenaro's connections, without bringing up the matter of the Great Key. Yet. The next string is Ba Lura's murder, and I haven't figured out how I can pull that one. Yet. The other string lies in astro-political analysis, and that I *can* do. Look." On the comconsole, Miles called up a schematic three-dimensional map of the Cetagandan empire, its wormhole routes, and its immediate neighbors.

"The Ba Lura could have foisted that decoy key onto any number of outlander delegations. Instead, it picked Barrayarans, or rather, its satrap-governor master did. Why?"

"Maybe we were the only ones there at the right time," Ivan suggested.

"Mm. I'm trying to *reduce* the random factors, please. If Yenaro's backer is the same as our man, we were picked in advance to be framed. Now." He waved at the map. "Picture a scenario where the Cetagandan empire breaks apart and the pieces begin an attempt to expand. Which, if any, benefit from trouble with Barrayar?"

Ivan's brows went up, and he leaned forward, staring at the glowing array of spheres and lines above the vid plate.

"Well . . . Rho Ceta is positioned to expand toward Komarr, or would be, if we weren't sitting on two-thirds of the wormhole jumps between. Mu Ceta just got a bloody nose, administered by us, when it attempted to expand past Vervain into the Hegen Hub.

Those are the two most obvious. These other three," Ivan pointed, "and Eta Ceta itself are all interior, I don't see any benefit to them."

"Then there's the other side of the nexus," Miles waved at the display. "Sigma Ceta, bordering the Vega Station groups. And Xi Ceta, giving onto Marilac. If they were seeking to break out, it might be expedient for them to have the empire's military resources tied up far away against Barrayar."

"Four out of eight. It's a start," Ivan conceded.

Ivan's analysis matched his own, then. Well, they'd both had the same strategic training; it stood to reason. Still Miles was obscurely comforted. It wasn't all the hallucination of his own over-driven imagination, if Ivan could see it too.

"It's a triangulation," said Miles. "If I can get any of the other lines of investigation to eliminate even part of the list, the final overlap ought to . . . well, it would be *nice* if it all came down to one."

"And then what?" Ivan demanded doggedly, his brows drawn down in suspicion. "What do you have in mind for *us* to do then?"

"I'm . . . not sure. But I do think you'd agree that a quiet conclusion to this mess would be preferable to a splashy one, eh?"

"Oh, yeah." Ivan chewed on his lower lip, eyeing the wormhole nexus map. "So when *do* we report?"

"Not . . . yet. But I think we'd better start documenting it all. Personal logs." So that anybody who came after them—Miles trusted not posthumously, but that was the unspoken thought—would at least have a chance of unraveling the events.

"I've been doing *that* since the first day," Ivan informed him grimly. "It's locked in my valise."

"Oh. Good." Miles hesitated. "When you talked to Colonel Vorreedi, did you plant the idea that Yenaro had a high-placed backer?"

"Not exactly."

"I'd like you to talk to him again, then. Try to direct his attention toward the satrap governors, somehow."

"Why don't you talk to him?"

"I'm . . . not ready. Not yet, not tonight. I'm still assimilating it all. And technically, he is my ImpSec superior here, or would be, if I were on active duty. I'd like to limit my, um . . ."

"Outright lies to him?" Ivan completed sweetly.

Miles grimaced, but did not deny it. "Look, I have an *access* in this matter that no other ImpSec officer could, due to my social position. I don't want to see the opportunity wasted. But it also limits me—I can't get at the routine legwork, the down-and-dirty details I need. I'm too conspicuous. I have to play to my own strengths, and get others to play to my weaknesses."

Ivan sighed. "All right. I'll talk to him. Just this once." With a tired grunt, he heaved himself out of his chair, and wandered toward the door. He looked back over his shoulder. "The trouble, coz, with your playing the spider in the center of this web, pulling all the strings, is that sooner or later all the interested parties are going to converge back along those strings to you. You do realize that, don't you? And what are you going to do *then*, O Mastermind?" He bowed himself out with all-too-effective irony.

Miles hunched down in his station chair, and groaned, and keyed up his list again.

The next morning, Ambassador Vorob'yev was called away from what was becoming his customary breakfast with Barrayar's young envoys in his private dining room. By the time he returned, Miles and Ivan had finished eating.

The ambassador did not sit down again, but instead favored Miles with a bemused look. "Lord Vorkosigan. You have an unusual visitor."

Miles's heart leapt. *Rian, here? Impossible . . .* His mind did a quick involuntary review of his undress greens, yes, his insignia were on straight, his fly was fastened—"Who, sir?"

"Ghem-colonel Dag Benin, of Cetagandan Imperial Security. He is an officer of middle rank assigned to internal affairs at the Celestial Garden, and he wants to speak privately with you."

Miles tried not to hyperventilate. *What's gone wrong . . . ? Maybe nothing, yet. Calm down.* "Did he say what about?"

"It seems he was ordered to investigate the suicide of that poor ba-slave the other day. And your, ah, erratic movements brought you to his negative attention. I thought you'd come to regret getting out of line."

"And . . . am I to talk to him, then?"

"We have decided to extend that courtesy, yes. We've shown him to one of the small parlors on the ground floor. It is, of course, monitored. You'll have an embassy bodyguard present. I don't suspect Benin of harboring any murderous intentions, it will merely be a reminder of your status."

We have decided. So Colonel Vorreedi, whom Miles still had not met, and probably Vorob'yev too, would be listening to every word. Oh, shit. "Very good, sir." Miles stood, and followed the ambassador. Ivan watched him go with the suffused expression of a man anticipating the imminent arrival of some unpleasant form of cosmic justice.

The small parlor was exactly that, a comfortably furnished room intended for private tête-à-têtes between two or three persons, with the embassy security staff as an invisible fourth. Ghem-Colonel Benin apparently had no objection to anything *he* had to say being recorded. A Barrayaran guard, standing outside the door, swung in behind Miles and the ambassador as they entered, and took up his post stolidly and silently. He was tall and husky even for a Barrayaran, with a remarkably blank face. He wore a senior sergeant's tabs, and insignia of commando corps, by which Miles deduced that the low-wattage expression was a put-on.

Ghem-Colonel Benin, waiting for them, rose politely as they entered. He was of no more than middle stature, so probably not over-stocked with haut-genes in his recent ancestry—the haut favored height. He had likely acquired his present post by merit rather than social rank, then, not necessarily a plus from Miles's point of view. Benin was very trim in the dark red Cetagandan dress uniform that was everyday garb for security staff in the Celestial Garden. He wore, of course, full formal face paint in the Imperial pattern rather than that of his clan, marking his primary allegiance; a white base with intricate black curves and red accents that Miles thought of as the bleeding-zebra look. But by association, it was a pattern that would command instant and profound respect and total, abject cooperation on eight planets. Barrayar, of course, was not one of them.

Miles tried to judge the face beneath the paint. Neither youthful and inexperienced nor aged and sly, Benin appeared to be a bit over forty-standard, young for his rank but not unusually so. The default expression of the face seemed to be one of attentive seriousness, though he managed a brief polite smile when Vorob'yev introduced him to Miles, and a brief relieved smile when Vorob'yev left them alone together.

"Good morning, Lord Vorkosigan," Benin began. Clearly well trained in the social arena, he managed to keep his glance at Miles's physique limited to one quick covert summation. "Did your ambassador explain to you why I am here?"

"Yes, Colonel Benin. I understand you were assigned to investigate the death of that poor fellow—if *fellow* is the right term—we saw so shockingly laid out on the floor of the rotunda the other day." *The best defense is a good offense.* "Did you finally decide it was a suicide?"

Benin's eyes narrowed. "Obviously." But an odd timbre in his voice undercut the statement.

"Well, yes, it was obvious from the exsanguination that the ba died on the spot, rather than having its throat cut elsewhere and the body transported. But it has occurred to me that if the autopsy showed the ba was stunned unconscious when it died, it would rather rule out suicide. It's a subtle test—the shock of death tends to cover the shock of stunning—but you can find the traces if you're looking. Was such a test done, do you know?"

"No."

Miles was not sure if he meant it wasn't done, or—no, Benin had to know. "Why not? If I were you, it's the first test I'd ask for. Can you get it done now? Though two days late is not ideal."

"The autopsy is over. The ba has been cremated," Benin stated flatly.

"What, already? Before the case was closed? Who ordered that? Not you, surely."

"Not—Lord Vorkosigan, this is not your concern. This is not what I came to talk with you about," Benin said stiffly, then paused. "Why this morbid interest in the Celestial Lady's late servant?"

"I thought it was the most interesting thing I'd seen since I came to Eta Ceta. It's in my line, you see. I've done civil security cases at home. Murder investigations—" well, one, anyway, "successfully, I might add." Yes, what *was* this Cetagandan officer's experience in such things? The Celestial Garden was such a well-ordered place. "Does this sort of thing happen here often?"

"No." Benin stared at Miles with intensified interest.

So the man might be well read, but lacked hands-on experience, at least since he'd been promoted to this post. He was damned quick at catching nuances, though. "It seems awfully premature to me, to cremate the victim before the case is closed. There are always late-occurring questions."

"I assure you, Lord Vorkosigan, Ba Lura was not carried unconscious into the funeral rotunda, dead or alive. Even the ceremonial guards would have noticed *that.*" Did the slight spin on his tone hint that perhaps the ceremonial guards were chosen for beauty rather than brains?

"Well, actually, I had a theory," Miles burbled on enthusiastically. "You're just the man to confirm or disprove it for me, too. *Has* anyone testified noticing the ba enter the rotunda?"

"Not exactly."

"Ah? Yes, and the spot where it lay dead—I don't know what kind of vid coverage you have of the building, but that area *had* to have been occluded. Or it could not have been, what, fifteen, twenty minutes before the body was discovered, right?"

Another thoughtful stare. "You are correct, Lord Vorkosigan. Normally, the entire rotunda is within visual scan, but because of the height and width of the catafalque, two—well, there is some blockage."

"Ah, ha! So how did the ba know exactly—no, let me rephrase that. Who all could have known about the blind spot at the late Empress's feet? Your own security, and who else? Just how high up did your orders come down from, Colonel Benin? Are you by chance under pressure from above to deliver a quick confirmation of suicide and close your case?"

Benin twitched. "A quick conclusion to this vile interruption of a most solemn occasion is certainly desirable. I desire it as ardently as anyone else. Which brings me to *my* questions for *you,* Lord Vorkosigan. If I may be permitted!"

"Oh. Certainly." Miles paused, then added, just as Benin opened his mouth, "Are you doing this on your own time, then? I admire your dedication."

"No." Benin took a breath, and composed himself again. "Lord Vorkosigan. Our records indicate you left the reception hall to speak privately with a haut-lady."

"Yes. She sent a ba servant with an invitation. I could hardly refuse. Besides . . . I was curious."

"I can believe that," muttered Benin. "What was the substance of your conversation with the haut Rian Degtiar?"

"Why—surely you monitored it." Surely they had not, or this interview would have taken place two days ago, before Miles had ever left the Celestial Garden—and been a lot less politely conducted, too. But Benin doubtless had a vid of Miles's exit from and entrance to the reception area, and testimony from the little ba escort as well.

"Nevertheless," said Benin neutrally.

"Well—I have to admit, I found the conversation extremely confusing. She's a geneticist, you know."

"Yes."

"I believe her interest in me—excuse me, I find this personally embarrassing. I believe her interest in me was genetic. I am widely rumored to be a mutant. But my physical disabilities are entirely teratogenic, damage done by a poison I encountered pre-natally. Not genetic. It's *very important* to me that be clearly understood." Miles thought briefly of his own ImpSec eavesdroppers. "The haut-women, apparently, collect unusual natural genetic variations for their research. The haut Rian Degtiar seemed quite disappointed to learn I held nothing of interest, genetically speaking. Or so I gathered. She talked all around the subject—I'm not sure but what she perceived her own interest as being rather, um, questionable. I'm afraid I don't find haut motivations entirely comprehensible." Miles smiled cheerfully. There. That was the vaguest convincing-sounding uncheckable bullshit he could come up with on the spur of the moment, and left a good deal of turning-room for what-ever the Colonel had got out of Rian, if anything.

"What *did* interest me, though, was the haut-lady's force-bubble," Miles added. "It never touched the ground. She had to be riding in a float-chair in there, I figured."

"They often do," said Benin.

"That's why I asked you about who saw the Ba Lura enter the chamber. Can anyone use a haut-bubble? Or are they keyed in some way to the wearer? And are they as anonymous as they look, or do you have some way of telling them apart?"

"They are keyed to the wearer. And each has its own unique electronic signature."

"Any security measure made by man can be unmade by man. If he has access to the resources."

"I am aware of this fact, Lord Vorkosigan."

"Hm. You see the scenario I'm driving at, of course. Suppose the ba was stunned elsewhere—a theory that hurried cremation has rendered uncheckable, alas—carried unconscious inside a haut-bubble to the blind spot, and had its throat cut, silently and without a struggle. The bubble glides on. It wouldn't have taken more than fifteen seconds. It wouldn't have required great physi-cal strength on the part of the murderer. But I don't know enough about the specs of the bubbles to judge the technical likelihood.

And I don't know if any bubbles went in and out—how much traffic *was* there in the funeral rotunda during the time-window we're talking about? There can't have been *that* much. Did any haut-lady bubbles enter and exit?"

Benin sat back, pursing his lips, regarding Miles with keen interest. "You have an alert way of looking at the world, Lord Vorkosigan. Five ba servants, four guards, and six haut-women crossed the chamber during the time in question. The ba have duties there, tending to the botanical arrangements and keeping the chamber perfectly clean. The haut-women frequently come to meditate and pay respects to the Celestial Lady. I have interviewed them all. None report noticing the Ba Lura."

"Then . . . the last one must be lying."

Benin tented his fingers, and stared at them. "It is not quite that simple."

Miles paused. "I despise doing internal investigations, myself," he said at last. "I trust you are documenting every breath you're taking, at this point."

Benin almost smiled. "That's entirely my problem, isn't it."

Miles was actually beginning to like the man. "You are, considering the venue, of rather low rank for an investigation of this sensitivity, aren't you?"

"That too . . . is my problem."

"Sacrificable."

Benin grimaced. Oh, yes. Nothing Miles had said yet was anything Benin hadn't thought of too—if he'd dared to speak it aloud. Miles decided to continue sprinkling the favors.

"You've won yourself quite a pretty problem, in this murder, I'd say, ghem-Colonel," Miles remarked. Neither of them were keeping up the pretense about the suicide anymore. "Still, if the method was as I guess, you can deduce quite a lot about the murderer. His rank must be high, his access to internal security great, and—excuse me—he has a *peculiar* sense of humor, for a Cetagandan. The insult to the Empress nearly borders on disloyalty."

"So says an examination of the method," said Benin, in a tone of complaint. "It's motive that troubles me. That harmless old ba has served in the Celestial Garden for decades. Revenge seems most unlikely."

"Mm, perhaps. So if Ba Lura is old news, maybe it's the murderer who's newly arrived. And consider—decades of standing around sopping up secrets—the ba was well placed to *know* things about persons of extraordinarily high rank. Suppose . . . the ba had been tempted, say, into a spot of blackmail. I would think that a close tracing of Ba Lura's movements these last few days might be revealing. For instance, did the ba leave the Celestial Garden at any time?"

"That . . . investigation is in progress."

"If I were you, I'd jump on that aspect. The ba might have communicated with its murderer." *Aboard his ship, in orbit, yes.* "The timing is peculiar, you see. To my eye, this murder shows every sign of having been rushed. If the murderer had had months to plan, he could have done a much better and quieter job. I think he had to make a lot of decisions in a hurry, maybe in that very hour, and some of them were, frankly, bad."

"Not bad enough," sighed Benin. "But you interest me, Lord Vorkosigan."

Miles trusted that wasn't too much of a double entendre. "This sort of thing is meat and drink to me. It's the first chance I've had to talk shop with anyone since I came to Eta Ceta." He favored Benin with a happy smile. "If you have any more questions for me, please feel free to stop by again."

"I don't suppose you would be willing to answer them under fast-penta?" Benin said, without much hope.

"Ah . . ." Miles thought fast, "with Ambassador Vorob'yev's permission, perhaps." Which would not, of course, be forthcoming. Benin's slight smile fully comprehended the delicacy of a refusal-without-refusing.

"In any case, I should be pleased to continue our acquaintance, Lord Vorkosigan."

"Any time. I'll be here nine more days."

Benin gave Miles a penetrating, unreadable look. "Thank you, Lord Vorkosigan."

Miles had about a million more questions for his new victim, but that was all he dared cram into the opening session. He wanted to project an air of professional interest, not frantic obsession. It was tempting, but dangerous, to think of Benin as an ally. But he was certainly a window into the Celestial Garden. Yeah, a window with eyes that looked back at you. But there had to be some reasonably subtle way to induce Benin to slap himself on the forehead and cry, *Say, I'd better take a closer look at those satrap governors!* He was definitely looking in the correct direction, up. And over his shoulder. A most uncomfortable position in which to work.

How much influence could the satrap governors, all near
Imperial relations, put on the Celestial Garden's security? Not too
much—they were surely regarded as potential threats. But one
might have been building up convenient contacts for a long time
now. One might, indeed, have been perfectly loyal till this new
temptation. It was a dangerous accusation; Benin had to be right
the first time. He wouldn't get a second chance.

Did anyone care about the murder of a ba slave? How much
interest did Benin have in abstract justice? If a Cetagandan
couldn't be one-up in any other way, holier-than-thou might do.
An almost aesthetic drive—the Art of Detection. How much risk
was Benin willing to run, how much did he have to lose? Did
he have a family, or was he some sort of pure warrior-monk,
totally dedicated to his career? To the ghem-Colonel's credit, by
the end of the interview Benin had been keeping his eyes on
Miles's face because he was interested in what Miles was saying,
not because he was not-looking at Miles's body.

Miles rose along with Benin, and paused. "Ghem-Colonel . . . may
I make a personal suggestion?"

Benin tilted his head in curious permission.

"You have good reason to suspect you have a little problem somewhere overhead. But you don't know where yet. If I were you, I'd
go straight to the top. Make personal contact with your Emperor.
It's the only way you can be sure you've capped the murderer."

Did Benin turn pale, beneath his face paint? No way to tell. "*That*
high over—Lord Vorkosigan, I can hardly claim casual acquaintance with my celestial master."

"This isn't friendship. It's business, and it's *his* business. If you
truly mean to be useful to him, it's time you began. Emperors are
only human." Well, Emperor Gregor was. The Cetagandan emperor
was haut-human. Miles hoped that still counted. "Ba Lura must
have been more to him than a piece of the furniture—it served
him for over fifty years. Make no accusations, merely request that
he protect your investigation from being quashed. Strike first, today,
before . . . someone . . . begins to fear your competence." *If you're
going to cover your ass, Benin, by God do it right.*

"I will . . . consider your advice."

"Good hunting." Miles nodded cheerfully, as if it wasn't *his*
problem. "Big game is the best. Think of the honor."

Benin bowed himself out with a small, wry smile, to be escorted
from the building by the embassy guard.

"See you around," Miles called.

"You may be sure of it." Benin's parting wave was almost, but not quite, a salute.

Miles's desire to dissolve into an exhausted puddle on the corridor floor was delayed by the arrival of Vorob'yev, doubtless from his listening post below-stairs, and another man. Ivan hovered behind them with an expression of morose anxiety.

The other man was middle-aged, middle-sized, and wearing the loose bodysuit and well-cut robes of a Cetagandan ghem-lord, in middle colors. They hung comfortably upon him, but his face was free of colored paint, and the haircut he sported was that of a Barrayaran officer. His eyes were . . . interested.

"A very well conducted interview, Lord Vorkosigan," said Vorob'yev, relieving Miles's mind. Slightly. An even wager who had interviewed whom, just now.

"Ghem-Colonel Benin obviously has a lot on his mind," said Miles. "Ah . . ." He glanced at Vorob'yev's companion.

"Allow me to introduce Lord Vorreedi," said the ambassador. "Lord Vorkosigan, of course. Lord Vorreedi is our particular expert in understanding the activities of the ghem-comrades, in all their multitude of arenas."

Which was diplomatic-talk for *Head Spy.* Miles nodded careful greetings. "Pleased to meet you at last, sir."

"And you," Vorreedi returned. "I regret not arriving sooner. The late empress's obsequies were expected to be rather more sedate than this. I didn't know of your keen interest in civil security, Lord Vorkosigan. Would you like us to arrange you a tour of the local police organizations?"

"I'm afraid time will not permit. But yes, if I hadn't been able to get into a military career, I think police work might have been my next choice."

A uniformed corporal from the embassy's ImpSec office approached, and motioned away his civilian-clothed superior. They conferred in low tones, and the corporal handed over a sheaf of colored papers to the protocol officer, who in turn handed them to the ambassador with a few words. Vorob'yev, his brows climbing, turned to Ivan.

"Lord Vorpatril. Some invitations have arrived for you this morning."

Ivan took the sheets, their colors and perfumes clashing, and leafed through them in puzzlement. "Invitations?"

"Lady Benello invites you to a private dinner, Lady Arvin invites you to a fire-pattern-viewing party—both tonight—and Lady Senden invites you to observe a court-dance practice, this afternoon."

"Who?"

"Lady Senden," the protocol officer supplied, "is Lady Benello's married sister, according to last night's background checks." He gave Ivan an odd look. "Just what did you do to merit this sudden popularity, Lord Vorpatril?"

Ivan held the papers gingerly, smiling thinly, by which Miles deduced he hadn't told the protocol officer quite *everything* about last night's adventure. "I'm not sure, sir." Ivan caught Miles's suffused gaze, and reddened slightly.

Miles craned his neck. "Do any of these women have interesting connections at the Celestial Garden, do you suppose? Or friends who do?"

"*Your* name isn't on these, coz," Ivan pointed out ruthlessly, waving the invitations, all hand-calligraphed in assorted colored inks. A faintly cheerful look was starting in his eyes, displacing his earlier glum dread.

"Perhaps some more background checks would be in order, my lord?" murmured the protocol officer to the ambassador.

"If you please, Colonel."

The protocol officer left with his corporal. Miles, with a grateful parting wave to Vorob'yev, tagged along after Ivan, who clutched the colored papers firmly and eyed him with suspicion.

"Mine," Ivan asserted, as soon as they were out of earshot. "You have ghem-Colonel Benin, who is more to your taste anyway."

"There are a lot of ghem-women here in the capital who serve as ladies-in-waiting to the haut-women in the Celestial Garden, is all," Miles said. "I'd . . . like to meet that ghem-lady I went walking with last night, for instance, but she didn't give me her name."

"I doubt many of Yenaro's crowd have celestial connections."

"I think this one was an exception. Though the people I *really* want to meet are the satrap governors. Face-to-face."

"You'd have a better chance at that at one of the official functions."

"Oh, yes. I'm planning on it."

Chapter Eight

The Celestial Garden was not quite so intimidating on the second visit, Miles assured himself. This time they were not lost in a great stream of galactic envoys, but were only a little party of three. Miles, Ambassador Vorob'yev, and Mia Maz were admitted through a side gate, almost privately, and escorted by a single servitor to their destination.

The trio made a good picture. Miles and the ambassador wore their ultra-formal House blacks again. Maz wore black linings and pure white over-robes, combining the two mourning colors, acknowledging the Cetagandan hue without over-stepping the boundaries of haut-privilege. No accident that it also displayed her own dark hair and lively complexion to advantage, and set off her two companions as well. Her dimple flashed with her smile of anticipation and pleasure, directed over Miles's head to Ambassador Vorob'yev. Miles, between them, felt like an unruly kid being escorted firmly by his two parents. Vorob'yev was taking no chances of unauthorized violations of etiquette today.

The offering of the elegiac poetry to the dead empress was not a ceremony normally attended by galactic delegates, with the exception of a very few high-ranking Cetagandan allies. Miles did not qualify on either count, and Vorob'yev had been forced to pull every string he owned to get them this invitation. Ivan had

ducked out, pleading weariness from the court-dance practice and
the fire-viewing parties of yesterday, and the excuse of four more
invitations for this afternoon and evening. It was a suspiciously
smug weariness. Miles had let him escape, his sadistic urge to
make Ivan sit along with him through what promised to be an
interminable afternoon and evening blunted by the reflection that
his cousin could do little to contribute to what was essentially
an information-gathering expedition. And Ivan might—just
might—pick up some useful new contacts among the ghem.
Vorob'yev had substituted the Vervani woman, to her obvious
delight, and Miles's benefit.

To Miles's relief the ceremony was not carried out in the
rotunda, with all its alarming associations, where the empress's
body still lay. Neither did the haut use anything so crass as an
auditorium, with people packed in efficient rows. Instead the servitor took them to a—dell, Miles supposed he might call it, a
bowl in the garden lined with flowers, plants, and hundreds of
little box-seat arrangements overlooking a complex array of daises
and platforms at the bottom. As befitted their rank, or lack of
it, the servitor placed the Barrayaran party in the last and highest
row, three quarters of the way around from the best frontal view.
This suited Miles—he could watch nearly the whole audience
without being over-looked himself. The low benches were flawless
wood, hand-smoothed to a high polish. Mia Maz, bowed gallantly
to her seat by Vorob'yev, patted her skirts and stared around,
bright-eyed.

Miles stared too, much less bright-eyed—he'd spent a great deal
of time the last day peering into his comconsole display, swotting
up background in hopes of finding an end to this tangle. The haut
were filtering in to their places, men in flowing snowy robes escorting white bubbles. The dell was beginning to resemble a great bank
of white climbing roses in a frenzy of bloom. Miles finally saw
the purpose of the box seats—it gave room for the bubbles. Was
Rian among them?

"Will the women speak first, or how do they organize this?"
Miles asked Maz.

"The women won't speak at all, today," said Maz. "They had their
own ceremony yesterday. They'll start with the men of lowest rank
and work up through the constellations."

Ending with the satrap governors. All of them. Miles settled
himself with the patience of a panther in a tree. The men he had

come to see were filing into the bottom of the bowl even now. If Miles had owned a tail, it would have twitched. As it was, he stilled a tapping boot.

The eight satrap governors, assisted by their highest-ranking ghem-officers, sank into seats around a raised reserved dais. Miles squinted, wishing for rangefinder binoculars—not that he could have carried them past the tight security. With a twinge of sympathy he wondered what ghem-Colonel Benin was doing right now, and if Cetagandan security went as frantic behind the scenes as Barrayaran security did at any ceremony involving Emperor Gregor. He could just picture them.

But he had what he'd come for—all eight of his suspects, artistically arranged on display. He studied his top four with particular care.

The governor of Mu Ceta was one of the Degtiar constellation, the present emperor's half-uncle, being half-brother to the late empress. Maz too watched closely as he settled his aged body creakily into his seat, and brushed away his attendants with jerky, irritated motions. The governor of Mu Ceta had been at his present post only two years, replacing the governor who had been recalled, and subsequently quietly exiled into retirement, after the Vervain invasion debacle. The man was very old, and very experienced, and had been chosen explicitly to calm Vervani fears of a re-match. Not, Miles thought, the treasonous type. Yet by haut Rian's testimony, every man in the circle had taken at least one step over the line, secretly receiving the unauthorized gene banks.

The governor of Rho Ceta, Barrayar's nearest neighbor, worried Miles a great deal more. The haut Este Rond was middle-aged and vigorous, haut-tall though unusually heavy. His ghem-officer stood well back from his governor's sweeping movements. Rond's general effect was bullish. And he was bullishly tenacious in his efforts, diplomatic and otherwise, to improve Cetaganda's trade access through the Barrayaran-controlled Komarr wormhole jumps. The Rond was one of the more junior haut-constellations, seeking growth. Este Rond was a hot prospect for sure.

The governor of Xi Ceta, Marilac's neighbor, wafted in, proud-nosed. The haut Slyke Giaja was what Miles thought of as a typical haut-lord, tall and lean and faintly effeminate. Arrogant, as befit a younger half-brother of the emperor. And dangerous. Young enough to be a possibility, though older than Este Rond.

The youngest suspect, the haut Ilsum Kety, governor of Sigma

Ceta, was a mere stripling of forty-five or so. In body type he was much like Slyke Giaja, who was in fact a cousin of his through their mothers, who were half-sisters though of different constellations. Haut family trees were even more confusing than the Vors'. It would take a full-time geneticist to keep track of all the semi-siblings.

Eight white bubbles floated into the basin, and took up an arc to the left of the circle of satrap governors. The ghem-officers took up a similar arc to the right. They, Miles realized, were going to get to *stand* through the entire afternoon's ceremony. Being a ghem-general wasn't all blood and beer. But could any of those bubbles be . . . ?

"Who are those ladies?" Miles asked Maz, nodding toward the octet.

"They are the satrap governors' consorts."

"I . . . thought the haut did not marry."

"There's no personal relationship implied in the title. They are appointed centrally, just like the governors themselves."

"Not by the governors? What's their function? Social secretaries?"

"Not at all. They are chosen by the empress, to be her representatives in all dealings having to do with the Star Crèche's business. All the haut living on a satrap planet send their genetic contracts through the consorts to the central gene bank here at the Celestial Garden, where the fertilizations and any genetic alterations take place. The consorts also oversee the return of the uterine replicators with the growing fetuses to their parents on the outlying planets. That has to be the strangest cargo run in the Cetagandan empire—once a year for each planet."

"Do the consorts travel back to Eta Ceta once a year, in that case, to personally accompany their charges?"

"Yes."

"Ah." Miles settled back, smiling fixedly. *Now* he saw how the Empress Lisbet had set up her scheme, the living channels she had used to communicate with each satrap governor. If every one of those consorts wasn't in on this plot to her eyebrows, he'd eat his boots. *Sixteen. I have sixteen suspects, not eight. Oh, God.* And he'd come here to cut *down* his list. But it followed logically that Ba Lura's murderer might not have had to borrow or steal a haut-lady's bubble. She might have owned one already. "Do the consort-ladies work closely with their satrap governors?"

Maz shrugged. "I really don't know. Not necessarily, I suppose. Their areas of responsibility are highly segregated."

A majordomo took center stage, and made a silent motion. Every voice in the dell went still. Every haut-lord dropped to his knees on padded rests thoughtfully provided in front of the benches. All the white bubbles bobbled—Miles still wondered how many of the haut-women cheated and cut corners at these ceremonies. After an anticipatory hush, the emperor himself arrived, escorted by guards in white and blood-red uniforms, zebra-faced, of terrible aspect if you took them seriously. Miles did, not for the face paint, but in certain knowledge of just how nervous and twitchy in the trigger-finger such an awesome responsibility could make a man.

It was the first time in his life Miles had seen the Cetagandan emperor in the flesh, and he studied the man as avidly as he had studied the satrap governors. Emperor the haut Fletchir Giaja was tall, lean, hawk-faced like his demi-cousins, his hair still untouched by gray despite his seventy-odd years. A survivor—he had succeeded to his rank at a fantastically young age for a Cetagandan, less than thirty, and held on through a wobbly youth to an apparently iron-secure mid-life. He seated himself with great assurance and grace of movement, serene and confident. Ringed by bowing traitors. Miles's nostrils flared, and he took a breath, dizzy with the irony. At another signal from the majordomo, everyone regained their seats, still in that remarkable silence.

The presentation of the elegiac poems in honor of the late haut Lisbet Degtiar began with the heads of the lowest-ranking constellations present. Each poem had to fit into one of half a dozen correct formal types, all mercifully short. Miles was extremely impressed with the elegance, beauty, and apparent deep feeling of about the first ten offerings. The recitation had to be one of those great formal ordeals, like taking an oath or getting married, in which the preparations wildly outmassed the moment of actualization. Great care was taken with movement, voice, and imperceptible variations of what to Miles's eye were identical white dress robes. But gradually, Miles began to be aware of stock phrases, repeated ideas; by the thirtieth man, his eyes were starting to glaze over. More than ever Miles wished Ivan by his side, suffering along with him.

Maz whispered an occasional interpretation or gloss, which helped fend off creeping drowsiness—Miles had not slept well last night. The satrap governors were all doing good imitations of men stuffed and mounted, except for the ancient governor of Mu Ceta, who slumped in open boredom, watching through sardonic slitted eyes as his juniors, i.e., everyone else there, performed with various degrees of flop-sweat. The older and more experienced men, as they came on, at least had better deliveries, if not necessarily better poems.

Miles meditated on the character of Lord X, trying to match it with one of the eight faces ranged before him. The murderer/traitor was something of a tactical genius. He had been presented with an unanticipated opportunity to gain power, had committed rapidly to an all-out effort, evolved a plan, and struck. How fast? The first satrap governor had arrived in person only ten days before Miles and Ivan had, the last only four days before. Yenaro, the embassy's ImpSec office had finally reported, had put his sculpture together in just two days from designs delivered from an unknown source, working his minions around the clock. Ba Lura could only have been suborned since its mistress's death, not quite three weeks ago.

The aged haut thought nothing of taking on plans that took decades to mature, with can't-lose security. Witness the old empress herself. They experienced time differently than Miles did, he was fairly sure. This whole chain of events smelled . . . young. Or young at heart.

Miles's opponent must be in an interesting frame of mind just now. He was a man of action and decision. But now he had to lie quiet and do nothing to draw attention to himself, even as it began to look more and more like Ba Lura's death was not going to pass as planned as a suicide. He had to sit tight on his bank and the Great Key till the funeral was over, and glide softly back to his planetary base—because he couldn't start the revolt from here; he'd prepared nothing in advance before he'd left home.

So would he send the Great Key on, or keep it with him? If he'd sent it back to his satrapy already, Miles was in deep trouble. Well, deeper trouble. Would the governor take the risk of losing the powerful tokens in transit? Surely not.

The droning amateur poets were getting to Miles. He found his subconscious mind not working along with the rest of it as it should, but going off on its own tangent. A poem of his own in honor of the late empress formed, unbidden, in his brain.

A Degtiar empress named Lisbet
Trapped a satrap lord neatly in his net.

Enticed into treason
For all the wrong reasons,
He'll soon have a crash with his kismet.

He choked down a genuinely horrible impulse to bounce down to the center of the dell and declaim his poetic offering to the assembled haut multitude, just to see what would happen.

Mia Maz glanced aside in concern at his muffled snort. "Are you all right?"

"Yes. Sorry," he whispered. "I'm just having an attack of limericks."

Her eyes widened, and she bit her lip; only her deepening dimple betrayed her. "*Shhh,*" she said, with feeling.

The ceremony went on uninterrupted. Alas, there was all too much time to evolve more verse, of equal artistic merit. He gazed out at the banks of white bubbles.

A beautiful lady named Rian
Hypnotized a Vor scion.
The little defective
Thinks he's a detective,
But instead will be fed to the lion. . . .

How did the haut live through these things? Had they bio-engineered their bladders to some inhuman capacity, along with all the other rumored changes?

Fortunately, before Miles could think of two rhymes for *Vorob'yev*, the first satrap governor arose to take his place on the speaker's dais. Miles came abruptly awake.

The satrap governors' poems were all excellent, all in the most difficult forms—and, Maz informed Miles in a whisper, mostly ghost-written by the best haut-women poets in the Celestial Garden. Rank hath its privileges. But try as he might, Miles could not read any useful sinister double meanings into them—his suspect was not using this moment to publicly confess his crimes, put the wind up his enemies, or any of the other really interesting possibilities. Miles was almost surprised. The placement of Ba Lura's body suggested Lord X had a weakness for the baroque in his plotting, when the simple would have done better. Making an Art of it?

The emperor sat through it with unruffled solemn calm. The

satrap governors all received polite nods of thanks from the chief
mourner for their elegant praises. Miles wondered if Benin had
taken his advice, and spoken with his master yet. He hoped so.

And then, abruptly, the literary ordeal was over. Miles suppressed
an impulse to applaud; that was apparently Not Done. The majordomo came out and made another cryptic gesture, at which everyone went to their knees again; the emperor and his guards
decamped, followed by the consort bubbles, the satrap governors,
and their ghem-officers. Then everyone else was freed—to find a
bathroom, Miles trusted.

The haut race might have divested itself of the traditional
meanings and functions of sexuality, but they were still human
enough to make the sharing of food part of life's basic ceremonies. In their own way. Trays of meat were sculpted into flowers.
Vegetables masqueraded as crustaceans, and fruit as tiny animals.
Miles stared thoughtfully at the plate of simple boiled rice on the
buffet table. Every grain had been individually hand-arranged in
an elaborate spiral pattern. He almost tripped over his own boots,
boggling at it. He controlled his bemusement and tried to refocus
on the business at hand.

The informal—by Celestial Garden standards—refreshments were
served in a long pavilion open as usual to the garden, presently
lit in a warm afternoon glow that invited relaxation. The haut-
ladies in their bubbles had evidently gone elsewhere—someplace
where they could drop their bubbles to eat, presumably. This was
the most exclusive of several post-poetry buffet sites scattered
around the Celestial Garden. The emperor himself was somewhere
at the other end of the graceful building. Miles wasn't quite sure
how Vorob'yev had got them in, but the man deserved a commen-
dation for extraordinary service. Maz, eyes alight, hand on
Vorob'yev's arm, was clearly in some sort of sociologist's heaven.

"Here we go," murmured Vorob'yev, and Miles went heads-up.
The haut Este Rond's party was entering the crowded pavilion.
The other haut, not knowing what to do about these out-of-place
outlanders, had been trying to pretend the Barrayarans were
invisible ever since they'd arrived. Este Rond did not have that
option. The beefy, white-robed satrap governor, his painted and
uniformed ghem-general by his side, paused to greet his Barrayaran neighbors.

A white-robed woman, unusual in this heavily male gathering, trailed the Rond's ghem-general. Her silver-blond hair was gathered in a looping queue down her back to her ankles, and she stood with downcast eyes, not speaking. She was much older than Rian, but certainly a haut-woman—*God* they aged well. She must be the Rond's ghem-general's haut-wife—any officer destined to such high planetary rank would have been expected to win one long ago.

Maz was giving Miles some inexplicable but urgent signal—a tiny head shake, and a *No, no!* formed silently on her lips. What was she trying to say? The haut-wife, apparently, did not speak unless spoken to—Miles had never seen anyone's body-language express such extraordinary reserve and containment, not even the haut Rian's.

Governor Rond and Vorob'yev exchanged elaborate courtesies, by which Miles gathered that the Rond had been their ticket in. Vorob'yev culminated his diplomatic coup by introducing Miles. "The lieutenant takes a very gratifying interest in the finer points of Cetagandan culture," Vorob'yev recommended him to the governor's attention.

The haut Rond nodded cordially; when Vorob'yev recommended someone it seemed even Cetagandan haut-lords attended.

"I was sent to learn, as well as serve, sir. It is my duty and my pleasure." Miles favored the haut-governor with a precisely calculated bow. "And I must say, I have certainly been having learning experiences." Miles tried by his edged smile to put as much double-spin on his words as possible.

The Rond smiled back, cool-eyed. But then, if Este Rond was Lord X, he ought to be cool. They exchanged a few empty pleasantries about the diplomatic life, then Miles ventured boldly, "Would you be so kind, haut Rond, as to introduce me to Governor haut Ilsum Kety?"

A razor-thin smile twitched the Rond's lips, and he glanced across the room at his fellow-governor and genetic superior. "Why, certainly, Lord Vorkosigan." If the Rond was going to be stuck with these outlanders, Miles gathered, he'd be happy to share the embarrassment.

The Rond shepherded Miles over. Vorob'yev was left talking with the Rho Cetan ghem-general, who was taking a sincere professional interest in his potential enemies. Vorob'yev shot Miles a warning not-quite-glower, just a slight creasing of his eyebrows; Miles opened his hand, down at his side, in an *I'll-be-good* promise.

As soon as they were out of the ambassador's earshot, Miles murmured to the Rond, "We know about Yenaro, you know."

"I beg your pardon?" said the Rond, in realistic-sounding bafflement, and then they arrived at the haut Ilsum Kety's little group.

Close-up, Kety seemed even taller and leaner than he had at a distance at the poetry-readings. He had cool chiseled features very much in the haut mold—hawk-noses had been the style ever since Fletchir Giaja had ascended the throne. A bit of silver-gray at the temples set off his dark hair. Since the man was only in his mid-forties, and haut to boot . . . by God, yes. The touch of frost was quite perfect, but it had to have been artificially produced, Miles realized with well-concealed inner amusement. In a world where the old men had it all, there was no social benefit to a youthful appearance when one actually *was* young.

Kety too was attended by his ghem-general, who also kept a haut-wife on standby. Miles tried not to let his eyes bug out too obviously. She was extraordinary even by haut-standards. Her hair was a rich dark chocolate color, parted in the middle and gathered in a thick braid that trailed down her back to actually coil upon the floor. Her skin was vanilla cream. Her eyes, widening slightly as she glanced down at Miles approaching by the Rond's side, were an astonishing light cinnamon color, large and liquid. A complete confection indeed, wholly edible and scarcely older than Rian. Miles was quietly grateful for his previous exposure to Rian, which helped a great deal toward keeping him on his feet and not crawling on his knees toward her right now.

Ilsum Kety clearly had no time for or interest in outlanders, but for whatever reason did not care or dare to offend the Rond; Miles managed a brief exchange of formal greetings with him. The Rond took the opportunity to skim Miles off his hands and escape to the buffet.

The irritated Kety was failing to perform his social duties. Miles took matters into his own hands, and directed a half-bow at Kety's ghem-general. The general, at least, was of the customary Cetagandan age for his position, i.e., antique. "General Chilian, sir. I have studied you in my history texts. It is an honor to meet you. And your fine lady. I don't believe I know her name." He smiled hopefully at her.

Chilian's brows, going up, drew back down in a slight frown. "Lord Vorkosigan," he acknowledged shortly. But he didn't take up the hint. After a tiny glint of distaste in Miles's direction, the haut-woman stood as if she weren't there, or at least wishing so. The two men seemed to treat her as if she were invisible.

So if Kety were Lord X, what must be going through his mind right now, as he found himself cornered by his intended victim? He'd planted the false rod on the Barrayaran party, set up the Ba Lura to tell Rian and convince her to make accusations of theft, killed the ba, and waited for the results. Which had been—a resounding silence. Rian had apparently done nothing, not said a word to anyone. Did Kety wonder if he'd killed Lura too soon after all, before it had made a chance to confess its loss? It must be very puzzling for the man. But nothing, not a twitch, showed on his haut face. Which would, of course, also be the case if the governor were totally innocent.

Miles smiled affably at the haut Ilsum Kety. "I understand we have a mutual hobby, governor," he purred.

"Oh?" said Kety unencouragingly.

"An interest in the Cetagandan Imperial regalia. Such a fascinating set of artifacts, and so evocative of the history and culture of the haut race, don't you think? And its future."

Kety stared at him blankly. "I would not regard that as a pastime. Nor a suitable interest for an outlander."

"It's a military officer's duty to know his enemies."

"I would not know. Those tasks belong to the ghem."

"Such as your friend Lord Yenaro? A slender reed for you to lean on, governor, I'm afraid you are about to find."

Kety's pale brow wrinkled. "Who?"

Miles sighed inwardly, wishing he could flood the entire pavilion with fast-penta. The haut were all so damned controlled, they looked like they were lying even when they weren't. "I wonder, haut Kety, if you would introduce me to Governor haut Slyke Giaja. As an Imperial relation of sorts myself, I can't help feeling he is something of my opposite number."

The haut Kety blinked, surprised into honesty. "I doubt *Slyke* would think so. . . ." By the look on his face he was balancing the annoyance to Prince Slyke Giaja of inflicting the outlander on him, versus the relief of being rid of Miles himself. Self-interest won, up to a point; the haut Kety motioned ghem-General Chilian nearer, and dispatched him to gain permission for the transfer. With a polite farewell and thank-you to Kety, Miles trailed after the ghem-general, hoping to take advantage of any indecision to press his suit. Imperial princes were not likely to make themselves so readily accessible as ordinary haut-governors.

"General . . . if the haut Slyke cannot speak with me, would you deliver a short message to him?" Miles tried to keep his voice even, despite his limping stride; Chilian was not shortening his steps in favor to the Barrayaran guest. "Just three words."

Chilian shrugged. "I suppose I can."

"Tell him . . . Yenaro is ours. Just that."

The general's brows rose at this cryptic utterance. "Very well."

The message, of course, would be repeated later to Cetagandan Imperial Security. Miles didn't mind the idea of Cetagandan Imperial Security taking a closer look at Lord Yenaro.

The haut Slyke Giaja was sitting with a small group of men, both ghem and haut, on the far side of the pavilion. Unusually, the party also included a white bubble, hovering near the Prince. Attendant upon it was a ghem-lady Miles recognized, despite the voluminous formal white robes she wore today—the woman who'd been sent to fetch him at Yenaro's party. The ghem-woman glanced across at him approaching, stared briefly, then looked resolutely away. So who was in the bubble? Rian? Slyke's consort? Someone else entirely?

Kety's ghem-general bent to murmur in his ear. Slyke Giaja glanced across at Miles, frowned, and shook his head. Chilian shrugged, and bent to murmur again. Miles, watching his lips move, saw his message or something very like it being delivered—the word *Yenaro* was quite distinctive. Slyke's face betrayed no expression at all. He waved the ghem-general away.

General Chilian returned to Miles's side. "The haut Slyke is too busy to see you at this time," he reported blandly.

"Thank you anyway," Miles intoned, equally blandly. The general nodded acknowledgment, and went back to his master.

Miles stared around, wondering how to leverage access to his next prospect. The Mu Cetan governor was not present—he'd probably departed directly from the garden amphitheater to take a nap.

Mia Maz drifted up to Miles, smiling, curiosity in her eyes. "Finding any good conversations, Lord Vorkosigan?" she asked.

"Not so far," he admitted ruefully. "Yourself?"

"I would not presume. I've mostly been listening."

"One learns more that way."

"Yes. Listening is the invisible conversational coup. I feel quite smug."

"What have you learned?"

"The haut topic at this party is each other's poetry, which they are slicing up along strict lines of dominance. By some coincidence everyone is agreeing that the men of higher rank had the better offerings."

"I couldn't tell the difference, myself."

"Oh, but we are not haut."

"Why were you wagging your eyebrows at me a while ago?" Miles asked.

"I was trying to warn you about a rare point of Cetagandan etiquette. How you are supposed to behave when you encounter a haut-woman outside of her bubble."

"It was . . . the first time I'd ever seen one," he lied strategically. "Did I do all right?"

"Hm, barely. You see, the haut-women lose the privilege of the force-shields when they marry out of the genome into the ghem-rank. They become as ghem-women—sort of. But the loss of the shield is considered a great loss of face. So the polite thing to do is to behave as if the bubble were still there. You must never directly address a haut-wife, even if she's standing right in front of you. Put all inquiries through her ghem-husband, and wait for him to transmit the replies."

"I . . . didn't say anything to them."

"Oh, good. And you must never stare directly at them, either, I'm afraid."

"I thought the men were being rude, to close the women out of the conversation."

"Absolutely not. They were being most polite, Cetagandan style."

"Oh. But the way they carry themselves, the women might as well still be in the bubbles. Virtual bubbles."

"That's the idea, yes."

"Do the same rules go for . . . haut-women who still have the privilege of their bubbles?"

"I have no idea. I cannot imagine a haut-woman talking face-to-face with an outlander."

Miles became aware of a ghostly gray presence at his elbow, and tried not to jump. It was the haut Rian Degtiar's little ba servant. The ba had passed into the room without a ripple, ignored by its inhabitants. Miles's heart began to race, a response he muffled in a polite nod at the servitor.

"Lord Vorkosigan. My lady wishes to speak with you," said the ba. Maz's eyes widened.

"Thank you, I would be pleased," Miles responded. "Ah . . ." He glanced around for Ambassador Vorob'yev, who was still being buttonholed by the Rho Cetan ghem-general. Good. Permissions not requested could not be denied. "Maz, would you be so kind as to tell the ambassador I've gone to speak with a lady. Mm . . . I may be some time at it. Go on without me. I'll catch up with you back at the embassy, if necessary."

"I don't think—" began Maz doubtfully, but Miles was already turning away. He shot her a smile over his shoulder and a cheerful little wave as he followed the ba out of the pavilion.

Chapter Nine

The little ba, its expression devoid as ever of any comment on its mistress's affairs, led Miles on a lengthy walk through the garden's winding paths, around ponds and along tiny, exquisite artificial streams. Miles almost stopped to gape at an emerald-green lawn populated by a flock of ruby-red peacocks the size of songbirds, slowly stalking about. A sunny spot on a ledge a little farther on was occupied by something resembling a spherical cat, or perhaps a bouquet of cat-fur, soft, white . . . yes, there was an animal in there; a pair of turquoise-blue eyes blinked once at him from the fuzz, and closed again in perfect indolence.

Miles did not attempt conversation or questions. He might not have been personally monitored by Cetagandan Imperial Security on his last trip to the Celestial Garden, when he'd been mixed in with a thousand other galactic delegates; this was certainly not the case today. He prayed Rian would realize this. Lisbet would have. He could only hope Rian had inherited Lisbet's safe zones and procedures, along with the Great Key and her genetic mission.

A white bubble waited in a cloistered walkway. The ba bowed to it and departed.

Miles cleared his throat. "Good evening, milady. You asked to see me? How may I serve you?" He kept his greeting as general as possible. For all he knew it was ghem-Colonel Benin and a voice-filter inside that damned blank sphere.

Rian's voice or a good imitation murmured, "Lord Vorkosigan. You expressed an interest in genetic matters. I thought you would care for a short tour."

Good. They were monitored, and she knew it. He suppressed the tiny part of himself that had been hoping against all reason for a love-affair cover, and answered, "Indeed, milady. All medical procedures interest me. I feel the corrections to my own damage were extremely incomplete. I'm always looking for new hopes and chances, whenever I have an opportunity to visit more advanced galactic societies."

He paced along beside her floating sphere, trying, and failing, to keep track of the twists and turns of their route through archways and other buildings. He managed a suitably admiring comment or two on the passing scenery, so their silence would not be too obvious. He'd walked about a kilometer from the Emperor's buffet, he gauged, though certainly not in a straight line, when they came to a long, low white building. Despite the usual charming landscaping, it had "biocontrol" written all over it, in the details of its window seals and door-locks. The air lock required complicated encodations from Rian, though once it had identified her, it admitted him under her aegis without a murmur of protest.

She led him through surprisingly un-labyrinthine corridors to a spacious office. It was the most utilitarian, least artistic chamber he'd yet seen in the Celestial Garden. One entire wall was glass, overlooking a long room that had a lot more in common with galactic-standard bio-labs than with the garden outside. Form follows function, and this place was bristling with function: purpose, not the languid ease of the pavilions. It was presently deserted, shut down, but for a lone ba servitor moving among the benches doing some sort of meticulous janitorial task. But of course. No haut genetic contracts were approved or, presumably, carried out during the period of mourning for the Celestial Lady, putative mistress of this domain. A screaming-bird pattern decorated the surface of a comconsole, and hovered above several cabinet-locks. He was standing in the center of the Star Crèche.

The bubble settled by one wall, vanishing without a pop. The haut Rian Degtiar rose from her float-chair.

Her ebony hair today was bound up in thick loops, tumbling no farther than her waist. Her pure white robes were only calf-length, two simple layers comfortably draped over a white bodysuit that covered her from neck to white-slippered toe. More woman, less icon, and yet . . . Miles had hoped repeated exposure to her beauty might build up an immunity in him to the mind-numbing effect of her. Obviously, he would need more exposure than this. Lots more. Lots and lots and—*stop it. Don't be more of a idiot than you have to be.*

"We can talk here," she said, gliding to a station chair beside the comconsole desk and settling herself in it. Her simplest movements were like dance. She nodded to another station chair across from hers, and Miles lurched into it with a strained smile, intensely conscious that his boots barely touched the floor. Rian seemed as direct as the ghem-generals' wives were closed. Was the Star Crèche itself a sort of psychological force-bubble for her? Or did she merely consider him so sub-human as to be completely non-threatening, as incapable as a pet animal of judging her?

"I . . . trust you are correct," Miles said, "but won't there be repercussions from your Security for bringing me in here?"

She shrugged. "If they wish, they can request the Emperor to reprimand me."

"They cannot, er, reprimand you directly?"

"No."

The statement was flat, factual. Miles hoped she was not being overly optimistic. And yet . . . by the lift of her chin, the set of her shoulders, it was clear that the haut Rian Degtiar, Handmaiden of the Star Crèche, firmly believed that within these walls *she* was empress. For the next eight days, anyway.

"I trust this is important. And brief. Or I'm going to emerge to find ghem-Colonel Benin waiting for an exit-interview."

"It's important." Her blue eyes seemed to blaze. "I know which satrap governor is the traitor, now!"

"Excellent! That was fast. Uh . . . how?"

"The Key was, as you said, a decoy. False and empty. As you knew." Suspicion still glinted in her eye, lighting upon him.

"By reason alone, milady. Do you have evidence?"

"Of a sort." She leaned forward intently. "Yesterday, Prince Slyke Giaja had his consort bring him to the Star Crèche. For a tour, he pretended. He insisted I produce the Empress's regalia, for his inspection. His face said nothing, but he gazed upon the collection for a long time, before turning away, as if satisfied. He congratulated me upon my loyal work, and left immediately there-after."

Slyke Giaja was certainly on Miles's short list. Two data points did not quite make a triangulation, but it was certainly better than nothing. "He didn't ask to see the Key demonstrated, to prove it worked?"

"No."

"He knew, then." *Maybe, maybe . . .* "I bet we gave him food for thought, seeing his decoy sitting there all demure. I wonder which way he's going to jump next? Does he realize *you* know it's a decoy, or does he think you've been fooled?"

"I could not tell."

It wasn't just him, Miles thought with glum relief; even the haut couldn't read other haut. "He must realize he has only to wait eight days, and the truth will come out the first time your successor tries to use the Great Key. Or if not the truth, certainly the accusa-tion against Barrayar. But is that his plan?"

"I don't know what his plan is."

"He wants to involve Barrayar somehow, that I'm sure of. Per-haps even provoke armed conflict between our states."

"This . . ." Rian turned one hand, curled as if around the stolen Great Key, "would be an outrage, but surely . . . not cause enough for war."

"Mm. This may only be Part One. This pis—angers you at us, logically Part Two ought to be something that angers us at you." An uncomfortable new realization. Clearly, Lord X—Slyke Giaja?—was not done yet. "Even if I'd handed the Key back in that first hour—which I don't think was in his script—we still could not have proved we didn't switch it. I wish we hadn't jumped the Ba Lura. I'd give anything to know what story it was *supposed* to have primed us with."

"I wish you hadn't either," said Rian rather tartly, settling back in her station chair and twitching her vest, the first un-purposive move Miles had ever seen her make.

Miles's lips twisted in brief embarrassment. "But—this is important—the consorts, the satrap governors' consorts. You never told me about them. They're in on this, aren't they? Why not on both sides?"

She nodded reluctant acknowledgment. "But I do not suspect any of them of being involved in this treason. That would be . . . unthinkable."

"But surely your Celestial Lady used them—why unthinkable? I mean, here a woman's got a chance to make herself an instant empress, right along with her governor. Or maybe even independently of her governor."

The haut Rian Degtiar shook her head. "No. The consorts do not belong to *them*. They belong to *us*."

Miles blinked, slightly dizzy. "Them. The men. Us. The women. Right?"

"The haut-women are the keepers. . . ." She broke off, evidently hopeless of explaining it to an outlander barbarian. "It cannot be Slyke Giaja's consort."

"I'm sorry. I don't understand."

"It's . . . a matter of the haut-genome. Slyke Giaja is attempting to take something to which he has no right. It is not that he attempts to usurp the emperor. That is his proper part. It's that he attempts to usurp the *empress*. A vileness beyond . . . The haut-genome is ours and ours alone. In this he betrays not the empire, which is nothing, but the haut, which is everything."

"But the consorts are in favor, presumably, of decentralizing the haut-genome."

"Of course. They are all my Celestial Lady's appointees."

"Do they . . . hm. Do they rotate every five years along with their governors? Or independently of them?"

"They are appointed for life, and removed only by the Celestial Lady's direct order."

The consorts seemed powerful allies in the heart of the enemy camp, if only Rian could activate them on her behalf. But she dared not do so, alas, if one of them was herself a traitor. Miles thought bad words to himself.

"The empire," he pointed out, "is the support of the haut. Hardly *nothing*, even from a genetic point of view. The, er, prey to predator ratio is quite high."

She did not smile at his weak zoological joke. He probably ought not to treat her to a recitation of his limericks, then, either. He tried again. "Surely the Empress Lisbet did not mean to instantly fragment the support of the haut."

"No. Not this fast. Maybe not even in this generation," admitted Rian.

Ah. That made more sense, a timing much more in an old haut-lady's style. "But now her plot has been hijacked to another's purpose. Someone with short-term, personal goals, someone she

did not foresee." He moistened his lips, and forged on. "I believe
your Celestial Lady's plans have fractured at their weak spot. The
emperor protects the haut-women's control of the haut-genome;
in turn you lend him legitimacy. A mutual support in both your
interests. The satrap governors have no such motive. You can't give
power away and keep it simultaneously."

Her exquisite lips thinned unhappily, but she did not deny the
point.

Miles took a deep breath. "It's not in Barrayar's interests for Slyke
Giaja to succeed in his power-grab. So far, I can serve you in this,
milady. But it's not in Barrayar's interests for the Cetagandan
Empire to be de-stabilized in the way your empress planned, either.
I think I see how to foil Slyke. But in turn you must give up your
attempt to carry out your mistress's posthumous vision." At her
astonished look he added weakly, "At least for now."

"How . . . would you foil Prince Slyke?" she asked slowly.

"Penetrate his ship. Retrieve the real Great Key. Replace it again
with the decoy, if possible. If we're lucky he might not even
realize the substitution till he got home, and then what could he
do about it? You hand over the real Great Key to your successor,
and it all passes away as smoothly as if it had never happened.
Neither party can accuse the other without incriminating himself."
Or herself. "I think it is, in all, the best outcome that can be
humanly achieved. Any other scenario leads to disaster, of one sort
or another. If we do nothing, the plot comes out in eight days
regardless, and Barrayar gets framed. If I try and fail . . . at least
I can't make it any worse." *Are you sure of that?*

"How could you get aboard Slyke's ship?"

"I have an idea or two. The governors' consorts—and their
ghem-ladies, and their servitors—can they go up and down from
orbit freely?"

One porcelain hand touched her throat. "More or less, yes."

"So you get a lady with legitimate access, preferably someone
relatively inconspicuous, to take me up. Not as myself, of course,
I'd have to be disguised somehow. Once I'm aboard, I can take
it from there. This gives us a problem of trust. Who could you
trust? I don't suppose you yourself could . . . ?"

"I haven't left the capital for . . . several years."

"You would not qualify as inconspicuous, then. Besides, Slyke
Giaja has to be keeping a close eye on you. What about that ghem-
lady you sent to meet me at Yenaro's party?"

Rian was looking decidedly unhappy. "Someone in the consort's train would be a better choice," she said reluctantly.

"The alternative," he pointed out coolly, "would be to let *Cetagandan* security do the job. Nailing Slyke would automatically clear Barrayar, and *my* problem would be solved."

Well . . . not quite. Slyke Giaja, if Lord X, was the man who'd somehow jiggered the orbital station's traffic control, and who'd known *just* what security blind spot would hold Ba Lura's body. Slyke Giaja had more security access than he bloody ought to. Was it so certain that Cetagandan security would be able to pull off a *surprise* raid on the Imperial prince's ship?

"How would *you* disguise yourself?" she asked.

He tried to convince himself her tone was merely taken aback, not scornful. "As a ba servitor, probably. Some of them are as short as I am. And you haut treat those people like they're invisible. Blind and deaf, too."

"No man would disguise himself as a ba!"

"So much the better, then." He grinned ironically at her reaction.

Her comconsole chimed. She stared at it in brief, astonished annoyance, then touched its code pad. The face of a fit-looking middle-aged man formed over the vid-plate. He wore a Cetagandan security officer's ordinary uniform, but he was no one Miles recognized. Gray eyes glinted like granite chips from freshly applied zebra-striped face paint. Miles quailed, and glanced around quickly—he was out of range of the vid-pickup, at least.

"Haut Rian." The man nodded deferentially.

"Ghem-Colonel Millisor," Rian acknowledged. "I ordered my comconsole blocked to incoming calls. This is not a convenient time to speak." She kept her eyes from darting to Miles.

"I used the emergency override. I've been trying to reach you for some time. My apologies, Haut, for intruding upon your mourning for the Celestial Lady, but she would have been the first to wish it. We have succeeded in tracking the lost L-X-10-Terran-C to Jackson's Whole. I need the authorization of the Star Crèche to pursue out of the Empire with all due force. I had understood that the recovery of the L-X-10-Terran-C was one of our late Lady's highest priorities. After the field tests she was considering it as an addition to the haut-genome itself."

"This *was* true, ghem-Colonel, but . . . well, yes, it still should be recovered. Just a moment." Rian rose, went to one of the cabinets, and unlocked it with the encode-ring, fished from its chain around her neck. She rummaged within, and removed a clear block about fifteen centimeters on a side with the scarlet bird pattern incised upon the top, returned to her desk, and placed it over the comconsole's read-pad. She tapped out some codes, and a light flashed briefly within the block. "Very well, ghem-Colonel. I leave it entirely to your judgment. You knew our late Lady's mind on this. You are fully authorized, and may draw your resources as needed from the Star Crèche's special fund."

"I thank you, Haut. I will report our progress." The ghem-colonel nodded, and keyed off.

"What was that all about?" Miles asked brightly, trying not to look too predatory.

Rian frowned at him. "Some old internal business of the haut-genome. It has nothing to do with you or Barrayar, or the present crisis, I assure you. Life does go on, you know."

"So it does." Miles smiled affably, as if fully satisfied. Mentally, he filed the conversation away verbatim. It might make a nice tidbit to distract Simon Illyan with later. He had a bad feeling he was going to need some major distractions for Illyan, when he got home.

Rian put the Great Seal of the Star Crèche carefully away again in its locked cabinet, and returned to her station-chair.

"So can you do it?" Miles pursued. "Have a lady you trust meet me, with a ba servitor's uniform and real IDs, the false rod, and some way to check the real one? And send her up to Prince Slyke's ship on some valid pretext, with me in her train? And *when*?"

"I'm . . . not sure when."

"We have to set the meeting in advance, this time. If I'm going to go wandering away from my embassy's supervision for several hours, you can't just call me away at random. I have to cover my own a— concoct a cover story for my own security, too. Do you have a copy of my official schedule? You must, or we could not have connected before. I think we should rendezvous outside the Celestial Garden, this time, for starters. I'm going to be going to something called the Bioestheties Exhibit tomorrow afternoon. I think I could make up an excuse to get away from there, maybe with Ivan's help."

"So soon . . ."

"Not soon enough, in my view. There's not much time left. And we have to allow for the possibility that the first attempt may have to be aborted for some reason. You . . . do realize, your evidence against Prince Slyke is suggestive only. Not conclusive."

"But it's all I have, so far."

"I understand. But we need all the margin we can get. In case we have to go back for a second pass."

"Yes . . . you're right . . ." She took a breath, frowning anxiously. "Very well, Lord Vorkosigan. I shall help you make this attempt."

"Do *you* have any guesses where on his ship Prince Slyke might be inclined to store the Great Key? It's a small object, and a big ship, after all. My first guess would be his personal quarters. Once aboard, is there any way of detecting the Great Key's location? I don't suppose we're so fortunate as to have a screamer circuit on it?"

"Not as such. Its internal power system is an old and very rare design, though. At short range, it might be possible to pick it up with an appropriate sensor. I will see that my lady brings you one, and anything else I can think of."

"Every little bit helps." There. They were in motion at last. He suppressed a wild impulse to beg her to throw it all over and flee away with him to Barrayar. Could he even smuggle her out of the Cetagandan Empire? Surely it was no more miraculous a task than the one now before him. Yes, and what would be the effect on his career, not to mention his father's, of installing a refugee Cetagandan haut-woman and close relative of Emperor Fletchir Giaja's in Vorkosigan House? And how much trouble would trail him? He thought fleetingly of the story of the Trojan War.

Still, it would have been flattering, if she had indeed been trying to suborn him, if she'd at least tried a little harder. She had not lifted a finger to attract him; not an eyebrow arched in false invitation. She seemed straightforward to the point of naiveté, to his own ImpSec-trained, naturally convoluted mind. When someone fell deeply and hopelessly in love with somebody, that somebody ought at least to have the courtesy to notice. . . .

The key word, boy, is hopelessly. Keep it in mind.

They shared no love, he and Rian, nor the chance of any. And no goals. But they did share an enemy. It would have to do.

Rian rose in dismissal; Miles scrambled up too, saying, "Has ghem-Colonel Benin caught up with you yet? He was assigned to investigate the death of Ba Lura, you know."

"So I understood. He has twice requested an audience with me. I have not yet granted his request. He seems . . . persistent."

"Thank God. We've still got a chance to get our stories straight."

Miles quickly summed up his own interview with Benin, with special emphasis on his fictional first conversation with Rian. "We need to make up a consistent account of this visit, too. I think he'll be back. I rather encouraged him, I'm afraid. I didn't guess Prince Slyke would give himself away to you so quickly."

Rian nodded, walked to the window-wall, and, pointing to various sites within the laboratory, gave Miles a brief description of the tour she'd given Prince Slyke yesterday. "Will that do?"

"Nicely, thanks. You can tell him I asked a lot of medical questions about . . . correcting various physical disabilities, and that you couldn't help me much, that I'd come to the wrong store." He could not help adding, "There's nothing wrong with my DNA, you know. All my damage was teratogenic. Outside your purview and all that."

Her face, always mask-like in its beauty, seemed to grow a shade more expressionless. Rattled, he added, "You Cetagandans spend an inordinate amount of time on appearances. Surely you've encountered false appearances before." *Stop it, shut up now.*

She opened a hand, acknowledging without agreeing or disagreeing, and returned to her bubble. Worn out, and not trusting his tongue any further, Miles paced silently beside it back to the main entrance.

They exited into a cool and luminous artificial dusk. A few pale stars shone in the apparently boundless dark blue hemisphere above. Sitting in a row on a bench across the entry walk from the Star Crèche were Mia Maz, Ambassador Vorob'yev, and ghem-Colonel Benin, apparently chatting amiably. They all looked up at Miles's appearance, and Vorob'yev's and Benin's smiles, at least, seemed to grow a shade less amiable. Miles almost turned around to flee back inside.

Rian evidently felt some similar emotion, for the voice from her bubble murmured, "Ah, your people are awaiting you, Lord Vorkosigan. I hope you found this educational, even if not to your needs. Good evening, then," and slipped promptly back into the sanctuary of the Star Crèche.

Oh, this whole thing is a learning experience, milady. Miles fixed a friendly smile on his face, and trod forward across the walkway to the bench, where his waiting watchers rose to greet him. Mia Maz had her usual cheerful dimple. Was it his imagination, or had Vorob'yev's diplomatic affability acquired a strained edge? Benin's expression was less easy to read, through the swirls of face paint.

"Hello," said Miles brightly. "You, uh, waited, sir. Thanks, though

I don't think you needed to." Vorob'yev's brows rose in faint, ironic disagreement.

"You have been granted an unusual honor, Lord Vorkosigan," said Benin, nodding toward the Star Crèche.

"Yes, the haut Rian is a very polite lady. I hope I didn't wear her out with all my questions."

"And were all your questions answered?" asked Benin. "You *are* privileged."

One could not mistake the bitter edge to *that* comment, though one could, of course, ignore it. "Oh, yes and no. It's a fascinating place, but I'm afraid its technologies hold no help for my medical needs. I think I'm going to have to consider more surgeries after all. I don't like surgeries; they're surprisingly painful." He blinked mournfully.

Maz looked highly sympathetic; Vorob'yev looked just a little saturnine. *He's beginning to suspect there's something screwy going on. Damn.*

In fact, both Benin and Vorob'yev looked like only the presence of the other was inhibiting him from pinning Miles to the nearest wall and twisting till some truth was emitted.

"If you are finished, then, I shall escort you to the gate," said Benin.

"Yes. The embassy car is waiting, Lord Vorkosigan," Vorob'yev added pointedly.

They all herded obediently after Benin down the path he indicated.

"The real privilege today was getting to hear all that poetry, though," Miles burbled on. "And how are you doing, ghem-Colonel? Are you making any progress on your case?"

Benin's lips twitched. "It does not simplify itself," he murmured.

I'll bet not. Alas, or perhaps fortunately, this was not the time or place for a couple of security men to let their hair down and talk shop frankly.

"Oh, my," said Maz, and they all paused to take in the show a curve in the path presented. A woodsy vista framed a small artificial ravine. Scattered in the dusk among the trees and along the streamlet were hundreds of tiny, luminous tree frogs, variously candy-colored, all singing. They sang in *chords*, pitch-perfect, one chord rising and dying away to be replaced by another; the creatures' luminosity rose and fell as they sang, so the progress of each pure note could be followed by the eye as well as the ear. The ravine's acoustics bounced the not-quite music around in a highly synergistic fashion. Miles's brain seemed to stop dead for a full three minutes at the sheer absurd beauty of it all, till some throat-clearing from Vorob'yev broke the spell, and the party moved on again.

Outside the dome, the capital city's night was warm, humid, and apricot-bright, rumbling with the vast subliminal noise of its life. Night and the city, stretching to the horizon and beyond.

"I am impressed by the luxury of the haut, but then I realize the size of the economic base that supports it," Miles remarked to Benin.

"Indeed," said Benin, with a small smirk. "I believe Cetaganda's per capita tax rate is only half that of Barrayar's. The Emperor cultivates his subjects' economic well-being as a garden, I have heard it said."

Benin was not immune to the Cetagandan taste for one-upmanship. Taxes were always a volatile civil issue at home. "I'm afraid so," Miles returned. "We have to match you militarily with less than a quarter of your resources." He bit his tongue to keep from adding, *Fortunately, that's not hard,* or something equally snide.

Benin was right, though, Miles reflected, as the embassy's aircar rose over the capital. One was awed by the great silver hemisphere, till one looked at the city extending for a hundred kilometers in all directions, not to mention the rest of the planet and the other seven worlds, and did a little math. The Celestial Garden was a flower, but its roots lay elsewhere, in the haut and ghem control of other aspects of the economy. The Great Key seemed suddenly a tiny lever, with which to try to move this world. *Prince Slyke, I think you are an optimist.*

Chapter Ten

"You've got to help me out on this one, Ivan," Miles whispered urgently.

"Oh?" murmured Ivan, in a tone of extreme neutrality.

"I didn't know Vorob'yev would be sending *him* along." Miles jerked his chin toward Lord Vorreedi, who had stepped away for some under-voiced conference of his own with their groundcar's driver, the uniformed embassy guard, and the plainclothes guard. The uniformed man wore undress greens like Miles and Ivan; the other two wore the bodysuits and calf-length robes of Cetagandan street wear, the protocol officer with more comfortable practiced ease.

Miles continued, "When I set up this rendezvous with my contact, I thought we'd get Mia Maz as our native guide again, what with this exhibition being the Ladies' Division or whatever they call it. You won't just need to cover my departure. You may need to distract them when I make my break."

The plainclothes guard nodded and strode off. Outer-perimeter man; Miles memorized his face and clothing. One more thing to keep track of. The guard headed toward the entrance to the exhibition . . . hall, it was not. When today's outing had first been described to Miles, he had pictured some cavernous quadrangular structure like the one that housed the District Agricultural Fair at Hassadar. Instead, the Moon Garden Hall, as it was styled, was another dome, a miniature suburban imitation of the Celestial Garden at the center of the city. Not too miniature—it was over three hundred meters in diameter, arcing over steeply sloping ground. Flocks of well-dressed ghem-types, both men and women, funneled toward its upper entrance.

"How the hell am I supposed to do that, coz? Vorreedi's not the distractible sort."

"Tell him I left with a lady, for . . . immoral purposes. You leave with immoral ladies all the time, why not me?" Miles's lips twisted in a suppressed snarl at Ivan's rolled eyes. "Introduce him to half a dozen of *your* girlfriends. I can't believe we won't run across some here. Tell them he's the man who taught you all you know about the Barrayaran Art of Love."

"He's not my type," said Ivan through his teeth.

"So use your initiative!"

"I don't have initiative. *I* follow orders, thank you. It's much safer."

"Fine. I *order* you to use your initiative."

Ivan breathed a bad word, by way of editorial. "I'm going to regret this, I know I am."

"Just hold on a little while longer. This will all be over in a few hours." *One way or another.*

"*That's* what you said day before yesterday. You lied."

"It wasn't my fault. Things were a little more complicated than I'd anticipated."

"You remember the time down at Vorkosigan Surleau when we found that old guerrilla weapons cache, and you talked me and Elena into helping you activate the old hovertank? And we ran it into the barn? And the barn collapsed? And my mother put me under house-arrest for two months?"

"We were ten years *old*, Ivan!"

"I remember it like yesterday. I remember it like day-before-yesterday, too."

"That old shed was practically falling down anyway. Saved the price of a demolition crew. For God's sake Ivan, this is serious! You can't compare it to—" Miles broke off as the protocol officer dismissed his men and, smiling faintly, turned back to the two young envoys. He shepherded them into the Moon Garden Hall.

Miles was surprised to see something so crass as a sign, even if made entirely of flowers, decorating an entry arch to a labyrinth of descending walkways spilling down the natural slope. *The 149th Annual Bioestheties Exhibition, Class A. Dedicated to the Memory of the Celestial Lady.* Which dedication had made it a mandatory stop on all polite funeral envoys' social calendars. "Do the haut-women compete here?" Miles asked the protocol officer. "I'd think this would be in their style."

"So much so that no one else could win if they did," said Lord Vorreedi. "They have their own annual bash, very privately, inside the Celestial Garden, but it's on hold till this period of official mourning is completed."

"So . . . these ghem-women exhibitors are, um, imitating their haut half-sisters?"

"Trying to, anyway. That's the name of the game, here."

The ghem-ladies' exhibits were arranged not in rows, but each set individually in its own curve or corner. Miles wondered briefly what kind of jockeying went on behind the scenes for favorable sites and spaces, and what kind of status-points one could win for obtaining the best ones, and if the competition went as far as assassinations. Character-assassinations, anyway, he judged from a few snatches of conversation from groups of ghem-ladies strolling about, admiring and critiquing.

A large tank of fish caught his eye. They were filmy-finned, their iridescent scales colored in the exact pattern of one of the ghem-clan's face paintings: bright blue, yellow, black and white. The fish swirled in a watery gavotte. It was not too remarkable, genetic-engineering-wise, except that the proud and hopeful exhibitor hovering nearby appeared to be a girl of about twelve. She seemed to be a mascot for her clan's ladies' more serious exhibits. *Give me six years, and watch out!* her small smile seemed to say.

Blue roses and black orchids were so routine, they were used merely as framing borders for the real entries. A young girl passed by, in tow of her ghem-parents, with a unicorn about half a meter high scampering after her on a golden leash. It wasn't even an exhibit . . . maybe a commercial product, for all Miles knew. Unlike Hassadar's District Agricultural Fair, utility did not seem to be a consideration. It might even count as a defect. The competition was for art; life was merely the medium, a bio-palette supplying effects.

They paused to lean on a balcony railing that gave a partial over-view down the hanging garden's slopes. A green flicker by his feet caught Miles's eye. An array of glossy leaves and tendrils was spiraling up Ivan's leg. Red blossoms slowly opened and closed, breathing a deep and delicate perfume, albeit the total effect was unfortunately mouth-like. He stared in fascination for a full minute before murmuring, "Uh, Ivan . . . ? Don't move. But look at your left boot."

As Miles watched, another tendril slowly wrapped itself around Ivan's knee and began hoisting. Ivan glanced down, lurched, and swore. "What the hell *is* it? Get it off me!"

"I doubt it's poisonous," said the protocol officer uncertainly. "But perhaps you had better hold still."

"I . . . think it's a climbing rose. Lively little thing, isn't it?" Miles grinned, and bent nearer, cautiously checking for thorns before extending his hands. They might be retractable or something. Colonel Vorreedi made a hesitant restraining motion.

But before he mustered the nerve to risk skin and flesh, a plump ghem-lady carrying a large basket hurried up the path. "Oh, there you are, you bad thing!" she cried. "Excuse me, sir," she addressed Ivan without looking up, kneeling by his boot and commencing to unwind her quarry. "Too much nitrogen this morning, I'm afraid . . ."

The rose let go its last tendril from around Ivan's boot with a regretful recoil, and was unceremoniously plunged into the basket with some other writhing escapees, pink and white and yellow. The woman, her eyes darting here and there at corners and under benches, hurried on.

"I think it liked you," said Miles to Ivan. "Pheromones?"

"Get stuffed," murmured Ivan back. "Or I'll dip *you* in nitrogen, and stake you out under the . . . good God, what is this?"

They'd rounded a corner to an open area displaying a graceful tree, with large fuzzy heart-shaped leaves filling two or three dozen branches that arced and drooped again, swaying slightly with the burden of the podded fruit tipping each branch. The fruit was mewing. Miles and Ivan stepped closer.

"Now . . . now *that* is just plain *wrong*," said Ivan indignantly.

Bundled upside down in each fruit pod was a small kitten, long and silky white fur fluffing out around each feline face, framing ears and whiskers and bright blue eyes. Ivan cradled one in his hand, and lifted it to his face for closer examination. With one blunt finger he carefully tried to pet the creature; it batted playfully at his hand with soft white front paws.

"Kittens like this should be out chasing string, not glued into

damned *trees* to score points for some ghem-bitch," Ivan opined
hotly. He glanced around the area; they were temporarily alone
and unobserved.

"Um . . . I'm not so sure they're glued in," said Miles. "Wait, I
don't think you'd better—"

Trying to stop Ivan from rescuing a kitten from a tree was
approximately as futile as trying to stop Ivan from making a pass
at a pretty woman. It was some kind of spinal reflex. By the glint
in his eye, he was bent on releasing all the tiny victims, to chase
after the climbing roses perhaps.

Ivan snapped the pod from the end of its branch. The kitten
emitted a squall, convulsed, and went still.

"Kitty, kitty . . . ?" Ivan whispered doubtfully into his cupped
hand. An alarming trickle of red fluid coursed from the broken
stem across his wrist.

Miles pulled back the pod-leaves around the kitten's . . . corpse,
he feared. There was no back half to the beast. Pink naked legs
fused together and disappeared into the stem part of the pod.

" . . . I don't think it was ripe, Ivan."

"That's *horrible!*" Ivan's breath rasped in his throat with his
outrage, but the volume was pitched way down. By unspoken
mutual consent, they sidled quickly away from the kitten-tree and
around the nearest unpeopled corner. Ivan glanced around frantically for a place to dispose of the tiny corpse, and so distance
himself from his sin and vandalism. "Grotesque!"

Miles said thoughtfully, "Oh, I don't know. It's not any more
grotesque than the original method, when you think about it. I
mean, have you ever watched a mother cat give birth to kittens?"

Ivan covered his full hand with the other, and glared at his
cousin. The protocol officer studied Ivan's dismay with a mixture
of exasperation and sympathy. Miles thought that if he had known
Ivan longer, the proportion of the first emotion to the second
would be much higher, but Vorreedi only said, "My lord . . . would
you like me to dispose of that for you . . . discreetly?"

"Uh, yes, please," said Ivan, looking very relieved. "If you don't
mind." He hastily palmed off the inert pod of fluff onto the
protocol officer, who hid it in a pocket handkerchief.

"Stay here. I'll be back shortly," he said, and went off to get rid
of the evidence.

"Good one, Ivan," growled Miles. "Want to keep your hands in
your pockets after this?"

Ivan scrubbed at the sticky substance on his hand with his own handkerchief, spat into his palm, and scrubbed again. *Out, out, damned spot. . . .* "Don't you start making noises like my mother. It wasn't my fault. . . . Things were a little more complicated than I'd anticipated." Ivan stuffed his handkerchief back in his pocket, and stared around, frowning. "This isn't fun anymore. I want to go back to the embassy."

"You have to hang on till I meet my contact, at least."

"And when will that be?"

"Soon, I suspect."

They strolled to the end of the aisle, where another little balcony gave an enticing view of the next lower section.

"Damn," said Ivan.

"What do you see?" asked Miles, tracking his gaze. He stretched to stand on tiptoe, but it wasn't enough to spot what had caught Ivan's negative attention.

"Our good buddy Lord Yenaro is here. Two levels down, talking to some women."

"It . . . could be a coincidence. This place is lousy with ghem-lords, with the award ceremony this afternoon. The winning women gain honor for their clan, naturally they want to cash in. And this is just the sort of artsy stuff that tickles his fancy, I think."

Ivan cocked an eyebrow at him. "You want to bet on that?"

"Nope."

Ivan sighed. "I don't suppose there's any way we can get him before he gets us."

"Don't know. Keep your eyes open, anyway."

"No lie."

They stared around some more. A ghem-lady of middle-age and dignified bearing approached them, and gave Miles an acknowledging, if not exactly friendly, nod. Her palm turned outward briefly, displaying to him a heavy ring, with a raised screaming-bird pattern filigreed with complex encodes.

"Now?" Miles said quietly.

"No." Her cultured voice was a low-pitched alto. "Meet me by the west entrance in thirty minutes."

"I may not be able to achieve precision."

"I'll wait." She passed on.

"Crap," said Ivan, after a moment's silence. "You're really going to try to bring this off. You will be the hell careful, won't you?"

"Oh, yes."

The protocol officer was taking a long time to find the nearest waste-disposal unit, Miles thought. But just as his nerves were stretching to the point of going to look for the man, he reappeared, walking quickly toward them. His smile of greeting seemed a little strained.

"My lords," he nodded. "Something has come up. I'm going to have to leave you for a while. Stay together, and don't leave the building, please."

Perfect. Maybe. "What sort of something?" asked Miles. "We spotted Yenaro."

"Our practical joker? Yes. We know he's here. My analysts judge him a non-lethal annoyance. I must leave you to defend yourselves from him, temporarily. But my outer-perimeter man, who is one of my sharpest fellows, has spotted another individual, known to us. A professional."

The term *professional*, in this context, meant a professional killer, or something along those lines. Miles nodded alertly.

"We don't know why he's here," Vorreedi went on. "I have some heavier backup on the way. In the meanwhile, we propose to . . . drop in on him for a short chat."

"Fast-penta is illegal here for anyone but the police and the imperials, isn't it?"

"I doubt this one would go to the authorities to complain," murmured Vorreedi, with a slightly sinister smile.

"Have fun."

"Watch yourselves." The protocol officer nodded, and drifted away, as-if-casually.

Miles and Ivan walked on, pausing to examine a couple more rooted floral displays that seemed less unnervingly uncertain of their kingdom and phylum. Miles counted minutes in his head. He could break away shortly, and reach his rendezvous right on time. . . .

"Well, *hello*, sweet thing," a musical voice trilled from behind them. Ivan turned around a beat faster than Miles. Lady Arvin and Lady Benello stood with arms linked. They unlinked arms and . . . oozed, Miles decided was the term, up on either side of Ivan, capturing one side each.

"Sweet thing?" Miles murmured in delight. Ivan spared him a brief glower before turning to his greeters.

"We heard you were here, Lord Ivan," the blonde, Lady Arvin, continued. Tall Lady Benello concurred, her cascade of amber curls bouncing with her nod. "What are you doing after-wards?"

"Ah . . . no particular plans," said Ivan, his head swiveling in an attempt to divide his attention precisely in half.

"Ooh," said Lady Arvin. "Perhaps you would care to have dinner with me, at my penthouse."

Lady Benello interrupted, "Or, if you're not in an urban mood, I know this place not far from here, on a lake. Each patron is rowed out to their own little tiny island, and a picnic is served, *al fresco*. It's *very* private."

Each woman smiled repellingly at the other. Ivan looked faintly hunted. "What a tough decision," he temporized.

"Come along and see Lady Benello's sister's pretties, while you think about it then, Lord Ivan," said Lady Arvin equably. Her eye fell on Miles. "You too, Lord Vorkosigan. We've been neglecting our most senior guest quite shamefully, *I* think. Upon discussion, we think this might be a regrettable oversight." Her hand tightened on Ivan's arm, and she peeked around his torso to give her red-haired companion a bright, meaningful smile. "This could be the solution to Lord Ivan's dilemma."

"In the dark all cats are gray?" Miles murmured. "Or at any rate, all Barrayarans?"

Ivan winced at the mention of felines. Lady Arvin looked blank, but Miles had a bad feeling the redhead had caught the joke. In any case, she detached herself from Ivan—was that a flash of triumph, crossing Lady Arvin's face?—and turned to Miles.

"Indeed, Lord Vorkosigan. Do you have any particular plans?"

"I'm afraid so," said Miles with a regret that was not entirely feigned. "In fact, I have to be going now."

"Right now? Oh, do come . . . see my sister's exhibit, at least." Lady Benello stopped short of linking arms with him, but seemed willing to walk by his side, even if it left her rival in temporary possession of Ivan.

Time. It wouldn't hurt to give the protocol officer a few more minutes to become fully engaged with his quarry. Miles smiled thinly, and allowed himself to be dragged along in the wake of the party, Lady Arvin in the lead towing Ivan. That tall redhead lacked the porcelain delicacy of the haut Rian. On the other hand, she was not nearly so . . . *impossible. The difficult we do at once. The impossible takes* . . .

Stop it. These women are users, you know that.

Oh, God, let me be used. . . .
Focus, boy, goddammit.

They walked down the switchback pathway, arriving at the next lower level. Lady Arvin turned in at a small circular open space screened by trees in tubs. Their leaves were glossy and jewel-like, but they were merely a frame for the display in the center. The display was a little baffling, artistically. It seemed to consist of three lengths of thick brocade, in subtle hues, spiraling loosely around each other from the top of a man-high pole to trail on the carpet below. The dense circular carpet echoed the greens of the bordering trees, in a complex abstract pattern.

"Heads up," murmured Ivan.

"I see him," breathed Miles.

Lord Yenaro, dark-robed and smiling, was sitting on one of the little curving benches that also helped frame the space.

"Where's Veda?" asked Lady Benello.

"She just stepped out," said Yenaro, rising and nodding greetings to all.

"Lord Yenaro has been giving my sister Veda a little help with her entry," Lady Benello confided to Miles and Ivan.

"Oh?" said Miles, staring around and wondering where the trap was this time. He didn't see it yet. "And, uh . . . just what is her entry?"

"I know it doesn't look very impressive," said Lady Benello defensively, "but that's not the point. The subtlety is in the smell. It's the cloth. It emits a perfume that changes with the mood of the wearer. I *still* wonder if we ought to have had it made up into a dress," this last comment seemed aimed at Yenaro. "We could have had one of the servitors stand here and model it all day."

"It would have seemed too commercial," Yenaro said to her. "This will score better."

"And, um . . . it's alive?" asked Ivan doubtfully.

"The scent glands in the cloth are as alive as the sweat glands in your body," Yenaro assured him. "Nevertheless, you are right, the display is a bit static. Step closer, and we'll hand-demonstrate the effects."

Miles sniffed, his paranoia-heightened awareness trying to individually check every volatile molecule that entered his nostrils. The dome was clouded with scents of every kind, drifting down from the displays upslope, not to mention the perfumes of the ghem-ladies and Yenaro in their robes. But the brocade did seem to be emitting a pleasant mixture of odors. Ivan didn't respond to the invitation to come closer either, Miles noticed. In addition to the perfumes, though, there was something else, a faint, oily acridity. . . .

Yenaro picked up a pitcher from the bench and walked toward the pole. "More zlati ale?" Ivan murmured dryly.

Recognition and memory zinged through Miles, followed by a wave of adrenaline that nearly stopped his heart before it began racing. "Grab that pitcher, Ivan! Don't let him spill it!"

Ivan did. Yenaro gave up his hold with a surprised snort. "Really, Lord Ivan!"

Miles dropped prone to the thick carpet, sniffing frantically. *Yes.*

"What are you *doing?*" asked Lady Benello, half-laughing. "The rug isn't part of it!"

Oh, yes it is. "Ivan," said Miles urgently, scrambling back to his feet. "Hand me that—*carefully*—and tell me what you smell down there."

Miles took the pitcher much more tenderly than he would have a basket of raw eggs. Ivan, with a look of some bewilderment, did as he was told. He sniffed, then ran his hand through the carpet, and touched his fingers to his lips. And turned white. Miles knew Ivan had reached the same conclusion he had even before he turned his head and hissed, "Asterzine!"

Miles tiptoed back well away from the carpet, lifted the pitcher's lid, and sniffed again. A faint odor resembling vanilla and oranges, gone slightly wrong, wafted up, which was exactly right.

And Yenaro had been going to dump it all, Miles was sure. At his own feet. With Lady Benello and Lady Arvin looking on. Miles thought of the fate of Lord X's, Prince Slyke's, last tool, the Ba Lura. *No. Yenaro doesn't know. He may hate Barrayarans, but he's not that frigging crazy. He was set up right along with us, this time. Third time's a charm, all right.*

When Ivan rose, his jaw set and his eyes burning, Miles motioned him over and handed him the pitcher again. Ivan took it gingerly, stepping back another pace. Miles knelt and tore off a few threads from the carpet's edge. The threads parted with a gum-like stretching, confirming his diagnosis. "Lord Vorkosigan!" Lady Arvin objected, her brows drawn down in amused puzzlement at the Barrayarans' bizarre barbarian behavior.

Miles traded the threads to Ivan for the pitcher again, and jerked his head toward Yenaro. "Bring *him.* Excuse us, please, ladies. Um . . . man-talk."

Rather to his surprise, this appeal actually worked; Lady Arvin only arched her brows, though Lady Benello pouted slightly. Ivan wrapped one hand around Yenaro's upper arm and guided him out of the display area. Ivan's grip tightened in silent threat when Yenaro tried to shrug him off. Yenaro looked angry and tight-lipped and just a little embarrassed.

They found an empty nook a few spaces down. Ivan stood himself and his captive with their backs to the path, shielding Miles from view. Miles gently set the pitcher down, stood, jerked up his chin, and addressed Yenaro in a low-pitched growl. "I will demonstrate what you almost did in just a moment. What I want to know now is just what the hell you *thought* you were doing?"

"I don't know what you're talking about," snapped Yenaro. "Let *go*, you lout!"

Ivan kept his hold, frowning fiercely. "Demonstrate first, coz."

"Right." The paving-stones were some cool artificial marble, and did not look flammable. Miles shook the threads off his finger, and motioned Ivan and Yenaro closer. He waited till there were no passersby in sight and said, "Yenaro. Take two drops on your fingers of that harmless liquid you were waving around, and sprinkle them on this."

Ivan forced Yenaro to kneel alongside Miles. Yenaro, with a cold glance at his captors, dipped his hand and sprinkled as ordered. "If you think—"

He was interrupted by a bright flash and a wave of heat that scorched Miles's eyebrows. The soft report, fortunately, was mostly muffled by their shielding bodies. Yenaro froze, arrested.

"And that was only about a gram of material," Miles went on relentlessly. "That whole carpet-bomb massed, what, about five kilos? You should know—I'm certain you carried it in here personally. When the catalyst hit, it would have gone up taking out this whole section of the dome, you, me, the ladies . . . it would have been quite the high point of the show."

"This is some sort of trick," grated Yenaro.

"Oh, it's a trick all right. But this time the joke was on you. You've never had any military training at all, have you? Or with your nose, you'd have recognized it too. Sensitized asterzine. Lovely stuff. Formable, dyeable, you can make it look like practically anything. And totally inert and harmless, till the catalyst hits it. Then . . ." Miles nodded toward the small scorched patch on the white pavement. "Let me put the question to you another way, Yenaro. What effect did your good friend the haut-governor *tell* you this was going to have?"

"He—" Yenaro's breath caught. His hand swept down across the dark and oily residue, then rose to his nose. He inhaled, frowning, then sat back rather weakly on his heels. His wide eyes lifted to meet Miles's gaze. "Oh."

"Confession," said Ivan meaningfully, "is good for the soul. And body."

Miles took a breath. "Once more, from the top, Yenaro. What did you *think* you were doing?"

Yenaro swallowed. "It . . . was supposed to release an ester. That would simulate alcohol poisoning. You Barrayarans are famous for that perversion. Nothing that you don't already do to yourselves!"

"Allowing Ivan and me to publicly stagger through the rest of the afternoon blind drunk, or a close approximation."

"Something like that."

"And yourself? Did you just ingest the antidote, before we showed up?"

"No, it was harmless! . . . supposed to be. I had made arrangements to go and rest, till it passed off. I thought it might be . . . an interesting sensation."

"Pervert," murmured Ivan.

Yenaro glared at him.

Miles said slowly, "When I was burned, that first night. All that hand-wringing on your part wasn't totally feigned, was it? You weren't expecting it."

Yenaro paled. "I expected . . . I thought perhaps the Marilacans had done something to the power adjustment. It was only supposed to shock, not injure."

"Or so you were told."

"Yes," Yenaro whispered.

"The zlati ale was your idea, though, wasn't it," growled Ivan.

"You knew?!"

"I'm not an idiot."

Some passing ghem glanced in puzzlement at the three men kneeling in a circle on the floor, though fortunately they passed on without comment. Miles nodded to the nearest bench, in the curve of the nook. "I have something to tell you, Lord Yenaro, and I think you had better be sitting down." Ivan guided Yenaro to it and firmly pushed him down. After a thoughtful moment, Ivan then poured the rest of the pitcher of liquid into the nearest tree-tub, before settling between Yenaro and the exit.

"This isn't just a series of gratifying tricks played on the dolt-ish envoys of a despised enemy, for you to chuckle at," Miles went on lowly. "You are being used as a pawn in a treason plot against the Cetagandan Emperor. Used, discarded, and silenced. It's begin-ning to be a pattern. Your last fellow-pawn was the Ba Lura. I trust you've heard what happened to *it*."

Yenaro's pale lips parted, but he breathed no word. After a moment he licked his lips and tried again. "This can't be. It's too crude. It would have started a blood feud between his clan and those of . . . all the innocent bystanders."

"No. It would have started a blood feud between their clans and *yours*. You were set up to take the fall for this one. Not only as an assassin, but as one so incompetent that he blew himself up with his own bomb. Following in your grandfather's footsteps, so to speak. And who would be left alive to deny it? The confusion would multiply within the capital, as well as between your Empire and Barrayar, while his satrapy made its break for independence. No, not crude. Downright elegant."

"The Ba Lura committed suicide. It was said."

"No. Murdered. Cetagandan Imperial Security is on to that one, too. They will unravel it in time. No . . . they will unravel it even-tually. I don't trust that it will be in time."

"It is impossible for a ba servitor to commit treason."

"Unless the ba servitor thinks that it is acting loyally, in a deliberately ambiguous situation. I don't think even the ba are so un-human that they cannot be *mistaken*."

" . . . No." Yenaro looked up at both the Barrayarans. "You must believe, I would have no regrets whatsoever if you two fell off a cliff. But I would not push you myself."

"I . . . so I judged," said Miles. "But for my curiosity—what were you to get out of the deal, besides a week's amusement in embarr-assing a couple of loutish barbarians? Or was this art for art's sake on your part?"

"He promised me a post." Yenaro stared at the floor again. "You don't understand, what it is to be without a post in the capital. You have no position. You have no status. You are . . . no one. I was tired of being no one."

"What post?"

"Imperial Perfumer." Yenaro's dark eyes flashed. "I know it doesn't sound very mighty, but it would have gained me entrance to the Celestial Garden, maybe the Imperial Presence itself. Where I would have worked among . . . the best in the empire. The top people. And I would have been *good*."

Miles had no trouble understanding ambition, no matter how arcane its form. "I imagine so."

Yenaro's lips twitched in half a grateful smile.

Miles glanced at his chrono. "God, I'm late. Ivan—can you handle this from here?"

"I think so."

Miles rose. "Good day, Lord Yenaro, and a better one than you were destined to have, I think. I may have used up a year's supply this afternoon already, but wish me luck. I have a little date with Prince Slyke now."

"Good luck," Yenaro said doubtfully.

Miles paused. "It *was* Prince Slyke, was it not?"

"No! I was talking about Governor the haut Ilsum Kety!"

Miles pursed his lips, and blew out his breath in a slow trickle. *I have just been either screwed or saved. I wonder which?* "Kety set you up . . . with all this?"

"Yes . . ."

Could Kety have sent his fellow governor and cousin Prince Slyke to scout out the Imperial Regalia for him, a stalking horse? Certainly. Or not. For that matter, could Slyke have set up Kety to operate Yenaro for him? Not impossible. *Back to square one. Damn, damn, damn!*

While Miles hovered in new doubt, the protocol officer rounded the corner. His hurried stride slowed as he spotted Miles and Ivan, and a look of relief crossed his face. By the time he strolled into the nook he was projecting the air of a tourist again, but he raked Yenaro with a knife-keen glance.

"Hello, my lords." His nod took all three in equally.

"Hello, sir," said Miles. "Did you have an interesting conversation?"

"Extraordinarily."

"Ah . . . I don't believe you've formally met Lord Yenaro, sir. Lord Yenaro, this is my embassy's protocol officer, Lord Vorreedi."

The two men exchanged more studied nods, Yenaro's hand going to his chest in a sketch of a sitting bow.

"What a coincidence, Lord Yenaro," Vorreedi went on. "We were just talking about you."

"Oh?" said Yenaro warily.

"Ah . . ." Vorreedi sucked his lip thoughtfully, then seemed to come to some internal decision. "Are you aware that you seem to be in the middle of some sort of vendetta at present, Lord Yenaro?"

"I—no! What makes you think so?"

"Hm. Normally, ghem-lords' personal affairs are not my business, only the official ones. But the, ah, chance of a good deed has come up so squarely in my path, I shall not avoid it. This time. I just had a short talk with a, ah, gentleman who informed me he was here today with the mission of seeing that you, in his precise phrasing, did not leave the Moon Garden Hall alive. He was a little vague about what method he proposed to use to accomplish this. What made him peculiar in this venue was that he was no ghem. A purely commercial artist. He did not know who had hired him, that information being concealed behind several layers of screening. Do you have any guesses?"

Yenaro listened to this recital shocked, tight-lipped, and thoughtful. Miles wondered if Yenaro was going through the same set of deductions he was. He rather thought so. The haut-governor, it appeared, whichever one it was, had sent Yenaro's ploy some backup. Just to make sure nothing went wrong. Such as Yenaro surviving his own bombing to accuse his betrayer.

"I . . . have a guess, yes."

"Would you care to share it?"

Yenaro regarded him doubtfully. "Not at this time."

"Suit yourself." Vorreedi shrugged. "We left him sitting in a quiet corner. The fast-penta should wear off in about ten minutes. You have that much lead-time to do—whatever you decide."

"Thank you, Lord Vorreedi," said Yenaro quietly. He gathered his dark robes about himself, and rose. He was pale, but admirably controlled, not shaking. "I think I will leave you now."

"Probably a good choice," said Vorreedi.

"Keep in touch, huh?" said Miles.

Yenaro gave him a brief, formal nod. "Yes. We must talk again." He strode away, glancing left and right.

Ivan chewed on his fingers. It was better than his blurting out everything to Vorreedi right here and now, Miles's greatest fear.

"Was that all true, sir?" Miles asked Colonel Vorreedi.

"Yes." Vorreedi rubbed his nose. "Except that I'm not so certain that it isn't any of our business. Lord Yenaro seems to be taking a great deal of interest in you. One can't help wondering if there might be some hidden connection. Sifting through that hired thug's hierarchy would be tedious and time-consuming for my department. And what would we find at the end?" Vorreedi's eye fell coolly on Miles. "Just how angry *were* you at getting your legs burned the other night, Lord Vorkosigan?"

"Not that angry!" Miles denied hastily. "Give me credit for a sense of proportion, at least, sir! No. It wasn't me who hired the goon." Though he had just as surely set up Yenaro for this, by attempting to play all those cute little head-games with his possible patrons, Kety, Prince Slyke, and the Rond. *You wanted a reaction, you got one.* "But . . . it's just a feeling, you understand. But I think pursuing this lead might be time and resources well spent."

"A feeling, eh?"

"You surely have trusted your intuition before, in your work, sir."

"Used, yes. Trusted, never. An ImpSec officer should be clear about the difference."

"I understand, sir."

They all rose to continue the tour of the exhibition, Miles carefully not glancing at the scorched spot on the pavement as they passed on. As they approached the west side of the dome, Miles searched the robed crowd for his contact-lady. There she was, sitting near a fountain, frowning. But he would never succeed in ditching Vorreedi now; the man was stuck like glue. He tried anyway. "Excuse me, sir. I have to speak to a lady."

"I'll come with you," said Vorreedi pleasantly.

Right. Miles sighed, hastily composing his message. The dignified ghem-lady looked up as he approached with his unwelcome companions. Miles realized he didn't know the woman's name.

"Pardon me, milady. I just wanted to let you know that I will not be able to accept your invitation to visit, uh, this afternoon. Please convey my deepest regrets to your mistress." Would she, and the haut Rian, interpret this as intended, as *Abort, abort abort!*? Miles could only pray so. "But if she can arrange instead a visit to the man's cousin, I think that would be most educational."

The woman's frown deepened. But she only said, "I will convey your words, Lord Vorkosigan."

Miles nodded farewell, mentally blessing her for avoiding the pitfall of any more complicated reply. When he looked back, she had already swept to her feet and was hurrying away.

Chapter Eleven

Miles had not entered the sacred confines of the Barrayaran embassy's ImpSec offices before, having stayed discreetly upstairs in the diplomatic corps' plusher territory. As he'd posited, it was on the second-lowest basement level. A uniformed corporal ushered him past security scanners and into Colonel Vorreedi's office.

It was not as austere as Miles expected, being decorated all about with small examples of Cetagandan art objects, though the powered sculptures were all turned off this morning. Some might be mementos, but the rest suggested the so-called protocol officer was a collector of excellent taste, if limited means.

The man himself was seated at a desk cleared in utilitarian bareness. Vorreedi was dressed as usual in the underlayers and robes of a middle-ranking ghem-lord of painfully sober preferences, subdued blues and grays. Except for the lack of face paint, in a crowd of ghem Vorreedi would practically disappear, though behind a Barrayaran ImpSec comconsole desk the effect of the ensemble was a little startling.

Miles moistened his lips. "Good morning, sir. Ambassador Vorob'yev told me you wanted to see me."

"Yes, thank you, Lord Vorkosigan." Vorreedi's nod dismissed the corporal, who withdrew silently. The doors slid shut behind him with a heavy sealing sound. "Do sit down."

Miles slipped into the station chair across the desk from Vorreedi, smiling in what he hoped seemed innocent good cheer. Vorreedi looked across at Miles with keen, undivided attention. Not good. Vorreedi was second in authority here only to Ambassador Vorob'yev, and like Vorob'yev, had been chosen as a top man for one of the most critical posts in the Barrayaran diplomatic corps. One might count on Vorreedi to be a very busy man, but never a stupid one. Miles wondered if Vorreedi's meditations this past night had been one-half so busy as his own. Miles braced himself for an Illyanesque opening shot, such as *What the hell are you up to, Vorkosigan, trying to start a damned war single-handed?!*

Instead, Colonel Vorreedi favored him with a long, thoughtful stare, before observing mildly, "Lieutenant Lord Vorkosigan. You are an ImpSec courier officer, by assignment."

"Yes, sir. When I am on duty."

"An interesting breed of men. Utterly reliable and loyal. They go here, go there, deliver whatever is asked of them without question or comment. Or failure, short of intervention by death itself."

"It's not usually that dramatic. We spend a lot of time riding around in jumpships. One catches up on one's reading."

"Mm. And to a man, these glorified mailmen report to Commodore Boothe, head of ImpSec Communications, Komarr. With one exception." Vorreedi's gaze intensified. "*You* are listed as reporting directly to Simon Illyan himself. Who reports to Emperor Gregor. The only other person I know of offhand in a chain of command that short is the Chief of Staff of the Imperial Service. It's an interesting anomaly. How do you explain it?"

"How do *I* explain it?" Miles echoed, temporizing. He thought briefly of replying, *I never explain anything*, except that was both 1) already evident and 2) clearly not the answer Vorreedi was looking for. "Why . . . every once in a while Emperor Gregor needs a personal errand run for himself or his household which is too trivial, or too inappropriate, to assign to working military personnel. Perhaps he wants, say, an ornamental breadfruit bush brought from the planet Pol to be planted in the garden of the Imperial Residence. They send me."

"That's a good explanation," Vorreedi agreed blandly. There was a short silence. "And do you have an equally good story for how you acquired this pleasant job?"

"Nepotism, obviously. Since I am clearly," Miles's smile thinned, "physically unfit for normal duties, this post was manufactured for me by my family connections."

"Hm." Vorreedi sat back, and rubbed his chin. "Now," he said distantly, "if you were a covert ops agent here on a mission from God," meaning Simon Illyan—same thing, from the ImpSec point of view, "you should have arrived with some sort of *Render all due assistance* order. Then a poor ImpSec local man might know where he stood with you."

If I don't get this man under control, he can and will nail my boots to the floor of the embassy, and Lord X will have no impediment at all to his baroque bid for chaos and empire. "Yes, sir," Miles took a breath, "and so would anyone else who saw it."

Vorreedi glanced up, startled. "Does ImpSec Command suspect a leak in my communications?"

"Not as far as I know. But as a lowly courier, I can't ask questions, can I?"

By the slight widening of his eyes, Vorreedi caught the joke. A subtle man indeed. "From the moment you set foot on Eta Ceta, Lord Vorkosigan, I have not noticed you *stop* asking questions."

"A personal failing."

"And . . . do you have any supporting evidence for your explanation of yourself?"

"Certainly." Miles stared thoughtfully into the air, as if about to pull his words from the thinnest part. "Consider, sir. All other ImpSec courier officers have an implanted allergy to fast-penta. It renders them interrogation-proof to illicit questioners, at fatal cost. Due to my rank and relations, that was judged too dangerous a procedure to do to me. Therefore, I am qualified for only the lowest-security sort of missions. It's all nepotism."

"Very . . . convincing."

"It wouldn't be much good if it weren't, sir."

"True." Another long pause. "Is there anything else you'd like to tell me—Lieutenant?"

"When I return to Barrayar, I will be giving a complete report of my m— excursion to Simon Illyan. I'm afraid you'll have to apply to him. It is definitely not within my authority to try to guess what he will wish to tell you."

There, whew. He'd told no lies at all, technically, even by implication. *Yeah. Be sure and point that out when they play a transcript of this conversation at your future court-martial.* But if Vorreedi chose to construe that Miles was a covert ops agent working on the highest levels and in utmost secrecy, it was no less than perfectly true. The fact that his mission here was spontaneously self-appointed and not assigned from above was . . . another order of problem altogether.

"I . . . could add a philosophical observation."

"Please do, my lord."

"You don't hire a genius to solve the most intractable imaginable problem, and then hedge him around with a lot of rules, nor try to micro-manage him from two weeks' distance. You turn him loose. If all you need is somebody to follow orders, you can hire an idiot. In fact, an idiot would be better suited."

Vorreedi's fingers drummed lightly on his comconsole desk. Miles felt the man might have tackled an intractable problem or two himself, in his past. Vorreedi's brows rose. "And do you consider yourself a genius, Lord Vorkosigan?" he asked softly. Vorreedi's tone of voice made Miles's skin crawl, it reminded him so much of his father's when Count Vorkosigan was about to spring some major verbal trap.

"My intelligence evaluations are in my personnel file, sir."

"I've read it. That's why we're having this conversation." Vorreedi blinked, slowly, like a lizard. "No rules at all?"

"Well, one rule, maybe. Deliver success or pay with your ass."

"You have held your current post for almost three years, I see, Lieutenant Vorkosigan. . . .Your ass is still intact, is it?"

"Last time I checked, sir." *For the next five days, maybe.*

"This suggests astonishing authority and autonomy."

"No authority at all. Just responsibility."

"Oh, dear." Vorreedi pursed his lips very thoughtfully indeed. "You have my sympathy, Lord Vorkosigan."

"Thank you, sir. I need it." Into the all-too-meditative silence that followed Miles added, "Do we know if Lord Yenaro survived the night?"

"He disappeared, so we think he has. He was last seen leaving the Moon Garden Hall with a roll of carpet over his shoulder." Vorreedi cocked an inquiring eye at Miles. "I have no explanation for the carpet."

Miles ignored the broad hint, responding instead with, "Are you so sure that disappearance equates with his survival? What about his stalker?"

"Hm." Vorreedi smiled. "Shortly after we left him he was picked up by the Cetagandan Civil Police, who still have him in close custody."

"They did this on their own?"

"Let's say they received an anonymous tip. It seemed the socially responsible thing to do. But I must say, the Civils responded to it with admirable efficiency. He appears to be of interest to them for some previous work."

"Did he have time to report in to his employers, before he was canned?"

"No."

So, Lord X was in an information vacuum this morning. He wouldn't like that one bit. The mis-fire of yesterday's plot must make him frantically frustrated. He wouldn't know what had gone wrong, or if Yenaro had realized his intended fate, though Yenaro's disappearance and subsequent non-communication would surely be a fat clue. Yenaro was now as loose a cannon as Miles and Ivan. Which of them would be first on Lord X's hit list after this? Would Yenaro go seeking protection to some authority, or would the rumor of treason frighten him off?

And what method could Lord X come up with for disposing of the Barrayaran envoys one-half so baroque and perfect as Yenaro had been? Yenaro was a masterpiece, as far as the art of assassination went, beautifully choreographed in three movements and a crescendo. Now all that elaborate effort was wasted. Lord X would be as livid at the spoiling of his lovely pattern as at the failure of his plot, Miles swore. And he was an anxious impatient artist who couldn't leave well enough alone, who had to add those clever little touches. The kind of person who, as a child given his first garden, would dig up the seeds to see if they'd sprouted yet. (Miles felt a tiny twinge of sympathy for Lord X.) Yes, indeed, Lord X, playing for great stakes and losing both time and his inhibitions, was now well and classically primed to make a major mistake.

Why am I not so sure that's such a great idea?

"More to add, Lord Vorkosigan?" said Vorreedi.

"Hm? No. Just, uh, thinking." *Besides, it would only upset you.*

"I would request, as the embassy officer ultimately responsible for your personal safety as an official envoy, that you and Lord Vorpatril end your social contacts with a man who is apparently involved in a lethal Cetagandan vendetta."

"Yenaro is of no further interest to me. I wish him no harm. My real priority is in identifying the man who supplied him with that fountain."

Vorreedi's brows rose in mild reproach. "You might have said so earlier."

"Hindsight," said Miles, "is always better."

"That's for damned sure," sighed Vorreedi, in a voice of experience. He scratched his nose, and sat back. "There is another reason I called you here this morning, Lord Vorkosigan. Ghem-Colonel Benin has requested a second interview with you."

"Has he? Same as before?" Miles kept his voice from squeaking.

"Not quite. He specifically requested to speak with both you and Lord Vorpatril. In fact, he's on his way now. But you can refuse the interview if you wish."

"No, that's . . . that's fine. In fact, I'd like to talk to Benin again. I, ah . . . shall I go fetch Ivan, then, sir?" Miles rose to his feet. Bad, bad idea to let the two suspects consult before the interrogation, but then, this wasn't Vorreedi's case. How fully had Miles convinced the man of his secret clout?

"Go ahead," said Vorreedi affably. "Though I must say . . ."

Miles paused.

"I do not see how Lord Vorpatril fits into this. He's no courier officer. And his records are as transparent as glass."

"A lot of people are baffled by Ivan, sir. But . . . sometimes, even a genius needs someone who can follow orders."

Miles tried not to scamper, hustling down the corridor to Ivan's quarters. The luxury of privacy their status had bought them was about to come to a screeching halt, he suspected. If Vorreedi didn't turn on the bugs in both their rooms after this, the man either had supernatural self-control or was brain dead. And the protocol officer was the voraciously curious type; it went with his job.

Ivan unlocked his door with a drawl of "Enter," at Miles's impatient knock. Miles found his cousin sitting up in bed, half-dressed in green trousers and cream shirt, leafing through a pile of hand-calligraphed colored papers with an abstracted and not particularly happy air.

"Ivan. Get up. Get dressed. We're about to have an interview with Colonel Vorreedi and ghem-Colonel Benin."

"Confession at last, thank God!" Ivan tossed the papers up in the air and fell backward on his bed with a *woof* of relief.

"No. Not exactly. But I need you to let me do most of the talking, and confirm whatever I assert."

"Oh, damn." Ivan frowned up at the ceiling. "What *now*?"

"Benin has to have been investigating Ba Lura's movements, the day before its death. I'm guessing he's traced the ba to our little encounter at the pod dock. I don't want to screw up his investigation. In fact, I want it to succeed, at least as far as identifying the Ba's murderer. So he needs as many real facts as possible."

"Real facts. As opposed to what other kind of facts?"

"We absolutely can't bring up any mention of the Great Key, or the haut Rian. I figure we can tell events exactly as they happened, just leave out that one tiny detail."

"You figure, do you? You must be using a different kind of math than the rest of the universe does. Do you realize how pissed Vorreedi and the Ambassador are going to be about our concealing that little incident?"

"I've got Vorreedi under control, temporarily. He thinks I'm on a mission from Simon Illyan."

"That means you aren't. I knew it!" Ivan groaned, and pulled a pillow over his face, and squashed it tight.

Miles pulled it out of his grasp. "I am now. Or I would be, if Illyan knew what I know. Bring that nerve disruptor. But don't pull it out unless I tell you to."

"I am not shooting your commanding officer for you."

"You're not shooting anybody. And anyway, Vorreedi's not my commander." That could be an important legal point, later. "I may want it for evidence. But not unless the subject comes up. We volunteer nothing."

"Never volunteer, yes, that's the ticket! You're catching on at last, coz!"

"Shut up. Get up." Miles threw Ivan's undress uniform jacket across his prostrate form. "This is important! But you have to stay absolutely cool. I may be completely off-base, and panicking prematurely."

"I don't think so. I think you're panicking post-maturely. In fact, if you were panicking any later it would be practically posthumously. I've been panicking for *days*."

Miles tossed Ivan his half-boots, with ruthless finality. Ivan shook his head, sat up, and began pulling them on.

"Do you remember," Ivan sighed, "that time in the back garden at Vorkosigan House, when you'd been reading all those military histories about the Cetagandan prison camps during the invasion, and you decided we had to dig an escape tunnel? Except it was you who did all the designing, and me and Elena who did all the digging?"

"We were about eight," said Miles defensively. "The medics were still working on my bones. I was still pretty friable then."

"—and the tunnel collapsed on me?" Ivan went on dreamily. "And I was under there for *hours?*"

"It wasn't hours. It was minutes. Sergeant Bothari had you out of there in practically no time."

"It seemed like hours to *me*. I can still taste the dirt. It got stuffed up my nose, too." Ivan rubbed his nose in memory. "Mother would still be having the fit, if Aunt Cordelia hadn't sat on her."

"We were stupid little *kids*. What has this got to do with anything?"

"Nothing, I suppose. I just woke up thinking about it, this morning." Ivan stood up, fastened his tunic, and pulled it straight. "I never believed I'd miss Sergeant Bothari, but I think I do now. Who's going to dig me out this time?"

Miles wanted to snap out a sharp rejoinder, but shivered instead. *I miss Bothari too.* He had almost forgotten how much, till Ivan's words hit the scar of his regret, that secret little pocket of anguish that never seemed to drain. Major mistakes . . . Dammit, a man walking a tight-wire didn't need someone shouting from the sidelines how far down the drop was, or what lousy balance he had. It wasn't as if he didn't know; but what he most needed was to forget. Even a momentary loss of concentration— of self-confidence—of forward momentum, could be fatal. "Do me a favor, Ivan. Don't try to think. You'll hurt yourself. Just follow orders, huh?"

Ivan bared his teeth in a non-smile, and followed Miles out the door.

They met with ghem-Colonel Benin in the same little conference room as before, but this time, Vorreedi rode shotgun personally, dispensing with the guard. The two colonels were just finishing the amenities and sitting down as Miles and Ivan entered, by which sign Miles hoped they'd had less time to compare notes than he and Ivan'd had. Benin was dressed again in his formal red uniform and lurid face paint, freshly and perfectly applied. By the time they'd all finished going through the polite greetings once more, and everyone was reseated, Miles had his breathing and heartbeat under control. Ivan concealed his nerves in an expression of blank benevolence that made him look, in Miles's opinion, remarkably sappy.

"Lord Vorkosigan," ghem-Colonel Benin began. "I understand you work as a courier officer."

"When I'm on duty." Miles decided to repeat the party line for Benin's benefit. "It's an honorable task, that's not too physically demanding for me."

"And do you like your duties?"

Miles shrugged. "I like the travel. And, ah . . . it gets me out of the way, an advantage that cuts two ways. You know about Barrayar's backward attitude to mutations." Miles thought of Yenaro's longing for a post. "And it gives me an official position, makes me somebody."

"I can understand *that*," conceded Benin.

Yeah, I thought you would.

"But you're not on courier duty now?"

"Not this trip. We were to give our diplomatic duties our undivided attention, and, it was hoped, maybe acquire a little polish."

"And Lord Vorpatril here is assigned to Operations, is that right?"

"Desk work," Ivan sighed. "I keep hoping for ship duty."

Not really true, Miles reflected; Ivan adored being assigned to HQ at the capital, where he kept up his own apartment and a social life that was the envy of his brother-officers. Ivan just wished his mother, *Lady* Vorpatril, might be assigned ship duty, someplace far away.

"Hm." Benin's hands twitched, as if in memory of sorting stacks of plastic flimsies. He drew breath, and looked Miles straight in the eyes. "So, Lord Vorkosigan—the funeral rotunda was *not* the first time you saw the Ba Lura, was it?"

Benin was trying for the rattling unexpected straight shot, to unnerve his quarry. "Correct," Miles answered, with a smile.

Expecting denial, Benin already had his mouth open for the second strike, probably the presentation of some telling piece of evidence that would give the Barrayaran the lie. He had to close it again, and start over. "If . . . if you wished to keep it a secret, why did you as much as flat tell me to look where I would be sure to find you? And," his tone sharpened with baffled annoyance, "if you didn't want to keep it a secret, why didn't you tell me about it in the first place?"

"It provided an interesting test of your competence. I wanted to know if it would be worth my while to persuade you to share your results. Believe me, my first encounter with the Ba Lura is as much a mystery to me as I'm sure it is to you."

Even from beneath the gaudy face paint, the look Benin gave Miles reminded him forcibly of the look he got all too often from superiors. He even capitalized it in his mind, The Look. In a weird backhanded way, it made him feel quite comfortable with Benin. His smile became slightly cheerier.

"And . . . how *did* you encounter the ba?" said Benin.

"What do you know so far?" Miles countered. Benin would, of course, keep something back, to cross-check Miles's story. That was quite all right, as Miles proposed to tell almost the whole truth, next.

"Ba Lura was at the transfer station the day you arrived. It left the station at least twice. Once, apparently, from a pod docking bay in which the security monitors were deactivated and unchecked for a period of forty minutes. The same bay and the same period in which you arrived, Lord Vorkosigan."

"Our first arrival, you mean."

" . . . Yes."

Vorreedi's eyes were widening and his lips were thinning. Miles ignored him, for now, though Ivan's gaze cautiously shifted to check him out.

"Deactivated? Torn out of the wall, I'd call it. Very well, ghem-Colonel. But tell me—was our encounter in the pod dock the first or second time the ba appeared to leave the station?"

"Second," Benin said, watching him closely.

"Can you prove that?"

"Yes."

"Good. It may be *very important* later that you can prove that." Ha, Benin wasn't the only one who could cross-check the truth of this conversation. Benin, for whatever reason, was being straight with him so far. Turn and turnabout. "Well, this is what happened from our point of view—"

In a flat voice, and with plenty of corroborative physical details, Miles described their confusing clash with the ba. The only item he changed was to report the ba reaching for its trouser pocket before he'd yelled his warning. He brought the tale up to the moment of Ivan's heroic struggle and his own retrieval of the loose nerve disruptor, and bounced it over to Ivan to finish. Ivan gave him a dirty look, but, taking his tone from Miles, offered a brief factual description of the ba's subsequent escape.

Since it lacked face paint, Miles could watch Vorreedi's face darken, out of the corner of his eye. The man was too cool and controlled to actually turn purple or anything, but Miles bet a blood pressure monitor would be beeping in plaintive alarm right now.

"And why did you not report this at our first meeting, Lord Vorkosigan?" Benin asked again, after a long, digestive pause.

"I might," said Vorreedi in a slightly choked voice, "ask you the same question, Lieutenant." Benin shot Vorreedi a raised-brow look, almost putting his face paint in danger of smudging.

Lieutenant, not *my lord*; Miles took the point. "The pod pilot reported to his captain, who will have reported to his commander." To wit, Illyan; in fact, the report, slogging through normal channels, should be reaching Illyan's desk right about now. Three days more for an emergency query to arrive on Vorreedi's desk from home, six more days for a reply and return-reply. It would all be over before Illyan could do a damned thing, now. "However, on my authority as senior envoy, I suppressed the incident for diplomatic reasons. We were sent with specific instructions to maintain a low profile and behave with maximum courtesy. My government considered this solemn occasion an important opportunity to send a message that we would be glad to see more normal trade and other relations, and an easing of tensions along our mutual borders. I did not judge that it would do anything helpful for our mutual tensions to open our visit with charges of an unmotivated armed attack by an Imperial slave upon the Barrayaran special representatives."

The implied threat was obvious enough; despite Benin's face paint, Miles could tell that one had hit home. Even Vorreedi looked as if he might be giving the pitch serious consideration.

"Can you . . . prove your assertions, Lord Vorkosigan?" asked Benin cautiously.

"We still have the captured nerve disruptor. Ivan?" Miles nodded to his cousin.

Gently, using only his fingertips, Ivan drew the weapon from his pocket and laid it gingerly on the table, and returned his hands demurely to his lap. He avoided Vorreedi's outraged eye. Vorreedi and Benin reached simultaneously for the nerve disruptor, and simultaneously stopped, frowning at each other.

"Excuse me," said Vorreedi. "I had not seen this before."

"Really?" said Benin. *How extraordinary*, his tone implied. "Go ahead." His hand dropped politely.

Vorreedi picked up the weapon and examined it closely, among other things checking to see that the safety lock was indeed engaged, before handing it equally politely to Benin.

"I'd be glad to return the weapon to you, ghem-Colonel," Miles went on, "in exchange for whatever information you are able to deduce from it. If it can be traced back to the Celestial Garden, that's not much help, but if it was something the Ba acquired en route, well . . . it might be revealing. This is a check that you can make more easily than I can." Miles paused, then added, "Who did the ba visit from the station the first time?"

Benin glanced up from his close contemplation of the nerve disruptor. "A ship moored off-station."

"Can you be more specific?"

"No."

"Excuse me, let me re-phrase that. Could you be more specific if you chose to?"

Benin set the disruptor down, and leaned back, his expression of attention to Miles, if possible, intensifying. He was silent for a long thoughtful moment before finally replying, "No, unfortunately. I could not."

Rats. The three haut-governors' ships moored off that transfer station were Ilsum Kety's, Slyke Giaja's and Este Rond's. This could have been the final line of his triangulation, but Benin didn't have it. Yet. "I'd be particularly interested in how traffic control, or what certainly passed for traffic control, came to direct us to the wrong, or at any rate the first, pod dock."

"Why do *you* think the ba entered your pod?" Benin asked in turn.

"Given the intense confusion of the encounter, I certainly would consider the possibility of it having been an accident. If it *was* arranged, I think something must have gone very wrong."

No shit, said Ivan's silent morose look. Miles ignored him.

"Anyway, ghem-Colonel, I hope this helps to anchor your timetable," Miles continued in a tone of finality. Surely Benin would be itching to run and check out his new clue, the nerve disruptor.

Benin didn't budge. "So what did you and the haut Rian *really* discuss, Lord Vorkosigan?"

"For that, I'm afraid you will have to apply to the haut Rian. She is Cetagandan to the bone, and so all your department." *Alas.* "But I think her distress at the death of the Ba Lura was quite genuine."

Benin's eyes flicked up. "When did *you* see enough of her to gauge the depth of her distress?"

"Or so I deduced." And if he didn't end this *now* he was going to put his foot in it so deep they'd need a hand-tractor to pull it out again. He had to play Vorreedi with the utmost delicacy; this was not quite the case with Benin. "This is fascinating, ghem-Colonel, but I'm afraid I'm out of time for this morning. But if you ever find out where that nerve disruptor came from, and where the ba went to, I would be more than glad to continue the conversation." He sat back, folded his arms, and smiled cordially.

What Vorreedi *should* have done was announce loudly that they had all the time in the world, and let Benin continue to be his stalking-horse—Miles would have, in his place—but Vorreedi himself was clearly itching to get Miles alone. Instead, the protocol officer rose, signaling the official end to the interview. Benin, on embassy grounds as a guest, on sufferance—not his normal mode, Miles was sure—acceded without comment, rising to take his farewells.

"I *will* be speaking with you again, Lord Vorkosigan," Benin promised darkly.

"I certainly hope so, sir. Ah—did you take my other piece of advice, too? About blocking interference?"

Benin paused, looking suddenly a little abstracted. "Yes, in fact."

"How did it go?"

"Better than I would have expected."

"Good."

Benin's parting semi-salute was ironic, but not, Miles felt, altogether hostile.

Vorreedi escorted his guest to the door, but turned him over to the hall guard and was back in the little room before Miles and Ivan could make good their escape.

Vorreedi pinned Miles by eye. Miles felt a momentary regret that his diplomatic immunity did not extend to the protocol officer as well. Would it occur to Vorreedi to separate the pair of them, and break Ivan? Ivan was practicing looking invisible, something he did very well.

Vorreedi stated dangerously, "I am not a mushroom, Lieutenant Vorkosigan."

To be kept in the dark and fed on horseshit, right. Miles sighed inwardly. "Sir, apply to my commander," meaning Illyan—Vorreedi's commander too, in point of fact—"be cleared, and I'm yours. Until then, my best judgment is to continue exactly as I have been."

"Trusting your instincts?" said Vorreedi dryly.

"It's not as if I had any clear conclusions to share yet."

"So . . . do your instincts suggest some connection between the late Ba Lura, and Lord Yenaro?"

Vorreedi had instincts too, oh, yes. Or he wouldn't be in *this* post. "Besides the fact that both have interacted with me? Nothing that I . . . trust. I'm after proof. Then I will . . . be somewhere."

"Where?"

Head down in the biggest privy you ever imagined, at the current rate. "I guess I'll know when I get there, sir."

"We too will speak again, Lord Vorkosigan. You can count on it." Vorreedi gave him a very abbreviated nod, and departed abruptly—probably to apprise Ambassador Vorob'yev of the new complications in his life.

Into the ensuing silence, Miles said faintly, "That went well, all things considered."

Ivan's lip curled in scorn.

They kept silence on the trudge back to Ivan's room, where Ivan found a new stack of colored papers waiting on his desk. He sorted through them, pointedly ignoring Miles.

"I have to reach Rian somehow," Miles said at last. "I can't afford to wait. Things are getting too damned tight."

"I don't want anything more to do with any of this," said Ivan distantly.

"It's too late."

"Yes. I know." His hand paused. "Huh. Here's a new wrinkle. This one has both our names on it."

"Not from Lady Benello, is it? I'm afraid Vorreedi will count her off-limits now."

"No. It's not a name I recognize."

Miles pounced on the paper, and tore it open. "Lady d'Har. A garden party. What does she grow in *her* garden, I wonder? Could it be a double meaning—referencing the Celestial Garden? Hm. Awfully short notice. It could be my next contact. God, I hate being at haut Rian's mercy for every setup. Well, accept it anyway, just in case."

"It's not my first choice of how to spend the evening," said Ivan.

"Did I say anything about a choice? It's a chance, we've got to take it." He went on nastily, "Besides, if you keep leaving your genetic samples all over town, your progeny could end up being featured in next year's art show. As bushes."

Ivan shuddered. "You don't think they would—that's not why—uh, could they?"

"Sure. Why, when you're gone, they could re-create the operative body parts that interest them, to perform on command, to any scale—quite the souvenir. And you thought that *kitten* tree was obscene."

"There's more to it than *that*, coz," Ivan stated with injured dignity. His voice faded in doubt. " . . . you don't think they'd really do something like that, do you?"

"There's no more ruthless passion than that of a Cetagandan artist in search of new media." He added firmly, "We're going to a garden party. I'm sure it's my contact with Rian."

"Garden party," conceded Ivan with a sigh. He stared off blankly into space. After a minute he commented offhandedly, "Y'know, it's too bad she can't just get the gene bank back from his ship. Then he'd have the key but no lock. *That'd* fox him up but good, I bet."

Miles sat down in Ivan's desk chair, slowly. When he'd got his breath back, he whispered, "Ivan—that's *brilliant*. Why didn't I think of that before?"

Ivan considered this. " 'Cause it's not a scenario that lets you play the lone hero in front of the haut Rian?"

They exchanged saturnine looks. For once, Miles's gaze shifted first. "I meant that as a rhetorical question," he said tightly. But he didn't say it very loudly.

Chapter Twelve

Garden party was a misnomer, Miles decided. He stared past Ambassador Vorob'yev and Ivan as the three of them exited from an ear-popping ride up the lift tube and into the apparently open air of the rooftop. A faint golden sparkle in the air above marked the presence of a lightweight force-screen, blocking unwanted wind, rain, or dust. Dusk here, in the center of the capital, was a silver sheen in the atmosphere, for the half-kilometer-high building overlooked the green rings of parkway surrounding the Celestial Garden itself.

Curving banks of flowers and dwarf trees, fountains, rivulets, walkways, and arched jade bridges turned the roof into a descending labyrinth in the finest Cetagandan style. Every turn of the walkways revealed and framed a different view of the city stretching to the horizon, though the best views were the ones that looked to the Emperor's shimmering great phoenix egg in the city's heart. The lift-tube foyer, opening onto it all, was roofed with arching vines and paved in an elaborate inlay of colored stones: lapis lazuli, malachite, green and white jade, rose quartz, and other minerals Miles couldn't even name.

Looking around, it gradually dawned on Miles why the protocol officer had them all wearing their House blacks, when Miles would have guessed undress greens to be adequate. It was not

159

possible to be overdressed here. Ambassador Vorob'yev was admitted on sufferance as their escort, but even Vorreedi had to wait in the garage below, tonight. Ivan, looking around too, clutched their invitation a little tighter.

Their putative hostess, Lady d'Har, stood on the edge of the foyer. Apparently being inside her home counted the same as being inside a bubble, for she was welcoming her guests. Even at her advanced age, her haut-beauty stunned the eye. She wore robes in a dozen fine layers of blinding white, sweeping down and swirling around her feet. Thick silver hair flowed to the floor. Her husband, ghem-Admiral Har, whose bulky presence would normally have dominated any room, seemed to fade into the background beside her.

Ghem-Admiral Har commanded half the Cetagandan fleet, and his duty-delayed arrival for the final ceremonies of the Empress's funeral was the reason for tonight's welcome-home party. He wore his Imperial blood-red dress uniform, which he could have hung with enough medals to sink him should he chance to fall in a river. He'd chosen instead to one-up the competition with the neck-ribbon and medallion of the deceptively simple-sounding Order of Merit. Clearing away the other clutter made this honor impossible for the viewer to miss. Or match. It was given, rarely, at the sole discretion of the Emperor himself. There were few higher awards to be had in the Cetagandan Empire. The haut-lady by his side was one of them, though. Lord Har would have pinned her to his tunic too, if he could, Miles felt, for all he had won her some forty years past. The Har ghem-clan's face paint featured mainly orange and green; the patterns lacked definition, crossing with the man's deeply age-lined features, and clashing horribly with the red of the uniform.

Even Ambassador Vorob'yev was awed by ghem-Admiral Har, Miles judged by the extreme formality of his greetings. Har was polite but clearly puzzled; *Why are these outlanders in my garden?* But he deferred to Lady d'Har, who relieved Ivan of his nervously proffered invitation with a small, cool nod, and directed them, in a voice age-softened to a honeyed alto, to where the food and drinks were displayed.

They strolled on. After he recovered from the shock of Lady d'Har, Ivan's head swiveled, looking for the young ghem-women he knew, without success. "This place is wall-to-wall old crusts," he whispered to Miles in dismay. "When we walked in, the average age here dropped from ninety to eighty-nine."

"Eighty-nine and a half, I'd say," Miles whispered back.

Ambassador Vorob'yev put a finger to his lips, suppressing the commentary, but his eyes glinted in amused agreement.

Quite. This was the real thing; Yenaro and his crowd were shabby little outsiders indeed, by comparison, excluded by age, by rank, by wealth, by . . . everything. Scattered through the garden were half-a-dozen haut-lady bubbles, glowing like pale lanterns, something Miles had not yet seen outside the Celestial Garden itself. Lady d'Har kept social contact with her haut-relatives, or former relatives, it appeared. *Rian, here?* Miles prayed so.

"I wish I could have got Maz in," Vorob'yev sighed with regret. "How *did* you do this, Lord Ivan?"

"Not me," denied Ivan. He flipped a thumb at Miles.

Vorob'yev's brows rose inquiringly.

Miles shrugged. "They told me to study the power-hierarchy. This is it, isn't it?" Actually, he was not so sure anymore.

Where did power lie, in this convoluted society? With the ghem-lords, he would have said once without hesitation, who controlled the weapons, the ultimate threat of violence. Or with the haut-lords, who controlled the ghem, through whatever oblique means. Certainly not with the secluded haut-women. Was their knowledge a kind of power, then? A very fragile sort of power. Wasn't *fragile power* an oxymoron? The Star Crèche existed because the Emperor protected it; the Emperor existed because the ghem-lords served him. Yet the haut-women had created the Emperor . . . created the haut itself . . . created the ghem, for that matter. Power to create . . . power to destroy . . . he blinked, dizzy, and munched on a canapé in the shape of a tiny swan, biting off its head first. The feathers were made with rice flour, judging from the taste, the center a spicy protein paste. Vat-grown swan meat?

The Barrayaran party collected drinks and began a slow circuit of the rooftop garden's walks, comparing views. They also collected stares, from the elderly ghem and haut scattered about; but none came up to introduce themselves, or ask questions, or attempt to start a conversation. Vorob'yev himself was only scouting, so far, Miles thought, but the man would surely pursue the evening's opportunities for contact-making soon. How Miles was to divest himself of the ambassador when his own contact turned up, he was not sure. Assuming this was where his contact was to meet him, and it wasn't all just his hyperactive imagination, or—

Or the next assassination attempt. They'd rounded some greenery to see a woman in haut-white, but with no haut-bubble, standing alone and staring out over the city. Miles recognized her from the heavy chocolate-dark braid falling down her back to her ankles, even at this three-quarters-turned view. The haut Vio d'Chilian. Was ghem-General Chilian here? Was Kety himself?

Ivan's breath drew in. Right. Except for their elderly hostess, this was the first time Ivan had seen a haut-woman outside her bubble, and Ivan lacked the ... inoculation of the haut Rian. Miles found he could view the haut Vio this time with scarcely a tremor. Were the haut-women a disease that you could only catch once, like the legendary smallpox, and if you survived it you were immune thereafter, however scarred?

"Who *is* she?" whispered Ivan, enchanted.

"Ghem-General Chilian's haut-wife," Vorob'yev murmured into his ear. "The ghem-general could order your liver fried for breakfast. *I* would send it to him. The free ghem-ladies can entertain themselves as they please with you, but the married haut are strictly off-limits. Understood?"

"Yes, sir," said Ivan faintly.

The haut Vio was staring as if hypnotized at the great glowing dome of the Celestial Garden. Longing for her lost life, Miles wondered? She'd spent years exiled in the hinterlands at Sigma Ceta with her ghem husband. What was she feeling, now? Happy? Homesick?

Some movement or sound from the Barrayarans must have broken her reverie, for her head turned toward them. For a second, just a second, her astonishing cinnamon eyes seemed copper-metallic with a rage so boundless, Miles's stomach lurched. Then her expression snapped into a smooth hauteur, as blank as the bubble she lacked, and as armored; the open emotion was gone so fast Miles was not sure the other two men had even seen it. But the look was not for them; it had been on her face even as she'd turned, before she could have identified the Barrayarans, blackly dressed in the shadows.

Ivan opened his mouth; *Please, no,* Miles thought, but Ivan had to try. "Good evening, milady. Wonderful view, eh?"

She hesitated a long moment—Miles pictured her fleeing—but then answered, in a low-pitched, perfectly modulated voice, "There is nothing like it in the universe."

Ivan, encouraged, brightened and moved forward. "Let me introduce myself. I'm Lord Ivan Vorpatril, of Barrayar. . . . And, uh, this

is Ambassador Vorob'yev, and this is my cousin, Lord Miles Vorkosigan. Son of You-know-who, eh?"

Miles winced. Watching Ivan babble in sexual panic would
normally be entertaining, if it wasn't so excruciatingly embarrassing.
It reminded Miles painfully of—himself. *Did I look like that much
of a fool, the first time I saw Rian?* He feared the answer was *yes*.

"Yes," said the haut Vio. "I know." Miles had seen people talk
to their potted plants with more warmth and expression than the
haut Vio turned on Ivan.

Give it up, Ivan, Miles urged silently. *This woman is married
to the first officer of a guy who maybe tried to kill us yesterday,
remember?* Unless Lord X *was* Prince Slyke after all—or the haut
Rond, or . . . Miles ground his teeth.

But before Ivan could dig himself any deeper, a man in
Cetagandan military uniform rounded the corner, his face paint
crinkling with his frown. Ghem-General Chilian. Miles froze, his
hand wrapping Ivan's forearm and biting deep in warning.

Chilian's gaze swept the Barrayarans, his nostrils flaring in suspicion. "Haut Vio," he addressed his wife. "Come with me, please."

"Yes, my lord," she said, her lashes sweeping down demurely,
and she escaped around Ivan with a bare nod of farewell. Chilian
brought himself to nod also, acknowledging the outlanders' existence; with an effort, Miles felt. The general glanced once back over
his shoulder as he whisked his wife away. So what sin had ghem-
General Chilian committed to win *her*?

"*Lucky* guy," sighed Ivan in envy.

"I'm not so sure," said Miles. Ambassador Vorob'yev just smiled
grimly.

They walked on, Miles's brain whirling around this new encounter. Was it accidental? Was it the start of a new setup? Lord X used
his human tools like long-handled forks, to keep the heat at a
distance. Surely the ghem-general and his wife were too close to
him, too obviously connected. Unless, of course, Lord X wasn't
Kety after all. . . .

A glow ahead brought Miles's gaze front and center. A haut-
bubble was approaching them along the evergreen-bounded walk.
Vorob'yev and Ivan stood aside to let it pass. Instead it stopped
in front of Miles.

"Lord Vorkosigan." The woman's voice was melodious even
through the filter, but it was not Rian's. "May I speak privately
with you?"

"Of course," said Miles, before Vorob'yev could put in an objection. "Where?" Tension shot through him. Was tonight to be his final assault already, upon the new target of Governor Ilsum Kety's ship? Too premature, still too uncertain . . . "And for how long?"

"Not far. We will be about an hour."

Not nearly long enough for a trip to orbit; this was something else, then. "Very well. Gentlemen, will you excuse me?"

Vorob'yev looked about as unhappy as his habitual control would allow. "Lord Vorkosigan . . ." His hesitation was actually a good sign; Vorreedi and he must have had a long and extraordinary talk. "Do you wish a guard?"

"No."

"A com link?"

"No."

"You *will* be careful?" Which was diplomatic for *Are you sure you know what the hell you're doing, boy?*

"Oh, yes, sir."

"What do we do if you're *not* back in an hour?" said Ivan.

"Wait." He nodded cordially, and followed the bubble down the garden path.

When they turned into a private nook, lit by low colored lanterns and screened by flowering bushes, the bubble rotated and abruptly blinked out. Miles found himself facing another haut beauty in white, riding in her float-chair like a throne. This woman's hair was honey-blond, intricately woven and tucked up around her shoulders, vaguely reminiscent of a gilt chain-mail neck guard. He would have guessed her age as forty-standard, which meant she was probably twice that.

"The haut Rian Degtiar instructs me to bring you," she stated. She moved her robes from the left side of the chair, uncovering a thickly padded armrest. "We have not much time." Her gaze seemed to measure his height, or shortness. "You can, um . . . *perch* here, and ride."

"How . . . fascinating." If only she *were* Rian . . . But this would test certain theories he had about the mechanical capacities of haut-bubbles, oh yes. "Uh . . . identification, milady?" he added almost apologetically. The last person he suspected of experiencing such a ride had ended up with its throat cut, after all.

She nodded, as if expecting this, and turned her hand outward, displaying the ring of the Star Crèche.

That was probably about as good as they could do, under the

circumstances. Cautiously, he approached, and eased himself aboard, grasping the back of the chair above her head for balance. Each was careful not to actually touch the other. Her long-fingered hand moved over the control panel embedded in the right arm-rest, and the force-field snapped on again. The pale white light reflected off the flowered bushes, bringing out their color, and cast a glow before them as they began to move down the path.

Their view was quite clear, scarcely impeded by an eggshell-thin, ghostly sphere of mist that marked the boundary of the force-field as seen from this side. Sound too was transmitted with high clarity, much better than the deliberately muffled reverse effect. He could hear voices, and the clink of glassware, from a balcony above. They passed Ambassador Vorob'yev and Ivan again, who stared curiously, uncertain, of course, if this was the same bubble they'd seen before. Miles squelched an absurd impulse to wave at them, going by.

They came not to the lift-tube foyer, as Miles had expected, but to the edge of the rooftop garden. Their silver-haired hostess was standing waiting. She nodded at the bubble, and coded open the force-screen, letting the bubble pass through onto a small private landing pad. The reflected glow off the pavement darkened, as the haut-woman blacked out her bubble. Miles stared upward at the shimmering night sky, looking for the lightflyer or aircar.

Instead, the bubble moved smoothly to the edge of the building and dropped straight over the side.

Miles clutched the seat-back convulsively, trying not to scream, fling his arms around his hostess-pilot's neck, or throw up all over her white dress. They were *free-falling*, and he *hated* heights . . . was this his intended death, his assassin sacrificing herself along with him? *Oh, God—!*

"I thought these things only went a meter in the air," he choked out, his voice, despite his best efforts, going high and squeaky.

"If you have enough initial altitude, you can maintain a con-trolled glide," she said calmly. Despite Miles's horrified first impres-sion, they were not actually dropping like a rock. They were arcing outward, across the boulevards far below, and the light-sparked green rings of parks, toward the dome of the Celestial Garden.

Miles thought wildly of the witch Baba Yaga, from the Barrayaran folk tales, who flew in a magic mortar. This witch didn't qualify as old and ugly. But he was not, at this moment, totally convinced she didn't eat bad children.

In a few minutes, the bubble decelerated again to a smooth

walking pace a few centimeters above the pavement outside one of the Celestial Garden's minor entrances. A movement of her finger brought back the white glow.

"Ah," she said, in a refreshed tone. "I haven't done that in *years*." She almost cracked a smile, for a moment nearly . . . human.

Miles was shocked when they passed through the Celestial dome's security procedures almost as if they weren't there, except for a swift exchange of electronic codes. No one stopped or searched the bubble. The sort of uniformed men who'd shaken down the galactic envoys with beady-eyed thoroughness stood back respectfully, with downcast gaze.

"Why don't they stop us?" Miles whispered, unable to overcome the psychological conviction that if he could see and hear them, they could see and hear him.

"Stop me?" repeated the haut-woman in puzzlement. "I am the haut Pel Navarr, Consort of Eta Ceta. I *live* here."

Their further progress was happily ground-hugging, if faster than the usual walking-pace, through the increasingly familiar precincts of the Celestial Garden to the low white building with the bio-filters on every window. The haut Pel's passage through its automated security procedures was almost as swift and perfunctory as through the dome entrance itself. They passed silently down a set of corridors, but turned in a different direction from the labs and offices at the building's heart, and went up one level.

Double doors parted to admit them to a large circular room done in subdued and subduing tones of silvery gray. Unlike any other place he'd seen in the Celestial Garden, it was devoid of living decorations, neither plant nor animal nor any of those disturbing creations in-between. Hushed, concentrated, undistracting . . . It was a chamber in the Star Crèche; he supposed he could dub it the Star Chamber. Eight women in white awaited them, sitting silently in a circle. His stomach should not still be turning over, dammit, the free fall was done.

The haut Pel brought her float-chair to a halt in a waiting empty gap in the circle, grounded it, and switched off the force-bubble. Eight extraordinary pairs of eyes focused on Miles.

No one, he thought, *should be exposed to this many haut-women at once*. It was some kind of dangerous overdose. Their beauty was varied; three were as silver-haired as the ghem-admiral's wife, one was copper-tressed, one was dark-skinned and hawk-nosed, with masses of blue-black ringlets tumbling down around her like a cloak. Two were blonde, his guide with her golden weave and another with hair as pale as oat straw in the sun, and as straight to the floor. One dark-eyed woman had chocolate-brown hair like the haut Vio, but in soft curling clouds instead of bound. And then there was Rian. Their massed effect went beyond beauty; where to, he was not sure, but *terror* came close. He slipped off the arm of the float chair and stood away from it, grateful for the propping effect of his stiff high boots.

"Here is the Barrayaran to testify," said the haut Rian.

Testify. He was here as a witness, then, not as the accused. A Key witness, so to speak. He stifled a slightly manic giggle. Somehow he did not think Rian would appreciate the pun.

He swallowed, and got his voice unlocked. "You have the advantage of me, ladies." Though he could make a good guess who they all were, at this point. His gaze swept the circle, and he blinked hard against the vertigo. "I have only met your Handmaiden." He nodded toward Rian. On a low table before her the Empress's entire formal regalia was laid out, including the Seal and the false Great Key.

Rian tilted her head in acknowledgment of the reasonableness of his request, and proceeded to go around the circle with a bewildering slug of haut names and titles—yes, here indeed sat the consorts of the eight satrap planets. With Rian the ninth, sitting in for the late Empress. The creative controllers of the haut-genome, of the would-be master race, were all met here in some extraordinary council.

The chamber was clearly set up for just this purpose; such meetings must also occur when the consorts journeyed home to escort the child-ships. Miles particularly focused on the consorts of Prince Slyke, Ilsum Kety, and the Rond. Kety's woman, the Consort of Sigma Ceta, was one of the silver-haired ones, closer to being contemporary with the late Empress than anyone else in the room. Rian introduced her as the haut Nadina. The oat-straw blonde served Prince Slyke of Xi Ceta, and the brown-curled woman was the Consort of Rho Ceta. Miles wondered anew at the significance of their titles, which named them all consorts of their planets, not of the men.

"Lord Vorkosigan," said the haut Rian. "I would like you to repeat for the consorts how you say you came into possession of the false Great Key, and all the subsequent events."

All? Miles did not blame her in the least for switching strategies from playing all cards close to her chest to calling in reinforcements.

It was not before time, in his opinion. But he disliked being taken by surprise. It would have been nice if she'd at least *consulted* him, first. *Yeah? How?*

"I take it you understood my message to abort the infiltration of Prince Slyke's ship," he countered.

"Yes. I expect you will explain why, in due order."

"Excuse me, milady. I do not mean to insult . . . anyone here. But if one of the consorts is a traitoress, in collusion with her satrap governor, this will pipeline everything we know straight to him. How do you *know* you are entirely among friends?"

There was enough tension in the room to go with any number of treasons, certainly. Rian raised a hand, as if to stem it. "He is an outlander. He cannot understand." She gave him a slow nod. "There is treason, we believe, yes, but not on *this* level. Further down."

"Oh . . . ?"

"We have concluded that even with the bank and Key in his hands, the satrap governor could not run the haut-genome by himself. The haut of his satrap would not cooperate with such a sudden usurpation, the overturning of all custom. He must plan to appoint a new consort, one under his own control. We think she has already been selected."

"Ah . . . do you know who?"

"Not yet," Rian sighed. "Not yet. She is someone, I fear, who does not wholly understand the goal of haut. It is all of a piece. If we knew which governor, we could guess which haut-woman he has suborned; if we knew which woman . . . well."

Dammit, this triangulation *had* to break soon. Miles chewed on his lower lip, then said slowly, "Milady. Tell me—if you can—something about how your force-bubbles are keyed to their individual operators, and why everyone is so damned convinced they're dead-secure. The keypad on those control panels looks like a palm-lock, but it can't just be a palm-lock; you can get around palm-locks."

"I cannot give *you* the technical details, Lord Vorkosigan," said Rian.

"I don't expect you to. Just the general logic of it."

"Well . . . they are keyed genetically, of course. One brushes one's hand across the pad, leaving a few skin cells. These are sucked in and scanned."

"Does it scan your entire genome? Surely that would take a lot of time."

"No, of course not. It runs through a tree of a dozen or so critical markers that individually identify a haut-woman. Starting with the presence of an X chromosome pair, and going down a branching list until confirmation is achieved."

"How much chance is there of duplicating the markers in two or more individuals?"

"We do not clone ourselves, Lord Vorkosigan."

"I mean, just of the dozen factors, just enough to fool the machine."

"Vanishingly small."

"Even among closely related members of one's own constellation?"

She hesitated, exchanging a glance with Lady Pel, who raised her brows thoughtfully.

"There's a reason I ask," Miles went on. "When ghem-Colonel Benin interviewed me, he let slip that six haut-bubbles had entered the funeral rotunda during the time period the Ba Lura's body must have been placed at the foot of the bier, and that it presented him with a major puzzle. He didn't tell me which six, but I bet you could get him to disgorge the list. It's a brute-force triage of a major data dump, but—suppose you ran the markers of those six through your records, and checked for accidental duplicates among living haut-women. If the woman is serving the satrap governor, she might have served him in that murder, too. You might finger your traitoress without ever having to leave the Star Crèche."

Rian, momentarily alert, sat back with a weary sigh. "Your reasoning is correct, Lord Vorkosigan. We could do that—if we had the Great Key."

"Oh," said Miles. "Yeah. That." He reverted from an eager parade-rest to a deflated at-ease. "For what it's worth, my strategic analysis and what little physical evidence I've wrung from ghem-Colonel Benin so far suggests either Prince Slyke or the haut Ilsum Kety. With the haut Rond a distant third. But as Rho Ceta and Mu Ceta would bear the brunt of it if open conflict with Barrayar was actually engineered, my own choice has settled pretty firmly between Slyke and Kety. Recent . . . events point to Kety." He glanced again around the circle. "Is there anything any of the consorts have seen or heard, or overheard, that would help pin him more certainly?"

A murmur of negatives; "Unfortunately, no," said Rian. "We have discussed that problem already this evening. Please begin."

On your head be it, milady. Miles took a deep breath, and launched into the full true account, minus most of his opinions, of his experiences on Eta Ceta from the moment the Ba Lura lurched into their personnel pod. He paused occasionally, to give Rian a chance to hint him away from anything she wanted to conceal. She appeared to want to conceal nothing, instead drawing him on with skillful questions and prompts to disgorge every detail.

Rian had seen, he slowly realized, that the secrecy problem cut two ways. Lord X could assassinate Miles, maybe Rian as well. But even the most megalomanic Cetagandan politician must find it excessively challenging to try to get away with disposing of all eight satrap consorts. His voice strengthened.

He felt his underlying assumptions slowly wringing inside-out. Rian seemed less and less like a damsel in distress all the time. In fact, he was beginning to wonder if he was trying to rescue the dragon. *Well, dragons need to be rescued too, sometimes. . . .* Nobody even blinked at his description of his near-assassination the day before. If anything, there was a subliminal murmur of appreciation for its elegance of form and style, and of faintly sympathetic disappointment at its foiling. The judges had no appreciation for the governor's originality in attempting to muscle in on their own territory, though. The Sigma and Xi Cetan consorts looked increasingly stony, exchanging a raised-brow glance or a nod of understanding now and then.

There was a long silence when he'd finished. Time to present Plan B? "I have a suggestion," Miles said boldly. "Recall all the duplicate gene banks from the satrap governors' ships. If they are all returned, you will have stripped him of his ability to carry out his larger plans. If he resists releasing it, you will have smoked him out."

"Bring them *back*," said the haut Pel in dismay. "Do you have any idea how much trouble we had getting them *up* there?"

"But he might take both bank and Key, and flee," objected the brown-curled Consort of Rho Ceta.

"No," said Miles. "That's the one thing he *can't* do. There are too many Imperially guarded wormhole jumps between him and home. Speaking militarily, open flight is impossible. He'd never make it. He cannot reveal a thing about any of this till he's safely in orbit around . . . Something Ceta. In a weird way, we have him cornered till the funeral is over." *Which will be all too soon, now.*

"That still leaves the problem of retrieving the real Key," said Rian.

"Once you have the bank back, you may be able to negotiate

the Key's return, in exchange for, say, amnesty. Or you can claim he stole it—perfectly true—and set your own security to get it back for you. Once the other governors are freed of the incriminating evidence they're holding, you may be able to cut him out of the herd, so to speak, with their goodwill. In any case, it will open up a lot of tactical options."

"He may threaten to destroy it," worried the Consort of Sigma Ceta.

"You must know Ilsum Kety better than anyone else here, haut Nadina," said Miles. "Would he?"

"He is . . . an erratic young man," she said reluctantly. "I am not yet convinced that he is guilty. But I know nothing about him that makes your accusations impossible."

"And your governor, ma'am?" Miles nodded to the Consort of Xi Ceta.

"Prince Slyke is . . . a determined and brilliant man. The plot you describe is not beyond his capacities. I'm . . . not sure."

"Well . . . you *can* re-create the Great Key, eventually, can't you?" Push or shove, the Empress's great plan would be canned for a generation. A very desirable outcome, from Barrayar's point of view. Miles smiled agreeably.

A faint groan went around the room. "Recovering the Great Key undamaged is the highest priority," Rian said firmly.

"He still wants to frame Barrayar," said Miles. "It may have started as cold-blooded astro-political calculation, but I'm pretty sure it's a personal motivation by now."

"If I recall the banks," said Rian slowly, "we will entirely lose this opportunity to distribute them."

The Consort of Sigma Ceta, the silver-haired Nadina, sighed, "I had hoped to live to see the Celestial Lady's vision of new growth carried out. She was right, you know. I have seen the stagnation increasing in my lifetime."

"Other opportunities will come," said another silver-haired lady.

"It must be done more carefully next time," said the brown-curled Consort of Rho Ceta. "Our Lady trusted the governors too much."

"I'm not so sure she did," said Rian. "I was only attempting to go as far as distributing inactive copies for backup. The Ba Lura felt our Mistress's desires keenly, but did not understand her subtlety. It wasn't *my* idea to attempt to distribute the Key now, and I'm not convinced it was hers, either. I don't know if the ba had a separate understanding with her, or just a separate misunderstanding. And now I never will." She bowed her head. "I apologize to the Council for my failure." Her tone of voice made Miles think of inward-turning knives.

"You did your best, dear," said the haut Nadina kindly. But she added more sternly, "However, you should not have attempted to handle it all alone."

"It was my charge."

"A little less emphasis on the *my*, and a little more emphasis on the *charge*, next time."

Miles tried not to squirm at the general applicability of this gentle correction.

A glum silence reigned, for a time.

"We may need to consider altering the genome to make the haut-lords more controllable," said the Rho Cetan consort.

"For renewed expansion, we need the opposite," objected the dark consort. "More aggression."

"The ghem-experiment, filtering favorable genetic combinations upward from the general population, surely suffices for *that*," said the haut Pel.

"Our Lady, in her wisdom, aimed at less uniformity, not more," conceded Rian.

"I believe we have long made a mistake in leaving the haut-males so entirely to their own devices," said the Rho Cetan consort stubbornly.

Said the dark one, "But how else should we select among them, if there is no free competition to sort them out?"

Rian held up a restraining hand. "The time for this larger debate . . . must be soon. But not now. I myself have been convinced by these events that further refinement must come before further expansion. But that," she sighed, "is a new Empress's task. *Now* we must decide what state of affairs she will inherit. How many favor the recall of the gene banks?"

The ayes had it. Several were slow in coming, but in some occult way a unanimous vote was achieved through nothing more than an exchange of unreadable glances. Miles breathed relief.

Rian's shoulders slumped wearily. "Then I so order you all. Return them to the Star Crèche."

"As what?" asked the haut Pel in a practical tone.

Rian stared into the air a moment, and replied, "As collections of human genomic materials from your various satrapies, requested by the Lady before her death, and received by us in trust for the Star Crèche's experimental files."

"That will do nicely on this end. The haut Pel nodded. "And on the other end?"

"Tell your governors . . . we discovered a serious error in the copy, which must be corrected before the genome can be released to them."

"Very good."

The meeting broke up, the women activating their float-chairs, though not yet their private bubbles, and leaving in twos and threes in a murmur of intense discussion. Rian and the haut Pel waited until the room emptied, and Miles perforce waited with them.

"Do you still want me to try to retrieve the Key for you?" Miles asked Rian. "Barrayar remains vulnerable until we nail the satrap governor with solid proof, data a clever man can't diddle. And I especially don't like the toehold he seems to have in your own security."

"I don't know," said Rian. "The return of the gene banks cannot take less than a day. I'll . . . send someone for you, as we did tonight."

"We'll be down to two days left, then. Not much margin. I'd rather go sooner than later."

"It cannot be helped." She touched her hair, a nervous gesture despite its grace.

Watching her, he searched his heart. The impact of his first mad crush was surely fading, in this drought of response, to be replaced by . . . what? If she had slaked his thirst with the least little drop of affection, he would be hers body and soul right now. In a way he was glad she wasn't faking anything, depressing as it was to be treated like a ba servitor, his loyalty and obedience assumed. Maybe his proposed disguise as a ba had been suggested by his subconscious for more than practical reasons. Was his back-brain trying to tell him something?

"The haut Pel will return you to your point of origin," Rian said.

He bowed. "In my experience, milady, we can never get back to exactly where we started, no matter how hard we try."

She returned nothing to this but an odd look, as he rode out again on the haut Pel's float-chair.

✧   ✧   ✧

Pel carried him through the Celestial Garden as before, in reverse. He wondered if she was as uncomfortable with their compressed proximity as he was. He made a stab at light conversation.

"Did the haut-ladies make all this plant and animal life in the garden? Competing, like the ghem bioestheties fair? I was particularly impressed by the singing frogs, I must say."

"Oh, no," said the haut Pel. "The lower life-forms are all ghem work. That's their highest reward, to have their art incorporated into the Imperial garden. The haut only work in human material."

He didn't recall seeing any monsters around. "Where?"

"We mostly field-test ideas in the ba servitors. It prevents the accidental release of any genomic materials through sexual routes."

"Oh."

"*Our* highest honor is for a favorable gene complex we have developed to be taken up into the haut-genome itself."

It was like some golden rule in reverse—never do unto yourself what you have not first tried on another. Miles smiled, rather nervously, and did not pursue the subject further. A groundcar driven by a ba servitor waited for the haut Pel's bubble at the side entrance to the Celestial Garden, and they were returned to Lady d'Har's penthouse by more normal routes.

Pel let him out of her bubble in another private nook, in an unobserved moment, and drifted away again. He pictured her reporting back to Rian—*Yes, milady, I released the Barrayaran back into the wild as you ordered. I hope he will be able to find food and a mate out there....* He sat on a bench overlooking the Celestial Garden, and meditated upon that view until Ivan and Ambassador Vorob'yev found him.

They looked, respectively, scared and angry. "You're late," said Ivan. "Where the hell did you go?"

"I almost called out Colonel Vorreedi and the guards," added Ambassador Vorob'yev sternly.

"That would have been . . . futile," sighed Miles. "We can go now."

"Thank God," muttered Ivan.

Vorob'yev said nothing. Miles rose, wondering how soon the ambassador and Vorreedi were going to stop taking *Not yet* for an answer.

Not yet. Please, not yet.

Chapter Thirteen

There was nothing he would have liked more than a day off, Miles reflected, but not *today*. The worst was the knowledge that he'd done this to himself. Until the consorts completed their retrieval of the gene banks, all he could do was wait. And unless Rian sent a car to the embassy to pick him up, a move so overt as to be vigorously resisted by both sets of Imperial Security, it was impossible for Miles to make contact with her again until the Gate-song Ceremonies tomorrow morning at the Celestial Garden. He grumbled under his breath, and called up more data on his suite's comconsole, then stared at it unseeing.

He wasn't sure it was wise to give Lord X an extra day either, for all that this afternoon would contain a nasty shock for him when his consort came to take away his gene bank. That would eliminate his last chance of sitting tight and gliding away with bank and Key, perhaps dumping his old centrally appointed and controlled consort out an airlock en route. The man must realize now that Rian would turn him in, even if it meant incriminating herself, before letting him get away. Assassinating the Handmaiden of the Star Crèche hadn't been part of the Original Plan, Miles was fairly sure. Rian had been intended to be a blind puppet, accusing Miles and Barrayar of stealing her Key. Lord X had a weakness for blind puppets. But Rian was loyal to the haut, beyond her own self-interest. No right-minded plotter could assume she would stay paralyzed for long.

Lord X was a tyrant, not a revolutionary. He wanted to take over the system, not change it. The late Empress was the real revolutionary, with her attempt to divide the haut into eight competing sibling branches, and may the best superman win. The Ba Lura might have been closer to its mistress's mind than Rian allowed. *You can't give power away and keep it simultaneously.* Except posthumously.

So what would Lord X do now? What *could* he do now, but fight to the last, trying anything he could think of to avoid being brought down for this? It was that or slit his wrists, and Miles didn't think he was the wrist-slitting type. He would still be searching for some way to pin it all on Barrayar, preferably in the form of a dead Miles who couldn't give him the lie. There was even still a faint chance he could bring that off, given the Cetagandan lack of enthusiasm for outlanders in general and Barrayarans in particular. Yes, this was a good day to stay indoors.

So would the results have been any better if Miles had publicly turned over the decoy Key and the truth on the very first day? No . . . then the embassy and its envoys would be mired right now in false accusations and public scandal, and no way to prove their innocence. If Lord X had picked any other delegation but Barrayar's upon which to plant his false Key—say, the Marilacans, the Aslunders, or the Vervani—his plan might yet be running along like clockwork. Miles hoped sourly that Lord X was Very, Very Sorry that he'd targeted Barrayar. *And I'm going to make you even sorrier, you sod.*

Miles's lips thinned as he turned his attention back to his comconsole. The satrap governors' ships were all to the same general plan, and a general plan, alas, was all the Barrayaran embassy data bank had available without tapping in to the secret files. Miles shuffled the holovid display though the various levels and sections of the ship. *If I were a satrap governor planning revolt, where would I hide the Great Key? Under my pillow?* Probably not.

The governor had the Key, but not the Key's key, so to speak; Rian still possessed that ring. If Lord X could open the Great Key, he could do a data dump, possess himself of a duplicate of the information-contents, and maybe, in a pinch, return the original, divesting himself of material evidence of his treasonous plans. Or even destroy it, hah. But if the Key were easy to get open, he should have done this already, when his plans first began to go seriously wrong. So if he was still trying to access the Key, it ought to be located in some sort of cipher lab. So where on this vast ship was a suitable cipher lab . . . ?

The chime of his door interrupted Miles's harried perusal. Colonel Vorreedi's voice inquired, "Lord Vorkosigan? May I come in?"

Miles sighed. "Enter." He'd been afraid all this comconsole activity would attract Vorreedi's attention. The protocol officer had to be monitoring from downstairs.

Vorreedi trod in, and studied the holovid display over Miles's shoulder. "Interesting. What is it?"

"Just brushing up on Cetagandan warship specs. Continuing education, officer-style, and all that. The hope for promotion to ship duty never dies."

"Hm." Vorreedi straightened. "I thought you might like to hear the latest on your Lord Yenaro."

"I don't think I own him, but—nothing fatal, I hope," said Miles sincerely. Yenaro might be an important witness, later; upon mature reflection Miles was beginning to regret not offering him asylum at the embassy.

"Not yet. But an order has been issued for his arrest."

"By Cetagandan Security? For treason?"

"No. By the civil police. For theft."

"It's a false charge, I'd lay odds. Somebody's trying to use the system to smoke him out of hiding. Can you find out who laid the charge?"

"A ghem-lord by the name of Nevic. Does that mean anything to you?"

"No. He's got to be a puppet. The man who put Nevic up to it is the man we want. The same man who supplied Yenaro with the plans and money for his fun-fountain. But now you have two strings to pull."

"You imagine it to be the same man?"

"Imagination," said Miles, "has nothing to do with it. But I need proof, stand-up-in-court type proof."

Vorreedi's gaze was uncomfortably level. "Why did you guess the charge against Yenaro would be treason?"

"Oh, well . . . I wasn't thinking. Theft is much better, less flashy, if what his enemy wants is for the civil police to drag Yenaro out into the open where he can get a clear shot at him."

Vorreedi's brows crimped. "Lord Vorkosigan . . ." But he appeared to think better of whatever he'd been about to say. He just shook his head and departed.

Ivan wandered in later, flung himself onto Miles's sofa, put up his booted feet on the armrest, and sighed.

"You still here?" Miles shut down his comconsole, which was by now making him cross-eyed. "I thought you'd be out making hay, or rolling in it, or whatever. Our last two days here and all. Or did you run out of invitations?" Miles jerked his thumb ceilingward, *We may be bugged.*

Ivan's lip curled, *Screw it.* "Vorreedi has laid on more bodyguards. It kind of takes the spontaneity out of things." He stared into the air. "Besides, I worry about where I put my feet, now. Wasn't it some queen of Egypt who was delivered in a rolled-up carpet? Could happen again."

"Could indeed," Miles had to agree. "Almost certainly will, in fact."

"Great. Remind me not to stand next to you."

Miles grimaced.

After a minute or two Ivan added, "I'm bored."

Miles chased him from his room.

The ceremony of Singing Open The Great Gates did not entail the opening of any gates, though it did involve singing. A massed chorus of several hundred ghem, both male and female, robed in white-on-white, arranged themselves near the eastern entrance inside the Celestial Garden. They planned to pass in procession around the four cardinal directions and eventually, later in the afternoon, finish at the north gate. The chorus stood to sing along an undulating area of ground with surprising acoustic properties, and the galactic envoys and ghem and haut mourners stood to listen. Miles flexed his legs, inside his boots, and prepared to endure. The open venue left lots of space for haut-lady bubbles, and they were out in force—some hundreds, scattered about the glade. How many haut-women *did* live here?

Miles glanced around his little delegation—himself, Ivan, Vorob'yev, and Vorreedi all in House blacks, Mia Maz dressed as before, striking in black and white. Vorreedi looked more Barrayaran, more officer-like, and, Miles had to admit, a lot more sinister out of his deliberately dull Cetagandan civvies. Maz rested one hand on Vorob'yev's arm and stood on tiptoe as the music started.

Breathtaking, Miles realized, could be a quite literal term—his lips parted and the hairs on the backs of his arms stood on end as the incredible sounds washed over him. Harmonies and dissonances followed one another up and down the scale with such precision, the listener could make out every word, when the voices were not simply wordless vibrations that seemed to crawl right up the spine and ring in the back-brain in a succession of pure emotions. Even Ivan stood transfixed. Miles wanted to comment, to express his astonishment, but breaking into the absolute concentration the music demanded seemed some sort of sacrilege. After about a thirty-minute performance, the music came to a temporary close, and the chorus prepared to move gracefully off to its next station, followed more clumsily by the delegates.

The two groups took different routes. Ba servitors under the direction of a dignified ghem-lord majordomo shepherded the delegates to a buffet, to both refresh and delay them while the chorus set up for its next performance at the southern gate. Miles stared anxiously after the haut-lady bubbles, which naturally did not accompany the outlander envoys, but floated off in their own mob in yet a third direction. He was getting less distracted by the diversions of the Celestial Garden. Could one finally grow to take it entirely for granted? The haut certainly seemed to.

"I think I'm getting used to this place," he confided to Ivan, as he walked along between him and Vorob'yev in the ragged parade of outlander guests. "Or . . . I could."

"Mm," said Ambassador Vorob'yev. "But when these pretty folks turned their pet ghem-lords loose to pick up some cheap new real estate out past Komarr, five million of *us* died. I hope that hasn't slipped your mind, my lord."

"No," said Miles tightly. "Not ever. But . . . even you are not old enough to remember the war personally, sir. I'm really starting to wonder if we'll ever see an effort like that from the Cetagandan Empire again."

"Optimist," murmured Ivan.

"Let me qualify that. My mother always says, behavior that is rewarded is repeated. And the reverse. I think . . . that if the ghem-lords fail to score any new territorial successes in our generation, it's going to be a long time till we see them try again. An expansionist period followed by an isolationist one isn't a new historical phenomenon, after all."

"Didn't know you'd taken up political science," said Ivan.

"Can you prove your point?" asked Vorob'yev. "In less than a generation?"

Miles shrugged. "Don't know. It's one of those subliminal gut-feel things. If you gave me a year and a department, I could probably produce a reasoned analysis, with graphs."

"I admit," said Ivan, "it's hard to imagine, say, Lord Yenaro conquering anybody."

"It's not that he couldn't. It's just that by the time he ever got a chance, he'd be too old to care. I don't know. After the next isolationist period, though, all bets are off. When the haut are done with ten more generations of tinkering with themselves, I don't know what they'll be." *And neither do they. That* was an odd realization. *You mean no one is in charge here?* "Universal conquest may seem like a crude dull game from their childhood after that. Or else," he added glumly, "they'll be unstoppable."

"Jolly thought," grumbled Ivan.

A delicate breakfast offering was set up in a nearby pavilion. On the other side of it, the float-cars with the white silk upholstery waited to convey refreshed funeral envoys the couple of kilometers across the Celestial Garden to the South Gate. Miles nabbed a hot drink, refused with concealed loathing the offer of a pastry tray—his stomach was knotting with nervous anticipation—and watched the movements of the ba servitors with hawk-like attention. *It has to break today. There's no more time. Come on, Rian!* And how the devil was he to take Rian's next report when he had Vorreedi glued to his hip? The man was noting his every eye-flicker, Miles swore.

The day wore on with a repeat of the cycle of music and food and transportation. A number of the delegates were looking glassily over-loaded with it all; even Ivan had stopped eating in self-defense at about stop three. When the contact did come, at the buffet after the fourth and last choral performance, Miles almost missed it. He was making idle chit-chat with Vorreedi, reminiscing about Keroslav District baking styles, and wondering how he was going to distract and ditch the man. Miles had reached the point of desperation of fantasizing slipping Ambassador Vorob'yev an emetic and siccing, so to speak, the protocol officer on his superior while Miles ducked out, when he saw out of the corner of his eye Ivan talking with a grave ba servitor. He did not recognize this ba; it was not Rian's favorite little creature, for it was young and had a brush of blond hair. Ivan's hands turned palm-out, and he shrugged, then he followed the servitor from the pavilion, looking puzzled. *Ivan? What the hell does she want Ivan for?*

"Excuse me, sir," Miles cut across Vorreedi's words, and around his side. By the time Vorreedi had turned after him, Miles had darted past another delegation and was halfway to the exit after Ivan. Vorreedi would follow, but Miles would just have to deal with that later.

Miles emerged, blinking, into the artificial afternoon light of the dome just in time to see the dark shadow and boot-gleam of Ivan's uniform disappear around some flowering shrubbery, beyond an open space featuring a fountain. He trotted after, his own boots scuffing unevenly on the colored stone walks threading the greenery. "Lord Vorkosigan?" Vorreedi called after him. Miles didn't turn around, but raised his hand in an acknowledging, but still rapidly receding, wave. Vorreedi was too polite to curse out loud, but Miles could fill in the blanks.

The man-high shrubbery, broken up by artistic groupings of trees, wasn't quite a maze, but nearly so. Miles's first choice of directions opened onto some sort of unpeopled water meadow, with the stream generated from the nearby fountain running like silver embroidery through its center. He ran back along his route, cursing his legs and his limp, and swung around the other end of the bushes.

In the center of a tree-shaded circle lined with benches, a haut-chair floated with its high back to Miles, its screen down. The blond servitor was gone already. Ivan leaned in toward the float-chair's occupant, his lips parted in fascination, his brows drawn down in suspicion. A white-robed arm lifted. A faint cloud of iridescent mist puffed into Ivan's surprised face. Ivan's eyes rolled back, and he collapsed forward across the seated occupant's knees. The force-screen snapped up, white and blank. Miles yelled and ran toward it.

The haut-ladies' float-chairs were hardly race cars, but they could move faster than Miles could run. In two turns through the shrubbery it was out of sight. When Miles cleared the last stand of flowers, he found himself facing one of the major carved-white-jade-paved walkways that curved through the Celestial Garden. Floating along it in both directions were half a dozen haut-bubbles, all now moving at the same dignified walking pace. Miles had no breath left to swear, but black thoughts boiled off his brain.

He spun on his heel, and ran straight into Colonel Vorreedi.

Vorreedi's hand descended on his shoulder and took a good solid grip on the uniform cloth. "Vorkosigan, what the hell is going on? And where is Vorpatril?"

"I'm . . . just about to go check on that right now, sir, if you'll permit me."

"Cetagandan Security had better know. I'll light up their lives if they've—"

"I . . . don't think Security can help us on this one, sir. I think I need to talk to a ba servitor. Immediately."

Vorreedi frowned, trying to process this. It obviously did not compute. Miles couldn't blame him. Until a week ago, he too had shared the universal assumption that Cetagandan Imperial Security was in charge here. *And so they are, in some ways. But not all ways.*

Speak of the devil. As Miles and Vorreedi turned to retrace their steps to the pavilion, a red-uniformed, zebra-faced guard appeared, striding rapidly toward them. Sheepdog, Miles judged, sent to round up straying galactic envoys. Fast, but not fast enough.

"My lords." The guard, a low-ranker, nodded very politely. "The pavilion is this way, if you please. The float-cars will take you to the South Gate."

Vorreedi appeared to come to a quick decision. "Thank you. But we seem to have mislaid a member of our party. Would you please find Lord Vorpatril for me?"

"Certainly." The guard touched a wrist com and reported the request in neutral tones, while still firmly herding Miles and Vorreedi pavilion-ward. Taking Ivan, for now, as merely a lost guest; that had to happen fairly often, since the garden was designed to entice the viewer on into its delights. *I give Cetagandan Security maybe ten minutes to figure out he's really disappeared, in the middle of the Celestial Garden. Then it all starts coming apart.*

The guard split off as they climbed the steps to the pavilion. Back inside, Miles approached the oldest bald servitor he saw. "Excuse me, Ba," he said respectfully. The ba glanced up, nonplused at not being invisible. "I must communicate immediately with the haut Rian Degtiar. It's an emergency." He opened his hands and stood back.

The ba appeared to digest this for a moment, then gave a half bow and motioned Miles to follow. Vorreedi came too. Around a corner in the semi-privacy of a service area, the ba pulled back its gray and white uniform sleeve and spoke into its wrist-com, a quick gabble of words and code phrases. Its non-existent eyebrows rose in surprise at the return message. It took off its wrist-com, handed it to Miles with a low bow, and retreated out of earshot. Miles wished Vorreedi, looming over his shoulder, would do the same, but he didn't.

"Lord Vorkosigan?" came Rian's voice from the com—unfiltered, she must be speaking from inside her bubble.

"Milady. Did you just send one of your . . . people, to pick up my cousin Ivan?"

There was a short pause. "No."

"I witnessed this."

"Oh." Another, much longer pause. When her voice came back again, it had gone low and dangerous. "I know what is happening."

"I'm glad somebody does."

"I will send *my* servitor for you."

"And Ivan?"

"*We* will handle that." The com cut abruptly. Miles almost shook it in frustration, but handed it back to the servitor instead, who took it, bowed again, and scooted away.

"Just what did you witness, Lord Vorkosigan?" Vorreedi demanded.

"Ivan . . . left with a lady."

"What, *again*? Here? *Now*? Does the boy have no sense of time or place? This isn't Emperor Gregor's Birthday Party, dammit."

"I believe I can retrieve him very discreetly, sir, if you will allow me." Miles felt a faint twinge of guilt for slandering Ivan by implication, but the twinge was lost in his general, heart-hammering fear. Had that aerosol been a knockout drug, or a lethal poison?

Vorreedi took a long, long minute to think this one over, his eye cold on Miles. Vorreedi, Miles reminded himself, was Intelligence, not Counter-intelligence; curiosity, not paranoia, was his driving force. Miles shoved his hands into his trouser pockets and tried to look calm, unworried, merely annoyed. As the silence lengthened, he dared to add, "If you trust nothing else, sir, please trust my competence. That's all I ask."

"Discreet, eh?" said Vorreedi. "You've made some interesting friends here, Lord Vorkosigan. I'd like to hear a lot more about them."

"Soon, I hope, sir."

"Mm . . . very well. But be prompt."

"I'll do my best, sir," Miles lied. It had to be today. Once away from his guardian, he wasn't coming back till the job was done.

Or we are all undone. He gave a semi-salute, and slipped away before Vorreedi could think better of it.

He went to the open side of the pavilion and stepped down into the artificial sunlight just as a float-car arrived that was not funerally decorated: a simple two-passenger cart with room for cargo behind. A familiar aged little bald ba was at the controls. The ba spotted Miles and swung closer, bringing its vehicle to a halt. They were intercepted by a quick-moving red-clad guard.

"Sir. Galactic guests may not wander the Celestial Garden unaccompanied."

Miles opened his palm at the ba servitor.

"My Lady requests and requires this man's attendance. I must take him," said the ba.

The guard looked unhappy, but gave a short, reluctant nod. "My superior will speak to yours."

"I'm sure." The ba's lips twitched in what Miles swore was a smirk.

The guard grimaced, and stepped away, his hand reaching for his com link. *Go, go!* thought Miles as he climbed aboard, but they were already moving. This time, the float-car took a shortcut, rising up over the garden and heading southwest in a straight line. They actually moved fast enough for the breeze to ruffle Miles's hair. In a few minutes, they descended toward the Star Crèche, gleaming pale through the trees.

A strange procession of white bubbles was bobbing toward what was obviously a delivery entrance at the back of the building. Five bubbles, one on each side and one above, were . . . *herding* a sixth, bumping it along toward the high, wide door and into whatever loading bay lay beyond. The bubbles buzzed like angry wasps whenever their force-fields touched. The ba brought its little float-car calmly down into the tail of this parade, and followed the bubbles inside. The door slid closed behind them and sealed with that solid clunk and cacophony of chirps that bespoke high security.

Except for being lined with colored polished stone in geometric inlays instead of gray concrete, the loading bay was utilitarian and normal in design. It was presently empty except for the haut Rian Degtiar, standing in full flowing white robes beside her own float-chair, waiting. Her pale face was tense.

The five herding bubbles settled to the floor and snapped off, revealing five of the consorts Miles had met in the council night before last. The sixth bubble remained stubbornly up, white and solid and impenetrable.

Miles swung out of his cart as it settled to the pavement, and limped hurriedly to Rian's side. "Is Ivan in there?" he demanded, pointing at the sixth bubble.

"We think so."

"What's happening?"

"Sh. Wait." She made a graceful, palm-down gesture; Miles gritted his teeth, jittering inside. Rian stepped forward, her chin rising.

"Surrender and cooperate," said Rian clearly to the bubble, "and mercy is possible. Defy us, and it is not."

The bubble remained defiantly up and blank. Stand-off. The bubble had nowhere to go, and could not attack. *But she has Ivan in there.*

"Very well," sighed Rian. She pulled a pen-like object from her sleeve, with a screaming-bird pattern engraved in red upon its side, adjusted some control, pointed it at the bubble, and pressed. The bubble winked out, and the float-chair fell to the floor with a reverberant thump, all power dead. A yelp floated from a cloud of white fabric and brown hair.

"I didn't know anyone could do that," whispered Miles.

"Only the Celestial Lady has the override," said Rian. She put the control back in her sleeve, and stepped forward again, and stopped.

The haut Vio d'Chilian had recovered her balance instantly. She now half-knelt, one arm under Ivan's black-uniformed arm, supporting his slumping form, the other hand holding a thin knife to his throat. It looked very sharp, as it pressed against his skin. Ivan's eyes were open, dilated, shifting; he was paralyzed, not unconscious, then. *And not dead. Thank God. Yet.*

The haut Vio d'Chilian, unless Miles missed his guess, would have no inhibitions whatsoever about cutting a helpless man's throat. He wished ghem-Colonel Benin were here to witness this.

"Move against me," said the haut Vio, "and your Barrayaran *servitor* dies." Miles supposed the emphasis was intended as a hautish insult. He was not quite sure it succeeded.

Miles paced anxiously to Rian's other side, making an arc around the haut Vio but venturing no closer. The haut Vio followed him with venomous eyes. Now directly behind her, the haut Pel gave Miles a nod; her float-chair rose silently into the air and slipped out a doorway to the Crèche. Going for help? For a weapon? Pel was the practical one . . . he had to buy time.

"Ivan!" Miles said indignantly. "*Ivan's* not the man you want!"

The haut Vio's brows drew down. "What?"

But of course. Lord X always used front men, and women, for his legwork, keeping his own hands clean. Miles had been galloping around doing the legwork; therefore, Lord X must have reasoned that Ivan was really in charge. "Agh!" Miles cried. "What did you think? That because he's taller, and, and cuter, he had to be running this show? It's the haut way, isn't it? You—you *morons! I'm* the brains of this outfit!" He paced the other way, spluttering. "I had you spotted from Day One, don't you know? But no! Nobody ever takes me seriously!" Ivan's eyes, the only part of him that apparently still worked, widened at this rant. "So you went and kidnapped the *wrong man.* You just blew your cover for the sake of grabbing the *expendable* one!" The haut Pel hadn't gone for help, he decided. She'd gone to the lav to fix her hair, and was going to take *forever* in there.

Well, he certainly had the undivided attention of everyone in the loading bay, murderess, victim, haut-cops and all. What next, handsprings? "It's been like this since we were little kids, y'know? Whenever the two of us were together, they'd always talk to *him* first, like I was some kind of idiot alien who needed an interpreter—" the haut Pel reappeared silently in the doorway, lifted her hand—Miles's voice rose to a shout, "Well, I'm sick of it, d'you hear?!"

The haut Vio's head twisted in realization just as the haut Pel's stunner buzzed. Vio's hand spasmed on the knife as the stunner beam struck her. Miles pelted forward as a line of red appeared at the blade's edge, and he grabbed for Ivan as she slumped unconscious. The stun nimbus had caught Ivan too, and his eyes rolled back. Miles let the haut Vio hit the floor on her own, as hard as gravity took her. Ivan he lowered gently.

It was only a surface cut. Miles breathed again. He pulled out his pocket handkerchief and dabbed at the sticky trickle of blood, then pressed it against the wound.

He glanced up at the haut Rian, and the haut Pel, who floated over to examine her handiwork. "She knocked him over with some kind of drug-mist. Stun on top of that—is he in medical danger?"

"I think not," said Pel. She dismounted from her float-chair, knelt, and rummaged through the unconscious haut Vio's sleeves, coming up with an assortment of objects which she laid out in a methodical row on the pavement. One was a tiny silvery pointed thing with a bulb on the end. The haut Pel waved it under her lovely nose, sniffing. "Ah. This is it. No, he's in no danger. It will wear off harmlessly. He'll be very sick when he wakes up, though."

"Maybe you could give him a dose of synergine?" Miles pleaded.

"We have that available."

"Good." He studied the haut Rian. *Only the Celestial Lady has the override.* But Rian had used it as one entitled, and no one had blinked, not even the haut Vio. *Have you grasped this yet, boy? Rian is the acting Empress of Cetaganda, until tomorrow, and every move she's made has been with full, real, Imperial authority. Handmaiden, ha.* Another one of those impenetrable, misleading haut titles that didn't say what it meant; you had to be in the know.

Assured of Ivan's eventual recovery, Miles scrambled to his feet and demanded, "What's happening now? How did you find Ivan? Did you get all the gene banks back, or not? What did you—"

The haut Rian held up a restraining hand, to stem the flood of questions. She nodded to the dead bubble-chair. "This is the Consort of Sigma Ceta's float-chair, but as you see, the haut Nadina is not with it."

"Ilsum Kety! Yes? What *happened*? How'd he diddle the bubble? How'd you detect it? How long have you known?"

"Ilsum Kety, yes. We began to know last night, when the haut Nadina failed to return with her gene bank. All the others were back and safe by midnight. But Kety apparently only knew that his consort would be missed at this morning's ceremonies. So he sent the haut Vio to impersonate her. We suspected at once, and watched her."

"Why *Ivan*?"

"That, I do not know yet. Kety *cannot* make a consort disappear without great repercussions; I suspect he meant to use your cousin to divest himself of guilt somehow."

"Another frame, yes, that would fit his *modus operandi*. You realize, the haut Vio . . . must have murdered the Ba Lura. At Kety's direction."

"Yes." Rian's eyes, falling on the prostrate form of the brown-haired woman, were very cold. "She too is a traitor to the haut. That will make her the business of the Star Crèche's own justice."

Miles said uneasily, "She could be an important witness, to clear Barrayar and me of blame in the disappearance of the Great Key.

Don't, um . . . do anything premature, till we know if that's needed, huh?"

"Oh, we have *many* questions for her, first."

"So . . . Kety still has his bank. And the Key. And a warning." *Damn.* Whose idiot idea had it been . . . ? Oh. Yes. *But you can't blame Ivan for this one. You thought recalling the gene banks was a great move. And Rian bought it too. Idiocy by committee, the finest kind.*

"And he has his consort, whom he knows he cannot let live. Assuming she still lives now. I did not think . . . I would be sending the haut Nadina to her death." The haut Rian stared at the far wall, avoiding both Miles's and Pel's eyes.

Neither did I. Miles swallowed sickness. "He can bury her in the chaos of his revolt, once it gets going. But he can't start his revolt yet." He paused. "But if, in order to arrange her death in some artistic way that incriminates Barrayar, he needs Ivan . . . I don't think she'll be dead yet. Saved, held prisoner on his ship, yes. Not dead yet." *Please, not dead yet.* "We know one other thing, too. The haut Nadina is successfully concealing information from him, or even actively misleading him. Or he wouldn't have tried what he just tried." Actually, that could also be construed as convincing evidence that the haut Nadina *was* dead. Miles bit his lip. "But now Kety's made enough overt moves to incriminate himself, for charges to stick to him and not to me, yes?"

Rian hesitated. "Maybe. He is clearly very clever."

Miles stared at the inert float-chair, sitting slightly canted, and looking quite ordinary without its magical electronic nimbus. "So are we. Those float-chairs. Somebody here must security-key them to their operators in the first place, right? Would I be making too silly a wild-ass guess if I suggested that person was the Celestial Lady?"

"That is correct, Lord Vorkosigan."

"So you have the override, and could encode this to anybody."

"Not to anybody. Only to any haut-woman."

"Ilsum Kety is expecting the return of this haut-bubble, after the ceremonies, with a haut-woman and a Barrayaran prisoner, yes?" He took a deep breath. "I think . . . we should not disappoint him."

Chapter Fourteen

"I found Ivan, sir." Miles smiled into the comconsole. The background beyond Ambassador Vorob'yev's head was blurred, but the sounds of the buffet winding down—subdued voices, the clink of plates—carried clearly over the com. "He's getting a tour of the Star Crèche. We'll be here a while yet—can't insult our hostess and all that. But I should be able to extract him and catch up with you before the party's over. One of the ba will bring us back."

Vorob'yev looked anything but happy at this news. "Well. I suppose it will have to do. But Colonel Vorreedi does not care for these spontaneous additions to the planned itinerary, regardless of the cultural opportunity, and I must say I'm beginning to agree with him. Don't, ah . . . don't let Lord Vorpatril do anything inappropriate, eh? The haut are not the ghem, you know."

"Yes, sir. Ivan's doing just fine. Never better." Ivan was still out cold, back in the freight bay, but the returning color to his face had suggested the synergine was starting to work.

"Just how did he obtain this extraordinary privilege, anyway?" asked Vorob'yev.

"Oh, well, you know Ivan. Couldn't let me score a coup he couldn't match. I'll explain it all later. Must go now."

"I'll be fascinated to hear it," the ambassador murmured dryly. Miles cut the com before his smile fractured and fell off his face.

"*Whew.* That buys us a little time. A very little time. We need to move."

"Yes," agreed his escort, the brown-haired Rho Cetan lady. She turned her float-chair and led him out of the side-office containing the comconsole; he had to trot to keep up.

They returned to the freight bay just as Rian and the haut Pel finished re-coding the haut Nadina's bubble-chair. Miles spared an anxious glance for Ivan, laid out on the tessellated pavement. He seemed to be breathing deeply and normally.

"I'm ready," Miles reported to Rian. "My people won't come looking for us for at least an hour. If Ivan wakes up . . . well, *you* should have no trouble keeping him under control." He licked lips gone dry. "If things go wrong . . . go to ghem-Colonel Benin. Or to your Emperor himself. No Imperial Security middlemen. Everything about this, especially the ways Governor Kety has been able to diddle what everyone fondly believed were diddle-proof systems, is screaming to me that he's suborned a connection high up, probably very high up, in your own security who's giving him serious aid and comfort. Being rescued by him could be a fatal experience, I suspect."

"I understand," said Rian gravely. "And I agree with your analysis. The Ba Lura would not have taken the Great Key to Kety for duplication in the first place if it had not been convinced that he was capable of carrying out the task." She straightened from the float-chair arm, and nodded to the haut Pel.

The haut Pel had filled her sleeves with most of the little items she had taken from the haut Vio. She nodded back, straightened her robes, and gracefully settled herself aboard. The little items did not, alas, include energy weapons, the power packs of which would set off security scanners. *Not even a stunner,* Miles thought with morbid regret. *I'm going into orbital battle wearing dress blacks and riding boots, and I'm totally disarmed. Wonderful.* He took his place again at Pel's left side, perched on the cushioned armrest, trying not to feel like the ventriloquist's dummy that he glumly fancied he resembled. The bubble's force-screen enclosed them, and Rian stood back, nodding. Pel, her right hand on the control panel, spun the bubble, and they floated quickly toward the exit, which dilated to let them pass; two other consorts exited simultaneously, and sped off in other directions.

Miles felt a brief pang in his heart that Pel and not Rian was his companion in arms. In his heart, but not in his head. It was essential not to place Rian, the most creditable witness of Kety's treason, in Kety's power. And . . . he liked Pel's style. She had already demonstrated her ability to think fast and clearly in an emergency. He still wasn't sure that drop over the side of the building night before last hadn't been for her amusement, rather than for secrecy. A haut-woman with a sense of humor, almost . . . too bad she was eighty years old, and a consort, and Cetagandan, and . . . *Give it up, will you? Ivan you aren't nor ever will be. But one way or another, Governor the haut Ilsum Kety's treason is not going to last the day.*

They joined Kety's party as it was making ready to depart at the south gate of the Celestial Garden. The haut Vio would have been sent to collect Ivan at the last possible moment, to be sure. Kety's train was large, as befit his governor's dignity: a couple of dozen ghem-guards, plus ghem-ladies, non-ba servitors in his personal livery, and rather to Miles's dismay, ghem-General Chilian. *Was* Chilian in on his master's treason, or was he due to be dumped along with the haut Nadina on the way home, and replaced with Kety's own appointee? He had to be one or the other; the commander of Imperial troops on Sigma Ceta could hardly be expected to stay neutral in the upcoming coup.

Kety himself gestured the haut Vio's bubble into his own vehicle for the short ride to the Imperial shuttleport, the exclusive venue for all such high official arrivals to and departures from the Celestial Garden. Ghem-General Chilian took another car; Miles and the haut Pel found themselves alone with Kety in a van-like space clearly designed for the lady-bubbles.

"You're late. Complications?" Kety inquired cryptically, settling back in his seat. He looked worried and stern, as befit an earnest mourner—or a man riding a particularly hungry and unreliable tiger.

Yeah, and I should have known he was Lord X when I first spotted that fake gray hair, Miles decided. This was one haut-lord who didn't want to wait for what life might bring him.

"Nothing I couldn't handle," reported Pel. The voice-filter, set to maximum blur, altered her tones into a fair imitation of the haut Vio's.

"I'm sure, my love. Keep your force-screen up till we're aboard."

"Yes."

Yep. Ghem-General Chilian definitely has an appointment with an unfriendly air lock, Miles decided. *Poor sucker.* The haut Vio, perhaps, meant to get back into the haut-genome one way or another. So was she Kety's mistress, or his master? Or were they a team? Two brains rather than one behind this plot could account for its speed, flexibility, and confusion all together.

The haut Pel touched a control, and turned to Miles. "When we get aboard, we must decide whether to look first for the haut Nadina or the Great Key."

Miles nearly choked. "Er . . ." He gestured toward Kety, sitting less than a meter from his knee.

"He cannot hear us," Pel reassured him. It seemed to be so, for Kety turned abstracted eyes to the passing view outside the luxurious lift-van's polarized canopy.

"The recovery of the Key," Pel went on, "is of the highest priority."

"Mm. But the haut Nadina, if she's still alive, is an important witness, for Barrayar's sake. And . . . she may have an idea where the Key is being kept. I think it's in a cipher lab, but it's a damned big ship, and there's a lot of places Kety may have tucked a cipher lab."

"Both it and Nadina will be close to his quarters," Pel said.

"He won't have her in the brig?"

"I doubt Kety will have wished many of his soldiers or servitors to know that he holds his consort prisoner. No. She will most likely be secreted in a cabin."

"I wonder where Kety figures to stage whatever fatal crime he's planned involving Ivan and the haut Nadina? The consorts move on pretty constricted paths. He won't site it on his own ship, nor his own residence. And he probably doesn't dare repeat the performance inside the Celestial Garden, that would be just *too* much. Something downside, I fancy, and tonight."

Governor Kety glanced at their force-bubble, and inquired, "Is he waking up yet?"

Pel touched her lips, then her controls. "Not yet."

"I want to question him, before. I must know how much they know."

"Time enough."

"Barely."

Pel killed her outgoing sound again.

"The haut Nadina first," Miles voted firmly.

"I . . . think you're right, Lord Vorkosigan," sighed Pel.

✧   ✧   ✧

Further dangerous conversation with Kety was blocked by the confusion of loading the shuttle to convey the portion of retinue that was going to orbit; Kety himself was busied on his com link. They did not find themselves alone with the governor again until the whole mob had disgorged into the shuttle hatch corridor aboard Kety's State ship, and gone about their various duties or pleasures. Ghem-General Chilian did not even attempt to speak with his wife. Pel followed at Kety's gesture. From the fact that Kety had dismissed his guards, Miles reasoned that they were about to get down to business. Limiting witnesses limited the murders necessary to silence them, later, if things went wrong.

Kety led them to a broad, tastefully appointed corridor obviously dedicated to upper-class residence suites. Miles almost tapped the haut Pel on the shoulder. "Look. Down the hall. Do you see?"

A liveried man stood guard outside one cabin door. He braced to attention at the sight of his master. But Kety turned in to another cabin first. The guard relaxed slightly.

Pel craned her neck. "Might it be the haut Nadina?"

"Yes. Well . . . maybe. I don't think he'd dare use a regular trooper for the duty. Not if he doesn't control their command structure yet." Miles felt a strong pang of regret that he hadn't figured out the schism between Kety and his ghem-general earlier. Talk about exploitable opportunities . . .

The door slid closed behind them, and Miles's head snapped around to see what they were getting into now. The chamber was clean, bare of decoration or personal effects: an unused cabin, then.

"We can put him here," said Kety, nodding to a couch in the sitting-room portion of the chamber. "Can you keep him under control chemically, or must we have some guards?"

"Chemically," responded Pel, "but I need a few things. Synergine. Fast-penta. And we'd better check him for induced fast-penta allergies first. Many important people are given them, I understand. I don't think you want him to die *here.*"

"Clarium?"

Pel glanced at Miles, her eyes widening in question; she did not know that one. Clarium was a fairly standard military interrogation tranquilizer—Miles nodded.

"That would be a good idea," Pel hazarded.

"No chance of his waking up before I get back, is there?" asked Kety in concern.

"I'm afraid I dosed him rather strongly."

"Hm. Please be more discreet, my love. We don't want excessive chemical residues left upon autopsy. Though with luck, there will not be enough left to autopsy."

"I'm reluctant to count on luck."

"*Good*," said Kety, with a peculiar exasperation. "You're learning at last."

"I'll await you," said Pel coolly, by way of a broad hint. As if the haut Vio would have done anything else.

"Let me help you lay him out," Kety said. "It must be crowded in there."

"Not for me. I'm using him for a footrest. The float-chair is . . . most comfortable. Let me . . . enjoy the privilege of the haut a little longer, my love." Pel sighed. "It has been so long. . . ."

Kety's lips thinned in amusement. "Soon enough, you shall have more privileges than the Empress ever had. And all the outworlders at your feet you may desire." He gave the bubble a short nod, and departed, striding quickly. Where would a haut-governor with an interrogation chemistry shopping list go? Sickbay? Security? And how long would it take?

"Now," said Miles. "Back up the corridor. We have to get rid of the guard—did you bring any of that stuff that the haut Vio used on Ivan?"

Pel pulled the tiny bulb from her sleeve and held it up.

"How many doses are left?"

Pel squinted. "Two. Vio over-prepared." She sounded faintly disapproving, as if Vio had lost style-points by this redundancy.

"I'd have taken a hundred, just in case. All right. Use it sparingly—not at all if you don't have to."

Pel floated her bubble out of the cabin again, and turned up the corridor. Miles slid around behind the float-chair, crouching with his hands gripping the high back and his boots slipping slightly on base which held the power pack. *Hiding behind a woman's skirts?* It was frustrating as hell to have his transportation—and everything else—under the control of a Cetagandan, even if the rescue mission *was* his idea. *But needs must drive.* Pel came to a halt before the liveried guard.

"Servitor," she addressed him.

"Haut." He nodded respectfully to the blank white bubble. "I am on duty, and may not assist you."

"This will not take long." Pel flicked off her force-screen. Miles heard a faint hiss, and a choking noise. The float-chair rocked. He popped up to find Pel with the guard slumped very awkwardly across her lap.

"Damn," said Miles regretfully, "we should have done this to Kety back in the first cabin—oh, well. Let me at that door pad."

It was a standard palm-lock, but set to whom? Very few, maybe Kety and Vio only, but the guard must be empowered to handle emergencies. "Move him up a little," Miles instructed Pel, and pressed the unconscious man's palm to the read-pad. "Ah," he breathed in satisfaction, as the door slid aside without alarm or protest. He relieved the guard of his stunner, and tiptoed inside, the haut Pel floating after.

"*Oh,*" huffed Pel in outrage. They had found the haut Nadina.

The old woman was sitting on a couch similar to the one in the previous cabin, wearing only her white bodysuit. The effects of a century or so of gravity were enough to sag even her haut body; taking away her voluminous outer wrappings seemed a deliberate indignity only barely short of stripping her naked. Her silver hair was clamped, half a meter from its end, in a device obviously borrowed from engineering and never designed for this purpose, but locked in turn to the floor. It was not physically cruel—the length of the rest of her hair still left her nearly two meters of turning room—but there was something deeply offensive about it. The haut Vio's idea, perhaps? Miles thought he knew how Ivan had felt, contemplating the kitten tree. It seemed a Wrong Thing to do to a little old lady (even one from a race as obnoxious as the haut) who reminded him of his Betan grandmother— well, not really, *Pel* actually seemed more like his Grandmother Naismith in personality, but—

Pel dumped the unconscious guard unceremoniously on the floor and rushed from her float-chair to her sister consort. "Nadina, are you injured?"

"Pel!" Anyone else would have fallen on her rescuer's neck in a hug; being haut, they confined themselves to a restrained, if apparently heartfelt, handclasp.

"Oh!" said Pel again, gazing furiously at the haut Nadina's situation. Her first action was to skin out of her own robes and donate about six underlayers to Nadina, who shrugged them on gratefully, and stood a little straighter. Miles completed a fast survey of the premises to be sure they were indeed alone, and returned to the women, who stood contemplating the hair-lock. Pel knelt and tugged at a few strands, which held fast.

"I've tried that," sighed the haut Nadina. "They won't come out even one hair at a time."

"Where is the key to its lock?"

"Vio had it."

Pel quickly emptied her sleeves of her mysterious arsenal; Nadina looked it over and shook her head.

"We'd better cut it," said Miles. "We have to go as quickly as possible."

Both women stared at him in shock. "Haut-women *never* cut their hair!" said Nadina.

"Um, excuse me, but this is an emergency. If we go at *once* to the ship's escape pods, I can pilot you both to safety before Kety awakes to his loss. Maybe even get away clean. Every second's delay costs us our very limited margin."

"No!" said Pel. "We must retrieve the Great Key first!"

He could not, unfortunately, send the two women off and promise to search for the Key on his own; he was the only qualified orbital pilot in the trio. They were going to have to stick together, blast it. One haut-lady was bad enough. Managing two was going to be worse than trying to herd cats. "Haut Nadina, do you know where Kety keeps the Great Key?"

"Yes. He took me to it last night. He thought I might be able to open it for him. He was very upset when I couldn't."

Miles glanced up sharply at her tone; there were no marks of violence on her face, at least. But her movements were stiff. Arthritis of age, or shock-stick trauma? He returned to the guard's unconscious body, and began searching it for useful items, code cards, weapons . . . ah. A folded vibra-knife. He palmed it out of sight, and returned to the ladies.

"I've heard of animals gnawing their legs off, to escape traps," he offered cautiously.

"Ugh!" said Pel. "Barrayarans."

"You don't understand," said Nadina earnestly.

He was afraid he did. They would stand here arguing about Nadina's trapped haut-hair until Kety caught up with them. . . . "Look!" He pointed at the door.

Pel jerked to her feet, and Nadina cried, "What?"

Miles snapped open the vibra-knife, grabbed the mass of silver hair, and sliced through it as close to the clamp as he could. "There. Let's *go*."

"Barbarian!" cried Nadina. But she wasn't going to go over the edge into hysterics; she shrieked her belated protest quite quietly, all things considered.

"A sacrifice for the good of the haut," Miles promised her. A tear stood in her eye; Pel . . . Pel looked as if she was secretly grateful the deed had been done by him and not her.

They all boarded the float-chair again, Nadina half across Pel's lap, Miles clinging on behind. Pel exited the chamber and raised her force-screen again. Float-chairs were supposed to be soundless, but the engine whined protest at this overload. It moved forward with a disconcerting lurch.

"Down this way. Turn right here," the haut Nadina directed. Halfway down the hall they passed an ordinary servitor, who stepped aside with a bow, and did not look back at them.

"Did Kety fast-penta you?" Miles asked Nadina. "How much does he know of what the Star Crèche suspects about him?"

"Fast-penta does not work on haut-women," Pel informed him over her shoulder.

"Oh? How about on haut-men?"

"Not *very* well," said Pel.

"Hm. Nevertheless."

"Down here." Nadina pointed to a lift tube. They descended a deck, and continued down another, narrower corridor. Nadina touched the silver hair piled in her lap, regarded the raggedly cut end with a deep frown, then let the handful fall with an unhappy, but rather final-sounding, snort. "This is all highly improper. I trust you are enjoying your opportunity for sport, Pel. And that it will be brief."

Pel made a non-committal noise.

Somehow, this was not the heroic covert ops mission that Miles had envisioned in his mind—blundering around Kety's ship in tow of a pair of prim, aging haut-ladies—well, Pel's allegiance to the proprieties was highly suspect, but Nadina appeared to be trying to make up for it. He had to admit, the bubble beat the hell out of his trying to disguise his physical peculiarities in the garb of a ba servitor, especially given that the ba appeared to be uniformly healthy and straight. Enough other haut-women were aboard that the sight of a passing bubble was unremarkable to staff and crew. . . .

No. We've just been lucky, so far.

They came to a blank door. "This is it," said Nadina.

No give-away guard this time; this was the little room that wasn't there. "How do we get in?" asked Miles. "Knock?"

"I suppose so," said Pel. She dropped her force-screen just long enough to do so, then raised it again.

"I meant that as a *joke*," said Miles, horrified. Surely no one was in there—he'd pictured the Great Key kept alone in some safe or coded compartment—

The door opened. A pale man with dark rings under his eyes, dressed in Kety's livery, pointed a device at the bubble, read off the electronic signature that resulted, and said, "Yes, haut Vio?"

"I . . . have brought the haut Nadina to try again," said Pel. Nadina grimaced in disapproving editorial.

"I don't think we're going to need her," said the liveried man, "but you can talk to the general." He stood aside to let them pass within.

Miles, who had been calculating how to knock the man out with Pel's aerosol again, started his calculations over. There were three men in the—floating cipher lab, yes. An array of equipment, festooned with temporary cables, cluttered every available surface. An even more whey-faced tech wearing the black undress uniform of Cetagandan military security sat before a console with the air of a man who'd been there for days, as evidenced by the caffeinated drink containers littered around him in a ring, and a couple of bottles of commercial painkillers sitting atop a nearby counter. But it was the third man, leaning over his shoulder, who riveted Miles's attention.

It wasn't ghem-General Chilian, as his mind had first tried to assume. This officer was a younger man, taller, sharp-faced, who wore the blood-red dress uniform of the Celestial Garden's own Imperial Security. He was not wearing his proper zebra-striped face paint, though. His tunic was rumpled and hanging open. Not the chief of security—Miles's mind ratcheted down the list he had memorized, weeks ago, in mis-aimed preparation for this trip—ghem-General Naru, yes, that was the man, third in command in that very inner hierarchy. Kety's deduced seduced contact. Called in, apparently, to lend his expertise in cracking the codes that protected the Great Key.

"All right," said the whey-faced tech, "start over with branch seven thousand, three-hundred and six. Only seven hundred more to go, and we'll have it, I swear."

Pel gasped, and pointed. Piled in a disorderly heap on the table beyond the console was not one but eight copies of the Great Key. Or one Great Key and seven copies . . .

Could Kety be attempting to carry out the late Empress Lisbet's vision after all? All the rest of the chaos of the past two weeks some confused misunderstanding? No . . . no. This had to be some other scam. Maybe he planned to send his fellow governors home with bad copies, or give Cetagandan Imperial Security seven more decoys to chase, or . . . a multitude of possibilities, as long as they advanced Kety's own personal agenda and no one else's.

Firing his stunner would set off every alarm in the place, making it a weapon of last resort. Hell, his victims, if clever—and Miles suspected he faced three very clever men—might jump him just to make him fire it.

"What *else* do you have up your sleeve?" Miles whispered to Pel.

"Nadina," Pel gestured to the table, "which one is the Great Key?"

"I'm not sure," said Nadina, peering anxiously at the clutter.

"Grab them *all.* Check *later*," urged Miles.

"But they could all be false," dithered Pel. "We must know, or it could all be for nothing." She fished in her bodice and pulled out a familiar ring on a chain, with a raised screaming-bird pattern. . . .

Miles choked. "For God's sake, you didn't bring that *here*? Keep it out of sight! After two weeks of trying to do what that ring does in a second, I guarantee those men wouldn't hesitate to kill you for it!"

Ghem-General Naru wheeled from his tech to face the pale glowing bubble. "Yes, Vio, what is it now?" His voice was bored, and dripping with open contempt.

Pel looked a little panicked; Miles could see her throat move, as she sub-vocalized some practice reply, then rejected it.

"We're not going to be able to keep this up for much longer," said Miles. "How about we attack, grab, and run?"

"How?" asked Nadina.

Pel held up her hand for silence from the on-board debating team, and essayed a temporizing reply to the general. "Your tone of voice is most improper, sir."

Naru grimaced. "Being back in your bubble makes you proud again, I see. Enjoy it while it lasts. We'll have all of those damned bitches pried out of their little fortresses after this. Their days of being cloaked by the Emperor's blindness and stupidity are numbered, I assure you, *haut* Vio."

Well . . . Naru wasn't in on this plot for the sake of the late Empress's vision of genetic destiny, that was certain. Miles could see how the haut-women's traditional privacies could come to be a deep, itching offense to a dedicated, properly paranoid security man. Was that the bribe Kety had offered Naru for his cooperation, the promise that the new regime would open the closed doors of the Star Crèche, and shine light into every secret place held by the haut-women? That he would destroy the haut-women's strange and fragile power-base, and put it all into the hands of the ghem-generals, where it obviously (to Naru) belonged? So was Kety stringing Naru along, or were they near-equal co-plotters? Equals, Miles decided. *This is the most dangerous man in the room, maybe even on the ship.* He set the stunner for low beam, in a forlorn hope of not setting off alarms on discharge.

"Pel," Miles said urgently, "get ghem-General Naru with your last dose of sleepy-juice. I'll try to threaten the others, get the drop on them, without actually firing. Tie them up, grab the Keys, and get out of here. It may not be elegant, but it's fast, and we're *out of time.*"

Pel nodded reluctantly, twitched her sleeves back, and readied the little aerosol bulb. Nadina gripped the chair-back: Miles prepared to spring away and take up a firing stance.

Pel dropped her bubble and squirted the aerosol toward Naru's startled face. Naru held his breath and ducked away, barely grazed by the iridescent cloud of drug. His breath puffed back out on a yell of warning.

Miles cursed, leapt, stumbled, and fired three times in rapid succession. He dropped the two scrambling techs; Naru nearly succeeded in rolling away again, but at least the beam nimbus brought the ghem-general to a twitching halt. Temporarily. Naru lumbered around on the deck like a warthog mired in a bog, his voice reduced to a garbled groan.

Nadina hurried to the table full of Keys, swept them into her outermost robe, and brought them back to Pel. Pel began trying the ring-key on each one. "Not that one . . . not that . . ."

Miles glanced at the door, which remained closed, would remain closed until an authorized hand pressed its palm-lock. Who would be so authorized? Kety . . . Naru, who was already in here . . . any others? *We're about to find out.*

"Not . . ." Pel continued. "Oh, what if they're *all* false? No . . ."

"Of course they are," Miles realized. "The real one must be, must be—" He began tracing cables from the cipher tech's comconsole. They led to a box, stuffed in behind some other equipment, and in the box was—another Great Key. But this one was braced in a com light-beam, carrying the signals that probed its codes. "—*here.*" Miles yanked it from its place and sprinted back to Pel. "We've got the Key, we've got Nadina, we've got the goods on Naru, we've got it all. Let's *go.*"

The door hissed open. Miles whirled and fired.

A stunner-armed man in Kety's livery stumbled backward. Thumps and shouts echoed from the corridor, as what seemed a dozen more men stood quickly out of the line of fire. "*Yes,*" cried Pel happily, as the cap of the real Great Key came off in her hand, demonstrating its provenance.

"Not now!" screeched Miles. "Put it back, Pel, put your force-screen up, *now!*"

Miles ducked aboard the float-chair; its force-screen snapped into place. A blast of massed stunner fire roiled through the doorway. The stunner fire crackled harmlessly around the sparkling sphere, only making it glitter a bit more. But the haut Nadina had been left outside. She cried out and stumbled backward, painfully grazed by the stun-nimbus. Men charged through the door.

"You have the Key, Pel!" cried the haut Nadina. "Flee!"

An impractical suggestion, alas; as his men secured the room and the haut Nadina, Governor Kety strolled through the door and closed it behind him, palm-locking it.

"Well," he drawled, eyes alight with curiosity at the carnage before him. "Well." He might at least have had the courtesy to curse and stamp, Miles thought sourly. Instead he looked . . . quite thoroughly in control. "What have we here?"

A Kety-liveried trooper knelt by ghem-General Naru, and helped straighten him and hold him up by his shoulders. Naru, struggling to sit, rubbed a shaking hand over his doubtless numb and tingling face—Miles had experienced the full unpleasantness of being stunned himself, more than once in his past—and essayed a mumbling answer. On the second try he managed slurred but intelligible speech. "'S the Consorts Pel and Nadina. An' the Barray'arn. *Tol* you those damned bubbles were a secur'ty menace!" He slumped back into the trooper's arms. "'S' all right, though. We have 'em all now."

"When that voyeur is tried for his treasons," said the haut Pel poisonously, "I shall ask the Emperor to have his eyes put out, before he is executed."

Miles wondered anew at the sequence of events here last night; how *had* they extracted Nadina from her bubble? "I think you're getting a little ahead of us, milady," he sighed.

Kety walked around the haut Pel's bubble, studying it. Cracking this egg was a pretty puzzle for him. Or was it? He'd done it once before.

Escape was impossible; the bubble's movements were physically blocked. Kety might besiege them, starve them out, if he didn't mind waiting—no. Kety couldn't wait. Miles grinned blackly, and said to Pel, "This float-chair has communication link capacity, doesn't it? I'm afraid it's time to call for help."

They had, by God, *almost* brought it off, almost made the entire affair disappear without a trace. But now that they'd identified and targeted Naru, the threat of secret aid for Kety from inside Cetagandan Imperial Security was neutralized. The Cetagandans should be able to unravel the rest of it for themselves. *If I can get the word out.*

Governor Kety motioned the two men holding the haut Nadina to drag her forward to what he apparently guessed was in front of the bubble, except that he was actually about forty degrees offsides. He relieved one guardsman of his vibra-knife, stepped behind Nadina, and lifted her thick silver hair. She squeaked in terror, but relaxed again when he only laid the knife very lightly against her throat.

"Drop your force-screen, Pel, and surrender. Immediately. I don't think I need to go into crude, tedious threats, do I?"

"No," whispered Pel in agreement. That Kety would slit the haut Nadina's throat now, and arrange the body later, was unquestionable. He'd gone beyond the point of no return some time ago.

"Dammit," grated Miles in anguish. "Now *he's* got it all. Us, the Great Key . . ." *The Great Key.* Chock full it was of . . . coded information. Information the value of which lay entirely in its secrecy and uniqueness. Everywhere else people waded through floods of information, information to their eyebrows, a clogging mass of data, signal and noise . . . all information was transmittable and reproducible. Left to itself, it multiplied like bacteria as long as there was money or power to be had in it, till it choked on its own reduplication and the boredom of its human receivers.

"The float-chair, your com link—it's all Star Crèche equipment. Can you download the Great Key from it?"

"Do *what*? Why . . ." said Pel, struggling with astonishment, "I suppose so, but the chair's com link is not powerful enough to transmit all the way back to the Celestial Garden."

"Don't worry about that. Patch it through to the commercial navigation's emergency communication net. There'll be a booster right outside this ship on the orbital transfer station. I have the standard codes for it in my head, they're made simple on purpose. Maximum emergency overrides—the booster'll split the signal and dump it into the on-board computers of every ship, commercial or military, navigating right now through the Eta Ceta star system, and every station. Supposed to be a cry-for-help system for ships in deep trouble, you see. So Kety'll have the Great Key. So will a couple thousand other people, and where is his sly little plot then? We may not be able to win, but we can take his victory from him!"

The look on Pel's face, as she digested this outrageous suggestion, transformed from horror to a fey delight, but then to dismay. "That will take—many minutes. Kety will never let—no! I have the solution for that." Pel's eyes lit with understanding and rage. "What are those codes?"

Miles rattled them off; Pel's fingers flashed over her control panel. A dicey moment followed while Pel arranged the opened Great Key in the light-beam reader. Kety cried from outside the bubble, "Now, Pel!" His hand tightened on the knife. Nadina closed her eyes and stood in dignified stillness.

Pel tapped the com link start code, dropped the bubble's force-screen, and sprang out of her seat, dragging Miles with her. "All right!" she cried, stepping away from the bubble. "We're out."

Kety's hand relaxed. The bubble's screen snapped back up. The force of it almost pushed Miles off his feet; he stumbled into the unwelcoming arms of the haut-governor's guards.

"That," said Kety coldly, eyeing the bubble with the Great Key inside, "is annoying. But a temporary inconvenience. Take them." He jerked his head at his guards, and stepped away from Nadina. "You!" he said in surprise, finding Miles in their grip.

"Me." Miles's lips peeled back on a white flash of teeth that had nothing to do with a smile. "Me all along, in fact. From start to finish." *And you are finished. Of course, I may be too dead to enjoy the spectacle. . . .* Kety dared not let any of the three interlopers live. But it would take a little time yet to arrange their deaths with civilized artistry. How much time, how many chances to—

Kety caught himself just before his fist delivered a jaw-cracking blow to Miles's face. "No. You're the breakable one, isn't that right," he muttered half to himself. He stepped back, nodded to a guard. "A little shock-stick on him. On them all."

The guard unshipped his standard military issue shock-stick, glanced at the white-robed haut consorts, and hesitated. He shot a covertly beseeching look at Kety.

Miles could almost see Kety grind his teeth. "All right, just the Barrayaran!"

Looking very relieved, the guard swung his stick with a will and belted Miles three times, starting with his face and skittering down his body to belly and groin. The first touch made him yell, the second took his breath away, and the third dropped him to the floor, blazing agony radiating outward and drawing his arms and legs in. Calculation stopped, temporarily. Ghem-General Naru, just being helped to his feet, chuckled in a tone of one happy to see justice done.

"General," Kety nodded to Naru, then to the bubble, "how long to get that open?"

"Let me see." Naru knelt to the unconscious whey-faced tech, and relieved him of a small device, which he pointed at the bubble. "They've changed the codes. Half an hour, once you get my men waked up."

Kety grimaced. His wrist com chimed. Kety's brows rose, and he spoke into it. "Yes, Captain?"

"Haut-governor," came the formal, uneasy voice of some subordinate. "We are experiencing a peculiar communication over emergency channels. An enormous data dump is being speed-loaded into our systems. Some kind of coded gibberish, but it has exceeded the memory capacity of the receiver and is spilling over into other systems like a virus. It's marked with an Imperial override. The initial signal appears to be originating from *our* ship. Is this . . . something you intend?"

Kety's brows drew down in puzzlement. Then his gaze rose to the white bubble, glowing in the center of the room. He swore, one sharp, heartfelt sibilant. "No. Ghem-General Naru! We have to get this force-screen down *now*!"

Kety spared a venomous glare for Pel and Miles that promised infinite retribution later, then he and Naru fell to frantic consultation. Heavy doses of synergine from the guards' med-kit failed to return the techs to immediate consciousness, though they stirred and groaned in a promising fashion. Kety and Naru were left to do it themselves. Judging by the wicked light in Pel's eyes, as she and the haut Nadina clung together, they were going to be way too late. The pain of the shock-stick blows were fading to pins and needles, but Miles remained curled up on the floor, the better not to draw further such attentions to himself.

Kety and Naru were so absorbed in their task and their irate arguments over the swiftest way to proceed, only Miles noticed when a spot on the door began to glow. Despite his pain, he smiled. A beat later, the whole door burst inward in a spray of melted plastic and metal. Another beat, to wait out anyone's hair-trigger reflexes.

Ghem-Colonel Benin, impeccably turned out in his blood-red dress uniform and freshly applied face paint, stepped firmly across the threshold. He was unarmed, but the red-clad squad behind him carried an arsenal sufficient to destroy any impediment in their path up to the size of a pocket dreadnought. Kety and Naru froze in mid-lurch; Kety's liveried retainers suddenly seemed to think better of drawing weapons, opening their hands palm-outward and standing very still. Colonel Vorreedi, equally impeccable in his House blacks, if not quite so cool in expression, stepped in behind Benin. In the corridor beyond, Miles could just glimpse Ivan looming behind the armed men, and shifting anxiously from foot to foot.

"Good evening, haut Kety, ghem-General Naru." Benin bowed with exquisite courtesy. "By the personal order of Emperor Fletchir Giaja, it is my duty to arrest you both upon the serious charge of treason to the Empire. And," contemplating Naru especially, Benin's smile went razor-sharp, "complicity in the murder of the Imperial Servitor the Ba Lura."

Chapter Fifteen

From Miles's eye-level, the deck sprouted a forest of red boots, as Benin's squad clumped in to disarm and arrest Kety's retainers and march them out with their hands atop their heads. Kety and Naru were taken along with them, sandwiched silently between some hard-eyed men who didn't look as though they were interested in listening to explanations.

At a growl from Kety, the procession paused in front of the entering Barrayarans. Miles heard Kety's voice, icy-cold: "Congratulations, Lord Vorpatril. I hope you may be fortunate enough to survive your victory."

"Huh?" said Ivan.

Oh, let him go. It would be too exhausting to try and sort out Kety about his confused inversion of Miles's little chain-of-command. Maybe Benin would have it straight. At a sharp word from their sergeant the security squad prodded their prisoners back into motion and clattered on down the corridor.

Four shiny black boots made their way through the mob and halted before Miles's nose. Speaking of explanations . . . Miles twisted his head and looked up the odd foreshortened perspective at Colonel Vorreedi and Ivan. The deck was cool beneath his stinging cheek, and he didn't really want to move, even supposing he could.

Ivan bent over him, giving an upside-down view up his nostrils, and said in a strained tone, "Are you all right?"

"Sh-sh-shock-stick. Nothing b-broken."

"Right," said Ivan, and hauled him to his feet by his collar. Miles hung a moment, shivering and twitching like a fish on a hook, till he found his unsteady balance. By necessity, he leaned on Ivan, who supported him with an un-commenting hand under his elbow.

Colonel Vorreedi looked him up and down. "I'll let the ambassador do the protesting about that." Vorreedi's distant expression suggested he thought privately that the fellow with the shock-stick had stopped too soon. "Vorob'yev is going to need all the ammunition he can get. You have created the most extraordinary public incident of his career, I suspect."

"Oh, Colonel," sighed Miles. "I predict there's going to b-be nothing p-public 'bout *this* incident. Wait 'n see."

Ghem-Colonel Benin, across the room, was bowing and scraping to the hauts Pel and Nadina, and supplying them with float-chairs, albeit lacking force-screens, extra robes, and ghem-lady attendants. Arresting them in the style to which they were accustomed?

Miles glanced up at Vorreedi. "Has Ivan, um, *explained* everything, sir?"

"I trust so," said Vorreedi, in a voice drenched with menace.

Ivan nodded vigorously, but then hedged, "Um . . . all I could. Under the circumstances."

Meaning, lack of privacy from Cetagandan eavesdroppers, Miles presumed. *All, Ivan? Is my cover still intact?*

"I admit," Vorreedi went on, "I am still . . . . assimilating it."

"What h-happened after I left the Star Crèche?" Miles asked Ivan.

"I woke up and you were *gone*. I think that was the worst moment of my life, knowing you'd gone haring off on some crazy self-appointed mission with no backup."

"Oh, but *you* were my backup, Ivan," Miles murmured, earning himself a glare. "And a good one too, as you have just demonstrated, yes?"

"Yeah, your favorite kind—unconscious on the floor where I couldn't inject any kind of sense into the proceedings. You took off to get yourself killed, or worse, and everybody would have blamed me. The last thing Aunt Cordelia said to me before we left was, 'And *try* to keep him out of trouble, Ivan.' "

Miles could hear Countess Vorkosigan's weary, exasperated cadences quite precisely in Ivan's parody.

"Anyway, as soon as I figured out what the hell was going on, I got away from the haut-ladies—"

"*How?*"

"God, Miles, they're just like my mother, only eight times over. Ugh! Anyway, the haut Rian insisted I go through ghem-Colonel Benin, which I was willing to do—*he* at least seemed like he had his head screwed on straight—"

Perhaps attracted by the sound of his name, Benin strolled over to listen in on this.

"—and God be praised he paid attention to me. Seemed to make more sense out of my gabble than I did at the time."

Benin nodded. "I was of course following the very unusual activities around the Star Crèche today—"

Around, not *in.* Quite.

"My own investigations had already led me to suspect something was going on involving one or more of the haut-governors, so I had orbital squads on alert."

"Squads, ha," said Ivan. "There's three Imperial battle cruisers surrounding this ship right now."

Benin smiled slightly, and shrugged.

"Ghem-General Chilian is a dupe, I believe," Miles put in. "Though you will p-probably wish to question him about the activities of his wife, the haut Vio."

"He has already been detained," Benin assured him.

Detained, not arrested, all right. Benin seemed exactly on track so far. But had he realized yet that all the governors had been involved? Or was Kety elected sole sacrifice? *A Cetagandan internal matter,* Miles reminded himself. It was not his job to straighten out the entire Cetagandan government, tempting as it would be to try. His duty was confined to extracting Barrayar from the morass. He smiled at the glowing white bubble still protecting the real Great Key. The hauts Nadina and Pel were consulting with some of Benin's men; it appeared that rather than attempting to get the force-screen down here they were making arrangements to transport it and its precious contents whole and inviolate back to the Star Crèche.

Vorreedi gave Miles a grim look. "One thing that Lord Vorpatril has not yet explained to my satisfaction, Lieutenant Vorkosigan, is why you concealed the initial incident involving an object of such obvious importance—"

"Kety was trying to frame Barrayar, sir. Until I could achieve independent corroborative evidence that—"

Vorreedi went on inexorably, "*From your own side.*"

"Ah." Miles briefly considered a relapse of shock-stick symptoms, rendering him unable to talk. No, alas. His own motives were obscure even to him, in retrospect. What *had* he started out wanting, before the twisting events had made sheer survival his paramount concern? Oh, yes, promotion. That was it.

Not this time, boy-o. Antique but evocative phrases like *damage control* and *spin doctoring* free-floated through his consciousness.

"In fact, sir, I did not at first recognize the Great Key for what it was. But once the haut Rian contacted me, events slid very rapidly from apparently trivial to extremely delicate. By the time I realized the full depth and complexity of the haut-governor's plot, it was too late."

"Too late for what?" asked Vorreedi bluntly.

What with the shock-stick residue and all, Miles did not need to feign a sick smile. But it seemed Vorreedi had drifted back to the conviction that Miles was not working as a covert ops agent for Simon Illyan after all. *That's what you want everybody to think, remember?* Miles glanced aside at ghem-Colonel Benin, listening in fascination.

"You would have taken the investigation away from me, you know you would have, sir. Everyone in the wormhole nexus thinks I'm a cripple who's been given a cushy nepotistic sinecure as a courier. That I might be competent for more is something Lieutenant Lord Vorkosigan would never, in the ordinary course of events, ever be given a chance to publicly prove."

To the world at large, true. But Illyan knew all about the pivotal role Miles had played in the Hegen Hub, and elsewhere, as did Miles's father Prime Minister Count Vorkosigan, and Emperor Gregor, and everyone else whose opinion really counted, back on Barrayar. Even Ivan knew about that extraordinary covert ops coup. In fact, it seemed the only people who didn't know were . . . the enemy he'd beaten. The Cetagandans.

So did you do all this only to shine in the haut Rian's beautiful eyes? Or did you have a wider audience in view?

Ghem-Colonel Benin slowly deciphered this outpouring. "You wanted to be a hero?"

"So badly you didn't even care for which *side*?" Vorreedi added in some dismay.

"I *have* done the Cetagandan Empire a good turn, it's true." Miles essayed a shaky bow in Benin's direction. "But it was Barrayar I was thinking of. Governor Kety had some nasty plans for Barrayar. Those, at least, I've derailed."

"Oh, yeah?" said Ivan. "Where would they, and you, be right now if we hadn't shown up?"

"Oh," Miles smiled to himself, "I'd already won. Kety just didn't know it yet. The only thing still in doubt was my personal survival," he conceded.

"Why don't you sign up for Cetagandan Imperial Security, then, coz," suggested Ivan in exasperation. "Maybe ghem-Colonel Benin would promote you."

Ivan, damn him, knew Miles all too well. "Unlikely," Miles said bitterly. "I'm too short."

Ghem-Colonel Benin's eyebrow twitched.

"Actually," Miles pointed out, "if I was free-lancing for anyone, it was for the Star Crèche, not for the Empire. I have not served the Cetagandan Empire, so much as the haut. Ask *them*." He nodded toward Pel and Nadina, getting ready to exit the room with their ghem-lady escorts fussing over their comfort.

"Hm." Ghem-Colonel Benin seemed to deflate slightly.

Magic words, apparently. A haut-consort's skirts made a stronger fortification behind which to hide than Miles would have thought possible, a few weeks ago.

The haut Nadina's bubble was hoisted into the air by some men with hand-tractors, and maneuvered out of the room. Benin glanced after it, turned again to Miles, and opened his hand in front of his chest in a sketch of a bow. "In any case, Lieutenant Lord Vorkosigan, my Celestial master the Emperor haut Fletchir Giaja requests you attend upon him in my company. Now."

Miles could decipher an Imperial command when he heard one. He sighed, and bowed in return, in proper honor of Benin's august order. "Certainly. Ah . . ." He glanced aside at Ivan and the suddenly agitated Vorreedi. He wasn't exactly sure he wanted witnesses for this audience. He wasn't exactly sure he wanted to be alone, either.

"Your . . . friends may accompany you," Benin conceded. "With the understanding that they may not speak unless invited to do so."

Which inviting would be done, if at all, solely by Benin's Celestial Master. Vorreedi nodded in partial satisfaction. Ivan began to practice looking blank with all his might.

They all herded out, surrounded and escorted—but not arrested, of course, that would violate diplomatic protocol—by Benin's Imperial guards. Miles found himself, still supported by Ivan, waiting to exit the doorway beside the haut Nadina.

"Such a nice young man," Nadina commented in a well-modulated undertone to Miles, nodding at Benin, whom they could glimpse out in the corridor directing his troopers. "So neatly turned-out, and he understands the proprieties. We'll have to see what we can do for him, don't you agree, Pel?"

"Oh, quite," Pel said, and floated on through.

After a lengthy walk through the great State ship, Miles cycled through the air lock into the Cetagandan security shuttle in the company of Benin himself, who had not let him out of his sight. Benin looked cool and alert as ever, but there was an underlying . . . well, *smugness* leaking through his zebra-striped facade. It must have given Benin a moment of supreme Cetagandan satisfaction, arresting his commanding officer for treason. The one-up high point of his career. Miles would have bet Betan dollars to sand Naru was the man who'd assigned the dapper and decorous Benin to close the case on the Ba Lura's death in the first place, setting him up to fail.

Miles ventured, "By the way, if I didn't say it before, congratulations on cracking your very tricky murder case, General Benin."

Benin blinked. "Colonel Benin," he corrected.

"That's what you think." Miles floated forward, and helped himself to the most comfortable window seat he could find.

"I don't believe I've seen this audience chamber before," Colonel Vorreedi whispered to Miles, his gaze flicking around to take in their surroundings. "It's not one ever used for public or diplomatic ceremonies."

Unusually, they had come not to a pavilion, but to a closed, low-lying building in the northern quadrant of the Celestial Garden. The three Barrayarans had spent an hour in an antechamber, cooling their heels while their internal tension rose. They were attended by half a dozen polite, solicitous ghem-guards, who saw to their physical comforts while courteously denying every request for outside communication. Benin had gone off somewhere with the hauts Pel and Nadina. In view of their Cetagandan company, Miles had not so much reported to Vorreedi as exchanged a few guarded remarks.

The new room reminded Miles a bit of the Star Chamber, simple, undistracting, deliberately serene, sound-baffled and cool in shades of blue. Voices had a curious deadened quality that hinted that the entire chamber was enclosed in a cone-of-silence. Patterns on the floor betrayed a large concealed comconsole table and station-chairs that could be raised for conferences, but for now, the supplicants stood.

Another guest was waiting, and Miles raised his brows in surprise. Lord Yenaro stood next to a red-clad ghem-guard. Yenaro looked pale, with dark greenish circles under his eyes, as if he had not slept for about two days. His dark robes, the same clothes Miles had last seen him wearing at the bioestheties exhibition, were rumpled and bedraggled. Yenaro's eyes widened in turn at the sight of Miles and Ivan. He turned his head away and tried not to notice the Barrayarans. Miles waved cheerfully, dragging a reluctantly polite return nod from Yenaro, and starting a very pained crease between his eyebrows.

And here came something to keep Miles's mind off his own lingering shock-stick pains right now. Or rather, someone.

Ghem-Colonel Benin entered first, and dismissed the Barrayarans' guards. He was followed by the hauts Pel, Nadina, and Rian in their float-chairs, shields down, who silently arranged themselves on one side of the room. Nadina had tucked the cut ends of her hair out of sight among her garments, the same robes Pel had shared and which Nadina had not stopped to change. They had all obviously been closeted for the past hour in a debriefing at the highest level, for last of all a familiar figure strode in, shedding more guards in the corridor outside.

Close-up, Emperor the haut Fletchir Giaja seemed even taller and leaner than when Miles had seen him at a distance at the elegy-reading ceremonies. And older, despite his dark hair. He was for the moment casually dressed, by Imperial standards, in a mere half a dozen layers of fine white robes over the usual masculine-loose but blinding-white bodysuit, befitting his status as chief mourner.

Emperors *per se* did not unnerve Miles, though Yenaro swayed on his feet as though he were about to faint, and even Benin moved with the most rigid formality. Emperor Gregor had been raised along with Miles practically as his foster-brother; somewhere in the back of Miles's mind the term *emperor* was coupled with such identifiers as *somebody to play hide-and-seek with*. In this context those hidden assumptions could be a psychosocial land mine. *Eight planets, and older than my father*, Miles reminded himself, trying to inculcate a proper deference to the illusion of power Imperial panoply sought to create. One chair at the head of the room rose from the floor to receive what Gregor would have sardonically dubbed The Imperial Ass. Miles bit his lip.

It was apparently going to be a most intimate audience, for Giaja beckoned Benin over and spoke to him in a low voice, and Benin subsequently dismissed even Yenaro's guard. That left the three Barrayarans, the two planetary consorts and Rian, Benin, the Emperor, and Yenaro. Nine, a traditional quorum for judgment.

Still, it was better than facing Illyan. Maybe the haut Fletchir Giaja was not disposed to razor-edged sarcasms. But anyone related to all those haut-women had to be dangerously bright. Miles swallowed against a babbling burst of explanations. *Wait for your straight lines, boy.*

Rian looked pale and grave. No clue there, Rian always looked pale and grave. A last pang of desire banked itself to a tiny, furtive ember in Miles's heart, secret and encysted like a tumor. But he could still be afraid for her. His chest was cold with that dread.

"Lord Vorkosigan," Fletchir Giaja's exquisite baritone broke the waiting silence.

Miles suppressed a quick glance around—it wasn't as though there were any other Lords Vorkosigan present, after all—stepped forward, and came to a precise parade rest. "Sir."

"I am still . . . unclear, just what *your* place was in these recent events. And how you came by it."

"My place was to have been a sacrificial animal, and it was chosen for me by Governor Kety, sir. But I didn't play the part he tried to assign to me."

The Emperor frowned at this less-than-straightforward reply. "Explain yourself."

Miles glanced at Rian. "Everything?"

She gave an almost imperceptible nod.

Miles closed his eyes in a brief, diffuse prayer to whatever sportive gods were listening, opened them again, and launched once more into the true description of his first encounter with the Ba Lura in the personnel pod, Great Key and all. At least it had the advantage of simultaneously getting in Miles's overdue confession to Vorreedi in a venue where the embassy's chief security officer was totally blocked from making any comment or reply. Amazing man, Vorreedi; he betrayed no emotion beyond one muscle jumping in his jaw.

"As soon as I saw the Ba Lura in the funeral rotunda with its throat cut," Miles went on, "I realized my then-unknown opponent had thrown me into the logically impossible position of having to prove a negative. There was no way, once I had been tricked into laying hands on the false Key, to prove that Barrayar had not effected a substitution, except by the positive testimony of the one eyewitness then lying dead on the floor. Or by positively locating the real Great Key. Which I set out to do. And if the Ba Lura's death was not a suicide, but rather a murder elaborately set up to pass as a suicide, it was clear someone high in the Celestial Garden's security was cooperating with the ba's killers, which made approaching Cetagandan Security for help quite dangerous at that point. But then somebody assigned ghem-Colonel Benin to the case, presumably with heavy hints that it would be well for his career to bring in a quick verdict confirming suicide. Somebody who seriously underestimated Benin's abilities," *and ambition,* "as a security officer. *Was* it ghem-General Naru, by the way?"

Benin nodded, a faint gleam in his eye.

"For . . . whatever reason, Naru decided ghem-Colonel Benin would make a suitable additional goat. It was beginning to be a pattern in their operations, as you must realize if you've collected testimony from Lord Yenaro here—?" Miles raised an inquiring eyebrow at Benin. "I see you found Lord Yenaro before Kety's agents did. I think I'm glad, in all."

"You should be," Benin returned blandly. "We picked him up— along with his very interesting carpet—last night. His account was critical in shaping my response to your cousin's, um, sudden onslaught of information and demands."

"I see." Miles shifted his weight, his parade rest growing rather bent. He rubbed his face, because it didn't seem like the time or place to rub his crotch.

"Does your medical condition require you to sit?" Benin inquired solicitously.

"I'll manage." Miles took a breath. "I tried, in our first interview, to direct ghem-Colonel Benin's attentions to the subtleties of his situation. Fortunately, ghem-Colonel Benin is a subtle man, and his loyalty to you," *or to the truth,* "outweighed whatever implied threats to his career Naru presented."

Benin and Miles exchanged guarded, appreciative nods.

"Kety tried to deliver me into the hands of the Star Crèche, accused by means of Ba Lura's false confession to the Handmaiden," Miles continued carefully. "But once again his pawns ad libbed against his script. I entirely commend the haut Rian for her cool and collected response to this emergency. The fact that she kept her head and did not panic allowed me to continue to try to clear Barrayar of blame. She is, um, a credit to the haut, you know." Miles regarded her anxiously for a cue. *Where are we?* But she remained as glassily attentive as if that now-absent force-bubble had become one with her skin. "The haut Rian acted throughout for the good of the haut, never once for her own personal aggrandizement or safety." Though one might argue, apparently, over where *the good of the haut* actually lay. "Your late August Mother chose her Handmaiden well, I'd say."

"That is hardly for you to judge, Barrayaran," drawled the haut Fletchir Giaja, whether in amusement, or dangerously, Miles's ear could not quite tell.

"Excuse me, but I didn't exactly volunteer for this mission. I was suckered into it. My *judgments* have brought us all here, one way or another."

Giaja looked faintly surprised, even a little nonplused, as if he'd never before had one of his gentle hints thrown back in his face. Benin stiffened, and Vorreedi winced. Ivan suppressed a grin, the merest twitch, and continued his Invisible Man routine.

The Emperor took another tack. "And how did you come to be involved with Lord Yenaro?"

"Um . . . from my point of view, you mean?" Presumably Benin had already presented him with Yenaro's own testimony; a cross-check was in order, to be sure. In carefully neutral phrasing, Miles described his and Ivan's three encounters with Yenaro's increasingly lethal practical jokes, with a lot of emphasis on Miles's clever (once proved) theories about Lord X. Vorreedi's face drained to an interesting greenish cast upon Miles's description of the go-round with the carpet. Miles added cautiously, "In my opinion, certainly proved by the incident with the asterzine bomb, Lord Yenaro was as much an intended victim as Ivan and myself. There is no treason in the man." Miles cut off a slice of smile. "He hasn't the nerve for it."

Yenaro twitched, but did not gainsay any of it. Yeah, slather on the suggestion of Imperial mercy due all 'round, maybe some would slop over on the one who needed it most.

At Benin's direction, Yenaro, in a colorless voice, confirmed

Miles's account. Benin called in a guard and had the ghem-lord taken out, leaving eight in this chamber of Imperial inquisition. Would they work their way down to one?

Giaja sat silent for a time, then spoke, in formally modulated cadences. "That suffices for my appraisal of the concerns of the Empire. We must now turn to the concerns of haut. Haut Rian, you may keep your Barrayaran creature. Ghem-Colonel Benin. Will you kindly wait in the antechamber with Colonel Vorreedi and Lord Vorpatril until I call you."

"Sire." Benin saluted his way out, shepherding the reluctant Barrayarans.

Obscurely alarmed, Miles put in, "But don't you want Ivan too, Celestial Lord? He witnessed almost everything with me."

"No," stated Giaja flatly.

That settled that. Well . . . until Miles and Ivan were out of the Celestial Garden, indeed, out of the Empire and halfway home, they wouldn't be any safer anyway. Miles subsided with a faint sigh; then his eyes widened at the abrupt change in the room's atmosphere.

Feminine gazes, formerly suitably downcast, rose in direct stares. Without awaiting permission, the three float-chairs arranged themselves in a circle around Fletchir Giaja, who himself sat back with a face suddenly more expressive; dryer, edgier, angrier. The glassy reserve of the haut vanished in a new intensity. Miles swayed on his feet.

Pel glanced aside at the motion. "Give him a chair, Fletchir," she said. "Kety's guard shock-sticked him in the best regulation form, you know."

In her place, yes.

"As you wish, Pel." The Emperor touched a control in his chair-arm; a station chair near Miles's feet rose from the floor. He fell more than sat in it, grateful and dizzy, on the edge of their circle.

"I hope you all see now," said the haut Fletchir Giaja more forcefully, "the wisdom of our ancestors in arranging that the haut and the Empire shall have only one interface. Me. Only one veto. Mine. Issues of the haut-genome *must* remain as insulated as possible from the political sphere, lest they fall into the hands of politicians who do not understand the goal of haut. That includes most of our gentle ghem-lords, as ghem-General Naru has perhaps proved to you, Nadina." A flash of subtle, savage irony there—Miles suddenly doubted his initial perception of gender issues on

Eta Ceta. What if Fletchir Giaja was haut first, and male second, and the consorts too were haut first, female second. . . . Who was in charge here, when Fletchir Giaja knew himself as a product of his mother's high art?

"Indeed," said Nadina, with a grimace.

Rian sighed wearily. "What can you expect from a half-breed like Naru? But it is the haut Ilsum Kety who has shaken my confidence in the Celestial Lady's vision. She often said that genetic engineering could only sow, that winnowing and reaping must still be done in an arena of competition. But Kety was not ghem, but *haut*. The fact that he could try what he tried . . . makes me think we have more work to do before the winnowing and reaping part."

"Lisbet always did have an addiction for the most primitive metaphors," Nadina recalled with faint distaste.

"She was right about the diversity issue, though," Pel said.

"In principle," Giaja conceded. "But this generation is not the time. The haut population can expand many times over into space presently held by servitor classes, without need for further territorial aggrandizement. The Empire is enjoying a necessary period of assimilation."

"The Constellations have been deliberately limiting their numerical expansion of late decades, to conserve their favored economic positions," observed Nadina disapprovingly.

"You know, Fletchir," Pel put in, "an alternate solution might be to require more constellation crosses by Imperial edict. A kind of genetic self-taxation. Novel, but Nadina is right. The Constellations have grown more miserly and luxurious with each passing decade."

"I thought the whole point of genetic engineering was to avoid the random waste of natural evolution, and replace it with the efficiency of reason," Miles piped up. All three haut-women turned to stare at him in astonishment, as if a potted plant had suddenly offered a critique of its fertilization routine. "Or . . . so it seems to me," Miles trailed off in a much smaller voice.

Fletchir Giaga smiled, faint, shrewd, and wintry. Belatedly, Miles began to wonder why he was being kept here, by Giaja's suggestion/command. He had a most unpleasant sensation of being in a conversation with an undertow of cross-currents which were streaming in three different directions at once. *If Giaja wants to send a message, I wish he'd use a comconsole.* Miles's whole body was throbbing in time with the pulsing of his headache, several hours past midnight of one of the longer days of his short life.

"I will return to the Council of Consorts with your veto," said Rian slowly, "as I must. But Fletchir, you must address the diversity issue more directly. If this generation is not the time, it is still certainly not too soon to begin planning. And the diversification issue. The single-copy method of security is too horrifyingly risky, as recent events also prove."

"Hm," Fletchir Giaja half-conceded. His eye fell sharply upon Miles. "Nevertheless—Pel—whatever possessed you to spill the contents of the Great Key across the entire Eta Ceta system? As a joke, it does not amuse."

Pel bit her lip; her eyes, uncharacteristically, lowered.

Miles said sturdily, "No joke, sir. As far as we knew, we were both going to die within a few minutes. The haut Rian stated that the highest priority was the recovery of the Great Key. The receivers got the Key but no lock; without the gene banks themselves it was valueless gibberish from their point of view. One way or another, we assured you would be able to recover it, in pieces maybe, even after our deaths, regardless of what Kety did subsequently."

"The Barrayaran speaks the truth," affirmed Pel.

"The best strategies run on rails like that," Miles pointed out. "Live or die, you make your goal." He shut up, as Fletchir Giaja's stare hinted that perhaps outlander barbarians had better not make comments that could be construed as a slur on his late mother's abilities, even when those abilities had been pitted against him.

You can't get anywhere with these people, or whatever they are. I want to go home, Miles thought tiredly. "What will happen to ghem-General Naru, anyway?"

"He will be executed," said the Emperor. To his credit, the bald statement clearly brought him no joy. "Security *must* be . . . secured."

Miles couldn't argue with that. "And the haut Kety? Will he be executed too?"

"He will retire, immediately, to a supervised estate, due to ill health. If he objects, he will be offered suicide."

"Er . . . forcibly, if necessary?"

"Kety is young. He will choose life, and other days and chances."

"The other governors?"

Giaja frowned annoyance at the consorts. "A little pragmatic blindness in that direction will close matters. But they will not find new appointments easy to come by."

"And," Miles glanced at the ladies, "the haut Vio? What about her? The others only tried to commit a crime. She actually succeeded."

Rian nodded. Her voice went very flat. "She too will be offered a choice. To replace the servitor she destroyed—de-sexed, depilated, and demoted to ba, her metabolism altered, her body thickened . . . but returned to a life inside the Celestial Garden, as she desired with a passion beyond reason. Or she may be permitted a painless suicide."

"Which . . . will she choose?"

"Suicide, I hope," said Nadina sincerely.

A multiple standard seemed at work in all this justice. Now that the thrill of the chase was over, Miles felt a nauseated revulsion at the shambles of the kill. *For this I laid my life on the line?*

"What about . . . the haut Rian? And me?"

Fletchir Giaja's eyes were cool and distant, light-years gone. "That . . . is a problem upon which I shall now retire and meditate."

The Emperor called Benin back in to escort Miles away, after a short murmured conference. But away to where? Home to the embassy, or head-first down the nearest oubliette? Did the Celestial Garden have oubliettes?

Home, it appeared, for Benin returned Miles to the company of Vorreedi and Ivan, and took them to the Western Gate, where a car from the Barrayaran embassy already waited. They paused, and the ghem-Colonel addressed Vorreedi.

"We cannot control what goes into your official reports. But my Celestial Master . . ." Benin paused to select a suitably delicate term, "*expects* that none of what you have seen or heard will appear as social gossip."

"That, I think I can promise," said Vorreedi sincerely.

Benin nodded satisfaction. "May I have your words upon your names in the matter, please."

He'd been doing his homework upon Barrayaran customs, it seemed. The three Barrayarans dutifully gave their personal oaths, and Benin released them into the dank night air. It was about two hours till dawn, Miles guessed.

The embassy aircar was blessedly shadowed. Miles settled into a corner, wishing he had Ivan's talent for invisibility, but wishing most of all that they could cut tomorrow's ceremonies and start home immediately. No. He'd come this far, might as well see it through to the bitter end.

Vorreedi had gone beyond emotion to silence. He spoke to Miles only once, in chill tones.

"What *did* you think you were doing, Vorkosigan?"

"I stopped the Cetagandan Empire from breaking up into eight aggressively expanding units. I derailed plans for a war by some of them with Barrayar. I survived an assassination attempt, and helped catch three high-ranking traitors. Admittedly, they weren't *our* traitors, but still. Oh. And I solved a murder. That's enough for one trip, I hope."

Vorreedi struggled with himself for a moment, then bit out helplessly, "*Are* you a special agent, or not?"

On a need-to-know list . . . Vorreedi didn't. Not really, not at this point. Miles sighed inwardly. "Well, if not . . . I *succeeded* like one, didn't I?"

Ivan winced. Vorreedi sat back with no further comment, but radiating exasperation. Miles smiled grimly, in the dark.

Chapter Sixteen

Miles woke from a late, uneasy doze to find Ivan cautiously shaking him by the shoulder.

He closed his eyes again, blocking out the dimness of his suite and his cousin. "Go *'way.*" He tried to pull the covers back up over his head.

Ivan renewed his efforts, more vigorously. "Now I know it was a mission," he commented. "You're having your usual post-mission sulks."

"I am not *sulking.* I am *tired.*"

"You look terrific, you know. Great blotch on the side of your face that goon left with his shock-stick. Goes all the way up to your eye. It'll show from a hundred meters. You should get up and look in the mirror."

"I hate people who are cheerful in the morning. What time is it? Why are you up? Why are you *here?*" Miles lost his clutch on his bedclothes as Ivan dragged them ruthlessly from his grip.

"Ghem-Colonel Benin is on his way here to pick you up. In an Imperial land-cruiser half a block long. The Cetagandans want you at the cremation ceremony an hour early."

"What? *Why?* He can't be arresting me from here, diplomatic immunity. Assassination? Execution? Isn't it a little late for that?"

"Ambassador Vorob'yev also wants to know. He sent me to rustle you up as swiftly as possible." Ivan propelled Miles toward his bathroom. "Start depilating. I've brought your uniform and boots from the embassy laundry. Anyway, if the Cetagandans really wanted to assassinate you, they'd hardly do it here. They'd slip something subtle under your skin that wouldn't go off for six months, and then would drop you mysteriously and untraceably in your tracks."

"Reassuring thought." Miles rubbed the back of his neck, surreptitiously feeling for lumps. "I bet the Star Crèche has some great terminal diseases. But I pray I didn't offend *them*."

Miles suffered Ivan to play valet, on fast-forward, with editorials. But he forgave his cousin all sins, past, present, and future, in exchange for the coffee bulb Ivan also shoved into his hand. He swallowed and stared at his face in the mirror, above his unfastened black tunic. The shock-stick contusion across his left cheek was indeed turning a spectacular polychrome, crowned by a blue-black circle under his eye. The other two hits were not as bad, as his clothing had offered some protection. He still would have preferred to spend the day in bed. In his cabin on the outbound ImpSec jumpship, heading home as fast as the laws of physics would allow.

They arrived at the embassy's lobby to find not Benin but Mia Maz waiting in her formal black and white funeral clothing. She had been keeping Ambassador Vorob'yev company when they'd dragged in last night—this morning, rather—and could not have had much more sleep than Miles. But she looked remarkably fresh, even chipper. She smiled at Miles and Ivan. Ivan smiled back.

Miles squinted. "Vorob'yev not here?"

"He's coming down as soon as he's finished dressing," Maz assured him.

"You . . . coming with me?" Miles asked hopefully. "Or . . . no, I suppose you have to be with your own delegation. This being the big finish and all."

"I'll be accompanying Ambassador Vorob'yev." Maz's smile escaped into a chipmunk grin, dimples everywhere. "Permanently. He asked me to marry him last night. I think it was a measure of his general distraction. In the spirit of the insanity of the moment, I said yes."

If you can't hire help . . . Well, that would solve Vorob'yev's quest for female expertise on the embassy's staff. Not to mention accounting for all that bombardment of chocolates and invitations.

"Congratulations," Miles managed. Though perhaps it ought to be *Congratulations* to Vorob'yev and *Good luck* to Maz.

"It still feels quite strange," Maz confided. "I mean, *Lady Vorob'yev*. How did your mother cope, Lord Vorkosigan?"

"You mean, being an egalitarian Betan and all? No problem. She says egalitarians adjust to aristocracies just fine, as long as they get to be the aristocrats."

"I hope to meet her someday."

"You'll get along famously," Miles predicted with confidence.

Vorob'yev appeared, still fastening his black tunic, at almost the same moment as ghem-Colonel Benin was escorted inside by the embassy guards. Correction. Ghem-General Benin. Miles smiled under his breath at the glitter of new rank insignia on Benin's blood-red dress uniform. *I called that one right, did I not?*

"May I ask what this is all about, ghem-General?" Vorob'yev didn't miss the new order.

Benin half-bowed. "My Celestial Master requests the attendance of Lord Vorkosigan at this hour. Ah . . . we *will* return him to you."

"Your word upon it? It would be a major embarrassment for the embassy were he to be mislaid . . . again." Vorob'yev managed to be stern at Benin while simultaneously capturing Maz's hand upon his arm and covertly stroking it.

"My word upon it, Ambassador," Benin promised. At Vorob'yev's reluctant nod of permission, he led Miles out. Miles glanced back over his shoulder, lonely for Ivan, or Maz, or somebody on his side.

The groundcar wasn't half a block long, but it was a very fine vehicle indeed, and not military issue. Cetagandan soldiers saluted Benin punctiliously, and settled him and his guest in the rear compartment. When they pulled away from the embassy, it felt something like riding in a house.

"May *I* ask what all this is about, ghem-General?" Miles inquired in turn.

Benin's expression was almost . . . crocodilian. "I am instructed that explanations must wait until you arrive at the Celestial Garden. It will take only a few minutes of your time, nothing more. I first thought that you would like it, but upon mature reflection, I think you will hate it. Either way, you deserve it."

"Take care your growing reputation for subtlety doesn't go to your head, ghem-General," Miles growled. Benin merely smiled.

✧   ✧   ✧

It was definitely an Imperial audience chamber, if a small one, not a conference chamber like the room last night. There was only one seat, and Fletchir Giaja was in it already. The white robes he wore this morning were bulky and elaborate to the point of half-immobilizing him, and he had two ba servitors waiting to help him with them when he rose again. He had his icon-look plastered back on his face again, his expression so reserved it resembled porcelain. Three white bubbles floated silently beyond his left hand. Another ba servitor brought a small flat case to Benin, who stood upon the Emperor's right.

"You may approach my Celestial Master, Lord Vorkosigan," Benin informed him.

Miles stepped forward, deciding not to kneel. He and the haut Fletchir Giaja were almost eye to eye as he stood.

Benin handed the case to the Emperor, who opened it. "Do you know what this is, Lord Vorkosigan?" Giaja asked.

Miles eyed the medallion of the Order of Merit on its colored ribbon, glittering on a bed of velvet. "Yes, sir. It is a lead weight, suitable for sinking small enemies. Are you going to sew me into a silk sack with it, before you throw me overboard?"

Giaja glanced up at Benin, who responded with a *Didn't I tell you so?* shrug.

"Bend your neck, Lord Vorkosigan," Giaja instructed him firmly. "Unaccustomed as you may be to doing so."

Was not Rian in one of those bubbles? Miles stared briefly at his mirror-polished boots, as Giaja slipped the ribbon over his head. He stepped back half a pace, tried and failed to keep his hand from touching the cool metal. He would not salute. "I . . . refuse this honor, sir."

"No, you don't," Giaja said in an observant tone, watching him. "I am given to understand by my keenest observers that you have a passion for recognition. It is a . . ."

Weakness that can be exploited—

"—an understandable quality that puts me much in mind of our own ghem."

Well, it was better than being compared to the hauts' other semi-siblings, the ba. Who were not the palace eunuchs they seemed, but rather some sort of incredibly valuable in-house science projects—the late Ba Lura might be better than half-sibling to Giaja himself, for all Miles knew. Sixty-eight percent shared chromosomal material, say. Quite. Miles decided he would have more respect for, not to mention caution of, the silent slippered ba after this. They were all in on this haut-business together, the putative servitors and their putative masters. No wonder the Emperor had taken Lura's murder so seriously.

"As far as recognition goes, sir, this is hardly something that I will be able to show around at home. More like, hide it in the bottom of the deepest drawer I own."

"Good," said Fletchir Giaja in a level tone. "As long as you lay all the matters associated with it alongside."

Ah. That was the heart of it. A bribe for his silence. "There is very little about the past two weeks that I shall take pleasure in remembering, sir."

"Remember what you will, as long as you do not recount it."

"Not publicly. But I have a duty to report."

"Your classified military reports do not trouble me."

"I . . ." He glanced aside at Rian's white bubble, hovering near. "Agree."

Giaja's pale eyelids swept down in an accepting blink. Miles felt very strange. Was it a bribe to accept a prize for doing exactly what he'd been going to do, or not do, anyway?

Come to think of it . . . would his own Barrayarans think he had struck some sort of bargain? The real reason he'd been detained for that unwitnessed chit-chat with the Emperor last night began to glimmer up at last in his sleep-deprived brain. *Surely they can't imagine Giaja could suborn me in twenty minutes of conversation. Could they?*

"You will accompany me," Giaja went on, "on my left hand. It's time to go." He rose, assisted by the ba, who gathered up his robes.

Miles eyed the hovering bubbles in silent desperation. His last chance . . . "May I speak with you one more time, haut Rian?" he addressed them generally, uncertain which was the one he sought.

Giaja glanced over his shoulder, and opened his long-fingered hand in a permissive gesture, though he himself continued on at the decorous pace enforced by his costume. Two bubbles waited, one followed, and Benin stood guard just outside the open door. Not exactly a private moment. That was all right. There was very little Miles wanted to say out loud at this point anyway.

Miles glanced back and forth uncertainly at the pale glowing spheres. One blinked out, and there Rian sat, much as he had first seen her, stiff white robes cloaked by the inkfall of shining hair. She still took his breath away.

She floated closer, and raised one fine hand to touch his left cheek. It was the first time they had touched. But if she asked, *Does it hurt?*, he swore 'he'd bite her.

Rian was not a fool. "I have taken much from you," she spoke quietly, "and given nothing."

"It's the haut way, is it not?" Miles said bitterly.

"It is the only way I know."

The prisoner's dilemma . . .

From her sleeve, she removed a dark and shining coil, rather like a bracelet. A tiny hank of silken hair, very long, wound around and around until it seemed to have no end. She thrust it at him. "Here. It was all I could think of."

That's because it is all you have that you truly own, milady. All else is a gift of your constellation, or the Star Crèche, or the haut, or your Emperor. You live in the interstices of a communal world, rich beyond the dreams of avarice, owning . . . nothing. Not even your own chromosomes.

Miles took the coil from her. It was cool and smooth in his hand. "What does this signify? To you?"

"I . . . truly do not know," she confessed.

Honest to the end. Does the woman even know how to lie? "Then I shall keep it. Milady. For memory. Buried very deep."

"Yes. Please."

"How will you remember me?" He had absolutely nothing on him that he could give away right now, he realized, except for whatever lint the embassy laundry had left in the bottoms of his pockets. "Or will it please you to forget?"

Her blue eyes glinted like sun on a glacier. "There is no danger of that. You will see." She moved gently away from him. Her force-screen took form around her slowly, and she faded like perfume. The two bubbles floated after the Emperor to seek their places.

The dell was similar in design to the one where the haut had held the elegiac poetry recitations, only larger, a wide sloping bowl open to the artificial sky of the dome. Haut-lady bubbles and haut- and ghem-lords in white filled its sides. The thousand or so galactic delegates in all their muted garbs crowded its circumference. In the center, ringed by a respectfully unpeopled band of grass and flowers, sat another round force-dome, a dozen meters or more in diameter. Dimly through its misted surface Miles could see a jumble of objects piled high around a pallet, upon which lay the slight, white-clad figure of the haut Lisbet Degtiar. Miles squinted, trying to see if he could make out the polished maplewood box of the Barrayaran delegation's gift, but Dorca's sword was buried somewhere out of sight. It hardly mattered.

But he was going to have a ringside seat, a nearly Imperial view of it all. The final parade, down an alley cleared to the center of the bowl, was arranged in inverse order of clout; the eight planetary consorts and the Handmaiden in their nine white bubbles, seven—count 'em folks, seven—ghem-governors, then the Emperor himself and his honor guard. Benin blended into ghem-General Naru's former place without a ripple. Miles limped along in Giaja's train, intensely self-conscious. He must present an astonishing sight, slight, short, sinister, his face looking as if he'd lost a spaceport bar fight the night before. The Cetagandan Order of Merit made a fine show against his House blacks, quite impossible to miss.

Miles supposed Giaja was using him to send some kind of signal to his haut-governors, and not a terribly friendly one. Since Giaja clearly had no plans to let out the details of the past two weeks' events, Miles could only conclude it was one of those *catch it if you can* things, intended to unnerve by doubt as much as knowledge, a highly delicate species of terrorism.

Yeah. Let 'em wonder. Well, not *them*—he passed the Barrayaran delegation near the front of the galactic mob. Vorob'yev stared at him stunned. Maz looked surprised but pleased, pointing at Miles's throat and saying something to her fiancé. Vorreedi looked wildly suspicious. Ivan looked . . . blank. *Thank you for your vote of confidence, coz.*

Miles himself stared for a moment when he spotted Lord Yenaro in the back row of ghem-lords. Yenaro was dressed in the purple and white garb of a Celestial Garden ghem-lord-in-waiting of the tenth rank, sixth degree, the lowest order. The lowest of the highest, Miles corrected himself. *Looks like he got that assistant perfumer's job after all.* And so the haut Fletchir Giaja brought another loose cannon under control. Smooth.

They all took their assigned places at the center of the bowl. A procession of young ghem-girls laid a final offering of flowers all around the central force-bubble. A chorus sang. Miles found himself attempting to calculate the price in labor alone of the entire month's ceremonies if one set the time of everyone involved at some sort of minimum wage. The sum was . . . celestial. He became increasingly aware that he hadn't had breakfast, or nearly enough coffee. *I will not pass out. I will not scratch my nose, or my ass. I will not—*

A white bubble drifted up in front of the Emperor. A short, familiar ba paced alongside it, carrying a compartmented tray. Rian's voice spoke from the bubble, ceremonial words; the ba laid the tray before Giaja's feet. Miles, at Giaja's left hand, stared down into the compartments and smiled sourly. The Great Key, the Great Seal, and all the rest of Lisbet's regalia, were returned to their source. The ba and the bubble retreated. Miles waited in mild boredom for Giaja to call forth his new Empress from somewhere in the mob of hovering haut-bubbles.

The Emperor motioned Rian and her ba to approach again. More formal phrases, so convoluted Miles took a full belated minute to unravel their meaning. The ba bowed and picked up the tray again on its mistress's behalf. Miles's boredom evaporated in a frisson of shock, muffled by intense bemusement. For once, he wished he were shorter, or had Ivan's talent for invisibility, or could magically teleport himself somewhere, anywhere, out of here. A stir of interest, even astonishment, ran through the haut and ghem audience. Members of the Degtiar constellation looked quite pleased. Members of other constellations . . . looked on politely.

The haut Rian Degtiar took possession of the Star Crèche again as a new Empress of Cetaganda, fourth Imperial Mother to be chosen by Fletchir Giaja, but now first in seniority by virtue of her genomic responsibility. Her first genetic duty would be to cook up her own Imperial prince son. God. Was she happy, inside that bubble?

Her new . . . not husband, mate, the Emperor—might never touch her. Or they might become lovers. Giaja might wish to emphasize his possession of her, after all. Though to be fair, Rian must have known this was coming before the ceremony, and she hadn't looked as tbough she objected. Miles swallowed, feeling ill, and horribly tired. Low blood sugar, no doubt.

Good luck to you, milady. Good luck . . . good-bye.

And Giaja's control extended itself, softly as fog. . . .

The Emperor raised his hand in signal, and the waiting Imperial engineers solemnly went into motion at their power station. Inside the great central force-bubble, a dark orange glow began, turning red, then yellow, then blue-white. Objects inside tilted, fell, then roiled up again, their forms disintegrating into molecular plasma. The Imperial engineers and Imperial Security had doubtless had a tense and sweaty night, arranging the Empress Lisbet's pyre with the utmost care. If that bubble burst now, the heat-effects would resemble a small fusion bomb.

It really didn't take very long, perhaps ten minutes altogether. A circle opened in the gray-clouded dome overhead, revealing blue sky. The effect was extremely weird, like a view into another dimension. A much smaller hole opened in the top of the force-bubble. White fire shot skyward as the bubble vented itself. Miles assumed the airspace over the center of the capital had been cleared of all traffic, though the stream diffused into faint smoke quickly enough.

Then the dome closed again, the artificial clouds scurrying away on an artificial breeze, the light growing brighter and cheerier. The force-bubble faded into nothingness, leaving only an empty circle of undamaged grass. Not even ash.

A waiting ba servitor brought the Emperor a colorful robe. Giaja traded off his outer layer of whites, and donned the new garment. The Emperor raised a finger, his honor guards again surrounded him, and the Imperial parade reversed itself out of the bowl. When the last major figure cleared the rim, the mourners gave a collective sigh, and the silence and rigid pattern broke in a murmur of voices and rustle of departing motion.

A large open float-car was waiting at the top of the dell to take the emperor . . . away, to wherever Cetagandan emperors went when the party was over. Would Giaja have a good stiff drink and kick off his shoes? Probably not. The attendant ba arranged the Imperial robes, and sat to the controls.

Miles found himself left standing beside the car as it rose. Giaja glanced over at him, and favored him with a microscopic nod. "Good-bye, Lord Vorkosigan."

Miles bowed low. "Until we meet again."

"Not soon, I trust," Giaja murmured dryly, and floated off, trailed by a gaggle of force-bubbles now turned all the colors of the rainbow. None paused as if to look back.

Ghem-General Benin, at Miles's elbow, almost cracked an expression. Laughing? "Come, Lord Vorkosigan. I will escort you back to your delegation. Having given your ambassador my personal word to return you, I must personally—*redeem* it, as you Barrayarans say. A curious turn of phrase. Do you use it in the sense of a soul in a religion, or an object in a lottery?"

"Mm . . . more in a medical sense. As in the temporary donation of a vital organ." Hearts and promises, all redeemed here today.

"Ah."

They came upon Ambassador Vorob'yev and his party, looking around as galactic delegates boarded float-cars for a ride to one last fantastical meal. The cars' white silk seats had all been replaced, in the last hour, by assorted colored silks, signifying the end of the official mourning. At no discernible signal, one came promptly to Benin. No waiting in line for them.

"If we left now," Miles noted to Ivan, "we could be in orbit in an hour."

"But—the ghem-ladies might be at the buffet," Ivan protested. "Women like food, y'know."

Miles was starving. "In that case, definitely leave straightaway," he said firmly.

Benin, perhaps mindful of his Celestial Master's last broad hint, supported this with a bland, "That sounds like a good choice, Lord Vorkosigan."

Vorob'yev pursed his lips; Ivan's shoulders slumped slightly.

Vorreedi nodded at Miles's throat, a glint of puzzled suspicion in his eyes. "What was *that* all about . . . Lieutenant?"

Miles fingered his silken collar with the Cetagandan Imperial Order of Merit attached. "My reward. And my punishment. It seems the haut Fletchir Giaja has a low taste for high irony."

Maz, who had obviously not yet been brought up to speed on the subtext of the situation, protested his lack of enthusiasm. "But it's an extraordinary honor, Lord Vorkosigan! There are Cetagandan ghem-officers who would gladly die for it!"

Vorob'yev explained coolly, "But rumors of it will hardly make him popular at home, love. Particularly circulating, as they must, without any real explanation attached. Even more particularly in light of the fact that Lord Vorkosigan's military assignment is in Barrayaran Imperial Security. From the Barrayaran point of view, it looks . . . well, it looks *very* strange."

Miles sighed. His headache was coming on again. "I know. Maybe I can get Illyan to classify it secret."

"About three thousand people just saw it!" Ivan said.

Miles stirred. "Well, that's your fault."

"Mine!"

"Yeah. If you'd brought me two or three coffee bulbs this morning, instead of only one, my brain might have been on-line, and I could've ducked faster and avoided this. Bloody slow reflexes. The implications are still dawning on me." For example: if he had *not* bowed his head to Giaja's silk collar in polite compliance, how dramatically would the chances have risen of his and Ivan's jumpship meeting some unfortunate accident while exiting the Cetagandan Empire?

Vorreedi's brows twitched. "Yes . . ." he said. "What *did* you and the Cetagandans talk about last night, after Lord Vorpatril and I were excluded?"

"Nothing. They never asked me anything more." Miles grinned blackly. "That's the beauty of it, of course. Let's see *you* prove a negative, Colonel. Just try. I want to watch."

After a long pause, Vorreedi slowly nodded. "I see."

"Thank you for that, sir," breathed Miles.

Benin escorted them all to the South Gate, and saw them out for the last time.

The planet of Eta Ceta was fading in the distance, though not fast enough to suit Miles. He switched off the monitor in his bunk aboard the ImpSec courier vessel, and lay back to nibble a bit more from his plain dry ration bar, and hope for sleep. He wore loose and wrinkled black fatigues, and no boots at all. He wriggled his toes in their unaccustomed freedom. If he played it right, he might be able to finesse his way through the entire two-week trip home barefoot. The Cetagandan Order of Merit, hung above his head, swayed slightly on its colored ribbon, gleaming in the soft light. He scowled meditatively at it.

A familiar double-knock sounded on his cabin door; for a moment he longed to feign sleep. Instead he sighed, and pushed himself up on his elbow. "Enter, Ivan."

Ivan had skinned out of his dress uniform and into fatigues as fast as possible also. And friction-slippers, hah. He had a sheaf of colored papers in his hand.

"Just thought I'd share these with you," Ivan said. "Vorreedi's clerk handed 'em to me just as we were leaving the embassy. Everything we're going to be missing tonight, and for the next week." He switched on Miles's disposal chute, in the wall. A yellow paper. "Lady Benello." He popped it in; it whooshed into oblivion. A green one. "Lady Arvin." Whoosh. An enticing turquoise one; Miles could smell the perfume from his bunk. "The inestimable Veda." Whoosh—

"I get the point, Ivan," Miles growled.

"And the food," Ivan sighed. "—*why* are you eating that disgusting rat bar? Even courier ship stores can do better than that!"

"I wanted something plain."

"Indigestion, eh? Your stomach acting up again? No blood leakage, I hope."

"Only in my brain. Look, why are you here?"

"I just wanted to share my virtuous divesting of my life of decadent Cetagandan luxury," Ivan said primly. "Sort of like shaving my head and becoming a monk. For the next two weeks, anyway." His eye fell on the Order of Merit, turning slowly on its ribbon. "Want me to put that down the disposer too? Here, I'll get rid of it for you—" He made to grab it.

Miles came up out of his bunk in a posture of defense like a wolverine out of its burrow. "Will you get out of here!"

"Ha! I *thought* that little bauble meant more to you than you were letting on to Vorreedi and Vorob'yev," Ivan crowed.

Miles stuffed the medal down out of sight, and out of reach, under his bedding. "I frigging earned it. Speaking of blood." Ivan grinned and stopped circling for a swoop on Miles's possessions, settling down into the tiny cabin's station chair.

"I've thought about it, you know," Miles went on. "What it's going to be like, ten or fifteen years from now, if I ever get out of covert ops and into a real line command. I'll have had more practical experience than any other Barrayaran soldier of my generation, and it's all going to be totally invisible to my brother officers. Classified. They'll all think I spent the last decade riding in jumpships and eating candy. How am I going to maintain authority over a bunch of overgrown backcountry goons—like you? They'll eat me alive."

"Well," Ivan's eye glinted, "they'll try, to be sure. I hope I'm around to watch."

Secretly, Miles hoped so too, but he would rather have had his fingernails removed with pliers, in the old-fashioned ImpSec interrogation style of a couple of generations ago, than say so out loud.

Ivan heaved a large sigh. "But I'm still going to miss the ghem-ladies. And the food."

"There's ladies and food at home, Ivan."

"True." Ivan brightened slightly.

"S'funny." Miles lay back on his bunk, shoving his pillow behind his shoulders to prop himself half-up. "If Fletchir Giaja's late Celestial Father had sent the haut-women to conquer Barrayar, instead of the ghem-lords, I think Cetaganda would own the planet right now."

"The ghem-lords were nothing if not crude," Ivan allowed. "But we were cruder." He stared at the ceiling. "How many more generations, d'you think, before we can no longer consider the haut-lords human?"

"I think the operative question is, how many generations till the haut-lords no longer regard *us* as human." *Well, I'm used to that even at home. Sort of a preview of things to come.* "I think . . . Cetaganda will remain potentially dangerous to its neighbors as long as the haut are in transition to . . . wherever they're going. Empress Lisbet and her predecessors," *and her heiresses,* "are running this two-track evolutionary race—the haut fully controlled, the ghem used as a source of genetic wild cards and pool of variations. Like a seed company keeping strains of wild plants even when they only sell a monoculture, to permit development in the face of the unexpected. The greatest danger to everybody else would be for the haut to lose control of the ghem. When the ghem are allowed to run the show—well, Barrayar knows what it's like when half a million practicing social Darwinists with guns are let loose on one's home planet."

Ivan grimaced. "Really. As your esteemed late grandfather used to tell us, in gory detail."

"But if . . . the ghem fail to be consistently militarily successful in the next generation or so—our generation—if their little expansionist adventures continue to be embarrassing and costly, like the Vervain invasion debacle, maybe the haut will turn to other areas of development than the military in their quest for superiority. Maybe even peaceful ones. Perhaps ones we can scarcely imagine."

"Good luck," snorted Ivan.

"Luck is something you make for yourself, if you want it." *And I want it more, oh yes.* Keeping one eye out for sudden moves from his cousin, Miles re-hung his medallion.

"You going to wear that? I dare you."

"No. Not unless I have a need to be really obnoxious sometime."

"But you're going to keep it."

"Oh, yes."

Ivan stared off into space, or rather, at the cabin wall, and into space beyond by implication. "The wormhole nexus is a big place, and constantly getting bigger. Even the haut would have trouble filling it all, I think."

"I hope so. Monocultures are dull and vulnerable. Lisbet knew that."

Ivan chuckled. "Aren't you a little short to be thinking of re-designing the universe?"

"Ivan." Miles let his voice grow unexpectedly chill. "Why should the haut Fletchir Giaja decide he needed to be polite to me? Do you *really* think this is just for my father's sake?" He ticked the medallion and set it spinning, and locked eyes with his cousin. "It's not a trivial trinket. Think again about all the things this means. Bribery, sabotage, and real respect, all in one strange packet . . . we're not done with each other yet, Giaja and I."

Ivan dropped his gaze first. "You're a frigging crazy man, you know that?" After an uncomfortable minute of silence, he hoisted himself from Miles's station-chair, and wandered away, muttering about finding some real food on this boat.

Miles settled back with slitted eyes, and watched the shining circle spin like planets.

Ethan of Athos

For those who listened in the beginning:
Dee, Dave, Laurie, Barbara, R.J., Wes,
and the patient ladies of the M.A.W.A

Chapter One

The birth was progressing normally. Ethan's long fingers carefully teased the tiny cannula from its clamp.

"Give me hormone solution C now," he ordered the medtech hovering beside him.

"Here, Dr. Urquhart."

Ethan pressed the hypospray against the circular end-membrane of the cannula, administering the measured dose. He checked his instrumentation: placenta tightening nicely, shrinking from the nutritive bed that had supported it for the last nine months. Now.

Quickly he broke the seals, unclamped the lid from the top of the canister, and passed his vibrascalpel through the matted felt of microscopic exchange tubing. He parted the spongy mass, and the medtech clamped it aside and closed the stopcock that fed it with the oxy-nutrient solution. Only a few clear yellow droplets beaded and brushed off on Ethan's gloved hands. Sterility obviously uncompromised, Ethan noted with satisfaction, and his touch with the scalpel had been so delicate that the silvery amniotic sac beneath the tubing was unscored. A pink shape wriggled eagerly within. "Not much longer," he promised it cheerfully.

A second cut, and he lifted the wet and vernix-covered infant from its first home. "Suction!"

The medtech slapped the bulb into his hand, and he cleared

the baby's nose and mouth of fluid before its first surprised inhalation. The child gasped, squawked, blinked, and cooed in Ethan's secure and gentle grip. The medtech wheeled the bassinet in close, and Ethan laid the infant under the warming light and clamped and cut the umbilical cord. "You're on your own now, boy," he told it.

The waiting engineering technician pounced on the uterine replicator that had incubated the fetus faithfully for three-quarters of a year. The machine's multitude of little indicator lights were now all darkened; the tech began disconnecting it from its bank of fellows, to take downstairs for cleaning and re-programming.

Ethan turned to the infant's waiting father. "Good weight, good color, good reflexes. I'd give your son an A-plus rating, sir."

The man grinned, and sniffed, and laughed, and brushed a surreptitious tear from the corner of one eye. "It's a miracle, Dr. Urquhart."

"It's a miracle that happens about ten times a day here at Sevarin." Ethan smiled.

"Do you ever get bored with it?"

Ethan gazed down with pleasure at the tiny boy, who was waving his fists and flexing in his bassinet. "No. Never."

Ethan was worried about the CJB-9. He quickened his pace down the quiet, clean corridors of the Sevarin District Reproduction Center. He was ahead of the shift change, having come in early especially to attend the birth. The last half hour of the night shift was the busiest, a crescendo of completing logs and signing off responsibilities to the yawning incomers. Ethan did not yawn, but did pause to punch two cups of black coffee from the dispenser in the rear of the medtech's station before joining the night shift team leader in his monitoring cubicle.

Georos waved greeting, his arm continuing in a smooth pounce on the proffered cup. "Thanks, sir. How was vacation?"

"Nice. My little brother got a week's leave from his army unit to coincide with it, so we were both home together for a change. South Province. Pleased the old man no end. My brother's got a promotion—he's first piccolo now in his regimental band."

"Is he going to stay in, then, past the two years' mandatory?"

"I think so. At least another two years. He's developing his musicianship, which is what he really wants anyway, and that extra slew of social duty credits in his bag won't hurt a bit."

"Mm," Georos agreed. "South Province, eh? I wondered why you weren't haunting us in your off-hours."

"It's the only way I can really vacate—get out of town," Ethan admitted wryly. He stared up at the rows of readouts lining the cubicle. The night team leader fell silent, sipping his coffee, watching Ethan over the rim, disturbingly silent after exhausting the small talk.

Uterine Replicator Bank 1 was on-line now. Ethan keyed directly to Bank 16, where the CJB-9 embryo dwelt.

"Ah, hell." The breath went out of him in a long sigh. "I was afraid of that."

"Yeah," agreed Georos, pursing his lips in sympathy. "Totally non-viable, no question. I took a sonic scan night before last—it's just a wad of cells."

"Couldn't they tell last week? Why hasn't the replicator been recycled? There are others waiting, God the Father knows."

"Waiting on paternal permission to flush the embryo." Georos cleared his throat. "Roachie scheduled the father to come in for a conference with you this morning."

"Aw . . ." Ethan ran his hand through his short dark hair, disarranging its trim professional neatness. "Remind me to thank our dear chief. Have you saved any more wonderful dirty work for me?"

"Just some genetic repairs on 5-B—possible enzyme deficiency. But we figured you'd want to do that yourself."

"True."

The night team leader began the routine report.

Ethan was almost late for the conference with the father of the CJB. During morning inspection he walked into one replicator chamber to find the tech in charge bopping happily through his duties to the loud and raucous strains of "Let's Stay Up All Night," a screechy dance tune currently popular among the undesignated set, blaring out of the stimu-speakers. The driving beat set Ethan's teeth on edge; this could scarcely be the ideal pre-natal sonic stimulation for the growing fetuses. Ethan left with the soothing strains of the classic hymn "God of Our Fathers, Light The Way" rendered by the United Brethren String Chamber Orchestra swelling gently through the room, and the grumpy tech yawning pointedly.

In the next chamber he found one bank of uterine replicators running 75% saturated in the waste toxins carried off by the exchange solution; the tech in charge explained he'd been waiting for it to hit the regulation 80% before doing the mandatory filter changes. Ethan explained, clearly and forcefully, the difference between minimum and optimum, and oversaw the filter changes and the subsequent drop back to a more reasonable 45% saturation.

The receptionist beeped him twice before penetrating his lecture to the tech on the exact shade of lemon-colored crystal brightness to be expected in an oxygen and nutrient exchange solution operating at peak performance. He dashed up to the office level and stood panting a moment outside his door, balancing the dignity of a spokesman for the Rep Center versus the discourtesy of making a patron wait. He took a deep breath that had nothing to do with his gallop upstairs, fixed a pleasant smile on his face, and pushed open the door with the DR. ETHAN URQUHART, CHIEF OF REPRODUCTIVE BIOLOGY raised in gold letters on its ivory plastic surface.

"Brother Haas? I'm Dr. Urquhart. No, no—sit down, make yourself comfortable," Ethan added as the man popped nervously to his feet, ducking his head in greeting. Ethan sidled around him to his own desk, feeling absurdly shielded.

The man was huge as a bear, red from long days in sun and wind; the hands that turned his cap around and around were thick with muscle and callus. He stared at Ethan. "I was expecting an older man," he rumbled.

Ethan touched his shaved chin, then became self-conscious of the gesture and put his hand down hastily. If only he had a beard, or even a mustache, people would not be constantly mistaking him for a 20-year-old despite his six-foot frame. Brother Haas was sporting a beard, about a two-week growth, scrubby by comparison to the luxuriant mustache that proclaimed him a long-standing designated alternate parent. Solid citizen. Ethan sighed. "Sit, sit," he gestured again.

The man sat on the edge of his chair, clutching his headgear in earnest supplication. His formal clothes were out of fashion and fit, but painfully clean and tidy; Ethan wondered how long the fellow'd had to scrub this morning to get *every speck* of dirt from under those horny nails.

Brother Haas slapped his cap absently against his thigh. "My boy, doctor—is—is there something the matter with my son?"

"Uh—didn't they tell you anything on the comlink?"

"No, sir. They just told me to come. So I signed out the ground car from my commune motor pool, and here I am."

Ethan glanced at the dossier on his desk. "You drove all the way up here from Crystal Springs this morning?"

The bear smiled. "I'm a farmer. I'm used to getting up early. Anyway, nothing's too much trouble for my boy. My first, y'know—" he ran a hand over his chin, and laughed, "well, I expect that's obvious."

"How did you end up here at Sevarin, instead of your district Rep Center at Las Sands?" asked Ethan curiously.

"It was for the CJB. Las Sands said they didn't have a CJB."

"I see." Ethan cleared his throat. "Any particular reason you decided on CJB stock?"

The farmer nodded firmly. "It was the accident last harvest decided me. One of our fellows tangled wrong-end-to with a thresher—lost an arm. Typical farm accident, but they said, if only he'd got to a doctor sooner, they mighta saved it. The commune's growing. We're right on the edge of the terraforming. We need a doctor of our own. Everybody knows CJBs make the best doctors. Who knows when I'll get enough social duty credits for a second son, or a third? I meant to get the best."

"Not all doctors are CJBs," said Ethan. "And most certainly not all CJBs are doctors."

Haas smiled polite disagreement. "What are you, Dr. Urquhart?"

Ethan cleared his throat again. "Well—in fact, I'm a CJB-8."

The farmer nodded confirmation to himself. "They said you were the best." He stared hungrily at the Rep doctor, as if he might trace the lineaments of his dream son in Ethan's face.

Ethan tented his hands together upon his desk, trying to look kindly and authoritative. "Well. I'm sorry they didn't tell you more over the comlink—there was no reason to keep you in the dark. As you no doubt suspected, there *is* a problem with your, uh, conceptus."

Haas looked up. "My son."

"Uh—no. I'm afraid not. Not this round." Ethan inclined his head in sympathy.

Haas's face fell, then he looked up again, lips compressed with hope. "Is it anything you can fix? I know you do genetic repairs— if it's the cost, well, my commune brethren will back me—I can clear the debt, in time—"

Ethan shook his head. "There are only a couple dozen common disorders we can do something about—some types of diabetes, for example, that can be repaired by one gene splice in a small group of cells, if you catch them at just the right stage of development. Some can even be pulled from the sperm sample when we filter out the defective X-chromosome-bearing portion. There are many more that can be detected in the early check, before the blastula is implanted in the replicator bed and starts forming its placenta. We routinely pull one cell then, and put it through an automated check. But the automated check only finds problems it's programmed to find—the hundred or so most common birth defects. It's not impossible for it to miss something subtle or rare—it happens half-a-dozen times a year. So you're not alone. We usually pull it, and just fertilize another egg—it's the most cost-effective solution, with only six days invested at that point."

Haas sighed. "So we start over." He rubbed his chin. "Dag said it was bad luck to start growing your father-beard before birthday. Guess he was right."

"Only a set-back," Ethan reassured his stricken look. "Since the source of the difficulty was in the ovum and not the sperm, the Center isn't even going to charge you for the month on the replicator." He made a hasty note to that effect in the dossier.

"Do you want me to go down to the paternity ward now, for a new sample?" asked Haas humbly.

"Ah—before you go, certainly. Save you another long drive. But there's one other little problem that needs to be ironed out first." Ethan coughed. "I'm afraid we can't offer CJB stock any more."

"But I came all the way here just for CJB!" protested Haas. "Damn it—I have a right to choose!" His hands clenched alarmingly. "Why not?"

"Well . . ." Ethan paused, careful of his phrasing. "Yours is not the first difficulty we've had with the CJB lately. The culture seems to be—ah—deteriorating. In fact, we tried very hard—all the ova it produced for a week were devoted to your order." No need to tell Haas how frighteningly scant that production was. "My best techs tried, I tried—part of the reason we took a chance on the current conceptus was that it was the only fertilization we achieved that was viable past the fourth cell division. Since then our CJB has stopped producing altogether, I'm afraid."

"Oh." Haas paused, deflated, then swelled with new resolve. "Who does, then? I don't care if I have to cross the continent. CJB is what I mean to have."

Ethan wondered glumly why resolution was classed as a virtue. More of a damned nuisance. He took a breath, and said what he'd hoped to avoid saying: "No one, I'm afraid, Brother Haas. Ours was the last working CJB culture on Athos."

Haas looked appalled. "No more CJBs? But where will we get our doctors, our medtechs—"

"The CJB *genes* are not lost," Ethan pointed out swiftly. "There are men all over the planet who carry them, and who will pass them on to their sons."

"But what happened to the, the cultures? Why don't they work any more?" asked Haas in bewilderment. "They haven't—been poisoned or anything, have they? Some damned Outlander vandalism—"

"No, no!" Ethan said. Ye gods, what a riot *that* fabulous rumor could start. "It's perfectly natural. The first CJB culture was brought by the Founding Fathers when Athos was first settled—it's almost two hundred years old. Two hundred years of excellent service. It's just—senescent. Old. Worn out. Used up. Reached the end of its life-cycle, already dozens of times longer than it would have lived in a, ah," it wasn't an obscenity, he was a doctor and it was correct medical terminology, "woman." He hurried on, before Haas could make the next logical connection. "Now, I'm going to offer a suggestion, Brother Haas. My best medtech—does superb work, most conscientious—is a JJY-7. Now, we happen to have a very fine JJY-8 culture here at Sevarin that we can offer you. I wouldn't mind having a JJY myself if only . . ." Ethan cut himself off, lest he tip into a personal bog and wallow in front of this patron. "I think you'd be very satisfied."

Haas reluctantly allowed himself to be talked into this substitute, and was sent off to the sampling room he had first visited with such high hopes a month before. Ethan sighed, sitting at his desk after the patron had departed, and rubbed the worry around his temples. The action seemed to spread the tension rather than dissipate it. The next logical connection . . .

Every ovarian culture on Athos was a descendant of those brought by the Founding Fathers. It had been an open secret in the Rep Centers for two years and more—how much longer could it be until the general public picked up on it? The CJB was not the first culture to die out recently. Some sort of bell curve, Ethan supposed; they were on the up-slope, and rising dizzily. Sixty percent of the infants growing cozily, placentas tucked in their soft nests of microscopic exchange tubing in the replicators downstairs, came from just eight cultures. Next year, if his secret calculations were borne out, it would be even worse. How long before there was not enough ovarian material to meet growth demand—or even population replacement? Ethan groaned, picturing his future unemployment prospects—if he wasn't ripped apart by angry mobs of ursine non-fathers before then. . . .

He shook himself from his depression. Something would be done before things came to that pass, surely. Something *had* to break.

The worry made an ominous bass note under Ethan's pleasant routine for three months after his return from vacation. Another ovarian culture, LMS-10, curled up and died altogether, and EEH-9's egg cell production declined by half. It would be the next to go, Ethan calculated. The first break in the downward slide arrived unexpectedly.

"Ethan?" Chief of Staff Desroches' voice had an odd edge, even over the intercom. His face bore a peculiar suffused look; his lips, framed by glossy black beard and mustache, kept twitching at the corners. Not at all the morose pout that had been threatening over the past year to become permanent. Ethan, curious, laid his micropipette down carefully on the lab bench and went to the screen.

"Yes, sir?"

"I'd like you to come up to my office right away."

"I just started a fertilization—"

"As soon as you're done, then," Desroches conceded with a wave of his hand.

"What's up?"

"The annual census ship docked yesterday." Desroches pointed upward, although in fact Athos's only space station rode in a synchronous orbit above another quadrant of the planet. "Mail's here. Your magazines were approved by the Board of Censors—you've got a year's back issues sitting on my desk. And one other thing."

"Another thing? But I just ordered the journal—"

"Not your personal property. Something for the Rep Center." Desroches' white teeth flashed. "Finish up and come see." The screen blanked.

To be sure. A year's back issues of *The Betan Journal of Reproductive Medicine* imported at hideous expense, although of the highest degree of interest, would scarcely make Desroches' black eyes dance with joy. Ethan scurried, albeit meticulously, through the fertilization, placed the pod in the incubation chamber from which, in six or seven days' time if things went well, the blastula would be transferred to a uterine replicator in one of the banks in the next room, and zipped upstairs.

A dozen brightly labeled data disks were indeed neatly stacked on the corner of the Chief's comconsole desk. The other corner was occupied by a holocube of two dark-haired young boys riding a spotted pony. Ethan scarcely glanced at either, his attention instantly overwhelmed by the large white refrigeration container squarely in the center. Its control panel lights burned a steady, reassuring green.

"L. Bharaputra & Sons Biological Supply House, Jackson's Whole", the shipping label read. "Contents: Frozen Tissue, Human, Ovarian, 50 units. Stack with heat exchange unit clear of obstruction. This End Up."

"We *got* them!" Ethan cried in delight and instant recognition, clapping his hands.

"At last." Desroches grinned. "The Population Council's going to have one hell of a party tonight, I'll bet—what a relief! When I think of the hunt for suppliers—the scramble for foreign exchange—for a while I thought we were going to have to send some poor son out there personally to get them."

Ethan shuddered, and laughed. "Whew! Thank the Father nobody had to go through *that*." He ran a hand over the big plastic box, eagerly, reverently. "Going to be some new faces around here."

Desroches smiled, reflective and content. "Indeed. Well—they're all yours, Dr. Urquhart. Turn your routine lab work over to your techs and get them settled in their new homes. Priority."

"I should say so!"

Ethan set the carton tenderly on a bench in the Culture Lab, and adjusted the controls to bring the internal temperature up somewhat. There would be a wait. He would only thaw twelve today, to fill the culture support units waiting, cold and empty, for new life. Soberly, he touched the darkened panel behind which the CJB-9 had dwelt so long and fruitfully. It made him feel sad, and strangely adrift.

The rest of the tissue must wait for thawing until Engineering installed the bank of new units along the other wall. He grinned, thinking of the frantic activity that must now be disrupting that department's placid routine of cleaning and repairs. Some exercise would be good for them.

While he waited, he carried his new journals to the comconsole for a scan. He hesitated. Since his promotion to department head last year, his censorship status had been raised to Clearance Level A. This was the first occasion he'd had to take advantage of it; the first chance to test the maturity and judgment supposed necessary to handle totally uncut, uncensored galactic publications. He moistened his lips, and nerved himself to prove that trust not misplaced.

He chose a disk at random, stuck it into the read-slot, and called up the table of contents. Most of the two dozen or so articles dwelt, predictably but disappointingly, on problems of reproduction in vivo in the human female, hardly apropos. Virtuously, he fought down an impulse to peek at them. But there was one article on early diagnosis of an obscure cancer of the vas deferens, and better still one encouragingly titled, "On an Improvement in Permeability of Exchange Membrances in the Uterine Replicator." The uterine replicator had originally been invented on Beta Colony—long famous for its leading-edge technologies—for use in medical emergencies. Most of its refinements still seemed to come from there, even at this late date, a fact not widely appreciated on Athos.

Ethan called up the entry and read it eagerly. It mostly seemed to involve some fiendishly clever molecular meshing of lipoproteins and polymers that delighted Ethan's geometric reason, at least on the second reading when he finally grasped it. He lost himself for a while in calculations about what it would take to duplicate the work here at Sevarin. He would have to talk to the head of Engineering. . . .

Idly, as he mentally inventoried resources, he called up the author's page. "On An Improvement . . ." came from a university hospital at some city named Silica—Ethan knew little of off-planet geography, but it sounded appropriately Betan. What ordered minds and clever hands must have come up with that idea. . . .

"Kara Burton, M.D., Ph.D., and Elizabeth Naismith, M.S. Bioengineering . . ." He found himself looking suddenly, on screen, at two of the strangest faces he had ever seen.

Beardless, like men without sons, or boys, but devoid of a boy's bloom of youth. Pale soft faces, thin-boned, yet lined and time-scored; the engineer's hair was nearly white. The other was thick-bodied, lumpy in a pale blue lab smock.

Ethan trembled, waiting for the insanity to strike him from their level, medusan gazes. Nothing happened. After a moment, he unclutched the desk edge. Perhaps then the madness that possessed galactic men, slaves to these creatures, was something only transmitted in the flesh. Some incalculable telepathic aura? Bravely, he raised his eyes again to the figures in the screen.

So. That was a woman—two women, in fact. He sought his own reaction; to his immense relief, he seemed to be profoundly unaffected. Indifference, even mild revulsion. The Sink of Sin did not appear to be draining his soul to perdition on sight, always presuming he had a soul. He switched off the screen with no more emotion than frustrated curiosity. As a test of his resolution, he would not indulge it further today. He put the data disk carefully away with the others.

The freezer box was nearly up to temperature. He readied the fresh buffer solution baths and set them super-cooling to match the current temperature of the box's contents. He donned insulated gloves, broke the seals, lifted the lid.

Shrink wrap? *Shrink wrap?*

He peered down into the box in astonishment. Each tissue sample should have been individually containerized in its own nitrogen bath, surely. These strange gray lumps were wrapped like so many packets of lunch meat. His heart sank in terror and bewilderment.

Wait, wait, don't panic—maybe it was some new galactic technology he hadn't heard of yet. Gingerly, searched the box for instructions, even rooting down among the packets themselves. Nothing. Look and guess time.

He stared at the little lumps, realizing at last that these were not cultured tissue at all, but the raw material itself. He was going to have to do the growth culturing personally. He swallowed. Not impossible, he reassured himself.

He found a pair of scissors, cut open the top packet, and dropped its contents, plop, into a waiting buffer bath. He contemplated it in some dismay. Perhaps it ought to be segmented, for maximum penetration of the nutrient solution—no, not yet, that would shatter the cellular structure in its frozen state. Thaw first.

He poked through the others, driven by growing unease. Strange, strange. Here was one six times the size of the other little ovoids, glassy and round. Here was one that looked revoltingly like a lump of cottage cheese. Suddenly suspicious, he counted packets. Thirty-eight. And those great big ones on the bottom—once, during his youthful army service, he had volunteered for K.P. in the butcher's department, fascinated by comparative anatomy even then. Recognition dawned like a raging sun.

"That," he hissed through clenched teeth, "is a *cow's* ovary!"

The examination was intense, and thorough, and took all afternoon. When he was done, his laboratory looked like a first-year zoology class had been doing dissections all over it, but he was quite, quite sure.

He practically kicked open the door to Desroches' office, and stood hands clenched, trying to control his ragged breathing.

Desroches was just donning his coat, the light of home in his eye; he never turned off the holocube until he was done for the day. He stared at Ethan's wild, disheveled face. "My God, Ethan, what is it?"

"Trash from hysterectomies. Leavings from autopsies, for all I know. A quarter of them are clearly cancerous, half are atrophied, five aren't even *human* for God's sake! *And every single one of them is dead.*"

"What?" Desroches gasped, his face draining. "You didn't botch the thawing, did you? Not you—!"

"You come look. Just come look," Ethan sputtered. He spun on his heel, and shot over his shoulder, "I don't know what the Population Council paid for this crud, but we've been *screwed.*"

Chapter Two

"Maybe," the senior Population Council delegate from Las Sands said hopefully, "it was an honest error. Maybe they thought the material was intended for medical students or something."

Ethan wondered why Roachie had dragged him along to this emergency session. Expert witness? Another time, he might have been awed by his august surroundings: the deep carpeting, the fine view of the capital, the long polished ripple-wood table and the grave, bearded faces of the elders reflected in it. Now he was so angry he barely noticed them. "That doesn't explain why there were 38 in a box marked 50," he snapped. "Or those damned cow ovaries—do they imagine we breed minotaurs here?"

The junior representative from Deleara remarked wistfully, "Our box was totally empty."

"Faugh!" said Ethan. "Nothing so completely screwed up could be either honest or an error—" Desroches, looking exasperated, motioned him down, and Ethan subsided. "Gotta be deliberate sabotage," Ethan continued to him in a whisper.

"Later," Desroches promised. "We'll get to that later."

The chairman finished recording the official inventory reports from all nine Rep Centers, filed them in his comconsole, and sighed. "How the hell did we pick this supplier, anyway?" he asked, semi-rhetorically.

The head of the procurement subcommittee dropped two tablets of medication into a glass of water, and laid his head on his arms to watch them fizz. "They were the lowest bidder," he said morosely.

"You put the future of Athos in the hands of the lowest bidder?" snarled another member.

"You all approved it, remember?" replied the procurement head, stung into animation. "You insisted on it, in fact, when you found the next bidder would only send thirty for the same price. Fifty different cultures promised for each Rep Center—you practically peed yourself with glee, as I recall—"

"Let us keep these proceedings official, please," the chairman warned. "We have no time to waste either apportioning or evading blame. The galactic census ship breaks orbit in four days, and is the only vector for our decisions until next year."

"We should have our own jump ships," remarked a member. "Then we wouldn't be treed like this, at the mercy of their schedule."

"Military's been begging for some for years," said another.

"So which Rep Centers do you want to trade in to pay for them?" asked a third sarcastically. "We and they are the two biggest items in the budget, next to the terraforming that grows the food for our children to eat while they're growing up—do you want to stand up and tell the people that their child-allotment is to be halved to give those clowns a pile of toys that produce nothing for the economy in return?"

"Nothing until now," muttered the second speaker cogently.

"Not to mention the technology we'd have to import—and what, pray tell, are we going to export to pay for it? It took all our surplus just to—"

"So make the jump ships pay for themselves. If we had them, we could export *something* and obtain enough galactic currency to—"

"It would directly contravene the purposes of the Founding Fathers to seek contact with that contaminated culture," interjected a fourth man. "They put us at the end of this long pipeline in the first place precisely to protect us from—"

The chairman tapped the table sharply. "Debates on larger issues belong in the General Council, gentlemen. We are met today to address a specific problem, and quickly." His flat, irritated tone did not invite contradiction. There was a general stirring and shuffling of notes and straightening of spines.

The junior member from Barca, poked by his senior, cleared his throat. "There is one possible solution, without going off-planet. We could grow our own."

"It's exactly because our cultures *won't* grow any more that we—" began another man.

"No, no, I understand that—none better," said the Barca man, a Chief of Staff like Deroches, hastily. "I meant, ah . . ." he cleared his throat again. "Grow some female fetuses of our own. They need not even be brought to term, quite. Then raid them for ovarian material and, er, begin again."

There was a revolted silence around the table. The chairman looked like a man sucking on a lemon. The member from Barca shrank in his seat.

The chairman spoke at last. "We're not that desperate yet. Although it may be well to have spoken what others will surely think of eventually."

"It needn't be public knowledge," the Barca man offered.

"I should hope not," agreed the chairman dryly. "The possibility is noted. Members will mark this section of the record classified. But I point out, for all, that this proposal does not address the other, perennial problem faced by this Council, and Athos: maintaining genetic variety. It had not pressed on our generation— until now—but we all knew it had to be faced in the future." His tones grew more mellow. "We would be shirking our responsibilities to ignore it now and let it be dumped on our grandsons in the form of a crisis."

There was a murmur of relief around the table, as logic safely propped emotional conviction. Even the junior member from Barca looked happier. "Quite." "Exactly." "Just so—" "Better to kill two chickens with one stone, if we can—"

"Immigration would help," put in another member, who doubled, one week a year, as Athos's Department of Immigration and Naturalization. "If we could get some."

"How many immigrants came on this year's ship?" asked the man across from him.

"Three."

"Hell. Is that an all-time low?"

"No, year before last there were only two. And two years before that there weren't any." The Immigration man sighed. "By rights we ought to be flooded with refugees. Maybe the Founding Fathers were just too thorough about picking a planet away from it all. I sometimes wonder if anyone out there has heard of us."

"Maybe the knowledge is suppressed, by, you know—*them*."

"Maybe the men trying to get here are turned away at Kline Station," opined Deroches.

"Maybe only a few are allowed to trickle in."

"It's true," agreed the immigration man, "the ones we do get tend to be a little—well—strange."

"No wonder, considering they're all products of that, uh, traumatic genesis. Not their fault."

The chairman tapped the table again. "We shall continue this later. We are agreed, then, to pursue our first choice of an off-planet supply of cultured tissue—"

Ethan, still fuming, steamed into speech. "Sirs! You're not thinking of going back to those scalpers—" Desroches pulled him firmly back into his seat.

"From some more reputable source," the chairman finished smoothly, with an odd look at Ethan. Not disapproval; a sort of smiling, silky smugness. "Gentlemen delegates?"

A murmur of approval rose around the table.

"The ayes have it; it is so moved. I think we also agree not to make the same mistake twice; no more sight-unseen purchases. It follows that we must now choose an agent. Dr. Desroches?"

Desroches stood. "Thank you, Mr. Chairman. I have given some thought to this problem. Of course, the ideal purchasing agent must first of all have the technical know-how to evaluate, choose, package, and transport the cultures. That narrows the possible choices considerably, right there. He must also be a man of proven integrity, not merely because he will be responsible for nearly all the foreign exchange Athos can muster this year—"

"All of it," the chairman corrected quietly. "The General Council approved it this morning."

Desroches nodded, "And not only because the whole future of Athos will depend on his good judgment, but also that he have the moral fibre to resist, er, whatever it is out there that, ah, he may encounter."

Women, of course, and whatever it was they did to men. Was Roachie volunteering, Ethan wondered? He certainly knew the technical end. Ethan admired his courage, even if his self-description was bordering on the swelled-headed. Probably needed it, to psyche himself up. Ethan did not begrudge it. For

Desroches to leave his two sons, on whom he doted, behind for a whole year . . .

"He should also be a man free of family responsibilities, that his absence not put too great a burden on his designated alternate," Desroches went on.

Every bearded face around the table nodded judiciously.

"—and finally, he should be a man with the energy and conviction to carry on regardless of the obstacles fate or, uh, whatever, may throw in his path." Desroches' hand fell firmly to Ethan's shoulder; the expression of smug approval on the chairman's face broadened to a smile.

Ethan's half-formed words of congratulation and commiseration froze in his throat. Running through his formerly-teeming brain was only one helpless, recycling phrase: *I'll get you for this, Roachie. . . .*

"Gentlemen, I give you Dr. Urquhart." Desroches sat, and grinned cheerily at Ethan. "*Now* stand up and talk," he urged.

The silence in Desroches' ground car on the drive back to Sevarin was long and sullen. Desroches broke it a little nervously. "Are you willing to admit you can handle it yet?"

"You set me up for that," growled Ethan at last. "You and the chairman had it all cooked up in advance."

"Had to. I figured you'd be too modest to volunteer."

"Modest, hell. You just figured I'd be easier to nail if I wasn't a moving target."

"I thought you were the best man for the job. Left to its own devices, God the Father knows what the committee would have picked. Maybe that idiot Frankin from Barca. Would you want to put the future of Athos in his hands?"

"No," Ethan began to agree reluctantly, then hardened. "Yes! Let *him* get lost out there."

Desroches grinned, teeth glinting in the faint tinted light from the control panel. "But the social duty credits you'll be getting— think of it! Three sons, a decade's accumulation in the normal course of events, earned in just one year. Generous, I think."

Ethan had a sudden poignant vision of a holocube for his own desk, filled with life and laughter. Ponies indeed, and long holidays sailing in the sunshine, passing on the subtleties of wind and water as his father had taught him, and the tumble, noise, and chaos of a home teeming with the future. . . . But he said glumly,

"*If* I succeed, and *if* I get back. And anyway, I have enough social duty credits for a son and a half. It would have meant a hell of a lot more if they'd coughed up enough credits to qualify my designated alternate."

"If you'll forgive my frankness, people like your foster brother are just the reason social duty credits may not be transferred," said Desroches. "He's a charming young man, Ethan, but even you must admit he's totally irresponsible."

"He's young," argued Ethan uneasily. "He just needs a bit more time to settle."

"Three years younger than you, I believe? Bull. He'll never settle as long as he can sponge off you. I think you'd do a lot better for yourself to find a qualified D.A. and make him your partner than try to make a D.A. out of Janos."

"Let's leave my personal life out of this, huh?" snapped Ethan, secretly stung; then added somewhat inconsistently, "which this mission is going to totally disrupt, by the way. Thanks heaps." He hunched down in the passenger side as the car knifed the night.

"It could be worse," said Desroches. "We really could have activated your Army Reserve status, made it a military order, and sent you out on a corpsman's pay. Fortunately, you saw the light."

"I didn't think you were bluffing."

"We weren't." Desroches sighed, and grew less jocular. "We didn't pick you casually, Ethan. You're not going to be an easy man to replace at Sevarin."

Desroches dropped Ethan off at the garden apartment he shared with his foster brother, and continued on out of town with a reminder of an early start at the Rep Center tomorrow. Ethan sighed acknowledgement. Four days. Two only allowed to orient his chief assistant to his sudden new duties and wind up his own personal affairs—should he make a will?—one day of briefing in the capital by the Population Council, and then report to the shuttleport. Ethan's brain balked at the impossibility of it all.

So much would simply have to be left hanging at the Rep Center. He thought suddenly of Brother Haas's JJY son, successfully started three months ago. Ethan had planned to personally officiate at his birthday, as he had personally seen to his fertilization; alpha and omega, to savor however briefly and vicariously the joyous fruits of his labors. He would be long gone before that date.

Approaching his door, he tripped over Janos's electric bike, dumped carelessly between the flower tubs. Much as Ethan admired Janos's fine idealistic indifference to material wealth, he wished he'd take better care of his things—but it had always been so.

Janos was the son of Ethan's own father's D.A.; the two had raised all their sons together, as they had run their business together, an experimental and ultimately successful fish farm on the South Province coast, as they had melded their lives together, seamlessly. Between son and foster-son no line was ever drawn. Ethan the eldest, bookish and inquisitive, destined from birth to higher education and higher service; Steve and Stanislaus, born each within a week of the other, each flatteringly bred from their father's partner's ovarian culture stock; Janos, boundlessly energetic, witty as quicksilver; Bret, the baby, the musical one. Ethan's family. He had missed them, achingly, in the army, in school, in his too-good-to-be-passed-up new job at Sevarin.

When Janos had followed Ethan to Sevarin, eager to trade country life for town life, Ethan had been comforted. No matter that it had interrupted Ethan's tentative social experimentation. Ethan, shy in spite of his achievements, loathed the singles scene and was glad of an excuse to escape it. They had fallen comfortably back into the pattern of their early teenage sexual intimacy. Ethan sought comfort tonight, more inwardly frightened than even his sarcastic banter with Desroches had revealed.

The apartment was dark, too quiet. Ethan made a rapid pass through all the rooms, then, reluctantly, checked the garage.

His lightflyer was gone. Custom-built, first fruits of a year's savings from his recently augmented salary as department head; Ethan had owned it all of two weeks. He swore, then choked back the oath. He really had intended to let Janos try it, once the newness had worn off. Too little grace time left to start an argument over trifles.

He returned to the apartment, dutifully considered bed. No— too little time. He checked the comconsole. No message, naturally. Janos had doubtless intended to be home before Ethan. He tried the comlink to the lightflyer's number; no answer. He smiled suddenly, punched up a city grid on the comconsole, and entered a code. The beacon was one of the little refinements of the luxury model—and there it was, parked not two kilometers away at Founders' Park. Janos partying nearby? Very well, Ethan would get out of his domestic rut and join him tonight, and doubtless startle him considerably by not being angry about the unauthorized borrowing.

The night wind ruffled his dark hair and chilled him awake as he neared Founders' Park on the purring electric bike. But it was the sight of the emergency vehicles' flashing yellow lights that froze his bones. God the Father—no, no; no need to assume that just because Janos and the rescue squad were in the same vicinity, there was some causal connection.

No ambulance, no city police, just a couple of garage tows. Ethan relaxed slightly. But if there was no blood on the pavement, why the fascinated crowd? He brought the bike to a halt near the grove of rustling oak trees, and followed the spectators upturned faces and the white fingers of the searchlights into the high leafy foliage.

His lightflyer. Parked in the top of a 25-meter-tall oak tree.

No—*crashed* in the top of the 25-meter oak tree. Vanes bent all to hell and gone, half-retracted wings crumpled, doors sprung open, gaping to the ground; his heart nearly failed him at the sight of the dangling empty pilot restraint harness hanging out. The wind sighed, the branches creaked ominously, and the crowd did a hasty prudent backstep. Ethan surged through them. No blood on the pavement . . .

"Hey, mister, you better not stand under there."

"That's my flyer," Ethan said. "It's in a damned tree . . ." He cleared his throat to bring his voice back down an octave to its normal range. There *was* a certain hypnotizing fascination to it. He tore himself away, whirled to grab the garageman by his jacket.

"The guy who was flying that—where . . . ?"

"Oh, they took him off hours ago."

"General Hospital?"

"Hell no. *He* was feeling no pain at all. His friend got a cut on the head, but I think they just sent him home in the ambulance. City police station, I imagine, for the driver. He was singing."

"Aw, sh—"

"You say you own this vehicle?" a man in a city parks department uniform accosted Ethan.

"I'm Dr. Ethan Urquhart, yes?"

The parks man pulled out a comm panel and punched up a half-completed form. "Do you realize that tree is nearly 200 years old? Planted by the Founders themselves—irreplaceable historic value. And it's split halfway down—"

"Got it, Fred," came a shout from on high.

"Lower away!"

"—responsibility for damages—"

A creak of strained wood, a rustle from above, an "Ah," from the crowd—a high-pitched rising whine as an antigrav unit suddenly failed to phase properly.

"Oh, shit!" came a yowl from the treetops. The crowd scattered with cries of warning.

Five meters per second, thought Ethan with hysterical irrelevancy. Times 25 meters times *how* many kilograms?

The nose-down impact on the granite cobblestones starred the gleaming red outer shell of the flyer with fracture lines from front to rear. In the sudden silence after the great crunch Ethan could quite clearly hear an elfin tinkle of expensive electronic instrumentation within, coming to rest a little out of phase with the main mass.

Janos's blond head turned, startled, at Ethan's tread upon the tiles of the Sevarin City Police Station.

"Oh, Ethan," he said plaintively. "I've had a *hell* of a day." He paused. "Uh—did you find your flyer?"

"Yeah."

"It'll be all right, just leave it to me. I called the garage."

The bearded police sergeant with whom Janos was dealing across the counter snickered audibly. "Maybe it'll hatch out some tricycles up there."

"It's down," said Ethan shortly. "And I've paid the bill for the tree."

"The tree?"

"Damages thereto."

"Oh."

"How?" asked Ethan. "The tree, I mean."

"It was the birds, Ethan," Janos explained.

"The birds. Force you down, did they?"

Janos laughed uneasily. Sevarin's avian population, all descendants of mutated chickens escaped from the early settlers and gone feral, were a diverse lean lot already hinting at speciation, but still not exactly great flyers. They were considered something of a municipal nuisance; Ethan glanced covertly at the police sergeant's face, and was relieved by a marked lack of concern at the birds' fate. He didn't think he could face a bill for chickens.

"Yeah, uh," said Janos, "you see, we found out we could tumble 'em—make a close pass, they'd go whipping around like a whirligig. Just like flying a fighter, and dive-bombing the enemy . . ." Janos's hands began to make evocative passes through the air, heroic starfighters.

Athos had had no military enemies in 200 years. Ethan gritted his teeth, maintained reason. "And ended up dive-bombing the tree in the dark instead. I suppose I can see how that could happen."

"Oh, it was before dark."

Ethan made a quick calculation. "Why weren't you at work?"

"It was your fault, really. If you hadn't left before dawn on that joy junket to the capital, I wouldn't have overslept."

"I reset the alarm."

"You know that's never enough."

True. Getting Janos upright and correctly aimed out the door in the morning was as exhausting as setting-up exercises.

"Anyway," Janos continued, "the boss got shitty about it. The upshot was, uh—I got fired this morning." He seemed to be finding his boots suddenly very interesting.

"Just for being late? That's unreasonable. Look, I'll talk to the guy in the morning—somehow—if you want, and—"

"Uh, don't—don't bother."

Ethan looked at Janos's sunny, even features more closely. No contusions, no bandages on those long lithe limbs, but he was definitely favoring his right elbow. It might just be from the flyer accident—but Ethan had seen that particular pattern of barked knuckles before.

"What happened to your arm?"

"The boss and his pet goon got a little rough, showing me out the door."

"Damn it! They can't—"

"It was after I took a swing at him," Janos admitted reluctantly, shifting.

Ethan counted to ten, and resumed breathing. No time. No time. "So you spent the afternoon getting drunk with—who?"

"Nick," said Janos, and hunched, waiting for the explosion.

"Mm. I suppose that accounts for the onslaught on the birds, then." Nick was Janos's buddy for all the competitive games that left Ethan cold; in his darker and more paranoid moments, Ethan occasionally suspected Janos of having something on the side with him. No time now. Janos unhunched, looking surprised, when no explosion came.

Ethan dug out his wallet and turned politely to the police sergeant. "What will it take to spring the Scourge of the Sparrows out of here, Officer?"

"Well, sir—unless you wish to make some further charge with respect to your vehicle . . ."

Ethan shook his head.

"It's all been taken care of in the night court. He's free to go."

Ethan was relieved, but astonished. "No charges? Not even for—"

"Oh, there were charges, sir. Operating a vehicle while intoxicated, to the public danger, damaging city property—and the fees for the rescue teams . . ." The sergeant detailed these at some length.

"Did they give you severance pay, then?" Ethan asked Janos, running a confused mental calculation from his foster brother's last known financial balance.

"Uh, not exactly. C'mon, let's go home. I've got a hell of a headache."

The sergeant counted back the last of Janos's personal property; Janos scribbled his name on the receipt without even glancing at it.

Janos made the noise of the electric bike an excuse not to continue the conversation during the ride home. This was a strategic error, as it allowed Ethan time to review his mental arithmetic.

"How'd you buy your way out of that?" Ethan asked, closing the front door behind him. He glanced across the front room at the digital; in three hours he was supposed to be getting up for work.

"Don't worry," said Janos, kicking his boots under the couch and making for the kitchen. "It's not coming out of your pocket this time."

"Whose, then? You didn't borrow money from Nick, did you?" Ethan demanded, following.

"Hell, no. He's broker than I am." Janos pulled a bulb of beer from the cupboard, bit the refrigeration tube, and drew. "Hair of the dog. Want one?" he offered slyly.

Ethan refused to be baited into a diversionary lecture on Janos's drinking habits, clearly the intent.

"Yeah."

Janos raised a surprised eyebrow, and tossed him a bulb. Ethan took it and flopped into a chair, legs stretched out. A mistake, sitting; the day's emotional exhaustion washed over him. "The fines, Janos."

Janos sidled off. "They took them out of my social duty credits, of course."

"Oh, God!" Ethan cried wearily. "I swear you've been going backwards ever since you got out of the damned army! *Anyone* could have enough credits to be a D.A. by now, without volunteering for *anything*." A red urge to take Janos and bash his head into the wall shook him, restrained only by the terrible effort required to stand up again. "I can't leave a baby with you all day if you're going to go on like this!"

"Hell, Ethan, who's asking you to? I got no time for the little shit-factories. They cramp your style. Well—not *your* style, I suppose. You're the one who's all hot for paternity, not me. Working at that Center overtime has turned your brain. You used to be fun." Janos, apparently recognizing he had crossed the line of Ethan's amazing tolerance at last, was retreating toward the bathroom.

"The Rep Centers are the heart of Athos," said Ethan bitterly. "All our future. But you don't care about Athos, do you? You don't care about anything but what's inside your own skin."

"Mm," Janos, judging from his brief grin about to try to turn Ethan's anger with an obscene joke, took in his dark face and thought better of it.

The struggle was suddenly too much for Ethan. He let his empty beer bulb drop to the floor from slack fingers. His mouth twisted in sardonic resignation. "You can have the lightflyer, when I leave."

Janos paused, shocked white. "Leave? Ethan, I never meant—"

"Oh. Not that kind of leave. This has nothing to do with you. I forgot I hadn't told you yet—the Population Council's sending me on some urgent business for them. Classified. Top secret. To Jackson's Whole. I'll be gone at least a year."

"Now who doesn't care?" said Janos angrily. "Off for a year without so much as a by-your-leave. What about me? What am I supposed to do while you're . . ." Janos's voice plowed into silence. "Ethan—isn't Jackson's Whole a *planet?* Out there? With—with—*them* on it?"

Ethan nodded. "I leave in four—no, three days, on the galactic census ship. You can have all my things. I don't know—what's going to happen out there."

Janos's chiseled face was drained sober. In a small voice he said, "I'll go clean up."

Comfort at last, but Ethan was asleep in his chair before Janos came out of the bathroom.

Chapter Three

Kline Station was an accretion of three hundred years; even so Ethan was unprepared for the size of it, and the complexity. It straddled a region of space where no less than six fruitful jump routes emerged within a reasonable sublight boost of each other. The dark star nearby hosted no planets at all, and so Kline Station rode a slow orbit far out of its gravity well, cresting the stygian cold.

Kline Station had been full of history even when Athos was first settled; it had been the jumping-off point for the Founding Fathers' noble experiment. A poor fortress, but a great place to do business, it had changed hands a number of times as one or another of its neighbors sought it as a guardian of its gates, not to mention a source of cash flow. Presently it maintained a precarious political independence based on bribery, determination, suppleness in business practice, and a stiffness in internal loyalty bordering on patriotism. A hundred thousand citizens lived in its mazy branches, augmented at peak periods of traffic by perhaps a fifth as many transients.

So much Ethan had learned from the crew of the census courier. The crew of eight was all male not, Ethan found, out of regular rule or respect for the laws of Athos, but from the disinclination of female employees of the Bureau to spend four months on the round-trip voyage without a downside leave. It gave Ethan a little breather, before being plunged into galactic culture. The crew was courteous to him, but not so encouraging as to break through Ethan's own timid reserve, and so he had spent much of the two months en route in his own cabin, studying and worrying.

As preparation, he'd decided to read all the articles by and about women in his *Betan Journals of Reproductive Medicine.* There was the ship's library, of course, but its contents certainly had not been approved by the Athosian Board of Censors, and Ethan was not really sure what degree of dispensation he was supposed to have on this mission. Better to stock up on virtue, he reasoned glumly; he was probably going to need it.

Women. Uterine replicators with legs, as it were. He was not sure if they were supposed to be inciters to sin, or sin was inherent in them, like juice in an orange, or sin was caught from them like a virus. He should have paid more attention during his boyhood religious instruction, not that the subject had ever been anything but mysteriously talked around. And yet, when he'd read one *Journal* edited of names as a scientific test, he'd found the articles indistinguishable as to the sex of the author.

This made no sense. Maybe it was only their souls, not their brains, that were so different? The one article he'd been sure was a man's work turned out to be by a Betan hermaphrodite, a sex which hadn't even existed when the Founding Fathers had fled to Athos, and where did they fit in? He lost himself, for a while, imagining the flap in Athosian Customs should such a creature present itself for entry, as the bureaucrats tried to decide whether to admit its maleness or exclude its femaleness—it would probably be referred to a committee for about a century, by which time the hermaphrodite would have conveniently solved the problem by dying of old age. . . .

Kline Station Customs were made nearly equally tedious by the most thorough microbiological inspection and control procedure Ethan had ever seen. Kline Station, it appeared, cared not if you were smuggling guns, drugs, or political refugees, as long as your shoes harbored no mutant fungi. Ethan's terror and—he admitted to himself—ravenous curiosity had mounted to a fever when he was at last permitted to walk through the flex tube from the courier into the rest of the universe.

The rest of the universe was disappointing at first glance, a dingy chilly freighter docking bay. The mechanical working side of Kline Station, to be sure, like the backside of a tapestry that probably made a fine show from some more intended perspective. Ethan puzzled over which of a dozen exits led to human habitation. The ship's crew was obviously busy, or out of sight; the microbial inspection team had dashed off as soon as its task was done, like as not to another job. A lone figure was leaning casually against a wall at the mouth of an exit ramp in the universal languid pose of idleness watching work. Ethan approached it for directions.

The crisp gray-and-white uniform was unfamiliar to Ethan, but obviously military even without the clue of the sidearm on the hip. Only a legal stunner, but it looked well-cared-for and not at all new. The slim young soldier looked up at Ethan's step, inventoried him, he felt, with one glance, and smiled politely.

"Pardon me, sir," Ethan began, and halted uncertainly. Hips too wide for the wiry figure, eyes too large and far apart above a small chiseled nose, jaw thin-boned and small, beardless skin fine as an infant's—it *might* have been a particularly elegant boy, but . . .

Her laughter pealed like a bell, entirely too loud for the reddening Ethan. "You *must* be the Athosian," she chuckled.

Ethan began to back away. Well, she didn't look like the middle-aged scientists portrayed in the *Betan Journal*. It was a perfectly natural mistake, surely. He had resolved earlier to avoid speaking to women as much as humanly possible, and here he was already— "How do I get out of here?" he mumbled, darting cornered glances around the docking bay.

She raised her eyebrows. "Didn't they give you a map?"

Ethan shook his head nervously.

"Why, that's practically criminal, turning a stranger loose in Kline Station without a map. You could go out looking for the commode and starve to death before you found your way back. Ah ha, the very man I'm looking for. Hi! Dom!" she hailed a courier crewman just now crossing the docking bay with a duffle slung over his shoulder. "Over here!"

The crewman changed course, his annoyance melting into the look of a man eager to please, if slightly puzzled. He stood straighter than Ethan had ever seen him, sucking in his gut. "Do I know you, ma'am—I hope?"

"Well, you ought to—you sat next to me in disaster drill class for two years. I admit it's been a while." She ran a hand through her dark cropped curls. "Picture longer hair. C'mon, the re-gen didn't change my face *that* much! I'm Elli."

His mouth made an "o" of astonishment. "By the gods! Elli Quinn? What have you done to yourself?"

She touched one molded cheekbone. "Complete facial regeneration. Do you like it?"

"It's fantastic!"

"Betan work, you know—the best."

"Yeah, but—" Dom's face puckered. "Why? It's not like you were so hard to look at, before you ran off to join the mercenaries." He gave her a grin that was like a sly poke in the ribs, although his hands were clasped behind his back like a boy's at a bakery window. "Or did you strike it rich?"

She touched her face again, less cheerfully. "No, I haven't taken up hijacking. It was sort of a necessity—caught a plasma beam to the head in a boarding battle out Tau Verde way, a few years back. I looked a little funny with no face at all, so Admiral Naismith, who does not do things by halves, bought me a new one."

"Oh," said Dom, quelled.

Ethan, who found his enthusiasm over the woman's facial aesthetics a trifle baffling, had no trouble sympathizing with this; any plasma burn was horrendous—this one must have come close to killing her. He eyed the face with a new medical interest.

"Didn't you start out with Admiral Oser's group?" asked Dom. "That's still his uniform, isn't it?"

"Ah. Allow me to introduce myself. Commander Elli Quinn, Dendarii Free Mercenary Fleet, at your service." She bowed with a flourish. "The Dendarii sort of annexed Oser, and his uniforms, and me—and it's been a step up in the world, let me tell you. But I, sir, have home leave for the first time in ten years, and intend to enjoy it. Popping up beside old classmates and giving them heart failure—flashing my credit rating in front of all the people who predicted I'd come to a bad end—speaking of coming to a bad end, you seem to have turned your passenger here loose without a map."

Dom eyed the mercenary officer suspiciously. "That wasn't intended as a pun, was it? I've been on this run four years, and I am so damned tired of coming back to a lot of half-witted bend-over jokes—"

The mercenary woman's laughter burst against the overhead

girders, her head thrown back. "The secret of your abandonment revealed, Athosian," she said to Ethan. "Should I take him in hand, then, being by virtue of my sex innocent of the suspicion of, er, unnatural lusts?"

"For all of me, you can," allowed Dom, shrugging. "*I* have a wife to get home to." He walked pointedly around Ethan.

"Good-oh. I'll look you up later, all right?" said the woman.

The crewman nodded to her, rather regretfully, and trod off up the exit ramp. Ethan, left alone with the woman, suppressed an urge to run after him begging protection. Recalling vaguely that economic servitude was one of the marks of the damned, he had a sudden horrible suspicion that she might be after his money—and he was carrying Athos's entire purse for the year. He became intensely conscious of her sidearm.

Amusement livened her strange face. "Don't look so worried. I'm not going to eat you," she snickered suddenly, "—conversion therapy not being my line."

"Glck," blurted Ethan, and cleared his throat. "I am a faithful man," he quavered. "To, to Janos. Would you like to see a picture of Janos?"

"I'll take your word for it," she replied easily. The amusement softened to something like sympathy. "I really have you spooked, don't I? What, am I by chance the first woman you've met?"

Ethan nodded. Twelve exits, and he had to pick this one. . . .

She sighed. "I believe you." She paused thoughtfully. "You could use a faithful native guide, though. Kline Station has a reputation for travelers' aid to uphold—it's good for business. And I'm a friendly cannibal."

Ethan shook his head with a paralyzed smile.

She shrugged. "Well, maybe when you get over your culture shock I'll run across you again. Are you going to have a long layover?" She pulled an object from her pocket, a tiny holovid projector. "You get one of these automatically when you get off a proper passenger ship—I don't need mine." A colorful schematic sprang into the air. "We're here. You want to be here, in the branch called Transients' Lounge—nice facilities, you can get a room—actually, you can get most anything, but I fancy you'd prefer the staid end of things. This section. Up this ramp and take the second cross-corridor. Know how to operate this thing? Good luck—" She pressed the map module into his hand, flashed a last smile, and vanished into another exit.

He gathered his meager belongings and found his way to the transients' area eventually, after only a few wrong turns. He passed many more women en route, infesting the corridors, the bubble-car tubes, the slidewalks and lift tubes and arcades, but thankfully none accosted him. They seemed to be everywhere. One had a helpless infant in her arms. He stifled a heroic impulse to snatch the child out of danger. He could hardly complete his mission with a baby in tow and besides, he couldn't possibly rescue them all. It also occurred to him, belatedly, as he dodged a squad of giggling children racing across his path to swoop like sparrows up a lift tube, that there was a 50% chance the infant was female anyway. It assuaged his conscience a little.

Ethan chose a room on the basis of price, after an alarming teleconference between the transient hostel's concierge, the Kline Station public computer system, a Transients' Ombudsman, and no less than four live human officials on ascending rungs of the station's governing hierarchy about the exchange rate to be assigned to Ethan's Athosian pounds. They were actually quite kind in computing the most favorable translation of his funds, via two currencies of which Ethan had never heard, into the maximum possible number of Betan dollars. Betan dollars were one of the harder and more universally acceptable currencies available. Still he ended with what seemed far fewer dollars than he had had pounds before, and he passed hastily over the proferred Imperial Suite in favor of an Economy Cabin.

Economy proved more cabinet than cabin. When he was asleep, Etlian assured himself, he wouldn't mind. Now, however, he was wide awake. He touched the pressure pad to inflate the bed and lay on it anyway, mentally reviewing his instructions and trying to ignore an odd myopic illusion that the walls were pressing inward.

When the Population Council had finally sat down to calculate it, returning the shipment to Jackson's Whole with Ethan to demand their money back cost more than the dubious refund, so Jackson's Whole was scrubbed. Ethan was at last, after much debate, given broad discretionary powers to choose another supplier on the basis of the freshest information available at Kline Station.

There were subsidiary instructions. Keep it under budget. Get the best. Go as far afield as needed. Don't waste money on unnecessary travel. Avoid personal contact with galactics; tell them nothing of Athos. Cultivate galactics to recruit immigrants; tell them all about the wonders of Athos. Don't make waves. Don't let them push you around. Keep an eye peeled for additional business opportunities. Personal use of Council funds will be considered peculation, and prosecuted as such.

Fortunately, the Chairman had spoken to Ethan privately after the committee briefing.

"Those your notes?" he nodded to the clutch of papers and discs Ethan was juggling. "Give them to me."

And he dropped them into his oubliette.

"Get the stuff and get back," he told Ethan. "All else is gas."

Ethan's heart lifted at the memory. He smiled slowly, sat up, tossed his map module in the air and caught it in a smooth swipe, pocketed it, and went for a walk.

In Transients' Lounge Ethan found the bright face of the tapestry at last by the simple expedient of taking a bubble car through the tubes to the most luxurious passenger dock, turning around, and walking back the other way. Framed in crystal and chrome were sweeping panoramas of the galactic night, of other branches of the Station shot with candy-colored lights, of the glittering wheels of the earliest sections turning forever for the sake of their obsolete centrifugal gravities. Not abandoned—nothing was ever wholly abandoned in this society—but some put to less urgent uses, others half-dismantled for salvage that Kline Station might grow, like a snake eating its tail.

Within the soaring transparent walls of Transients' Lounge rioted a green fecundity of vines, trees in tubs, air ferns, orchids, muted tinkling chimes, bizarre fountains running backward, upside down, spiraling around the dizzy catwalks, lively intricate trickery with the artificial gravity. Ethan paused to stare in fascination for fifteen minutes at one fountain, sheeting water suspended in air, running endlessly in the form of a moebius strip. A breath away, across the transparent barrier, a cold that could turn all to stone in an instant lurked in deathly silence. The artistic contrast was overwhelming, and Ethan was not the only downsider transient who stood transfixed in open wonder.

Bordering the parks section were cafes and restaurants where, Ethan calculated, if he only ate once a week he might dine, and hostelries where patrons who could afford the restaurants four times a day dwelt. And theaters, and feelie-dream booths, and an arcade which, according to its directory, offered travelers the solace of some eighty-six officially established religions. Athos's, of course, was not among them. Ethan passed what was obviously the funeral procession of some philosophic person who spurned cryogenic storage in favor of microwave cremation—Ethan, eyes still full of the endless dark beyond the trees, thought he could understand a preference for fire over ice—and some mysterious ceremony whose principals, a woman wrapped in red silk and a man in spangled blue, were pelted with rice by giggling friends who then tied dozens of strings around the pair's wrists.

Coming to the core of the section, Ethan got down to business. Here were the consuls, embassies, and offices of commercial agents from a score of planets who shipped through the nexus of Kline Station's local space. Here, presumably, he would get a lead on a biological supplier who could fulfill Athos's needs. Then buy a ticket for the chosen planet, then—but Kline Station itself was sensory overload enough for one day.

Dutifully, Ethan at least peeked into the Betan Embassy. Unfortunately, its commercial directory computer interface was manned by what was obviously a female expediter. Ethan withdrew hastily without speaking to her. Perhaps he'd try later, during another shift. He pointedly ignored the collection of consuls representing the great syndicated houses of Jackson's Whole. Ethan did resolve to send House Bharaputra a stiff note of complaint, though, later.

Passing back through from this direction, Ethan's chosen hostel did indeed look staid. He estimated he'd walked a couple of kilometers through various levels from the luxury docks, but a curiosity that grew rather than faded with each new sight and discovery drew him out of Transients' Lounge entirely, into the Stationers' own sections. Here the decor diminished from staid to utilitarian.

The odors from a small cafeteria, tucked between a customized plastics fabricator and a pressure suit repair facility, reminded Ethan suddenly that he hadn't eaten since leaving shipboard. But there were a great many women within. He reversed the impulse and withdrew, feeling very hungry. A random walk led him down two more little tubes into a narrow, rather grubby commercial arcade. He was not far from the docking area by which he'd entered Kline Station.

His wanderings were arrested by the smell of overused frying grease drifting from one doorway. He peered into the dimly-lit interior.

A number of men in a kaleidoscope of Stationer work uniforms were lounging at tables and along a counter in attitudes of repose. It was evidently some sort of break room. There were no women present at all. Ethan's oppressed spirits lifted. Perhaps he could relax here, even get something to eat. He might even strike up a conversation. Indeed, remembering his instructions from the Athosian Department of Immigration, he had a duty to do so. Why not start now?

Ignoring a queasy subliminal feeling of unease—this was no time to let his shyness rule him—he entered, blinking. More than a break room. Judging from the alcoholic smell of the beverages, these men must be off-duty altogether. It was some sort of recreational facility, then, though it resembled an Athosian club not at all. Ethan wondered wistfully if one could get artichoke beer here. Being Stationer, it would more likely be based on algae or something. He suppressed a homesick twinge, moistened his lips, and walked boldly up to a group of half-a-dozen men in color-coded coveralls clustered around the counter. Stationers must be used to seeing Transients far more bizarrely dressed than his plain casual Athosian shirt, jacket, trousers, and shoes, but for a moment he wished for the doctor's whites he wore at the Rep Center, all clean and crisp from the laundry, that always lent him their reassuring sense of official identity.

"How do you do," Ethan began politely. "I represent the Bureau of Immigration and Naturalization of the Planet Athos. If I may, I'd like to tell you about the pioneering opportunities for settlement still available there—"

The sudden dead silence of his audience was interrupted by a large worker in green coveralls. "Athos? The Planet of the Fags? You on the level?"

"Can't be," said another, in blue. "Those guys never stick their noses off their home dirtball."

A third man, all in yellow, said something extremely coarse.

Ethan took a breath and began again, valiantly. "I assure you, I am indeed on the level. My name is Ethan Urquhart; I am myself a doctor of reproductive medicine. A crisis has arisen recently in our birth rate—"

Green-coveralls gave a bark of laughter. "I'll bet! Let me tell you what you're doing wrong, buddy—"

The coarse one, from whom alcoholic esters were wafting in high concentration, said something depressingly one-track. Green-coveralls chortled and patted Ethan familiarly on the stomach.

"You're in the wrong store, Athosian. Beta Colony's the place to go for a change-of-sex operation. After that, you can get knocked up in no time."

One-track repeated himself. Ethan turned to him, his outrage and confusion taking refuge in stiff formality. "Sir, you seem to have some sadly narrow preconceptions about my planet. Personal relationships are a matter of individual preference, and entirely private. In fact there are many communes, strict interpreters of the Founding Fathers, who take vows of chastity. They are highly respected—"

"Yeech!" cried Green-coveralls raucously. "That's even *worse!*" A roar of laughter went up from his co-workers.

Ethan felt his face flush. "Excuse me. I am a stranger here. This is the only place I've seen on Kline Station that is free of women, and I thought some reasonable discourse might be possible. It's a very serious—"

One-track made a loud remark in the same vein.

Ethan wheeled around and slugged him.

Then froze, horror-stricken at his own dreadful breach of control. This wasn't the behavior of an ambassador—he must apologize at once—

"Free of women?" One-track snarled, scrambling back to his feet, his eyes red and drunken and feral. "Is that why you came in here—bloody procuring? I'll show you—"

Ethan found himself secured abruptly from behind by two of One-track's burlier friends. He trembled, suppressing a terrified impulse to struggle and break free. If he stayed cool maybe he could still—

"Hey, fellows, take it easy," Green-coveralls began anxiously. "He's obviously just a transient—"

The first blow doubled Ethan over, his breath whistling between clenching teeth. The two pinioning him straightened him up again. "—what we do to your type," wham! "around here!"

Ethan found he had no breath left with which to apologize. He hoped desperately One-track wasn't going to make a very long speech. But One-track continued, punctuating Ethan regularly.

"—bloody—damned—nosing around our—"

A light, sardonic alto voice interrupted. "Aren't you a little worried by the odds? What if he gets loose, and gangs up on the six of you?"

Ethan twisted his head around; it was the mercenary woman,

Commander Quinn. She bounced lightly on her feet, head cocked alertly.

Green-coveralls swore reverently under his breath; One-track just swore. "Come on, Zed," said Green-coveralls, laying a hand on his comrade's arm, although never taking his eyes from the woman's face, "That's enough, I'm thinking."

One-track shook himself free. "And what's this dirt-sucker to you, Sweetie?" he snapped.

One corner of the woman's carved mouth twisted up; Blue-coverall's lips parted in entrancement. "Suppose I say I'm his military advisor?" she said.

"Fag-loving women," One-track swore, "are worse than the fags themselves—" and continued in crudeness.

"Zed," muttered Blue-coveralls, "can it. She's not a tech, she's a troop. Combat vet—look at her insignia—" There was a stir in the back of the room, as several neutral observers made prudent exits.

"All drunks are a pain," drawled the woman to the air, "but aggressive drunks are just plain disgusting."

One-track shoved toward her, mouthing confused obscenities. She waited in stillness until he crossed some invisible boundary. There was a sudden buzz and a flash of blue light. Ethan realized as the weapon spun in her hand and melted soundlessly back into its holster that the pause had been for stunner nimbus; all others in the group were out of range and untouched.

"Take a nap," she sighed. She glanced up at the two men still holding Ethan. "That your friend?" she nodded to the prone One-track, unconscious on the floor. "You should be more choosy. Friends like that can get you killed."

Ethan was hastily dropped. His knees buckled as he folded over his aching belly. The mercenary woman pulled him back to his feet. "C'mon, pilgrim. Let me take you back where you belong."

"I should have said, 'Why, are you missing yours?'," Ethan decided. "That's what I should have said to him. Or maybe—"

Commander Quinn's lips curved. Ethan wondered irritably why everyone around here seemed to find Athosians so amusing, except for the ones who acted as if he were offering them a dose of leprosy. A sudden new fear put him so off-balance he very nearly clutched the mercenary's arm. "Oh, God the Father. Are those constables?"

A pair of men were nearing them in the corridor. Their uniforms were pine green slashed with sky blue, and an intimidating array of equipment hung from their utility belts. Ethan felt a sudden stab of guilt. "Maybe I should turn myself in—get it over with. I did assault that man—"

Commander Quinn's mouth quivered with amusement. "Not unless you're incubating some rare new plant virus under your fingernails. Those guys are Biocontrol—the ecology cops. Underfoot all over Kline Station," she paused to exchange polite nods with the men, who passed on, and added under her breath, "bunch of compulsive hand-washers." She continued after a meditative moment, "Don't cross them, though. They have unlimited powers of search and seizure—you could find yourself being forcibly deloused, with no appeal."

Ethan thought about that. "I suppose station ecology is much less resilient than planetary."

"Balanced on a wire, between fire and ice," she agreed. "Some places have religion. Here we have safety drills. By the way, if you ever see a patch of frost forming anywhere but a docking bay, report it at once."

They re-entered Transients' Lounge. Her eyes were too penetrating, edgy with seriousness, for her quirking mouth, and they made Ethan hideously uneasy. "Hope that little incident doesn't put you off Stationers," she said. "What say I take you to dinner, to make up for my fellow citizens' bad manners?"

Was this some sort of proposition, a ploy to get him alone and helpless? He edged farther from her, as she paced softly beside him like a predatory cat.

"I—I'm not ungrateful," he stammered, his voice rising in pitch, "but, uh, I have a stomach ache," quite true, "thank you anyway," there was a lift tube to the next level, the one his hostel was on, "good-bye!"

He bolted for the tube, leaped in. Reaching upward did nothing to speed his ascent. His last shreds of dignity kept him from flapping his arms. He offered her a strained smile through the crystal sides of the tube as her level fell away in dreamy slowness, distorted, foreshortened, blinked out.

He nipped out of the tube at his exit and darted behind a sort of free-form sculpture with plants nearby in the mallway. He peered through the leaves. She did not chase him. He unwound eventually, slumping on a bench for a long, numb time. Safe at last.

He heaved a sigh and got to his feet, and dragged off up the mall. His little cubicle seemed newly attractive. Something very bland to eat from the room service console, a shower, and bed. No more exploratory adventures. Tomorrow he would get right to business. Gather his data, choose the supplier, and ship out on the first available transport . . .

A man dressed in some planetary fashion of dull neutrality, plain gray tunic and trousers, approached Ethan on the esplanade, smiling. "Dr. Urquhart?" He grasped Ethan's arm.

Ethan smiled back in uncertain courtesy. Then stiffened, his mouth opening to cry indignant protest as the hypospray prickled his arm. A heartbeat, and his mouth slackened, the cry unspent. The man guided him gently toward a bubble car in the tubeway.

Ethan's feet felt vague, like balloons. He hoped the man wouldn't let go, lest he bob helplessly up to the ceiling and hang upside down with things falling out of his pockets on the passersby. The mirrored canopy of the bubble car closed over his unfocused gaze like a nictitating membrane.

Chapter Four

◥◥◥◥◥◥◥

Ethan came to awareness in a hostel room much larger and more luxurious than his own. His reason flowed with slow clarity, like honey. The rest of him floated in a sweet, languid euphoria. Distantly, under his heart, or down in his throat, something whined and cried and scratched frantically like an animal locked in a cellar, but there was no chance of its getting out. His viscous logic noted indifferently that he was bound tightly to a hard plastic chair, and certain muscles in his back and arms and legs burned painfully. So what.

Far more intriguing was the man emerging from the bathroom, rubbing his damp reddened face vigorously with a towel. Gray eyes like granite chips, hard-bodied, average height, much like the fellow who'd picked Ethan off the mall and who even now sat on a nearby float chair, watching his prisoner closely.

Ethan's kidnapper was of so ordinary an appearance Ethan could hardly keep him before his mind even when he was looking directly at him. But Ethan had the oddest insight, like X-ray vision, that his bones contained not marrow but ice stone-hard as that outside the Station. Ethan wondered how he manufactured red blood cells with this peculiar medical condition. Maybe his veins ran liquid nitrogen. They were both utterly charming, and Ethan wanted to kiss them.

"Is he under, Captain?" asked the man with the towel.

"Yes, Colonel Millisor," replied the other. "A full dose."

The man with the towel grunted and flung it on the bed, next to the contents of Ethan's pockets, and all his clothes, arrayed there. Ethan noticed his own nakedness for the first time. There were a few Kline Station tokens, a comb, an empty raisin wrapper, his map module, his credit chit for his Betan funds for purchasing the new cultures—the creature under his heart howled, unheard, at that sight. His captor poked among the spoils. "This stuff scan clean?"

"Ha. Almost," said the cold captain. "Take a look at this." He picked up Ethan's map module, cracked open its back, and fixed an electron viewer over its microscopic circuit board. "We shook him down in the loading zone. See that little black dot? It was caused by a bead of acid in a polarized lipid membrane. When my scanner beam crossed it, it depolarized and dissolved, and burned out—whatever had been there. Tracer for sure, probably an audio recorder as well. Very neat, tucked right in the standard map circuitry, which incidentally masked the bug's electronic noise with its own. He's an agent, all right."

"Were you able to trace the link back to its home base?"

The captain shook his head. "No, unfortunately. To find it was to destroy it. But we blinded them. They don't know where he is now."

"And who is 'they'? Terrence Cee?"

"We can hope."

The leader, the one Ethan's kidnapper had named Colonel Millisor, grunted again, and approached Ethan to stare into his eyes. "What's your name?"

"Ethan," said Ethan sunnily. "What's yours?"

Millisor ignored this open invitation to sociability. "Your full name. And your rank."

This struck an old chord, and Ethan barked smartly, "Master Sergeant Ethan CJB-8 Urquhart, Blue Regiment Medical Corps, U-221-767, *sir!*" He blinked at his interrogator, who had drawn back in startlement. "Retired," he added after a moment.

"Aren't you a doctor?"

"Oh, yes," said Ethan proudly. "Where does it hurt?"

"I hate fast-penta," growled Millisor to his colleague.

The captain smiled coldly. "Yes, but at least you can be sure they're not holding anything back."

Millisor sighed, lips compressed, and turned to Ethan again. "Are you here to meet Terrence Cee?"

Ethan stared back, confused. See Terrence? The only Terrence he knew was one of the Rep Center techs. "They didn't send him," he explained.

"Who didn't send him?" Millisor asked sharply, all attention.

"The Council."

"Hell," the captain worried. "Could he have found himself some new backing, so soon after Jackson's Whole? He can't have had time, or the resources! I took care of every—"

Millisor held up a hand for silence, probed Ethan again. "Tell me everything you know about Terrence Cee."

Dutifully, Ethan began to do so. After a few moments Millisor, his face reflecting increasing frustration, cut him off with a sharp chop of his hand. "Stop."

"Must have been some other fellow," opined the cold captain. His leader shot him a look of exasperation. "Try another subject. Ask him about the cultures," the captain suggested placatingly.

Millisor nodded. "The human ovarian cultures shipped to Athos from Bharaputra Biologicals. What did you do with them?"

Ethan began to describe, in detail, all the tests he'd put the material through that memorable afternoon. To his growing dismay, his captors didn't look at all pleased. Horrified, then mystified, then angry, but not happy. And he so wanted to make them happy. . . .

"More garbage," the cold captain interrupted. "What is all this nonsense?"

"Can he be resisting the drug?" asked Millisor. "Increase the dose."

"Dangerous, if you still mean to put him back on the street with a gap in his memory. We're running short of time for that scenario to pass."

"That scenario may have to be changed. If that shipment has arrived on Athos and been distributed already, we may have no choice but to call in a military strike. And deliver it in less than seven months, or instead of a limited commando raid to torch their Reproduction Centers, we'll be forced to sterilize the whole damned planet to be sure of getting it all."

"Small loss," shrugged the cold captain.

"Big expense. And increasingly hard to keep covert."

"No survivors, no witnesses."

"There are always survivors at a massacre. Among the victors, if nowhere else." The granite chips sparked, and the captain looked uncomfortable. "Dose him."

A prickle in Ethan's arm. Methodical and relentless, they asked him detailed questions about the shipment, his assignment, his superiors, his organization, his background. Ethan babbled. The room expanded and shrank. Ethan felt as if he were being turned inside out, with his stomach lining exposed to the world and his eyes twisted around and staring at each other. "Oh, I love you all," he crooned, and retched violently.

He came to with his head under the shower. They gave him a different drug, replacing his euphoria with disjointed terror, and badgered him endlessly about Terrence Cee, the shipment, his mission, together and by turns.

Their frustration and hostility mounting, they gave him a drug that vastly increased the firing rate of his sensory nerves, and applied instruments to his skin in areas of high nerve density that left no mark but induced incredible agony. He told them everything, anything, whatever they asked—he would gladly have told them what they wanted to hear, if only he could have guessed what it was—but they were merciless and unmoved, surgical in their concentration. Ethan became plastic, frantic, until at last all sensation was obliterated in a series of uncontrollable convulsions that nearly stopped his heart. At this they desisted.

He hung in his chair, breath shallow and shocky, staring at them through dilated eyes.

The leader glared back, disgusted. "Damnation, Rau! This man is a total waste of time. The shipment that he unpacked on Athos is definitely not what was sent from Bharaputra's laboratory. Terrence Cee has pulled a switch somehow. It could be anywhere in the galaxy by now."

The captain groaned. "We were so close to wrapping up the entire case on Jackson's Whole! No, damn it! It has to be Athos. We all agreed, it *had* to be Athos."

"It may still be Athos. A plan within a plan—within a plan. . . ." Millisor rubbed his neck wearily, looking suddenly much older than Ethan's first estimate. "The late Dr. Jahar did too good a job. Terrence Cee is everything Jahar promised—except loyal. . . . Well, we'll get no more out of this one. You sure that wasn't just a speck of dirt in that circuit board?"

The captain started to look indignant, then frowned at Ethan as though he were something he had found sticking to the bottom of his boot. "It wasn't dirt. But that's sure as hell not any agent of Terrence Cee's. Think he has any use as a stalking-goat?"

"If only he were an agent," said Millisor regretfully, "it would be worth a try. Since he evidently isn't, he has no value at all." He glanced at his chronometer. "My God, have we been at this seven hours? It's too late now to blank him and turn him loose. Have Okita take him out and arrange an accident."

The docking bay was cold. A few safety lights splashed color on walls and silvered the silhouettes of silent equipment isolated in the thick stretches of dimness. The metal catwalks arched through a high, echoing hollowness, emerging from shadows, converging in darkness, a spider's skyway. Mysterious mechanical bundles dangled from the girders like a spider's preserved victims.

"This should be high enough," muttered the man called Okita. He was almost as average-looking as Captain Rau, but for the compact density of his muscles. He manhandled Ethan to his knees. "Here. Drink up."

He forced a tube into Ethan's mouth and squeezed the bulb, for the nth time. Ethan choked, and perforce swallowed the burning, aromatic liquid. The dense man let Ethan drop. "Absorb that a minute," Okita told him, as though he had some choice in the matter.

Ethan clung to the mesh flooring of the catwalk, dizzy and belching, and stared through it at the metal floor far below. It seemed to gleam and pulsate in slow, seasick waves. He thought of his smashed lightflyer.

Captain Rau's chosen henchman leaned against the safety railing and sniffed reflectively, also looking down. "Falls are funny things," he mused. "Freaky. Two meters are enough to kill you. But I heard of a case where a fellow fell 300 meters and survived. Depends on just how you hit, I guess." The bland eyes flickered over the bay, checking entrances, checking for Ethan knew not what. "They run their gravity a little light here. Better break your neck first," Okita decided judiciously. "Just to be sure."

Ethan could not press his fingers through the narrow mesh to cling, though he tried. For an insane moment he thought of trying to bribe his assassin-to-be with his Betan credit chit, that his captors had carefully returned to his pockets along with all their other contents before sending them off like a pair of lovers looking for a dark place to tryst. Like a drunk and his loyal friend trying to guide him back to his hostel before he wandered drunkenly into the maze of the station and got lost. Ethan reeked of alcoholic esters, and his mumbled whimperings for help had been unintelligible to the amused passers-by in the populated corridors. His tongue seemed less thick now, but this place was unpopulated in the extreme.

A surge of loyalty and nausea shook him. No. He would die with his purse intact. Besides, Okita looked remarkably unbribable. Ethan didn't think he'd even be interested in delaying his execution for a little rape. At least the money could be taken from his crumpled body and returned to Athos. . . .

Athos. He did not want to die, dared not die. The terrifying scraps of conversation he'd overheard between his interrogators worried him like savage dogs. Bomb the Rep Centers? Banks of helpless babies crashing down, flames shooting up to boil away their gentle waterbeds—he shuddered, and shivered, and moaned, but could not drive his half-paralyzed muscles to his straining will. Vile, inhuman plans—so reasonably discussed, so casually dispatched . . . all insane here . . .

The dense man sniffed, and stretched, and scratched, and sighed, and checked his chronometer for the third time. "All right," he said at last. "Your biochemistry should be muddled enough by now. Time for your flying lesson, boy-o."

He grasped Ethan by the scruff of his neck and the seat of his pants, and boosted him up to the railing.

"Why are you doing this to me?" squeaked Ethan in a last desperate attempt to communicate.

"Orders," grunted the dense man with finality. Ethan stared into the bored, flat eyes, and gave himself up for murdered for the crime of being innocent.

Okita yanked his head back over the railing by the hair, and folded his hand around the squeeze bottle. The murky ceiling of the docking bay, crossed by girders above, blurred in Ethan's eyes. The cold metal rail bit his neck.

Okita studied the positioning, cocking his head and narrowing his eyes. "Right." Bracing Ethan's arching body against the railing with his knees, he raised doubled fists for a powerful blow.

The catwalk shook, a rattling jar. The panting figure raising the stunner in both hands did not pause to cry warning, but simply fired. She seemed to have dropped out of the sky. The shock of the stunner nimbus scarcely made any difference in Ethan's inventory of discomfort. But Okita was caught square on, and followed the momentum of his aimed blow over the railing. His legs, picking up speed, tilted up and slid past Ethan's nose, like a ship sinking bow-first.

"Aw, *shit*," yelled Commander Quinn, and bounded forward. The stunner clattered across the catwalk and spun over the side to whistle through the air and burst to sizzling shards far below. Her clutching swipe was just too late to connect with Okita's trouser leg. Blood winked from her torn fingernail. Okita followed the stunner, headfirst.

Ethan slithered bonelessly down to crouch on the mesh. Her boots, at his eye level, arched to tiptoe as she peered down over the side. "Gee, I feel really bad about that," she remarked, licking her bleeding finger. "I've never killed a man by accident before. Unprofessional."

"You again," Ethan croaked.

She gave him a cat's grin. "What a coincidence."

The body splayed on the deck below stopped twitching. Ethan stared down whitely. "I'm a doctor. Shouldn't we go down there and, um . . ."

"Too late, I think," said Commander Quinn. "But I wouldn't get too misty-eyed over that creep. Quite aside from what he almost did to you just now, he helped kill eleven people on Jackson's Whole, five months ago, just to cover up the secret I'm trying to find out."

His syrup-slow logic spoke. "If it's a secret people are killed just for knowing, wouldn't it make a lot more sense to try to *avoid* finding it out?" He clutched his shredded acuity. "Who are you really, anyway? Why are you following me?"

"Technically, I'm not following you at all. I'm following Ghem-colonel Luyst Millisor, and the so-charming Captain Rau, and their two goons—ah, one goon. Millisor is interested in you, therefore I am too. Q.E.D.—Quinn Excites Dismay."

"Why?" he whimpered wearily.

She sighed. "If I had arrived at Jackson's Whole two days ahead of them instead of two days behind them, I could tell you. As for the rest—I really am a commander in the Dendarii Mercenaries, and everything I've told you is true, except that I'm not on home leave. I'm on assignment. Think of me as a rent-a-spy. Admiral Naismith is diversifying our services."

She squatted beside him, checked his pulse, eyes and eyelids, battered reflexes. "You look like death warmed over, Doctor."

"Thanks to you. They found your tracer. Decided *I* was a spy. Questioned me . . ." He found he was shivering uncontrollably.

Her lips made a brief grim line. "I know. Sorry. I did save your life just now, I hope you noticed. Temporarily."

"Temporarily?"

She nodded toward the deck below. "Colonel Millisor is going to be quite excited about you, after this."

"I'll go to the authorities—"

"Ah—hm. I hope you'll think better of that. In the first place, I don't think the authorities would be able to protect you quite well enough. Secondly, it would blow my cover. Until now I don't think Millisor suspected I existed. Since I have an awful lot of friends and relatives around here, I'd just as soon keep it that way, Millisor and Rau being—what they are. You see my point?"

He felt he ought to argue with her. But he was sick and weak— and, it also occurred to him, still very high in the air. Green vertigo plucked at him. If she decided to send him after Okita . . . "Yeah," he mumbled. "Uh, what—what are you going to do with me?"

She planted her hands on her hips and frowned thoughtfully down upon him. "Not sure yet. Don't know if you're an ace or a joker. I think I'll keep you up my sleeve for a while, until I can figure out how best to play you. With your permission," she added in palpable afterthought.

"Stalking-goat," he muttered darkly.

She quirked an eyebrow at him. "Perhaps. If you can think of a better idea, trot it out."

He shook his head, which made shooting pains ricochet around inside his skull and yellow pinwheels counter-rotate before his eyes. At least she didn't seem to be on the same side as his recent captors. *The enemy of my enemy—my ally. . . ?*

She hoisted him to his feet and pulled his arm across her shoulders to thread their way down stairs and ladders to the docking bay floor. He noticed for the first time that she was several centimeters shorter than himself. But he had no inclination to spot her points in a free-for-all.

When she released him he sank to the deck in a dizzy stupor. She poked around Okita's body, checking pulse points and damages. Her lips thinned ironically. "Huh. Broken neck." She sighed, and stood regarding the corpse and Ethan with much the same narrow calculation.

"We could just leave him here," she said. "But I rather fancy giving Colonel Millisor a mystery of his own to solve. I'm tired of being on the damn defensive, lying low, always one move behind. Have you ever given thought to the difficulty of getting rid of a body on a space station? I'll bet Millisor has. Bodies don't bother you, do they? What with your being a doctor and all, I mean."

Okita's fixed stare was exactly like that of a dead fish, glassily reproachful. Ethan swallowed. "I actually never cared much for that end of the life-cycle," he explained. "Pathology and anatomy and so forth. That's why I went for Rep work, I guess. It was more, um . . . hopeful." He paused a while. His intellect began to crunch on in spite of himself. "*Is* it hard to get rid of a body on a space station? Can't you just shove it out the nearest airlock, or down an unused lift tube, or something?"

Her eyes were bright with stimulation. "The airlocks are all monitored. Taking anything out, even an anonymous bundle, leaves a record in the computers. And it would last *forever* out there. Same objection applies to chopping it up and putting it down an organics disposer. Eighty or so kilos of high-grade protein leaves too big a blip in the records. Besides, it's been tried. Very famous murder case, a few years back. The lady's still in therapy, I believe. It would definitely be noticed."

She flopped down beside him to sit with her chin on her knees, arms wrapped around her boots and flexing, not rest but nervous energy contained. "As for stashing it whole anywhere inside the Station—well, the safety patrols are nothing compared to the ecology cops. There isn't a cubic centimeter of the Station that doesn't get checked on a regular schedule. You *could* keep moving it around, but . . .

"I think I have a better idea. Yes. Why not? As long as I'm going to commit a crime, let it be a perfect one. Anything worth doing is worth doing well, as Admiral Naismith would say . . ."

She rose to make a wandering circuit of the docking bay, selecting bits of equipment with the faintly distracted air of a housekeeper choosing vegetables at the market.

Ethan lay on the floor in misery, envying Okita, whose troubles were over. He had been on Kline Station, he estimated, just about a day, and had yet to have his first meal. Beaten up, kidnapped, drugged, nearly murdered, and now rapidly becoming accessory-after-the-fact to a crime which if not exactly a murder was surely the next best thing. Galactic life was every bit as bad as anything he had imagined. And he had fallen into the hands of a madwoman, to boot. The Founding Fathers had been right.... "I want to go home," he moaned.

"Now, now," Commander Quinn chided, plunking down a float pallet next to Okita's body and rolling a squat cylindrical shipping canister off it. "That's no way to be, just when my case is showing signs of cracking open at last. You just need a good meal," she glanced at him, "and about a week in a hospital bed. Afraid I shan't be able to supply that, but as soon as I finish cleaning up here I will take you to a place you can rest a bit while I get the next phase started. All right?"

She unlatched the shipping canister and, with some difficulty, folded Okita's body into it. "There. That doesn't look too coffin-like, does it?" She made a rapid but thorough pass over the impact area with a sonic scrubber, emptied its receptacle bag in with Okita, hopped the canister back onto the pallet with a hand-tractor, and replaced everything else where she had found it. Lastly, and somewhat mournfully, she collected all the pieces of her stunner.

"So. That gives the project its first deadline. Pallet and drum must be returned here within eight hours, before the next scheduled docking, or they'll be missed."

"Who were those men?" he asked her, as she had him crawl onto the pallet and settle himself for the ride. "They were insane. I mean, everyone I've met here is crazy, but they—they were talking about bombing Athos's reproduction clinics! Killing all the babies—maybe killing everyone!"

"Oh?" she said. "That's a new wrinkle. First I've heard of that scenario. I am extremely sorry I didn't get to listen in on that interrogation, and I hope you will, ah, fill me in on what I missed. I've been trying to plant a bug in Millisor's quarters for three weeks, but his counter-intelligence equipment is, unfortunately, superb."

"You mainly missed a lot of screaming," said Ethan morosely.

She looked rather embarrassed. "Ah—yes. I'm afraid I didn't think they'd need to use anything but fast-penta."

"Stalking-goat," Ethan grumbled.

She cleared her throat, and sat cross-legged beside him with the control lead in her hand. The pallet rose into the air like a magic carpet.

"Not—not too high," Ethan choked, scrambling for a non-existent hand-hold. She brought it back down to a demure ten centimeters altitude, and they started off at a walking pace.

She spoke slowly, seeming to choose her words with great care. "Ghem-Colonel Luyst Millisor is a Cetagandan counter-intelligence officer. Captain Rau, and Okita, and another brawn by the name of Setti, are his team."

"Cetagandan! Isn't that planet pretty far from here to be interested in, um," he glanced at the Stationer woman, "us? This nexus, I mean."

"Not far enough, evidently."

"But why, in God the Father's name, should they want to destroy Athos? Is Cetaganda—controlled by women or something?"

A laugh escaped her. "Hardly. I'd call it a typical male-dominated totalitarian state, only slightly mitigated by their rather artistic cultural peculiarities. No. Millisor is not, per se, interested in either Athos or the Kline Station nexus. He's chasing—something else. The big secret. The one I was hired to find out."

She paused to maneuver the float pallet around a tricky ascending corner. "Apparently there was, on Cetaganda, a long-range, military-sponsored genetics project. Until about three years ago, Millisor was the security chief for that project. And the security was tight. In 25 *years*, no one had been able to find out what they were up to, beyond the fact that it seemed to be the one-man show of a certain Dr. Faz Jahar, a moderately bright Cetagandan geneticist who vanished from view about the time it started. Do you have any idea how incredibly long that is to keep a secret in this business? The thing has really been Millisor's life work, as well as Jahar's.

"In any event, something went wrong. The project went up in smoke—literally. The laboratory blew up one night, taking Jahar with it. And Millisor and his merry men have been chasing *something* around the galaxy ever since, blowing people away with the careless abandon of either homicidal lunatics, or—men scared out of their wits. And, ah, while I'm not sure I'd vouch for Captain Rau, ghem-Colonel Millisor does not strike me as a madman."

"You couldn't prove it by me," said Ethan glumly. There was still something not quite right with his vision, and tremula came and went in his muscles.

They came to a large hatch in the corridor wall. RENOVATION, said a bright sign. DO NOT ENTER. AUTHORIZED PERSONNEL ONLY.

Commander Quinn did something Ethan could not quite see to the control box, and the hatch slid open. She floated the pallet through. There came a voice, and a laugh, from the corridor they had just vacated. She closed the hatch quickly, leaving them in total darkness.

"There," she muttered, switching on a hand light. "Nobody saw us. Undeserved luck. Bloody time for it to start averaging out."

Ethan blinked at his surroundings. An empty rectangular basin was the centerpiece for a large airy chamber full of columns, pierced lattices, mosaics, and elaborate arches.

"It's supposed to be an exact replica of some famous palace on Earth," Commander Quinn explained. "The Elhamburger or something. A very wealthy shipper was having it done—all finished, in fact—when his assets were suddenly tied up in litigation. The suits have been going on for four months now, and the place is still padlocked. You can babysit our friend here till I get back." She rapped on the lid of the canister.

Ethan decided that all that was needed to make his day complete would be for it to rap back. But she had grounded the pallet and was piling up some cushions. "No blankets," she muttered. "I gotta keep my jacket. But if you sort of burrow in here, you should be warm enough."

It was like falling into a bank of clouds. "Burrow," Ethan whispered. "Warm . . ."

She dug into her jacket pocket. "And here's a candy bar to tide you over."

He snatched it; he couldn't help himself.

"Ah, one other thing. You can't use the plumbing. It would register on the computer monitors. I know this sounds terrible, but—if you've gotta go, use the canister." She paused. "It's not, after all, like he didn't deserve it."

"I'd rather die," said Ethan distinctly around a mouthful of nuts and goo. "Uh—are you going to be gone long?"

"At least an hour. Hopefully not more than four. You can sleep, if you like."

Ethan jerked himself awake. "Thank you."

"And now," she rubbed her hands together briskly, "phase two of the search for the L-X-1O Terran-C."

"The what?"

"That was the code name of Millisor's research project. Terran-C for short. Maybe some part of whatever they were working on originated on Earth."

"But Terrence Cee is a man," said Ethan. "They kept asking me if I was here to meet *him*."

She was utterly still for a moment. "Oh . . . ? How strange. How very strange. I never knew that." Her eyes were bright as mirrors. Then she was gone.

Chapter Five

⟨≈≈≈⟩

Ethan awoke with a startled gasp as something landed on his stomach. He thrashed up, looking around wildly. Commander Quinn stood before him in the wavering illumination of her hand light. The fingers of her other hand tapped a nervous, staccato rhythm on her empty stunner holster. Ethan's hands encountered a bulky bundle of cloth in his lap, which proved to be a set of Stationer coveralls wrapped around a matching pair of boots.

"Put those on," she ordered, "and hurry. I think I've found a way to get rid of the body, but we have to get there before shift change if I'm going to catch the right people on duty."

He dressed. She helped him impatiently with the unfamiliar tabs and catches, then made him sit again on the float pallet. It all made him feel like a backward four-year-old. After a quick reconnoiter by the mercenary woman, they left the chamber as unseen as they had entered it, and drifted off through the maze of the Station.

At least he no longer felt as if his brains were suspended in syrup in a jar, Ethan thought. The world parted around him now with no more than natural clarity, and colors did not flash fire in his eyes, nor leave scorched trails across his retinas. This was fortunate, as the Stationer coveralls Quinn had brought him to wear over his Athosian clothes were bright red. But waves of nausea still pulsed slowly in his stomach like moon-raised tides. He slouched, trying to lower his center of gravity still further onto the moving float pallet, and ached for something more than the three hours sleep the mercenary woman had allowed him.

"People are going to see us," he objected as she turned down a populated corridor.

"Not in that outfit." She nodded toward the coveralls. "Along with the float pallet it's the next best thing to a cloak of invisibility. Red is for Docks and Locks—they'll all think you're a porter in charge of the pallet. As long as you don't open your mouth or act like a downsider."

They passed into a large chamber where thousands of carrots were aligned in serried ranks, their white beards of roots dripping in the intermittent misting from the hydroponics sprayers, their fluffy green tops glowing in the grow-lights. The air of the room through which, Quinn assured him, they were taking a short cut, tasted cool and moist with a faint underlying tang of chemicals.

His stomach growled. Quinn, guiding the float pallet, glanced over at him. "I don't think I should have eaten that candy bar," Ethan muttered darkly.

"Well, for the gods' sakes don't throw up in *here*," she begged him. "Or use the—"

Ethan swallowed firmly. "No."

"Do you think a carrot would settle your stomach?" she asked solicitously. She reached over, tipping the pallet terrifyingly, and plucked one from the passing row. "Here."

He took the damp hairy thing dubiously, and after a moment stuffed it into one of the coverall's many closured pockets. "Maybe later."

They rose past a dozen stacked banks of growing vegetables to take an exit high in the chamber wall. NO ADMITTANCE, it said in glowing green letters. Quinn ignored the admonition with a verve bordering, Ethan thought, on the anti-social. He glanced back at the door as it hissed closed behind them. NO ADMITTANCE, it repeated on this side. So, they had committees on Kline Station too. . . .

She brought the pallet down in the next cross-corridor beside a door marked ATMOSPHERE CONTROL. NO ADMITTANCE. AUTHORIZED PERSONNEL ONLY, by which Ethan reasoned it must be their destination.

Commander Quinn unfolded herself from a half-lotus. "Now,

whatever happens, try not to talk. Your accent would give you away at once. Unless you'd rather stay out here with Okita until I'm ready for you."

Ethan shook his head quickly, struck by a vision of himself trying to explain to some passing authority that he was *not*, despite appearances, a murderer searching for a place to bury the body.

"All right. I can use the extra pair of hands. But be prepared to move on my order when the chance comes." She led on through the airseal doors, float pallet following like a dog on a leash.

It was like stepping into a chamber beneath the sea. Viridescent lines of light and shadow waved and scintillated across the floor, the walls—Ethan gaped at the walls. Three-story-high transparent barriers held back clear water stuffed with greenery and pierced with brilliant light. Millions of tiny silver bubbles galloped merrily through the minute fronds of aquatic plants, now pausing, now streaming on. An amphibian fully half a meter long pushed through this underwater jungle to stare at Ethan through its beady eyes. Its skin was black and shiny as patent leather, striped in scarlet. It shot away in a spray of silver to vanish in the green lace.

"Oxy-CO_2 exchange for the Station," Commander Quinn explained in an undertone. "The algae is bioengineered for maximum oxygen generation and CO_2 absorption. But of course, it grows. So to save having the chambers down half the time while we, ah, bale hay, the newts—specially bred—crop it for us. But then, naturally, you end up with a lot of newts. . . ."

She broke off as a blue-suited technician shut down a monitor at a control station and turned to frown at them. She waved at him cheerily. "Hi, Dale, remember me? Elli Quinn. Dom told me where to look you up."

His frown flipped to a grin. "Yes, he told me he'd seen you. . ." He advanced as if he might hug her, but settled on bashful handshake instead.

They exchanged small talk while Ethan, unintroduced, tried not to shift about nervously, or open his mouth or act like a downsider. The first two were easy enough, but what was it that marked a downsider in Stationer eyes? He stood by the float pallet and tried desperately to act like nobody at all.

Quinn ended what seemed to Ethan an unnecessarily lengthy digression about the Dendarii Mercenaries with the remark, "And do you know, those poor troops have never tasted fried newt legs!"

The tech's eyes glinted with a humor baffling to Ethan. "What!

Can there be a soul in the universe so deprived? No cream of newt soup, either, I suppose?"

"No newt creole," confided Commander Quinn with mock horror. "No newts 'n chips."

"No newt provençal?" chorused the tech. "No newt stew? No newt mousse in aspic? No slither goulash, no newt chowder?"

"Bucket 'o newts is unknown to them," confirmed Quinn. "Newt caviar is a delicacy unheard of."

"No newt nuggets?"

"Newt nuggets?" echoed the commander, looking suddenly really nonplused.

"Latest thing," explained the tech. "They're really boned leg meat, chopped, reformed, and fried."

"Oh," said the mercenary woman. "I'm relieved. For a moment there I was picturing some form of, er, newt organettes."

They both burst into laughter. Ethan swallowed and looked around surreptitiously for some kind, any kind, of basin. A couple of the slick black creatures swam to the barrier and goggled at him.

"Anyway," Quinn went on to the tech, "I thought if you were about due for the culling this shift you might spare me a few, to freeze and take back with me. Assuming you're not short, of course."

"We are never," he groaned, "short of newts. Help yourself. Take a hundred kilos. Take two. Three."

"A hundred would be plenty. All I can afford to ship. Make it a treat for officers only, eh?"

He chuckled, and led her up a ladder to an access port. Ethan skittishly followed her come-along gesture, bringing up the float pallet.

The tech picked his way delicately across a mesh catwalk. Beneath them the waters hissed and rushed in little eddies; a fresh draft from below cooled Ethan's skin and cleared his aching head. He kept one hand on the safety railing. Some of the whirlpools below suggested powerful suction pumpers at work somewhere in the silver-green. Another water chamber was visible beyond this one, and beyond that another, retreating out of sight.

The catwalk widened to a platform. The hiss became a roar as the tech pulled back a cover above an underwater cage. The cage roiled with black and scarlet shapes, slipping and splashing over each other.

"Oh, lord yes," yelled the tech. "Full house. Sure you don't want to feed your whole army?"

"Would if I could," called Quinn back. "Tell you what, though. I'll trot the excess down to Disposal for you, once I pick out my choice. Does Transients' Lounge need any?"

"No orders this shift. Help yourself."

He opened a housing over a control box, did something; the newt trap rose slowly, draining water, compressing the wriggling black and scarlet mass. Another motion at the controls, a buzz, a blue light. Ethan could feel the nimbus of a powerful stun beam even where he stood. The mass stopped writhing and lay still and shining.

The tech heaved a large green plastic carton from a stack of identical ones and positioned it on a digital scale under a trap door in the bottom of the cage. He aligned a chute and opened the trap. Dozens of limp newts slithered down into the carton. As the digital readout approached 100 kilograms he slowed the flow, tossing a last black body in by hand. He then removed the carton with a hand-tractor, replaced it with another, and repeated the process. A third carton did not quite make it to full capacity. The tech entered the exact biomass removed from the system into his computer log.

"Want me to help you pack your canister?" he offered.

Ethan blanched, but the mercenary woman said lightly, "Naw, go on back down to your monitors. I'm going to sort through these by hand a bit, I think—no point in shipping any but the best."

The tech grinned, and started back across the catwalk. "Find 'em some nice juicy ones," he called. Quinn gave him a friendly wave as he vanished back through the access port.

"Now," she turned back to Ethan, her face gone intent, "let's make these numbers match. Help me get that dirt-sucker up on this scale."

It wasn't easy; Okita had stiffened, wedged in the canister. The mercenary woman stripped him of clothes and a variety of lethal weapons and made them into a compact bundle.

Ethan shook off the paralysis of his confusion to attempt a task he at last felt sure of, and weighed the corpse. Whatever this madness was he had fallen into, it threatened Athos. His original impulse to escape the mercenary woman was becoming, in his gradually clearing head, an equally strenuous desire not to let her out of his sight until he could discover, somehow, everything she knew about it.

"Eight-one-point-four-five kilograms," he reported in his best clipped scientific tone, the one he used for visiting VIPs back at Sevarin. "Now what?"

"Now get him into one of these cartons and fill it to, ah, 100.62 kilos with newts," she instructed with a glance at the first carton's readout. When this was done—the last fraction of a kilo was accomplished by her pulling a vibra-knife from her jacket and adding slightly less than half a newt—she switched data discs and sealed the carton.

"Now 81.45 kilos of newts into that shipping canister," she instructed. It came out even, leaving them with three cartons and a canister as before.

"Will you please tell me what we're doing?" Ethan begged.

"Turning a rather difficult problem into a much simpler one. Now instead of an extremely incriminating drum full of dead downsider, all we have to get rid of is 80 or so kilos of stunned newts."

"But we haven't got rid of the body," Ethan pointed out. He stared down into the bright waters. "Are you going to dump the newts back in?" he asked hopefully. "Can they swim all right, stunned?"

"No, no, no!" said Quinn, looking quite shocked. "That would unbalance the system! It's very finely tuned. The whole point of this exercise is to keep the computer records straight. As for the body—you'll see."

"All set?" called the tech as they floated out of the access port, canister, cartons and all stacked on the pallet.

"No, darn it," said Quinn. "I realized when I was about half-way through that I'd grabbed the wrong size shipping canister. I'll have to come back later. Look, give me the receipt and I'll still run this load down to Disposal for you. I want to look up Teki there anyway."

"Oh, sure, all right," said the tech, brightening. "Thanks." He punched up the records, put them on a data disk, and handed it over. Commander Quinn retreated with all seemly haste.

"Good." She slumped as the airseal doors slid shut behind them, the first hint of weariness Ethan had seen in her. "I'll get to oversee the final act myself." She added to Ethan's bewildered look, "We could have just left them to go down to Disposal on the regular schedule, but I kept having this horrible vision of a last-minute order arriving from Transients' Lounge and Dale opening a carton to fill it. . . ."

"An order for newts?" Ethan floundered.

She snickered. "Yes, but up there they're sold to the downsiders as Premium Fresh Frog Legs, on the restaurant menus. We stiff 'em for a sweet price, too."

"Is—is that, er, ethical?"

She shrugged. "Gotta make a profit somewhere. Snob appeal keeps the demand up. You can hardly give the wee beasties away on the Stationer side, everybody's so sick of them. But Biocontrol refuses to diversify the weed-grazers on account of the system working at max efficiency for oxygen generation as is. And everyone has to agree, the oxygen comes first. The newts are just a by-product."

They re-mounted the float pallet and drifted off down the corridor. Ethan glanced sideways at the mercenary woman's abstracted profile. He must try . . .

"What kind of genetics project?" he asked suddenly. "Millisor's thing, I mean. Don't you know any more about it than that?"

She spared him a thoughtful glance. "Human genetics. And in truth, I know very little more than that. Some names, a few code words. God only knows what they were up to. Making monsters, maybe. Or raising supermen. The Cetagandans have always been a bunch of aggressive militarists. Maybe they meant to raise battalions of mutant super-soldiers in vats like you Athosians and take over the universe or something."

"Not likely," remarked Ethan. "Not battalions, anyway."

"Why not? Why not clone as many as you want, once you've made the mold?"

"Oh, certainly, you could produce quantities of infants—although it would take enormous resources to do so. Highly trained techs, as well as equipment and supplies. But don't you see, that's just the beginning. It's nothing, compared to what it takes to raise a child. Why, on Athos it absorbs most of the planet's economic resources. Food of course—housing—education, clothing, medical care—it takes nearly all our efforts just to maintain population replacement, let alone to increase. No government could possibly afford to raise such a specialized, non-productive army."

Elli Quinn quirked an eyebrow. "How odd. On other worlds,

people seem to come in floods, and they're not necessarily impoverished, either."

Ethan, diverted, said, "Really? I don't see how that can be. Why, the labor costs alone of bringing a child to maturity are astronomical. There must be something wrong with your accounting."

Her eyes screwed up in an expression of sudden ironic insight. "Ah, but on other worlds the labor costs aren't added in. They're counted as free."

Ethan stared. "What an absurd bit of double thinking! Athosians would never sit still for such a hidden labor tax! Don't the primary nurturers even get social duty credits?"

"I believe," her voice was edged with a peculiar dryness, "they call it women's work. And the supply usually exceeds the demand— non-union scabs, as it were, undercutting the market."

Ethan was increasingly puzzled. "Are not most women combat soldiers, then, like you? Are there men Dendarii?"

She hooted, then lowered her voice as a passer-by stared. "Four-fifths of the Dendarii are men. And of the women, three out of four are techs, not troops. Most military services are skewed that way, except for ones like Barrayar that have no women at all."

"Oh," said Ethan. After a disappointed pause he added, "You are an atypical sample, then." So much for his nascent Rules of Female Behavior. . . .

"Atypical." She was still a moment, then snorted. "Yeah, that's me all over."

They passed through an archway framing airseal doors labeled ECOBRANCH: RECYCLING. Ethan ate his carrot as they threaded the corridors, stripping off roots and top and, after a glance around his immaculate white surroundings, stuffing them back in his pocket. By the time he had crunched down the last mouthful they arrived at a door marked ASSIMILATION STATION B: AUTHORIZED PERSONNEL ONLY.

They entered a brightly-lit chamber lined with banks of intimidating-looking monitors. A lab bench and sink in the center seemed half-familiar to Ethan, for it was jammed with equipment for organic analysis. A number of color-coded conduits with access ports—for sampling?—crowded one end of the room. The other end was entirely occupied by a strange machine connected to the larger system by pipes; Ethan could not begin to guess its function.

A pair of legs in pine-green trousers with sky-blue piping were sticking out between a couple of the conduits. A high-pitched voice muttered unintelligibly. After a few more savage sibilants there was a clang and the whine of a sealing mechanism, and the legs' owner wriggled out and stood.

She wore plastic gloves to her armpits, and was clutching an unidentifiable crumpled metal object perhaps a third of a meter long that dripped vile-smelling brown liquid. *F. Helda,* read the nametag over her left breast pocket, *Biocontrol Warden.* Her face was red and angry, and terrified Ethan. Her voice cleared, "—unbelievable stupid downsider jerks . . ." She broke off as she saw Ethan and his companion. Her eyes narrowed and her frown deepened. "Who are you? You don't belong in here. Can't you read?"

Dismay flashed in Quinn's eyes. She recovered and smiled winningly. "I just brought down the newt cull from Atmosphere. A little favor for Dale Zeeman."

"Zeeman should do his own work," the ecotech woman snapped, "not entrust it to some ignorant downsider. I'll write him up for this—"

"Oh, I'm Stationer born and bred," Quinn assured her hastily. "Let me introduce myself—Elli Quinn's the name. Maybe you know my cousin Teki—he works in this department. As a matter of fact, I rather thought he'd be here."

"Oh," said the woman, only slightly mollified. "He's in A Station. But don't you go over there now, they're cleaning the filters. He won't have time to chat until after the system is back up. Work shifts are not the place for personal visiting, you know—"

"What in the world is that?" Quinn diverted her lecture with a nod at the metal object.

Ecotech Helda's clutch tightened on the tortured metal as if she might strangle it. Her chill toward her unauthorized visitors struggled with her need to vent her rage, and lost. "My latest present from Transients' Lounge. You wonder how illiterates can afford space travel—damn it, even illiterates have no excuse, the rules are demonstrated on the holovid! It *was* a perfectly good emergency oxygen canister, until some asshole stuffed it down an organics disposer. He must have had to smash it flat first to fit it in. Thank the gods it was discharged, or it might have blown out a pipe. Unbelievable stupidity!"

She stalked across the room to fling it into a bin with a number of other obviously non-organic bits of trash. "I hate downsiders," she growled. "Careless, dirty, inconsiderate animals . . ." She stripped off the gloves and disposed of them, mopped the drips with a sonic scrubber and antiseptic, and turned to the sink to scrub her hands with violent thoroughness.

Quinn nodded toward the big green cartons. "Can I help you get these out of the way?" she asked brightly.

"There was absolutely no point in bringing them down ahead of schedule," said the ecotech. "I have an interment scheduled in five minutes, and the degrader is programmed to break down all the way to simple organics and vent to Hydroponics. It will just have to wait. You can take yourselves off and tell Dale Zeeman—" she broke off as the door slid open.

Half a dozen somber Stationers followed a covered float pallet through the door. Quinn motioned Ethan silently to an inconspicuous seat on their own float pallet as the procession entered the chamber. Ecotech Helda hastily straightened her uniform and composed her features to an expression of grave sympathy.

The Stationers gathered around while one of them intoned a few platitudes. Death was a great leveler, it seemed. The turns of phrase were different, but the sense would have passed at an Athosian funeral, Ethan thought. Maybe galactics weren't so wildly different after all . . .

"Do you wish a final view of the deceased?" Helda inquired of them.

They shook their heads, a middle-aged man among them remarking, "Ye gods, the funeral was enough." He was shushed by a middle-aged woman beside him.

"Do you wish to stay for interment?" asked Helda, formally and unpressingly.

"Absolutely not," said the middle-aged man. At a look of embarrassed disapproval from his female companion, he added firmly, "I saw Grandpa through five replacement operations. I did my bit when he was alive. Watching him get ground up to feed the flowers won't add a thing to my karma, love."

The family filed out, and the ecotech returned to her original aggressively businesslike demeanor. She stripped the corpse—it was an exceedingly ancient man—and took the clothes to the corridor, where presumably someone had lingered to collect them. Returning, she checked a data file, donned gloves and gown, wrinkled her lip, and attacked the deceased with a vibra-knife.

Ethan watched with a professional fascination as a dozen mechanical replacement parts clanked into a tray—a heart, several tubes, bone pins, a hip joint, a kidney. The tray was taken to a washer, and the body to the strange machine at the end of the room.

Helda unsealed a large hatch and swung it down, and shifted the body on its catch basin onto it. She clamped the catch basin to the inner side, swung it up—there was a muffled thump from within—and resealed it. The ecotech pressed a few buttons, lights lit, and the machine whined and hissed and grunted with a demure even rhythm that suggested normal operation.

While Helda was occupied in the other end of the room, Ethan risked a whisper. "What's happening in there?"

"Breaking the body down to its components and returning the biomass to the Station ecosystem," Quinn whispered back. "Most clean animal mass—like the newts—is just broken down into higher organics and fed to the protein culture vats—that's where we grow steak meat, and chicken and such for human consumption—but there's a sort of prejudice against disposing of human bodies that way. Smacks of cannibalism, I guess. And so that your next kilo cube of pork doesn't remind you too much of your late Uncle Neddie, the humans get broken down much finer and fed to the plants instead. A purely aesthetic choice—it all goes round and round in the end—logically, it doesn't make any difference."

His carrot had turned to lead in his stomach. "But you're going to let them put Okita—"

"Maybe I'll turn vegetarian for the next month," she whispered. "Sh."

Helda glanced irritably at them. "What are you hanging about for?" She focused on Ethan. "Have you no work to do?"

Quinn smiled blandly, and rapped the green cartons. "I need my float pallet."

"Oh," said the ecotech. She sniffed, hitched up one sharp, bony shoulder, and turned away to tap a new code into the degrader's control panel. Stamping back with a hand tractor, she lifted the top carton and locked it into position on the hatch. It flipped up; there was a slithery rumble from within the machine. The hatch flopped down again, and the first carton was replaced by the second. Then the third. Ethan held his breath.

The third carton emptied with a startling thump.

"What the hell . . . ?" muttered the ecotech, and reached for the seals. Commander Quinn turned white, her fingers twitching over her empty stunner holster.

"Look, is that a cockroach?" cried Ethan loudly in what he prayed might pass for a Stationer accent.

Helda whirled. "Where?"

Ethan pointed to a corner of the room away from the degrader. Both the ecotech and the commander went to inspect. Helda got down on her hands and knees and ran a finger worriedly along a seam between floor and wall. "Are you sure?" she said.

"Just a movement," he murmured, "in the corner of my eye . . ."

She frowned fiercely at him. "More like a damned hangover in the corner of your eye. Slovenly muscle-brain."

Ethan shrugged helplessly.

"Better call Infestation Control anyway," she muttered. She hit the start button on the degrader on her way to the comconsole, and jerked her thumb back over her shoulder. "Out."

They complied immediately. Floating down the corridor Commander Quinn said, "My gods, Doctor, that was inspired. Or— you didn't really see a roach, did you?"

"No, it was just the first thing that popped into my head. She seemed like the sort of person who is bothered by bugs."

"Ah." Her eyes crinkled in amused approval.

He paused. "Do you have a roach problem here?"

"Not if we can help it. Among other things, they've been known to eat the insulation off electrical wiring. You think about fire on a space station a bit, and you'll see why you got her attention."

She checked her chronometer. "Ye gods, we've got to get this float pallet and canister back to Docking Bay 32. Newts, newts, who will buy my newts . . . ? Ah ha, the very thing."

She made a sharp right turn into a cross corridor, nearly dumping Ethan, and speeded up. After a moment she brought the pallet to a halt before a door marked "Cold Storage Access 297-C."

Inside they found a counter, and a plump, bored-looking young woman on duty eating little fried morsels of something from a bag.

"I'd like to rent a vacuum storage locker," Quinn announced.

"This is for Stationers, ma'am," the counter girl began, after a hungry, wistful look at the mercenary woman's face. "If you go up to Transients' Lounge, you can get—"

Quinn slapped an ID down on the counter. "A cubic meter will do, and I want it in removable plastic. Clean plastic, mind you."

The counter girl glanced at the ID. "Ah. Oh." She shuffled off, and returned a few minutes later with a big plastic-lined case.

The mercenary woman signed and thumbprinted, and turned to Ethan. "Let's lay them in nicely, eh? Impress the cook, when he thaws 'em out."

They packed the newts in neat rows. The counter girl, looking on, wrinkled her nose, then shrugged and returned to her comconsole where the holovid was displaying something that looked suspiciously more like play than work.

They were just in time, Ethan gauged; some of their amphibian victims were beginning to twitch. He almost felt worse about them than he did about Okita. The counter girl bore the box off.

"They won't suffer long, will they?" Ethan asked, looking back over his shoulder.

Commander Quinn snorted. "I should die so quick. They're going into the biggest freezer in the universe—outside. I think I really will ship them back to Admiral Naismith, later, when things calm down."

"'Things,'" echoed Ethan. "Quite. I think you and I should have a talk about 'things.'" His mouth set mulishly.

Hers turned up on one side. "Heart to heart," she agreed cordially.

Chapter Six

After sneaking the float pallet back to its docking bay, Commander Quinn brought him by a round-about route to a hostel room not much larger than Ethan's own. This hostel lay, Ethan was dimly aware, in yet another section of Transients' Lounge, although he was not quite sure where they had recrossed that unmarked border. Quinn had dropped behind several times, or parked him abruptly in some cul-de-sac while she scouted ahead, or once wandered off quite casual-seeming, her arm draped across the shoulders of some uniformed Stationer acquaintance as she gesticulated gaily with her free hand. Ethan prayed she knew what she was doing.

She at any rate seemed to feel he had been successfully smuggled to some kind of home base, for she relaxed visibly when the hostel room doors sealed shut behind them, kicking off her boots and stretching and diving for the room service console.

"Here. Real beer." She handed him a foaming tumbler, after pausing to squirt something into it from her Dendarii issue medkit. "Imported."

The aroma made his mouth water, but he stood suspiciously, without raising it to his lips. "What did you put in it?"

"Vitamins. Look, see?" She snapped a squirt out of the air from the same vial, and washed it down with a long swallow from her own tumbler. "You're safe here for now. Drink, eat, wash, what-you-will."

He glanced longingly toward the bathroom. "Won't double use show up on the computer monitors? What if someone asks questions?"

She smirked. "It will show that Commander Quinn is entertaining a handsome Stationer acquaintance in her room, at length. Nobody'd dare ask anything. Relax."

The implications were anything but relaxing, but Ethan was by that time ready to risk his life for a shave; his stubbled chin was perilously close to pretending to paternal honors to which he had no right.

The bathroom, alas, had no second exit. He gave up and drank his beer while he washed. If Millisor and Rau had not found useful intelligence in him, he doubted Commander Quinn could either, no matter what she'd doctored his drink with.

He was horrified by the haggard face that stared back at him from the mirror. Sandpaper chin, red-rimmed eyes, skin blotched and puffy—no patron in his right mind would trust his infant to that ruffian. Fortunately, a few minutes work returned him to his normal reassuringly squeaky-clean neatness; merely tired, not degraded. There was even a sonic scrubber that cleaned his clothes while he showered.

He emerged to find Commander Quinn occupying the room's sole float chair, her jacket off, feet propped up and luxuriating in their decompression. She opened her eyes and gestured him toward the bed. He stretched himself out nervously, the pillow to his back; but there was no other choice of seating. He found a fresh beer and a tray of edibles, anonymous Stationer tidbits, ready to hand. He tried not to think about the food's possible sources.

"So," she began. "There seems to be an awful lot of interest focused on this shipment of biologicals Athos ordered. Suppose you start there."

Ethan swallowed a bite and gathered all his resolve. "No. We trade information. Suppose *you* start there." His burst of assertiveness ran down in the face of her bland raised eyebrows, and he added weakly, "If you don't mind."

She cocked her head and smiled. "Very well." She paused to wash down a bite of her own. "Your order was filled, apparently, by Bharaputra Laboratories' top genetics team. They spent a couple of months at it, under need-to-know security. This probably saved several lives, later. The order was sent off on a non-stop freight run to Kline Station, where it sat in a warehouse for two months waiting for the yearly census courier to take it to Athos. Nine big white freezer boxes—" she described them in precise detail, right down to the serial numbers. "Is that what you got?"

Ethan nodded grimly.

She went on. "Just about the time the shipment was leaving Kline Station for Athos, Millisor and his team arrived on Jackson's Whole. They went through Bharaputra's lab like—well, professionally speaking, it was a very successful commando raid." Her lips closed on some angrier private judgement. "Millisor and his team escaped right through House Bharaputra's private army, vaporizing the laboratory and all its contents behind them. The contents included most of the genetics team, quite a few innocent bystanders, and the technical records of the work done on your shipment. I gather they must have spent some time questioning the Bharaputra people before they crisped them, because they got it all. Pausing only to murder the wife and burn down the house of one of the geneticists, Millisor and company vanished from the planet, to turn up under new identities here just three weeks too late to catch your shipment.

"So then I arrived on Jackson's Whole, innocently asking questions about Athos. House Bharaputra Security about had a colonic spasm. Fortunately, I was finally able to persuade them I had no connection with Millisor. In fact, they think I'm working for them, now." She smiled slowly.

"The Bharaputrans?"

Her smile became a grimace. "Yes. They hired me to assassinate Millisor and his team. A lucky break for me, since now I'm not racing one of their own hit squads to the target. I seem to have made a start in spite of myself. They'll be so pleased." She sighed, and drank again. "Your turn, Doctor. What was in those boxes to be worth all those lives?"

"Nothing!" He shook his head in bewilderment. "Valuable, yes, but not worth killing for. The Population Council had ordered 450 live ovarian cultures, to produce egg cells, you know, for children—"

"I know how children are produced, yes," she murmured.

"They were to be certified free of genetic defects, and taken only from sources in the top 20 intelligence percentiles. That's all. A week's routine work for a good genetics team such as you describe. But what we got was *trash!*" He detailed the shipment received with increasingly irate fervor, until she cut him off.

"All right, Doctor! I believe you. But what left Jackson's Whole was not trash, but something very special. Somebody therefore took your shipment somewhere in transit and replaced it with garbage—"

"Very odd garbage, when you think about it," Ethan began slowly, but she was going on.

"What somebody, then, and when? Not you, not me—although I suppose you've only my word for that—and not, obviously, Millisor, although he would have liked to."

"Mlllisor seemed to think it was this Terrence Cee—person, or whatever he is."

She sighed. "Whatever-he-is had plenty of time for it. It could have been switched on Jackson's Whole, or on shipboard en route to Kline Station, or anytime before the census courier left for Athos—ye gods, do you have any idea how many ships dock at Kline Station in the course of two months? And how many connections they in turn make? No wonder Millisor has been going around looking like his stomach hurts. I'll get a copy of the Station docking log anyway, though. . . ." She made a note.

Ethan used the pause to ask, "What is a *wife?*"

She choked on her beer. For all that she waved it about, Ethan noticed that its level was dropping very slowly. "I keep forgetting about you. . . . Ah, wife. A marriage partner—a man's female mate. The male partner is called a husband. Marriage takes many forms, but is most commonly a legal, economic, and genetic alliance to produce and raise children. Do you copy?"

"I think so," he said slowly. "It sounds a little like a designated alternate parent." He tasted the words. "Husband. On Athos, to husband is a verb meaning to conserve resources. Like stewardship." Did this imply the male maintained the female during gestation? So, this supposedly organic method had hidden costs that might make a real Rep Center seem cheap, Ethan thought with satisfaction.

"Same root."

"What does it mean 'to wife,' then?"

"There is no parallel verb. I think the root is just some old word meaning simply, 'woman.' "

"Oh." He hesitated. "Did the geneticist whose house was burned and his—his *wife* have any children?"

"A little boy, who was in nursery school at the time. Strangely enough, Millisor didn't bother to torch it, too. Can't imagine how he overlooked that loose thread. The wife was pregnant." She bit rather savagely into a protein cube.

Ethan shook his head in frustration. "Why? Why, why, why?"

She smiled elliptically. "There are moments when I think you might be a man after my own heart—that was a joke," she added as Ethan lurched, recoiling. "Yes. Why. My very own assigned question. Millisor seemed convinced that what Bharaputra's labs produced was actually intended for Athos, in spite of the subsequent diversion. Now, if nothing else, I've learned in the past few months that what Millisor thinks had better be taken into account. Why Athos? What does Athos have that nobody else does?"

"Nothing," said Ethan simply. "We're a small, agriculturally based society with no natural resources worth shipping. We're not on a nexus route to anywhere. We don't go around bothering anyone."

"'Nothing,'" she noted. "Think of a scenario where a planet with 'nothing' would be at a premium . . . You have privacy, I suppose. Other than that, only your insistence upon reproducing yourselves the hard way sets you apart." She sipped her beer. "You say Millisor was talking about attacking your Reproduction Centers. Tell me about them."

Ethan needed little encouragement to wax enthusiastic about his beloved job. He described Sevarin and its operations, and the dedicated cadre of men who made it work. He explained the beneficent system of social duty credits that qualified potential fathers. He ran down abruptly when he found himself describing the personal troubles that prevented him from achieving his own heart's desire for a son. This woman was getting entirely too easy to talk to—he wondered anew what was in his beer.

She leaned back in her chair and whistled tunelessly a moment. "Damn that diversion anyway. But for that, I'd say the cuckoo's-egg scenario had the most appeal. It accounted so nicely for Millisor's activities. . . . Rats."

"The what scenario?"

"Cuckoo's-egg. Do you have cuckoos on Athos?"

"No . . . Is it a reptile?"

"An obnoxious bird. From Earth. Principally famous for laying its eggs in other birds' nests and skipping out on the tedious work of raising them. Now found galaxy-wide mainly as a literary allusion, since by some miracle nobody was dumb enough to export them off-planet. All the rest of the vermin managed to follow mankind into space readily enough. But do you see what I mean by a cuckoo's-egg scenario?"

Ethan, seeing, shivered. "Sabotage," he whispered. "Genetic sabotage. They thought to plant their monsters on us, all unawares . . ." He caught himself up. "Oh. But it wasn't the Cetagandans who sent the shipment, was it? Uh—rats. It wouldn't work anyway. We have ways of weeding out gene defects . . ." He subsided, more puzzled than ever.

"The shipment may have incorporated material stolen from the Cetagandan research project, though. Thus accounting for Millisor's passion for retrieving or destroying it."

"Obviously, but—why should Jackson's Whole want to do that to us? Or are they enemies of Cetaganda?"

"Ah—hm. How much do you know about Jackson's Whole?"

"Not much. They're a planet, they have biological laboratories, they submitted a bid to the Population Council in response to our advertisement year before last. So did half a dozen other places."

"Yes, well—next time, order from Beta Colony."

"Beta Colony was the high bid."

She ran a finger unconsciously across her lips; Ethan thought of plasma burns. "I'm sure, but you get what you pay for. . . . Actually, that's misleading. You can get what you pay for on Jackson's Whole too, if your purse is deep enough. Want to have a young clone made of yourself, grown to physical maturity in vitro, and have your brain transferred into it? There's a 50% chance the operation will kill you, and a 100% guarantee it kills—whatever individual the clone might have been. No Betan med center would touch a job like that—clones have full civil rights there. House Bharaputra will."

"Ugh," said Ethan, revolted. "On Athos, cloning is considered a sin."

She raised her eyebrows. "Oh, yeah? What sin?"

"Vanity."

"Didn't know that was a sin—oh, well. The point is, if somebody offered House Bharaputra enough money, they'd have cheerfully filled your boxes with—dead newts, for instance. Or eight-foot-tall bioengineered super-soldiers, or anything else that was asked for." She fell silent, sipping her beer.

"So what do we do next?" he prodded bravely.

She frowned. "I'm thinking. I didn't exactly plan this Okita scenario in advance, y'know. I don't have orders for active interference in the affair—I was just supposed to observe. Professionally speaking, I suppose I shouldn't have rescued you. I should have just watched, and sent off a regretful report on the radius of your splatter to Admiral Naismith."

"Will he, ah, be annoyed with you?" Ethan inquired nervously, with a skewed paranoid flash of her admiral sternly ordering her to restore the original balance by sending him to join Okita.

"Naw. He has unprofessional moments himself. Terribly impractical, it's going to kill him one of these days. Though so far he seems able to make things come out all right by sheer force of will." She speared the last tidbit on the platter, finished her beer, and rose. "So. Next I watch Millisor some more. If he has more back-up team than what I've spotted so far, his search for you and Okita should smoke them out. You can lie low in here. Don't leave the room."

Imprisoned again, although more comfortably. "But what about my clothes, my luggage, my room . . ." his Economy Cabin, unoccupied, ticking up his bill nonetheless, "my mission!"

"You absolutely must not go near your room!" She sighed. "It's eight months till your return ship to Athos, right? Tell you what— you help me with my mission, I'll help you with yours. You do what I tell you, you might even live to complete it."

"Always assuming," said Ethan, chapped, "that ghem-Colonel Millisor doesn't outbid House Bharaputra or Admiral Naismith for your services."

She shrugged on her jacket, a lumpy thing with lots of pockets that seemed to have a deal more swing than accounted for by the weight of the fabric. "You can get one thing straight right now, Athosian. There are some things money can't buy."

"What, mercenary?"

She paused at the door, her lips curving up despite her sparking eyes. "Unprofessional moments."

The first day of his semi-voluntary incarceration passed sleeping off the exhaustion, terror, and biochemical cocktails of the preceding 24 hours. He came to muzzy consciousness once just as Commander Quinn was tiptoeing out of the room, but sank back. The second time he awoke, much later, he found her asleep stretched out on the floor dressed in uniform trousers and shirt, her jacket hung ready-to-hand. Her eyes slitted open to follow him as he staggered to the bathroom.

He found on the second day that Commander Quinn did not lock him in during the long hours of her absences. He dithered in the hallway for twenty minutes, upon discovering this, trying to evolve some rational program for his freedom besides being immediately gobbled up by Millisor, who was by now doubtless tearing the Station apart looking for him. The whirr of a cleaning robot rounding the corner sent him spinning back into the room, heart palpitating. Maybe it wouldn't hurt to let the mercenary woman protect him a little longer.

By the third day he had recovered enough of his native tone of mind to begin serious worrying about his predicament, although not yet enough physical energy to try doing anything about it. Belatedly, he began boning up on galactic history through the comconsole library.

By the end of the next day he was becoming painfully aware of the inadequacy of a cultural education that consisted of two very general galactic histories, a history of Cetaganda, and a fiction holovid titled "Love's Savage Star" that he had stumbled onto and been too stunned to switch off. Life with women did not just induce strange behavior, it appeared; it induced *very* strange behavior. How long before the emanations or whatever it was from Commander Quinn would make him start acting like that? Would ripping open her jacket to expose her mammary hypertrophy really cause her to fixate upon him like a newly hatched chick on its mother hen? Or would she carve him to ribbons with her vibra-knife before the hormones or whatever they were cut in?

He shuddered, and cursed the study time he'd wasted on timidity during the two months voyage to Kline Station. Innocence might be bliss, but ignorance was demonstrably hell; if his soul was to be offered up on the altar of necessity, by God the Father Athos should have the full worth of it. He read on.

The opposite of nirvana in his spiritual descent, Ethan decided, was tizzy; and by the sixth day he had achieved it.

"What the hell is Millisor doing out there?" he demanded of Commander Quinn during one of her brief stop-ins.

"He's not doing as much as I'd hoped," she admitted. She slumped in her chair, winding a curl of her dark hair around and around her finger. "He hasn't reported you or Okita missing to the Station authorities. He hasn't revealed hidden reserves of personnel. He's made no move to leave the Station. The time he's spending maintaining his cover identity suggests he's digging in for a long stay. Last week I'd thought he was just waiting for the return ship from Athos that you came on, but now it's clear there's something more. Something even more important than an AWOL subordinate."

Ethan paced, his voice rising. "How long am I going to have to stay in here?"

She shrugged. "Until something breaks, I suppose." She smiled sourly. "Something might, although not for our side. Millisor and Rau and Setti have been searching the Station themselves, real quiet-like—they keep coming back to this one corridor near Ecobranch. I couldn't figure out why, at first. Now, Okita's clothes scanned clean of bugs, but just to be sure I mailed 'em off to Admiral Naismith. So I knew it couldn't be that. I finally got hold of the technical specs for that section. The damned protein-culture vats are behind that corridor wall. I think Okita may have had some sort of inorganic code-response-only tracer implanted internally. Some poor sod is going to break a tooth on it in his Chicken Kiev any day now. I just hope to the gods it won't be a transient who will sue the Station . . . So much for the perfect crime." She heaved a sigh. "Millisor hasn't figured it out yet, though—he's still eating meat."

Ethan was getting mortally tired of salads himself. And of this room, and of the tension, indecision, and helplessness. And of Commander Quinn, and the casual way she ordered him around. . . .

"I have only your say-so that the Station authorities can't help me," he broke out suddenly. "*I* didn't shoot Okita. *I* haven't done anything! I don't even have an argument with Millisor—it's you who seems to be carrying on a private war with him. He'd never have thought I was a secret agent in the first place if Rau hadn't found your bug. It's you who's been getting me in deeper and deeper, to serve your spying."

"He'd have picked you up in any case," she observed.

"Yes, but all I needed was to convince Millisor that Athos didn't have his stuff. His interrogation might have done that, if your interference hadn't aroused his suspicions. Hell, he'd be welcome to come inspect our Rep Centers if he wants."

She raised her eyebrows, a gesture Ethan found increasingly irritating. "You really think you could negotiate that with him? Personally, I'd rather import a new plague bacillus."

"At least he's male," Ethan snapped.

She laughed; Ethan's temper rose to the boiling point. "How long are you going to keep me locked up in here?" he demanded again.

She paused, visibly. Her eyes widened, narrowed; she tamped out her smile. "You're not locked up," she pointed out mildly. "You can leave any time. At your own risk, of course. I shall be saddened, but I shall survive."

He slowed in his frenetic pacing. "You're bluffing. You can't let me go. I've learned too much."

Her feet came down from the desktop, and she stopped twisting her hair. She stared at him with a discomforting expressionlessness, like someone calculating the narrowness of slide necessary to prepare a biological specimen for slice mounting. When she spoke again, her voice grated like gravel. "I should say you haven't learned bloody enough."

"You don't want me to tell the Station authorities about Okita, do you? That puts your neck on the line with your own people—"

"Oh, hardly my neck. They would of course have a shit fit if they found out what we did with the body—to which I might point out you were a willing accessory. Contamination is a much more serious charge than mere murder. Nearly up there with arson."

"So? What can they do, deport me? That's not a punishment, that's a *reward*!"

Her eyes slitted, concealing their sharpening light. "If you leave, Athosian, don't expect to come bleating back to me for protection. I have no use for quitters, quislings—or queers."

He supposed she was insulting him. He took it as intended. "Well, I have no use for a sly, tricky, arrogant, overbearing— woman!" he sputtered.

She spread her hand invitingly toward the door, pursing her lips. Ethan realized he had just had the last word. His credit chit was in his pocket, his shoes were on his feet. Nostrils flaring, he marched out the door, head held high. His back crawled in expectation of a stunner beam, or worse. None came.

It was very, very quiet in the corridor when the airseal doors had hissed shut. Had the last word really been what he'd wanted? And yet—he'd rather face Millisor, Rau, and Okita's ghost together than crawl back into his prison and apologize to Quinn.

Determination. Decision. Action. That was the way to solve

problems. Not running away and hiding. He would seek out and confront Millisor face-to-face. He stomped off down the corridor.

By the time he reached the mallway exit from the hostel he was walking normally, and he had revised his plan to the more sane and sensible one of calling Millisor from the safe distance of a public comconsole. He could be tricky himself. He would not approach his own hostel. If necessary, he might even abandon his personal gear, and purchase a ticket off-Station—to Beta Colony?— at the last moment before boarding, thus escaping the whole crowd of insane secret agents. By the time he got back to Kline Station, they might even have chased each other off to some other part of the galaxy.

He removed himself a couple of levels from Quinn's hostel and found a comconsole booth.

"I wish to reach a transient, ghem-Colonel Luyst Millisor," he told the computer. He spelled the name out carefully. His voice, he noted with self-approval, scarcely quavered.

No such individual is registered at Kline Station, the holoscreen flashed back.

"Er . . . Has he checked out?" Gone, and Commander Quinn stringing him along all this time . . . ?

No such individual registered within the past 12-month cycle, the holoscreen murmured brightly.

"Um, um—how about a Captain Rau?"

No such individual . . .

"Setti?"

No such individual . . .

He stopped short of mentioning Okita, and stood blankly. Then it came to him; Millisor was the man's real name. But here on Kline Station he was doubtless using an assumed one, with forged identity cards to match. Ethan had not the first clue what the alias might be. Dead end.

At a loss, he wandered down the mall. He could, he supposed, just return to his room and let Millisor find *him,* but whether he'd get a chance to negotiate or even get a word out before being scragged by Okita's vengeful comrades was a very moot point.

The variegated passers-by scarcely ruffled his self absorption, but two approaching faces were extraordinary. A pair of plainly-dressed men of average height had brilliant designs painted upon their faces, completely masking their skin. Dark red was the base color of one, slashed with orange, black, white, and green in an intricate pattern, obviously meaningful. The other was chiefly brilliant blue, with yellow, white, and black swirls outlining and echoing eyes, nose, and mouth. They were deep in conversation with each other. Ethan stared covertly, fascinated and delighted.

It wasn't until they passed nearly shoulder to shoulder with him that Ethan's eye teased out the features beneath the markings. He suddenly realized that he did know what the face paint meant, from his recent reading. They were marks of rank for Cetagandan ghem-lords.

Captain Rau looked up at the same moment square into Ethan's face. Rau's mouth opened, his eyes widening in the blue mask, his hand reaching swiftly for a pouch on his belt. Ethan, after a second of confounded paralysis, ran.

There was a shout behind him. A God-the-Father *nerve disruptor* bolt crackled past his head. Ethan glanced back over his shoulder. Rau had only missed, it appeared, because Millisor had knocked the lethal weapon upward. They were yelling at each other even as they began pursuit. Ethan now remembered clearly just how terrifying the Cetagandans could be.

Ethan dove head-first into an Up lift tube and swam as frantically as any salmon through its languid field, hand over hand down the emergency grips. Jostled rising passengers swore at him in surprise.

He exited on another level, ran, took another lift, changed again, and again, with many a panicked backward glance. Here across a crowded shop, there through a deserted construction zone— AUTHORIZED PERSONNEL ONLY—twist, turn, double and dive. He crossed out of Transients' Lounge somewhere, for gadgets on the walls that had long lists of instructions and prohibitions beside them in the tourist ghetto here were nearly anonymous.

He went to ground at last in an equipment closet, and lay gasping for breath on the floor. He seemed to have lost his pursuers. He had certainly lost himself.

Chapter Seven

He sat in a sour huddle for an hour after he caught his breath and his heart stopped hammering. So, running away and hiding was no way to solve problems? Any action was better than rotting in Quinn's cell-like hostel room? He meditated glumly on just how fast one could re-evaluate one's moral position in the flash and crackle from the silvered bell-muzzle of a nerve disruptor. He stared into the closet's dimness. At least Quinn's prison had had a bathroom.

He would have to go to the Station authorities, now. There was no going back to Quinn, she'd made that clear, and no illusion left of his ability to negotiate a separate peace with the Cetagandan crazies. He beat his head gently on the wall a few times in token of his self-esteem, unfolded from his crouch, and began to search his hidey hole.

A locker full of Stationer work coveralls made him suddenly conscious of his own downsider apparel, followed by another and more horrid thought; had Quinn planted another bug on him? She'd certainly had plenty of opportunity. He stripped to the skin and traded his Athosian clothes for some red coveralls and boots that were only a little too large. The boots chafed his feet, but he dared not retain even his socks. He only needed the camouflage long enough to sneak to—make that, locate and sneak to—the nearest Station Security post. It wasn't stealing; he would give the coveralls back at the first opportunity.

He slipped out of the closet and took a left down the empty corridor, trying to imitate the rolling purposeful stride of a Stationer while fixing the closet's number in his memory so that he might retrieve his clothes later. He passed two women in blue coveralls floating a loaded pallet, but they were obviously in a hurry. Ethan couldn't nerve himself to stop them for directions. A Stationer such as his red suit proclaimed him to be would have known the way. It was bound to seem peculiar to them even without his accent.

He was just beginning to seriously question his original assumption that if he didn't know where he was, neither would his pursuers, when a scream, a thud, and a rattling crash snapped his attention to the cross-corridor just ahead. Two float pallets had collided. Crying and swearing mingled with a clatter of plastic boxes cascading from one pallet and an ear-splitting, screeching twitter. Balls of yellow feathers exploded from a spilled box into the air, darting, swerving, and ricocheting off the walls.

A woman was screaming— "The gravity! The gravity!" Ethan recognized the voice with a start. It was the bony green-and-blue uniformed ecotech, Helda, from the Assimilation Station. She was glaring at him, scarlet-faced. "The gravity! Wake up, you twit, they're getting away!" She scrambled out from under the boxes and staggered toward him, panting.

As Ethan struggled with his conscience whether or not to blow his incognito by volunteering medical assistance—the other three people involved all seemed to be moving, sitting up, and complaining at healthy volume—Helda yanked open a cover on the wall beside Ethan's head and turned a rheostat. The frantically fluttering songbirds beat their wings in vain as they were sucked to the deck. Ethan's knees nearly buckled as his weight more than doubled. He found himself and the ecotech braced against each other.

"Oh, gods, you again," snarled Helda. "I might have known. Are you on duty?"

"No," squeaked Ethan.

"Good. Then you can help me pick up these damned birds before they spread toxoplasmosis all over the Station."

Ethan recognized the disease, a mildly contagious, slow subviral life-form that attacked RNA, and fell willingly to hands and knees to crawl after her and pluck up the dozen or so hysterical birds pinned by their own weight. Only when the last bird was stuffed back into its box and the lid tied down with the ecotech's belt did she pay the least attention to the bitterly complaining human accident victims now lying flat on the deck and panting for breath. When she turned the gravity dial back to standard Ethan felt he might take off and fly himself, so great was the relief.

One of the victims shakily sitting up wore a pine-green and blue uniform like Helda's. Blood runneled down his face from a cut on his forehead. Ethan gauged it at a glance as spectacular but superficial. Clean pressure over the wound—not from his hands, he'd been handling the birds—would take care of it in a trice. The two white-faced teenagers from the other pallet, one male, one that Ethan's now-practiced eye identified immediately as female, clutched each other and stared at the blood in horror, obviously under the impression that they'd near-killed the man.

Ethan, holding his hands in loose fists to remind himself to touch nothing, put some gruff authority into his voice and directed the frightened boy to make a pad and stop the bleeding. The girl was crying that her wrist was broken, but Ethan would have bet Betan dollars it was merely sprained. Helda, holding her hands identically to Ethan's, elbowed open a comlink in the wall and called for help. Her first concern was for a decontamination team from her own department, her second for Station Security, and a distant third for a medtech for the injured.

Ethan blew out his breath in relief at his lucky break. Instead of his having to hunt for Station Security, it would be coming to him. He could fling himself upon Security's mercy and get unlost at the same time.

The decontamination team arrived first. Airseal doors cordoned off the area, and the team began going over walls, floors, ceilings and vents with sonic scrubbers, x-ray sterilizers, and potent disinfectants.

"You'll have to deal with Security, Teki," Helda directed her assistant as she stepped into the sealed passenger pallet the decontamination team had produced. "See that they throw the book at those two joyriders."

The two teenagers paled still further, scarcely reassured by a secretive shake of his head directed at them by Teki.

"Well, come along," Helda snapped at Ethan.

"Huh? Uh . . ." Monosyllablic grunts might conceal his accent, but were lousy for eliciting information. Ethan dared a, "Where to?"

"Quarantine, of course."

Quarantine? *For how long?* He must have mouthed the words aloud, for the decon man shooing him toward the float pallet said soothingly, "We're just going to scrub you down and give you a shot. If you've got a heavy date, you can call her from there. We'll vouch for you."

Ethan wanted to disabuse the decon man of this last dreadful misapprehension, but the ecotech's presence inhibited him. He allowed himself to be chivvied into the pallet. He seated himself across from the woman with a fixed smile.

The canopy was closed and sealed, shutting off all sound from the exterior. Ethan pressed his face longingly to the transparent surface as the pallet rose and drifted past the two arriving Security patrolmen in their orange and black uniforms. He doubted they could hear him if he screamed.

"Don't touch your face," Helda reminded him absently, glancing back for one last look at the disaster scene. It seemed to be under control now, the decon team having taken charge of her float pallet of birds and reopened the airseal doors.

Ethan displayed his closed fists in token of his understanding.

"You do seem to have grasped sterile technique," Helda admitted grudgingly, settling back and glowering at him. "For a while there I thought Docks and Locks was now hiring the mentally handicapped."

Ethan shrugged. Silence fell. Silence lengthened. He cleared his throat. "What was that?" he asked gruffly, with a jerk of his chin back to indicate the recent accident.

"Couple of stupid kids playing starfighter with a float pallet. Their parents will hear from me. You want speed, take a tube car. Float pallets are for work. Or do you mean the birds?"

"Birds."

"Condemned cargo. You should have heard the freighter captain scream when we impounded them. As if he had a civil right to spread disease all over the galaxy. Although it could have been worse." She sighed. "It could have been beef again."

"Beef?" croaked Ethan.

She snorted. "A whole bleeding herd of live beef, being transported somewhere for breeding. Crawling with microvermin. I had to cut them in half to fit them in the disposer. Worst mess you ever saw. We broke *them* down to atoms, you can bet. The owners sued the Station." Her eyes glinted. "They lost." She added after a moment, "I hate messes."

Ethan shrugged again, hoping the gesture would be taken for sympathy. This frightening female was the last person on the Station he wished to surrender to, bar Millisor. He trusted devoutly that Ecobranch did not dispose of diseased human transients in the same cavalier fashion.

"Did Docks and Locks clear up that trash dump in Bay 13 yet?" she inquired suddenly.

"Er, ah . . ." Ethan cleared his throat.

She frowned. "*What* is the matter with you? Do you have a cold?"

Ethan wouldn't have dared admit to harboring viruses. "Strained my voice yesterday," he muttered.

"Oh." She settled back like a disappointed bird-dog. The monologue having now fallen officially to her, she stared around for another topic of conversation. "Now *that's* a disgusting sight." She jerked her thumb to the side; Ethan saw nothing but a couple of passing Stationers. "You wonder how someone can stand to let herself go like that."

"What?" muttered Ethan, totally bewildered.

"That fat girl."

Ethan looked back over his shoulder. The obesity in question was so clinically mild as to be nearly invisible to his eye, given the extra padding of the female build.

"Biochemistry," Ethan suggested placatingly.

"Ha. That's just an excuse for lack of self-discipline. She probably gorges at night on fancy imported downsider food." Helda brooded a moment. "Revolting stuff. You don't know *where* it's been. Now, *I* never eat anything but clean vat lean, and salads—none of those high-fat, gooey dressings, either—" a lengthy dissertation upon her diet and digestion more than filled the time until the float pallet stopped at their destination.

Ethan waited until she'd exited before unpeeling himself from the farthest corner of his seat. He poked his head cautiously out.

The quarantine processing area had a hospitalish smell that pierced him with homesickness for Sevarin. A distressed lump rose in his throat, which he swallowed back down.

"This way, sir." A male ecotech in a sterile gown motioned him ahead. A couple more techs promptly began going over the passenger pallet with x-ray sterilizers. Ethan was directed down a corridor from the off-loading zone to a sort of locker room, the gowned tech following behind sweeping up his invisible septic footprints with a sonic scrubber.

The tech gave him a brief, accurate lecture on how to take a decontamination shower, and absconded with his red suit and boots muttering, "No underwear? Some people!"

Ethan's IDs and credit chit were in the red coveralls' pocket. Ethan nearly cried. But there was no help for it. He showered thoroughly, dried, scratched his itching nose at last, then hovered naked and alone about the chamber for what seemed a very long time. He was just meditating on the pros and cons of running howling nude back down the corridor when the gowned tech returned.

"Hello." The tech dropped his folded coveralls and boots on a bench, pressed a hypospray against his arm, said, "See Records on your way out. It's the other way," and wandered off. "Goodbye."

Ethan pounced on the clothes. His wallet was still in the pocket, or at any rate back in the pocket. He sighed relief, dressed, squared his shoulders in preparation for full confession, and at a guess from the tech's cryptic speech went on down the corridor in the direction opposite his entry.

He was just thinking himself lost again when he saw an open arched door and beyond it a room with a manned computer interface. The young man from the bird pallet, Teki, now pale and interesting with a white plastic bandage across his forehead, arrived at the doorway at the same time as Ethan. He paused rather breathlessly, and with a bright nod let Ethan enter first. The bony Helda stood by the counter within, tapping one foot, with her arms folded.

She fixed Teki with a cold look. "It's about time you got off that comconsole. I thought I told you to tell your girlfriend not to call you at work."

"It wasn't Sara," said Teki righteously. "It was a relative. With a *business* message." Sensibly re-directing Helda's attention, he seized on Ethan. "Look, here's our helper."

Ethan swallowed and approached, wondering how to begin. He wished the woman wasn't there.

"Good-oh," said the green-and-blue uniformed man running the computer interface. "Just let me have your card, please." He held out his hand.

He wanted some standard Stationer ID, Ethan supposed. He took a deep breath, nerved himself, and glanced up at the frowning woman. His confession became an "Er, ah—don't have it with me . . ."

Her frown deepened. "You're supposed to have it with you at all times, Docks-and-Locks."

"Off duty," Ethan offered desperately. "My other coveralls." If he could just get away from this terrible female, he'd go straight to Security. . . .

She inhaled.

Teki cut in. "Aw, c'mon, Helda, give the guy a break. He did help us out with those blasted tweetybirds." Winking, he took Ethan by the arm and towed him toward the chamber's other exit. "Just go get it and bring it back, all right?"

The woman said, "Well!" but the counterman nodded.

"Don't mind Helda," whispered the young man to Ethan as he pushed him past the inner door, through a UV-and-filtered-air lock, and out a final airseal. "She drives everybody crazy. That fat kid of hers emigrated downside just to get away from her. I don't suppose she said thanks for the help?"

Ethan shook his head.

"Well, *I* thank you." He nodded cheerfully; the airseal doors hissed closed on his smile.

"Help," said Ethan in a tiny voice. He turned around. He was in another standard Station corridor, identical to a thousand others. He squeezed his eyes shut briefly in spiritual pain, sighed, and started walking.

Two hours later he was still walking, certain he was circling. Station Security posts, frequent and highly visible in Transients' Lounge, disappeared here in the Stationers' own areas. Or maybe like the equipment in the walls they were merely cryptically marked, and he was walking right past them. Ethan swore softly under his breath as another blister rubbed up by his ill-fitting boots popped.

Glancing down a cross-corridor, he gave a joyous start. The stuff on the walls had labels, lists, and locks again. He turned that way. A few more junctions, another door, and he found himself in a public mallway. Not far along it, beside a fountain, shimmered a directory.

"You are here," he muttered, tracing through the holovid. Colored light licked over his finger. Nearest Security post, there: he looked up to match the map with a mirrored booth on the balcony at the farthest end of the mall. Just one level below this mallway was his own hostel. Quinn's hostel was over a bit, up two. He wondered anxiously where the one in which the Cetagandans had questioned him was. Not far away enough, he was sure. He steeled himself and hobbled up the mall, glancing out of the corner of his eye for men in bright face paint or women in crisp gray-and-white uniforms.

KLINE STATION SECURITY, glowed the legend atop the booth. The mirroring was one-way. From inside there was a fine view overlooking the mall, Ethan found upon entering. Banks of monitors and com links filled the little room. A Security person sat, feet up, eating little fried morsels of something from a bag and gazing idly down at the colorful concourse.

A Security *woman*, Ethan corrected himself with an inward moan. Young and dark-haired, in her orange-and-black quasi-military uniform she bore a faint, generic resemblance to Commander Quinn.

He cleared his throat. "Uh, excuse me . . . Are you on duty?"

She smiled. "Alas, yes. From the time I put on this uniform to the time I take it off at the end of my shift, plus whenever they beep me after. But I get off at 2400," she added encouragingly. "Would you care for a newt nugget?"

"Uh, no—no thank you," Ethan replied. He smiled back in nervous uncertainty. Her smile became blinding. He tried again. "Did you hear anything about a fellow firing a nerve disruptor in one of the mallways this morning?"

"Gods, yes! Is it gossip in Docks and Locks already?"

"Oh . . ." Ethan realized where some of the disjointedness in this conversation was coming from; the red coveralls were misleading her. "I'm not a Stationer."

"I can tell by your accent," she agreed cordially. She sat up and rested her chin on his hand. Her eyes positively twinkled. "Earning your way across the galaxy as a migrant worker, are you? Or did you get stranded?"

"Uh, neither . . ." Ethan continued smiling, since she did. Was this some expected part of exchanges between the sexes? Neither Quinn nor the ecotech had used such intense facial signals, but Quinn admitted herself atypical and the ecotech was definitely weird. His mouth was beginning to hurt. "But about that shooting . . ."

"Oh, have you talked to anybody that was there?" Some of her glowing manner fell away, and she sat up more alertly. "We're looking for more witnesses."

Caution asserted itself. "Uh—why?"

"It's the charge. Of course the fellow claims he fired by accident, showing off the weapon to his friend. But the tipster who called in the incident claimed he shot at a man, who ran away. Well, the tipster vanished, and the rest of the so-called witnesses were the usual lot—full of contagious drama, but when you pin 'em down they always turn out to have been facing the other way or zipping their boot or something at the actual moment the disruptor went off." She sighed. "Now, if it's proved the fellow with the disruptor was firing *at* someone, he gets deported, but if it was an accident all we can do is confiscate the illegal weapon, fine him, and let him go. Which we'll have to do in another twelve hours if this intent-to-harm business can't be substantiated."

Rau under arrest? Ethan's smile became beatific. "What about his friend?"

"Vouches for him, of course. He shook down clean, so there was nothing to be done with *him.*"

Millisor on the loose, if he understood the Security woman correctly. Ethan's smile faded. And Setti, whom Ethan had never seen and would not recognize if he walked right into him. Ethan took a breath. "My name is Urquhart."

"Mine's Lara," said the Security woman.

"That's nice," said Ethan automatically. "But—"

"It was my grandmother's name," the Security woman confided. "I think family names give such a nice sense of continuity, don't you? Unless you happen to get stuck with something like Sterilla, which happened to an unfortunate friend of mine. She shortens it to Illa."

"Uh—that wasn't exactly what I meant."

She tilted her head, chipper. "Which wasn't?"

"I beg your pardon?"

"What thing that you said wasn't what you meant?"

"Er . . ."

"—quhart," she finished. "It's a nice name, I don't think you should be shy about it. Or did you get teased about it as a kid or something?"

He stood with his mouth open, awash. But before the conversational thread could become more raveled, another, older Security woman shot down the lift tube that connected the booth to an upper level. She exited the tube with an authoritative thump.

"No socializing on duty, Corporal, may I remind you—again," she called over her shoulder as she went to a locker. "Wrap it up, we've got a call."

The Security girl made a moue at her superior's back, and whispered to Ethan, "2400, all right?" She came to her feet, and something like attention, as her officer pulled a pair of sidearms in holsters from the wall cabinet. "Serious, ma'am?"

"We're wanted for a search cordon, levels C7 and 8. A prisoner just vanished from Detention."

"Escaped?"

"They didn't say escaped. They said, vanished." The officer's mouth twisted dryly. "When Echelon insists on weasel-words, I get suspicious. The prisoner was that dirt sucker they pried loose from the nerve disruptor this morning. Now, I had a look at his weapon. Best military issue, and not new." She buckled on her heavy-duty stunner, and handed its twin to her corporal.

"Yeah, so? Army surplus." The corporal straightened her uniform, checked her face in a small mirror, then checked her weapon with equal care.

"Yeah, not so. I'll bet you Betan dollars to anything you choose he's another gods-please-damn unregistered military espionage agent."

"Not that plague again. Is it just one, or a bunch?"

"I hope it's not a bunch. That's the worst. Unpredictable, violent, don't care about the law, don't care about *public safety* for the gods' sakes, and after you half break your neck handling them with gloves you still get reprimanded at some embassy's request and all your carefully amassed case evidence gets tossed into the vacuum—" She turned to make shooing motions at Ethan. "Out, out, we've got to lock up here." She added to her corporal, "You stick tight by me, you hear? No heroics."

"Yes, ma'am."

And Ethan found himself locked out on the balcony as Station Security, in a pair, hurried out of sight. The corporal glanced back over her shoulder at his tentative raised hand and "Ah—ah . . ." and gave him a friendly little wave of her fingers.

Over three corridors. Up two levels. Through the maze within a maze of Quinn's hostel. The familiar door. Ethan moistened his lips, and knocked.

And knocked again.

And stood . . .

The door hissed open. His relief was swallowed by surprise as a cleaning robot dodged around him. The room beyond was as anonymous and pristine as if never occupied.

"Where'd she go?" he wailed, rhetorically to relieve his feelings.

But the cleaning robot paused. "Please rephrase your question, sir or madam," it spoke from a grille in its maroon plastic housing.

He turned to it eagerly. "Commander Quinn—the person who had this room—where did she go?"

"The previous occupant checked out at 1100, sir or madam. The previous occupant left no forwarding address with this hostel, sir or madam."

Eleven hundred? She must have gone within minutes of the time he'd stormed out, Ethan calculated. "Oh, God the Father . . ."

"Sir or madam," chirped the robot politely, "please rephrase your question."

"I wasn't talking to you," said Ethan, running his hands through his hair. He felt like tearing it out in clumps.

The robot hovered. "Do you require anything else, sir or madam?"

"No—no . . ."

The robot whirred away up the corridor.

Down two levels. Over three corridors. The Security team had not yet returned. Their booth was still locked.

Ethan plunked down beside the fountain and waited. This time he would really turn himself in, for sure. If Rau had got himself on the wrong side of the law by firing at Ethan, Ethan must therefore be on the right side, correct? He had nothing to fear from Security.

Of course, if they couldn't keep Rau the arrestee in their secure area, how likely was it they could keep Rau the assassin out? Ethan studiously ignored this whisper from his logic as a fear planted by Quinn. Security was his best chance. Indeed, now that he had irrevocably offended Quinn, Security was his only chance.

"Dr. Urquhart?" A hand fell on Ethan's shoulder.

Ethan jumped half a meter, and whirled. "Who wants t'know?" he demanded hoarsely.

A blond young man fell back a pace in consternation. He was of middle height, wire-muscled and slight, dressed in an unfamiliar downsider fashion, a sleeveless knit shirt, loose trousers bunched at the ankles into the tops of comfortable-looking boots of some butter-soft leather. "Excuse me. If you're Dr. Ethan Urquhart of Athos, I've been looking all over for you."

"Why?"

"I hoped you might help me. Please, sir, don't go—" he held out a hand as Ethan flinched away. "You don't know me, but I'm very interested in Athos. My name is Terrence Cee."

Chapter Eight

After a moment's stunned silence Ethan sputtered, "What do you want of Athos?"

"Refuge, sir," said the young man. "For I'm surely a refugee." Tension rendered his smile false and anxious. He grew more urgent as Ethan backed away slightly. "The census courier's manifest listed one of your titles as ambassador-at-large. You can give me political asylum, can't you?"

"I—I—" Ethan stammered. "That was just something the Population Council threw in at the last minute, because no one was sure what I'd find out here. I'm not really a diplomat, I'm a doctor." He stared at the young man, who stared back with a kind of beaten hunger. The automatic part of Ethan totted up the symptoms of fatigue Cee presented: gray in the hollows of his skin, bloodshot sclera, a barely observable tremula in his smooth corded hands. A horrid realization shook Ethan. "Look, uh—you aren't by chance asking me to protect you from ghem-Ccolonel Millisor, are you?"

Cee nodded.

"Oh—oh, no. You don't understand. It's just me, out here. I don't have an embassy or anything like that. I mean, real embassies have security guards, soldiers, a whole intelligence corps—"

Cee's smile twisted. "Does the man who arranged Okita's last accident really need them?"

Ethan stood with his mouth open, his utter dismay robbing him of reply.

Cee went on. "There are many of them—Millisor can command the resources of Cetaganda against me—and I'm alone. The only one left. The sole survivor. Alone, it isn't a question whether they'll kill me, only how soon." His beautiful structured hands opened in pleading. "I was sure I'd eluded them, and it was safe to double back. Only to find Millisor—the fearless vampire hunter himself!—" the young man's mouth thinned in bitterness, "squatting across the last gateway. I beg you, sir. Grant me asylum."

Ethan cleared his throat nervously. "Ah—just what do you mean by 'vampire hunter'?"

"It's how he views himself." Cee shrugged. "To him all his crimes are heroics, for the good of Cetaganda, because somebody has to do the dirty work—his exact thought, that. He's proud to do it. But he doesn't have to nerve himself to do the dirty work on me. He hates and fears me worse than any hell, in his secretive little soul—ha! As if his secrets were more vital or vile than anyone else's. As if I gave a damn for his secrets, or his soul."

Wanly, Ethan recognized the seasick symptoms of talk at cross-purposes again. He stretched for some bottom to this floating conversation. "What are you?"

The young man drew back, his face suddenly shuttered with suspicion. "Asylum. Asylum first, and then you can have it all."

"Huh?"

The suspicion turned to despair before Ethan's eyes. The excitement that hope had lent Cee evaporated, leaving a bleak dryness. "I understand. You see me as *they* do. A medical monstrosity, put together from graveyard bits, cooked in a vat. Well," he inhaled resolution, "so be it. But I'll have vengeance on ghem-Captain Rau, at least, before my death. That much I swear to Janine."

Ethan seized upon the one intelligible item in all this, and with as much dignity he could muster said, "If by a 'vat' you are referring to a uterine replicator, I'll have you know I was incubated in a uterine replicator myself, and it is every bit as good as any other method of generation. Better. So I'll thank you not to insult my origins, or my life's work."

Some of the same floating confusion that Ethan was sure must be in his own face crossed Cee's. Why not. Misery, Ethan thought with acid satisfaction, loves company.

The young man—boy, really, for take away the aging effects of exhaustion upon him and he was surely younger than Janos—seemed about to speak, then shook his head and turned away.

Necessity, thought Ethan frantically, is the uterine replicator of invention. "Wait!" he cried. "I grant you the asylum of Athos!" He might as well have promised the remission of Cee's sins as well, since he had about as much power to effect one as the other. But Cee turned back anyway, hope flaring again in his blue eyes, hot like a gas jet. "Only," Ethan went on, "you have to tell me where you took the ovarian cultures the Population Council ordered from Bharaputra Laboratories."

It was Terrence Cee's turn to stand in open-mouthed dismay now. "Didn't Athos receive them?"

"No."

The breath hissed from the blond man's mouth as though he had been struck in the stomach. "Millisor! He must have got them! But no—but how—he could not conceal—"

Ethan cleared his throat gently. "Unless you think your Colonel Millisor would spend seven hours interrogating me—quite unpleasantly—as to their whereabouts for a practical joke, I don't think so."

It was actually quite refreshing to see somebody else look as agitated as he felt, Ethan thought. Cee turned to his new protector, his arms spread wide in bewilderment.

"But Dr. Urquhart—if you don't have them, and I don't have them, and Millisor doesn't have them—where'd they go?"

Ethan thought he finally understood Elli Quinn's stated dislike of being on the damned defensive. He'd had a belly full of it himself. Dump enough shit on it, he thought savagely, and even the fragile seed of resolution in his timid heart might blossom into something greater. He smiled pleasantly at the blond young man. Cee really did look like a shorter, thinner Janos. It was the coloration that did it. But Cee's mouth held no hint of the petulance that sometimes marred Janos's when set in anger or weariness.

"Suppose," suggested Ethan, "we pool our information and find out?"

Cee gazed up at him—he was several centimeters shorter than Ethan—and asked, "Are you truly Athos's senior intelligence agent?"

"In a sense," murmured Athos's only agent of any description, "yes."

Cee nodded. "It would be a pleasure, sir." He took a deep breath. "I must have some purified tyramine, then. I used the last of my supply on Millisor three days ago."

Tyramine was an amino acid precursor of any number of endogenous brain chemicals, but Ethan had never heard of it as a truth drug. "I beg your pardon?"

"For my telepathy," said Cee impatiently.

The floor seemed to drop away under Ethan. Far, far away. "The whole psionics hypothesis was definitively disproved hundreds of years ago," he heard his own voice say distantly. "There is no such thing as mental telepathy."

Terrence Cee touched his forehead in a gesture that reminded Ethan of a patient describing a migraine.

"There is now," he said simply.

Ethan stood blinded by the dawning of a new age. "We are standing," he croaked at last, "in the middle of a bleeding public mallway in one of the most closely monitored environments in the galaxy. Before Colonel Millisor leaps out a lift tube, don't you think we'd better, uh, find some quieter place to talk?"

"Oh. Oh, yes, of course, sir. Is your safe house nearby?"

"Er . . . Is yours?"

The young man grimaced. "As long as my cover identity holds."

Ethan gestured invitingly, and Cee led off. Safe house, Ethan decided, must be a generic espionage term for any hideout, for Cee took him not to a home but to a cheap hostel reserved for transients with Stationer work permits. Here were housed clerks, housekeepers, porters, and other lower-echelon employees of the service sector whose function Ethan could only guess at, such as the two women in bright clothing and gaudy make-up almost Cetagandan in its unnatural coloration, who started to accost Cee and himself and shouted some unintelligible insult after them when they brushed hastily by.

Cee's quarters were a near-clone of Ethan's own neglected Economy Cabin, plain and cramped. Ethan wondered rather fearfully if Cee was reading his mind right now—apparently not, for the Cetagandan expatriate gave no sign of realizing his mistake yet.

"I take it," said Ethan, "that your powers are intermittent."

"Yes," replied Cee. "If my escape to Athos had gone as I'd originally planned, I meant never to use them again. I suppose your government will demand my services as the price of its protection, now."

"I—I don't know," answered Ethan honestly. "But if you truly possess such a talent, it would seem a shame not to use it. I mean, one can see the applications right away."

"Can't one, though," muttered Cee bitterly.

"Look at pediatric medicine—what a diagnostic aid for pre-verbal patients! Babies who can't answer, Where does it hurt? What does it feel like? Or for stroke victims or those paralyzed in accidents who have lost all ability to communicate, trapped in their bodies. God the Father," Ethan's enthusiasm mounted, "you could be an absolute savior!"

Terrence Cee sat down rather heavily. His eyes widened in wonder, narrowed in suspicion. "I'm more often regarded as a menace. No one I've met who knew my secret ever suggested any use for me but espionage."

"Well—were they espionage agents themselves?"

"Now that you mention it—yes, for the most part."

"So, there you are. They see you as what they would be, given your gift."

Cee gave him a very odd look, and smiled slowly. "Sir, I hope you're right." His posture became less closed, some part of the tension uncoiling in his lean muscles, but his blue eyes remained intent upon Ethan. "Do you realize that I am not a human being, Dr. Urquhart? I'm an artificial genetic construct, a composite from a dozen sources, with a sensory organ squatting like a spider in my brain that no human being ever had. I have no father and no mother. I wasn't born, I was made. And that doesn't horrify you?"

"Well, er—where did the men who made you get all your other genes? From other people, surely?" asked Ethan.

"Oh, yes. Carefully selected strains, all politically purified." Wormwood could not have set Cee's mouth in a tighter line.

"So," said Ethan, "if you count back, let me see, four generations, *every* human being is a composite from as many as sixteen different sources. They're called ancestors, but it comes to the same thing. Your mix was just marginally less random, that's all. Now, I do know genetics. With the exception of that new organ you claim, I can flat guarantee the 'just marginally.' That is not the test of your humanity."

"So what is the test of humanity?"

"Well—you have free will, obviously, or you could not be oppos-ing your creators. Therefore you are not an automaton, but a child of God the Father, answerable to Him according to your abilities," Ethan catechized.

If Ethan had sprouted wings and flapped up to the ceiling Cee could not be staring at him in more shaken astonishment. It seemed as though these perfectly obvious facts had never before been presented to him.

Cee strained forward. "What am I to you, then, if not a monster?"

Ethan scratched his chin reflectively. "We all remain children of the Father, however we may otherwise be orphaned. You are my brother, of course."

"Of course . . . ?" echoed Cee. His legs and arms drew in, making his body a tight ball. Tears leaked between his squeezed eyelids. He scrubbed his face roughly on his trouser knee, smearing the tears' reflective sheen across his flushed face. "Damn it," he whispered, "I'm the ultimate weapon, the super agent. I survived it all. How can you make me weep now?" Suddenly savage, he added, "If I find out you're lying to me, I swear I will kill you."

In another man's mouth they might have seemed empty words. Coming from Cee's ragged edginess, the threat was stomach-knotting. "You're obviously extremely tired," Ethan, alarmed, offered in solace. Cee had not yet quite regained his self-control, though he was clearly trying, breathing carefully as a yogi. Ethan hunted around the room and handed him a tissue. "And I'd think looking at the world through Millisor's eyes, if that's what you've been doing lately, would be something of a strain."

"You've got that straight," choked Cee. "I've had to go in and out of his mind since this thing," he made the migraine gesture again, "got fully developed in my head when I was thirteen years old."

"Ick," said Ethan, in heartfelt candor. "Well, that's it, then."

Cee emitted a surprised laugh that did more for his self-control than the breathing exercise had. "How can you know?"

"I don't know anything about how your telepathy works, but I've met the man." Ethan rubbed his lips thoughtfully. "How old are you?" he asked suddenly.

"Nineteen."

There was no adolescent defiance in the reply. Cee was merely stating a fact, as if his youth had never been an object in any test put to him. The insight chilled Ethan, like sighting the tip of an iceberg. "Ah—I don't suppose you'd care to tell me a little more about yourself? Speaking as your Immigration Officer, as it were."

✧   ✧   ✧

The work had been based on a natural mutation of the pineal gland, Terrence Cee explained. How the migrant witch-woman, deformed, impoverished, and quite mad, had first caught the attention of Dr. Faz Jahar, Cee did not know. But she had been swept from her slum hovel into the university laboratory of the alert young medico. Jahar knew somebody who knew somebody who knew a high-ranking army ghem-lord and could make him look and listen; and so Jahar tapped a researcher's dream, unlimited secret government funding. The madwoman vanished into classified oblivion, and was never seen alive again. To be sure, none of her previous acquaintances ever inquired after her.

Cee's recitation was cool and distant now, on-track, as something practiced too many times and overtrained. Ethan was not sure if the previous breakdown or current excess of Cee's self-control was more unnerving.

The telepathy complex was refined in vitro, twenty generations in five years. The first three human experiments to have it spliced into their chromosomes died before they ever outgrew their uterine replicators. Four more died in infancy and early childhood of inoperable brain cancers, three of some subtler failure to thrive.

"Is this disturbing you?" Cee, glancing up, inquired of Ethan.

Ethan, greenish-white and curled into a corner, said "No . . . go on."

The specifications of the matrix genetic blueprints—Ethan would have called them children—were made more rigid. Jahar tried again. L-X-1O-Terran-C was the first survivor. His early test results proved ambiguous, disappointing. Funding was cut. But Jahar, after so much human sacrifice, refused to give up.

"I suppose," said Cee, "Faz Jahar was as much of a parent as I ever had. He believed in me—no. He believed in his own work, within me. When the nurses and the extra technicians were dropped out of his budget, he tutored me himself. He even tutored Janine."

"Who is Janine?" asked Ethan after a moment, as Cee fell silent.

"J-9-X-Ceta-G was—my sister, if you will," said Cee at last. His inward gaze did not meet Ethan's eyes. "Although we shared few genes besides those for the pineal receptor organ. She was the only other survivor among Jahar's early creations. Or perhaps she was my wife. I'm not sure if Jahar intended her from the beginning as a co-progenitor of his new model human, or if she was merely an experimental trifle—he encouraged sex between us, as we grew older—but she was never trained as an intelligence agent. Millisor always thought of her as a sort of potential brood-mare for some nest of spylets—he had these secret, sexually-charged fantasies about her. . . ." Ethan was relieved when Cee broke off, sparing him a guided tour of Millisor's questionable sexuality.

Dr. Faz Jahar's fortunes took an abrupt upward turn when Terrence Cee hit puberty. Completion of his brain growth and change in his biochemical balance at last activated the frustratingly quiescent organ. Cee's telepathic abilities became demonstrable, reliable, repeatable.

There were limitations. The organ could only be kicked into a state of electrical receptivity upon the ingestion of high doses of the amino acid tyramine. Receptivity faded as Cee's body metabolized the excess and returned him to his original biochemical balance. Telepathic range was limited to a few hundred meters at best. Reception was blocked by any barrier that interfered with the electrical signals emitted by the target brains.

Some minds could be experienced more clearly than others, some could barely be picked up at all even when Cee was actually touching his target's body. This seemed to be a problem of fit, or match, between sender and receiver, for some minds that registered as no more than a formless, mushy sense of life to Terrence came through in hallucinatory clarity—subvocalization, sensory input, the stream of conscious thought, and all—to Janine, and vice versa.

Too many individuals within target range created interference with each other. "Like being at a party where everything is too loud," said Cee, "and straining to pick out one conversation."

Dr. Jahar had primed Terrence Cee all his short life for his destiny in service to Cetaganda, and at first Cee had been content, even proud, to fulfill it. The first hairline cracks in his resolve came as he became familiar with the true minds of the hard-edged security personnel who surrounded the project. "Their insides didn't match their outsides," explained Cee. "The worst ones were so far gone in their corruptions, they didn't even smell it anymore."

The cracks propagated with each new experimental assignment in counter-intelligence.

"Millisor's deadliest mistake," Cee said thoughtfully, "was having us probe the minds of suspected intellectual dissidents while he interrogated them on their loyalty. I never knew people like them were possible, before."

Cee began military training with carefully selected private tutors.

There was talk of using him as a field agent, on safe assignments or ones vital enough to justify risking his expensive person. There was no talk at all of ever admitting him to the ghem-comrades, the tightly-knit society of men who controlled the officer corps and the military junta that in turn controlled the planet of Cetaganda, its conquests, and its client outposts.

Cee's telepathy gave him no secret window into the subconscious minds of his subjects. The only memories he could probe were those the subjects were presently calling to mind. This made using Cee for mere surveillance, in the hopes of catching something valuable on the fly-by, rather wasteful of the telepath's time. Organized interrogations were much more efficient. The interrogations Cee attended became wider in scope, and often much uglier.

"I understand completely," said Ethan with a small shiver.

It was Janine, perhaps, who first began thinking of their creators as their captors. The dream of flight, never spoken aloud, fed back and forth between them during the rare occasions when both their powers were activated at the same time. Both began siphoning off and hoarding their tyramine tablets. Escape plans were laid, debated, and honed in utter silence.

The death of Dr. Faz Jahar was an accident. Cee became quite passionate trying to convince Ethan, who hadn't questioned the point, of the truth of this. Perhaps the escape might have gone better if they hadn't tried to destroy the laboratory and bring the four new children with them. It had complicated things. But Janine had insisted that none be left behind. When she and Terrence were made to sit in more frequently on more intensive interrogations of political prisoners, Cee gave up arguing that part of the plan with her.

If only Jahar hadn't tried to save his notes and gene cultures, he wouldn't have gone up with the bomb. If only the little children hadn't panicked and cried out, the guard might not have spotted them; if only they hadn't tried to run, he might not have fired. If only Terrence and Janine had chosen a different route, a different planet, a different city, different identities, in which to lose themselves.

The coolness of Cee's recitation froze altogether, his voice going flat, drained of emotion and self. He might have been denouncing the past decisions of some figure of ancient history, instead of his own, except that he began to rock, unconsciously, in cadence with his words. Ethan found his foot tapping along, and stilled it.

If only he had not left the apartment that afternoon to pick a little money off the spacers at cards down by the shuttleport docks and get groceries. If only he had arrived back a little earlier, and Captain Rau a little later. If only Janine had not gambled her life against Captain Rau's nerve disruptor to warn him. If only. If only. If only.

Cee discovered the altered consciousness of the berserker within himself in the battle to keep her body, every cell harboring the genetic secret, from falling back into Millisor's hands. It was a full day before Cee was able to get her corpse cryogenically frozen, much too long to beat brain-death even if there had been no disruptor damage.

He hoped anyway. All his will was focused now on the single obsession of making as much money as he could as quickly as possible. Terrence Cee, who had embraced a near-honest poverty for the sake of Janine's scruples while she lived, now plumbed the twisted uses of his power to their limits to amass the wealth needed to serve her corpse. Enough for the passage of a man and a heavy cyro-carton to the laboratories of Jackson's Whole where, it was whispered, enough money could buy *anything*.

But even a great deal of money could not buy life back from that death. Alternatives were gently suggested. Would the honored customer perhaps wish a clone made of his wife? A copy could be produced which even the most expert could not tell from the original. He would not even have to wait seventeen years for the copy to grow to maturity; things could be speeded up amazingly. The copy's personality could even be recreated with a surprising degree of verisimilitude, for the right price—perhaps even improved upon, were there aspects of the original not quite to the honored customer's taste. The clone herself would not know the difference.

"All I needed to get her back," said Cee, "was a mountain of money and the ability to convince myself that lies were truth." He paused. "I had the money."

Cee was silent for a long time. Ethan stirred uneasily, embarrassed as a stranger in the presence of death.

"Not to be pushy or anything," he prodded at last, "but I trust you were about to explain the connection of all this with the order for 450 live human ovarian cultures that Athos sent to Bharaputra Laboratories?" He smiled winningly, hoping that Terrence Cee was not about to clam up just before the pay-off.

Cee glanced at Ethan sharply, and rubbed his forehead and

temples in unconscious frustration. In a little while he answered, "Athos's order came into the genetics section of Bharaputra Labs while I was going around and around with them about Janine. I'd never heard of the planet before. It sounded so strange and distant to me—I thought, if only I could get there, maybe I could lose Millisor and my past forever. After Janine's remains were—" he swallowed painfully, his eyes flinching away from Ethan's, "were cremated, I left Jackson's Whole and started on a roundabout route designed to bury my trail. I lined up a job here to give me a cover identity while I waited for the next ship to Athos.

"I got here five days ago. Out of pure habit, I checked the transients' register for Cetagandan nationals. And found Millisor had been set up here for three months as an art and artifacts broker. I couldn't imagine how I'd spotted him before he spotted me, until I maneuvered close enough to read him. He'd pulled everyone off transient surveillance to hunt for you and Okita. They're at least a week behind in covering the exits, and with one man short they're going to be a long time catching up. I believe I owe you more than one thank you, Doctor. What did you do with Okita, anyway?"

Ethan refused to be diverted. "What did you have Bharaputra Laboratories do to Athos's order?" He experimented with giving Cee a stern and fishy stare.

Cee moistened his lips. "Nothing. Millisor just thinks I did. I'm sorry it got him all wound up.

"I'm not quite as dense as I appear," said Ethan gently. Cee made a vague I-never-suggested-it gesture. "I happen to have independent information that Bharaputra's top genetics team spent two months assembling an order that could have been put together in a week." He glanced around at the tiny, sparse room. "I also note that you appear to be minus a mountain of money." Ethan gentled his voice still further. "Did you have them make an ovarian culture from your *wife's* remains, instead of having her cloned, when you realized cloning could not bring back what was essential in her? And then bribe them to slip the culture into our order, meaning to follow it on to Athos?"

Cee twitched. His mouth opened; he finally whispered, "Yes, sir."

"Complete with the gene complex for this pineal mutation?"

"Yes, sir. Unaltered." Cee stared at the floor. "She liked children. She was beginning to dare to want them, when we thought we were safe, before Rau caught up with us the final time. It was the last thing—the last thing I could do for *her.* Anything else would have merely been for myself. Can you see that, sir?"

Ethan, moved, nodded. At that moment he would have cheerfully decked any Athosian fundamentalist who dared to argue that Cee's tragic fixation upon his forbidden female could have no honor in it. He trembled at his own radical emotion. And yet, something did not add up. He almost had it . . .

The door buzzer blatted.

They both jumped. Cee's hand checked his jacket for some hidden weapon. Ethan merely paled.

"Does anyone know you're here?" Cee asked.

Ethan shook his head. But he had promised this young man the protection of Athos, such as it was. "I'll answer it," he volunteered. "You, er—cover me," he added as Cee started to object. Cee nodded, and slipped to one side.

The door hissed open.

"Good evening, Ambassador Urquhart." Elli Quinn, framed in the aperture, beamed at him. "I heard the Athosian Embassy might be in the market for security guards—soldiers—an intelligence corps. Look no further, Quinn is here, all three in one. I'm offering a special discount on daring rescues to any customer who places his order before midnight. It's five minutes till," she added after a moment. "You going to invite me in?"

Chapter Nine

"You again," groaned Ethan. He gave Commander Quinn a malignant glower as her exact words—his exact words—registered. "Where'd you plant the bug, Quinn?"

"On your credit chit," she answered promptly. "It was the one item you slept with." She rocked on her toes, and cocked her head to peer around Ethan's shoulder. "Won't you introduce me to your new friend? Pretty please?"

Ethan bleated under his breath.

"Exactly," Quinn nodded. "And I must say you're the best stalking-goat I ever ran. The way troubles flock to you is just astonishing."

"I thought you had no use for—ah—queers," said Ethan coldly.

She grinned evilly. "Well, now, don't take that too much to heart. To tell the truth, I was starting to wonder just how I was ever going to shift you out from under my bed. I was really very pleased with your initiative."

Ethan's lip curled, but until she took her booted foot off the door groove the safety seals would refuse to close. He stepped aside with what grace he could choke up.

Terrence Cee's right hand smoothed his jacket, tensely. "Is she a friend?"

"No," said Ethan curtly.

"Yes." Commander Quinn nodded vigorously, turning her best smile on the new target.

Cee, Ethan noted irritably, showed the same silly startlement that all galactic males displayed upon their first encounter with Commander Quinn; but to Ethan's relief he seemed to recover far more quickly, his eyes jumping from her face to her holster to her boots and other likely weapons check-points. Quinn's eyes mapped Cee's inventory of her against Cee himself, and crinkled smugly in the knowledge of where to look for *his* weapons. Ethan sighed. Was the mercenary woman always destined to be one step ahead of them?

The doorseals hissed shut and Quinn seated herself with her hands resting demurely on her knees, away from whatever arsenal she carried. "Tell this nice young man who I am, Ambassador Doctor Urquhart."

"Why?" Ethan grumped.

"Oh, c'mon. You owe me a favor, after all."

"What!" Ethan inhaled in preparation for fully expressing his outrage, but Quinn went on.

"Sure. If I hadn't primed my cousin Teki to ease you on out of quarantine you'd still be hung up in there with no ID, legal prisoner of the handwashers. And you and Mr. Cee here would never have met."

Ethan's jaw snapped shut. "Introduce yourself," he finally fumed.

She gave him a gracious nod and turned to Cee, her studied ease not quite concealing an intent excitement. "My name is Elli Quinn. I hold the rank of Commander in the Dendarii Free Mercenary Fleet, and the post of a field agent in the Fleet intelligence section. My orders were to observe ghem-Colonel Millisor and his group and discover their mission. Thanks largely to Ambassador Urquhart here, I have finally done so." Her eyes sparked satisfaction.

Terrence Cee stared at them both in new suspicion. It made Ethan boil, after all his careful work to coax Cee's damaged spirit to trust him a little.

"Who are you working for?" asked Cee.

"Admiral Miles Naismith commands me."

Cee brushed this aside impatiently. "Who is *he* working for, then?"

Ethan wondered why this question had never occurred to him.

Commander Quinn cleared her throat. "One of the reasons, of

course, for hiring a mercenary agent instead of using your own in-house people is precisely so that if the mercenary is captured, he cannot reveal where all his reports went."

"In other words, you don't know."

"That's right."

Cee's eyes narrowed. "I can think of another reason for hiring a mercenary. What if you want to do an in-house check of your own people? How can I be sure you're not working for the Cetagandans yourself?"

Ethan gasped at this horrific, logical idea.

"In other words, might Colonel Millisor's superiors just be evaluating him for his next promotion?" Quinn's smile grew quizzical. "I hope not, because they would be awfully unhappy with that last report of mine—" by which vagueness Ethan gathered that she had no intention of publicly reclaiming Okita as her kill. This generosity failed to fill him with gratitude.

"—the only guarantee I can offer you is the same one I'm relying on myself. I don't think Admiral Naismith would accept a contract from the Cetagandans."

"Mercenaries get rich by taking their contracts from the highest bidder," said Cee. "They don't care who."

"Ah—hm. Not precisely. Mercenaries get rich by winning with the least possible loss. To win, it helps if you can command the best possible people. And the very best do care who. True, there are moral zombies and outright psychos in the business—but not on Admiral Naismith's staff."

Ethan barely restrained himself from quibbling with this last assertion.

Well-launched, she continued, forgetting her carefully non-threatening posture and rising to pace about in all her nervous concentration. "Mr. Cee, I wish to offer you a commission in the Dendarii Free Mercenary Fleet. Based on your telepathic gift alone—if proved—I can personally guarantee you a tech/spec lieutenancy on the Intelligence Staff. Maybe something more, given your experience, but I'm sure I can deliver a lieutenancy. If you were indeed bred and born for military intelligence, why not make that destiny your own? No secret power structures like the ghem-lords make or break you in the Dendarii. You rise on merit alone. And however strange you think yourself, there you will find a comrade who is stranger still—"

"I'll bet," muttered Ethan.

"—live births, replicator births, genetically altered marginal habitat people—one of our best ship captains is a genetic hermaphrodite."

She wheeled, she gestured; she would swoop down like a hawk if she could, Ethan felt, and carry off his new charge.

"I might point out, Commander Quinn, that Mr. Cee asked for the protection of *Athos.*"

She didn't even bother to be sarcastic. "Yes, there you are," she said quickly. "If it's Millisor you fear, what better place to find protection than in the middle of an army?"

Furthermore, Ethan thought, Commander Quinn was unfairly good-looking when she was flushed with excitement. . . . He peeked fearfully at Cee, and was relieved to find him looking cold and unmoved. If that pitch had been aimed with such passion at him, he might be ready to run out and sign up himself. Did the Dendarii need ship's surgeons?

"I presume," Cee said dryly, "they would wish to debrief me first."

"Well," she shrugged, "sure."

"Under drugs, no doubt."

"Ah—well, it *is* mandatory for all Intelligence volunteers. In spite of all good conscious intent, it's possible to be a plant and not know it."

"Interrogation with all the trimmings, in short."

She looked more cautious. "Well, we have all the trimmings in stock, of course. If needed."

"To be used. If needed."

"Not on our *own* people."

"Lady," he touched his forehead, "when this thing is activated I *am* the other people."

Some of her energy drained away in doubt for the first time. "Ah. Hm."

"And if I choose not to go with you—what will you do then, Commander Quinn?"

"Oh—well . . ." She looked, Ethan thought, exactly like a cat pretending not to stalk a mouse. "You're not off Kline Station yet. Millisor's still out there. I might be able to do you a favor or two yet—"

Was this a threat or a bribe?

"In return, you might care to give me some more information about Millisor and Cetagandan Intelligence. Just so I have *something* to take back to Admiral Naismith."

Ethan pictured a cat proudly depositing a dead mouse on its owner's pillow.

Cee must have been picturing something similar, for he inquired sardonically, "Would my dead body do?"

"Admiral Naismith," Quinn assured him, "wouldn't like that *nearly* so well."

Cee snorted. "What do you blindlings know of men's real minds? What can any of you really tell? When I look at you blind like this, what can I know?"

Quinn hesitated in real thought. "Well, that's the way we must judge people all the time," she offered slowly. "We measure actions, as well as words and appearances. We make imaginative guesses. We place faith, if you will." She nodded toward Ethan, who, prodded by honest conscience, nodded back even though he had no wish to prop any argument of hers.

Cee paced. "Both actions and lies may be compelled, against the real will. By fear, or other things. I know." He turned, turned again. "I must know. I must *know*." He stopped, fixed them both with a stare like a man trying to penetrate black midnight. "Get me some tyramine. Then we talk. When I can know what you *really* are."

Ethan wondered if the dismay in his own face matched Quinn's. They looked at each other, not needing telepathy to picture the other's thoughts: Quinn, doubtless stuffed with secret Dendarii intelligence procedures; himself, well—Cee was bound to find out eventually what a mistake he'd made seeking protection from Ethan. Perhaps it had better not be the hard way. Ethan sighed regret for the demise of his flatteringly exalted image in Cee's eyes. But a fool is twice a fool who tries to conceal it. "All right by me," he conceded mournfully.

Quinn was chewing her lip, abstracted. "That's obsolete," she muttered, "and so's that, and they have to have changed that by now—and Millisor knows all *that* already. And all the rest is purely personal." She looked up. "All right."

Cee appeared nonplused. "You agree?"

Quinn's mouth quirked. "The first time the ambassador and I have agreed on anything, I think?"

She raised her eyebrows at Ethan, who muttered, "Humph."

"Do you have access to purified tyramine?" Cee demanded of them. "On hand?"

"Oh, any pharmacy would stock it," Ethan said. "It has some clinical uses in—"

"There's a problem with going to a pharmacy," Cee began grimly, when Quinn burst out in a tone of sudden enlightenment. "Oh. *Oh.*"

"Oh, what?" asked Ethan.

"Now I understand why Millisor went to such trouble to penetrate the commercial computer network, but didn't bother trying to get into the military one. I didn't see how he could have possibly got 'em mixed up." The satisfaction of a puzzle solved glowed attractively in her dark eyes.

"Huh?" said Ethan.

"It's a trap, right?" said Quinn.

Cee nodded confirmation.

She explained to Ethan, "Millisor has the commercial computer network flagged. I bet if anybody on Kline Station purchases purified tyramine, whistles go off in Millisor's listening post, and up pops Rau, or Setti or somebody—cautiously, on account of there are sure to be false alarms—and—oh, yes. Very neat." She nodded professional approval.

She sat a moment, absently scratching one perfect front tooth with a fingernail. An ex-nail biter, Ethan diagnosed. "I may have a way around that," she murmured.

Ethan had never manned an espionage listening post before, and he found the gadgetry fascinating. Terrence Cee seemed coolly familiar with the principles if not the particular models. The Dendarii apparently went in heavily for microminiaturization along Betan lines. Only the need to interface with gross human eyes and fingers bloated the control pad, propped open on the table between Cee and Ethan, to the size of a small notebook.

The view displayed by the little holovid plate of the Station arcade where Quinn now stood tended to jump rather disorientingly with movements of her head, since the vid pick-up surfaces were concealed in her tiny bead earrings. But with concentration and a little practice Ethan found himself absorbed in the display with almost the illusion of being an eyewitness to the scene half the Station away. Cee's darkened hostel room faded from his consciousness, although Cee himself intent beside Ethan, remained a distracting presence.

"Nothing can go wrong, if you do exactly what I tell you and don't try to ad lib," Quinn was explaining to her cousin Teki, who was looking smart in a fresh pine-green and sky-blue uniform. The white bandage on Teki's forehead from yesterday's float pallet accident had been replaced by a clear permeable plastic one. Ethan noted with approval no sign of redness or swelling around the neatly sealed cut. "Remember, it's the *absence* of a signal that calls for an abort," Quinn went on. "I'll be nearby in case of emergencies, but try not to look at me. If you don't see me wave from the balcony, just turn right around and take the stuff back and tell them you wanted the other, the, um . . ."

"Tryptophan," Ethan muttered, "for sleep."

"Tryptophan," Quinn continued, "for sleep. Then just go home. Don't try to look for me. I'll get in touch with you later."

"Elli, has this got something to do with that fellow you were so hot to spring from quarantine yesterday?" said Teki. "You promised you'd explain it later."

"It's not later enough yet."

"It's got something to do with the Dendarii Mercenaries, doesn't it?"

"I'm on leave."

Teki grinned. "You in love, then? At least he's an improvement over the crazy dwarf."

"Admiral Naismith," said Quinn stiffly, "is not a dwarf. He's nearly five feet tall. And I am not 'in love' with him, you low-minded twit; I merely admire his brilliance." The view jiggled as she bounced on her heels. "Professionally."

Teki hooted, but cautiously. "All right, so if this isn't something for the dwarf, what is it? You're not smuggling drugs or some damn thing, are you? I don't mind doing you a favor, but I'm not risking my job even for you, coz."

"You're on the side of the angels, I assure you," Quinn told him impatiently. "And if you don't want to be late for your precious job, it's time to shove off."

"Oh, all right." Teki shrugged good-naturedly. "But I demand the whole fairy-tale later, you hear?" He turned to saunter off up the arcade, adding a last word over his shoulder. "But if it's all so legal, moral, and non-fattening, why do you keep saying, 'Nothing can go wrong'?"

"Because nothing *can* go wrong." Quinn invoked the phrase like a charm under her breath, and waved him off.

In a few minutes she sauntered after him. Ethan and Cee were treated to a leisurely window-shopping tour of the arcade. Only an occasional, offhand pan around reassured them that the cousin was still in sight. Teki entered the pharmaceutical dispensary. Quinn moved up, adjusting the directional audio pick-up in her hair clip, pausing to mull over a display of medications against nausea due to weightlessness.

"Hm," the pharmacist was saying. "We don't get much call for that one. . . ." He tapped out a code on his computer interface. "Half-gram or one-gram tablets, sir?"

"Uh—one-gram, I guess," answered Teki.

"Coming up," the man replied. There was a long pause. The sound of more tapping; a muttered curse from the pharmacist. The sound of a fist pounding lightly on the casing of the control panel. A plaintive beep from the computer. More tapping, in a repeat of the previous pattern.

"Millisor's trap at work?" Ethan whispered to Cee.

"Almost certainly. Time delay," Cee muttered back.

"I'm sorry, sir," said the pharmacist to Teki. "There seems to be a glitch. If you'll have a seat, I'll retrieve your order manually. It will just be a few minutes."

Quinn dared a look toward the counter. The pharmacist pulled out a thick index book, blew off a fine layer of dust, and thumbing through the thin pages exited by a rear door.

Teki sighed and flopped down on a padded bench. He glanced up at Quinn; her gaze immediately broke away from the dispensing counter to focus in apparent fascination upon a rack of contraceptives. Ethan flushed in embarrassment and stole a glance at Cee, whose concentration appeared unruffled. Ethan returned his gaze straightly to the holovid. The galactic man was no doubt used to these things, having by his own admission lived intimately with a woman for several years. He probably saw nothing wrong. Personally, Ethan wished Quinn would go back to the spacesick pills.

"Rats," breathed Quinn. "That was quick."

Another dizzying glance, up at the new customer hastily entering the dispensary. Average height, blandly dressed, compact as a bomb—Rau.

Rau slowed down abruptly, cased the counter, spotted Teki, and drifted down the display aisle breathing deeply and quietly. He fetched up on the opposite side of the contraceptive rack from Quinn. She must have given him one of her dazzling smiles, for a startled answering smile was jerked involuntarily from his lips before he retreated across the room and away from her distracting face.

The pharmacist returned at last and fed Teki's credit card to the computer which, working properly now, tasted it and gave it back with a demure burp. Teki gathered up his package and left. Rau was not more than four paces behind him.

Teki wandered slowly down the arcade, with many a furtive glance toward the empty balcony on the far end. He finally seated himself by the standard fountain-and-green-plants display in the middle, and waited a good long time. Rau seated himself nearby, pulled out a hand-viewer, and began to read. Quinn window-shopped interminably.

Teki glanced at the balcony, checked his chronometer in frustration, and stared down the arcade at Quinn, who took no apparent notice of him. After a few more minutes of fuming foot-tapping, Teki got up and started to leave.

"Oh, sir," called Rau, smiling. "You forgot your package!" He held it up invitingly.

"Gods fly away with you, Teki!" Quinn whispered fiercely under her breath. "I said no ad libs!"

"Oh. Er—thank you." Teki took the package back from death's polite hand, and stood a moment blinking indecisively. Rau nodded and returned to his hand-viewer. Teki sighed aggrievedly and trudged back up the arcade to the dispensary.

"Excuse me," Teki called to the pharmacist. "But is it tyramine or tryptophan that's the sleep aid?"

"Tryptophan," said the pharmacist.

"Oh, I'm sorry. It was the tryptophan I wanted."

There was a slightly murderous silence. Then, "Quite, sir," said the pharmacist coldly. "Right away."

"It wasn't a total loss," said Quinn, pulling out her earrings and attaching them carefully to their holders in the monitor case. "At least I confirmed that Rau is hiding out in Millisor's listening post. But I'd kinda figured that anyway."

She added the hair clip, sealed the case, and slipped it into her jacket. Hooking a chair under herself with one foot, she sat with her elbows on Terrence Cee's little fold-out table. "I suppose they'll follow Teki around for the next week, now. So much the better. I like to see my adversaries overworked. Just so he doesn't try to call me, nothing can go wrong."

Nothing can go right, either, thought Ethan with a sideways look at Terrence Cee's face. Cee had been almost hopeful when the tyramine seemed within their grasp. Now he was closed and cold and suspicious once again.

Quite aside from his own ill-advised pledge to protect Cee, Ethan could not walk away from this frenetic tangle as long as Millisor remained a threat to Athos. And whatever their separate ends might be, Cee's and Quinn's and his own, the untangling would surely take all their combined resources.

"I suppose I could try to steal some," said Quinn unenthusiastically, evidently also conscious of Cee's renewed frigidity. "Although Kline Station is not the easiest place for that sort of tactic . . ." She trailed off in thought.

"Is there any particular reason it has to be purified tyramine?" Ethan asked suddenly. "Or do you just need so many milligrams of tyramine in your bloodstream, period?"

"I don't know," said Cee. "We always just used the tablets."

Ethan's eyes narrowed. He rummaged the little wall-desk nearby for a note panel, and began to tap out a list.

"What now?" asked Quinn, craning her neck.

"A prescription, by God the Father," said Ethan, tapping on in growing excitement. "Tyramine occurs naturally in some foods, you know. If you choose a menu with a high concentration of it— Millisor can't possibly have every food outlet on the Station bugged—nothing illegal about going grocery shopping, is there? You'll probably have to hit the import shops for a lot of this. I don't think much of it is room service console standard fare."

Quinn took the list and read it, her eyebrows rising. "All of this stuff?"

"As much as you can get."

"You're the doctor," she shrugged, getting to her feet. Her smile grew lopsided. "I think Mr. Cee is going to need one."

Two hours of strained silence later, Quinn returned to Cee's hostel room lugging two large bags.

"Party time, gentlemen," she called, dumping the bags on the table. "What a feast."

Cee quailed visibly at the mass of edibles.

"It—seems rather a lot," remarked Ethan.

"You didn't say how much," Quinn pointed out. "But he only has to eat and drink until he switches on." She lined up claret, burgundy, champagne, sherry, and dark and light beer bulbs in a soldierly row. "Or passes out." Around the liquids in an artistic fan she placed yellow cheese from Escobar, hard white cheese from Sergyar, two kinds of pickled herring, a dozen chocolate bars, sweet and dill pickles. "Or throws up," she concluded.

The hot fried chicken liver cubes alone were native produce from the Kline Station culture vats. Ethan thought of Okita and gulped. He picked up a few items and blanched at the price tags.

Quinn caught his grimace, and sighed. "Yes, you were right about having to hit the import shops. Do you have any idea how this is going to look on my expense account?" She bowed Terrence Cee toward the smorgasbord. "Bon appetit."

She kicked off her boots and lay down on Cee's bed with her hands locked behind her neck and an expression of great interest on her face. Ethan pulled the plastic seal off a liter squeeze bottle of claret, and helpfully offered up the cups and utensils the room service console produced.

Cee swallowed doubtfully, and sat down at the table. "Are you sure this will work, Dr. Urquhart?"

"No," said Ethan frankly. "But it seems like a pretty safe experiment."

An audible snicker drifted from the bed. "Isn't science wonderful?" said Quinn.

Chapter Ten

For courtesy's sake Ethan shared the wine, although he gave the chicken livers, pickles, and chocolate a pass. The claret was rotgut despite its price, although the burgundy was not bad and the champagne—for dessert—was quite tasty. A slightly gluey disembodiment warned Ethan that courtesy had gone far enough. He wondered how Cee, still dutifully nibbling and sipping across the table, was holding up.

"Can you feel anything yet?" Ethan inquired of him anxiously. "Can I get you anything? More cheese? Another cup?"

"A spacesick sack?" asked Quinn helpfully. Ethan glared at her, but Cee merely waved away the offers, shaking his head.

"Nothing yet," he said. His hand unconsciously rubbed his neck. Ethan diagnosed incipient headache. "Dr. Urquhart, are you quite sure that no part of the shipment of ovarian cultures Athos received could have been what Bharaputra sent?"

Ethan felt he'd answered that question a thousand times. "I unpacked it myself, and saw the other boxes later. They weren't even cultures, just raw dead ovaries."

"Janine—"

"If her, um, donation was cultured for egg cell production—"

"It was. They all were."

"Then it wasn't there. None were."

355

"I saw them packed myself," said Cee. "I watched them loaded at the shuttleport docks on Jackson's Whole."

"That narrows down the time and place they could have been switched, a little," observed Quinn. "It had to have been on Kline Station, during the two months in warehouse. That only leaves, ah, 426 suspect ships to trace." She sighed. "A task, unfortunately, quite beyond my means."

Cee swirled burgundy in a plastic cup, and drank again. "Beyond your means, or simply of no interest to you?"

"Well—all right, both. I mean, if I really wanted to trace it, I'd let Millisor do the legwork, and just follow him. But the shipment is only of interest because of that one gene complex in one culture which, if I understand things correctly, you also contain. A pound of your flesh would serve my purposes just as well—better. Or a gram, or a tube of blood cells . . ." she trailed off, inviting Cee to pick up on the hint.

Cee sidestepped. "I can't wait for Millisor to trace it. As soon as his team catches up on their backlog, they'll find me here on Kline Station."

"You have a little margin yet," she pointed out. "I'll wager they're going to waste quite a few man-hours following poor innocent Teki around while he does the housework. Maybe it'll bore them to death," she said hopefully, "sparing me the bother of completing a certain odious task I promised House Bharaputra."

Cee glanced at Ethan. "Doesn't Athos want the shipment back?"

"We'd written it off. Although retrieving it would save purchasing another, I'm afraid it would be a false economy if Millisor followed it to Athos with an army at his back and genocide on his mind. He's so obsessed with this idea that Athos must have it—I'd actually like to see him find the damned thing, just to be sure Athos was rid of him." Ethan gave Cee an apologetic shrug. "Sorry."

Cee smiled sadly. "Never apologize for honesty, Dr. Urquhart." He went on more urgently. "But don't you see, the gene complex *cannot* be allowed to fall back into their hands. Next time they'll be more careful to make their telepaths true slaves. And then there will be no limits to the corruptions of their use."

"Can they really make men without free will?" said Ethan, chilled. The old catch-phrase, "Abomination in the eyes of God the Father" seemed illuminated with real and disquieting meaning. "I must say I don't like that idea, followed to its logical conclusion. Machines made of flesh . . ."

Quinn spoke lazily from the bed in a tone, Ethan was becoming aware, that concealed fast-moving thought. "Seems to me the genie's out of the bottle anyway, whether Millisor gets the stuff back or not. Millisor thinks in terms of counter-intelligence from a lifetime of habit. He's only going through so much exercise to be sure nobody *else* gets it. Now that Cetaganda knows it can be done, they'll duplicate the research in time. Twenty-five years, fifty years, whatever it takes. By then maybe there had better be a race of free telepaths to oppose them." Her eyes probed Cee as if already locating a good spot for a biopsy.

"And what makes you think your Admiral Naismith's employer would be any improvement over the Cetagandans?" asked Cee bitterly.

She cleared her throat. The telepath had been reading her mind ever since he'd started asking questions, Ethan realized, and she already knew it. "So, send a duplicate tissue sample of yourself to every government in the galaxy if you like." She grinned wolfishly. "Millisor would have a stroke, giving you your revenge and getting Athos off the hook at the same time. I *like* efficiency."

"To make a hundred races of slaves?" asked Cee. "A hundred mutant minorities, all feared and hated and controlled by whatever ruthless force seems necessary to their uneasy captors? And hunted to their deaths when that control fails?"

Ethan had never found himself clinging to a cusp of human history before. The trouble with the position, he found, was that in whatever direction you looked there fell away a glassy, uncontrollable slide down to a strange future you would then have to live in. He had never wanted to pray more, nor been less sure that it would do any good.

Cee shook his head, drank again. "For myself, I'm done with it. No more. I'd have walked into the fire three years ago, but for Janine."

"Ah," said Quinn. "Janine."

Cee looked up with piercing eyes. Not nearly drunk, Ethan thought. "You want a pound of flesh, mercenary? That's the price that will buy it. Find me Janine."

Quinn pursed her lips. "Mixed in, you say, with the rest of Athos's mail-order brides. Tricky." She wound a strand of hair around her finger. "You realize, of course, that my mission here is finished. I've done my job. And I could stun you where you sit, take my tissue sample, and be gone before you came to."

Cee stirred uneasily. "So?"

"So, just so you realize that."

"What do you want of me?" Cee demanded. Anger edged his voice. "To trust you?"

Her lips thinned. "You don't trust anybody. You never had to. Yet you demand that others trust you."

"Oh," said Cee, looking suddenly enlightened. "That."

"You breathe one word of *that*," she smiled through clenched teeth, "and I'll arrange an accident for you like Okita never dreamed of."

"Your Admiral's personal secrets are of no interest to me," said Gee stiffly. "They're hardly relevant to this situation anyway."

"They're relevant to me," Quinn muttered, but she gave him a small nod, conditional acceptance of this assurance of privacy.

Every sin that Ethan had ever committed or contemplated rose unbidden to his mind. He took Quinn's unspoken point. So, evidently, did Cee, for he turned the subject by turning to Ethan.

Ethan suddenly felt terribly naked. Everything that he least wanted to be caught thinking about seemed to race through his consciousness. Cee's marvelous physical attractiveness, for example, the nervous intelligent leanness of him, the electric blue eyes— Ethan damned his own weakness for blonds, and yanked his thoughts back from a slide to the sexual. Watching himself be mentally undressed in Ethan's thoughts would hardly impress Gee with Ethan's cool diplomatic medical professionalism. Ethan envied Quinn's bland, unfailing control.

But it could be worse. He could think about just how gossamer-thin was the shield of Athos's protection he had supposedly thrown over Cee, on the basis of which the telepath had revealed so damagingly much. How betrayed was Cee going to feel when he discovered that the asylum of Athos consisted of Ethan's wits, period? Ethan reddened, utterly ashamed, and stared at the floor.

He was going to lose Cee to Quinn and the glamour of the Dendarii Mercenaries before he even got a chance to tell him about Athos—the beautiful seas, the pleasant cities, the ordered communes and the patchwork terraformed farmlands, and beyond them the vast wild desolate wastes with their fascinating extremes of climate and people—the saintly, if grubby, contemplative hermits, the outlaw Outlanders . . . Ethan pictured himself taking Cee sailing on the South Province coast, checking the underwater fences of his father's fish farm—did Cetaganda have oceans?—salt sweat and salt water, hot hard work and cold beer and blue shrimp afterward.

Cee shivered, as a man forcing himself awake from some bright but dangerous narcotic dream. "There are oceans on Cetaganda," he whispered, "but I never saw them. My whole life was corridors."

Ethan's red went to scarlet. He felt transparent as glass.

Quinn, watching him, emitted a sour chuckle of perfect understanding. "I predict your talent will not make you popular at parties, Cee."

Cee appeared to pull himself back on track by force of will. Ethan was relieved.

"If you can give me asylum, Dr. Urquhart, why not Janine's seed as well? And if you can't protect her, how do you figure to . . ."

Ethan was not relieved. But lies were pointless now. "I haven't even figured out how to get my own tail out of this mess yet," he admitted ruefully, "let alone yours." He eyed Quinn. "But I'm not quitting."

A wave of her index finger indicated a touché. "I might point out, gentlemen, that before any of us can do anything at all about that genetic shipment we must first find the damn thing. Now, there seems to be a missing element in this equation. Let's try to narrow it down. If none of us nor Millisor has it, who else might?"

"Anyone who found out what it was," answered Cee. "Rival planetary governments. Criminal organizations. Free mercenary fleets."

"Watch who you put in the same breath, Cee," Quinn muttered.

"House Bharaputra must have known," said Ethan.

Quinn smiled with half her mouth. "And they fit two categories out of the three, being both a government and a criminal organization. . . . Ahem. Pardon my prejudices. Yes. Certain individuals in House Bharaputra did know what it was. They all became smoking corpses. I fear that House Bharaputra no longer knows what it hatched. Internal evidence: Bharaputra didn't exactly take me into their entire confidence, but I submit that if they'd known, my assignment would have been to return Millisor and company to them alive for questioning and not, as explicitly requested, dead." She caught Cee's eye. "You doubtless knew their minds better than I. Does my reasoning hold?"

"Yes," Cee admitted reluctantly.

"We're going in circles," Ethan observed.

Quinn twisted her hair. "Yeah."

"What about some individual entrepreneur," suggested Ethan, "stumbling on the knowledge by accident. A ship's crewman, say . . ."

"Aargh," groaned Quinn. "I said to narrow the range of possibilities, not widen them! Data. Data." She swung to her feet, studied Cee. "You done for now, Mr. Cee?"

Cee was hunched over, his hands pressing his head. "Yes, go. No more now."

Ethan was concerned. "Are you experiencing pain? Does it have a localized pattern?"

"Yes, never mind, it's always like this." Cee stumbled to his bed, rolled over, curled up.

"Where are you going?" Ethan asked Quinn.

"First, to empty my regular information traps; second, to try a little oblique interrogation of the warehouse personnel. Although what the human supervisor of an automated system is likely to remember after five to seven months about one shipment out of thousands . . . Oh, well. It's a loose end I can nail down. You may as well stay here, it's as safe as anyplace." A jerk of her head implied, *And you can keep an eye on our friend in the bed.*

Ethan ordered up three-fourths of a gram of salicylates and some B-vitamins from the room service console, and pressed them on the pale telepath. Cee took them and rolled back up with a never-mind-me gesture that failed to reassure Ethan. But Cee's clenched glazed stupor at last relaxed into sleep.

Ethan watched over him, chafing anew at his own helplessness. He had nothing to offer, nothing half so clever as Quinn's bags of tricks. Nothing but an insistent conviction that they all had hold of the problem by the wrong end.

Quinn's return woke Ethan, asleep on the floor. He creaked to his feet and let her in, rubbing sand out of his eyes. It was time for another shave, too; maybe he could borrow some depilatory from Cee.

"How did it go? What did you find out?" he asked.

She shrugged. "Millisor continues to maintain his cover routine. Rau's back at the listening post. I could call in an anonymous tip to Station Security where to look for him, but if he slipped out of Detention again I'd just have to track him down someplace new. And the warehouse supervisor can drink premium aquavit by the liter and talk for hours without remembering anything." She smothered a slightly aromatic belch herself.

Cee awoke to their voices and sat up on the edge of his bed. "Oh," he muttered, and lay back down rather more carefully, blinking. After a moment he sat up again. "What time is it?"

"Nineteen-hundred hours," said Quinn.

"Oh, hell." Cee jerked to his feet. "I've got to get to work."

"Should you go out at all?" asked Ethan anxiously.

Quinn frowned judiciously. "He'd probably better maintain his cover for the time being. It's worked so far."

"I'd better maintain my income," said Cee, "if I'm ever to buy a ticket off this vacuum-packed rat warren."

"I'll buy you a ticket," offered Quinn.

"Going your way," said Cee.

"Well, naturally."

Cee shook his head and stumbled to the bathroom.

Quinn dialed orange juice and coffee from the room service console. Ethan, scooting around the table to reserve a place for Cee, accepted both gratefully.

Quinn sipped from an insulated bulb of shimmering black liquid. "Well, my shift was a bust, Doctor, but how about yours? Did Cee say anything new?"

This was mere polite conversation, Ethan gauged. She had probably recorded every snore they'd emitted.

"We slept, mostly." Ethan drank. The coffee was hot and vile, some cheap synthetic. Ethan considered that it was being charged to Cee, and made no comment. "But I've been thinking about the problem of tracking the shipment. It seems to me we've been going at it wrong way round. Look at the internal evidence of what actually arrived on Athos."

"Trash, you said, to fill up the boxes."

"Yes, but—"

A peeping noise, as from a captive baby chick, sounded from Quinn's rumpled gray and white jacket. She patted the pockets, muttering, "What the hell—oh gods, Teki, I told you not to call me at work . . ." She pulled out a small beeper, and checked a glowing numeric readout.

"What is that?" asked Ethan.

"My emergency call-back signal. A very few people have the code. Supposedly not traceable, but Millisor has some equipment that— hm, that's not Teki's console number."

She swung around in her chair to Terrence Cee's comconsole. "Don't talk, Doctor, and stay out of range of the 'vid pick-up."

The face of a perky auburn-haired young woman wearing blue Stationer coveralls appeared over the holovid plate.

"Oh." Quinn sounded relieved. "It's you, Sara." She smiled.

Sara did not smile. "Hello, Elli. Is Teki with you?"

A tiny spurt of coffee shot out the bulb's mouthpiece as Quinn's hand tightened convulsively. Her smile became fixed. "With me? Did he say he was going to see me?"

Sara's eyes narrowed. "Don't play games with me, Elli. You can tell him *I* was at the Blue Fern Bistro on time. And I'm not going to wait more than three hours for any guy, even one wearing a spiffy green and blue uniform." She frowned at Quinn's gray-and-whites. "I'm not as taken with uniforms as he is. I'm going ho— out. I'm going out, and you can tell him that a party doesn't need him to get started." Her hand moved toward the cut-off control.

"Wait, Sara! Don't cut me off! Teki's not with me, honest!" Quinn, who'd seemed about to climb into the vid, relaxed slightly as the girl's hand hesitated. "What's this all about? I last saw Teki just before his work shift. I know he got to Ecobranch all right. Was he supposed to meet you after?"

"He said he was going to take me to dinner, and to the null-gee ballet, for my birthday. It started an hour ago." The girl sniffed, anger masking distress. "At first I thought he was working late, but I called and they said he left on time."

Quinn glanced at her chronometer. "I see." Her hands flexed, gripping the desk edge. "Have you called his home, or any of his other friends yet?"

"I called everywhere. Your father gave me your number." The girl frowned again in renewed suspicion.

"Ah." Quinn's fingers drummed on her stunner holster, now refilled with a shiny lightweight civilian model. "Ah." Ethan, jolted by the thought of Quinn having a father, struggled to pay attention.

Quinn's eyes snapped up to the girl in the vid. Her voice became lower in register, with a clipped hard edge. This one, Ethan thought involuntarily, really has commanded in combat. "Have you called Station Security?"

"Station Security!" The girl recoiled. "Elli, what for?"

"Call them now, and tell them everything you've told me. File a missing person report on Teki."

"For a fellow who's late for a date? Elli, they'll laugh at me. You're laughing at me, aren't you?" she said uncertainly.

"I'm dead serious. Ask to speak with Captain Arata. Tell him Commander Quinn sent you. He won't laugh."

"But Elli—"

"Do it now! I have to go. I'll check back with you as soon as I can."

The girl's image dissolved in sparkling snow. Invective hissed under Quinn's breath.

"What's going on?" asked Cee, emerging from the bathroom fastening the wrists of his green coveralls.

"I think Millisor has picked up Teki for questioning," said Quinn. "In which case my cover has just gone up in smoke. Damn it! There was no logical reason for Millisor to do that! Is he thinking with his gonads now? That's not like him."

"The logic of desperation, maybe," said Cee. "He was very upset by the disappearance of Okita. Even more upset by Dr. Urquhart's reappearance. He, um—had some very strange theories about Dr. Urquhart."

"On the basis of which," said Ethan, "you went to a great deal of trouble to find me. I'm sorry I'm not the super-agent you were expecting."

Cee gave him a rather odd look. "Don't be."

"I meant to push Millisor off-balance." Quinn bit through a fingernail with an audible snap. "But not that far off. I gave them no reason to take Teki. Or I wouldn't have, if he'd done what I told him and turned around immediately—I knew better than to involve a non-professional. Why didn't I listen to myself? Poor Teki won't know what hit him."

"You didn't have any such scruples about involving me," remarked Ethan, miffed.

"You were involved already. And besides, I didn't use to baby-sit you when you were a toddler. And besides . . ." she paused, shooting *him* a look strangely akin to the one Cee had just given him, "you underestimate yourself," she finished.

"Where are you going?" asked Ethan in alarm as she stalked toward the door.

"I'm going to—" she began determinedly. Her hand, reaching for the door control, hesitated and fell back. "I'm going to think this through."

She turned and began to pace. "Why are they holding him so

long?" she asked. Ethan was not quite sure if the question was addressed to him, Cee, or the air. "They could've drained him of everything he knew in fifteen minutes. Let him wake up on a tube car thinking he'd dozed off on the way home, and no one the wiser, not even me."

"They found out everything I knew in fifteen minutes," Ethan pointed out, "but that didn't stop them."

"Yes, but their suspicions were aroused, sorry, you were quite right, by finding my bug on you. I deliberately put nothing on Teki so that couldn't happen again. Besides, they can check Teki in Kline Station records back to his conception. You were a man without a past, or at least with an inaccessible one, leaving lots of room for paranoid fantasies to grow."

"As a result of which it took them seven hours to convince themselves they were right the first time," said Ethan.

Cee spoke. "And since Okita's disappearance they think you are an agent who successfully resisted seven hours of interrogation. They may be even less willing to take 'I don't know' for an answer now."

"In that case," said Quinn grimly, "the sooner I get Teki out of there the better."

"Excuse me," said Ethan, "but out of where?"

"Odds are, Millisor's quarters. Where you were questioned. Their quiet room, the one I've never been able to bug." She ran her hands through her hair wildly. "How the hell am I going to do this? A frontal assault on a defended cube in the middle of a pack of innocent civilians in the delicate mechanical environment of a space station . . . ? Doesn't sound too efficient."

"How did you rescue Dr. Urquhart?" asked Cee.

"I waited—patiently—for him to come out. I waited a long time for the best opportunity."

"Quite a long time, yes," Ethan agreed cordially. They exchanged tight smiles.

She paced back and forth like a frenzied tigress. "I'm being stampeded. I know I am. I can feel it. Millisor is reaching out for me through Teki. And Millisor's a man with no inhibitions about applying leverage. Q.E.D.—Quinn Eats Dirt. Gods. Don't panic, Quinn. What would Admiral Naismith do in the same situation?" She stood still, facing the wall.

Ethan envisioned diving Dendarii starfighters, waves of space-armored assault troops, ominous lumbering high-energy weapons platforms jockeying for position.

"Never do yourself," muttered Quinn, "what you can con an expert into doing for you. That's what he'd say. Tactical judo from the space magician himself." Her straight back held the dynamism of zen meditation. When she turned her face was radiant with jubilation. "Yes, that's exactly what he'd do! Sneaky little dwarf, I love you!" She saluted an invisible presence and dove for the comconsole.

Cee glanced dismayed inquiry at Ethan, who shrugged helplessly.

The image of an alert-looking clerk in pine green and sky blue materialized above the vid plate.

"Ecobranch Epidemiology Hotline. May I help you?" the clerk intoned politely.

"I'd like to report a suspected disease vector," said Quinn in her most brusque, no-nonsense manner.

The clerk arranged a report panel at her elbow, poised her fingers over it. "Human or animal?"

"Human."

"Transient or Stationer?"

"Transient. But he may even now be transmitting it to a Stationer."

The clerk looked even more seriously interested. "And the disease?"

"Alpha-S-D-plasmid-3."

The clerk's tapping hand paused. "Alpha-S-D-plasmid-2 is a sexually transmitted soft tissue necrosis that originated on Varusa Tertius. Is that what you mean?"

Quinn shook her head. "This is a new and much more virulent mutant strain of Varusan Crotch-rot. They haven't even bioengineered the counter-virus last I heard. Hadn't you people heard of it yet? You're fortunate."

The clerk's eyebrows rose. "No, ma'am." She tapped furiously, and made several adjustments to her recording equipment. "And the name of the suspected vector?"

"Ghem-lord Harman Dal, a Cetagandan art and artifacts broker. He has a new agency in Transients' Lounge, just licensed a few weeks ago. He comes in contact with a lot of people."

Harman Dal, Ethan gathered, was Millisor's alias.

"Oh, dear," said the clerk. "We're certainly glad to get this report. Ah . . ." the clerk paused, groping for phrasing. "And how did you come to know about this individual's disease?"

Quinn's stern gaze broke from the clerk's face to her own feet, to distant corners of the room, to her twisting hands. She positively shuffled. She'd have blushed if she'd had a chance to hold her breath long enough. "How would you think?" she muttered to her belt buckle.

"Oh." The clerk did blush. "Oh. Well, in that case we are extremely grateful that you chose to come forward. I assure you all such epidemiological matters are handled in the strictest confidence. You must see one of our own quarantine physicians at once—"

"Absolutely," agreed Quinn, feigning nervous eagerness. "Can I come down now? But—but I'm terribly afraid that if you don't hurry, Dal is going to put three patients on your hands instead of just two."

"I assure you, ma'am, our department is adept at handling delicate situations. Please place your ID so the machine can read it—"

Quinn did so, promised again to report directly to Quarantine, was reassured of anonymity and gratitude, and broke off.

"There, Teki," she sighed. "Help is on the way. I've signed my real name to a criminal act, but the price was right."

"Being sick is against the law here?" asked Ethan in startlement.

"No, but lodging a false report of a disease vector definitely is. When you see all the machinery it sets in motion you'll realize why they discourage practical jokers. But I'd rather face criminal charges than plasma fire any day. I'll put the fine on my expense account."

Cee's face bore awed delight. "Will Admiral Naismith approve?"

"He may give me a medal." Quinn winked at him, cheerful again. "Now. Ecobranch may get more resistance from their new patient than they expect. Best they get a little low-profile back-up, eh? Can you handle a stunner, Mr. Cee?"

"Yes, Commander."

Ethan waved a hesitant hand. "I had Athosian Army basic training," he heard himself volunteering insanely.

Chapter Eleven

In the event, it was Ethan and not Cee whom Quinn chose to accompany her person on what she dubbed "the second wave of this assault." She left the telepath stationed by the lift tubes at the end of Millisor's transient hostel corridor, arming him with the second stunner of her matching pair.

"Stay out of sight and pick off anybody who bolts," she instructed him, "and don't be shy about firing. With a stunner you can always apologize for mistakes later."

Ethan lifted an eyebrow at this as he turned to pace her down the corridor.

"All right, almost always," she muttered, glancing back over her shoulder to check Cee's concealment in the confusion of potted plants, mirrors, and angled conversation niches that formed the decor of the lift tube foyer. Millisor's chosen hostel was clearly meant for a class of traveler beyond Ethan's budget.

About this time Ethan realized a fatal flaw in the attack plan. "You didn't give me a stunner," he whispered urgently to Quinn.

"I only had two," she murmured back impatiently. "Here. Take my medkit. You can be the medic."

"What am I supposed to do, hit Rau over the head with it?"

She grinned briefly. "If you get the chance, sure. Meantime, Teki's going to be needing an antidote to whatever they've pumped him

367

full of. You'll probably be wanting the fast-penta antagonist. It's right in there next to the fast-penta. Unless things have gone really ugly, in which case I leave it up to your medical expertise."

"Oh," said Ethan, mollified. It almost made sense.

He was just opening his mouth with a newly-marshalled objection when Quinn bundled him into the limited and inadequate concealment of a door niche. Coming down the corridor from the opposite end, toward the bulk freight lift, were three silhouettes leading a sealed passenger pallet with the Ecobranch logo of a stylized fern and water blazoned on the front. Passing into the soft, luxurious light—Ethan sensed someone had done some careful psychological studies of the response of the human brain to selected optical wavelengths—the three figures resolved into a burly Station Security man and two ecotechs, one male, one female.

One bony, angular female whose very walk—stalk—radiated all the personal warmth and charm of a hatchet . . .

"God the Father," squeaked Ethan, "It's Horrible Helda—"

"Don't *panic*," Quinn hissed at him, pushing him back into the niche. It was scarcely 20 centimeters deep, not enough to hide one person, let alone two. "Just turn your back and pretend to be doing something normal and they'll scarcely notice you. Here, turn around, put your hand on the wall beside my head," she arranged him hastily, "lean in, keep your voice down—"

"What am I pretending to be doing?"

"Cuddling. Now shut up and let me listen. And don't look at me like that or I'll start giggling. Though a few well-placed giggles might add conviction . . ."

Doing something normal? Ethan had never felt more abnormal in his life. His shoulderblades crawled in expectation of some lethal outburst from Millisor's room, just across the hall. It didn't help that he couldn't see what was coming. Quinn, of course, had a fine view, with the added bonus that her face was partly concealed by Ethan's arm and her body shielded from stray shots by his.

"Only one Security troop for their back-up?" Quinn muttered, eyes glinting between fluttering eyelashes. "Glad we came."

A muffled peeping sound broke from her jacket. Her hand dove to wring it to silence. She lifted her beeper just far enough out to eye the numeric readout. Her lip curled.

"What is it?" whispered Ethan in her ear.

"That bastard Millisor's room comconsole number," she murmured back sweetly, curling her other hand realistically around the back of Ethan's neck. "So, he squeezed my code out of Teki. Probably wants me to call him up so he can make threats at me. Let him sweat."

Ethan, growing desperate, pressed artistically close to her, oozing around to one side and winning himself a better view.

Eeotech Helda stabbed the door buzzer to Millisor's room and checked a report panel in her hand. "Ghem-lord Harman Dal? Transient Dal?"

There was no response.

"Is he home?" asked the other ecotech.

For answer Helda pointed to a sealed panel in the wall. Ethan guessed its colored lights must encode some sort of life-support usage reading, for the other ecotech said, "Ah. And with company, too. Maybe this is for real."

Helda buzzed again. "Transient Dal, this is Kline Station Biocontrol Warden Helda. I require you to open this door at once or find yourself in violation of Biocontrol Regulations 176b and 2a."

"At least give him time to get his pants on," the other ecotech said. "I mean, this has gotta be embarrassing."

"Let him be embarrassed," said Helda shortly. "The dirtsucker deserves it, bringing his filthy—" she struck the buzzer again.

At the third no-response she pulled a device from her jacket and held it over the door locking mechanism. The device's lights twinkled; nothing happened.

"Gods," said the other ecotech, startled, "they've blocked the emergency override circuits!"

"Now that's a violation of fire-safety regulations," said the burly Security man happily, and tapped out a quick note on his report panel. At a look of inquiry from the other ecotech he explained his sudden good cheer. "You Biocontrol guys may be able to barge over every Transient civil rights guarantee on hearsay evidence but *I* gotta have documented justification or my tail goes on the line." He sighed envy.

"Dal, unblock this door at once!" Helda yelled furiously into the intercom.

"We could cut off his food service from down below," suggested the other ecotech. "He'd have to come out eventually."

Helda ground her teeth. "I'm not waiting that long for some infected dirt-sucker to decide to get cooperative with me." She moved to a sealed locked panel a little farther down the wall marked FIRE CONTROL: AUTHORIZED PERSONNEL ONLY and stuck her ID card in its read-slot. Its transparent doors hissed obediently apart. They wouldn't have dared do otherwise, Ethan thought. She pressed a complex series of bright keypads.

A muffled hissing roar, and faint cries, penetrated from the sealed door to Millisor's room. Helda smiled satisfaction.

"What's she doing?" Ethan whispered in Quinn's shell-like ear.

Quinn was grinning ferociously. "Fire control. Downside, you have automatic sprinkler systems that fling water on fires. Very inefficient. Here we seal the room and pump out the air. Real fast. No oxygen, no oxidation. Millisor either wasn't smart enough or wasn't stupid enough to sabotage the fire control vents . . ."

"Er . . . isn't that rather hard on anyone trapped inside?"

"Normally there's an alarm to evacuate the room first. Helda overrode it."

The unlocking device pressed over the door mechanism by the other ecotech twinkled and beeped. Frantic pounding came from the interior.

"Now Millisor wants to open it, and can't, because of the pressure differential," Quinn whispered.

After a good long pause Helda reversed the airflow. The doorseals parted with an audible pop and whoosh. Millisor and Rau, noses bleeding, stumbled gasping into the corridor, swallowing and working their jaws in an effort to equalize inner-ear pressure.

"Helda didn't even give the poor fellows a chance to tell her about their hostage." Quinn smirked. "*Efficient* lady . . ."

Millisor finally got his breath. "Are you insane?" he snarled at the three Stationer officials. He focused on the Security man. "My diplomatic immunity—"

The Security man jerked his thumb at Helda. "She's in charge here."

"Where is your warrant?" cried Millisor angrily. "This space is legally paid for and possessed, and furthermore I hold a Class IV diplomatic waiver. You have no right to restrict or impede my movements for anything except a major felony charge—"

Ethan could not tell if the bluster was feigned or real, Harman Dal or ghem-Colonel Millisor talking.

"The rights you cite are for transients versus Security," said Helda sharply. "A biocontrol emergency abrogates them all. Now step into the float pallet."

Ethan and Quinn had been playing the part of goggling bystand-ers. About this time Rau's eye fell on them; a hand on his superior's arm stemmed the next argument. Millisor's head swivelled, and his mouth shut with a snap. There was something chilling about so much rage being so abruptly controlled. Not quenched, but banished from the surface, conserved for some future moment. Thought boiled in Millisor's eyes.

"Hey," the Security man said, sticking his head into the recently evacuated room, "there's a third guy in here. Tied to a chair, naked."

"That's disgusting," said Helda. She treated Millisor to a with-ering glare.

The glare failed its intended effect, bouncing off Millisor's furious introspection. Rau stirred nervously. His hand twitched toward his jacket, but both Millisor and Quinn shook their heads at him, each from their different perspective.

"He's bleeding," said the Security man, advancing into the room and, with a glance back at Millisor and Rau, meditatively loos-ing his stunner in its holster.

"It's the nose," called Helda. "Always makes it look like a slaugh-ter, but I guarantee you nobody ever died of a bloody nose."

"My friend here is a doctor," Quinn chirped, inserting herself into the group with a quick wriggle. "Can we help?"

"Oh, yes," called the Security man, sounding relieved.

Quinn grabbed Ethan by the hand and thrust him past her into the room, never taking her smiling gaze off Millisor and Rau. Her stunner had found its way into her other hand, somehow. The Security man glanced back at her and nodded gratefully. Helda grudgingly snapped on plastic gloves and followed to view the scene of debauch for herself.

Ethan approached Millisor's trussed prey anxiously. The Secu-rity man knelt beside the chair and poked tentatively at the wires binding Teki's ankles. They had cut through and his skin oozed blood. Teki's clothes were laid out on the bed in the familiar search array. Wires also bound his wrists, and the skin puffed up redly along their tight lines. Blood from his nose masked his lower face. Teki's head bled, but his eyes were open and smiling, unnaturally bright. He giggled as the Security man touched his ankle. The Security man jumped back in startlement, eyed him with grow-ing grimness, and pulled out his report panel with the air of a swordsman unsheathing his steel. "I don't like the looks of this," he stated.

Helda, coming up behind Ethan, stopped short. "By all the gods! Teki! I always thought you were an idiot, but this goes beyond all—"

"I'm off-shift," said Teki in a small, dignified voice. "I don't hafta put up with you off-shift, Helda." He twitched against his bonds, starting a new trickle of blood across his feet.

Helda's voice stumbled to silence as she got a better view. But not for long. *"What is this?"*

"Is he drugged, Doctor?" asked the Security man as Ethan knelt beside Teki. "What with? Was this a, a private act that got out of hand, or something chargeable?" His thick fingers poised hopefully over his report panel.

"Drugged and tortured," said Ethan shortly, opening Quinn's medkit. "Kidnapped, too." There was a vibra-scalpel; a touch, and the ankle wires parted with a ping.

"Raped?"

"I doubt it."

Helda, closing in, turned her head at the sound of Ethan's voice and stared at him. "You're no doctor," she gasped. "You're that moron from Docks and Locks again. My department wants a word with you!"

Teki yelped with laughter, causing Ethan to drop the sterile sponge he'd been applying to his ankle. "Joke's on you, Helda! He really is a doctor." He leaned toward Ethan, nearly tipping the chair, and confided conspiratorially, "Don't let on you're an Athosian, or she'll pop an artery. She hates Athos." He nodded happily, then, exhausted, let his head loll sideways again.

Helda recoiled. "An Athosian? *Is* this some kind of joke?" She glared anew at Ethan.

Ethan, absorbed in his work, jerked his head at Teki. "Ask him, he's the one full of truth serum." Teki's pulse was racing, his extremities cold, but he was not quite shocky. Ethan released the wrists. Reassuringly, Teki did not fall over, but sat up on his own. "But for your information, madam, I am indeed Dr. Ethan Urquhart of Athos. *Ambassador* Doctor Urquhart, on a special mission for the Population Council."

He hadn't really expected to impress her, but to his surprise she drew back whitely. "Oh?" she said in a neutral tone.

"Don't tell her that, Doc," Teki urged anew. "Ever since her son sneaked off to Athos nobody dares to mention the place. She can't even nag him long-distance there—their censorship guys send back any vids from a woman. She can't get at him at *all.*" Teki dissolved in giggles. "I bet he's happy as a clam."

Ethan cringed at the thought of getting drawn into some family squabble. The Security man looked equally dubious, but asked, "How old was the boy?"

"Thirty-two," Teki snickered.

"Oh." The Security man lost interest.

"Do you possess an antidote to that—so-called truth serum, *Doctor?*" Helda inquired frostily. "If so I suggest you administer it, and we'll sort the rest of this out down in Quarantine."

Ethan slowed. His words fell from him one by one, like drops of cold honey. "Where you possess dictatorial powers, and where you . . ." He looked up to catch her frigid, frightened eyes. Time stopped. "You . . ."

Time sprang forward. "Quinn!" Ethan bellowed.

At her prompt appearance, herding Millisor and Rau before her with jabs from her stunner, Ethan jumped to his feet. He felt like running around in tight circles, or tearing his hair out in great clumps, or grabbing her by her gray-and-white jacket and shaking her until her teeth rattled. His clenched hands beat the air. His words tumbled over one another in his excitement.

"I kept trying to tell you, but you never stopped to listen. Pretend you're the agent, or whatever, on Kline Station trying to grab Athos's shipment. You make an impromptu decision to replace the frozen tissue, with substitute material. We know it's impromptu, because if it had been planned you could have brought real cultures with you and nobody would ever have known a switch had been made, right? Where, where, in God the Fathers name even on Kline Station, are you going to come up with 450 human ovaries? Not even 450. Three hundred eighty-eight and six cows' ovaries. I don't think even you could pull 'em out of your jacket, Commander Quinn."

Quinn opened her mouth, closed it, and looked extremely thoughtful. "Go on, Doctor."

Millisor had dropped his Harmon Dal act and, oblivious now to Quinn's stunner, stood with his attention rapt on Ethan. Rau watched his leader anxiously for some signal to action. The other ecotech looked bewildered; the Security man, although his eyebrows were up in equal puzzlement, was absorbing every word.

Ethan gabbled on. "Forget the 426 suspect ships. Trace backwards from one ship, the census courier to Athos. Method, motive, and opportunity, by God! Who has ready access to every corner and cubbyhole on Kline Station, who could pass in and out of a guarded transfer warehouse with no question asked? Who has access to human cadavers every day? Cadavers from which a few grams of selected tissues will never be missed, because the bodies are biochemically destroyed immediately after the theft? But not quite enough cadavers, eh Helda, before it was time for the census courier to leave for Athos? Hence the cow ovaries, thrown in out of desperation to make up the numbers, and the short-changed boxes, and the empty box." Ethan paused, panting.

"You're insane," choked Helda. Her face had gone from white to red to white again. Millisor's stunned eyes devoured her. Quinn looked like a woman taken by a beatific vision. The Security's man's fingers were locked on his report panel in a sort of overloaded paralysis.

"Not as crazy as you are," said Ethan. "What did you hope to accomplish?"

"Redundant question," snapped Millisor. "We know what she accomplished. Forget the window-dressing, and find out where—" A sharp gesture from Quinn's stunner reminded him that his status had been reversed from interrogator to prisoner.

"You're all coming to Quarantine—"

"It's over, Helda," said Ethan. "I bet if I look around your Assimilation Station I'll even find a shrink-wrap sealer."

"Oh, yes," chorused Teki helpfully. "We use it to seal suspected contaminants, to store them for later analysis. It's under the wet bench. I sealed my shoes up once, on a slow day. I tried to seal water, to make balloons to drop down the lift tubes, but it didn't work—"

"Shut *up*, Teki!" snarled Helda desperately.

"It's not as bad as what Vernon did with the white mice—"

"Stop," growled Millisor in exasperation out of the corner of his mouth. Teki subsided and sat blinking.

Ethan spread his hands and asked Helda more gently and urgently, "Why? I have to understand."

The concentrated venom in her posture broke into speech almost despite her will. "Why? You even need to ask why? It was to cut you motherless unnatural bastards off, that's why. I meant to get the next shipment too, if there was one, and the next, and the next, until—" She was choking now. On her rage? No, Ethan realized, his buoyant intellectual triumph turning sickly-sour in his stomach; on tears. "Until I'd hooked Simmi out of there, and he came to his senses and came home and got a real woman, I swear I wouldn't criticize a hair on her head this time, I'll never be allowed to even see my own grandchildren on that dreadful dirty planet . . ." She turned her back and stood stiff-legged, defiant but for her hands over her red, smeared face, ugly and helpless and snorting.

Ethan thought he understood how a propaganda-stuffed young soldier must feel the first time in combat, stumbling by some sudden chance over his enemy's human face. He had gloried for a red moment in his power to break her. Now he stood foolishly with the pieces in his hands. Not at all heroic.

"Ye gods," muttered the Security man, in awe touched with glee, "I have to arrest an eco-cop . . . ?"

Teki giggled. The other ecotech, clearly taken aback by Helda's confession, looked as though he didn't know whether to argue or try to become invisible.

"But what did you do with the *other*?" Millisor rocked forward, teeth clenched.

"Other what?" Helda sniffed.

"The frozen human ovarian cultures you took out of the boxes for Athos," Millisor ground out, carefully, like a man speaking in words of one syllable to a mutant.

"Oh. I threw them out."

The veins stood out on the Cetagandan's forehead. Ethan could name each one. Millisor seemed to be having trouble breathing. "Idiot bitch," he panted. "Idiot bitch, do you know what you've done . . . ?"

Quinn's laughter rang over them all like morning bells. "Admiral Naismith will love it!"

The ghem-colonel's steel self-control broke at last. "Idiot bitch!" he screamed, and launched himself toward Helda, clawed hands outstretched. Both Quinn's and the Security man's stunner beams caught him in a neat cross-fire, and he crashed as trees do.

Rau just stood shaking his head and muttering over and over, "Shit. Shit. Shit . . ."

"Attempted assault," the Security man paused to croon over his report panel, "on a Biocontrol Warden carrying out her duties . . ."

Rau sidled toward the door.

"Don't forget breaking Detention," Quinn added helpfully. "This here's the fellow," she gestured at Rau, "that you were all looking for who evaporated out of C-9 the other day. And I bet if you search this room you'll find all sorts of military goodies that Kline Station Customs never authorized."

"Quarantine first," said the other ecotech, after a nervous glance at his still emotionally incapacitated superior.

"But surely Ambassador Urquhart will wish to lay charges for the admitted theft and destruction of Athosian property," suggested Quinn. "Who's going to arrest whom?"

"We're *all* gonna go to Quarantine, where I can make you all hold still till I get to the bottom of this," said the Security man firmly. "People who disappear out of C-9 will find that slipping Quarantine is quite another matter."

"Too true," murmured Quinn.

Rau's lip rippled silently as another pair of heavily-armed Security officers appeared in the doorway, cutting off retreat. The room seemed suddenly crowded. Ethan hadn't seen the burly Security man call for reinforcements, but it must have been some time earlier. His estimation of the slow-seeming man went up a notch.

"Yes, sir?" said one of the new officers.

"Took you long enough," said the Security man. "Search that one," he pointed to Rau, "and then you can help us run 'em all to Quarantine. These three are accused of vectoring communicable disease. That one's been fingered as the jailbreak from C-9. This one's accused of theft by that one, who appears to be wearing a Station code-uniform to which he is not entitled, and who also claims that one over there was kidnapped. I'll have a printout as long as I am tall of charges for the one out cold on the floor when he wakes up. Those three are all gonna need first aid—"

Ethan, reminded, slipped up to Teki and pressed the hypospray of fast-penta antagonist into his arm. He felt almost sorry for the young man as his foolish grin was rapidly replaced by the expression of a man with a terminal hangover. The Security team in the meanwhile were shaking all sorts of glittering mysterious objects out of the unresisting Rau.

"—and the pretty lady in the gray outfit who seems to know so much about everybody else's business I'm holding as a material witness," the Security man concluded. "Ah—where is she?"

Chapter Twelve

❧❧❧

In Quarantine, Rau followed the supine form of his still-stunned superior off for whatever short-arm inspection Biocontrol demanded without a word. He had said nothing, in fact, since they'd left the hostel room under heavy guard, but had remained close to Millisor with a sort of grim loyalty, like a dog refusing to leave its encoffined master.

Ethan wasn't sure what tests were required for detecting Alpha-S-D-plasmid-2—or its mythical mutation-3—but from the dour look on Rau's face he suspected they were rather invasive. He'd have felt better if Rau had shown the least sign of possessing a sense of humor. The light in Rau's eyes as he glanced back one last time at Ethan was like reflections off knife blades.

Ethan was in turn carried off to an office for a long, long talk with Security in the persons of the burly arresting officer and a female officer who was apparently his administrative superior. Partway through they were joined by a third Security man, introduced as Captain Arata, a neurasthenic Eurasian type with lank black hair, pale skin, and eyes like needles, who said little and listened much.

Ethan's first impulse to tell all and throw himself upon their mercy was blunted almost at once by the problem of Okita. He managed not to mention Okita. Cetaganda's psionics breakthrough was modified, under the wilting effect of those three pairs of Stationer eyes, to the vaguer news that "a culture in Athos's ovarian shipment had been doctored on Jackson's Whole with some altered genetic material stolen from Cetaganda." Ethan avoided touching on Cee altogether. It would have made things so complicated. . . .

"Then," said the Security woman, "Ecotech Helda actually did Athos a favor, albeit unintentionally. She saved your gene pool from contamination, in fact."

She was, Ethan realized, obliquely pressing him to drop charges against Helda, to save Kline Station from public embarrassment. He thought of the quantities of trade that passed through their supposedly secure switching warehouses. The realization that they were sweating as hard as he was felt wonderfully invigorating, and he took the offensive instantly.

Security became extremely polite. The half-dozen or so little charges the burly officer had worked up against Ethan were matched against Ethan's ambassadorial status and somehow made to evaporate. No vandalism like Helda's, they assured him, would ever be permitted to happen again. Ecotech Helda was of a sufficient age to take an early retirement, with no questions asked. Ambassador Urquhart need not concern himself with ghem-lord Harmon Dal, or Colonel Millisor as Ethan named him; he and his assistants were definitely slated for deportation on the first ship available, for the proven felony of kidnapping.

"By the way, Mr. Ambassador," Captain Arata put in, "do you have any idea where the ghem-lord's third and fourth employees are?"

"You mean you haven't arrested Setti yet?" asked Ethan.

"We're working on it," said Arata. His cool, controlled face gave Ethan no clue as to what that meant.

"You'd better ask Colonel Millisor when he wakes up, then. As for the other one—ah—you'd better ask Commander Quinn."

"And just where *is* Commander Quinn, Mr. Ambassador?"

Ethan sighed. "On her way back to the Dendarii Mercenaries, probably." With her draftee Cee in tow, no doubt. How long would the rootless young man survive, cut off from his own dreams? Longer than he would live if Millisor caught up with him, Ethan had to admit in all honesty. Let it go. Let it go.

Arata sighed too. "Slippery witch," he muttered. "We'll see about that. She still owes me some information."

And then Ethan was free to go. Thank you for your kind assistance, Mr. Ambassador. If there is any little thing Kline Station can do to help make your stay more pleasant, please ask. They made no further mention of Helda; he made no further mention of Helda. Have a nice day, Mr. Ambassador.

In the corridor leading to the exit locks Ethan paused. "Come to think of it, Captain Arata, there is a favor you can do me."

"Yes, sir?"

"Colonel Millisor is under guard, right? If he's awake, would it be possible for me to speak to him briefly?"

Arata gave him a look of sharp speculation. "I'll check, sir."

Ethan accompanied the Security captain out of the administrative section and through two more sterility-locks. There they found a gowned ecotech just exiting a glassed-in room. The ecotech killed a lighted "Do Not Enter" sign on the room's door and began peeling out of his protective garb. An armed Security guard, within, passed out a similar set of garments rolled up in a wad, which the ecotech tossed in the general direction of a laundry receptacle.

"What's the status of your patient?" Captain Arata inquired.

The ecotech took in Arata's rank insignia. "Alert and oriented. Some residual tremors from stunner trauma, headache likewise. He has chronically elevated blood pressure, stress-induced gastritis, a liver showing pre-cirrhotic degeneration, and a slightly enlarged prostate that will probably have to be watched over the next few years. In short, his health is normal for a man of his age. What he does *not* have is Alpha-S-D-plasmid-2, -3, -29, or any other number. He doesn't have so much as a head cold. Somebody was jerking us around, Captain, with that vector report, and I hope you'll find out who. I don't have time for this sort of nonsense."

"We're working on it," said Captain Arata.

Ethan followed Arata into the now-unsealed room. Arata motioned the guard to a station outside the door, and himself took up a stance of polite but firm parade rest just within. It was probably not worthwhile requesting him to wait out of earshot, Ethan reflected; the room was undoubtedly monitored.

Ethan approached the bed on which Millisor, dressed in an ordinary patient gown, lay—restrained, Ethan noted with relief, and edged closer. Millisor made no move. His hands lay relaxed, as if having tested his bonds once was sufficient for his logic. He watched Ethan with cool calculation. It all made Ethan feel a dreadful coward, like some gawker poking at a trussed-up predator that braver hunters had captured.

"Uh, good afternoon, Colonel Millisor," Ethan began inanely.

"Good afternoon, Dr. Urquhart." Millisor returned an ironic nod of his head like an abbreviated bow. He seemed drained now of personal animosity—professional, like Quinn. Of course, he'd exhibited no personal animosity when he'd ordered Ethan's execution, either.

"I, uh—just wanted to be absolutely and finally sure, before you left, that you clearly understood that Athos does not have, and never at any time did have, the shipment of genetic material from Jackson's Whole," Ethan said.

"The probabilities would now seem to lean that way," agreed Millisor. "I doubt everything, you see."

Ethan thought this over. "Encountering the truth must be horribly confusing for you, then."

Millisor's lips twitched dryly. "Fortunately, it happens very seldom." His gaze narrowed. "So, what do you think of Terrence Cee, now that you've met him?"

Ethan jumped guiltily. "Who?"

"Come, Doctor. I know he's here. I can feel the shape of him in the tactical situation. Did you find him attractive, Athosian? Many people do. I have often wondered if his, ah, gift, truly only worked one way."

It was a nasty thought, particularly as Ethan had found Cee very attractive indeed. He jittered. Millisor was now staring with covert interest at Arata, alert for reactions on the Security officer's part to the new turn in the conversation. Ethan hurried to cut off any unnecessary extension of Millisor's secret hit list. "I haven't discussed Mr. Cee with—with anyone. Just in case you were wondering."

Millisor's eyebrows rose in disbelief. "As a favor to me?"

"As a favor to them," Ethan corrected.

Millisor accepted this with a little provisional nod. "But Cee is on Kline Station. Where, Doctor?"

Ethan shook his head. "I truly do not know. If you choose not to believe that, it's your problem."

"Then your pet mercenary knows. It comes to the same thing. Where is she?"

"She's not mine!" Ethan denied, horrified. "I don't have anything to do with Commander Quinn. She's on her own. You have a problem with her, you take it up with her, not me."

Arata, without moving a muscle, became more intent.

"On the contrary," said Millisor, "she has all my admiration. Much that I could not account for now is entirely clear. I wouldn't mind hiring her myself."

"Uh—I don't think she's available."

"All mercenaries have price tags. Maybe not money alone. Rank, power, pleasure."

"No," said Ethan firmly. "She seems to be in love with her C.O. I've seen the phenomenon in Athos's army—hero-worship of certain senior officers by their juniors—some seniors abuse their advantage, others don't. I don't know which category her admiral falls in, but in either case I don't think you can match the bid."

Arata nodded silent agreement, looking faintly bleak.

"I too know the phenomenon," sighed the ghem-lord. "Well. That's too bad." A chill seemed to waft from the man in the bed which made Ethan wonder if his defense of Quinn's honor had perhaps been untimely. But Millisor was safely immobilized.

"I confess, Doctor, you puzzle me," Millisor went on. "If you and Cee were not co-conspirators, then you could only have been his victim. I fail to see your advantage in continuing to protect the man after what he tried to do to Athos."

"He didn't try to do anything to Athos, except immigrate there. Hardly a crime. From what I've seen of the galaxy so far, it made perfectly good sense. I can hardly wait to go home myself."

Millisor's eyebrows rose nearly to his hairline, one of the few gestures currently available to him. "By God! I begin to believe you really are as naive a fool as your file proclaims you, Doctor! I thought you knew what had been done to your shipment."

"Yes, so he put his wife in it. A little necrophiliac, maybe. Considering his upbringing, the only wonder is that the man isn't a lot stranger still."

Millisor actually laughed out loud. Ethan felt no urge to chuckle along. He regarded the ghem-lord uneasily.

Miilisor sighed. "Let me present you with two facts. Obsolete facts, since that idiot Stationer female committed her mindless act of sabotage. One. The gene-complex, ah, in question—" he glanced at Arata, "was recessive, and would not appear in phenotype until found in both halves of the genotype. Two. Every single one of the cultures bound for Athos had had the complex spliced into them. Think it through, Doctor."

Ethan did.

In the first generation, the ovarian cultures would contribute their recessive, hidden alleles to the children—and at the rate the old cultures were dying off, very soon all the children—born on Athos. But not until the second generation reached puberty would the functional telepathic organ appear in its statistical one-half of the population, from breeding back to the double-recessive cultures. In the third generation, half the remaining population would pass from latent to functional, and so on, the telepathic majority edging out the non-telepathic minority in perpetual half-increments.

But by then even the non-telepaths would bear the genes in their bodies, potential fathers of telepathic sons. The entire population would be permeated with the gene complex, too late, impossible to eradicate.

The question, *Why Athos?* was answered at last. Of course Athos. Only Athos.

The audacity, the perfection, the beauty—and the enormity—of Cee's plot took Ethan's breath away. It all fit, with the over-powering self-evidence of a mathematical proof. It even accounted for Cee's missing mountain of money.

"Now who cannot recognize truth?" mocked Millisor softly.

"Oh," said Ethan, in a very small voice.

"The most insidious thing about the little monster is his charm," Millisor went on, watching Ethan closely. "We built him that way on purpose, not knowing then that the limits of his talent would render him unsuitable as a field agent. Although from the trouble he subsequently gave us we may have been wrong on that point as well. But do not mistake charm for virtue, Doctor. He is danger-ous, utterly devoid of loyalty to the humanity from which he sprang, but of which he is not a part—"

Ethan wondered if that should be understood as Humanity = Cetaganda.

"—a virus of a man, who would make the whole universe over in his twisted image. Surely you of all men understand that lethal contagions demand vigorous counter-measures. But ours is the controlled violence of surgery. You must not swallow the virus's propaganda. We are not the butchers he would have you believe us to be."

Millisor's hands turned in their restraints, opened in pleading. "Help us. You must help us."

Ethan stared at Millisor's bonds, shaken. "I'm sorry . . ." God the Father, was he actually apologizing to Millisor? "No, Colonel. I remember Okita. I can understand a man being a killer, I think. But a *bored* killer?"

"Okita is only a tool. The surgeon's knife."

"Then your service has turned a man into a thing." An old quote drifted through Ethan's memory: *By their fruits you shall know them. . . .*

Millisor's eyes narrowed; he did not pursue the argument, but rather, with a glance at Arata, inquired, "And just what did you do to Sergeant Okita, Dr. Urquhart?"

Ethan glanced at Arata too, sorry he'd brought up the subject. "I didn't do anything to him. Maybe he met with an accident. Or perhaps he deserted." Or considering Okita's ultimate fate, perhaps "desserted" might be the better term . . . Ethan squelched that line of thought. "In any case, I can't help you. Even if I wanted to betray Cee to you—if that's what you're asking me to do—I really don't know where he is."

"Or where he is headed?" said Millisor suggestively.

Ethan shook his head. "Anywhere, for all I know. Anywhere but Athos, that is."

"Alas, yes," murmured Millisor. "Before, Cee was tied to that shipment. If I had the one, I had a string to the other. Now that the shipment is destroyed, a very poor second choice to our recovering it, he is entirely unleashed. Anywhere," Millisor sighed. "Anywhere . . ."

The ghem-colonel, Ethan reminded himself firmly, was the one who was tied down. He had his feet under him; it was up to him to end this interview before the smooth spy plucked any more information from him.

Ethan paused in his strategic retreat out the door. "I will leave you with one last thought, though, Colonel. If you had made that pitch to me when we first met, instead of doing what you did, you might have convinced me, and had it all."

Millisor's hands clenched and jerked against their bonds at last.

And so Ethan returned to his own hostel room, rented his first day on Kline Station and never occupied since. He thanked his spotty luck that he had paid for it in advance, for his personal effects were all as he had left them. He bathed, shaved, trimmed, changed back in to his own clothes at last, and ate a light meal from the room service console.

He sighed over his coffee. Pushing two weeks—he would have to look up the date, having lost track—expended on this adventure, as Quinn's stalking-goat, as Millisor's moving target, Cee's pawn, anybody's ping pong ball, and what did he have to show for it? An education? Once he returned his red coveralls and boots, he would have no more tangible souvenir than the learning. He pulled out his credit chit and regarded it. Quinn's microscopic bug was presumably still on it somewhere. If he shouted into it, might he cause a feedback squeal in her left ear? But she was gone, with no word of farewell. Anyhow, people who talked to their credit cards would doubtless make their neighbors uneasy, even on Kline Station.

He lay down wearily, only to find his nerves still too strung up to allow sleep. Was it day, or night? On Kline Station, who could say? He wasn't sure if he missed Athos's diurnal rhythm or its weather more. He wanted rain, or a brisk polar front to blow the cobwebs out of his brains. He could turn up the air conditioning, but it would still smell the same.

After nearly an hour spent comparing all the things he should have said and done this last fortnight with the actual events, he gave up in disgust, dressed, and went out. If sleep was to elude him, he might at least be doing something useful with his time. Athos was paying an ungodly enough sum for it.

He strolled back to the Transients' Lounge level where the embassies and consuls were concentrated and began doing some serious shopping for legitimate biological supply houses. Most of the more technically advanced planets offered something. Beta Colony offered nineteen separate sources, from purely commercial ventures to a government-sponsored gene pool at Silica University stocked entirely by invited donations from talented and gifted citizens. As much as Ethan cringed at taking any more of Quinn's advice on anything, Beta Colony did seem to be the best destination. He would not be disappointed, the woman expediting the commercial directory interface assured him. He exited feeling he had done a good day's work at last, and a little smug. He had dealt with the female expeditor just as he would have dealt with a man. It could be done; wasn't hard at all.

He returned to his room for a quick snack, then sat down to his comconsole for a little comparison-shopping for the best price on a round-trip ticket to Beta Colony. The straightest route was via Escobar, giving him a chance to check out another potential source at no added cost to the Population Council. At least half the committee would be pleased with him, about as good odds as he was likely to obtain.

All his decisions made at last, his weariness washed over him. He lay down to rest for a minute.

Hours later, an insistent chiming from his comconsole hooked him to mushy consciousness. One foot was asleep, from lying at an odd angle with his shoes on, and it tingled numbly as he stumbled to press the "Receive" keypad.

Terrence Cee's face materialized over the holovid plate. "Dr. Urquhart?"

"Well. I didn't expect to hear from you again." Ethan rubbed sleep from his face. "I thought you'd have no further use for the asylum of Athos. You and Quinn both being the practical sort."

Cee winced, looking distinctly unhappy. "In fact, I'm about to leave," he said in a dull voice. "I wanted to see you one more time, to—to apologize. Can you meet me in Docking Bay C-8 right away?"

"I suppose," said Ethan. "Are you off to the Dendarii Mercenaries with Quinn, then?"

"I can't talk any more now. I'm sorry." Cee's image turned to sparkling snow, then emptiness.

Quinn was hanging over Cee's shoulder, perhaps, inhibiting his frankness. Ethan suppressed an impulse to call Security and tell Captain Arata where to look for her. He and Quinn were even now, help averaging harm. His mystery was solved; she had the intelligence coup she wanted. Let it end so.

As he exited his hostel to the mall a man, who had been idly seated by the central pool feeding the goldfish with pellets from a credit-card-operated dispenser placed nearby, rose and approached him.

Ethan stifled an urge to run back up the mall in screaming paranoia. The man couldn't be Setti. He was altogether the wrong racial type for a Cetagandan: tall, dark-skinned with a high-bridged nose, and wearing a pink silk jacket gaudy with embroidery.

"Dr. Urquhart?" the man inquired politely.

Ethan kept some distance between them. If this was another damned spy of some sort, he swore he would put him head first into the pool. . . . "Yes?"

"I wonder if I might request a small service of you."

"Request away."

The man produced a small flat oblong from his jacket, a little holovid projector. "Should you see him again, I wish you would give this message capsule to ghem-Colonel Ruyst Millisor. The message is activated by entering his military serial number."

Definitely the pool. "Colonel Millisor is under arrest by Kline Station Security. You want to get a message to him, go see them."

"Ah." The man smiled. "Perhaps I shall. Still, who can say what chances the turning of the great wheel may bring us? Take it anyway. If no opportunity arises to deliver it, throw it away." He tried to press the little oblong on Ethan, who foiled him by backing up. Rather than chase Ethan skipping backwards down the mall, the man paused, shaking his head. He laid the message capsule down on a bench Ethan had put between them. "I leave it to your discretion, sir." He bowed with a flourish of his hand reminiscent of a genuflection, and turned to go.

"I'm not touching it," Ethan stated flatly. The man smiled over his shoulder as he stepped into a nearby lift tube. "I'll take it to Security!' Ethan shouted. The man cupped his hand to his ear and shook his head, rising up the crystal tube. "I'll— I'll—" Ethan swore under his breath as the pink apparition ascended out of sight.

Ethan circled the bench, watching the little oblong from the corner of his eye. With a wordless growl, he finally pocketed it. He would take it to Captain Arata, then, at the first opportunity, and let him worry about it. He glanced at his chronometer, and hurried on.

He had to take a tube-car to the docking bay, which was in a freight section on the opposite side of the Station from Transients' Lounge. This time he had a map ready to hand, and made no wrong turns.

The docking bay was extremely quiet. A single flex tube was activated, indicating a small ship on the other side, perhaps a fast courier hired especially for the occasion. In any case, not a commercial run lading other cargo. Quinn's expense account must be elastic indeed, Ethan reflected.

Terrence Cee, dressed in his green Stationer coveralls, sat wanly on a packing case, alone in the middle of the bay. He looked up as Ethan stepped out of a ramp corridor. "You came quickly, Dr. Urquhart."

Ethan glanced at the flex tube. "I figured you were catching a scheduled run of some sort. I didn't realize you'd be traveling in this much style."

"I thought perhaps you wouldn't come at all."

"Because—why? Because I'd found out the whole truth about that shipment?" Ethan shrugged. "I can't say I approve of what you tried to do. But given the obvious problems your—your race, I guess—would suffer as a minority anywhere else, I think I can understand why."

A melancholy smile lit Cee's face, then was gone. "You do? But of course. You would." He shook his head. "I should have said, I hoped you would not come."

Ethan followed the direction of his nod.

Quinn stood in the shadows by a girder. But she was an unusually frazzled-looking Quinn. Her crisp jacket was gone, and she wore only a black T-shirt and her uniform trousers. Her boots were gone, too. And, Ethan realized as she moved into the light, her stunner holster was empty.

She moved because she was prodded by a man in the orange and black uniform of Kline Station Security. So they'd caught up with her at last. Ethan nearly chuckled. Watching her wriggle out of this one ought to be just fascinating. . . .

His humor drained away as he caught a better look at the weapon with which the compact, bland-faced man was poking her spine. A lethal nerve disruptor. Altogether non-regulation for Security.

At the ring of footsteps Ethan turned his head the other way, to find Millisor and Rau walking toward them.

Chapter Thirteen

Ethan and Quinn were shoved together within the potential radius of fire from the bell-muzzle of the nerve disruptor, held in the tense hand of the man in the Security uniform. Cee was segregated from them under Rau's stunner. It needed nothing more than that to give Ethan a silent appreciation of their relative status.

Quinn looked even worse close up, with a split swollen lip, and white and shaking from either pain or the aftereffects of low stun. She seemed shorter without her boots. Cee stumbled like a corpse looking only for a place to lie down; congealed, cold, the blue light of his eyes extinguished.

"What happened?" Ethan whispered to Quinn. "How did *they* ever find you when Security couldn't?"

"I forgot the damned beeper," she hissed back through clenched teeth. "Should've shoved it down the first trash vent we passed. I knew it was compromised! But Cee was arguing with me, and I was in a hurry, and—oh, hell, what's the use . . ." She bit her lip in frustration, winced, and licked it tenderly. Her eyes returned again and again to their opponents, adding up the unfavorable odds, rejecting the sum and trying again with no better luck.

Millisor walked around them, smooth and smug. "So glad you could make it, Dr. Urquhart. We could have arranged accidents for you and the commander separately, but having you both together allows us a rather exquisite opportunity for—efficiency."

"Vengeance?" quavered Ethan. "But we never tried to kill you."

"Oh, no," Millisor protested. "Vengeance has nothing to do with it. You both simply know too much to live."

Rau grinned nastily. "Tell them the rest, Colonel," he urged.

"Ah, yes. With your sense of humor, Commander, you will particularly like this one. Observe, if you will, all those unused flex tubes on the outer wall. Sealed at both ends, they make a very private little compartment. Just the spot for a couple with rather odd tastes in adventure to arrange a tryst. How unfortunate that, in the sound sleep following their exertions—"

Rau waved his stunner cheerfully, by way of indicating just how that sound sleep was to be achieved.

"—the flex tube is vented into space in preparation for locking in the auto-conveyer from a freighter hold. Said freighter being due in this docking bay immediately after my courier departs. Shall we leave you two entirely nude, I wonder?" he mused, "or merely naked from the waist down, suggesting fumbling passionate hurry?"

"God the Father," Ethan moaned in horror, "the Population Council will think I was depraved enough to make love to a woman in a flex tube!"

"Gods forbid," Quinn, looking equally appalled, echoed under her breath, "that Admiral Naismith would think I was stupid enough to make love to anything in a flex tube!"

Terrence Cee's eyes roved over the docking bay, as if seeking death as desperately as Quinn's eyes sought escape. He made a little jerky motion; Rau's stunner instantly drew a bead on him.

"Dream on, mutant," Rau growled. "We aren't giving you a chance. One wrong move and you'll be carried aboard stunned." His lips drew back unpleasantly. "You don't want to miss the show your friends are going to put on for us, do you?"

Cee's hands clenched and unclenched, despair and rage struggling for ascendancy in him, both equally impotent. "I'm sorry, Doctor," he whispered. "They held a nerve disruptor to the commander's head, and I knew they weren't bluffing. I thought maybe you wouldn't come, just for a call from me. I should have let them shoot her then. Sorry. Sorry . . ."

Quinn's lips turned sardonically upward, breaking to bleed again. "You don't have to apologize quite that fervently, Cee. . . . Your resisting wouldn't have saved him anyway."

"You don't have to apologize at all," said Ethan firmly. "I'd have done the same myself, in all probability."

The man with the nerve disruptor waved them apart, driving Ethan and Quinn to the outer wall, and along it toward the bay's far end.

"Who is that guy, anyway?" Ethan asked Quinn with a jerk of his head. "Setti?"

"You guessed it. I should have shot him in the back when I had the chance, and collected the other half of my bounty from House Bharaputra," Quinn replied in a disgusted undertone. She added thoughtfully, "If I jumped that goon, d'you think you could make it across the bay to one of those corridors before Rau stunned you?"

It was fifty meters or more across the cavernous chamber. "No," said Ethan frankly.

"How about a dash for the cover of that flex-tube?"

"Then what? Make faces at them till they walked over and shot me?"

"All right," she snarled impatiently, "you come up with a better idea."

Ethan's hands twitched in his pockets, and encountered a little oblong. "May be we could buy some more time with this?" he said, pulling out the message capsule.

"What the hell's that?"

"It was the weirdest thing. On my way here this man came up to me in the mall and pushed it on me—he said it was a message for Millisor. It's activated by Milhisor's military service number, and I should give it to him if I saw him—"

Quinn froze, her hand clenched on his arm. "What color was he?"

"Huh?"

"The man, the man!"

"Pink. That is, he had this pink suit."

"Not the suit, the man!"

"Interesting—sort of a coffee-color. Extremely elegant. I wish I could've got some of those skin genes for Athos—"

"Hey," Setti began, moving toward them with a frown.

"Giveittome, giveittome," Quinn gabbled, grabbing the message capsule out of Ethan's hand. "Lessee. 672-191-, oh gods, is it 142 or 124?" Her shaking index finger jabbed at the tiny keypad, then agonized in hesitation. "421 and pray. Here, Setti!" Quinn cried, and tossed the message capsule at the startled Cetagandan, whose left hand snaked out in an easy, automatic catch. "Down!" she yelled in Ethan's ear, kicked his feet out from under him, and dropped atop his head.

There was a moment's puzzled silence. The tiny hum of a holovid forming its image sounded insect-thin.

"Aw, rats," Quinn groaned, her weight slumping on Ethan. "Wrong again."

Ethan rather muffled, complained, "What the devil do you think you're—"

The shock wave blew them both ten meters across the docking bay floor, to fetch up in a tangle of arms and legs against the outer bulkhead. Except for the ringing in his ears, Ethan could not at first hear a thing. His bones seemed to reverberate like a struck gong, and his vision darkened.

"Thought that had to be the case," Quinn muttered in shaky satisfaction. She stood up, fell down, stood up again and bounced off the wall, blinking rapidly, her hands feeling in front of her.

Alarms seemed to be shrieking like mad things all over the place. Emergency lights came on with a brilliant glare—Ethan was relieved to realize he hadn't been struck blind—and the distant booms of airseals shutting followed one another like dominos filling.

Closer, quieter, and much more ominous was a hissing, rising to a whistling, of air escaping around the nearest flex-tube seal, damaged in the explosion. Icy fog boiled in a cloud around it.

Even Ethan had the sense to start away from it, crawling on his hands and knees. The gravity wavered nauseatingly. A melted patch in the metal deck was just ceasing to bubble. Ethan skirted it. Of Setti there was no sign anywhere.

"By God," Ethan muttered dizzily, "she *is* good at getting rid of bodies. . . ."

He looked up across an interminable metallic desert to see Terrence Cee, running like a deer, brought down in a flying tackle by Rau. Millisor, dashing up behind, took aim to give the telepath a swift kick in the head, thought better of it, and hopped to his other foot to deliver a blow to Cee's less-valuable solar plexus instead. Millisor and Rau each grabbed an arm, dragging Cee from his crouch toward the activated flex tube beyond which their ship waited.

Ethan staggered to his feet and began running toward them. He hadn't the least idea what he was going to do when he got there. Except stop them, somehow. That was the only clear imperative. "God the Father," he moaned, "there had better be a reward in heaven for this sort of thing . . ."

He had the advantage of a shorter angle to cross, against Millisor's and Rau's disadvantage of their writhing burden. Ethan found himself standing, legs spread apart, blocking the entrance to the flex tube. Perfectly positioned for a fast draw, barring the minor hitch of being weaponless. *Help,* he thought. "Stop!" he cried.

To his surprise, they did, cautious. Rau had lost his stunner somewhere, but Millisor pulled a vicious, glittering little needler from his jacket and took aim at Ethan's chest. Ethan pictured its tiny needles expanding on impact and whirling like razors through his abdomen. His autopsy would be the godawfullest mess . . .

Terrence Cee yanked away from Rau and spun to stand in front of Ethan, his arms spread wide in a futile gesture of protection. "No!"

"You think I have to keep you alive just because the cultures are gone, mutant?" Millisor, furious, cried at him. "Dead will do, by God!" He raised his weapon in both hands. "What the—" he lurched as his feet rose from the floor, his hands clutching out for lost balance.

Ethan grabbed Cee. His stomach seemed to be floating away independently of the rest of him. He looked around hysterically, to spot Quinn clinging to the far wall near one of the corridor entrances, the cover plate forcibly torn off an environmental engineering control panel beside her.

Millisor's body undulated in midair, compensating expertly for his unwanted spin, and he brought his weapon back to steady aim. Quinn, yelling helplessly, tore the cover plate the rest of the way off its cabinet and flung it toward them. It spun wickedly through the air, but it was obvious before it was halfway across the bay that it was going to miss Millisor. The Cetagandan's grip tightened on his needler trigger—

Millisor's body, haloed for a blinding instant like some burning martyr, convulsed in the booming blue crackle of a plasma bolt. Ethan's head jerked at the pungent stench of burnt meat and fabric and boiling plastics. He blinked red and purpled afterimages of the dancing, dying silhouette of the ghem-lord.

The needler spun away, and Rau lost his grip on the floor in an aborted grab for it. The Cetagandan captain swam frantically in air, swiveling his head in urgent search for the source of this devastating new attack. Quinn's cover plate, rebounding off the far wall, winged by nearly taking Ethan's head with it.

"There he is!" Cee, grappling in midair with Ethan, pointed with a shout at the catwalks and girders. A pink blur moved along them, aimed something at Rau. "No! He's my meat!" Cee cried. With a berserker yell, Cee launched himself off Ethan toward Rau. "Kill you, bastard!"

The only benefit Ethan could see coming from this insane outbreak of martial spirit was that he, Ethan, was pushed toward the outer bulkhead wall. He managed to catch a grip on a projection without breaking a wrist, halting his mindless momentum.

"No, Terrence! If somebody's firing at Cetagandans, the thing to do is get *out* of the way!" But this voice of reason whipped away in the wind. Wind? The air leak must be widening—explosive decompression at any moment, surely . . .

Cee's and Rau's struggling forms sank to the deck like a pebble dropping through oil, as Quinn gradually turned up a little gravity. Ethan's own body stopped flapping like a flag in the breeze, and he found himself hanging, though still lightly, entirely too far above the deck. He began to climb down hastily, before Quinn decided to try something like Helda's trick with the birds.

Rau threw the smaller, lighter Cee bouncing and skidding along the deck, and whirled to dash for his ship's flex tube. Two steps, and he flared, melted, and burned like a wax image in a brilliant plasma cross-fire, coming from not one but two sources among the girders. He fell with a meaty thunk, and, horribly, lived a moment more, writhing and screaming soundlessly through fleshless black jaws. Cee, on hands and knees, watched open-mouthed, as though himself dismayed by the completeness of his vicarious revenge.

Ethan started across the deck toward the telepath. On the Station side of the bay, two men swung out of the network of girders and catwalks. One was the pink apparition from the mallway, a second was another dark-skinned man dressed in shimmering brown in a similar highly-decorated style. They closed on Quinn, who, so far from welcoming her rescuers, started back up the wall like a busy spider.

Each of the dark men grabbed an ankle and yanked her down, careless of what her head struck on the way. An attempted karate kick on her part was foiled by brown-silk and turned into what would have been a nasty fall in higher gravity and still didn't look exactly pleasant. Pink-suit pinioned her arms from behind, and brown-silk took the fight out of her with a breath-stopping blow to her stomach.

One on each side, they hustled her away up the corridor ramp toward the emergency exit as pressure-suited Stationer damage control squads began to pour into the chamber from several other entrances.

"They're—they're snatching Quinn!" Ethan cried to Cee. "Who are they? What are they?" He danced from foot to foot in an agony of bewilderment, pulling Cee up.

Cee squinted after them. "Jackson's Whole? Bharaputrans, here? We've got to go after her!"

"Preferably while there's still air to breathe—"

Clinging to each other, they proceeded in a sort of bounding hobble as rapidly as they could across the docking bay and up the ramp.

At the emergency airseal they had to wait for terrifying seconds, working their jaws to protect their ears against the now rapidly decreasing air pressure, while the trio ahead of them cycled through and vacated the personnel lock that permitted escape from blocked chambers. Jabbing at the control button in a panicked tattoo, or even leaning on it, did nothing to hasten the process, Ethan found; the door opened only when it was damn good and ready.

They fell through, then had to wait again while pressure equalized and Quinn's assailants gained a lengthening head start. Ethan gasped in relief. He had been entirely mistaken about Stationer air; it smelled just great, better than any air he'd ever had.

"How the devil," Ethan panted to Cee as they waited, "did Millisor and Rau ever get out of Quarantine? I thought even a virus couldn't escape it."

"Setti sprang them," Cee panted back. "He came in either along with, or pretending to be, the guard taking them to their deportation dock, I'm not sure which. They walked right out the door. All the documentation and IDs perfect, of course. I don't think even Quinn realizes how far into the Station computer network they'd penetrated in the time they were here."

The emergency airseal lock hissed open at last, and Ethan and Cee staggered up the corridor in hot pursuit of a quarry now out of sight. They bumped to a halt at the first cross-corridor.

Cee, his arm flung out, turned in a circle a couple of times like a damaged clockwork mechanism. "That way," he pointed to their left.

"You sure?"

"No."

They galloped down it anyway. At the next cross-corridor they were rewarded by the sound of a familiar alto voice, raised in protest, wafting from the right. They followed on, to come out in a stark freight lift-tube foyer.

The man in chocolate-brown silk had Quinn shoved up facing a wall, her arms twisted behind her. Her toes stretched and sought the floor, without success.

"Come on, Commander," the man in pink was saying, "We haven't got time for this. Where is it?"

"Wouldn't dream of keeping you," she replied in a rather smeary voice, as her face was being squashed sideways into the wall. "Ow! Hadn't you better run off to your embassy before Security gets here? They'll be all over the place after that bomb blast."

The man in pink whirled, raising his plasma gun, as Ethan and Cee skidded into the foyer. "Wait," Cee said, his hand restraining Ethan's arm.

"Friends!" Quinn shrieked, twitching. "Friends, friends, don't fire, we're all friends here!"

"We are?" Ethan, winded and dizzy, dubiously absorbed the tableau before him.

"Mercenaries who take money for contracts they can't carry out don't have friends," growled brown-silk. "At least, not for long."

"I was *working* on it," argued Quinn. "You goons have no appreciation of subtlety. Besides, you can litter the place with corpses and run off to the protection of your House consul. No skin off you if you're deported and declared persona non grata on Kline Station forever. Not only do I have to play by different rules, but I wanna be able to come back here someday. Let's try for a little finesse, huh?"

"You've had nearly six months for finesse. Baron Luigi wants the House's money back," said pink-silk. "That's the only subtlety I have to appreciate."

Brown-silk lifted Quinn a few more centimeters.

"Ow, ow, all right, no problem!" yammered Quinn. "Your credit chit is in my right inner jacket pocket. Help yourselves."

"And just where is your jacket?"

"Millisor took it off me. It's back in the docking bay. Ow, no, honest!"

There was a disgusted pause. "It *could* be the truth," mused pink-silk.

"Docking bay's crawling with Station Security by now," brown-silk pointed out. "It could be a trick."

"Look, fellas, let's be reasonable about this, huh?" said Quinn. "Luigi's deal was half in advance and half on delivery. Now, I already took care of Okita. That's one-quarter right there."

"We have only your word for that. *I* haven't seen a body," said pink-silk.

"Finesse, Gen'ral, finesse."

"Major," pink-silk corrected automatically.

"And it was I who took out Setti in the docking bay just now. That's half. Seems to me we're even."

"With our bomb," said brown-silk.

"You gonna argue with results? Look, are we allies, or not?"

"Not," said brown-silk, and elevated her slightly more.

Voices, and a clatter of boots and equipment, echoed down the corridor from the direction of the docking bay. Pink-silk shoved his plasma arc into a holster out of sight under his embroidered jacket. "Time's up."

"Are you going to let this slide?" demanded brown-silk.

Pink-silk shrugged. "Call it even at half-pay. You right-handed or left-handed, Quinn?"

"Right-handed."

"Take the Baron's interest out of her left arm, and let's go."

Brown-silk, quite deliberately, let Quinn drop, achieved an arm-bar, and popped her left elbow.

The muffled cartilaginous crack was quite audible. Quinn made no other sound. Again, Cee restrained Ethan's forward lurch. The pair of Bharaputrans stepped delicately into the nearest lift-tube, and sank from sight.

"Damn, I thought they'd never leave," Quinn sighed. "The last thing I need is for Security to catch up with those guys and start comparing notes." She slithered greenly to a seat on the floor, her back propped against the wall. "I want to go back to combat duty. I don't think I like this Intelligence stuff as well as Admiral Naismith said I would."

Ethan cleared his throat. "You, ah—need a doctor, Commander?"

She grinned wanly. "Yeah. Do you?"

"Yeah." Ethan sat down rather heavily beside her. His ears still rang, and the chamber walls seemed to pulsate. He mulled over her comment. "This isn't by chance your first Intelligence assignment, is it?"

"Yep."

"Just my luck." The floor beckoned; never had friction plating looked so soft and inviting.

"Security's coming," she observed. She glanced up at Cee, hovering in anxious but helpless solicitude. "What do you say we do them a favor, and simplify the scenario for them? Get gone, Mr. Cee. If you walk and don't run, those green coveralls will carry you right past 'em. Go to work or something."

"I—I . . ." Terrence Cee spread his hands. "What can I ever do to repay you? Either of you?"

She winked. "Never fear, I'll think of something. Meantime, I haven't seen any telepaths around here today. Have you, Doctor?"

"Not a one," agreed Ethan blandly.

Terrence Cee shook his head in frustration, glanced up the corridor, and faded into the Up lift tube.

When Security finally arrived, they arrested Quinn.

Chapter Fourteen

Ethan stepped through the weapons detector without eliciting a beep or blink of false accusation, and breathed more easily. Kline Station Security Detention was a stark, intimidating environment, gleaming and efficient, without any of the usual Stationer attempts to soften the ambience with plants or artistic displays. The effect was doubtless designed; it certainly worked. Ethan felt guilty just visiting the Minimum Security block.

"Commander Quinn is in Number Two Detention Infirmary, Ambassador Urquhart," the guard assigned to be his guide informed him. "This way, please."

Up some lift-tubes, down some corridors. Station life, Ethan decided, must exert powerful evolutionary pressures to develop a good sense of direction. Not to mention sensitivity to subtleties of status. Colorblindness could prove a mortal handicap here. The Security uniforms, as all other work uniforms, were color coded, and furthermore the proportion of orange to black varied with rank. The ordinary guard wore orange picked out with black; he paused to give a snappy salute, casually returned, to a white-haired man whose sleek black uniform was barely highlighted with orange piping. One might study the entire Station heirarchy in nuances of hue.

Captain Arata, who was just now exiting the Infirmary as Ethan

399

and his guide approached, wore mostly black, with broad orange bands on collar and sleeves and an orange stripe down his trouser legs. He also wore a frustrated frown.

"Ah, Ambassador Urquhart." The frown was put away and replaced with a slightly ironic smile. "Come to visit our star boarder, have you? You needn't have troubled, she'll be a free woman shortly. Her credit check passed—astonishingly enough— her fines are paid, and she waits only for her medical release."

"That's all right, Captain—it's no trouble," said Ethan. "I just wanted to ask her a question."

"As did I," sighed Arata. "Several. I trust you will have better luck getting answers. These past few weeks, when I wanted a date, all she wanted to do was trade information under the counter. Now I want information, and what do I get? A date." He brightened slightly. "We will doubtless talk shop. If I worm any more out of her, maybe I'll be able to charge our night out to the department." He nodded at Ethan; an inviting silence fell.

"Good luck," said Ethan, cordially unhelpful. He had handled the Security post-mortem of yesterday's terrifying affair in the docking bay by climbing onto his ambassadorial status and referring all questions ruthlessly to the ever-inventive Quinn. She had stitched truth to lies to produce a fabulous beast of a story that nevertheless held up on every checkable point. In her version, for example, Millisor and Rau had been attempting to kidnap her, to program her as a double agent to penetrate the Dendarii Mercenaries for Cetagandan Intelligence. The Bharaputrans were accused of all the crimes they had in fact committed, and a few they hadn't—Okita who? Most of Security's energies were now diverted to the consulate where the Bharaputran hit squad was still holed up, negotiating the terms of their deportation. Terrence Cee had vanished utterly from the scenario. Ethan wouldn't have dared add or subtract a word.

"How unfortunate," Arata murmured, permitting a little of the needle-sharpness to flash in his eyes, "that *I* require a court order to use fast-penta."

Ethan smiled blandly. "Quite." They bowed each other farewell.

The guard turned Ethan over to the infirmary doctor. Except for the coded locks on the doors, Quinn's cell might have been any hospital room. Any Stationer hospital room, that is. Ethan was beginning to miss openable windows, taken for granted on Athos, with a starved passion.

Not wishing to state his real mission straight off, Ethan began with that thought.

"How do you feel about windows that open?" he asked Quinn. "Downside, I mean."

"Paranoid," she answered promptly. "I keep looking around for things to seal them up with. Aren't you going to ask how I am?"

"You're fine," Ethan said absently, "except for the dislocated elbow and the contusions. I asked the doctor. Oral analgesics and no violent exercise for a few days."

In fact, she looked well. Her color was good, and her movements, except for the immobilized left arm, were only a little stiff. She sat up on, rather than in, her bed. She had escaped her patient gown, itself a uniform of sickness, and was back in her gray-and-whites, although minus the jacket and with slippers in place of boots.

"Suits me." Her eyes crinkled. "And how do you feel about women now, Dr. Urquhart?"

"Oh—" he paused, "somewhat the way you feel about windows, I'm afraid. Did you ever get used to windows, or learn to enjoy them?"

"Rather. But then, I've been accused of being a thrill-seeker." Her grin tilted. "I'll never forget my first trip downside, after I'd signed on with the Dendarii Mercenaries—the Oseran Mercenaries, they were back then, before Admiral Naismith took over. I'd dreamed all my life of experiencing a real planetary climate. Mountain mists, ocean breezes, that sort of thing. The directory said the planet's climate was 'temperate,' which I took as a synonym for mild. We landed for emergency re-supply in the middle of a bloody blizzard. It was a year before I volunteered for downside duty again."

"I can imagine." Ethan laughed, and relaxed a little, and sat down.

Her head tilted to match her smile. "Yes, so you can. One of your more surprising charms, coming from your background. Being able to make an effort of the imagination, that is, and see through a different person's eyes."

Ethan shrugged, embarrassed. "I've always liked learning new things, finding out how things work. Molecular biology was the best. Curiosity is not a theological virtue, though."

"Mm, true. Are there carnal virtues?"

Ethan puzzled over this unusual thought. "I—don't know. It

seems like there ought to be. Perhaps they're called something else. I'm sure there are no new virtues under the sun—or new vices, either." Before Quinn could point out that they were under no sun—for surely the distant cinder Kline Station orbited could not be so called—Ethan hurried on. "Speaking of things carnal—I, uh—that is, before you go back to the Dendarii Mercenaries, I wanted to ask you if—um—I have what you may think a rather unusual request. If it doesn't offend you?" he inquired nervously.

He had her entire attention, her head cocked, eyes bright, a smile pressed out straight. "Before you say what it is, how can I tell? But I believe I've heard it all, so go on, by all means."

He was closer to the door than she; besides, she had one hand tied behind her back, so to speak, and there was a guard outside to defend him. How much trouble could he possibly get into? He took a breath.

"I plan to go on to complete my mission of collecting new ovarian cultures for Athos. Probably to Beta Colony, as you recommended, and the government gene repository that stocks the donations from its outstanding citizens—their seed catalog sounded quite attractive."

She nodded judicious approval, her eyes full of amused expectation.

"However," Ethan went on, "there's no reason I can't begin now. Speaking of outstanding or, um, extraordinary sources. What I mean is, um—would you care to donate an ovary to Athos, Commander Quinn?"

There was a moment's dumbfounded silence. "By the gods," she said in a rather weak voice, "I *hadn't* heard it all."

"The operation is quite painless," Ethan assured her earnestly. "Kline Station has quite nice tissue culturing facilities, too—I've spent the morning checking them out. It's not a common request, but it's quite within their capabilities. And you did say you'd help me with my mission if I helped you with yours."

"I did? Oh. So I did . . ."

An anxious new thought struck Ethan. "You do have one to spare, don't you? I'd understood women all had two ovaries, in analogue to male testes. You haven't donated before, or had an accident—combat or something—I'm not asking for your only one, am I?"

"No, I'm still fully equipped with all my original parts." She laughed; Ethan was subtly reassured. "I was just a little taken aback.

That—that wasn't the proposition I was expecting, is all. Excuse me. I fear I am become incurably low-minded."

"You can't help that, I'm sure," Ethan said tolerantly. "Being female, and all that."

She opened her mouth, closed it, and shook her head. "Not touching that one with a stick," she muttered cryptically. "Well," she took a breath, let it run out, "well . . ." She cocked her head at him. "And just who would make use of my, um, donation?"

"Anyone who chose," Ethan answered. "In time, the culture would be divided and a subculture placed on file in each Reproduction Center on Athos. This time next year, you could have a hundred sons. As soon as I get my designated alternate problems straightened out, I rather fancied—I, uh—" Ethan found himself turning inexplicably red under her level gaze, "I rather fancied having all my sons from the same culture, you see. I'll have earned four sons altogether by then. I never had a double-brother, from the same culture as me. The practice seems to give a family a certain attractive unity. Diversity in unity, as it were . . ." He became conscious that he was babbling, and ran down.

"A hundred sons," she mused. "But no daughters?"

"Well—no. No daughters. Not on Athos." He added timidly, "Are daughters as important to a woman as sons are to a man?"

"There is a certain—ease, in the thought," she admitted. "There is no room for either daughters or sons in my line of work, however."

"Well, there you are."

"Well. There I am." The semi-permanent amusement lurking in her eyes had given way to a meditative seriousness. "I could never see them, could I? My hundred sons. They would never know who I was."

"Only a culture number. EQ-1. I—I might be able to push my Clearance Level A censorship status far enough to, say, send you a holocube someday, if—if that's something you would like. You could never come to Athos, nor send a message—at least, not under your own identity. You might fudge your sex, and get it past the censors that way . . ." He'd been associating with Quinn and her rough-and-ready approach to authority too long, Ethan reflected, upon the ease with which this anti-social suggestion fell from his lips. He cleared his throat.

Her eyes glinted, amusement rampant again. "What a positively revolutionary idea."

"You know I'm not a revolutionary," Ethan replied with some dignity. He paused. "Although—I'm afraid home is going to look a little different, when I go back. I don't want to change out of all fit."

She glanced around the room, and by implication beyond its walls to the surrounding Station, her former home. "Your instincts are sound, sir, although I suspect futile. Change is a function of time and experience, and time is implacable."

"An ovarian culture can defeat time for 200 years—maybe longer now, as we refine our methods of caring for them. You could be having children long after your own death."

"I could have been dead yesterday. I could be dead this time next month, for that matter. Or this time next year."

"That's true of anybody."

"Yeah, but my odds are about six times worse than average. My insurance has it calculated to the third decimal place, y'know." She sighed. "Well. Here we are." Her lips curved. "And I thought Tav Arata was cheeky. Dr. Urquhart, you've topped them all."

Ethan's shoulders slumped with disappointment, as he saw his imagined string of dark-haired sons with mirror-bright eyes fading back into the realm of ungraspable dream. "I'm sorry. I didn't mean to give offense. I'll go." He began to rise.

"You give up too easily," she remarked to the air.

He sat back down hastily. His hands clasped each other between his knees, to keep his fingers from nervous drumming. He searched his mind for supplication. "The boys would be excellently cared for. Certainly mine would be. We screen our paternal applicants very carefully. A man who does not live up to his trust may have his sons repossessed, a shame and disgrace all strive to avoid."

"What's in it for me, though?"

Ethan thought this over carefully. "Nothing," he had to admit honestly at last. He had a sudden impulse to offer her money— a mercenary, after all—no. That felt all wrong, somehow, he could not say why. He slumped again.

"Nothing." She shook her head ruefully. "What woman could resist that appeal? Did I ever tell you that one of my other hobbies was banging my head against brick walls?"

He glanced at her forehead, startled, then realized this was a joke.

She nibbled her last unbitten fingernail, without biting through. "You sure Athos can take a hundred little Quinns?"

"More than that, in time. It might liven the place up. . . . Perhaps it would improve our military.

Quinn looked bemused indeed. "What can I say? Dr. Urquhart, you're on."

Ethan lit with joy.

Ethan met Quinn by pre-arrangement at a cafe in a small arcade near the Stationer edge of Transients' Lounge. She had arrived before him, and sat sipping something blue from a small stemmed glass, which she lifted to him in toast as he threaded the tables toward her.

"How are you feeling?" he asked as he sat down beside her.

She rubbed the right side of her abdomen pensively. "Fine. You were quite correct, I didn't feel a thing. Still don't. Not even a scar to show for my charity." She sounded faintly disappointed.

"The ovary took the culturing treatment just fine," he assured her. "The cells are dividing nicely. It will be ready for freezing for transport in 48 hours. And then, I guess, I'm off to Beta Colony. When will you be leaving?" A faint speculation—hope?—that they might possibly be traveling on the same ship crossed his mind.

"I'm leaving tonight. Before I get into any more trouble with the Station authorities," she replied, dashing Ethan's nascent scenario of further conversations. He never had had time to ask her about all the planets she had undoubtedly seen in her military pilgrimages. "I also want to be long, long gone before any Cetagandan follow-up on Millisor's death arrives. Though it seems they are going to get directed back to Jackson's Whole—I wish them all joy of each other." She stretched and grinned, like a cat full of bird after a successful hunt and picking a few feathers from its teeth.

"I'd just as soon avoid meeting any more Cetagandans myself," said Ethan. "If I can."

"Shouldn't be too difficult. For your peace of mind, I might mention that before his death ghem-Colonel Millisor managed to send off a confirmation of Helda's destruction of the Bharaputran cultures to his superiors. I doubt the Cetagandans will show any further interest in Athos. Although Mr. Cee is another matter, since the same report also confirmed his presence here on Kline Station.

"But I've got a stack of reports myself that will give Admiral Naismith something to meditate on for months. I'm glad I don't have to decide what to do with it all. I lack but one item to make his day complete—and here it comes, I trust, now." She nodded past Ethan's shoulder, and he turned in his seat.

Terrence Cee was making his way toward them.

His green Stationer coveralls were inconspicuous enough, although his wiry blond intensity turned an older female head or two, Ethan noted.

He sat down with them, nodding at Quinn, smiling briefly at Ethan. "Good afternoon, Commander, Doctor."

Quinn smiled back. "Good afternoon, Mr. Cee. Can I buy you a drink? Burgundy, sherry, champagne, beer . . ."

"Tea," said Cee. "Just tea."

Quinn put the order on her credit card in the table's auto-waiter. The Station, it seemed, did not import all comforts. The real thing—a pleasant aromatic black variety grown and processed on Kline Station—appeared promptly, steaming in a transparent mug. Ethan ordered some too, the business hiding the little discomfort Cee's presence induced in him. The telepath could have no further interest in Athos now either.

Cee sipped; Quinn sipped. "Well," Quinn said. "Did you bring it?"

Cee nodded, sipped again, and laid three thin data discs and an insulated box perhaps half the size of Ethan's hand upon the table. They all disappeared into Quinn's jacket. At Ethan's look of inquiry, Quinn shrugged, "We all trade in flesh here, it seems," by which Ethan understood the box contained the promised tissue sample from the telepath.

"I thought Terrence was going back to the Dendarii Mercenaries with you," said Ethan, surprised.

"I've tried to talk him into it—by the way, the offer remains open, Mr. Cee."

Terrence Cee shook his head. "When Millisor was breathing down my neck, it seemed the only exit. You've given me a little space to make a choice, Commander Quinn—for which I thank you." A movement of his finger toward the packets secreted in her jacket indicated the tangible form of his thanks.

"I am too kind," Quinn sighed wryly. "If you change your mind later, you can still look us up, you know. Look for a heap of trouble with a squiggly-minded little man on top of it, and tell him Quinn sent you. He'll take you in."

"I'll remember," Cee promised noncommittally.

"Ah, well—I won't be traveling alone." Quinn smiled smugly. "I scrounged up another recruit to keep me company on the trip back. Interesting fellow—a migrant worker. He's knocked around all over the galaxy. You should meet him, Mr. Cee. He's about your height—skinny—blond, too." She lifted her stemmed glass in toast, and tossed off the rest of her blue drink. "Confusion to the enemy."

"Thank you, Commander," Cee said sincerely.

"Where, ah—were you thinking of going now, if not the Dendarii Mercenaries?" Ethan asked him.

Cee spread his hands. "There are a multitude of choices. Too many, really, and all about equally meaningless . . . excuse me." He remembered to feign good cheer. "Some direction away from Cetaganda." He nodded toward Quinn's left jacket pocket. "I trust you won't have any trouble smuggling that package out. It should go into a proper freeze-box as soon as possible. A very small one, maybe. It might be better if a freeze-box does not appear on your luggage manifest."

She smiled slowly, scratching one tooth—her fingernails were all neatly filed down again—and murmured, "A very small one, or—hm. I think I may have an ideal solution to that little problem, Mr. Cee."

Ethan watched with interest as Quinn dropped the enormous white freezer transport box down upon the counter of Cold Storage Access 297-C. It banged, startling the attention of the counter girl dreaming over a holovid drama. The figures of the girl's private play vanished in smoke, and she hastily removed an audio plug from her ear.

"Yes, ma'am?"

"I've come for my newts," said Quinn. She reached around and shoved her thumb-printed authorization into the read-slot in the counter's computer.

"Oh, yes, I remember you," said the girl. "A cubic meter in plastic. Do you want it quick-thawed?"

"Don't want it thawed at all, I'm shipping them frozen, thanks," said Quinn. "Eighty kilos of newts would be a little icky after four weeks' travel warm, I fear."

The girl wrinkled her nose. "I think they're icky at any temperature."

"I assure you, they will be appreciated in direct ratio to their distance from their source." Quinn grinned.

The corridor doors hissed open behind them. Ethan and Terrence Cee stepped out of the way as a float pallet entered piloted by a green-and-blue uniformed ecotech and bearing half a dozen small sealed canisters.

"Oh, oh, priority," said the counter girl. "Excuse me, ma'am."

Ethan recognized the ecotech with a pleasant start; it was Teki, presumably from his work station just around the corner. Teki recognized Quinn and Ethan at the same moment. Cee, not known to the ecotech, didn't register, and stepped smoothly into the background.

"Ah, Teki!" said Quinn. "I was just about to step around and say goodbye. You're fully recovered from your little adventure of last week, I trust?"

Teki snorted. "Yeah, getting kidnapped and worked over by a gang of homicidal lunatics is my idea of a real fun time, sure. Thanks."

Quinn's mouth quirked. "Has Sara forgiven you for standing her up?"

Teki's eyes twinkled, and he failed to suppress a slow smirk. "Well, yes—once she was finally convinced it wasn't a put-on, she got real, um, sympathetic." He attempted sternness. "But damn, I knew it had to be something for the dwarf! You can tell me now, can't you Elli?"

"Sure. Just as soon as it gets declassified."

Teki groaned. "Not fair! You promised!"

She shrugged, helpless. He frowned grudgingly, then, palpably, let the grudge go: "Goodbye? You leaving soon?"

"In a few hours."

"Oh!" Teki looked genuinely disappointed. He glanced at Ethan. "Afternoon, Mr. Ambassador. Say, I'm, uh—sorry about what Helda did to your stuff. Hope you won't take it as representative of our department. She's on medical leave—they're calling it a nervous breakdown. I'm acting head of Assimilation Station B now," he added with a bit of shy pride. He held out a green sleeve for inspection, circled by two blue bands in place of his previous one. "At least till she gets back." On closer look, Ethan found the second band to be but lightly tacked in place.

"It's all right," said Ethan. "You stitch that armband on good and tight—I'm assured her medical leave will be permanent."

"Oh, yeah?" Teki brightened still more. "Look, let me throw this shit out—" he gestured to the little canisters on his float pallet, "and I'll be with you—you all can come around to Station B for a couple of minutes, can't you?"

"Only a couple," warned Quinn. "I can't stay long, if I'm to make my ship."

Teki waved in a gesture of understanding. "Come on back," he invited, maneuvering his float pallet past the counter and through the airseal doors behind them that the counter girl had keyed open for him.

"Gotta wait for my stuff," Quinn excused herself but Ethan, curious, trailed along. Cee drifted behind, inconspicuous and quiet, a lonely figure still, odd man out. Ethan smiled over his shoulder, trying to include him in the group.

"So tell me more about Helda," said Teki to Ethan. "Is it really true she mailed all that stolen tissue to Athos?"

Ethan nodded. "I'm still not sure what she hoped to accomplish. I don't think she even knew. Maybe it was just to have something in the shipping cartons to pass casual inspection—I mean, empty boxes would show obvious tampering. She managed to create a mystery almost in spite of herself."

Teki shook his head, as if still unable to believe it all.

"What is all this?" Ethan gestured toward the float pallet.

"Samples, of some contaminated stuff we confiscated and destroyed today—they go into cold storage, for proof later in case of lawsuits, or further outbreaks, or whatever."

They entered a chill white room featuring quantities of robotic equipment and an airlock: a chamber on the very skin of the Station, Ethan realized.

Teki tapped instructions rapidly into a control console, inserted a data disc, placed the canister into a high-tensile-strength plastic bag with a coded label, and attached the bag to a robotic device. The device rose and floated into the airlock, which hissed shut and began to cycle.

Teki touched a control on the wall, and a panel slid back, revealing a small transparent barrier like the great ones in Transients' Lounge. Crowding projections of bits of the Station blocked most of the spectacular galactic view. It was the Station equivalent of a back alley, Ethan decided, except that it was brightly lit. Teki watched carefully as the robot exited the airlock and floated through the vacuum across a long grid of metal columns all tethered about with bags and boxes.

"It's like the universe's biggest closet," mused Teki. "Our own private storage locker. We really ought to clean house and destroy all the really old stuff that was thrown out there in Year One, but it's not like we're running out of room. Still, if I'm going to be an Assimiliation Station head, I could organize something . . . responsibility . . . no more playing around . . .."

The ecotech's words became a buzzing drone in his ears as Ethan's attention was riveted on a collection of transparent plastic bags tethered a short way down the grid. Each bag seemed to contain a jumble of little white boxes of a familiar type. He had seen just such a little box readied for Quinn's donation at a Station biolab that morning. How many boxes? Hard to see, hard to count. More than twenty, surely. More than thirty. He could count the bags that contained them, though; there were nine.

"Thrown out," he whispered. "Thrown—*out?*"

The robot reached the end of a column and attached its burden thereto. Teki's attention was all on the working device; he moved off to monitor it as it cycled back through the airlock. Ethan reached back, grabbed Cee by the arm, bundled him forward, and pointed silently out the window.

Cee looked annoyed, then looked again. He stiffened, his lips parting. He stared as if his eyes might devour the distance, and the barrier. The telepath began to swear under his breath, so softly that Ethan could hardly make out the words; his hands clenched, unclenched, and splayed against the transparency.

Ethan gripped Cee's arm harder. "Is it them?" he whispered. "Could it be?"

"I can make out the Bharaputra House logo on the labels," breathed Cee. "I saw them packed."

"She must have put them out here herself," muttered Ethan. "Left no record in the computer—I bet a search would list that bin as empty. She threw them *out*. She really literally did throw them *out. Out there.*"

"Could they still be all right?" asked Cee.

"Stone frozen—why not . . . ?"

They stared at each other, wild in surmise.

"We've got to tell Quinn," Ethan began.

Cee's hands clamped down over Ethan's wrists. "No!" he hissed. "She has hers. Janine—those are mine."

"Or Athos's."

"No." Cee was trembling white, his eyes blazing like blue pinwheels. "Mine."

"The two," said Ethan carefully, "need not be mutually exclusive."

In the loaded silence that followed, Cee's face flared in an exaltation of hope.

Chapter Fifteen

Home. Ethan's eye teased him as he stared eagerly through the shuttle window. Could he make out the patchwork farmlands, name cities, rivers, roads yet? Cumulus clouds were scattered over the bays and islands off the South Province coast, dappling the bright morning with shade, obscuring his certainty. But yes, there was an island the shape of a crescent moon, there the silver thread of a small river where the coastline looped.

"My father's fish farm is in that bay there," he pointed out to Terrence Cee in the seat beside him. "Just behind that crescent-shaped outer island."

Cee's blond head craned. "Yes, I see."

"Sevarin is north, and inland. The shuttleport where we'll be landing is at the capital, north one district from that. You can't see it yet."

Cee settled back in his seat, looking reflective. The first whispers of the upper atmosphere carried a hum from the shuttle's engines. A hymn, to Ethan's ears.

"Will you be getting a hero's welcome?" Cee asked Ethan.

"Oh, I doubt it. My mission was secret, after all. Not strictly, in the military sense you're familiar with, but done quietly, on account of not wanting to start a public panic or cause a crisis of confidence in the Rep Centers. Although I imagine some of the

Population Council will be there. I'd like you to meet Dr. Desroches. And some of my family—I called my father from the space station, so I know he'll be waiting. I told him I was bringing a friend," Ethan added, hoping to ease Cee's obvious nervousness. "He seemed quite pleased to hear it."

He was nervous himself. How *was* he going to explain Cee to Janos? He had run through several hundred practice introductions in his mind, during the two-month leg of their journey from Kline Station, until he had wearied of worrying. If Janos was going to be jealous, or hard-nosed about it, let him get down to work and earn his designated alternate status. It might be just the stimulus needed to kick him into action at last; given Janos's own personal proclivities, he was unlikely to believe that Cee had shown every sign of being a prime candidate for one of the Chaste Brotherhoods. Ethan sighed.

Cee regarded his hands meditatively, and glanced up at Ethan. "And will they view you as a hero, or a traitor, in the end?"

Ethan surveyed the shuttle. His precious cargo, nine big white freezer cartons, was not consigned to the chances of the cargo hold, but strapped to the seats all around them. The only other passengers, the census statistician and his assistant and three members of the galactic census courier's crew heading for downside leave, hung together protectively at the far end, out of earshot.

"I wish I knew," said Ethan. "I pray about it daily. I haven't prayed on my knees since I was a kid, but on this I do. Don't know if it helps."

"You're not going to change your mind and switch back at the last minute? The last minute is coming up fast."

As fast as the ground below. They were dropping through the cloud layer now, white fog beading on the window and flaring off in the wind of their passage. Ethan thought of the other cargo, secreted in his personal luggage, compressed and concealed: the 450 ovarian cultures he had purchased on Beta Colony for the sake of assuring any possible future Cetagandan follow-up of his activities—and indeed, of assuring the Population Council itself—that the original Bharaputran cultures had never been found. Cee had helped him make the switch, hours and hours spent in the census courier's cargo hold changing labels, doctoring records. Or maybe it had been Ethan helping Cee. They were both in it together now, anyway, to the neck and beyond.

Ethan shook his head. "It was a decision that somebody had

to make. If not me, then the Population Council. There are only two choices in the long run that don't risk race war or genocide: all, or nothing. I am convinced you were right on that score. And the committee—well—I feared they would be constitutionally incapable of anything but a split decision. You're right in your perception—as always—I tremble at our future. But even in fear and trembling, I'm willing to reach for it. It ought to be— interesting."

If Ethan felt a spasm of guilt, it was for the 451st culture, EQ-l, whose container he held on his lap. If he were unable to complete his scheme, of all the Sons born to Athos in the next generation, only his would not bear the hidden alleles, the recessive telepathy time-bomb. But his grandsons would get them, he assuaged his conscience. It would all average out in the long run. May he live to see it; may he live to nurture it.

"But you retained the chance to change your mind," Cee noted. A jerk of his chin in the direction of the cargo bay and Ethan's luggage indicated the cause of his unease.

"I'm afraid I'm hopelessly economical," Ethan apologized. "I should have been a housekeeper, I sometimes think. The Betan cultures were just too good to jettison into the vacuum. But if I get my old job back, or better still advance to head a Rep Center, there may be a chance—I'd like to try my hand at gene splicing the telepathy complex into the genuine Betan cultures and slipping them back into Athos's gene pool, if I can do it in secrecy. As soon as I become adept at the operation, this one too." He lifted EQ-1 from his lap, then set it back carefully, his conscience quieted still further. "I did promise Commander Quinn a hundred sons. And as a Rep Center chief, I would have a seat on the Population Council. Maybe even a shot at the chairmanship, someday."

There was a small crowd in the Athosian shuttleport docking bay in spite of the close secrecy surrounding Ethan's mission. Most of them turned out to be representatives from the nine District Reproduction Centers, eager to carry off their new cultures. Ethan was nearly trampled in the rush for the freezer boxes. But the Chairman of the Population Council was there, and Dr. Desroches, and best of all Ethan's father.

"Did you have any trouble?" the chairman asked Ethan.

"Oh," Ethan clutched EQ-1, "nothing we couldn't handle . . ."

Desroches grinned. "Told you so," he murmured to the chairman.

Ethan and his father embraced, not once but several times, as if to assure each other of their continued vitality. Ethan's father was a tall, tanned, wind-wrinkled man; Ethan could smell the salt sea lingering even in his best clothes, and inhaled pleasurable memories therefrom.

"You're so pale," Ethan's father complained, holding him at arm's length and looking him up and down. "God the Father, boy, it's like getting you back from the dead in more ways than one." His father embraced him again.

"Well, I've been indoors for a year." Ethan smiled. "Kline Station didn't have a sun to speak of, I was only on Escobar for a week, and Beta Colony had too much sun—nobody goes aboveground there unless they want to be fried. I'm healthier than I look, I assure you. In fact, I feel great. Uh—" he looked around surreptitiously one more time, "where's Janos?" Sudden fear shot through him at his father's grave look.

Ethan's father took a deep breath. "I'm sorry to have to tell you this, son—but we all agreed it would be better to tell you first thing. . . ."

God the Father, thought Ethan, *Janos has gone and killed himself in my lightflyer . . .*

"Janos isn't here."

"I can see that." Ethan's heart seemed to rise and choke his words.

"He got kind of wild, after you left—nobody to be a restraining influence on him, Spiri says, though I take it as a man's duty to restrain himself, and Janos was old enough to start playing a man's part—Spiri and I had a bit of an argument about it, in fact, though it's all settled now—"

The docking bay seemed to spin around Ethan's center of gravity, just below his stomach. "What *happened?*"

"Well—Janos ran off to the Outlands with his friend Nick about two months after you left. He says he's not coming back—no rules or restrictions out there, he says, nobody keeping score on you." Ethan's father snorted. "No future, either, but he doesn't seem to care about that. Though give him ten years, and he may find he's had a bellyfull of freedom. Others have. I calculate it'll take him at least that long, though. He always was the thickest of you boys."

"Oh," said Ethan in a very small voice. He tried to look properly grieved. He tried very hard, twitching the corners of his mouth back down by main force. "Well—" he cleared his throat, "perhaps it's for the best. Some men just aren't cut out for paternity. Better they should realize it before and not after they become responsible for a son."

He turned to Terrence Cee, his grin escaping control at last. "Here, Dad, I want you to meet someone—I brought us an immigrant. Only one, but altogether a remarkable person. He's endured much, to make it to refuge here. He's been a good traveling companion for the last eight months, and a good friend."

Ethan introduced Cee; they shook hands, the slight galactic, the tall waterman. "Welcome, Terrence," said Ethan's father. "A good friend of my son's is a son to me. Welcome to Athos."

Emotion broke through Cee's habitual closed coolness; wonder, and something like awe. "You really mean that . . . Thank you. Thank you, sir."

Two of the three moons rose together that night over Athos's Eastern Sea. The little breakers murmured beyond the dunes. The second floor verandah of Ethan's father's house gave a fine view over the moon-spangled waters of the bay. The breeze cooled Ethan's blush, as the darkness concealed its color.

"You see, Terrence," Ethan explained shyly to Cee, "the fastest way to gain your paternal rights, and Janine's sons, is to devote all your time to public works until you gain enough social duty credits for designated alternate status. There's plenty to do—everything from road repair to parks maintenance to work for the government—maybe sharing some of your galactic expertise—to all kinds of charity work. Old men's homes, orphanages for the bereft and repossessed, animal care, disaster relief services—although the army handles most of that—the choices are endless."

"But how shall I support myself meanwhile?" objected Cee. "Or is support included?"

"No, you must support yourself. To gain designated alternate points the work must be over and above the regular economy—it's really a kind of labor tax, if you want to think of it that way. But I thought—if you will allow me—I can support you. I make plenty for two as a Rep Center department head—and Desroches and the Chairman have hinted that I may get the Chief of Staff post at the new Rep Center for the Red Mountain district, when it goes into place year after next. By then, with diligence, you'll have your D.A. status. And then it can go really fast, because," Ethan took a breath, "as a designated alternate parent, you can become a Primary Nurturer to my sons. And being a Primary Nurturer is, bar none, the fastest way to accumulate social duty credits toward paternity." Ethan faltered. "I admit, it's not a very adventurous life, compared to the one you've led. Sitting in a garden, rocking a cradle—someone else's cradle, at that. Though it would be good practice for your own, and of course I would be happy to stand as designated alternate parent to your sons."

Cee's voice came out of the darkness. "Is hell an adventure, compared to heaven? I've been to the bottom of the pit, thank you. I have no wish to descend again for *adventure's* sake." His tone mocked the very word. "Your garden sounds just fine to me."

He sighed long. There was a pause. Then, "Wait a minute, though. I got the impression the mutual D.A. business, outside the communal brotherhoods, was sort of like married couples—is sex entailed in all this?"

"Well . . ." said Ethan. "No, not necessarily. D.A. arrangements can be, and are, entered into by brothers, cousins, fathers, grandfathers—anyone qualified and willing to act as a parent. Parenthood shared between lovers is just the most common variety. But here you are on Athos, after all, for the rest of your life. I thought, perhaps, in time, you might grow accustomed to our ways. Not to rush you or anything, but if you find yourself getting used to the idea, you might, uh, let me know . . ." Ethan trailed off.

"By God the Father," Cee's voice was amused, assured. And had Ethan really feared he would surprise the telepath? "I just might."

Ethan paused in front of the bathroom mirror before turning out the light, and studied his own face. He thought of Elli Quinn, and EQ-1. In a woman, one saw not charts and graphs and numbers, but the genes of one's own children personified and made flesh. So, every ovarian culture on Athos cast a woman's shadow, unacknowledged, ineradicably there.

And what had she been like, Dr. Cynthia Jane Baruch, 200 years dead now, and how much had she secretly shaped Athos, all unbeknownst to the founding fathers who had hired her to create their ovarian cultures? She who had cared enough to put herself in them? The very bones of Athos were molded to her pattern. His bones.

"Salute, Mother," Ethan whispered, and turned away to bed. Tomorrow began the new world, and the work thereof.

Labyrinth

Labyrinth

Miles contemplated the image of the globe glowing above the vid plate, crossed his arms, and stifled queasiness. The planet of Jackson's Whole, glittering, wealthy, corrupt . . . Jacksonians claimed their corruption was entirely imported—if the galaxy were willing to pay for virtue what it paid for vice, the place would be a pilgrimage shrine. In Miles's view this seemed rather like debating which was superior, maggots or the rotten meat they fed off. Still, if Jackson's Whole didn't exist, the galaxy would probably have had to invent it. Its neighbors might feign horror, but they wouldn't permit the place to exist if they didn't find it a secretly useful interface with the sub-economy.

The planet possessed a certain liveliness, anyway. Not as lively as a century or two back, to be sure, in its hijacker-base days. But its cutthroat criminal gangs had senesced into Syndicate monopolies, almost as structured and staid as little governments. An aristocracy, of sorts. Naturally. Miles wondered how much longer the major Houses would be able to fight off the creeping tide of integrity.

House Dyne, detergent banking—launder your money on Jackson's Whole. House Fell, weapons deals with no questions asked. House Bharaputra, illegal genetics. Worse, House Ryoval, whose motto was "Dreams Made Flesh," surely the damndest—

Miles used the adjective precisely—procurer in history. House Hargraves, the galactic fence, prim-faced middlemen for ransom deals—you had to give them credit, hostages exchanged through their good offices came back alive, mostly. And a dozen smaller syndicates, variously and shiftingly allied.

Even we find you useful. Miles touched the control and the vid image vanished. His lip curled in suppressed loathing, and he called up his ordnance inventory for one final check of his shopping list. A subtle shift in the vibrations of the ship around him told him they were matching orbits—the fast cruiser *Ariel* would be docking at Fell Station within the hour.

His console was just extruding the completed data disk of weapons orders when his cabin door chimed, followed by an alto voice over its com, "Admiral Naismith?"

"Enter." He plucked off the disk and leaned back in his station chair.

Captain Thorne sauntered in with a friendly salute. "We'll be docking in about thirty minutes, sir."

"Thank you, Bel."

Bel Thorne, the *Ariel's* commander, was a Betan hermaphrodite, man/woman descendant of a centuries-past genetic-social experiment every bit as bizarre, in Miles's private opinion, as anything rumored to be done for money by House Ryoval's ethics-free surgeons. A fringe effort of Betan egalitarianism run amok, hermaphroditism had not caught on, and the original idealists' hapless descendants remained a minority on hyper-tolerant Beta Colony. Except for a few stray wanderers like Bel. As a mercenary officer Thorne was conscientious, loyal, and aggressive, and Miles liked him/her/it—Betan custom used the neuter pronoun—a lot. *However . . .*

Miles could smell Bel's floral perfume from here. Bel was emphasizing the female side today. And had been, increasingly, for the five days of this voyage. Normally Bel chose to come on ambiguous-to-male, soft short brown hair and chiselled, beard-less facial features counteracted by the gray-and-white Dendarii military uniform, assertive gestures, and wicked humor. It worried Miles exceedingly to sense Bel soften in his presence.

Turning to his computer console's holovid plate, Miles again called up the image of the planet they were approaching. Jackson's Whole looked demure enough from a distance, mountainous, rather cold—the populated equator was only temperate—ringed in the vid by a lacy schematic net of colored satellite tracks, orbital transfer stations, and authorized approach vectors. "Have you ever been here before, Bel?"

"Once, when I was a lieutenant in Admiral Oser's fleet," said the mercenary. "House Fell has a new baron since then. Their weaponry still has a good reputation, as long as you know what you're buying. Stay away from the sale on neutron hand grenades."

"Heh. For those with strong throwing arms. Fear not, neutron hand grenades aren't on the list." He handed the data disk to Bel.

Bel sidled up and leaned over the back of Miles's station chair to take it. "Shall I grant leaves to the crew while we're waiting for the baron's minions to load cargo? How about yourself? There used to be a hostel near the docks with all the amenities, pool, sauna, great food . . ." Bel's voice lowered. "I could book a room for two."

"I'd only figured to grant day passes." Necessarily, Miles cleared his throat.

"I *am* a woman, too," Bel pointed out in a murmur.

"Among other things."

"You're so hopelessly monosexual, Miles."

"Sorry." Awkwardly, he patted the hand that had somehow come to rest on his shoulder.

Bel sighed and straightened. "So many are."

Miles sighed too. Perhaps he ought to make his rejection more emphatic—this was only about the seventh time he'd been round with Bel on this subject. It was almost ritualized by now, almost, but not quite, a joke. You had to give the Betan credit for either optimism or obtuseness . . . or, Miles's honesty added, genuine feeling. If he turned round now, he knew, he might surprise an essential loneliness in the hermaphrodite's eyes, never permitted on the lips. He did not turn round.

And who was he to judge another, Miles reflected ruefully, whose own body brought him so little joy? What did Bel, straight and healthy and of normal height, if unusual genital arrangements, find so attractive in a little half-crippled part-time crazy man? He glanced down at the gray Dendarii officer's uniform he wore. The uniform he had won. *If you can't be seven feet tall, be seven feet smart.* His reason had so far failed to present him with a solution to the problem of Thorne, though.

"Have you ever thought of going back to Beta Colony, and seeking one of your own?" Miles asked seriously.

Thorne shrugged. "Too boring. That's why I left. It's so very safe, so very narrow. . . ."

"Mind you, a great place to raise kids." One corner of Miles's mouth twisted up.

Thorne grinned. "You got it. You're an almost perfect Betan, y'know? Almost. You have the accent, the in-jokes . . ."

Miles went a little still. "Where do I fail?"

Thorne touched Miles's cheek; Miles flinched.

"Reflexes," said Thorne.

"Ah."

"I won't give you away."

"I know."

Bel was leaning in again. "I could polish that last edge . . ."

"Never mind," said Miles, slightly flushed. "We have a mission."

"Inventory," said Thorne scornfully.

"That's not a mission," said Miles, "that's a cover."

"Ah ha." Thorne straightened up. "At last."

"At last?"

"It doesn't take a genius. We came to purchase ordnance, but instead of taking the ship with the biggest cargo capacity, you chose the *Ariel*—the fleet's fastest. There's no deader dull routine than inventory, but instead of sending a perfectly competent quarter-master, you're overseeing it personally."

"I do want to make contact with the new Baron Fell," said Miles mildly. "House Fell is the biggest arms supplier this side of Beta Colony, and a lot less picky about who its customers are. If I like the quality of the initial purchase, they could become a regular supplier."

"A quarter of Fell's arms are Betan manufacture, marked up," said Thorne. "Again, ha."

"And while we're here," Miles went on, "a certain middle-aged man is going to present himself and sign on to the Dendarii Mercenaries as a medtech. At that point all Station passes are cancelled, we finish loading cargo as quickly as possible, and we leave."

Thorne grinned in satisfaction. "A pick-up. Very good. I assume we're being well-paid?"

"Very. If he arrives at his destination alive. The man happens to be the top research geneticist of House Bharaputra's Laboratories. He's been offered asylum by a planetary government capable of protecting him from the long arms of

Baron Luigi Bharaputra's enforcers. His soon-to-be-former employer is expected to be highly irate at the lack of a month's notice. We are being paid to deliver him to his new masters alive and not, ah, forcibly debriefed of all his trade secrets.

"Since House Bharaputra could probably buy and sell the whole Dendarii Free Mercenary Fleet twice over out of petty cash, I would prefer we not have to deal with Baron Luigi's enforcers either. So we shall be innocent suckers. All we did was hire a bloody medtech, sir. And we shall be irate ourselves when he deserts after we arrive at fleet rendezvous off Escobar."

"Sounds good to me," conceded Thorne. "Simple."

"So I trust," Miles sighed hopefully. Why, after all, shouldn't things run to plan, just this once?

The purchasing offices and display areas for House Fell's lethal wares were situated not far from the docks, and most of House Fell's smaller customers never penetrated further into Fell Station. But shortly after Miles and Thorne placed their order—about as long as needed to verify a credit chit—an obsequious person in the green silk of House Fell's uniform appeared, and pressed an invitation into Admiral Naismith's hand to a reception in the Baron's personal quarters.

Four hours later, giving up the pass cube to Baron Fell's major-domo at the sealed entrance to the station's private sector, Miles checked Thorne and himself over for their general effect. Dendarii dress uniform was a gray velvet tunic with silver buttons on the shoulders and white edging, matching gray trousers with white side piping, and gray synthasuede boots—perhaps just a trifle effete? Well, he hadn't designed it, he'd just inherited it. Live with it.

The interface to the private sector was highly interesting. Miles's eye took in the details while the majordomo scanned them for weapons. Life-support—in fact, all systems—appeared to be run separately from the rest of the station. The area was not only sealable, it was detachable. In effect, not Station but Ship—engines and armament around here somewhere, Miles bet, though it could be lethal to go looking for them unescorted. The majordomo ushered them through, pausing to announce them on his wrist com: "Admiral Miles Naismith, commanding, Dendarii Free Mercenary Fleet. Captain Bel Thorne, commanding the fast cruiser *Ariel,*

Dendarii Free Mercenary Fleet." Miles wondered who was on the other end of the com.

The reception chamber was large and gracefully appointed, with iridescent floating staircases and levels creating private spaces without destroying the illusions of openness. Every exit (Miles counted six) had a large green-garbed guard by it trying to look like a servant and not succeeding very well. One whole wall was a vertigo-inducing transparent viewport overlooking Fell Station's busy docks and the bright curve of Jackson's Whole bisecting the star-spattered horizon beyond. A crew of elegant women in green silk saris rustled among the guests offering food and drink.

Gray velvet, Miles decided after one glance at the other guests, was a positively demure choice of garb. He and Bel would blend right into the walls. The thin scattering of fellow privileged customers wore a wide array of planetary fashions. But they were a wary bunch, little groups sticking together, no mingling. Guerrillas, it appeared, did not speak to mercenaries, nor smugglers to revolutionaries; the Gnostic Saints, of course, spoke only to the One True God, and perhaps to Baron Fell.

"Some party," commented Bel. "I went to a pet show with an atmosphere like this once. The high point was when somebody's Tau Cetan beaded lizard got loose and ate the Best-In-Show from the canine division."

"Hush." Miles grinned with one corner of his mouth. "This is business."

A green-sari'd woman bowed silently before them, offering a tray. Thorne raised a brow at Miles—*do we . . . ?*

"Why not?" Miles murmured. "We're paying for it, in the long run. I doubt the baron poisons his customers, it's bad for business. Business is emperor, here. Laissez-faire capitalism gone completely over the edge." He selected a pink tid-bit in the shape of a lotus and a mysterious cloudy drink. Thorne followed suit. The pink lotus, alas, turned out to be some sort of raw fish. It squeaked against his teeth. Miles, committed, swallowed it anyway. The drink was potently alcoholic, and after a sip to wash down the lotus he regretfully abandoned it on the first level surface he could find. His dwarfish body refused to handle alcohol, and he had no desire to meet Baron Fell while either semi-comatose or giggling uncontrollably. The more metabolically fortunate Thorne kept beverage in hand.

A most extraordinary music began from somewhere, a racing

rich complexity of harmonics. Miles could not identify the instrument—instruments, surely. He and Thorne exchanged a glance, and by mutual accord drifted toward the sound. Around a spiraling staircase, backed by the panoply of station, planet, and stars, they found the musician. Miles's eves widened. *House Ryoval's surgeons have surely gone too far this time. . . .*

Little decorative colored sparkles defined the spherical field of a large null-gee bubble. Floating within it was a woman. Her ivory arms flashed against her green silk clothes as she played. All *four* of her ivory arms. . . . She wore a flowing, kimono-like belted jacket and matching shorts, from which the second set of arms emerged where her legs should have been. Her hair was short and soft and ebony black. Her eyes were closed, and her rose-tinted face bore the repose of an angel, high and distant and terrifying.

Her strange instrument was fixed in air before her, a flat polished wooden frame strung across both top and bottom with a bewildering array of tight gleaming wires, soundboard between. She struck the wires with four felted hammers at blinding speed, both sides at once, her upper hands moving at counterpoint to her lowers. Music poured forth in a cascade.

"Good God," said Thorne, "it's a quaddie."

"It's a what?"

"A quaddie. She's a long way from home."

"She's—not a local product?"

"By no means.

"I'm relieved. I think. Where the devil does she come from, then?"

"About two hundred years ago—about the time hermaphrodites were being invented," a peculiar wryness flashed across Thorne's face, "there was this rush of genetic experimentation on humans, in the wake of the development of the practical uterine replicator. Followed shortly by a rush of laws restricting such, but meanwhile, somebody thought they'd make a race of free-fall dwellers. Then artificial gravity came in and blew them out of business. The quaddies fled—their descendants ended up on the far side of nowhere, way beyond Earth from us in the Nexus. They're rumored to keep to themselves, mostly. Very unusual, to see one this side of Earth. H'sh." Lips parted, Thorne tracked the music.

As unusual as finding a Betan hermaphrodite in a free mercenary fleet, Miles thought. But the music deserved undivided attention, though few in this paranoid crowd seemed to even be noticing it. A shame. Miles was no musician, but even he could sense an intensity of passion in the playing that went beyond talent, reaching for genius. An evanescent genius, sounds woven with time and, like time, forever receding beyond one's futile grasp into memory alone.

The outpouring of music dropped to a haunting echo, then silence. The four-armed musician's blue eyes opened, and her face came back from the ethereal to the merely human, tense and sad.

"Ah," breathed Thorne, stuck its empty glass under its arm, raised hands to clap, then paused, hesitant to become conspicuous in this indifferent chamber.

Miles was all for being inconspicuous. "Perhaps you can speak to her," he suggested by way of an alternative.

"You think?" Brightening, Thorne tripped forward, swinging down to abandon the glass on the nearest handy floor and raising splayed hands against the sparkling bubble. The hermaphrodite mustered an entranced, ingratiating smile. "Uh . . ." Thorne's chest rose and fell.

Good God, Bel, tongue-tied? Never thought I'd see it. "Ask her what she calls that thing she plays," Miles supplied helpfully.

The four-armed woman tilted her head curiously, and starfished gracefully over her boxy instrument to hover politely before Thorne on the other side of the glittering barrier. "Yes?"

"What do you call that extraordinary instrument?" Thorne asked.

"It's a double-sided hammer dulcimer, ma'am—sir . . ." her servant-to-guest dull tone faltered a moment, fearing to give insult, "Officer."

"Captain Bel Thorne," Bel supplied instantly, beginning to recover accustomed smooth equilibrium. "Commanding the Dendarii fast cruiser *Ariel.* At your service. How ever did you come to be here?"

"I had worked my way to Earth. I was seeking employment, and Baron Fell hired me." She tossed her head, as if to deflect some implied criticism, though Bel had offered none.

"You are a true quaddie?"

"You've heard of my people?" Her dark brows rose in surprise. "Most people I encounter here think I am a *manufactured* freak." A little sardonic bitterness edged her voice.

Thorne cleared its throat. "I'm Betan, myself. I've followed the history of the early genetics explosion with a rather more personal interest." Thorne cleared its throat again, "Betan hermaphrodite, you see," and waited anxiously for the reaction.

Damn. Bel never waited for reactions, Bel sailed on and let the chips fall anyhow. *1 wouldn't interfere with this for all the world.* Miles faded back slightly, rubbing his lips to wipe off a twitching grin as all Thorne's most masculine mannerisms reasserted themselves from spine to fingertips and outward into the aether.

Her head tilted in interest. One upper hand rose to rest on the sparkling barrier not far from Bel's. *"Are* you? You're a genetic too, then."

"Oh, yes. And tell me, what's your name?"

"Nicol."

"Nicol. Is that all? I mean, it's lovely."

"My people don't use surnames."

"Ah. And, uh, what are you doing after the party?"

At this point, alas, interference found them. "Heads up, *Captain,"* Miles murmured. Thorne drew up instantly, cool and correct, and followed Miles's gaze. The quaddie floated back from the force barrier and bowed her head over her hands held palm-to-palm and palm-to-palm as a man approached. Miles too came to a polite species of attention.

Georish Stauber, Baron Fell, was a surprisingly old man to have succeeded so recently to his position, Miles thought. In the flesh he looked older than the holovid Miles had viewed of him at his own mission briefing. The baron was balding, with a white fringe of hair around his shiny pate, jovial and fat. He looked like somebody's grandfather. Not Miles's; Miles's grandfather had been lean and predatory even in his great age. And the old Count's title had been as real as such things got, not the courtesy-nobility of a Syndicate survivor. Jolly red cheeks or no, Miles reminded himself, Baron Fell had climbed a pile of bodies to attain this high place.

"Admiral Naismith. Captain Thorne. Welcome to Fell Station," rumbled the baron, smiling.

Miles swept him an aristocratic bow. Thorne somewhat awkwardly followed suit. Ah. He must copy that awkwardness next time. Of such little details were cover identities made. And blown.

"Have my people been taking care of your needs?"

"Thank you, yes." So far the proper businessmen.

"So glad to meet you at last," the baron rumbled on. "We've heard a great deal about you here."

"Have you," said Miles encouragingly. The baron's eyes were strangely avid. *Quite a glad-hand for a little tin-pot mercenary, eh?* This was a little more stroke than was reasonable even for a high-ticket customer. Miles banished all hint of wariness from his return smile. *Patience. Let the challenge emerge, don't rush to meet what you cannot yet see.* "Good things, I hope."

"Remarkable things. Your rise has been as rapid as your origins are mysterious."

Hell, hell, what kind of bait was this? Was the baron hinting that he actually knew "Admiral Naismith's" real identity? This could be sudden and serious trouble. No—fear outran its cause. Wait. Forget that such a person as Lieutenant Lord Vorkosigan, Barrayaran Imperial Security, ever existed in this body. *It's not big enough for the two of us anyway, boy.* Yet why was this fat shark smiling so ingratiatingly? Miles cocked his head, neutrally.

"The story of your fleet's success at Vervain reached us even here. So unfortunate about its former commander."

Miles stiffened. "I regret Admiral Oser's death."

The baron shrugged philosophically. "Such things happen in the business. Only one can command."

"He could have been an outstanding subordinate."

"Pride is so dangerous," smiled the baron.

Indeed. Miles bit his tongue. *So he thinks I "arranged" Oser's death. So let him.* That there was one less mercenary than there appeared in this room, that the Dendarii were now through Miles an arm of the Barrayaran Imperial Service so covert most of them didn't even know it themselves . . . it would be a dull Syndicate baron who couldn't find profit in those secrets somewhere. Miles matched the baron's smile and added nothing.

"You interest me exceedingly," continued the baron. "For example, there's the puzzle of your apparent age. And your prior military career."

If Miles had kept his drink, he'd have knocked it back in one gulp right then. He clasped his hands convulsively behind his back instead. Dammit, the pain lines just didn't age his face enough. If the baron was indeed seeing right through the pseudo-mercenary to the twenty-three-year-old Security lieutenant— and yet, he usually carried it off—

The baron lowered his voice. "Do the rumors run equally true about your Betan rejuvenation treatment?"

So *that's* what he was on about. Miles felt faint with relief. "What interest could you have in such treatments, my lord?" he gibbered lightly. "I thought Jackson's Whole was the home of practical immortality. It's said there are some here on their third cloned body."

"I am not one of them," said the baron rather regretfully.

Miles's brows rose in genuine surprise. Surely this man didn't spurn the process as murder. "Some unfortunate medical impediment?" he said, injecting polite sympathy into his voice. "My regrets, sir."

"In a manner of speaking." The baron's smile revealed a sharp edge. "The brain transplant operation itself kills a certain irreducible percentage of patients—"

Yeah, thought Miles, *starting with 100% of the clones, whose brains are flushed to make room. . . .*

"—another percentage suffer varying sorts of permanent damage. Those are the risks anyone must take for the reward."

"But the reward is so great."

"But then there are a certain number of patients, indistinguishable from the first group, who do not die on the operating table by accident. If their enemies have the subtlety and clout to arrange it. I have a number of enemies, Admiral Naismith."

Miles made a little who-would-think-it gesture, flipping up one hand, and continued to cultivate an air of deep interest.

"I calculate my present chances of surviving a brain transplant to be rather worse than the average," the baron went on. "So I've an interest in alternatives." He paused expectantly.

"Oh," said Miles. Oh, indeed. He regarded his fingernails and thought fast. "It's true, I once participated in an . . . unauthorized experiment. A premature one, as it happens, pushed too eagerly from animal to human subjects. It was not successful."

"No?" said the baron. "You appear in good health."

Miles shrugged. "Yes, there was some benefit to muscles, skin tone, hair. But my bones are the bones of an old man, fragile." *True.* "Subject to acute osteoinflammatory attacks—there are days when I can't walk without medication." *Also true, dammit.* A recent and unsettling medical development. "My life expectancy is not considered good." *For example, if certain parties here ever figure out who "Admiral Naismith" really is, it could go down to as little as fifteen minutes.* "So unless you're extremely fond of pain and think you would enjoy being crippled, I fear I must dis-recommend the procedure."

The baron looked him up and down. Disappointment pulled down his mouth. "I see."

Bel Thorne, who knew quite well there was no such thing as the fabled "Betan rejuvenation treatment," was listening with well-concealed enjoyment and doing an excellent job of keeping the smirk off its face. Bless its little black heart.

"Still," said the baron, "your . . . scientific acquaintance may have made some progress in the intervening years."

"I fear not," said Miles. "He died." He spread his hands helplessly. "Old age."

"Oh." The baron's shoulders sagged slightly.

"Ah, there you are, Fell," a new voice cut across them. The baron straightened and turned.

The man who had hailed him was as conservatively dressed as Fell, and flanked by a silent servant with "bodyguard" written all over him. The bodyguard wore a uniform, a high-necked red silk tunic and loose black trousers, and was unarmed. Everyone on Fell Station went unarmed except Fell's men; the place had the most strictly-enforced weapons regs Miles had ever encountered. But the pattern of calluses on the lean bodyguard's hands suggested he might not need weapons. His eyes flickered and his hands shook just slightly, a hyper-alertness induced by artificial aids—if ordered, he could strike with blinding speed and adrenalin-insane strength. He would also retire young, metabolically crippled for the rest of his short life.

The man he guarded was also young—some great lord's son? Miles wondered. He had long shining black hair dressed in an elaborate braid, smooth dark olive skin, and a high-bridged nose. He couldn't be older than Miles's real age, yet he moved with a mature assurance.

"Ryoval," Baron Fell nodded in return, as a man to an equal, not a junior. Still playing the genial host, Fell added, "Officers, may I introduce Baron Ryoval of House Ryoval. Admiral Naismith, Captain Thorne. They belong to that Illyrican-built mercenary fast cruiser in dock, Ry, that you may have noticed."

"Haven't got your eye for hardware, I'm afraid, Georish." Baron Ryoval bestowed a nod upon them, of a man being polite to his social inferiors for the principle of it. Miles bowed clumsily in return.

Dropping Miles from his attention with an almost audible thump, Ryoval stood back with his hands on his hips and regarded the null-gee bubble's inhabitant. "My agent didn't exaggerate her charms."

Fell smiled sourly. Nicol had withdrawn—recoiled—when Ryoval first approached, and now floated behind her instrument, fussing with its tuning. Pretending to be fussing with its tuning. Her eyes glanced warily at Ryoval, then returned to her dulcimer as if it might put some magic wall between them.

"Can you have her play—" Ryoval began, and was interrupted by a chime from his wrist com. "Excuse me, Georish." Looking slightly annoyed, he turned half-away from them and spoke into it. "Ryoval. And this had better be important."

"Yes, m'lord," a thin voice responded. "This is Manager Deem in Sales and Demonstrations. We have a problem. That creature House Bharaputra sold us has savaged a customer."

Ryoval's greek-statue lips rippled in a silent snarl. "I told you to chain it with duralloy."

"We did, my lord. The chains held, but it tore the bolts right out of the wall."

"Stun it."

"We have."

"Then punish it suitably when it awakes. A sufficiently long period without food should dull its aggression—its metabolism is unbelievable."

"What about the customer?"

"Give him whatever comforts he asks for. On the House."

"I . . . don't think he'll be in shape to appreciate them for quite some time. He's in the clinic now. Still unconscious."

Ryoval hissed. "Put my personal physician on his case. I'll take care of the rest when I get back downside, in about six hours. Ryoval out." He snapped the link closed. "Morons," he growled. He took a controlled, meditative breath, and recalled his social manner as if booting it up out of some stored memory bank. "Pardon the interruption, please, Georish."

Fell waved an understanding hand, as if to say, *Business.*

"As I was saying, can you have her play something?" Ryoval nodded to the quaddie.

Fell clasped his hands behind his back, his eyes glinting in a falsely benign smile. "Play something, Nicol."

She gave him an acknowledging nod, positioned herself, and closed her eyes. The frozen worry tensing her face gradually gave way to an inner stillness, and she began to play, a slow, sweet theme that established itself, rolled over, and began to quicken.

"Enough!" Ryoval flung up a hand. "She's precisely as described."

Nicol stumbled to a halt in mid-phrase. She inhaled through pinched nostrils, clearly disturbed by her inability to drive the piece through to its destined finish, the frustration of artistic incompletion. She stuck her hammers into their holders on the side of the instrument with short, savage jerks, and crossed her upper and lower arms both. Thorne's mouth tightened, and it crossed its arms in unconscious echo. Miles bit his lip uneasily.

"My agent conveyed the truth," Ryoval went on.

"Then perhaps your agent also conveyed my regrets," said Fell dryly.

"He did. But he wasn't authorized to offer more than a certain standard ceiling. For something so unique, there's no substitute for direct contact."

"I happen to be enjoying her skills where they are," said Fell. "At my age, enjoyment is much harder to obtain than money."

"So true. Yet other enjoyments might be substituted. I could arrange something quite special. Not in the catalog."

"Her *musical* skills, Ryoval. Which are more than special. They are unique. Genuine. Not artificially augmented in any way. Not to be duplicated in your laboratories."

"My laboratories can duplicate anything, sir." Ryoval smiled at the implied challenge.

"Except originality. By definition."

Ryoval spread his hands in polite acknowledgment of the philosophical point. Fell, Miles gathered, was not just enjoying the quaddie's musical talent, he was vastly enjoying the possession of something his rival keenly wanted to buy, that he had absolutely no need to sell. One-upmanship was a powerful pleasure. It seemed even the famous Ryoval was having a tough time coming up with a better—and yet, if Ryoval could find Fell's price, what force on Jackson's Whole could save Nicol? Miles suddenly realized he knew what Fell's price could be. Would Ryoval figure it out too?

Ryoval pursed his lips. "Let's discuss a tissue sample, then. It would do her no damage, and you could continue to enjoy her unique services uninterrupted."

"It would damage her uniqueness. Circulating counterfeits always brings down the value of the real thing, you know that, Ry." Baron Fell grinned.

"Not for some time," Ryoval pointed out. "The lead time for a mature clone is at least ten years—ah, but you know that." He reddened and made a little apologetic bow, as if he realized he'd just committed some faux pas.

By the thinning of Fell's lips, he had. "Indeed," said Fell coldly.

At this point Bel Thorne, tracking the interplay, interrupted in hot horror, "You can't sell her tissues! You don't own them. She's not some Jackson's Whole construct, she's a freeborn galactic citizen!"

Both barons turned to Bel if the mercenary were a piece of furniture that had suddenly spoken. Out of turn. Miles winced.

"He can sell her contract," said Ryoval, mustering a glassy tolerance. "Which is what we are discussing. A *private* discussion."

Bel ignored the hint. "On Jackson's Whole, what practical difference does it make if you call it a contract or call it flesh?"

Ryoval smiled a little cool smile. "None whatsoever. Possession is rather more than nine points of the law, here."

"It's totally illegal!"

"Legal, my dear—ah—you are Betan, aren't you? That explains it," said Ryoval. "And illegal, is whatever the planet you are on chooses to call so and is able to enforce. I don't see any Betan enforcers around here to impose their peculiar version of morality on us all, do you, Fell?"

Fell was listening with raised brows, caught between amusement and annoyance.

Bel twitched. "So if I were to pull out a weapon and blow your head off, it would be perfectly legal?"

The bodyguard tensed, balance and center-of-gravity flowing into launch position.

"Quash it, Bel," Miles muttered under his breath.

But Ryoval was beginning to enjoy baiting his Betan interruptor. "You have no weapon. But legality aside, my subordinates have instructions to avenge me. It is, as it were, a natural or virtual law. In effect you'd find such an ill-advised impulse to be illegal indeed."

Baron Fell caught Miles's eyes and tilted his head just slightly. Time to intervene. "Time to move on, Captain," Miles said. "We aren't the baron's only guests here."

"Try the hot buffet," suggested Fell affably.

Ryoval pointedly dropped Bel from his attention and turned to Miles. "Do stop by my establishment if you get downside, Admiral. Even a Betan could stand to expand the horizons of his experience. I'm sure my staff could find something of interest in your price range."

"Not any more," said Miles. "Baron Fell already has our credit chit."

"Ah, too bad. Your next trip, perhaps." Ryoval turned away in easy dismissal.

Bel didn't budge. "You can't sell a galactic citizen down there," gesturing jerkily to the curve of the planet beyond the viewport. The quaddie Nicol, watching from behind her dulcimer, had no expression at all on her face, but her intense blue eyes blazed.

Ryoval turned back, feigning sudden surprise. "Why, Captain, I just realized. Betan—you must be a genuine genetic hermaphrodite. You possess a marketable rarity yourself. I can offer you an eye-opening employment experience at easily twice your current rate of pay. And you wouldn't even have to get shot at. I guarantee you'd be extremely popular. Group rates."

Miles swore he could see Thorne's blood pressure skyrocketing as the meaning of what Ryoval had just said sunk in. The hermaphrodite's face darkened, and it drew breath. Miles reached up and grasped Bel by the shoulder, hard. The breath held.

"No?" said Ryoval, cocking his head. "Oh, well. But seriously, I would pay well for a tissue sample, for my files."

Bel's breath exploded. "My clone-siblings, to be—be—some sort of sex-slaves into the next century! Over my dead body—or yours—you—"

Bel was so mad it was stuttering, a phenomenon Miles had never seen in seven years' acquaintance including combat.

"So Betan," smirked Ryoval.

"Stop it, Ry," growled Fell.

Ryoval sighed. "Oh, very well. But it's so easy."

"We can't win, Bel," hissed Miles. "It's time to withdraw." The bodyguard was quivering.

Fell gave Miles an approving nod.

"Thank you for your hospitality, Baron Fell," Miles said formally. "Good day, Baron Ryoval."

"Good day, Admiral," said Ryoval, regretfully giving up what was obviously the best sport he'd had all day. "You seem a cosmopolitan sort, for a Betan. Perhaps you can visit us sometime without your moral friend, here."

A war of words should be won with words. "I don't think so," Miles murmured, racking his brain for some stunning insult to withdraw on.

"What a shame," said Ryoval. "We have a dog-and-dwarf act I'm sure you'd find *fascinating*."

There was a moment's absolute silence.

"Fry 'em from orbit," Bel suggested tightly.

Miles grinned through clenched teeth, bowed, and backed off. Bel's sleeve clutched firmly in his hand. As he turned he could hear Ryoval laughing.

Fell's majordomo appeared at their elbows within moments. "This way to the exit, please, officers," he said, smiling. Miles had never before been thrown out of any place with such exquisite politeness.

Back aboard the *Ariel* in dock, Thorne paced the wardroom while Miles sat and sipped coffee as hot and black as his own thoughts.

"Sorry I lost my temper with that squirt Ryoval," Bel apologized gruffly.

"Squirt, hell," said Miles. "The brain in that body has got to be at least a hundred years old. He played you like a violin. No. We couldn't expect to count coup on him. I admit, it would have been nice if you'd had the sense to shut up." He sucked air to cool his scalded tongue.

Bel made a disturbed gesture of acknowledgement and paced on. "And that poor girl, trapped in that bubble—I had one chance to talk to her, and I blew it—I *blithered*. . . ."

She really had brought out the male in Thorne, Miles reflected wryly. "Happens to the best of us," he murmured. He smiled into his coffee, then frowned. No. Better not to encourage Thorne's interest in the quaddie after all. She was clearly much more than just one of Fell's house servants. They had one ship here, a crew of twenty; even if he had the whole Dendarii fleet to back him he'd want to think twice about offending Baron Fell in Fell's own territory. They had a mission. Speaking of which, where was their blasted pick-up? Why hadn't he yet contacted them as arranged?

The intercom in the wall bleeped.

Thorne strode to it. "Thorne here."

"This is Corporal Nout at the portside docking hatch. There's a . . . woman here who's asking to see you."

Thorne and Miles exchanged a raised-brows glance. "What's her name?" asked Thorne.

An off-side mumble, then, "She says it's Nicol."

Thorne grunted in surprise. "Very well. Have her escorted to the wardroom."

"Yes, Captain." The corporal failed to kill his intercom before turning away, and his voice drifted back, ". . . stay in this outfit long enough, you see one of *everything*."

Nicol appeared in the doorway balanced in a float chair, a hovering tubular cup that seemed to be looking for its saucer, enameled in a blue that precisely matched her eyes. She slipped it through the doorway as easily as a woman twitching her hips, zipped to a halt near Miles's table, and adjusted the height to that of a person sitting. The controls, run by her lower hands, left her uppers entirely free. The lower body support must have been custom-designed just for her. Miles watched her maneuver with great interest. He hadn't been sure she could even live outside her null-gee bubble. He expected her to be weak. She didn't look weak. She looked determined. She looked at Thorne.

Thorne looked all cheered up. "Nicol. How nice to see you again."

She nodded shortly. "Captain Thorne. Admiral Naismith." She glanced back and forth between them, and fastened on Thorne. Miles thought he could see why. He sipped coffee and waited for developments.

"Captain Thorne. You are a mercenary, are you not?"

"Yes. . . ."

"And . . . pardon me if I misunderstood, but it seemed to me you had a certain . . . empathy, for my situation. An understanding of my position."

Thorne rendered her a slightly idiotic bow. "I understand you are dangling over a pit."

Her lips tightened, and she nodded mutely.

"She got herself into it," Miles pointed out.

Her chin lifted. "And I intend to get myself out of it."

Miles turned a hand palm-out, and sipped again.

She readjusted her float chair, a nervous gesture ending at about the same altitude it began.

"It seems to me," said Miles, "that Baron Fell is a formidable protector. I'm not sure you have anything to fear from Ryoval's, er, carnal interest in you as long as Fell's in charge."

"Baron Fell is dying." She tossed her head. "Or at any rate, he thinks he is."

"So I gathered. Why doesn't he have a clone made?"

"He did. It was all set up with House Bharaputra. The clone was fourteen years old, full-sized. Then a couple of months ago, somebody assassinated the clone. The baron still hasn't found out for sure who did it, though he has a little list. Headed by his half-brother."

"Thus trapping him in his aging body. What a . . . fascinating tactical maneuver," Miles mused. "What's this unknown enemy going to do next, I wonder? Just wait?"

"I don't know," said Nicol. "The Baron's had another clone started, but it's not even out of the replicator yet. Even with growth accelerators it'd be years before it would be mature enough to transplant. And . . . it has occurred to me that there are a number of ways the baron could die besides ill health between now and then."

"An unstable situation," Miles agreed.

"I want out. I want to buy passage out."

"Then why, he asked," said Miles dryly, "don't you just go plunk your money down at the offices of one of the three galactic commercial passenger lines that dock here, and buy a ticket?"

"It's my contract," said Nicol. "When I signed it back on Earth, I didn't realize what it would mean once I got to Jackson's Whole. I can't even buy my way out of it, unless the baron chooses to let me. And somehow, it seems to cost more and more just to live here. I ran a calculation . . . it gets much worse before my time is up."

"How much time?" asked Thorne.

"Five more years."

"Ouch," said Thorne sympathetically.

"So you, ah, want us to help you jump a Syndicate contract," said Miles, making little wet coffee rings on the table with the bottom of his mug. "Smuggle you out in secret, I suppose."

"I can pay. I can pay more right now than I'll be able to next year. This wasn't the gig I expected, when I came here. There was talk of recording a vid demo . . . it never happened. I don't think it's ever going to happen. I have to be able to reach a wider audience, if I'm ever to pay my way back home. Back to my people. I want . . . *out* of here, before I fall down that gravity well." She jerked an upper thumb in the general direction of the planet they orbited. "People go downside here, who never come up again." She paused. "Are you *afraid* of Baron Fell?"

"No!" said Thorne, as Miles said, "Yes." They exchanged a sardonic look.

"We are inclined to be careful of Baron Fell," Miles suggested. Thorne shrugged agreement.

She frowned, and maneuvered to the table. She drew a wad of assorted planetary currencies out of her green silk jacket and laid it in front of Miles. "Would this bolster your nerve?"

Thorne fingered the stack, flipped through it. At least a couple thousand Betan dollars worth, at conservative estimate, mostly in middle denominations, though a Betan single topped the pile, camouflaging its value to a casual glance. "Well," said Thorne, glancing at Miles, "and what do we mercenaries think of that?"

Miles leaned back thoughtfully in his chair. The kept secret of Miles's identity wasn't the only favor Thorne could call in if it chose. Miles remembered the day Thorne had helped capture an asteroid mining station and the pocket dreadnought *Triumph* for him with nothing but sixteen troops in combat armor and a hell of a lot of nerve. "I encourage creative financing on the part of my commanders," he said at last. "Negotiate away, Captain."

Thorne smiled, and pulled the Betan dollar off the stack. "You have the right idea," Thorne said to the musician, "but the amount is wrong."

Her hand went uncertainly to her jacket and paused, as Thorne pushed the rest of the stack of currency, minus the single, back at her. "What?"

Thorne picked up the single and snapped it a few times. "This is the right amount. Makes it an official contract, you see." Bel extended a hand to her; after a bewildered moment, she shook it. "Deal," said Thorne happily.

"Hero," said Miles, holding up a warning finger, "beware, I'll call in my veto if you can't come up with a way to bring this off in dead secret. That's my cut of the price."

"Yes, *sir*," said Thorne.

Several hours later, Miles snapped awake in his cabin aboard the *Ariel* to an urgent bleeping from his comconsole. Whatever he had been dreaming was gone in the instant, though he had the vague idea it had been something unpleasant. Biological and unpleasant. "Naismith here."

"This is the duty officer in Nav and Com, sir. You have a call originating from the downside commercial com net. He says to tell you it's Vaughn."

Vaughn was the agreed-upon code name of their pick-up. His real name was Dr. Canaba. Miles grabbed his uniform jacket and shrugged it on over his black T-shirt, passed his hands futilely through his hair, and slid into his console station chair. "Put him through."

The face of a man on the high side of middle age materialized above Miles's vid plate. Tan-skinned, racially indeterminate features, short wavy hair graying at the temples; more arresting was the intelligence that suffused those features and quickened the brown eyes. *Yep, that's my man,* thought Miles with satisfaction. *Here we go.* But Canaba looked more than tense. He looked distraught.

"Admiral Naismith?"

"Yes. Vaughn?"

Canaba nodded.

"Where are you?" asked Miles.

"Downside."

"You were to meet us up here."

"I know. Something's come up. A problem."

"What sort of problem? Ah—is this channel secure?"

Canaba laughed bitterly. "On this planet, nothing is secure. But I don't think I'm being traced. But I can't come up yet. I need . . . help."

"Vaughn, we aren't equipped to break you out against superior forces—if you've become a prisoner—"

He shook his head. "No, it's not that. I've . . . lost something. I need help to get it back."

"I'd understood you were to leave everything. You would be compensated later."

"It's not a personal possession. It's something your employer wants very badly. Certain . . . samples, have been removed from my . . . power. They won't take me without them."

Dr. Canaba took Miles for a mercenary hireling, entrusted with minimum classified information by Barrayaran Security. So. "All I was asked to transport was you and your skills."

"They didn't tell you everything."

The hell they didn't. Barrayar would take you stark naked, and be grateful. What was this?

Canaba met Miles's frown with a mouth set like iron. "I *won't* leave without them. Or the deal's off. And you can whistle for your pay, mercenary."

He meant it. Damn. Miles's eyes narrowed. "This is all a bit mysterious."

Canaba shrugged acknowledgment. "I'm sorry. But I *must* . . . Meet with me, and I'll tell you the rest. Or go, I don't care which. But a certain thing must be accomplished, must be . . . expiated."
He trailed off in agitation.

Miles took a deep breath. "Very well. But every complication you add increases your risk. And mine. This had better be worth it."

"Oh, Admiral," breathed Canaba sadly, "it is to me. It is to me."

Snow sifted through the little park where Canaba met them, giving Miles something new to swear at if only he hadn't run out of invective hours ago. He was shivering even in his Dendarii-issue parka by the time Canaba walked past the dingy kiosk where Miles and Bel roosted. They fell in behind him without a word.

Bharaputra Laboratories were headquartered in a downside town Miles frankly found worrisome: guarded shuttleport, guarded Syndicate buildings, guarded municipal buildings, guarded walled residential compounds; in between, a crazy disorder of neglected aging structures that didn't seem to be guarded by anyone, occupied by people who *slunk*. It made Miles wonder if the two Dendarii troopers he'd detailed to shadow them were quite enough. But the slithery people gave them a wide berth; they evidently understood what guards meant. At least during the daylight.

Canaba led them into one of the nearby buildings. Its lift tubes were out-of-order, its corridors unheated. A darkly-dressed maybe-female person scurried out of their way in the shadows, reminding Miles uncomfortably of a rat. They followed Canaba dubiously up the safety ladder set in the side of a dead lift tube, down another corridor, and through a door with a broken palm-lock into an empty dirty room, grayly lit by an unpolarized but intact window. At least they were out of the wind.

"I think we can talk safely here," said Canaba, turning and pulling off his gloves.

"Bel?" said Miles.

Thorne pulled an assortment of anti-surveillance detectors from its parka and ran a scan, as the two guards prowled the perimeters. One stationed himself in the corridor, the second near the window.

"It scans clean," said Bel at last, as if reluctant to believe its own instruments. "For now." Rather pointedly, Bel walked around Canaba and scanned him too. Canaba waited with bowed head, as if he felt he deserved no better. Bel set up the sonic baffler.

Miles shrugged back his hood and opened his parka, the better to reach his concealed weapons in the event of a trap. He was finding Canaba extraordinarily hard to read. What were the man's motivations anyway? There was no doubt House Bharaputra had assured his comfort—his coat, the rich cut of his clothing beneath it, spoke of that—and though his standard of living surely would not drop when he transferred his allegiance to the Barrayaran Imperial Science Institute, he would not have nearly the opportunities to amass wealth on the side that he had here. So, he wasn't in it for the money. Miles could understand that. But why work for a place like House Bharaputra in the first place unless greed overwhelmed integrity?

"You puzzle me, Dr. Canaba," said Miles lightly. "Why this midcareer switch? I'm pretty well acquainted with your new employers, and frankly, I don't see how they could out-bid House Bharaputra." There, that was a properly mercenary way to put it.

"They offered me protection from House Bharaputra. Although, if *you're* it . . ." He looked doubtfully down at Miles.

Ha. And, hell. The man really was ready to bolt. Leaving Miles to explain the failure of his mission to Chief of Imperial Security Illyan in person. "They bought our services," said Miles, "and therefore you command our services. They want you safe and happy. But we can't begin to protect you when you depart from a plan designed to maximize your safety, throw in random factors, and ask us to operate in the dark. I need full knowledge of what's going on if I'm to take full responsibility for the results."

"No one is asking you to take responsibility."

"I beg your pardon, doctor, but they surely have."

"Oh," said Canaba. "I . . . see." He paced to the window, back. "But will you do what I ask?"

"I will do what I can."

"Happy," Canaba snorted. "God . . ." He shook his head wearily, inhaled decisively. "I never came here for the money. I came here because I could do research I couldn't do anywhere else. Not hedged round with outdated legal restrictions. I dreamed of breakthroughs . . . but it became a nightmare. The freedom became slavery. The things they wanted me to do. . . ! Constantly interrupting the things I wanted to do. Oh, you can always find someone to do anything for money, but they're second-raters. These labs are full of second-raters. The very best can't be bought. I've done things, unique things, that Bharaputra won't develop because the profit would be too small, never mind how many people it would benefit—I get no credit, no standing for my work—every year, I see in the literature of my field galactic honors going to lesser men, because I cannot publish my results . . ." He stopped, lowered his head. "I doubtless sound like a megalomaniac to you."

"Ah . . ." said Miles, "you sound quite frustrated."

"The frustration," said Canaba, "woke me from a long sleep. Wounded ego—it was only wounded ego. But in my pride, I rediscovered shame. And the weight of it stunned me, stunned me where I stood. *Do* you understand? Does it matter if you understand? Ah!" He paced away to the wall, and stood facing it, his back rigid.

"Uh," Miles scratched the back of his head ruefully, "yeah. I'd be glad to spend many fascinating hours listening to you explain it to me—on my ship. Outbound."

Canaba turned with a crooked smile. "You are a practical man, I perceive. A soldier. Well, God knows I need a soldier now."

"Things are that screwed up, eh?"

"It . . . happened suddenly. I thought I had it under control."

"Go on," sighed Miles.

"There were seven synthesized gene-complexes. One of them is a cure for a certain obscure enzyme disorder. One of them will increase oxygen-generation in space station algae twenty-fold. One of them came from outside Bharaputra Labs, brought in by a man—we never found out who he really was, but death followed him. Several of my colleagues who had worked on his project were murdered all in one night, by the commandos who pursued him— their records destroyed—I never told anyone I'd borrowed an unauthorized tissue sample to study. I've not unravelled it fully yet, but I can tell you, it's absolutely unique."

Miles recognized that one, and almost choked, reflecting upon the bizarre chain of circumstances that had placed an identical tissue sample in the hands of Dendarii Intelligence a year ago. Terrence See's telepathy complex—and the main reason *why* His Imperial Majesty suddenly wanted a top geneticist. Dr. Canaba was in for a little surprise when he arrived at his new Barrayaran laboratory. But if the other six complexes came anywhere near matching the value of the known one, Security Chief Illyan would peel Miles with a dull knife for letting them slip through his fingers. Miles's attention to Canaba abruptly intensified. This side-trip might not be as trivial as he'd feared.

"Together, these seven complexes represent tens of thousands of hours of research time, mostly mine, some of others—my life's work. I'd planned from the beginning to take them with me. I bundled them up in a viral insert and placed them, bound and dormant, in a live . . ." Canaba faltered, "organism, for storage. An organism, I thought, that no one would think to look at for such a thing."

"Why didn't you just store them in your own tissue?" Miles asked irritably. "Then you couldn't lose 'em."

Canaba's mouth opened. "I . . . never thought of that. How elegant. Why didn't I think of that?" His hand touched his forehead wonderingly, as if probing for systems failure. His lips tightened again. "But it would have made no difference. I would still need to . . ." he fell silent. "It's about the organism," he said at last. "The . . . creature." Another long silence.

"Of all the things I did," Canaba continued lowly, "of all the interruptions this vile place imposed on me, there is one I regret the most. You understand, this was years ago. I was younger, I thought I still had a future to protect. And it wasn't all my doing—guilt by committee, eh? Spread it around, make it easy, say it was *his* fault, *her* doing . . . well, it's mine now."

You mean it's *mine* now, thought Miles grimly. "Doctor, the more time we spend here, the greater the chance of compromising this operation. Please get to the point."

"Yes . . . yes. Well, a number of years ago, House Bharaputra Laboratories took on a contract to manufacture a . . . new species. Made to order."

"I thought it was House Ryoval that was famous for making people, or whatever, to order," said Miles.

"They make slaves, one-off. They are very specialized. And small—their customer base is surprisingly small. There are many rich men, and there are, I suppose, many depraved men, but a House Ryoval customer has to be a member of both sets, and the overlap isn't as large as you'd think. Anyway, our contract was supposed to lead to a major production run, far beyond Ryoval's capabilities. A certain sub-planetary government, hard-pressed by its neighbors, wanted us to engineer a race of super-soldiers for them."

"What, again?" said Miles. "I thought that had been tried. More than once."

"This time, we thought we could do it. Or at least, the Bharaputran hierarchy was willing to take their money. But the project suffered from too much input. The client, our own higher-ups, the genetics project members, everybody had ideas they were pushing. I swear it was doomed before it ever got out of the design committee."

"A super-soldier. Designed by committee. Ye gods. The mind boggles." Miles's eyes were wide in fascination. "So then what happened?"

"It seemed to . . . several of us, that the physical limits of the merely human had already been reached. Once a, say, muscle system has been brought to perfect health, stimulated with maximum hormones, exercised to a certain limit, that's all you can do. So we turned to other species for special improvements. I, for instance, became fascinated by the aerobic and anaerobic metabolism in the muscles of the thoroughbred horse—"

"What?" said Thorne, shocked.

"There were other ideas. Too many. I swear, they weren't all mine."

"You mixed human and animal genes?" breathed Miles.

"Why not? Human genes have been spliced into animals from the crude beginnings—it was almost the first thing they tried. Human insulin from bacteria and the like. But till now, no one dared do it in reverse. I broke the barrier, cracked the codes . . . It looked good at first. It was only when the first ones reached puberty that all the errors became fully apparent. Well, it was only the initial trial. They were meant to be formidable. But they ended up monstrous."

"Tell me," Miles choked, "were there any actual combat-experienced soldiers on the committee?"

"I assume the client had them. They supplied the parameters," said Canaba.

Said Thorne in a suffused voice, "*I* see. They were trying to re-invent the *enlisted* man."

Miles shot Thorne a quelling glower, and tapped his chrono. "Don't let us interrupt, doctor."

There was a short silence. Canaba began again. "We ran off ten prototypes. Then the client . . . went out of business. They lost their war—"

"Why am I not surprised?" Miles muttered under his breath.

"—funding was cut off, the project was dropped before we could apply what we had learned from our mistakes. Of the ten proto-types, nine have since died. There was one left. We were keeping it at the labs due to . . . difficulties, in boarding it out. I placed my gene complexes in it. They are there still. The last thing I meant to do before I left was kill it. A mercy . . . a responsibility. My expiation, if you will."

"And then?" prodded Miles.

"A few days ago, it was suddenly sold to House Ryoval. As a novelty, apparently. Baron Ryoval collects oddities of all sorts, for his tissue banks—"

Miles and Bel exchanged a look.

"—I had no idea it was to be sold. I came in in the morning and it was gone. I don't think Ryoval has any idea of its real value. It's there now, as far as I know, at Ryoval's facilities."

Miles decided he was getting a sinus headache. From the cold, no doubt. "And what, pray, d'you want us soldiers to do about it?"

"Get in there, somehow. Kill it. Collect a tissue sample. Only then will I go with you."

And stomach twinges. "What, both ears and the tail?"

Canaba gave Miles a cold look. "The left gastrocnemius muscle. That's where I injected my complexes. These storage virus aren't virulent, they won't have migrated far. The greatest concentration should still be there."

"I see." Miles rubbed his temples, and pressed his eyes. "All right. We'll take care of it. This personal contact between us is very dangerous, and I'd rather not repeat it. Plan to report to my ship in forty-eight hours. Will we have any trouble recognizing your critter?"

"I don't think so. This particular specimen topped out at just over eight feet. I . . . want you to know, the fangs were *not* my idea."

"I . . . see."

"It can move very fast, if it's still in good health. Is there any help I can give you? I have access to painless poisons . . ."

"You've done enough, thank you. Please leave it to us professionals, eh?"

"It would be best if its body can be destroyed entirely. No cells remaining. If you can."

"That's why plasma arcs were invented. You'd best be on your way."

"Yes." Canaba hesitated. "Admiral Naismith?"

"Yes. . . ."

"I . . . it might also be best if my future employer didn't learn about this. They have intense military interests. It might excite them unduly."

"Oh," said Miles/Admiral Naismith/Lieutenant Lord Vorkosigan of the Barrayaran Imperial Service, "I don't think you have to worry about that."

"Is forty-eight hours enough for your commando raid?" Canaba worried. "You understand, if you don't get the tissue, I'll go right back downside. I will not be trapped aboard your ship."

"You will be happy. It's in my contract," said Miles. "Now you'd better get gone."

"I must rely on you, sir." Canaba nodded in suppressed anguish, and withdrew.

They waited a few minutes in the cold room, to let Canaba put some distance between them. The building creaked in the wind; from an upper corridor echoed an odd shriek, and later, a laugh abruptly cut off. The guard shadowing Canaba returned. "He made it to his ground car all right, sir."

"Well," said Thorne, "I suppose we'll need to get hold of a plan of Ryoval's facilities, first—"

"I think not," said Miles.

"If we're to raid—"

"Raid, hell. I'm not risking my men on anything so idiotic. I said I'd slay his sin for him. I didn't say how."

The commercial comconsole net at the downside shuttleport seemed as convenient as anything. Miles slid into the booth and fed the machine his credit card while Thorne lurked just outside the viewing angle and the guards, outside, guarded. He encoded the call.

In a moment, the vid plate produced the image of a sweet-faced receptionist with dimples and a white fur crest instead of hair. "House Ryoval, Customer Services. How may I help you, sir?"

"I'd like to speak to Manager Deem, in Sales and Demonstrations," said Miles smoothly, "about a possible purchase for my organization."

"Who may I say is calling?"

"Admiral Miles Naismith, Dendarii Free Mercenary Fleet."

"One moment, sir."

"You really think they'll just sell it?" Bel muttered from the side as the girl's face was replaced by a flowing pattern of colored lights and some syrupy music.

"Remember what we overheard yesterday?" said Miles. "I'm betting it's *on* sale. Cheap." He must try not to look too interested.

In a remarkably short time, the colored glop gave way to the face of an astonishingly beautiful young man, a blue-eyed albino in a red silk shirt. He had a huge livid bruise up on side of his white face. "This is Manager Deem. May I help you, Admiral?"

Miles cleared his throat carefully. "A rumor has been brought to my attention that House Ryoval may have recently acquired from House Bharaputra an article of some professional interest to me. Supposedly, it was a prototype of some sort of new improved fighting man. Do you know anything about it?"

Deem's hand stole to his bruise and palpated it gently, then twitched away. "Indeed, sir, we do have such an article."

"Is it for sale?"

"Oh, ye—I mean, I think some arrangement is pending. But it may still be possible to bid on it."

"Would it be possible for me to inspect it?"

"Of course," said Deem with suppressed eagerness. "How soon?"

There was a burst of static, and the vid image split, Deem's face abruptly shrinking to one side. The new face was only too familiar. Bel hissed under its breath.

"I'll take this call, Deem," said Baron Ryoval.

"Yes, my lord." Deem's eyes widened in surprise, and he cut out. Ryoval's image swelled to occupy the space available.

"So, Betan." Ryoval smiled. "It appears I have something you want after all."

Miles shrugged. "Maybe," he said neutrally. "If it's in my price range."

"I thought you gave all your money to Fell."

Miles spread his hands. "A good commander always has hidden reserves. However, the actual value of the item hasn't yet been established. In fact, its existence hasn't even been established."

"Oh, it exists, all right. And it is . . . impressive. Adding it to my collection was a unique pleasure. I'd hate to give it up. But for you," Ryoval smiled more broadly, "it may be possible to arrange a special cut rate." He chuckled, as at some secret pun that escaped Miles.

A special cut throat is more like it. "Oh?"

"I propose a simple trade," said Ryoval. "Flesh for flesh."

"You may overestimate my interest, Baron."

Ryoval's eyes glinted. "I don't think so."

He knows I wouldn't touch him with a stick if it weren't something pretty compelling. So. "Name your proposal, then."

"I'll trade you even, Bharaputra's pet monster—ah, you should see it, Admiral!—for three tissue samples. Three tissue samples that will, if you are clever about it, cost you nothing." Ryoval held up one finger. "One from your Betan hermaphrodite," a second finger, "one from yourself," a third finger, making a W, "and one from Baron Fell's quaddie musician."

Over in the corner, Bel Thorne appeared to be suppressing an apoplectic fit. Quietly, fortunately.

"That third could prove extremely difficult to obtain," said Miles, buying time to think.

"Less difficult for you than me," said Ryoval. "Fell knows my agents. My overtures have put him on guard. You represent a unique opportunity to get in under that guard. Given sufficient motivation, I'm certain it's not beyond you, mercenary."

"Given sufficient motivation, very little is beyond me, Baron," said Miles semi-randomly.

"Well, then. I shall expect to hear from you within—say—twenty-four hours. After that time my offer will be withdrawn." Ryoval nodded cheerfully. "Good day, Admiral." The vid blanked.

"Well, then," echoed Miles.

"Well, what?" said Thorne with suspicion. "You're not actually seriously considering that—vile proposal, are you?"

"What does he want my tissue sample for, for God's sake?" Miles wondered aloud.

"For his dog and dwarf act, no doubt," said Thorne nastily.

"Now, now. He'd be dreadfully disappointed when my clone turned out to be six feet tall, I'm afraid." Miles cleared his throat. "It wouldn't actually hurt anyone, I suppose. To take a small tissue sample. Whereas a commando raid risks lives."

Bel leaned back against the wall and crossed its arms. "Not true. You'd have to fight me for mine. And *hers.*"

Miles grinned sourly. "So."

"So?"

"So let's go find a map of Ryoval's flesh pit. It seems we're going hunting."

House Ryoval's palatial main biologicals facility wasn't a proper fortress, just some guarded buildings. Some bloody big guarded buildings. Miles stood on the roof of the lift-van and studied the layout through his night-glasses. Fog droplets beaded in his hair. The cold damp wind searched for chinks in his jacket much as he searched for chinks in Ryoval's security.

The white complex loomed against the dark forested mountain-side, its front gardens floodlit and fairy-like in the fog and frost. The utility entrances on the near side looked more promising. Miles nodded slowly to himself and climbed down off the rented lift-van, artistically broke-down on the little mountain side-trail overlooking Ryoval's. He swung into the back, out of the piercing wind.

"All right, people, listen up." His squad hunkered around as he set up the holovid map in the middle. The colored lights of the display sheened their faces, tall Ensign Murka, Thorne's second-in-command, and two big troopers. Sergeant Laureen Anderson was the van driver, assigned to outside back-up along with Trooper Sandy Hereld and Captain Thorne. Miles harbored a secret Barrayan prejudice against taking female troops inside Ryoval's, that he trusted he concealed. It went double for Bel Thorne. Not that one's sex would necessarily make any difference to the adventures that might follow in the event of capture, if even a tenth of the bizarre rumors he'd heard were true. Nevertheless . . . Laureen claimed to be able to fly any vehicle made by man through the eye of a needle, not that Miles figured she'd ever done anything so domestic as thread a needle in her life. She would not question her assignment.

"Our main problem remains, that we still don't know where exactly in this facility Bharaputra's creature is being kept. So first we penetrate the fence, the outer courts, and the main building, here and here." A red thread of light traced their projected route at Miles's touch on the control board. "Then we quietly pick up an inside employee and fast-penta him. From that point on we're racing time, since we must assume he'll be promptly missed.

"The key word is quietly. We didn't come here to kill *people*, and we are not at war with Ryoval's employees. You carry your stunners, and keep those plasma arcs and the rest of the toys packed till we locate our quarry. We dispatch it fast and quietly, I get my sample," his hand touched his jacket, beneath which rested the collection case that would keep the tissue alive till they got back to the *Ariel*. "Then we fly. If anything goes wrong before I get that very expensive cut of meat, we don't bother to fight our way out. Not worth it. They have peculiar summary ways of dealing with murder charges here, and I don't see the need for any of us to end up as spare parts in Ryoval's tissue banks. We wait for Captain Thorne to arrange a ransom, and then try something else. We hold a lever or two on Ryoval in case of emergencies."

"Dire emergencies," Bel muttered.

"If anything goes wrong after the butcher-mission is accomplished, it's back to combat rules. That sample will then be irreplaceable, and must be got back to Captain Thorne at all costs. Laureen, you sure of our emergency pickup spot?"

"Yes, sir." She pointed on the vid display.

"Everybody else got that? Any questions? Suggestions? Last minute observations? Communications check, then, Captain Thorne."

Their wrist coms all appeared to be in good working order. Ensign Murka shrugged on the weapons pack. Miles carefully pocketed the blueprint map cube, that had cost them a near-ransom from a certain pliable construction company just a few hours ago. The four members of the penetration team slipped from the van and merged with the frosty darkness.

They slunk off through the woods. The frozen crunchy layer of plant detritus tended to slide underfoot, exposing a layer of slick mud. Murka spotted a spy eye before it spotted them, and blinded it with a brief burst of microwave static while they scurried past. The useful big guys made short work of boosting Miles over the wall. Miles tried not to think about the ancient pub sport of dwarf tossing. The inner court was stark and utilitarian, loading docks with big locked doors, rubbish collection bays, and a few parked vehicles.

Footsteps echoed, and they ducked down in a rubbish bay. A red-clad guard passed, slowly waving an infra-red scanner. They crouched and hid their faces in their infra-red blank ponchos, looking like so many bags of garbage no doubt. Then it was tip-toe up to the loading docks.

Ducts. The key to Ryoval's facility had turned out to be ducts, for heating, for access to power-optics cables, for the com system. Narrow ducts. Quite impassable to a big guy. Miles slipped out of his poncho and gave it to a trooper to fold and pack.

Miles balanced on Murka's shoulders and cut his way through the first ductlet, a ventilation grille high on the wall above the loading dock doors. Miles handed the grille down silently, and after a quick visual scan for unwanted company, slithered through. It was a tight fit even for him. He let himself down gently to the concrete floor, found the door control box, shorted the alarm, and raised the door about a meter. His team rolled through, and he let the door back down as quietly as he could. So far so good; they hadn't yet had to exchange a word.

They made it to cover on the far side of the receiving bay just before a red-coveralled employee wandered through, driving an electric cart loaded with cleaning robots. Murka touched Miles's sleeve, and looked his inquiry—*This one?* Miles shook his head, *Not yet.* A maintenance man seemed less likely than an employee from the inner sanctum to know where their quarry was kept, and they didn't have time to litter the place with the unconscious bodies of false trials. They found the tunnel to the main building, just as the map cube promised. The door at the end was locked as expected.

It was up on Murka's shoulders again. A quick zizz of Miles's cutters loosened a panel in the ceiling, and he crawled through— the frail supporting framework would surely not have held a man of greater weight—and found the power cables running to the door lock. He was just looking over the problem and pulling tools out of his pocketed uniform jacket when Murka's hand reached up to thrust the weapons pack beside him and quietly pull the panel back into place. Miles flung himself to his belly and pressed his eye to the crack as a voice from down the corridor bellowed, "Freeze!"

Swear words screamed through Miles's head. He clamped his jaw on them. He looked down on the tops of his troopers' heads. In a moment, they were surrounded by half-a-dozen red-clad black-trousered armed guards. "What are you doing here?" snarled the guard sergeant.

"Oh, shit!" cried Murka. "*Please,* mister, don't tell my CO you caught us in here. He'd bust me back to private!"

"Huh?" said the guard sergeant. He prodded Murka with his weapon, a lethal nerve disruptor. "Hands up! Who are you?"

"M'name's Murka. We came in on a mercenary ship to Fell Station, but the captain wouldn't grant us downside passes. Think of it—we come all the way to Jackson's Whole, and the sonofabitch wouldn't let us go downside! Bloody pure-dick wouldn't let us see Ryoval's!"

The red-tunic'd guards were doing a fast scan-and-search, none to gently, and finding only stunners and the portion of security-penetration devices that Murka had carried.

"I made a bet we could get in even if we couldn't afford the front door." Murka's mouth turned down in great discouragement. "Looks like I lost."

"Looks like you did," growled the guard sergeant, drawing back.

One of his men held up the thin collection of baubles they'd stripped off the Dendarii. "They're not equipped like an assassination team," he observed.

Murka drew himself up, looking wonderfully offended. "We aren't!"

The guard sergeant turned over a stunner. "AWOL, are you?"

"Not if we make it back before midnight." Murka's tone went wheedling. "Look, m'CO's a right bastard. Suppose there's any way you could see your way clear that he doesn't find out about this?" One of Murka's hands drifted suggestively past his wallet pocket.

The guard sergeant looked him up and down, smirking. "Maybe."

Miles listened with open-mouthed delight. *Murka, if this works I'm promoting you. . . .*

Murka paused. "Any chance of seeing inside first? Not the girls even, just the place? So I could say that I'd seen it."

"This isn't a whorehouse, soldier boy!" snapped the guard sergeant.

Murka looked stunned. "What?"

"This is the *biologicals* facility."

"Oh," said Murka.

"You *idiot*," one of the troopers put in on cue. Miles sprinkled silent blessings down upon his head. None of the three so much as flicked an eyeball upward.

"But the man in town told me—" began Murka.

"What man?" said the guard sergeant.

"The man who took m'money," said Murka.

A couple of the red tunic'd guards were beginning to grin. The guard sergeant prodded Murka with his nerve disruptor. "Get going, soldier boy. Back that way. This is your lucky day."

"You mean we get to see inside?" said Murka hopefully.

"No," said the guard sergeant, "I mean we aren't going to break both your legs before we throw you out on your ass." He paused and added more kindly, "There's a whorehouse back in town." He slipped Murka's wallet out of his pocket, checked the name on the credit card and put it back, and removed all the loose currency. The guards did the same to the outraged-looking troopers, dividing the assorted cash up among them. "They take credit cards, and you've still got till midnight. Now move!"

And so Miles's squad was chivied, ignominiously but intact,

down the tunnel. Miles waited till the whole mob was well out of earshot before keying his wrist com. "Bel?"

"Yes," came back the instant reply.

"Trouble. Murka and the troops were just picked up by Ryoval's security. I believe the boy genius has just managed to bullshit them into throwing them out the back door, instead of rendering them down for parts. I'll follow as soon as I can, we'll rendezvous and regroup for another try." Miles paused. This was a total bust. They were now worse off than when they'd started. Ryoval's security would be stirred up for the rest of the long Jacksonian night. He added to the com, "I'm going to see if I can't at least find out the location of the critter before I withdraw. Should improve our chances of success next round."

Bel swore in a heartfelt tone. "Be careful."

"You bet. Watch for Murka and the boys. Naismith out."

Once he'd identified the right cables it was the work of a moment to make the door slide open. He then had an interesting dangle by his fingertips while coaxing the ceiling panel to fall back into place before he dropped from maximum downward extension, fearful for his bones. Nothing broke. He slipped across the portal to the main building and took to the ducts as soon as possible, the corridors having been proved dangerous. He lay on his back in the narrow tube and balanced the blueprint holocube on his belly, picking out a new and safer route not necessarily passable to a couple of husky troopers. And where did one look for a monster? A closet?

It was about the third turn, inching his way through the system dragging the weapon pack, that he became aware that the territory no longer matched the map. Hell and damnation. Were these changes in the system since its construction, or a subtly sabotaged map? Well, no matter, he wasn't really lost; he could still retrace his route.

He crawled along for about thirty minutes, discovering and disarming two alarm sensors before they discovered him. The time factor was getting seriously pressing. Soon he would have to—ah, there! He peered through a vent grille into a dim room filled with holovid and communications equipment. *Small Repairs,* the map cube named it. It didn't look like a repairs shop. Another change since Ryoval had moved in? But a man sat alone with his back to Miles's wall. Perfect, too good to pass up.

Breathing silently, moving slowly, Miles eased his dart-gun out of the pack and made sure he loaded it with the right cartridge, fast-penta spiked with a paralyzer, a lovely cocktail blended for the purpose by the *Ariel*'s medtech. He sighted through the grille, aimed the needle-nose of the dart gun with tense precision, and fired. Bullseye. The man slapped the back of his neck once and sat still, hand falling nervelessly to his side. Miles grinned briefly, cut his way through the grille, and lowered himself to the floor.

The man was well-dressed in civilian-type clothes—one of the scientists, perhaps? He lolled in his chair, a little smile playing around his lips, and stared with unalarmed interest at Miles. He started to fall over.

Miles caught him and propped him back upright. "Sit up now, that's right, you can't talk with your face in the carpet now, can you?"

"Nooo . . ." The man bobbled his head and smiled agreeably.

"Do you know anything about a genetic construct, a monstrous creature, just recently bought from House Bharaputra and brought to this facility?"

The man blinked and smiled. "Yes."

Fast-penta subjects did tend to be literal, Miles reminded himself. "Where is it being kept?"

"Downstairs."

"Where exactly downstairs?"

"In the sub-basement. The crawl-space around the foundations. We were hoping it would catch some of the rats, you see." The man giggled. "Do cats eat rats? Do rats eat cats. . . ?"

Miles checked his map-cube. Yes. That looked good, in terms of the penetration team getting in and out, though it was still a large search area, broken up into a maze by structural elements running down into the bedrock, and specially-set low-vibration support columns running up into the laboratories. At the lower edge, where the mountainside sloped away, the space ran high-ceilinged and very near the surface, a possible break-out point. The space thinned to head-cracking narrowness and then to bedrock at the back where the building wedged into the slope. All right. Miles opened his dart case to find something that would lay his victim out cold and non-questionable for the rest of the night. The man pawed at him and his sleeve slipped back to reveal a wrist com almost as thick and complex as Miles's own. A light blinked on it. Miles looked at the device, suddenly uneasy. This room . . . "By the way, who are you?"

"Moglia, Chief of Security, Ryoval Biologicals," the man recited happily. "At your service, sir."

"Oh, indeed you are." Miles suddenly-thick fingers scrabbled faster in his dart case. Damn, damn, *damn.*

The door burst open. "Freeze, mister!"

Miles hit the tight-beam alarm/self-destruct on his own wrist com and flung his hands up, and the wrist com off, in one swift motion. Not by chance, Moglia sat between Miles and the door, inhibiting the trigger reflexes of the entering guards. The com melted as it arced through the air—no chance of Ryoval security tracing the outside squad through it now, and Bel would at least know something had gone wrong.

The security chief chuckled to himself, temporarily fascinated by the task of counting his own fingers. The red-clad guard sergeant, backed by his squad, thundered into what was now screamingly obvious to Miles as the Security Operations Room, to jerk Miles around, slam him face-first into the wall, and begin frisking him with vicious efficiency. Within moments he had separated Miles from a clanking pile of incriminating equipment, his jacket, boots, and belt. Miles clutched the wall and shivered with the pain of several expertly-applied nerve jabs and the swift reversal of his fortune.

The security chief, when un-penta'd at last, was not at all pleased with the guard sergeant's confession about the three uniformed men he had let go with a fine earlier in the evening. He put the whole guard shift on full alert, and sent an armed squad out to try to trace the escaped Dendarii. Then, with an apprehensive expression on his face very like the guard-sergeant's during his mortified admission—compounded with sour satisfaction, contemplating Miles, and drug-induced nausea—he made a vid call.

"My lord?" said the security chief carefully.

"What is it, Moglia?" Baron Ryoval's face was sleepy and irritated.

"Sorry to disturb you sir, but I thought you might like to know about the intruder we just caught here. Not an ordinary thief, judging from his clothes and equipment. Strange-looking fellow, sort of a tall dwarf. He squeezed in through the ducts." Moglia held up tissue-collection kit, chip-driven alarm-disarming tools, and Miles's weapons, by way of evidence. The guard sergeant bundled Miles, stumbling, into range of the vid pick-up. "He was asking a lot questions about Bharaputra's monster."

Ryoval's lips parted. Then his eyes lit, and he threw back his head and laughed. "I should have guessed. Stealing when you should be buying, Admiral?" he chortled. "Oh, very good, Moglia!"

The security chief looked fractionally less nervous. "Do you know this little mutant, my lord?"

"Yes, indeed. He calls himself Miles Naismith. A mercenary— bills himself as an admiral. Self-promoted, no doubt. Excellent work, Moglia. Hold him, and I'll be there in the morning and deal with him personally."

"Hold him how, sir?"

Ryoval shrugged. "Amuse yourselves. Freely."

When Ryoval's image faded, Miles found himself pinned between the speculative glowers of both the security chief and the guard sergeant.

Just to relieve feelings, a burly guard held Miles while the security chief delivered a blow to his belly. But the chief was still to ill to really enjoy this as he should. "Came to see Bharaputra's toy soldier, did you?" he gasped, rubbing his own stomach.

The guard sergeant caught his chief's eye. "You know, I think we should give him his wish."

The security chief smothered a belch, and smiled as at a beatific vision. "Yes . . ."

Miles, praying they wouldn't break his arms, found himself being frog-marched down a complex of corridors and lift tubes by the burly guard, followed by the sergeant and the chief. They took a last lift-tube to the very bottom, a dusty basement crowded with stored and discarded equipment and supplies. They made their way to a locked hatch set in the floor. It swung open on a metal ladder descending into obscurity.

"The last thing we threw down there was a rat," the guard sergeant informed Miles cordially. "Nine bit its head right off. Nine gets very hungry. Got a metabolism like an ore furnace."

The guard forced Miles onto the ladder and down it a meter or so by the simple expedient of striking at his clinging hands with a truncheon. Miles hung just out of range of the stick, eyeing the dimly-lit stone below. The rest was pillars and shadows and a cold dankness.

"Nine!" called the guard sergeant into the echoing darkness. "Nine! Dinner! Come and catch it!"

The security chief laughed mockingly, then clutched his head and groaned under his breath.

Ryoval had said he'd deal with Miles personally in the morning;

surely the guards understood their boss wanted a live prisoner. Didn't they? Didn't he? "Is this the dungeon?" Miles spat blood and peered around.

"No, no, just a basement," the guard sergeant assured him cheerily. "The dungeon is for the *paying* customers. Heh, heh, heh." Still chortling at his own humor, he kicked the hatch closed. The chink of the locking mechanism rained down; then silence.

The bars of the ladder bit chill through Miles's socks. He hooked an arm around an upright and tucked one hand into the armpit of his black T-shirt to warm it briefly. His gray trousers had been emptied of everything but a ration bar, his handkerchief, and his legs.

He clung there for a long time. Going up was futile; going down, singularly uninviting. Eventually the startling ganglial pain began to dull, and the shaking physical shock to wear off. Still he clung. Cold.

It could have been worse, Miles reflected. The sergeant and his squad could have decided they wanted to play Lawrence of Arabia and the Six Turks. Commodore Tung, Miles's Dendarii chief of staff and a certified military history nut, had been plying Miles with a series of classic military memoirs lately. How had Colonel Lawrence escaped an analogous tight spot? Ah, yes, played dumb and persuaded his captors to throw him out in the mud. Tung must have pressed that book-fax on Murka, too.

The darkness, Miles discovered as his eyes adjusted, was only relative. Faint luminescent panels in the ceiling here and there shed a sickly yellow glow. He descended the last two meters to stand on solid rock.

He pictured the newsfax, back home on Barrayar—*Body of Imperial Officer Found in Flesh-Czar's Dream Palace. Death From Exhaustion?* Dammit, this wasn't the glorious sacrifice in the Emperor's service he'd once vowed to risk, this was just embarrassing. Maybe Bharaputra's creature would eat the evidence.

With this morose comfort in mind, he began to limp from pillar to pillar, pausing, listening, looking around. Maybe there was another ladder somewhere. Maybe there was a hatch someone had forgotten to lock. Maybe there was still hope.

Maybe there was something moving in the shadows just beyond that pillar. . . .

Miles's breath froze, then eased again, as the movement materialized into a fat albino rat the size of an armadillo. It shied as it saw him and waddled rapidly away, its claws clicking on the rock. Only an escaped lab rat. A bloody big rat, but still, only a rat.

The huge rippling shadow struck out of nowhere, at incredible speed. It grabbed the rat by its tail and swung it squealing against a pillar, dashing out its brains with a crunch. A flash of a thick claw-like fingernail, and the white furry body was ripped open from sternum to tail. Frantic fingers peeled the skin away from the rat's body as blood splattered. Miles first saw the fangs as they bit and tore and buried themselves in the rat's tissues.

They were functional fangs, not just decorative, set in a pro-truding jaw, with long lips and a wide mouth; yet the total effect was lupine rather than simian. A flat nose, ridged, powerful brows, high cheekbones. Hair a dark matted mess. And yes, fully eight feet tall, a rangy, tense-muscled body.

Climbing back up the ladder would do no good; the creature could pluck him right off and swing him just like the rat. Levi-tate up the side of a pillar? Oh, for suction-cup fingers and toes, something the bioengineering committee had missed somehow. Freeze and play invisible? Miles settled on this last defense by default—he was paralyzed with terror.

The big feet, bare on the cold rock, also had claw-like toenails. But the creature was dressed, in clothes made of green lab-cloth, a belted kimono-style coat and loose trousers. And one other thing.

They didn't tell me it was female.

She was almost finished with the rat when she looked up and saw Miles. Bloody-faced, bloody-handed, she froze as still as he.

In a spastic motion, Miles whipped the squashed ration bar from his trouser thigh-pocket and extended it toward her in his out-stretched hand. "Dessert?" He smiled hysterically.

Dropping the rat's stripped carcass, she snatched the bar out of his hand, ripped off the cover, and devoured it in four bites. Then she stepped forward, grabbed him by an arm and his black T-shirt, and lifted him up to her face. The clawed fingers bit into his skin, and his feet dangled in the air. Her breath was about what he would have guessed. Her eyes were raw and burning. "Water!" she croaked.

They didn't tell me she talked.

"Um, um—water," squeaked Miles. "Quite. There ought to be water around here—look, up at the ceiling, all those pipes. If you'll, um, put me down, good girl, I'll try and spot a water pipe or something. . . ."

Slowly, she lowered him back to his feet and released him. He backed carefully away, his hands held out open at his sides. He cleared his throat, and tried to bring his voice back down to a low, soothing tone. "Let's try over here. The ceiling gets lower, or rather, the bedrock rises . . . over near that light panel, there, that thin composite plastic tube—white's the usual color for water. We don't want gray, that's sewage, or red, that's the power-optics . . ." No telling what she understood; tone was everything with creatures. "If you, uh, could hold me up on your shoulders like Ensign Murka, I could have a go at loosening that joint there . . ." He made pantomime gestures, uncertain if anything was getting through to whatever intelligence lay behind those terrible eyes.

The bloody hands, easily twice the size of his own, grabbed him abruptly by the hips and boosted him upward. He clutched the white pipe, inched along it to a screw-joint. Her thick shoulders beneath his feet moved along under him. Her muscles trembled; it wasn't all his own shaking. The joint was tight—he needed tools—he turned with all his strength, in danger of snapping his fragile finger bones. Suddenly the joint squeaked and slid. It gave, the plastic collar was moving, water began to spray between his fingers. One more turn and it sheared apart, and water arched in a bright stream down onto the rock beneath.

She almost dropped him in her haste. She put her mouth under the stream, wide open, let the water splash straight in and all over her face, coughing and guzzling even more frantically than she'd gone at the rat. She drank, and drank, and drank. She let it run over her hands, her face and head, washing away the blood, and then drank some more. Miles began to think she'd never quit, but at last she backed away and pushed her wet hair out of her eyes, staring down at him. She stared at him for what seemed like a full minute, then suddenly roared, "Cold!"

Miles jumped. "Ah . . . cold . . . right. Me too, my socks are wet. Heat, you want heat. Lessee. Uh, let's try back this way, where the ceiling's lower. No point here, the heat would all collect up there out of reach, no good . . ." She followed him with all the intensity of a cat tracking a . . . well . . . rat, as he skittered around pillars to where the crawl space's floor rose to genuine crawl-height, about four feet. There, that one, that was the lowest pipe he could find. "If we could get this open," he pointed to a plastic pipe about as big around as his waist, "it's full of hot air being pumped along under pressure. No handy joints though, this time." He stared at his puzzle, trying to think. This composite plastic was extremely strong.

She crouched and pulled, then lay on her back and kicked up at it, then looked at him quite woefully.

"Try this." Nervously, he took her hand and guided it to the pipe, and traced long scratches around the circumference with her hard nails. She scratched and scratched, then looked at him again as if to say, *This isn't working!*

"Try kicking and pulling again now," he suggested.

She must have weighed three hundred pounds, and she put it all behind the next effort, kicking then grabbing the pipe, planting her feet on the ceiling and arching with all her strength. The pipe split along the scratches. She fell with it to the floor, and hot air began to hiss out. She held her hands, her face to it, nearly wrapped herself around it, sat on her knees and let it blow across her. Miles crouched down and stripped off his socks and flopped them over the warm pipe to dry. Now would be a good opportunity to run, if only there was anywhere to run to. But he was reluctant to let his prey out of his sight. His prey? He considered the incalculable value of her left calf muscle, as she sat on the rock and buried her face in her knees.

They didn't tell me she wept.

He pulled out his regulation handkerchief, an archaic square of cloth. He'd never understood the rationale for the idiotic handkerchief, except, perhaps, that where soldiers went there would be weeping. He handed it to her. "Here. Mop your eyes with this."

She took it, and blew her big flat nose in it, and made to hand it back.

"Keep it," Miles said. "Uh . . . what do they call you, I wonder."

"Nine," she growled. Not hostile; it was just the way her strained voice came out of that big throat. ". . . What do they call you?"

Good God, a complete sentence. Miles blinked. "Admiral Miles Naismith." He arranged himself cross-legged.

She looked up, transfixed. "A soldier? A *real officer?*" And then more doubtfully, as if seeing him in detail for the first time, "You?"

Miles cleared his throat firmly. "Quite real. A bit down on my luck just at the moment," he admitted.

"Me, too," she said glumly, and sniffed. "I don't know how long I've been here in this basement, but that was my first drink."

"Three days, I think," said Miles. "Have they not, ah, given you any food, either?"

"No." She frowned; the effect, with the fangs, was quite over-powering. "This is worse than anything they did to me in the lab, and I thought that was bad."

It's not what you don't know that'll hurt you, the old saying went. *It's what you do know that isn't so.* Miles thought of his map cube; Miles looked at Nine. Miles pictured himself taking this entire mission's carefully-worked-out strategy plan delicately between thumb and forefinger and flushing it down a waste-disposal unit. The ductwork in the ceiling niggled at his imagination. Nine would never fit through it. . . .

She clawed her wild hair away from her face and stared at him with renewed fierceness. Her eyes were a strange light hazel, adding to the wolfish effect. "What are you *really* doing here? Is this another test?"

"No, this is real life." Miles's lips twitched. "I, ah, made a mistake."

"Guess I did too," she said, lowering her head.

Miles pulled at his lip and studied her through narrowed eyes. "What sort of life have you had, I wonder?" he mused, half to himself.

She answered literally. "I lived with hired fosterers till I was eight. Like the clones do. Then I started to get big and clumsy and break things—they brought me to live at the lab after that. It was all right, I was warm and had plenty to eat."

"They can't have simplified you too much if they seriously intended you to be a soldier. I wonder what your IQ is?"

"A hundred and thirty-five."

Miles fought off stunned paralysis. "I . . . see. Did you ever get . . . any training?"

She shrugged. "I took a lot of tests. They were . . . OK. Except for the aggression experiments. I don't like electric shocks." She brooded a moment. "I don't like experimental psychologists, either. They lie a lot." Her shoulders slumped. "Anyway, I failed. We all failed."

"How can they know if you failed if you never had any proper training?" Miles said scornfully. "Soldiering entails some of the most complex, cooperative learned behavior ever invented—I've been studying strategy and tactics for years, and I don't know half yet. It's all up *here*." He pressed his hands urgently to his head.

She looked across at him sharply. "If that's so," she turned her huge hands over, staring at them, "then why did they do *this* to me?"

Miles stopped short. His throat was strangely dry. *So, admirals lie too. Sometimes, even to themselves.* After an unsettled pause he asked, "Did you never think of breaking open a water pipe?"

"You're punished, for breaking things. Or I was. Maybe not you, you're human."

"Did you ever think of escaping, breaking out? It's a soldier's duty, when captured by the enemy, to escape. Survive, escape, sabotage, in that order."

"Enemy?" She looked upward at the whole weight of House Ryoval pressing overhead. "Who are my friends?"

"Ah. Yes. There is that . . . point." And where would an eight-foot-tall genetic cocktail with fangs run to? He took a deep breath. No question what his next move must be. Duty, expediency, survival, all compelled it. "Your friends are closer than you think. Why do you think I came here?" *Why, indeed?*

She shot him a silent, puzzled frown.

"I came for you. I'd heard of you. I'm . . . recruiting. Or I was. Things went wrong, and now I'm escaping. But if you came with me, you could join the Dendarii Mercenaries. A top outfit— always looking for a few good men, or whatever. I have this master-sergeant who . . . who *needs* a recruit like you." Too true. Sergeant Dyeb was infamous for his sour attitude about women soldiers, insisting that they were too soft. Any female recruit who survived his course came out with her aggression highly developed. Miles pictured Dyeb being dangled by his toes from a height of about eight feet. . . . He controlled his runaway imagination in favor of concentration on the present crisis. Nine was looking . . . unimpressed.

"Very funny," she said coldly, making Miles wonder for a wild moment if she'd been equipped with the telepathy complex—no, she pre-dated that—"but I'm not even human. Or hadn't you heard?"

Miles shrugged carefully. "Human is as human does." He forced himself to reach out and touch her damp cheek. "Animals don't weep, Nine."

She jerked, as from an electric shock. "Animals don't lie. Humans do. All the time."

"Not *all* the time." He hoped the light was too dim for her to see the flush in his face. She was watching his face intently.

"Prove it." She tilted her head as she sat cross-legged. Her pale gold eyes were suddenly burning, speculative.

"Uh . . . sure. How?"

"Take off your clothes."

". . . what?"

"Take off your clothes, and lie down with me as *humans* do. Men and women." Her hand reached out to touch his throat.

The pressing claws made little wells in his flesh. "Blrp?" choked Miles. His eyes felt wide as saucers. A little more pressure, and those wells would spring forth red fountains. *I am about to die. . . .*

She stared into his face with a strange, frightening, bottomless hunger. Then abruptly, she released him. He sprang up and cracked his head on the low ceiling, and dropped back down, the stars in his eyes unrelated to love at first sight.

Her lips wrinkled back on a fanged groan of despair. "Ugly," she wailed. Her clawed nails raked across her cheeks leaving red furrows. "Too *ugly* . . . animal . . . you *don't* think I'm human—" She seemed to swell with some destructive resolve.

"No, no, no!" gibbered Miles, lurching to his knees and grabbing her hands and pulling them down. "It's not that. It's just, uh—how old are you, anyway?"

"Sixteen."

Sixteen. God. He remembered sixteen. Sex-obsessed and dying inside every minute. A horrible age to be trapped in a twisted, fragile, abnormal body. God only knew how he had survived his own self-hatred then. No—he remembered how. *He'd* been saved by one who loved him. "Aren't you a little young for this?" he tried hopefully.

"How old were you?"

"Fifteen," he admitted, before thinking to lie. "But . . . it was traumatic. Didn't work out at all in the long run."

Her claws turned toward her face again.

"Don't *do* that!" he cried, hanging on. It reminded him entirely too much of the episode of Sergeant Bothari and the knife. The Sergeant had taken Miles's knife away from him by superior force. Not an option open to Miles here. "Will you *calm down?*" he yelled at her.

She hesitated.

"It's just that, uh, an officer and gentleman doesn't just fling himself onto his lady on the bare ground. One . . . one sits down. Gets comfortable. Has a little conversation, drinks a little wine, plays a little music . . . slows down. You're hardly warm yet. Here, sit over here where it's warmest." He positioned her nearer the broken duct, got up on his knees behind her, tried rubbing her neck and shoulders. Her muscles were tense—they felt like rocks under his thumbs. Any attempt on his part to strangle her would clearly be futile.

I can't believe this. Trapped in Ryoval's basement with a sex-starved teenage werewolf. There was nothing about this in any of my Imperial Academy training manuals. . . . He remembered his mission, which was to get her left calf muscle back to the *Ariel* alive. *Dr. Canaba, if I survive you and I are going to have a little talk about this. . . .*

Her voice was muffled with grief and the odd shape of her mouth. "You think I'm too tall."

"Not at all." He was getting hold of himself a bit; he could lie faster. "I adore tall women, ask anyone who knows me. Beside, I made the happy discovery some time back that height difference only matters when we're standing up. When we're lying down it's, ah, less of a problem. . . ." A rapid mental review of everything he'd ever learned by trial and error, mostly error, about women was streaming uninvited through his mind. It was harrowing. What did women *want?*

He shifted around and took her hand, earnestly. She stared back equally earnestly, waiting for . . . *instruction.* At this point the realization came over Miles that he was facing his first virgin. He smiled at her in total paralysis for several seconds. "Nine . . . you've never done this before, have you?"

"I've seen vids." She frowned introspectively. "They usually start with kisses, but . . ." a vague gesture toward her misshapen mouth, "maybe you don't want to."

Miles tried not to think about the late rat. She'd been systematically starved, after all. "Vids can be very misleading. For women—especially the first time—it takes practice to learn your own body responses, woman friends have told me. I'm afraid I might hurt you." *And then you'll disembowel me.*

She gazed into his eyes. "That's all right. I have a very high pain threshold."

But I don't.

This was mad. She was mad. *He* was mad. Yet he could feel a creeping fascination for the—proposition—rising from his belly to his brain like a fey fog. No doubt about it, she was the tallest female thing he was every likely to meet. More than one woman of his acquaintance had accused him of wanting to go mountain-climbing. He could get that out of his system once for all. . . .

Damn, I do believe she'd clean up good. She was not without a certain . . . charm was *not* the word—whatever beauty there was to be found in the strong, the swift, the leanly athletic, the functioning form. Once you got used to the *scale* of it. She radiated a smooth heat he could feel from here—*animal magnetism?* the suppressed observer in the back of his brain supplied. Power? Whatever else it was, it would certainly be *astonishing.*

One of his mother's favorite aphorisms drifted through his head. *Anything worth doing,* she always said, *is worth doing well.*

Dizzy as a drunkard, he abandoned the crutch of logic for the wings of inspiration. "Well then, doctor," he heard himself muttering insanely, "let us experiment."

Kissing a woman with fangs was indeed a novel sensation. Being kissed back—she was clearly a fast learner—was even more novel. Her arms circled him ecstatically, and from that point on he lost control of the situation, somehow. Though some time later, coming up for air, he did look up to ask, "Nine, have you ever heard of the black widow spider?"

"No . . . what is it?"

"Never mind," he said airily.

It was all very awkward and clumsy, but sincere, and when he was done the water in her eyes was from joy, not pain. She seemed enormously (how else?) pleased with him. He was so unstrung he actually fell asleep for a few minutes, pillowed on her body.

He woke up laughing.

"You really do have the most elegant cheekbones," he told her, tracing their line with one finger. She leaned into his touch, cuddled up equally to him and the water pipe. "There's a woman on my ship who wears her hair in a sort of woven braid in the back— it would look just great on you. Maybe she could teach you how."

She pulled a wad of her hair forward and looked cross-eyed at it, as if trying to see past the coarse tangles and filth. She touched his face in turn. "You are very handsome, Admiral."

"Huh? Me?" He ran a hand over the night's beard stubble, sharp features, the old pain lines . . . *she must be blinded by my putative rank, eh?*

"Your face is very . . . alive. And your eyes see what they're looking at."

"Nine . . ." He cleared his throat, paused. "Dammit, that's not a name, that's a number. What happened to Ten?"

"He died." *Maybe I will too,* her strange-colored eyes added silently, before her lids shuttered them.

"Is Nine all they ever called you?"

"There's a long biocomputer code-string that's my actual designation."

"Well, we all have serial numbers," Miles had two, now that he thought about it, "but this is absurd. I can't call you Nine, like some robot. You need a proper name, a name that fits you." He leaned back onto her warm bare shoulder—she was like a furnace; they had spoken truly about her metabolism—and his lips drew back on a slow grin. "Taura."

"Taura?" Her long mouth gave it a skewed and lilting accent. ". . . it's too beautiful for me!"

"Taura," he repeated firmly. "Beautiful but strong. Full of secret meaning. Perfect. Ah, speaking of secrets . . ." Was now the time to tell her about what Dr. Canaba had planted in her left calf? Or would she be hurt, as someone falsely courted for her money—or his title—Miles faltered. "I think, now that we know each other better, that it's time for us to blow out of this place."

She stared around, into the grim dimness. "How?"

"Well, that's what we have to figure out, eh? I confess, ducts rather spring to my mind." Not the heat pipe, obviously. He'd have to go anorexic for months to fit in, besides, he'd cook. He shook out and pulled on his black T-shirt—he'd put on his trousers immediately after he'd woken; that stone floor sucked heat remorselessly from any flesh that touched it—and creaked to his feet. God. He was getting too old for this sort of thing already. The sixteen-year-old, clearly, possessed the physical resilience of a minor goddess. What was it he'd gotten into at sixteen? Sand, that was it. He winced in memory of what it had done to certain sensitive body folds and crevices. Maybe cold stone wasn't so bad after all.

She pulled her pale green coat and trousers out from under herself, dressed, and followed him in a crouch until the space was sufficient for her to stand upright.

They quartered and re-quartered the underground chamber. There were four ladders with hatches, all locked. There was a locked vehicle exit to the outside on the downslope side. A direct breakout might be simplest, but if he couldn't make immediate contact with Thorne it was a twenty-seven-kilometer hike to the nearest town. In the snow, in his sock feet—her bare feet. And if they got there, he wouldn't be able to use the vidnet anyway because his credit card was still locked in the Security Ops office upstairs. Asking for charity in Ryoval's town was a dubious proposition. So, break straight out and be sorry later, or linger and try to equip themselves, risking recapture, and be sorry sooner? Tactical decisions were such fun.

Ducts won. Miles pointed upward to the most likely one. "Think you can break that open and boost me in?" he asked Taura.

She studied it, nodded slowly, the expression closing on her face. She stretched up and moved along to a soft metal clad joint, slipped her claw-hard fingernails under the strip, and yanked it off. She worked her fingers into the exposed slot and hung on it as if chinning herself. The duct bent open under her weight. "There you go," she said.

She lifted him up as easily as a child, and he squirmed into the duct. This one was a particularly close fit, though it was the largest he had spotted as accessible in this ceiling. He inched along it on his back. He had to stop twice to suppress a residual, hysteria-tinged laughing fit. The duct curved upward, and he slithered around the curve in the darkness only to find that it split here into a Y, each branch half-sized. He cursed and backed out.

Taura had her face turned up to him, an unusual angle of view.

"No good that way," he gasped, reversing direction gymnastically at the gap. He headed the other way. This too curved up, but within moments he found a grille. A tightly-fitted, unbudgable, unbreakable, and with his bare hands uncuttable grille. Taura might have the strength to rip it out of the wall, but Taura couldn't fit through the duct to reach it. He contemplated it for a few moments. "Right," he muttered, and backed out again.

"So much for ducts," he reported to Taura. "Uh . . . could you help me down?" She lowered him to the floor, and he dusted himself futilely. "Let's look around some more."

She followed him docilely enough, though something in her expression hinted she might be losing faith in his admiralness. A bit of detailing on a column caught his eye, and he went to take a closer look in the dim light.

It was one of the low-vibration support columns. Two meters in diameter, set deep in the bedrock in a well of fluid, it ran straight up to one of the labs, no doubt, to provide an ultra-stable base for certain kinds of crystal generation projects and the like. Miles rapped on the side of the column. It rang hollow. *Ah yes, makes sense, concrete doesn't float too well, eh?* A groove in the side

outlined . . . an access port? He ran his fingers around it, probing. There was a concealed . . . something. He stretched his arms
and found a twin spot on the opposite side. The spots yielded
slowly to the hard pressure of his thumbs. There was a sudden
pop and hiss, and the whole panel came away. He staggered, and
barely kept from dropping it down the hole. He turned it sideways and drew it out.

"Well, well," Miles grinned. He stuck his head through the port,
looked down and up. Black as pitch. Rather gingerly, he reached
his arm in and felt around. There was a ladder running up the
damp inside, for access for cleaning and repairs; the whole column could apparently be filled with fluid of whatever density
at need. Filled, it would have been self-pressure-sealed and
unopenable. Carefully, he examined the inner edge of the hatch.
Openable from either side, by God. "Let's go see if there's any
more of these, further up."

It was slow going, feeling for more grooves as they ascended
in the blackness. Miles tried not to think about the fall, should
he slip from the slimy ladder. Taura's deep breathing, below him,
was actually rather comforting. They had gone up perhaps three
stories when Miles's chilled and numbing fingers found another
groove. He's almost missed it; it was on the opposite side of the
ladder from the first. He then discovered, the hard way, that he
didn't have nearly the reach to keep one arm hooked around the
ladder and press both release catches at the same time. After a
terrifying slip, trying, he clung spasmodically to the ladder till his
heart stopped pounding. "Taura?" he croaked. "I'll move up, and
you try it." Not much up was left. The column ended a meter or
so above his head.

Her extra arm length was all that was needed—the catches
surrendered to her big hands with a squeak of protest.

"What do you see?" Miles whispered.

"Big dark room. Maybe a lab."

"Makes sense. Climb back down and put that lower panel back
on. No sense advertising where we went."

Miles slipped through the hatch into the darkened laboratory
while Taura accomplished her chore. He dared not switch on a
light in the windowless room, but a few instrument readouts on
the benches and walls gave enough ghostly glow for his dark-
adapted eyes that at least he didn't trip over anything. One glass
door led to a hallway. A heavily electronically-monitored hallway.

With his nose pressed to the glass Miles saw a red shape flit past a cross-corridor; guards here. What did they guard?

Taura oozed out of the access hatch to the column—with difficulty—and sat down heavily on the floor, her face in her hands. Concerned, Miles nipped back to her. "You all right?"

She shook her head. "No. Hungry."

"What, already? That was supposed to be a twenty-four-hour rat—er, ration bar." Not to mention the two or three kilos of meat she'd had for an appetizer.

"For you, maybe," she wheezed. She was shaking.

Miles began to see why Canaba dubbed his project a failure. Imagine trying to feed a whole army of such appetites. Napoleon would quail. Maybe the raw-boned kid was still growing. Daunting thought.

There was a refrigerator at the back of the lab. If he knew lab techs . . . ah, ha. Indeed, in among the test tubes was a package with half a sandwich and a large, if bruised, pear. He handed them to Taura. She looked vastly impressed, as if he'd conjured them from his sleeve by magic, and devoured them at once, and grew less pale.

Miles foraged further for his troop. Alas, the only other organics in the fridge were little covered dishes of gelatinous stuff with unpleasant multi-colored fuzz growing in them. But there were three big shiny walk-in wall freezers lined up in a row. Miles peered through a glass square in one thick door, and risked pressing the wall pad that turned on the light inside. Within were row on row on row of labelled drawers, full of clear plastic trays. Frozen samples of some kind. Thousands—Miles looked again, and calculated more carefully—hundreds of thousands. He glanced at the lighted control panel by the freezer door. The temperature inside was that of liquid nitrogen. Three freezers . . . *Millions* of. . . . Miles sat down abruptly on the floor himself. "Taura, do you know where we *are*?" he whispered intensely.

"Sorry, no," she whispered back, creeping over.

"That was a rhetorical question. *I* know where we are."

"Where?"

"Ryoval's treasure chamber."

"What?"

"That," Miles jerked his thumb at the freezer, "is the baron's hundred-year-old tissue collection. My God. Its value is almost incalculable. Every unique, irreplaceable, mutant bizarre bit he's begged, bought, borrowed or stolen for the last three-fourths of a century, all lined up in neat little rows, waiting to be thawed and cultured and cooked up into some poor new slave. This is the living heart of his whole human biologicals operation." Miles sprang to his feet and pored over the control panels. His heart raced, and he breathed open-mouthed, laughing silently, feeling almost as if he was about to pass out. "Oh, shit. Oh, God." He stopped, swallowed. Could it be done?

These freezers had to have an alarm system, monitors surely, piped up to Security Ops at the very least. Yes, there was a complex device for opening the door—that was fine, he didn't want to open the door. He left it untouched. It was systems readout he was after. If he could bugger up just one sensor. . . . Was the thing broadcast-output to several outside monitor locations, or did they run an optic thread to just one? The lab benches supplied him with a small hand light, and drawers and drawers of assorted tools and supplies. Taura watched him in puzzlement as he darted here, there, taking inventory.

The freezer monitor *was* broadcast output, inaccessible; could he hit it on the input side? He levered off a smoke-dark plastic cover as silently as he could. There, *there,* the optic thread came out of the wall, pumping continuous information about the freezer's interior environment. It fit into a simple standard receiver plug on the more daunting black box that controlled the door alarm. There'd been a whole drawer full of assorted optic threads with various ends and Y-adaptors. . . . Out of the spaghetti-tangle he drew what he needed, discarding several with broken ends or other damage. There were three optical data recorders in the drawer. Two didn't work. The third did.

A quick festoon of optic thread, a swift unplugging and plugging, and he had one freezer talking to two control boxes. He set the freed thread to talking to the datacorder. He simply had to chance the blip during transfer. If anyone checked they'd find all seemed well again. He gave the datacorder several minutes to develop a nice continuous replay loop, crouching very still with even the tiny hand light extinguished. Taura waited with the patience of a predator, making no noise.

One, two, three, and he set the datacorder to talking to all three control boxes. The real thread plugs hung forlornly loose. Would it work? There were no alarms going off, no thundering herd of irate security troops. . . .

"Taura, come here."

She loomed beside him, baffled.

"Have you ever met Baron Ryoval?" asked Miles.

"Yes, once . . . when he came to buy me."

"Did you like him?"

She gave him an are-you-out-of-your-mind? look.

"Yeah, I didn't much care for him either." Restrained murder, in point of fact. He was now meltingly grateful for that restraint. "Would you like to rip his lungs out, if you could?"

Her clawed hands clenched. "Try me!"

"Good!" He smiled cheerily. "I want to give you your first lesson in tactics." He pointed. "See that control? The temperature in these freezers can be raised to almost 200 degrees centigrade, for heat sterilization during cleaning. Give me your finger. One finger. Gently. More gently than that." He guided her hand. "The least possible pressure you can apply to the dial, and still move . . . Now the next," he pulled her to the next panel, "and the last." He exhaled, still not quite able to believe it.

"And the lesson is," he breathed, "it's not how much force you use. It's where you apply it."

He resisted the urge to scrawl something like *The Dwarf Strikes Back* across the front of the freezer with a flow pen. The longer the baron in his mortal rage took to figure out who to pursue, the better. It would take several hours to bring all that mass in there from liquid nitrogen temperature up to *well-done,* but if no one came in till morning shift, the destruction would be absolute.

Miles glanced at the time on the wall digital. Dear God, he'd spent a lot of time in that basement. Well-spent, but still . . . "Now," he said to Taura, who was still meditating on the dial, and her hand, with her gold eyes glowing, "we have to get out of here. Now we *really* have to get out of here." Lest her next tactics lesson turn out to be, Don't blow up the bridge you're standing on, Miles allowed nervously.

Contemplating the door-locking mechanism more closely, plus what lay beyond—among other things, the sound-activated wall-mounted monitors in the halls featured automatic laser fire—Miles almost went to turn the freezer temperatures back down. His chip-driven Dendarii tools, now locked in the Security Ops office, might barely have handled the complex circuitry in the pried-open control box. But of course, he couldn't get at his tools without his tools . . . a nice paradox. It shouldn't surprise Miles, that Ryoval saved his most sophisticated alarm system for this lab's one and only door. But it made the room a much worse trap than even the sub-basement.

He made another tour of the lab with the filched hand light, checking drawers again. No computer-keys came to hand, but he did find a big, crude pair of cutters in a drawer full of rings and clamps, and bethought him of the duct grille that had lately defeated him in the basement. So. The passage up to this lab had merely been the illusion of progress toward escape.

"There's no shame in a strategic retreat to a better position," he whispered to Taura when she balked at re-entering the support column's dark tube. "This is a dead-end, here. Maybe literally." The doubt in her tawny eyes was strangely unsettling, a weight in his heart. *Still don't trust me, eh? Well, maybe those who have been greatly betrayed need great proof.* "Stick with me, kid," he muttered under his breath, swinging into the tube. "We're going places." Her doubt was merely masked under lowered eyelids, but she followed him, sealing the hatch behind them.

With the hand light, the descent was slightly less nasty than the ascent into the unknown had been. There were no other exits to be found, and shortly they stood on the stone they had started from. Miles checked the progress of their ceiling waterspout, while Taura drank again. The splattering water ran off in a flat greasy trickle downslope; given the vast size of the chamber, it would be some days before the pool collecting slowly against the lower wall offered any useful strategic possibilities, though there was always the hope it might do a bit to undermine the foundations.

Taura boosted him back into the duct. "Wish me luck," he murmured over his shoulder, muffled by the close confines.

"Goodbye," she said. He could not see the expression on her face; there was none in her voice.

"See you later," he corrected firmly.

A few minutes of vigorous wriggling brought him back to his grille. It opened onto a dark room stacked with stuff, part of the basement proper, quiet and unoccupied. The snip of his cutters, biting through the grille, seemed loud enough to bring down Ryoval's entire security force, but none appeared. Maybe the security chief was sleeping off his drug hangover. A scrabbling noise, not of Miles's own making, echoed thinly through the duct and Miles froze. He flashed his light down a side-branching tube. Twin red jewels flashed back, the eyes of a huge rat. He briefly considered trying to clout it and haul it back to Taura. No. When they got back to the *Ariel,* he'd give her a steak dinner. Two steak dinners. The rat saved itself by turning and scampering away.

The grille parted at last, and he squeezed into the storage room. What time was it, anyway? Late, very late. The room gave onto a corridor, and on the floor at the end, one of the access hatches gleamed dully. Miles's heart rose in serious hope. Once he'd got Taura, they must next try to reach a vehicle. . . .

This hatch, like the first, was manual, no sophisticated electronics to disarm. It re-locked automatically upon closing, however. Miles jammed it with his clippers before descending the ladder. He aimed his light around—"Taura!" he whispered. "Where are you?"

No immediate answer; no glowing gold eyes flashing in the forest of pillars. He was reluctant to shout. He slapped down the rungs and began a silent fast trot through the chamber, the cold stone draining the heat through his socks and making him long for his lost boots.

He came upon her sitting silently at the base of a pillar, her head turned sideways resting on her knees. Her face was pensive, sad. Really, it didn't take long at all to begin reading the subtleties of feeling in her wolfish features.

"Time to march, soldier girl," Miles said.

Her head lifted. "You came back!"

"What did you think I was going to do? Of course I came back. You're my recruit, aren't you?"

She scrubbed her face with the back of a big paw—hand, Miles corrected himself severely—and stood up, and up. "Guess I must be." Her outslung mouth smiled slightly. If you didn't have a clue what the expression was, it could look quite alarming.

"I've got a hatch open. We've got to try to get out of this main building, back to the utility bay. I saw several vehicles parked there earlier. What's a little theft, after—"

With a sudden whine, the outside vehicle entrance, downslope to their right, began to slide upward. A rush of cold dry air swept through the dankness, and a thin shaft of yellow dawn light made the shadows blue. They shielded their eyes in the unexpected glare. Out of the bright squinting haze coalesced half-a-dozen red-clad forms, double-timing it, weapons at the ready.

Taura's hand was tight on Miles's. *Run,* he started to cry, and bit back the shout; no way could they outrun a nerve disruptor beam, a weapon which at least two of the guards now carried. Miles's breath hissed out through his teeth. He was too infuriated even to swear. They'd been so *close.* . . .

Security Chief Moglia sauntered up. "What, still in one piece, Naismith?" He smirked unpleasantly. "Nine must have finally realized it's time to start cooperating, eh, Nine?"

Miles squeezed her hand hard, hoping the message would be properly understood as, *Wait.*

She lifted her chin. "Guess so," she said coldly.

"It's about time," said Moglia. "Be a good girl, and we'll take you upstairs and feed you breakfast after this."

Good, Miles's hand signalled. She was watching him closely for cues, now.

Moglia prodded Miles with his truncheon. "Time to go, dwarf. Your friends have actually made ransom. Surprised me."

Miles was surprised himself. He moved toward the exit, still towing Taura. He didn't look at her, did as little as possible to draw unwanted attention to their, er, togetherness, while still maintaining it. He let go of her hand as soon as their momentum was established.

What the hell. . . ? Miles thought as they emerged into the blinking dawn, up the ramp and onto a circle of tarmac slick with glittering rime. A most peculiar tableau was arranged there.

Bel Thorne and one Dendarii trooper, armed with stunners, shifted uneasily—not prisoners? Half a dozen armed men in the green uniform of House Fell stood at the ready. A float truck emblazoned with Fell's logo was parked at the tarmac's edge. And Nicol the quaddie, wrapped in white fur against the frost, hovered in her float chair at the stunner-point of a big green-clad guard. The light was gray and gold and chilly as the sun, lifting over the dark mountains in the distance, broke through the clouds.

"Is that the man you want?" the green-uniformed guard captain asked Bel Thorne.

"That's him." Thorne's face was white with an odd mixture of relief and distress. "Admiral, are you all right?" Thorne called urgently. Its eyes widened, taking in Miles's tall companion. "What the hell's *that?*"

"*She* is Recruit-trainee Taura," Miles said firmly, hoping 1) Bel would unravel the several meanings packed in that sentence and 2) Ryoval's guards wouldn't. Bel looked stunned, so evidently Miles had got at least partly through; Security Chief Moglia looked suspicious, but baffled. Miles was clearly a problem Moglia thought he was about to get rid of, however, and he thrust his bafflement aside to deal with the more important person of Fell's guard captain.

"What *is* this?" Miles hissed at Bel, sidling closer until a red-clad guard lifted his nerve disruptor and shook his head. Moglia and Fell's captain were exchanging electronic data on a report panel, heads bent together, evidently the official documentation.

"When we lost you last night, I was in a panic," Bel pitched its voice low toward Miles. "A frontal assault was out of the question. So I ran to Baron Fell to ask for help. But the help I got wasn't quite what I expected. Fell and Ryoval cooked up a deal between them to exchange Nicol for you. I swear, I only found out the details an hour ago!" Bel protested at Nicol's thin-lipped glower in its direction.

"I . . . see." Miles paused. "Are we planning to refund her dollar?"

"*Sir*," Bel's voice was anguished, "we had *no idea* what was happening to you in there. We were expecting Ryoval to start beaming up a holocast of obscene and ingenious tortures, starring you, at any minute. Like Commodore Tung says, on hemmed-in ground, use subterfuge."

Miles recognized one of Tung's favorite Sun Tzu aphorisms. On bad days Tung had a habit of quoting the 4000-year-dead general in the original Chinese; when Tung was feeling benign they got a translation. Miles glanced around, adding up weapons, men, equipment. Most of the green guards carried stunners. Thirteen to . . . three? Four? He glanced at Nicol. Maybe five? *On desperate ground*, Sun Tzu advised, *fight*. Could it get much more desperate than this?

"Ah . . ." said Miles. "Just what the devil did we offer Baron Fell in exchange for this extraordinary charity? Or is he doing it out of the goodness of his heart?"

Bel shot him an exasperated look, then cleared its throat. "I promised you'd tell him the real truth about the Betan rejuvenation treatment."

"Bel . . ."

Thorne shrugged unhappily. "I thought, once we'd got you back, we'd figure something out. But I never thought he'd offer Nicol to Ryoval, I swear!"

Down in the long valley, Miles could see a bead moving on the thin gleam of monorail. The morning shift of bioengineers and technicians, janitors and office clerks and cafeteria cooks, was due to arrive soon. Miles glanced at the white building looming above, pictured the scene to come in that third floor lab as the guards deactivated the alarms and let them in to work, as the first one through the door sniffed and wrinkled his nose and said plaintively, "What's that awful *smell?*"

"Has 'Medtech Vaughn' signed aboard the *Ariel* yet?" Miles asked.

"Within the hour."

"Yeah, well . . . it turns out we didn't need to kill his fatted calf after all. It comes with the package." Miles nodded toward Taura.

Bel lowered its voice still further. "*That's* coming with us?"

"You'd better believe it. Vaughn didn't tell us everything. To put it mildly. I'll explain later," Miles added as the two guard captains broke up their tete-a-tete. Moglia swung his truncheon jauntily, heading toward Miles. "Meantime, you made a slight miscalculation. This isn't hemmed-in ground. This is *desperate* ground. Nicol, I want you to know, the Dendarii don't give refunds."

Nicol frowned in bewilderment. Bel's eyes widened, as it checked out the odds—calculating them thirteen to three, Miles could tell.

"Truly?" Bel choked. A subtle hand signal, down by its trouser seam, brought the trooper to full alert.

"Truly desperate," Miles reiterated. He inhaled deeply. "Now! Taura, attack!"

Miles launched himself toward Moglia, not so much actually expecting to wrestle his truncheon from him as hoping to maneuver Moglia's body between himself and the fellows with the nerve disruptors. The Dendarii trooper, who had been paying attention to details, dropped one of the nerve disruptor wielders with his first stunner shot, then rolled away from the second's return fire. Bel dropped the second nerve disruptor man and leapt aside. Two red guards, aiming their stunners at the running hermaphrodite, were lifted abruptly by their necks. Taura cracked their heads together, unscientifically but hard; they fell to hands and knees, groping blindly for their lost weapons.

Fell's green guards hesitated, not certain just whom to shoot, until Nicol, her angel's face alight, suddenly shot skyward in her float chair and dropped straight down again on the head of her guard, who was distracted by the fight. He fell like an ox. Nicol flipped her floater sideways as green-guard stunner fire found her, shielding herself from its flare, and shot upwards again. Taura picked up a red guard and threw him at a green one; they both went down in a tangle of arms and legs.

The Dendarii trooper closed on a green guard hand-to-hand, to shield himself from stunner blast. Fell's captain wouldn't buy the maneuver, and ruthlessly stunned them both, a sound tactic with the numbers on his side. Moglia got his truncheon up against Miles's windpipe and started to press, meanwhile yelling into his wrist com, calling for back-up from Security Ops. A green guard screamed as Taura yanked his arm out of its shoulder socket and swung him into the air by the dislocated joint at another one aiming his stunner at her.

Colored lights danced before Miles's eyes. Fell's captain, focusing on Taura as the biggest threat, dropped to stunner fire from Bel Thorne as Nicol whammed her float chair into the back of the last green guard left standing.

"The float truck!" Miles croaked. "Go for the float truck!" Bel cast him a desperate look and sprinted toward it. Miles fought like an eel until Moglia got a hand down to his boot, drew a sharp, thin knife, and pressed it to Miles's neck.

"Hold still!" snarled Moglia. "That's better . . ." He straightened in the sudden silence, realizing he'd just pulled domination from disaster. "*Everybody* hold still." Bel froze with its hand on the float-truck's door pad. A couple of the men splayed on the tarmac twitched and moaned.

"Now stand away from—glk," said Moglia.

Taura's voice whispered past Moglia's ear, a soft, soft growl. "Drop the knife. Or I'll rip your throat out with my bare hands."

Miles's eyes wrenched sideways, trying to see around his own clamped head, as the sharp edge sang against his skin.

"I can kill him, before you do," croaked Moglia.

"The little man is mine," Taura crooned. "You gave him to me yourself. He came *back* for me. Hurt him one little bit, and I'll tear your head off and then I'll drink your blood."

Miles felt Moglia being lifted off his feet. The knife clattered to the pavement. Miles sprang away, staggering. Taura held Moglia by his neck, her claws biting deep. "I still want to rip his head off," she growled petulantly, remembrance of abuse sparking in her eyes.

"Leave him," gasped Miles. "Believe me, in a few hours he's going to be suffering a more artistic vengeance than anything we can dream up."

Bel galloped back to stun the security chief at can't miss range while Taura held him out like a wet cat. Miles had Taura throw the unconscious Dendarii over her shoulder while he ran around to the back of the float truck and released the doors for Nicol, who zipped her chair inside. They tumbled within, dropped the doors, and Bel at the controls shot them into the air. A siren was going off somewhere in Ryoval's.

"Wrist com, wrist com," Miles babbled, stripping his unconscious trooper of the device. "Bel, where is our drop shuttle parked?"

"We came in at a little commercial shuttleport just outside Ryoval's town, about forty kilometers from here."

"Anybody left manning it?"

"Anderson and Nout."

"What's their scrambled com channel?"

"Twenty-three."

Miles slid into the seat beside Bel and opened the channel. It took a small eternity for Sergeant Anderson to answer, fully thirty or forty seconds, while the float-truck streaked above the treetops and over the nearest ridge.

"Laureen, I want you to get your shuttle into the air. We need an emergency pick-up, soonest. We're in a House Fell float truck, heading—" Miles thrust his wrist under Bel's nose.

"North from Ryoval Biologicals," Bel recited. "At about two hundred sixty kilometers per hour, which is all the faster this crate will go."

"Home in on our screamer," Miles set the wrist com emergency signal. "Don't wait for clearance from Ryoval's shuttleport traffic control, 'cause you won't get it. Have Nout patch my com through to the *Ariel*."

"You got it, sir," Anderson's thin voice came cheerily back over his com.

Static, and another few seconds excruciating delay. Then an excited voice, "Murka here. I thought you were coming out right behind us last night! You all right, sir?"

"Temporarily. Is 'Medtech Vaughn' aboard?"

"Yes, sir."

"All right. Don't let him off. Assure him I have his tissue sample with me."

"Really! How'd you—"

"Never mind how. Get all the troops back aboard and break from the station into free orbit. Plan to make a flying pick-up of the drop shuttle, and tell the pilot-officer to plot a course for the Escobar wormhole jump at max acceleration as soon as we're clamped on. Don't wait for clearance."

"We're still loading cargo. . . ."

"Abandon any that's still unloaded."

"Are we in serious shit, sir?"

"Mortal, Murka."

"Right, sir. Murka out."

"I thought we were all supposed to be as quiet as mice here on Jackson's Whole," Bel complained. "Isn't this all a bit splashy?"

"The situation's changed. There'd be no negotiating with Ryoval for Nicol, or for Taura either, after what we did last night. I struck a blow for truth and justice back there that I may live to regret, briefly. Tell you about it later. Anyway, do you really want to stick around while I explain to Baron Fell the real truth about the Betan rejuvenation treatment?"

"Oh," Thorne's eyes were alight, as it concentrated on its flying, "I'd pay money to watch that, sir."

"Ha. No. For one last moment back there, all the pieces were in our hands. Potentially, anyway." Miles began exploring the readouts on the float-truck's simple control panel. "We'd never get everybody together again, never. One maneuvers to the limit, but the golden moment demands action. If you miss it, the gods damn you forever. And vice versa. . . . Speaking of action, did you see Taura take out *seven* of those guys?" Miles chortled in memory. "What's she going to be like after basic training?"

Bel glanced uneasily over its shoulder, to where Nicol had her float chair lodged and Taura hunkered in the back along with the body of the unconscious trooper. "I was too busy to keep count."

Miles swung out of his seat, and made his way into the back to check on their precious live cargo.

"Nicol, you were great," he told her. "You fought like a falcon. I may have to give you a discount on that dollar."

Nicol was still breathless, ivory cheeks flushed. An upper hand shoved a strand of black hair out of her sparkling eyes. "I was afraid they'd break my dulcimer." A lower hand stroked a big box-shaped case jammed into the float-chair's cup beside her. "Then I was afraid they'd break Bel. . . ."

Taura sat leaning against the truck wall, a bit green.

Miles knelt beside her. "Taura dear, are you all right?" He gently lifted one clawed hand to check her pulse, which was bounding. Nicol gave him a rather strange look at his tender gesture. Her float chair was wedged as far from Taura as it could get.

"Hungry," Taura gasped.

"Again? But of course, all that energy expenditure. Anybody got a ration bar?" A quick check found an only-slightly-nibbled rat bar in the stunned trooper's thigh pocket, which Miles immediately liberated. Miles smiled benignly at Taura as she wolfed it down; she smiled back as best she could with her mouth full. *No more rats for you after this,* Miles promised silently. *Three steak dinners when we get back to the* Ariel, *and a couple of chocolate cakes for dessert. . . .*

The float-truck jinked. Taura, reviving somewhat, extended her feet to hold Nicol's dented cup in place against the far wall and keep it from bouncing around. "Thank you," said Nicol warily. Taura nodded.

"Company," Bel Thorne called over its shoulder. Miles hastened forward.

Two aircars were coming up fast behind them. Ryoval's security. Doubtless beefed up tougher than the average civilian police car—yes. Bel jinked again as a plasma bolt boiled past, leaving bright green streaks across Miles's retinas. Quasi-military and seriously annoyed, their pursuers were.

"This is one of Fell's trucks, we ought to have *something* to fling back at them." There was nothing in front of Miles that looked like any kind of weapons-control.

A *whoomp,* a scream from Nicol, and the float-truck staggered in air, righted itself under Bel's hands. A roar of air and vibration—Miles cranked his head around frantically—one top back corner of the truck's cargo area was blown away. The rear door was fused shut on one side, whanging loose along the opposite edge. Taura still braced the float chair; Nicol now had her upper hands wrapped around Taura's ankles. "Ah," said Thorne. "No armor."

"What did they think this was going to be, a peaceful mission?" Miles checked his wrist com. "Laureen, are you in the air yet?"

"Coming, sir."

"Well, if you've ever itched to red-line it, now's your chance. Nobody's going to complain about your abusing the equipment this time."

"*Thank* you, sir," she responded happily.

They were losing speed and altitude. "Hang on!" Bel yelled over its shoulder, and suddenly reversed thrust. Their closing pursuers shot past them, but immediately began climbing turns. Bel accelerated again; another scream from the back as their live cargo was thus shifted toward the now-dubious rear doors.

The Dendarii hand stunners were of no use at all. Miles clambered into the back again, looking for some sort of luggage compartment, gun rack, anything—surely Fell's people did not rely only on the fearsome reputation of their House for protection. . . .

The padded benches along each side of the cargo compartment, upon which Fell's guard squad had presumably sat, swung up on storage space. The first was empty, the second contained personal luggage—Miles had a brief flash of strangling an enemy with someone's pajama pants, flinging underwear into thruster air-intakes—the third compartment was also empty. The fourth was locked.

The float-truck rocked under another blast, part of the top peeled away in the wind, Miles grabbed for Taura, and the truck plummeted downward. Miles's stomach, and the rest of him, seemed to float upward. They were all flattened to the floor again as Bel pulled up. The float truck shivered and lurched, and all, Miles and Taura, the unconscious trooper, Nicol in her float chair, were flung forward in a tangle as the truck plowed to a tilted stop in a copse of frost-blackened scrub.

Bel, blood streaming down its face, clambered back to them crying "Out, out, out!" Miles stretched for the new opening in the roof, jerked his hand back at the burning touch of hot slagged metal and plastics. Taura, standing up, stuck her head out through the hole, then crouched back down to boost Miles through. He slithered to the ground, looked around. They were in an unpeopled valley of native vegetation, flanked by ropy, ridgy hills. Flying up the slot toward them came the two pursuing aircars, swelling, slowing—coming in for a capture, or just taking careful aim?

The *Ariel*'s combat drop shuttle roared up over the ridge and descended like the black hand of God. The pursuing aircars looked suddenly *much* smaller. One veered off and fled; the second was smashed to the ground not by plasma fire but by a swift swat from a tractor beam. Not even a trickle of smoke marked where it went down. The drop shuttle settled demurely beside them in a deafening crackling crush of shrubbery. Its hatch extended and unfolded itself in a sort of suave, self-satisfied salute.

"Show-off," Miles muttered. He pulled the woozy Thorne's arm over his shoulder, Taura carried the stunned man, Nicol's battered cup stuttered through the air, and they all staggered gratefully to their rescue.

Subtle noises of protest emanated from the ship around him as Miles stepped into the *Ariel*'s shuttle hatch corridor. His stomach twitched queasily from an artificial gravity not quite in synch with overloaded engines. They were on their way, breaking orbit already. Miles wanted to get to Nav and Com as quickly as possible, though the evidence so far suggested that Murka was carrying on quite competently. Anderson and Nout hauled in the downed trooper, now moaning his way to consciousness, and turned him over to the medtech waiting with a float pallet. Thorne, who had acquired a temporary plas dressing for the forehead cut during the shuttle flight, sent Nicol in her damaged float chair after them and wisked off toward Nav and Com. Miles turned to encounter the man he least wanted to see. Dr. Canaba hovered anxiously in the corridor, his tanned face strained.

"You," said Miles to Canaba, in a voice dark with rage. Canaba stepped back involuntarily. Miles wanted, but was too short, to pin Canaba to the wall by his neck, and regretfully dismissed the idea of ordering Trooper Nout to do it for him. Miles pinned Canaba with a glare instead. "You cold-blooded double-dealing son-of-a-bitch. You set me up to murder a sixteen-year-old girl!"

Canaba raised his hands in protest. "You don't understand—"

Taura ducked through the shuttle hatch. Her tawny eyes widened in a surprise only exceeded by Canaba's. "Why, Dr. Canaba! What are you doing here?"

Miles pointed to Canaba. "You, stay there," he ordered thickly. He tampered his anger down and turned to the shuttle pilot. "Laureen?"

"Yes, sir?"

Miles took Taura by the hand and led her to Sergeant Anderson. "Laureen, I want you to take Recruit-trainee Taura here in tow and get her a square meal. All she can eat, and I do mean all. Then help her get a bath, a uniform, and orient her to the ship."

Anderson eyed the towering Taura warily. "Er . . . yes, sir."

"She's had a hell of a time," Miles felt compelled to explain, then paused and added, "Do us proud. It's important."

"Yes, sir," said Anderson sturdily, and led off, Taura following with an uncertain backward glance to Miles and Canaba.

Miles rubbed his stubbled chin, conscious of his stains and stink, fear-driven weariness stretching his nerves taut. He turned to the stunned geneticist. "All right, doctor," he snarled, "make me understand. Try real hard."

"I couldn't leave her in Ryoval's hands!" said Canaba in agitation. "To be made a victim, or worse, an agent of his, his merchandised depravities . . ."

"Didn't you ever think of asking us to rescue her?"

"But," said Canaba, confused, "why should you? It wasn't in your contract—a mercenary—"

"Doctor, you've been living on Jackson's Whole too damn long."

"I knew that back when I was throwing up every morning before going to work." Canaba drew himself up with a dry dignity. "But Admiral, you don't understand." He glanced down the corridor in the direction Taura had gone. "I couldn't leave her in Ryoval's hands. But I can't possibly take her to Barrayar. They kill mutants there!"

"Er . . ." said Miles, given pause. "They're attempting to reform those prejudices. Or so I understand. But you're quite right. Barrayar is not the place for her."

"I had hoped, when you came along, not to have to do it, to kill her myself. Not an easy task. I've known her . . . too long. But to leave her down there would have been the most vile condemnation . . ."

"That's no lie. Well, she's out of there now. Same as you." *If we can keep so. . . .* Miles was frantic to get to Nav and Com and find out what was happening. Had Ryoval launched pursuit yet? Had Fell? Would the space station guarding the distant wormhole exit be ordered to block their escape?

"I didn't want to just abandon her," dithered Canaba, "but I couldn't take her with me!"

"I should hope not. You're totally unfit to have charge of her. I'm going to urge her to join the Dendarii Mercenaries. It would seem to be her genetic destiny. Unless you know some reason why not?"

"But she's going to die!"

Miles stopped short. "And you and I are not?" he said softly after a moment, then more loudly, "Why? How soon?"

"It's her metabolism. Another mistake, or concatenation of mistakes. I don't know when, exactly. She could go another year, or two, or five. Or ten."

"Or fifteen?"

"Or fifteen, yes, though not likely. But early, still."

"And yet you wanted to take from her what little she had? Why?"

"To spare her. The final debilitation is rapid, but very painful, to judge from what some of the other . . . prototypes, went through. The females were more complex than the males, I'm not certain . . . But it's a ghastly death. Especially ghastly as Ryoval's slave."

"I don't recall encountering a lovely death yet. And I've seen a variety. As for duration, I tell you we could all go in the next fifteen minutes, and where is your tender mercy then?" He *had* to get to Nav and Com. "I declare your interest in her forfeit, doctor. Meanwhile, let her grab what life she can."

"But she was my project—I must answer for her—"

"No. She's a free woman now. She must answer for herself."

"How free can she ever be, in that body, driven by that metabolism, that face—a freak's life—better to die painlessly, than to have all that suffering inflicted on her—"

Miles spoke through his teeth. With emphasis. "No. It's. Not."

Canaba stared at him, shaken out of the rutted circle of his unhappy reasoning at last.

That's right, doctor, Miles's thought glittered. *Get your head out of your ass and look at me. Finally.*

"Why should . . . you care?" asked Canaba.

"I like her. Rather better than I like you, I might add." Miles paused, daunted by the thought of having to explain to Taura about the gene complexes in her calf. And sooner or later they'd have to retrieve them. Unless he could fake it, pretend the biopsy was some sort of medical standard operating procedure for Dendarii induction—no. She deserved more honesty than that.

Miles was highly annoyed at Canaba for putting this false note between himself and Taura and yet—without the gene complexes, would he have indeed gone in after her as his boast implied? Extended and endangered his assigned mission just out of the goodness of his heart, yeah? Devotion to duty, or pragmatic ruthlessness, which was which? He would never know, now. His anger receded, and exhaustion washed in, the familiar post-mission down—too soon, the mission was far from over, Miles reminded himself sternly. He inhaled. "You can't save her from being alive, Dr. Canaba. Too late. Let her go. Let *go.*"

Canaba's lips were unhappily tight, but, head bowing, he turned his hands palm-out.

✧   ✧   ✧

"Page the Admiral," Miles heard Thorne say as he entered Nav and Com, then "Belay that," as heads swivelled toward the swish of the doors and they saw Miles. "Good timing, sir."

"What's up?" Miles swung into the com station chair Thorne indicated. Ensign Murka was monitoring ship's shielding and weapons systems, while their Jump pilot sat at the ready beneath the strange crown of his headset with its chemical cannulae and wires.

Pilot Padget's expression was inward, controlled and meditative; his consciousness fully engaged, even merged, with the *Ariel*. Good man.

"Baron Ryoval is on the com for you," said Thorne. "Personally."

"I wonder if he's checked his freezers yet?" Miles settled in before the vid link. "How long have I kept him waiting?"

"Less than a minute," said the com officer.

"Hm. Let him wait a little longer, then. What's been launched in pursuit of us?"

"Nothing, so far," reported Murka.

Miles's brows rose at this unexpected news. He took a moment to compose himself, wishing he'd had time to clean up, shave, and put on a fresh uniform before this interview, just for the psychological edge. He scratched his itching chin and ran his hands through his hair, and wriggled his damp sock toes against the deck matting, which they barely reached. He lowered his station chair slightly, straightened his spine as much as he could, and brought his breathing under control. "All right, bring him up."

The rather blurred background to the face that formed over the vid plate seemed faintly familiar—ah yes, the Security Ops room at Ryoval Biologicals. Baron Ryoval had arrived personally on that scene as promised. It took only one glance at the dusky, contorted expression on Ryoval's youthful face to fill in the rest of the scenario. Miles folded his hands and smiled innocently. "Good morning, Baron. What can I do for you?"

"*Die,* you little mutant!" Ryoval spat. "You! There isn't going to be a bunker deep enough for you to burrow in. I'll put a price on your head that will have every bounty hunter in the galaxy all over you like a second skin—you'll not eat or sleep—I'll have you—"

Yes, the baron had seen his freezers all right. Recently. Gone entirely was the suave contemptuous dismissal of their first encounter. Yet Miles was puzzled by the drift of his threats. It seemed the baron expected them to escape Jacksonian local space. True, House Ryoval owned no space fleet, but why not rent a dreadnought from Baron Fell and attack now? That was the ploy Miles had most expected and feared, that Ryoval and Fell, and maybe Bharaputra too, would combine against him as he attempted to carry off their prizes.

"Can you afford to hire bounty hunters now?" asked Miles mildly. "I thought your assets were somewhat reduced. Though you still have your surgical specialists, I suppose."

Ryoval, breathing heavily, wiped spittle from his mouth. "Did my dear little brother put you up to this?"

"Who?" said Miles, genuinely startled. Yet another player in the game . . . ?

"Baron Fell."

"I was . . . not aware you were related," said Miles. "*Little* brother?"

"You lie badly," sneered Ryoval. "I knew he had to be behind this."

"You'll have to ask him," Miles shot at random, his head spinning as the new datum rearranged all his estimates. *Damn* his mission briefing, which had never mentioned this connection, concentrating in detail only on House Bharaputra. Half-brothers only, surely—yes, hadn't Nicol mentioned something about "Fell's half-brother"?

"I'll have your head for this," foamed Ryoval. "Shipped back frozen in a box. I'll have it encased in plastic and hang it over my—no, better. Double the money for the man who brings you in alive. You will die slowly, after infinite degradation—"

In all, Miles was glad the distance between them was widening at high acceleration.

Ryoval interrupted his own tirade, dark brows snapping down in sudden suspicion. "Or was it Bharaputra who hired you? Trying to block me from cutting in on their biologicals monopoly at the last, not merging as they promised?"

"Why, now," drawled Miles, "would Bharaputra really mount a plot against the head of another House? Do you have personal evidence that they do that sort of thing? Or—who did kill your, ah, brother's clone?" The connections were locking into place at last. Ye gods. It seemed Miles and his mission had blundered into the middle of an on-going power struggle of byzantine complexity. Nicol had testified that Fell had never pinned down the killer of his young duplicate. . . . "Shall I guess?"

"You know bloody well," snapped Ryoval. "But which of them hired you? Fell, or Bharaputra? *Which?*"

Ryoval, Miles realized, knew absolutely nothing yet of the real Dendarii mission against House Bharaputra. And with the atmosphere among the Houses being what it apparently was, it could be quite a long time before they got around to comparing notes. The longer the better, from Miles's point of view. He began to suppress, then deliberately released, a small smile. "What, can't you believe it was just my personal blow against the genetic slave trade? A deed in honor of my lady?"

This reference to Taura went straight over Ryoval's head; he had his ideé-fixe now, and its ramifications and his rage were an effective block against incoming data. Really, it should not be at all hard to convince a man who had been conspiring deeply against his rivals, that those rivals were conspiring against him in turn.

"Fell, or Bharaputra?" Ryoval reiterated furiously. "Did you think to conceal a theft for Bharaputra with that wanton destruction?"

Theft? Miles wondered intently. Not of Taura, surely—of some tissue sample Bharaputra had been dealing for, perhaps? Oh *ho*. . . .

"Isn't it obvious?" said Miles sweetly. "You gave your brother the motive, in your sabotage of his plans to extend his life. And you wanted too much from Bharaputra, so they supplied the method, placing their super-soldier inside your facility where I could rendezvous with her. They even made you pay for the privilege of having your security screwed! You played right into our hands. The master plan, of course," Miles buffed his fingernails on his T-shirt, "was mine."

Miles glanced up through his eyelashes. Ryoval seemed to be having trouble breathing. The baron cut the vid connection with an abrupt swat of his shaking hand. Blackout.

Humming thoughtfully, Miles went to get a shower.

He was back in Nav and Com in fresh gray-and-whites, full of salicylates for his aches and contusions and with a mug of hot black coffee in his hands as antidote to his squinting red eyes, when the next call came in.

So far from breaking into a tirade like his half-brother, Baron Fell sat silent a moment in the vid, just staring at Miles. Miles, burning under his gaze, felt extremely glad he'd had the chance to clean up. So, had Baron Fell missed his quaddie at last? Had Ryoval communicated to him yet any part of the smouldering paranoid misconceptions Miles had so lately fanned to flame? No pursuit had yet been launched from Fell Station—it must come soon, or not at all, or any craft light enough to match the *Ariel*'s acceleration would be too light to match its firepower. Unless Fell planned to call in favors from the consortium of Houses that ran the Jumppoint Station. . . . One more minute of this heavy silence, Miles felt, and he would break into uncontrollable blither. Fortunately, Fell spoke at last.

"You seem, Admiral Naismith," Baron Fell rumbled, "whether accidentally or on purpose, to be carrying off something that does not belong to you."

Quite a few somethings, Miles reflected, but Fell referred only to Nicol if Miles read him right. "We were compelled to leave in rather a hurry," he said in an apologetic tone.

"So I'm told." Fell inclined his head ironically. He must have had a report from his hapless squad commander. "But you may yet save yourself some trouble. There was an agreed-upon price for my musician. It's of no great difference to me, if I give her up to you or to Ryoval, as long as I get that price."

Captain Thorne, working the *Ariel*'s monitors, flinched under Miles's glance.

"The price you refer to, I take it, is the secret of the Betan rejuvenation technique," said Miles.

"Quite."

"Ah . . . hum." Miles moistened his lips. "Baron, I cannot."

Fell turned his head. "Station commander, launch pursuit ships—"

"Wait!" Miles cried.

Fell raised his brows. "You reconsider? Good."

"It's not that I *will* not tell you," said Miles desperately, "it's just that the truth would be of no use to you. None whatsoever. Still, I agree you deserve some compensation. I have another piece of information I could trade you, more immediately valuable."

"Oh?" said Fell. His voice was neutral but his expression was black.

"You suspected your half-brother Ryoval in the murder of your clone, but could not chain any evidence to him, am I right?"

Fell looked fractionally more interested. "All my agents and Bharaputra's could not turn up a connection. We tried."

"I'm not surprised. Because it was Bharaputra's agents who did the deed." Well, it was possible, anyway.

Fell's eyes narrowed. "Killed their own product?" he said slowly.

"I believe Ryoval struck a deal with House Bharaputra to betray you," said Miles rapidly. "I believe it involved the trade of some unique biological samples in Ryoval's possession; I don't think cash alone would have been worth their risk. The deal was done on the highest levels, obviously. I don't know how they figured to divide the spoils of House Fell after your eventual death—maybe they didn't mean to divide it at all. They seem to have had some ultimate plan of combining their operations for some larger monopoly of biologicals on Jackson's Whole. A corporate merger of sorts." Miles paused to let this sink in. "May I suggest you may wish to reserve your forces and favors against enemies more, er, intimate and immediate than myself? Besides, you have all our credit chit but we have only half our cargo. Will you call it even?"

Fell glowered at him for a full minute, the face of a man thinking in three different directions at once. Miles knew the feeling. He then turned his head, and grated out of the corner of his mouth, "Hold pursuit ships."

Miles breathed again.

"I thank you for this information, Admiral," said Fell coldly, "but not very much. I shall not impede your swift exit. But if you or any of your ships appear in Jacksonian space again—"

"Oh, Baron," said Miles sincerely, "staying far, far away from here is fast becoming one of my dearest ambitions."

"You're wise," Fell growled, and moved to cut the link.

"Baron Fell," Miles added impulsively. Fell paused. "For your future information—is this link secured?"

"Yes."

"The true secret of the Betan rejuvenation technique—is that there is none. Don't be taken in again. I look the age I do, because it is the age I am. Make of it what you will."

Fell said absolutely nothing. After a moment a faint, wintry smile moved his lips. He shook his head and cut the com.

Just in case, Miles lingered on in sort of a glassy puddle in one corner of Nav and Com until the Com Officer reported their final clearance from Jumppoint Station traffic control. But Miles calculated Houses Fell, Ryoval, and Bharaputra were going to be too busy with each other to concern themselves with him, at least for a while. His late transfer of information both true and false among the combatants—to each according to his measure—had the feel of throwing one bone to three starving, rabid dogs. He almost regretted not being able to stick around and see the results. Almost.

Hours after the jump he woke in his cabin, fully dressed but with his boots set neatly by his bed, with no memory of how he'd got there. He rather fancied Murka must have escorted him. If he'd fallen asleep while walking alone he'd surely have left the boots on.

Miles first checked with the duty officer as to the *Ariel's* situation and status. It was refreshingly dull. They were crossing a blue star system between jump points on the route to Escobar, unpeopled and empty of everything but a smattering of routine commercial traffic. Nothing pursued them from the direction of Jackson's Whole. Miles had a light meal, not sure if it was breakfast, lunch, or dinner, his bio-rhythm being thoroughly askew from shiptime after his downside adventures. He then sought out Thorne and Nicol. He found them in Engineering. A tech was just polishing out the last dent in Nicol's float chair.

Nicol, now wearing a white tunic and shorts trimmed with pink piping, lay sprawled on her belly on a bench watching the repairs. It gave Miles an odd sensation to see her out of her cup. It was like looking at a hermit crab out of its shell, or a seal on the shore. She looked strangely vulnerable in one-gee, yet in null gee she'd looked so right, so clearly at ease, he'd stopped noticing the oddness of the extra arms very quickly. Thorne helped the tech fit the float cup's blue shell over its reconditioned antigrav mechanism, and turned to greet Miles as the tech proceeded to lock it in place.

Miles sat down-bench from Nicol. "From the looks of things," he told her, "you should be free of pursuit from Baron Fell. He and his half-brother are going to be fully occupied avenging themselves on each other for a while. Makes me glad I'm an only child."

"Hm," she said pensively.

"You should be safe," Thorne offered encouragingly.

"Oh—no, it's not that," Nicol said. "I was just thinking about my sisters. Time was I couldn't wait to get away from them. Now I can't wait to see them again."

"What are your plans now?" Miles asked.

"I'll stop at Escobar, first," she replied. "It's a good nexus crossing. From there I should be able to work my way back to Earth. From Earth I can get to Orient IV, and from there I'm sure I can get home."

"Is home your goal now?"

"There's a lot more galaxy to be seen out this way," Thorne

pointed out. "I'm not sure if Dendarii rosters can be stretched to include a ship's musician, but—"

She was shaking her head. "Home," she said firmly. "I'm tired of fighting one-gee all the time. I'm tired of being alone. I'm starting to have nightmares about growing legs."

Thorne sighed faintly.

"We do have a little colony of downsiders living among us now," she added suggestively to Thorne. "They've fitted out their own asteroid with artificial gravity—quite like the real thing downside, only not as drafty."

Miles was faintly alarmed—to lose a ship commander of proven loyalty—

"Ah," said Thorne in a pensive tone to match Nicol's. "A long way from my home, your asteroid belt."

"Will you return to Beta Colony, then, someday?" she asked. "Or are the Dendarii Mercenaries your home and family?"

"Not quite that passionate, for me," said Thorne. "I mainly stick around due to an overwhelming curiosity to see what happens next." Thorne favored Miles with a peculiar smile.

Thorne helped load Nicol back into her blue cup. After a brief systems check she was hovering upright again, as mobile—more mobile—than her legged companions. She rocked and regarded Thorne brightly.

"It's only three more days to Escobar orbit," said Thorne to Nicol rather regretfully. "Still—seventy-two hours. 4,320 minutes. How much can you do in 4,320 minutes?"

Or how often, thought Miles dryly. *Especially if you don't sleep.* Sleep, per se, was not what Bel had in mind, if Miles recognized the signs. Good luck—to both of them.

"Meanwhile," Thorne maneuvered Nicol into the corridor, "let me show you around my ship. Illyrican-built—that's out your way a bit, I understand. It's quite a story, how the *Ariel* first fell into Dendarii hands—we were the Oseran Mercenaries, back then—"

Nicol made encouraging noises. Miles suppressed an envious grin, and turned the other way up the corridor, to search out Dr. Canaba and arrange the discharge of his last unpleasant duty.

Bemusedly, Miles set aside the hypospray he'd been turning over in his hands as the door to sickbay sighed open. He swivelled in the medtech's station chair and glanced up as Taura and Sergeant Anderson entered. "My *word,*" he murmured.

Anderson sketched a salute. "Reporting as ordered, sir." Taura's hand twitched, uncertain whether to attempt to mimic this military greeting or not. Miles gazed up at Taura and his lips parted with involuntary delight. Taura's transformation was all he'd dreamed of and more.

He didn't know how Anderson had persuaded the stores computer to so exceed its normal parameters, but somehow she'd made it disgorge a complete Dendarii undress kit in Taura's size: crisp gray-and-white pocketed jacket, gray trousers, polished ankle-topping boots. Taura's face and hair were clean enough to outshine her boots. Her dark hair was now drawn back in a thick, neat, and rather mysterious braid coiling up the back of her head—Miles could not make out where the ends went—and glinting with unexpected mahogany highlights.

She looked, if not exactly well-fed, at least less rawly starving, her eyes bright and interested, not the haunted yellow flickers in bony caverns he'd first seen. Even from this distance he could tell that re-hydration and the chance to brush her teeth and fangs had cured the ketone-laced breath that several days in Ryoval's sub-basement on a diet of raw rats and nothing had produced. The dirt-encrusted scale was smoothed away from her huge hands, and—inspired touch—her clawed nails had been, not blunted, but neatened and sharpened, and then enamelled with an iridescent pearl-white polish that complemented her gray-and-whites like a flash of jewelry. The polish had to have been shared out of some personal stock of the sergeant's.

"Outstanding, Anderson," said Miles in admiration.

Anderson smirked proudly. "That about what you had in mind, sir?"

"Yes, it was." Taura's face reflected his delight straight back at him. "What did you think of your first wormhole jump?" he asked her.

Her long lips rippled—what happened when she tried to purse them, Miles guessed. "I was afraid I was getting sick, I was so dizzy all of a sudden, till Sergeant Anderson explained what it was."

"No little hallucinations, or odd time-stretching effects?"

"No, but it wasn't—well, it was quick, anyway."

"Hm. It doesn't sound like you're one of the fortunates—or unfortunates—to be screened for jump pilot aptitudes. From the talents you demonstrated on Ryoval's landing pad yesterday morning, Tactics should be loathe to lose you to Nav and Com." Miles paused. "Thank you, Laureen. What did my page interrupt?"

"Routine systems checks on the drop shuttles, putting them to bed. I was having Taura look over my shoulder while I worked."

"Right, carry on. I'll send Taura back to you when she's done here."

Anderson exited reluctantly, clearly curious. Miles waited till the doors swished closed to speak again. "Sit down, Taura. So your first twenty-four hours with the Dendarii have been satisfactory?"

She grinned, settling herself carefully in a station chair, which creaked. "Just fine."

"Ah." He hesitated. "You understand, when we reach Escobar, you do have the option to go your own way. You're not compelled to join us. I could see you got some kind of start, downside there."

"What?" Her eyes widened in dismay. "No! I mean . . . do I eat too much?"

"Not at all! You fight like four men, we can bloody well afford to feed you like three. But. . . I need to set a few things straight, before you make your trainee's oath." He cleared his throat. "I didn't come to Ryoval's to recruit you. A few weeks before Bharaputra sold you, do you remember Dr. Canaba injecting something into your leg? With a needle, not a hypospray."

"Oh, yes." She rubbed her calf half-consciously. "It made a knot."

"What, ah, did he tell you it was?"

"An immunization."

She'd been right, Miles reflected, when they'd first met. Humans did lie a lot. "Well, it wasn't an immunization. Canaba was using you as a live repository for some engineered biological material. Molecularly bound, dormant material," he added hastily as she twisted around and looked at her leg in disquiet. "It can't activate spontaneously, he assures me. My original mission was only to pick up Dr. Canaba. But he wouldn't leave without his gene complexes."

"He planned to take me with him?" she said in thrilled surprise. "So I should thank *him* for sending you to me!"

Miles wished he could see the look on Canaba's face if she did. "Yes and no. Specifically, no." He rushed roughly on before his nerve failed him. "You have nothing to thank him for, nor me either. He meant to take only your tissue sample, and sent me to get it."

"Would you rather have left me at—is that why Escobar—" she was still bewildered.

"It was your good luck," Miles plunged on, "that I'd lost my men and was disarmed when we finally met. Canaba lied to me, too. In his defense, he seems to have had some dim idea of saving you from a brutal life as Ryoval's slave. He sent me to kill you, Taura. He sent me to slay a monster, when he should have been begging me to rescue a princess in disguise. I'm not too pleased with Dr. Canaba. Nor with myself. I lied through my teeth to you down in Ryoval's basement, because I thought I had to, to survive and win."

Her face was confused, congealing, the light in her eyes fading. "Then you didn't . . . really think I was human—"

"On the contrary. Your choice of test was an excellent one. It's much harder to lie with your body than with your mouth. When I, er, demonstrated my belief, it had to be real." Looking at her, he still felt a twinge of lurching, lunatic joy, somatic residual from that adventure-of-the-body. He supposed he always would feel something—male conditioning, no doubt. "Would you like me to demonstrate it again?" he asked half-hopefully, then bit his tongue. "No," he answered his own question. "If I am to be your commander—we have these non-fraternization rules. Mainly to protect those of lower rank from exploitation, though it can work both—ahem!" He was digressing dreadfully. He picked up the hypospray, fiddled with it nervously, and put it back down.

"Anyway, Dr. Canaba has asked me to lie to you again. He wanted me to sneak up on you with a general anesthetic, so he could biopsy back his sample. He's a coward, you may have noticed. He's outside now, shaking in his shoes for fear you'll find out what he intended for you. I think a local zap with a medical stunner would suffice. I'd sure want to be conscious and watching if he were working on *me*, anyway." He flicked the hypospray contemptuously with one finger.

She sat silent, her strange wolfish face—though Miles was getting used to it—unreadable. "You want me to let him . . . cut into my leg?" she said at last.

"Yes."

"Then what?"

"Then nothing. That will be the last of Dr. Canaba for you, and Jackson's Whole and all the rest of it. That, I promise. Though if you're doubtful of my promises, I can understand why."

"The last . . ." she breathed. Her face lowered, then rose, and her shoulders straightened. "Then let's get it over with." There was no smile to her long mouth now.

✧   ✧   ✧

Canaba, as Miles expected, was not happy to be presented with a conscious subject. Miles truly didn't care how unhappy Canaba was about it, and after one look at his cold face, Canaba didn't argue. Canaba took his sample wordlessly, packaged it carefully in the biotainer, and fled with it back to the safety and privacy of his own cabin as soon as he decently could.

Miles sat with Taura in sickbay till the medical stun wore off enough for her to walk without stumbling. She sat without speaking for a long time. He watched her still features, wishing beyond measure he knew how to re-light those gold eyes.

"When I first saw you," she said softly, "it was like a miracle. Something magic. Everything I'd wished for, longed for. Food. Water. Heat. Revenge. Escape." She gazed down at her polished claws, "Friends . . ." and glanced up at him, ". . . touching."

"What else do you wish for, Taura?" Miles asked earnestly.

Slowly she replied. "I wish I were normal."

Miles was silent too. "I can't give you what I don't possess myself," he said at length. The words seemed to lie in inadequate lumps between them. He roused himself to a better effort. "No. Don't wish that. I have a better idea. Wish to be yourself. To the hilt. Find out what you're best at, and develop it. Hopscotch your weaknesses. There isn't time for them. Look at Nicol—"

"So beautiful," sighed Taura.

"Or look at Captain Thorne, and tell me what 'normal' is, and why I should give a damn for it. Look at me, if you will. Should I kill myself trying to overcome men twice my weight and reach in unarmed combat, or should I shift the ground to where their muscle is useless, 'cause it never gets close enough to apply its strength? I haven't got *time* to lose, and neither have you."

"Do you know how little time?" demanded Taura suddenly.

"Ah . . ." said Miles cautiously, "do you?"

"I am the last survivor of my creche mates. How could I not know?" Her chin lifted defiantly.

"Then don't wish to be normal," said Miles passionately, rising to pace. "You'll only waste your precious time in futile frustration. Wish to be great! That at least you have a fighting chance for. Great at whatever you are. A great trooper, a great sergeant. A great quartermaster, for God's sake, if that's what comes with ease. A great musician like Nicol—only think how horrible if she were wasting her talents trying to be merely normal." Miles paused self-consciously in his pep talk, thinking, *Easier to preach than practice.* . . .

Taura studied her polished claws, and sighed. "I suppose it's useless for me to wish to be beautiful, like Sergeant Anderson."

"It is useless for you to try to be beautiful *like* anyone but yourself," said Miles. "Be beautiful like Taura, ah, that you can do. Superbly well." He found himself gripping her hands, and ran one finger across an iridescent claw, "Though Laureen seems to have grasped the principle. You might be guided by her taste."

"Admiral," said Taura slowly, not releasing his hands, "are you actually my commander yet? Sergeant Anderson said something about orientation, and induction tests, and an oath. . . ."

"Yes, all that will come when we make fleet rendezvous. Till then, technically, you're our guest."

A certain sparkle was beginning to return to her gold eyes. "Then—till then—it wouldn't break any Dendarii rules, would it, if you showed me again how human I am? One more time?"

It must be, Miles thought, akin to the same drive that used to propel men to climb sheer rock faces without an antigrav belt, or jump out of ancient aircraft with nothing to stop them going splat but a wad of silk cloth. He felt the fascination rising in him, the death-defying laugh. "Slowly?" he said in a strangled voice. "Do it right this time? Have a little conversation, drink a little wine, play a little music? Without Ryoval's guard squad lurking over-head, or ice cold rock under my . . ."

Her eyes were huge and gold and molten. "You did say you liked to practice what you were great at."

Miles had never realized how susceptible he was to flattery from tall women. A weakness he must guard against. Sometime.

They retired to his cabin and practiced assiduously till halfway to Escobar.

Afterword

The stories in this volume are grouped by an internal series chronology that I could scarcely have imagined when I wrote the first of them. Not only did I not know then how important certain ideas were going to be to my later work, I didn't realize just how long "later" was going to run. It is not quite serendipity that they also form a thematic unit, all touching variously on meditations of mine regarding human evolution, reproduction, bioethics, and gender issues.

Ethan of Athos was my third novel, written in 1985 (published 1986), *Cetaganda* my eleventh, written in 1995 (published 1996), making these two stories slices of my thinking on these issues exactly a decade apart. "Labyrinth" fell in between, written in 1988 to be part of a planned novella collection, *Borders of Infinity*, which was published by Baen Books in late 1989. The story also appeared in *Analog* magazine that August with delightful cover and interior art by Frank Kelly Freas, an artist whose work always signaled "Fun fiction here!" to me back when I read *Analog* in my teens. Other readers must have agreed, because "Labyrinth" won the *Analog* reader's poll for best novella that year.

At the time I wrote *Ethan of Athos*, I had not yet sold any novels, though two completed works were making the rounds of New York publishers. I had, however, made my first short story sale, and on the boost to my morale so provided, I embarked on my third novel. I was groping around for the magic trick by which I might break in, and among the advice I collected was "Try something short. The editors are less daunted by thinner manuscripts on their slush piles, and maybe they'll read it sooner!" So I was determined to keep the length under strict control. I still wasn't sure I would be able to sell the books as a series, although I quite liked the universe I had begun to develop, so I also wanted the next thing to be series-optional, not dependent on the two prior books but connectable to them if some editor *did* see the light. But more importantly—in the course of my first novel, *Shards of Honor,* I had tossed off as a mere sidebar the idea of the uterine replicator. Upon consideration, this appeared to me more and more a piece of technology that really did have the potential to change the world, and I wanted to explore some of those possible changes.

Extra-uterine gestation is not a new idea in SF. Aldous Huxley first used it way back in the early thirties in *Brave New World*, but being who and where he was, used it mainly as part of a metaphoric exploration of specifically British class issues. I was a child of another country and time, with a very different worldview, and other issues interested me a lot more. Primary among my beliefs was that, given humanity as I knew it, there wasn't going to be just *one* way any new tech would be applied—and that the results were going to be even more chaotic than the causes.

One obvious consequence of the uterine replicator was the possibility of a society where women's historical monopoly on reproduction would be broken. All-male societies exist in our world—armies, prisons, and monasteries to name three—but all must re-supply their populations from the larger communities in which they are embedded. This technology could break that dependence. I discarded armies and prisons as containing skewed, abnormally violent populations, and instead considered monasteries as a possible model for an all-male society both benign and, provably, viable over generations.

About this time—the winter of 1984–85—I went to a New Year's Eve party given by a nurse friend, and fell into a conversation about some of these nascent ideas with two men. One was an unmarried and notably macho surgeon, the other a hospital administrator with two children of his own. The two men took, interestingly, opposite sides of the argument of whether such an all-male colony could ever be workable. The macho surgeon rejected the notion out of hand; the man who'd actually *had* some-thing to do with raising his own children was intrigued, and not so inclined to sell his gender short. (The surgeon, note, did not perceive that he was slandering his gender; in bragging about what he could not possibly do in the way of menial women's work, he was positioning himself and his fellows as ineluctably on the high-status end of human endeavor.) It was clear, in any case, that the topic was a hot one, of enormous intrinsic interest to a wide range of people.

A decade later, in *Cetaganda*, I explored disparate consequences of the same reproductive technologies in a very different social milieu. The Cetagandan haut use replicators and associated genetic engineering to construct their race's entire genome as a commu-nity property under strict central control. Although spread among many individuals, the genome becomes conceptualized as a work of art being consciously sculpted by its haut-women guardians. Where this is finally going, even the haut women do not have the hubris to guess—one of their few saving graces.

In addition, *Cetaganda* allowed me to do something a writer can pull off especially nicely in a series—critique or comment upon the assumptions of earlier books. I had originally tossed off the Cetagandans as mostly-offstage and rather all-purpose bad guys to stir up some plot action for my heroes. But the Barrayarans had started out as bad guys too, from a certain point of view. The closer I came to them, the more complicated their picture grew. No one is a villain in their own eyes; when I brought the story closer to the Cetagandans, they, too, became more complex and ambiguous. I was very pleased with the effect.

"Labyrinth" returned the themes to ground level; after all, these are people's *lives* we are discussing here, which come in one size only, Individual. The "masses" are a mere abstraction, a fiction with even less weight than an author's musings, an intellectual construct of extremely dubious morality. And lives are not interchangeable. Or, as I told my daughter back when she was learning to drive: "State Farm will buy me a new car. They can't buy me a new daughter." (Not yet, anyway . . .)

The novella also allowed me to ring the changes through still another social milieu: in this case, Jackson's Whole, and what it might do with the new biological options. On this planet, laissez-faire capitalism has gone completely over the top, as the rule of law enforced by governments with guns is replaced by the rule of guys with enough money to hire guns. Here, the only limits of biotechnology are "whatever money can buy." For chaotic results, this serves up a smorgasbord to make an adventure author's mouth water. Since Miles is the master of chaos, this was a character and a setting made to bring out the most in each other, and indeed they did, both here and in later tales.

One future technology, three societies, three results: more to come, as my time and ingenuity permit. Yet in all these different societies, the test of humanity comes out the same, and it has nothing to do with genetics. No one can be guilty of their own birth, no matter what form it takes. We need not fear our technology if we do not mistake the real springs of our humanity. It's not how we get here that counts; it's what we do after we arrive.

Lois McMaster Bujold
June 2001

MILES VORKOSIGAN/NAISMITH:

HIS UNIVERSE AND TIMES

Chronology	Events	Chronicle
Approx. 200 years before Miles's birth	Quaddies are created by genetic engineering.	*Falling Free*
During Beta-Barrayaran War	Cordelia Naismith meets Lord Aral Vorkosigan while on opposite sides of a war. Despite difficulties, they fall in love and are married.	*Shards of Honor*
The Vordarian Pretendership	While Cordelia is pregnant, an attempt to assassinate Aral by poison gas fails, but Cordelia is affected; Miles Vorkosigan is born with bones that will always be brittle and other medical problems. His growth will be stunted.	*Barrayar*
Miles is 17	Miles fails to pass physical test to get into the Service Academy. On a trip, necessities force him to improvise the Free Dendarii Mercenaries into existence; he has unintended but unavoidable adventures for four months. Leaves the Dendarii in Ky Tung's competent hands and takes Elli Quinn to Beta for rebuilding of her damaged face; returns to Barrayar to thwart plot against his father. Emperor pulls strings to get Miles into the Academy.	*The Warrior's Apprentice*
Miles is 20	Ensign Miles graduates and immediately has to take on one of the duties of the Barrayaran nobility and act as detective and judge in a murder case. Shortly afterwards, his first military assignment ends with his arrest. Miles has to rejoin the Dendarii to rescue the young Barrayaran emperor. Emperor accepts Dendarii as his personal secret service force.	"The Mountains of Mourning" in *Borders of Infinity* *The Vor Game*

Chronology	Events	Chronicle
Miles is 22	Miles and his cousin Ivan attend a Cetagandan state funeral and are caught up in Cetagandan internal politics.	*Cetaganda*
	Miles sends Commander Elli Quinn, who's been given a new face on Beta, on a solo mission to Kline Station.	*Ethan of Athos*
Miles is 23	Now a Barrayaran Lieutenant, Miles goes with the Dendarii to smuggle a scientist out of Jackson's Whole. Miles's fragile leg bones have been replaced by synthetics.	"Labyrinth" in *Borders of Infinity*
Miles is 24	Miles plots from within a Cetagandan prison camp on Dagoola IV to free the prisoners. The Dendarii fleet is pursued by the Cetagandans and finally reaches Earth for repairs. Miles has to juggle both his identities at once, raise money for repairs, and defeat a plot to replace him with a double. Ky Tung stays on Earth. Commander Elli Quinn is now Miles's right-hand officer. Miles and the Dendarii depart for Sector IV on a rescue mission.	"The Borders of Infinity" in *Borders of Infinity* *Brothers in Arms*
Miles is 25	Hospitalized after previous mission, Miles's broken arms are replaced by synthetic bones. With Simon Illyan, Miles undoes yet another plot against his father while flat on his back.	*Borders of Infinity*
Miles is 28	Miles meets his clone brother Mark again, this time on Jackson's Whole.	*Mirror Dance*
Miles is 29	Miles hits thirty; thirty hits back.	*Memory*

Chronology	Events	Chronicle
Miles is 30	Emperor Gregor dispatches Miles to Komarr to investigate a space accident, where he finds old politics and new technology make a deadly mix.	*Komarr*
Miles is 31	The Emperor's wedding sparks romance and intrigue on Barrayar, and Miles plunges up to his neck in both.	*A Civil Campaign*